Also by Julie Lessman

WINDS of CHANGE

a Heart Revealed

A NOVEL

JULIE LESSMAN

Revell

a division of Baker Publishing Group
Grand Rapids, Michigan

© 2011 by Julie Lessman

Published by Revell
a division of Baker Publishing Group
P.O. Box 6287, Grand Rapids, MI 49516-6287
www.revellbooks.com

Printed in the United States of America

Library of Congress Cataloging-in-Publication Data is on file at the Library of Congress, Washington, DC.

ISBN 978-0-8007-3416-9

Unless otherwise indicated, Scripture used in this book, whether quoted or paraphrased by the characters, is taken from the King James Version of the Bible.

Scripture quotations labeled NKJV are from the New King James Version. Copyright © 1982 by Thomas Nelson, Inc. Used by permission. All rights reserved.

This book is a work of fiction. Names, characters, places, and incidents are the product of the author's imagination or are used fictitiously. Any resemblance to actual events, locales, or persons, living or dead, is coincidental.

11 12 13 14 15 16 17   7 6 5 4 3 2 1

To my amazing son, Matt—
whose uncommon kindness, gentle strength,
and love of sports provided the perfect framework
for the hero of this book.
May Sean O'Connor touch the hearts and lives
of my readers just a glimmer as deeply and powerfully
as our son has touched ours.

And thus the secrets of his heart are revealed;
and so, falling down on his face, he will worship God
and report that God is truly among you.

—1 Corinthians 14:25 NKJV

Prologue

Dublin, Ireland, 1916

She heard it before she felt it. Harsh air sucking through clenched teeth, the grunt of an arm raised, the soft swish of a hand slicing the air.

"I want the truth—"

And then she felt it. The crack of his knuckles when her jaw met the back of his hand, the thud of her head against the wall, the putrid rise of nausea as it climbed in her throat.

"Did you sleep with him?"

"No, I swear—"

"Liar!"

Cruel hands rattled her shoulders while the vile stench of whiskey smothered her air. The taste of blood and vomit soured her tongue, forcing the words to heave from her throat. "It was an innocent comment, I swear, from a friend and nothing more—"

He wrenched her arm and her scream pierced the night before he jerked her close, his foul breath hot against her skin. "You think I'm stupid, do ya? I see the way he looks at you, the way they all look at you . . ."

"It doesn't matter, Rory—you're the one I love—only you!" The air seized in her lungs as she waited for her words to take effect. Blood pulsing in her brain, she licked her lips and forced her gaze to his, watching as his rage slowed and simmered into lust. Her body quivered as she pressed in close, tracing his mouth with shaky fingers. The violent throb of her pulse betrayed the casual huskiness of her whisper. "You . . . I only want you . . . forever and ever."

He stared, the crazed look in his eye finally fading into the smoldering obsession she had mistaken for love. Jerking her close, he devoured her with his mouth, his lips hard and cruel as they plumbed the depths of his desire. He shoved her to the wall, pinning her there with a possessive gaze while his hands took the liberties allowed to a husband. "Mine . . . you're all mine, Emma, and no other man can ever have you—do you hear?"

His breathing quickened as taut arms swallowed her up. "Don't you know how much I love you?" he whispered, his voice pleading as the dark bristle of his late-day beard ground against her cheek. He jerked away to cup her face in his hands, all of his fury suddenly chased away by the lovesick look in his eyes. A gentle smile lifted the corners of his mouth, transforming his handsome face into the lost little boy she'd fallen in love with. "Emma, my beautiful, beautiful Emma, I'm sorry for hitting you, love, and I swear from now on, I'll give you all the love you deserve."

His kiss was gentler this time, and her eyes fluttered closed. Mrs. Rory Malloy—the envy of every girl on O'Connell Street. Her sweat-soaked blouse shivered against her skin. Every lass's dream . . . and one woman's nightmare. Rory's whispers of love tickled her ear, but all she could hear was her father's curse, ricocheting off the battered walls of her mind.

I pray to God you get what you deserve . . .

With a gentle stroke of her cheek, Rory carried her into their bedroom. He closed the door with the tip of his shoe, severing the light as surely as he'd severed the hope from her soul.

Not to worry, Da . . . I did.

1

Boston, Massachusetts, July 4, 1931

lways a bridesmaid, never a bride . . . and the saints be praised! Blessed relief curved Emma Malloy's mouth into a gentle smile. She inhaled a deep breath of rose-scented air while Charity O'Connor Dennehy tucked an arm to her waist, palm resting against the pink chiffon of Emma's bridesmaid dress. With a contented sigh that merged with Emma's own, the two best friends studied Charity's youngest sister, Katie, laughing as her new husband slipped the garter from her leg.

"Brides and babies have to be some of God's most beautiful creatures." Charity's tone was wistful. She rested her head against Emma's, the two of them lost in a sea of noisy guests celebrating Katie and Luke's wedding in a cozy back room of Kearney's Café.

Ivy garland from the O'Connor garden looped its way along a lace-covered table where a crystal vase of yellow roses presided over cake and punch. Long rectangular tables were cloaked in a wide array of tablecloths on loan from the other three O'Connor sisters, all sporting crystal bud vases abloom with roses in varying shades as different as the sisters themselves. Dusty pink for twenty-seven-year-old Lizzie—the color of the shy blush that often tinged her cheeks—blended nicely with the vibrant scarlet blooms that her older sister Charity seemed to prefer. Creamy white tea roses called to mind the innocence and sincerity of Charity's eldest sister, Faith, while Katie's bridal bouquet of lemon-yellow roses bespoke the joy and promise of a new beginning.

Emma couldn't help but smile at the thought of four sisters who "cloaked" each other—and her—as well with a mantle of love and support as beautifully woven as any lace tablecloth. From Katie's independent zest for life and Lizzie's soft-spoken gentleness, to Faith's solid faith and Charity's quirky humor, Emma felt more like a sister than a friend in this family that she now claimed as her own. A sigh feathered her lips as she leaned in, tilting her own chin-length brunette curls against Charity's golden marcel waves. "Mmm . . . brides and babies, yes," she repeated reverently, the softest hint of brogue in her tone. "And sure, when it comes to brides, our Katie is one of the most beautiful."

Indeed, rising from the chair to stand next to her new husband, Katie glowed like the crystal chandelier overhead, her cheeks as soft and dewy as the delicate bouquet in her hand.

"Oh—look! She's getting ready to throw the bouquet." Charity tugged Emma closer while a surge of young women pressed forward with outstretched arms. Turning her back to the crowd, Katie launched the bouquet over her shoulder in a wide sweep.

Plunk. Emma stared at her feet in shock, where Katie's bouquet nestled neatly between her satin Mary Jane pumps. Pandemonium erupted with little-girl shrieks and flying limbs. Emma blinked, too stunned to move.

In a blur, Charity snatched the flowers from the jaws of death and thrust them in her hands. "It's yours, Mrs. Malloy, married or not. And may it bring you the happiness you so richly deserve."

Heat gorged Emma's cheeks. *The happiness she so richly deserves?* She gulped, the action almost painful for the guilt clogging her throat. *Oh, Charity, that's blasphemy . . .*

10

"Hey, no fair—she's already married," ten-year-old Gabriella objected. The O'Connor's tomboy foster child crossed her arms in indignation, the spray of freckles on her heart-shaped face all bunched in a frown. Eyes the same deep mahogany of her hair narrowed considerably, ready to take Emma on.

Charity tweaked a dark banana curl on her foster-sister's shoulder. "The flowers will be dead tomorrow, Gabe. Let the woman have some happiness, will you?"

"But . . . but I can't . . . ," Emma managed with another hard swallow.

"They're flowers, Emma, not a death sentence, so enjoy them." Charity cocked a brow. "Did you even have a bouquet when you took your vows?"

Emma shook her head, avoiding Charity's eyes.

"Well then, consider it the bouquet you never had at your own wedding, all right?"

"But . . . but . . . they should go to somebody who's not . . ." Emma thrust the bouquet back at Charity, her voice a strained whisper, "married."

"There's nobody more 'not married' than you, Mrs. Malloy, cheating sot of a husband notwithstanding." Charity cupped an arm around her friend's shoulder. "Enjoy the flowers, will you, Emma? They may well be the only decent thing you'll ever see out of a marriage."

Cheeks burning, Emma hid her discomfort with her nose buried in the bouquet, the scent of the flowers far sweeter than the memory of her past. At thirty-one years of age, she was quite certain that Charity was right. Over eleven years ago, a handsome Irishman named Rory Malloy had dashed her hopes of happiness with a pan of hot grease that scarred her face during a drunken fit. Suddenly, she was no longer the comely Irish lass who had turned his head, but an albatross as disfigured and scarred as their love had proven to be. She closed her eyes, lost in the satiny spray of roses in her hand. Grazing the ribboned stem of the bouquet with her thumb, she felt the prick of a forgotten thorn and sighed, reminded of just how painful marriage could be.

From the moment Rory had put the ring on her finger, it seemed her happily-ever-after had quickly dissolved into a murky nightmare of physical and emotional abuse, finally ending when he moved in with another woman. The pain of her sham marriage had convinced Emma once and for all that for some women—at least women like her—marriage was *not* a good thing. She sighed as Luke dipped his bride back to smother her throat with kisses. "I don't think I've ever seen Katie happier or more beautiful. The perfect bride, I'd say."

A throaty chuckle quivered the chiffon bodice of Charity's bridesmaid gown. She pulled back to give Emma a mischievous smile. "You mean the perfect distraction when Luke discovers 'our Katie' is anything but the 'perfect' wife."

Emma's fingers playfully nipped at Charity's waist. "Stop that, Mrs. Dennehy. Katie and Luke were made for each other, and everyone knows it."

Charity sighed and studied the happy couple. "I suppose. I guess it's the 'iron sharpening iron' Scripture in play. Luke agreed Katie can continue to work with him three days a week at the BCAS while Lizzie watches Kit, but everybody knows he's bent on having a family, so I suspect Katie's tenure will be short-lived. Five to ten says sparks will fly when he tries to lower the boom after the honeymoon."

"Lower the boom?" Emma repeated with a lift of her brows. Her eyes flicked to Luke as he tugged his fifteen-month-old daughter "Kitty Kat" out of the arms of Katie's sister, Lizzie, with a tickle of Kitty's ribs. Husky baby giggles echoed in the room as he planted a kiss on her tummy.

"Yeah, you know, like Mitch did with me over ten years ago? We get married, he buys the store for you and me to manage, and then, *boom!* I get pregnant with the twins, and my working days are over. And in the blink of an eye, you're saddled with a store to manage all by yourself while I'm locked in an ivory tower like Rapunzel with a shoulder-length bob." Charity shot an affectionate scowl at her husband who was deep in a conversation with her brothers, Sean and Steven, then returned her knowing gaze to the newlyweds. "Trust me, Mrs. Malloy, as much as those two like to have their own way, this will be a marriage where sparks will fly."

Emma bumped Charity's shoulder with a teasing grin. "Yes, *Rapunzel*, but apparently it's worked for you and Mitch. Besides, I thought 'sparks' were a good thing."

Charity's grin bordered on wicked. "Oh, they are, my friend—that is, if you learn how to channel the heat. And trust me, with those two, there will be *plenty* of heat. Let's face it—you don't just marry an Irishman, you marry a stubborn streak and an Irish temper."

"Not all Irishmen are like that," Emma defended, brow puckering at the mere mention of "temper." Despite the heat of the room, a chill iced her spine at the memory of Rory's "Irish temper" before she'd left him in Dublin over ten years ago. *Deliver me from men with tempers . . .*

Charity's eyes narrowed. "Name one."

With a heft of her chin, Emma rose to the challenge. "Well, your brother, Sean, for one. He doesn't have a lick of a temper and he's the sweetest, most easygoing man I've ever met."

Charity's gaze honed in on her unmarried brother across the room who stood, arms folded and hip cocked to the wall, chatting with his brothers-in-law.

Emma's gaze followed and then paused. *Odd . . .* Sean's trademark smile was absent and his manner unusually stiff, a stark contrast to the others, who were laughing over something Mitch was saying. Emma frowned.

"Oh, I'll go along with that, but remember he's Irish, Emma, so what Sean doesn't have in temper, he makes up for in stubbornness." She leaned in, as if Sean were close enough to hear. "And although no one ever sees it, trust me—there's a temper lurking inside of that easygoing brother of mine. I only saw it once, mind you, when he was thirteen, but suffice it to say that it was that very 'temper' that effectively bashed in Herman Finkel's head."

"What?" Emma turned, her eyes wide. "What on earth happened?"

Charity pursed her lips as she studied her brother. "Well,

Sean was walking me home from school one day when we passed the park where Herman was heckling Becky Landers." Charity rolled her eyes. "God give me the grace to understand why little boys feel the need to torment the little girls they like . . ." Pausing, she shot a narrow gaze at her husband. "Big boys too, come to think of it." She shook her head as if to dispel the thought. "Well, anyway, I had this sneaky feeling that Sean had a secret crush on Becky because as we all know, men are *so* obvious, when all of a sudden Herman tosses a snowball her way. Saints preserve us, Sean leveled the poor kid like a runaway train, knocking him flat. I'm telling you, Emma, before Sean was through, poor Herman had a split lip, black eyes, and a chipped tooth."

"No!" Emma's mouth slacked open.

"Yes," Charity said, conspiracy thick in her tone. "Our gentle, nonconfrontational Sean O'Connor—the man who wouldn't hurt a fly—suddenly pummeling poor Herman like Jack Dempsey on a bad day. That night, Mr. Finkel threatened Father with the police." A secret smile formed on Charity's lips. "I don't think I've ever seen Father so angry. Not sure what he said or did to Sean other than confiscate profits from his paper route for a solid year, but whatever it was, I never saw Sean lose his temper again." A twinkle lit in Charity's eyes as she gave Emma a smug look. "But as we all know, 'still waters run deep.' So for all his squalling about being a confirmed bachelor until the day he dies, when my brother says he has no interest in women, Herman Finkel is living proof that Sean is lying through his teeth."

Emma bit back a grin. "Poor Sean—desperate to remain a bachelor and he has you as a sister—the Queen of Romance."

Charity slid Emma a narrow gaze. "It's for his own good, Emma, and you know it. Look at the man—he's at his own sister's wedding, for pity's sake, and he looks like his tie is too tight. Somebody has to put him out of his misery, because I won't rest until I see both of my brothers happily wed."

"He does look pretty miserable," Emma said with a chew of her lip.

"Of course he's miserable—he hates weddings even more than being home sick with the flu. Which validates his stubbornness and neatly lumps him right in with every other Irish man."

Emma shook her head. "I don't know—I've known Sean for eleven years now, and I've never seen it. He's the peacemaker, the buffer, the Rock of Gibraltar everyone relies on. Seems like he always accommodates others just to keep everyone happy."

A low chuckle escaped Charity's lips. "Oh, he's a rock all right, right along with the rest of them, starting with Father and Mitch and right on down to Katie's new husband. Trust me, Mount Rushmore has nothing on these guys, which," Charity said with a nod in Katie and Luke's direction, "brings me right back to the inevitable sparks between Katie and Luke. I mean, really, how appropriate is it for them to get married on the Fourth of July?"

"Mmm," Emma said, studying the happy couple with a tilt of her head. "Practically perfect except for missing the fireworks display at Revere Beach. I know how much Katie loves fireworks, so it's a shame she'll miss them this year."

Folding her arms, Charity nudged her elbow against Emma's while mischief glinted in her blue eyes. "Well, judging from the way Luke's been looking at her all day, I'd say Katie will have all the fireworks she can handle."

"Sean!" The room stilled at the booming sound of the groom's voice, edged with laughter. All eyes turned to the men by the wall, including Emma's, who followed the lightning thrust of Luke McGee's hand while her smile remained buried in Katie's bouquet.

Lost in conversation, Sean glanced up in surprise. Ever the athlete, he instinctively reached to catch whatever Luke was tossing his way. Whistles and cheers rose as he blinked at the pretty, lacy garter clutched in his upraised fist. Split-second realization forced color into his cheeks. And then, with a skewed smile and an innocent slant of heavy blond brows, the garter slipped through his fingers to the floor. "Whoops . . ."

Charity's husband, Mitch, retrieved the unwanted garter with a deft swipe of his hand and bobbled it with a grin. He shoved it into Sean's breast pocket next to the white silk handkerchief and rose boutonniere. "Sorry, old boy, but this one belongs to you, and everybody here knows it. And I don't mind saying, we all think it's long, *long* overdue."

Sean plucked the garter from his pocket and slipped it on his arm, all embarrassment apparently forgotten as he grinned at his brothers-in-law. "I do believe I detect a bit of jealousy from the ranks of the married. Well, unlike you poor slobs, it will take more than trickery from Luke McGee and a bit of lace to get me to the altar."

"Yeah, like four sisters and a mother on a round-the-clock novena," Mitch said with a chuckle, slapping him on the back. "Face it, Sean—your bachelor days are numbered."

Shouts and laughter erupted as Luke ushered Katie toward the door with a suitcase in his hand. Katie's sister, Lizzie, followed behind, eyes moist as she snuggled a sleepy Kit.

"Now you give me a call when you get to New York, Katie, you hear?" Marcy O'Connor squeezed her daughter in a tearful hug. "So I know you're okay?"

Patrick O'Connor shook Luke's hand and shot his wife an off-center smile. "For pity's sake, Marcy, Katie Rose is a married woman now, not a youngster underfoot who has to check in. Leave the newlyweds be." He swooped Katie up in a ferocious hug and winked at his new son-in-law. "Besides, she's Luke's problem now, not ours."

"Father!" Mock indignation laced Katie's tone as she gave her father a playful smack.

"It's all under control, Mr. O'Connor," Luke said with an easy grin. He pressed a firm hand against the small of Katie's back, totally ignoring the sudden lift of her brow. "And we will call tonight, Mrs. O'Connor, rest assured. Thank you all for everything."

"Do we get calls too?" Charity asked with a dance of her brows.

Katie laughed and deposited a gentle kiss on Kit's cheek,

now sound asleep against Lizzie's shoulder. "Nope, only Lizzie so we can check in on Kit." She dispensed hugs to all three of her sisters and Emma. "You and Faith will have to wait till I get back because we'll be *very* busy. Luke has a full agenda planned, lots of things he wants me to see and do in his old hometown."

"Uh-huh . . . I'm quite sure he does," Charity said with a tease in her tone.

"Charity!" Emma's cheeks tinged pink, along with Faith, Lizzie, and Katie's, who sneaked a quick glance at Luke while he conversed with her parents.

Faith tweaked the back of Charity's neck. "Ignore her, Katie, we all know she's got a one-track mind. Just make sure Luke takes you to the Empire State Building, you hear? It opened a couple of months ago, and it's supposed to be fabulous."

"Oh, yes," Emma breathed, "you'll have to tell us all about it. It's the tallest building in the world and even has an observatory on the eighty-sixth floor with incredible views of the city." She sighed and gave Katie a tight hug. "Why, that high up, your head's sure to be in the clouds."

A grin tugged at Katie's lips. "It already is, Emma." Her eyes grew misty as she touched a gentle hand to Emma's cheek and then to her sisters'. "I love you all so much, and I can't thank you enough for your prayers and support. What does one do without sisters, I wonder?"

Emma smiled and squeezed Katie's hand. "One prays for friends who are just as dear."

"Taxi's waiting, you two," Steven said with a grin, bobbling his father's car keys in hand.

"Ready, Katie?" Luke cupped a secure hand to Katie's waist.

"Hey, McGee . . ." Sean and his brothers-in-law forged forward to give Katie a hug before slapping Luke on the back. Sean flicked the garter on his arm with a chuckle. "Trust me—you'll pay for this dearly in our next game on the court."

Luke delivered a cocky smile on the way to the door.

"Lookin' forward to it, Sean. Now that we're related, I won't have to take it so easy on you."

Emma smiled when Charity and her entire family shadowed Katie and Luke out the door. A gentle sigh floated from her lips. *Family. I wonder if they know how truly blessed they are?*

"Sweet tea in Georgia, a solid week without Mr. Priss in the office—imagine that!" Bobbie Sue Dulay, one of Luke's employees from the Boston Children's Aid Society sauntered over to Emma with a purse under her arm. "Talk about a week off with pay."

Emma grinned up at the older silver-haired woman who far exceeded Emma in girth, height, and humor. "Yes, Katie tells me he can be pretty particular about things in the office."

"Humph. That's the toad callin' the frog homely for sure. If I didn't know better, I suspec' those two of being twins separated at birth." Bobbie Sue shook her head as she watched the newlyweds duck out the door. "Yep, a marriage made in heaven for shore, if you're in mind for a little spice in your life."

A marriage made in heaven. Against her will, the smile stiffened on Emma's face. She worked hard to appear attentive while Bobbie Sue prattled on, but somehow her thoughts wandered to Rory. Heaven had had nothing to do with what she and Rory had shared, and for the first time in a long while, a hint of melancholy stole into her mood. Luke and Katie had it all—a marriage made in heaven, a family to love, and the blessings of God—and at the thought, a rare malaise settled on Emma Malloy. Like Katie and Luke, Emma had spoken vows too, and given an oath. She swallowed hard as she absently nodded at something Bobbie Sue said. Yet, love like that would never be hers, she realized, and although she had accepted that long, long ago, that didn't stop the sting of tears that suddenly pricked in her eyes.

"Are you okay?" A crease popped in Bobbie Sue's brow as she bent to study Emma's face, freckles all bunched in a frown. "Why, honey, you're bubbling like you're fixing to cry."

Emma blinked, then drew in a deep breath and forced a

smile. "Come on, Bobbie Sue, let's get some wedding cake, shall we? And don't mind me," she said with a quick swipe at her eyes. She linked arms with the woman, then squared her shoulders as they strolled to the other side of the room. "I'm notorious for crying over weddings." Her smile was unnaturally bright as she ignored the stab in her heart.

Especially my own.

"Well, the wedding was a hit, Marcy. You and Katie did a wonderful job, and on a shoestring budget, no less." Emma bent to slip off her heels and massage her feet.

Despite a room in shambles from wilted flowers, spilled punch, and crumbs on the floor, a sense of satisfaction could be seen in each of the faces around the table. The silence in Kearney's back room was a welcome relief from noisy well-wishers and shrieking cousins who'd spent the last two hours running wild. Now that guests had departed and all children had been shipped off to neighbors for safekeeping, nothing was left but cleanup.

Marcy O'Connor tucked a stray curl behind her ear, her honey-colored bob laced with almost invisible strands of silver, and Emma couldn't help but think she seemed more of an older sister than the mother of her three daughters in the room. Her tone was tired but content. "Thanks, Emma. And a hit, indeed. Especially with Patrick, who's lost more than one night's sleep worrying about the cost of this wedding. I swear the man used to enjoy the sleep of the dead, but not anymore. At least not since this awful depression started two years ago. I'm just grateful Katie and Luke suggested a cake and punch reception here rather than a dinner at a hotel or an expensive hall. And with Luke getting this room free and Collin and Brady printing the invitations and programs as a gift, not to mention you girls providing flowers and cakes, Patrick O'Connor may actually sleep tonight."

Lizzie grinned. "He should. Four daughters married and no more weddings to pay for—maybe he'll sleep for days."

"Oh, that sounds so good, doesn't it?" Charity said with a scrunch of her nose, head propped in her hand.

Faith chuckled. "No more daughters, true, but that doesn't necessarily mean no more weddings to pay for, does it, Mother?"

Marcy chewed on her lip and chanced a peek across the room. Patrick and the other men appeared to be glued to the radio he'd insisted on bringing so he wouldn't miss the Yankees game during cleanup. Her voice lowered to a whisper. "No . . . not necessarily."

Charity leaned in, arms on the table and lips parted in a faint smile. She squinted. "You *have* discussed adopting Gabe with Father, haven't you, Mother?"

A faint hint of color washed into Marcy's cheeks as her gaze darted to her husband and back. "Hush, Charity, will you? I'll tell your father when the time is right." Her lips crooked to the right. "And trust me, after paying for his fourth daughter's wedding—cake reception or no—would *not* be the right time for Patrick O'Connor. I'll just give the poor man a month or so to get over the shock of this expense, and then I'll ease him into it slowly." She sighed and rose to her feet. "Well, we best get busy. Mr. Kearney needs this room for a recital tonight. Did everybody bring a change of clothes, I hope? He said we could use the storage area in back as a dressing room."

Emma jumped up and pushed in her chair. "Not me, Marcy, but that's okay. I rather enjoy wearing this lovely dress you made." She picked her bride's bouquet up from the table and gave it a gentle sniff. "Would you like me to unplug the radio and ramrod the men?"

A tired grin plucked at Marcy's lips. "Yes, Emma, please. And don't you dare do too much, you hear? We'll be out to help in a bit."

"Yes, ma'am." Emma headed toward the men while Marcy and her daughters shuffled off to the storage room with high heels in hand and laughter on their lips.

"Yeah, well, he may be the 'Sultan of Swat,' but it will be a cold day in the devil's kitchen before I forgive that man for leaving Boston." Patrick O'Connor puffed on his pipe with a vengeance, smoke curling up past his handsome face, which was screwed up in a frown. He leaned over the radio, the gray in his temples glinting as he squinted to listen to the play-by-play.

Steven looped an arm around his father's shoulder. "Come on, Pop, Babe Ruth transformed the dead-ball era into the Golden Age of Baseball, and you know it. And a record of sixty home runs? Face it, the guy doesn't need to be forgiven, he needs to be canonized."

"Canonized?" Faith's husband, Collin, scowled. "After he deserted the Red Sox for the Yankees?"

"I'm with Steven," Sean said. "And don't forget he saved baseball's rump when fans stayed away in droves after the White Sox threw the Series in 1919. Face it, Pop—baseball needed a hero, and the Babe is it."

"Ahem." Emma quietly cleared her throat, and seven sets of male eyes blinked up as if she were the Babe himself. "I have orders to start you gentlemen on cleanup." A smile played on her lips. "And be warned—I've been authorized to unplug the radio, *if* necessary."

The corners of Sean's mouth edged up, easing the strain she'd noticed in his face earlier. "Now there's a fearsome threat—sweet Emma Malloy terrorizing us with a timid smile."

Color flooded her cheeks as she hiked her chin in true Charity fashion, biting back an answering grin. "I suggest you put the Babe to bed, gentlemen, before the true threat to your happy homes come bounding out of the back room." She gave them an uncustomary wink and spun on her heel, shooting a smile over her shoulder.

"You've been spending too much time with my wife, Emma," Mitch said in a dry tone. "And just for the record, Sean, there's nothing timid about Emma when it comes to running the store. In fact, she can be as fearsome a taskmaster as Charity when she wants to be."

Sean loosened his tie, then rolled up the shirtsleeves of his white dress shirt. He gave Emma a cheeky grin, wondering what it was about Emma Malloy that always lifted his spirits. "Oh yeah, I'll bet—a regular bully. I'm sure she has everybody quaking in their boots."

Another soft blush stole into Emma's cheeks as she pivoted to face him, her teasing smile calming his belligerent mood. With a rare hint of the vamp, she tossed lustrous folds of rich, chestnut hair over one shoulder and assessed him through stunning gray eyes as pure and clear as any mountain stream. "One does not have to 'bully' subordinates to get what one wants, Mr. O'Connor, as you should well know from managing your own store." One manicured brow hiked high despite the glimmer of a twinkle in her eye. "Or maybe you don't."

Before he could respond, she whirled around and slipped out the door, and for the first time today, he felt a full-fledged grin slide across his lips. He didn't know how she did it, but the woman had a knack for soothing his soul more than any person alive, and Sean wished he could bottle it.

Subordinates. His smile suddenly went sour at the thought of Andy, Mort, and Ray. Not only were they the best employees he'd had in eleven years as manager of Kelly's Hardware, but they were men he respected who had become good friends as well. His lips flattened into a hard line. Men who depended on him to provide jobs to take care of their families in this dire economy. His bad mood returned with a vengeance as he joined his best friend, Pete, to dismantle a trellis archway his mother had asked him to build for pictures.

"Hey, the wedding's over, O'Connor, wipe that scowl off your face," Pete said with a squint. "What's eating you, anyway? I haven't seen you this out of sorts since Howie Devlin's older sister cornered you in a booth at Robinson's."

With a grunt, Sean ripped off a branch of his mother's trailing cottage roses twined through the white latticework. In the process, he knocked over a milk bottle of water hidden beneath the white satin draped around the base. Water gushed, and he groaned, squatting to mop it up with the satin.

Pete grabbed the material around the other leg and started helping, peering up beneath bushy brows that framed the concern in his eyes. "What's going on, buddy? First, you're at your own sister's wedding in one of the worst moods I've ever seen, then you're like a bull in a china shop—two things as out of character as the Good Humor man running kids down with his truck. What's up with you anyway? This isn't like you."

Sean vented with a blast of air that started at the base of his lungs and rose like a pot ready to boil over. "Let's just write it off as a bad day at work, okay? I'll tell ya what though, Pete, there are days I'd like nothing more than to give Old Man Kelly a piece of my mind." He wadded the satin and hurled it off to the side. "*And* my fist." Rising, he reached for another branch, then quickly jerked away. "Blasted rosebush," he muttered, scowling at the back of his forearm, which now ran red with blood from a lengthy cut.

Pete handed him a piece of the soggy satin. "Here, you're a train wreck waiting to happen, you know that? Why don't you go have Kearney patch you up and then maybe you need to visit the speakeasy downstairs—you could use a cold one bad."

"Oh yeah, wouldn't that be rich—thrown in the brig by my own brother, the prohibition agent. No, thanks, I'd rather take it out on you on the court, Murph, if it's all the same to you."

Pete's lips slanted. "Get yourself a brew, O'Connor. I'd rather not test our friendship."

"Yeah, yeah. How about you disarm the trellis while I get this patched up? And trust me—I may just give some serious thought to that beer." Heading for the door, Sean cocked his arm to check the bleeding right before he ran headlong into Emma.

Emma jolted, hand to her chest. "Goodness, Sean, what did you do?"

The bucket in her hands wavered, causing soapy water to surge over the side.

He lifted his arm and vented a heavy sigh while several drops of blood splattered on the floor. "Apparently I'm a hazard when it comes to dismantling rose limbs from Mother's trellis," he said with a dry grin. "You wouldn't know where I could get a bandage for this, would you, Emma? I suspect she'd be none too happy if I dripped blood on this white shirt."

Emma chewed on her lip, masking a smile. "No, but I can certainly check with Mr. Kearney. But first, we need to wash off that nasty wound." She immediately set the bucket down and squeezed out a clean, soapy rag, clenching her teeth as she gingerly patted the blood away.

Laugh lines fanned at the side of Sean's face, easing the deep ridge in his brow. Eyes the same clear blue as Charity's assessed her with a hint of a smile, merging with a spray of freckles and a tan to give him the carefree air of a mischievous Huck Finn. "I think I'll live, Mrs. Malloy."

She met the twinkle in his eye with one of her own. "Not if you bleed all over that shirt, Sean O'Connor—your mother will have your head. Hold out your arm." With short, gentle strokes, she cleaned the deep scratch and patted it dry, wincing at the rugged line that seemed to go on forever. "Goodness, what did you do, roll around in it?"

He flicked the lacy garter that pinched against his rather intimidating bicep. "Nope, didn't have to. Not with this jinx on my arm. In fact, I think I'm going to get rid of this albatross right now." He reached up and jerked the garter off, dragging it down the craggy wound as it oozed fresh blood. With a squint of his eyes, he arced the garter into the wastebasket across the room with a neat, clean swish. "Yes! Two points for me and zero for marriage." He held out his arm with an easy grin. "Patch me up, Mrs. Malloy—that was a mighty close call."

Shaking her head, she hurried out the door, shooting him a warning look tempered by a faint smile. "Don't move! I'll fetch some bandages from Mr. Kearney." Moments later, she returned with supplies in hand. "This may sting," she warned, eyes on the scratch as she re-cleaned the wound and then applied a salve. "You really don't plan to ever get married?" she asked, unable to resist posing the question to a man who seemed so suited to a true depth of love, so prone to giving, and so destined for a marriage that would be happy. She wrapped a length of gauze around his arm.

"Nope. Marriage isn't for everybody, Emma." His voice softened to just above a whisper. "You should know that."

She carefully tied the bandage with a knot while the comment heated her cheeks. Her eyes flicked up to meet his, tugging a frail sigh from her lips. She attempted a smile. "But you would be such a natural, Sean. I feel it in my bones."

He gave her nose a playful tap. "Could be arthritis, you know, ever think of that? Oh sure, I guess I'm a 'natural' at some things—a natural clown, a natural athlete, a natural at losing at chess. But marriage?" A faint shiver shook his broad shoulders. "Trust me—the only thing that feels natural about that is staying far away from it."

"Which at the ripe, old age of thirty-four, I'd say you've managed to do very nicely." She glanced up with a tilt of her head and a curious smile. "No more problems with Miss Rose Kelly, I take it?"

Sean threaded a hand through light, sandy hair, disrupting his neat slicked-back style with a carefree, tousled look that partially fell in his eyes. She noted the slight shift of his lips as they quirked to the right. "Ah . . . the boss's daughter. Funny you should mention that. Remember that summer she cornered me in the back room?"

Emma nodded and smiled.

"Well, I told her I was 'seeing someone,' just like we discussed, and thank goodness, that seemed to do the trick. She stopped coming into the store all the time, and the next thing I hear, she's engaged to that rich dandy her father wanted her to marry. So things *were* just great . . ." He absently rubbed his sore arm, eyes trained on the hardwood floor now littered with cake crumbs, rose petals, and confetti. His eyes flinched, then peered up with concern. "That is . . . until two weeks ago."

Emma paused, hands immersed in the soapy water as she rinsed out the bloody rag. "What happened two weeks ago?" she asked with a pinch of brows.

"Nothing—*yet*—other than she's been coming into the store more times in a week than I've seen her in the last year. You know, the same thing as before—smiling, flirting . . . browsing." He cuffed the back of his neck, his usual easy smile suddenly flat. "Now I ask you, Emma, why in tarnation does a twenty-two-year-old woman with a rock on her hand the size of the Blarney Stone and a wedding a month away need to browse in a hardware store?"

Emma blinked. "I don't know, maybe she's on the hunt for the perfect wedding gift for her fiancé." She wrung out the wet cloth, her curiosity as piqued as Sean's.

"Yeah, a length of rope and level so she can keep him in line."

She cocked her head. "Maybe she knows he needs a particular tool. Is he handy?"

One blond brow jagged high. "Handy? The only thing handy about J. Chester Connealy is his bankroll. The man wouldn't know a pliers from a wrench, which certainly explains how Rose locked him into this marriage. She can squeeze a man in a death hold tighter than any woman I've ever seen, and the poor guy probably never saw it coming."

Emma gave him a patient smile. "I'm sure he's in love with her, Sean. After all, men are not prone to put a ring on a woman's finger unless they are."

"Yeah, well, I wish he'd hurry up and marry her then. Every time she comes in the store, I get this queasy feeling. Like she's sizing me up more than the inventory."

"Could be your imagination, you know." Emma worked her lip to temper her smile, but the tease slipped out in her tone. "Or maybe a bit of panic due to a deathly fear of females."

He studied her, lips pursed. "Maybe. But either way, Rose Kelly makes me downright nervous. Always has. From the moment her father brought her into the store at the age of fifteen, she's had this . . . this way around me. Staring at me, asking me questions, buzzing around, closer than a shadow." He shivered. "And when she cornered me in the supply room two summers ago and kissed the daylights out of me, well, you can certainly understand why I'm just a wee bit skittish when it comes to the boss's daughter."

"Yes . . . yes, I completely understand." She hesitated. "Well, I guess you could always pray about it, you know."

A haze of color whooshed into his tan cheeks as he stood up tall, obviously uneasy with the idea of praying anywhere but at the dinner table and mass. He swallowed hard and grabbed the bucket from her hand. "Uh . . . I'll get fresh water for you, Emma, but you go right ahead and give it your best shot, okay?"

"Oh, no you don't," she said, wrenching the bucket back. She nodded at his sisters and mother as they exited the storage room. "You better finish helping the men or you'll be taken to task for loafing. *I'll* get the fresh water." Her gazed flitted to the blotches of blood on the floor. "Mmm . . . and a mop too, come to think of it."

He nodded and started toward the men before turning halfway with a jag in his brow. His smile slanted off-kilter. "And about the prayer, Mrs. Malloy, feel free to give it your all. But I'm giving you fair warning—if Rose Kelly gets within a hairbreadth of me before or after she strolls down that aisle, I'll be looking to level some blame, you hear?"

He strode away and she found herself shaking her head with a smile, not blaming Rose Kelly one little bit—the man had way too much charm for his own good. She hefted the bucket in her hand and shot a glance over her shoulder while he casually strolled across the room. "Oh, I hear you, Sean O'Connor," she said with a quirk of her lips. "And let's hope the Almighty does too."

"We done yet?" Sean wiped the sweat from his brow with the side of his upper sleeve, the throb from his arm a perfect match for the throb in his head—the one connected to Mr.

Kelly and the layoffs he'd threatened that morning. He scanned the hall where tables had been stored away and recital chairs now filled a room that sparkled and shined with soap and lemon oil, and would give anything if he could just go home and sleep for days. But that wasn't an option, not when he had three employees and an employer depending on him to staunch the red ink. No, he needed to study the books until he came up with a way to keep the store in the black. And not just to eke out a profit like he'd managed to do the last few years of these, the worst of economic times, but enough black ink to carry Mr. Kelly's other store as well. *And* its shiftless manager. Sean's lips settled into a grim line at the thought of Mr. Kelly's nephew, Lester, whose work ethic was nonexistent . . . kind of like Mr. Kelly's compassion during these lean times. The crease in Sean's brow deepened as he jerked at his tie, yanking it loose like he wished he could do to Mr. Kelly's tightfisted greed.

"Well, *you're* done, anyway." Charity folded her arms, lips pursed as she studied her older brother. "Somebody needs to go home and take a nap, I think. You're starting to worry me, Sean, with that permanent scowl." She placed a hand to his forehead, gaze squinted. "You're not getting sick, are you?"

He swatted her hand away with a roll of his eyes and then forced a tight smile. "I'm fine. Just a little crabby because I have to go back into work, that's all."

"A *little*?" Mitch lifted a trash can overflowing with rose limbs, wadded decorations, and miles of paper streamers. One edge of his mouth crooked up. "You're starting to make Collin look like a good sport on the court."

Faith's husband, Collin, stretched with a groan, muscled arms high overhead as he shot his brother-in-law a lopsided grin. "Or you every day of your life."

Chuckling, Charity stood on tiptoe to brush her lips against her husband's. "Come on, Collin, Mitch isn't *that* bad. Every other day at the most."

Mitch's eyelids thinned to a glare. "Hey—shouldn't you be back in the kitchen washing dishes? Your mouth is liable to get you into trouble, little girl."

Clasping her hands behind her back, Charity rolled on her heels with a gleam in her eyes. "Nope, Lizzie, Mother, and Faith have everything under control, I assure you. Besides, I'm waiting for Emma to get back with a clean bucket and rags so I can help her wipe down the walls and chairs." Her gaze shifted to Sean. "*And* get the crab to go home."

Sean ignored her jibe. "I'll leave when the work's done and not before."

"Well, then, you better get busy, O'Connor, because here's the soap and rags." Pete strolled up and clunked several buckets onto the floor, then handed out rags all around. "Stole these from sweet Emma Malloy, who got waylaid in the hall. Figured she'd be awhile."

"What do you mean 'waylaid'?" Sean honed in on Pete with a razor-thin stare.

Pete glanced up, rag in hand. "I don't know, some guy she knows, I guess . . . or at least I hope she knows him the way he's hanging all over her."

"What?" His body went stiff and his headache kicked up a notch. "Are you sure it wasn't some drunk who stumbled up from the speakeasy?"

"I don't know, maybe. Hey, wait . . . where ya going?"

Sean bolted for the door, not even bothering to answer Pete's question. He couldn't if he'd wanted to, not for the thickening of his throat and the blood pounding in his brain. *Waylaid . . . drunk . . . hanging all over her.* Fury pulsed in his veins as he thought of sweet, innocent Emma. *So help me, if that bum lays a hand on her . . .*

He turned the corner and saw them, a single shadow at the end of the hall, two people twined as the drunk swallowed her up in his arms. Something he hadn't tasted in a long time poisoned his tongue like bile, and in several fatal clips of his pulse, he descended on them, ripping the drunk off Emma and slamming him to the wall. "Keep your filthy hands to yourself," he shouted, his temple throbbing with rage. "She's a married woman, you lowlife."

The guy shoved him back, and Sean's anger flared like

bacon grease on a gas stove, dousing all reason. He fisted the man's shirt and rammed him again. Emma screamed when the man's body thudded with a loud crack, buckling against the wood-slatted wall.

"Sean, stop it!" Terror rang in her voice, but he dismissed it, slinging her hand away when she tried to hold him back.

The drunk retaliated with a curse and another angry shove, and like a pin pulled from a grenade, Sean's temper detonated in an iron-fisted punch that doubled the man to his knees.

Emma's scream barely penetrated his brain.

"Get up, you coward," Sean hissed, hands clenched at his sides.

The man peered up, trailing the back of his wrist across the blood on his lip. His eyes burned with anger as he lumbered to his feet. "You're either unhinged, stupid, or both—"

Heat scorched through him, and he was vaguely aware of someone jerking his sleeve. "Sean, stop!" Emma cried again, but he ignored it.

With a harsh grunt, he plowed the man's jaw with his fist. "Nope, just a man who defends women from drunks like you." The instant his knuckles connected with skin, something snapped in his brain, unleashing a rage so dark and sinister that it seemed to own him. The same rage that had compelled him to give up boxing at Pop Clancy's gym at the age of sixteen, despite Pop's contention he was a natural in the ring. "Killer instinct," Pop had called it, and the very words had twisted Sean's gut, forcing him to walk away forever. It was that rage that had gotten him in trouble as a boy. And during the war, the same rage that had almost ruined him as a man. And now, like hard-grain alcohol in the bloodstream of a drunk, it took control again, suffocating everything but the driving need to avenge, the need to defend, the need to kill . . .

"Sean!"

His brother's shout couldn't pierce his stupor, but the impact of Steven's hold did as he gripped Sean from behind and jerked him back. "What the devil are you doing?"

He didn't know. All he knew was for several awful moments,

he'd been in a hell worse than anything he'd experienced during the war, a place where demons took control and rational thinking was as cold and comatose as his body felt right now. Chest heaving, the air burned in his lungs as he stared, his vision clearing to see Emma bent over a man with blood on his face.

"Martin, are you all right?" Her voice was broken, scared, a woman who'd witnessed too much brutality in her own life. "Steven, please—can you help me get him up?"

Sean extended a hand and Emma flinched away, her face as pale as the battered man on the floor. "No, please—Steven can do it." The fear in her eyes sliced through his heart like the rose thorns had slashed through his skin, and when she spoke, her shocked disapproval choked the life from his soul. "You've done more than enough."

"I'm sorry, Emma, but I thought he was bothering you—"

She spun around, heat replacing the coolness in her gaze. "He was *hugging* me, Sean," she rasped, the sound as foreign as the judgment in her eyes. "An innocent thank-you from a friend for getting him a job with one of my suppliers."

"Emma, I'm sorry . . ."

"Don't tell me, tell him."

He swallowed hard, the shame in his throat as thick as the disgust in Martin's eyes. "Martin, I . . . I'm sorry. I didn't realize—"

"No, you sure didn't."

"Please—I'd like to make it up to you—what can I do?" The anger had fled, leaving him steeped in remorse and grateful there was no one else in the hall to witness his shame.

Martin acknowledged Steven when he helped him to his feet, then leveled a hard gaze on Sean. "You can get out of here and leave me alone."

Sean nodded and stepped back to make room for Steven as he assisted Martin to the door.

When his brother brushed past, his eyes were troubled and his voice low. "Are you crazy? What were you thinking?" he whispered, and Sean looked away. But not before he saw the damage he'd done in Emma's eyes. Shock. Disbelief. Apprehension.

Fear.

What *had* he been thinking? That maybe, after all these years, his rage had finally been laid to rest? That his worst memory was dead and gone, nothing more now than his worst nightmare? But he'd been wrong. He stared at the trio as they disappeared down the hall, his body numb and his mind even worse.

His worst nightmare. He sagged against the wall and put a hand to his eyes. And God help him . . . he was wide awake.

2

B-but our b-baby is gone . . ." Marcy's voice warbled into a heartrending sob, and Patrick tucked her close as they sat on the sunporch, staring at an empty backyard where they'd raised six children.

He absently stroked his wife's hair as he thought of his youngest daughter—the "handful" he'd butted heads with since she could walk. Well, she'd be butting heads with Luke now, he thought with a dog-eared smile, blinking to dispel the wetness in his own eyes.

"Why do babies have to grow up and go away?" Marcy lamented, her voice nasal and her tone more than a bit melancholy.

He pressed a kiss to her head. "So we can enjoy that wonderful world of grandparenting, my love, where the expenses and problems of babies belong to our children instead of to us."

"B-but . . . I . . . l-love . . . b-babies," she said in a pitiful wail.

A smile curved his lips. "I know you do, darlin', and no woman born was ever better with babies than you. But each of your daughters *have* married fine young men, so if you must weep, my love, weep for your two sons. They're a far cry from ending up as lucky as their father."

She turned in his arms then, lip quivering and eyes glossy with tears. "Oh, Patrick . . . we are so blessed."

She fell against him in renewed weeping, and he grinned outright. *Blessed.* An appropriate word, indeed, he thought with a gentle squeeze of her waist. God had given him thirty-six years with a woman who still took his breath away, and six children that brought a gleam to his eye. Pulling back, he lifted her chin with the pads of his fingers, and then cupped her face in his hands. "Yes, we are, Mrs. O'Connor, incredibly so." A rush of emotion overtook him, and he leaned in to feather the corner of her lips with his own, his words warm against her mouth. "I love you, Marceline, in every way humanly possible." He fondled her blond hair seasoned by silver, reveling in its silky feel as his fingers wove in. "As a wife and a mother . . ."

Sky-blue eyes blinked back—eyes that still had the power to make his heart race—and gratitude swelled in his chest. He nuzzled the lobe of her ear.

"As a friend and a helpmate . . ." His lips trailed to hers, caressing her mouth with kisses that were slow and deliberate. "And most definitely, Mrs. O'Connor," he whispered against her skin, "as a woman who holds my heart in the palm of her hand." He kissed her full on the mouth, his moan merging with hers.

"Aren't you two a little old for that stuff?"

Marcy jolted in his arms, but Patrick held on tight, eyelids lifting enough to give Gabriella Dawn a withering stare. "What do you want, young lady—we're busy."

She folded her arms and pursed her lips. "Too busy to be a foster parent? I'm guessing the Boston Society for the Care of Girls might want to know about that."

A groan rumbled in Patrick's chest as he released his wife. "This better be good."

"Steven won't let me have a piece of wedding cake."

Patrick eyed her with a dubious stare. "And how many have you had today?"

"Four," Steven said as he strolled into the room. "Not counting the top layer you put on ice that I just caught her trying to sneak."

"*Four* pieces of cake?" Marcy said, mouth gaping in shock.

Gabe blinked. "Of course—it was wonderful, my first wedding cake ever. Nobody bakes like you, Mrs. O'Connor, you know that."

"Flattery will get you nowhere, young lady," Patrick said, his romantic mood now "on ice" as well. "No more cake."

"But what about tomorrow? I can have a piece then, can't I . . . please?" Panic paled her cheeks, making her generous spray of freckles all the more noticeable.

"Nope." Steven plopped in the chair. His blue eyes, a deeper shade than his mother's, twinkled with a smile that was matter-of-fact. "Sorry, Gabe. All that's left is Luke and Katie's top tier in the icebox. Collin, Brady, and I polished off the rest . . . along with you, of course."

A painful groan erupted from Gabe's throat as she slumped against the love seat. "But why can't I have some of the top tier? Luke won't mind—he loves me."

"We all love you, darling," Marcy said in a soothing tone. She tugged Gabe into her lap, giving her a tight squeeze. "But the cake in the icebox is off-limits, do you hear? It's an O'Connor tradition—Luke and Katie will eat it when they get home from the honeymoon, as part of their first meal in their new apartment. Celebration of their new life together as a family—Katie, Luke, and Kitty." A smile flickered on Marcy's lips. "And any other little ones who happen along . . ."

Steven grinned. "That's something I gotta see—Katie Rose having a baby. Heaven help us all. She's practically all thumbs with little Kit as it is. Can't imagine her with a newborn."

"Hush, Steven, Katie Rose will make a perfectly wonderful mother. She's just a little hesitant because it's been Lizzie who's watched Kitty since Luke moved back to Boston. But that will all change when Katie gets pregnant and quits the BCAS to stay home full-time."

"Katie's gonna quit all right, but not to stay home." Gabe leaned back against Marcy's chest, settling in with a cross of skinny legs on Patrick's lap.

Patrick hiked a brow. "Comfy?"

She ignored him and propped her hands behind her neck. "She's gonna be a lawyer."

"Not anymore, dear," Marcy said. "She's a married woman now."

Steven ruffled a hand through his dark hair and put his feet up on the ottoman. "You sure about that, Mother? I think Katie may still have plans for law school."

Marcy frowned. "Well, I know she'd still like to go, but I just assumed it was out of the question since she's married now and likely to have a baby of her own."

"Maybe, but all I know is when I was sorting through the mail a few weeks ago, Katie got a letter from Portia Law School." Steven stifled a yawn.

Patrick sat up, disrupting Gabe's feet. "What? Did she tell you what it was?"

"Nope, and when I asked, she just shoved the letter in her pocket and smiled, telling me that some dreams never die. So naturally I assumed she was still planning to go."

"Oh, she's going," Gabe said. She closed her eyes and adjusted her feet on Patrick's lap.

"Excuse me?" Patrick shifted her legs to a different position. "How do you know that?"

"Because we share a room, remember? Or did. I saw the letter on her dresser, welcoming her to Portia Law School this fall."

"What?" Patrick straightened in unison with Marcy. He jiggled Gabe's leg, forcing her to open her eyes. "Does Luke know?"

"Nope."

Marcy swiveled Gabe's chin. "How do you know?"

Gabe's rosebud mouth eased into a smirk. "Because when Katie found me reading the letter, she snatched it away and made me promise not to tell Luke. She said it was a surprise."

"Oh, it'll be a surprise all right," Steven said with a chuckle.

Marcy shook her head, a hand to her brow. "Oh, Katie Rose . . ."

"Let it go, Marcy," Patrick said. He slipped an arm around his wife's shoulder and drew her close. "It's their problem now, not ours. They'll work it out."

"But Katie has to learn you can't have secrets in a marriage—it can hurt a relationship."

"Yes, darlin', I know," Patrick said with a dry smile. "All too well. But that's a lesson for her husband to impart, not us. And if ever a man was up to the task, it's Luke McGee."

Marcy slumped against Patrick's shoulder. "I suppose . . ."

"So, Gabe . . . up for a Nehi at Robinson's?" Steven rose, muscled arms stretched high.

Wiry limbs scrambled as Gabe shrieked to her feet. "Honest, Steven, you mean it?"

"Sure, squirt. But you gotta promise to keep your mitts off Katie and Luke's cake. Deal?"

"Deal! Let's go."

"Hold on, young lady," Marcy said with a grip of the sash at the back of Gabe's pale pink dress. "Not before you change from your good clothes."

"But I don't wanna cha—"

The words garbled in her throat when Steven squeezed the nape of her neck, forcing a hunch of Gabe's shoulders. "No change, no Nehi. It's that simple, squirt. Why should I buy a soda for a kid who doesn't respect her foster parents?"

"Okay, okay, but I swear you people are in cahoots."

Marcy tugged Gabe back to deposit a quick kiss to her cheek. "We don't swear in this house, Gabriella Dawn, and we are not in cahoots. We are in a family, and that includes you, understood? Now, scoot and have a good time." Gabe tore out of the sunporch with a whoop and a holler, and Marcy called after her. "And you mind Steven, you hear?"

"Oh, she'll mind, or else." Steven said with a smile. He shook his head. "And you always thought Katie was the 'handful,' Pop. No wonder you two look so tired."

"Speaking of tired," Patrick said with a squint, "what was wrong with Sean today? You would have sworn he was blood-related with Mitch, given the grouchy mood he was in. Did something happen at work?"

Steven's smile disappeared. A noisy gust of air escaped his mouth as he perched on the arm of the sofa across the way with a fold of his arms. "I don't know, Pop, but whatever happened put him in the foulest mood I've ever seen." Steven peered up, a crimp in his brow that clearly indicated his concern. "I had to pull him off some poor guy who gave Emma a hug out in the hall. Apparently Sean lost his temper because he thought the guy was a drunk who was manhandling her, so he took several swings at him."

"What?" Marcy bolted up, hand to her throat. "Sean doesn't even have a temper."

"Well, he does now," Steven said. "Started pummeling Emma's friend, Martin, like he used to pummel those kids in the ring at Clancy's, remember, Pop?"

Patrick nodded, an uneasy feeling gnawing in his gut. "Did he hurt him?" he whispered, eyes trained on Steven.

"Naw, scared him mostly, because I'll tell you what, he scared the tar out of me, railing on the poor guy like some madman. I got to him on the second swing, but even so, Martin left with a swollen lip, bruised jaw, and a black eye that will have him thinking twice before he ever hugs another woman again."

"Did you get a chance to talk to Sean? Ask him what happened?" Patrick studied the son whose own bad temper was buried deep, but definitely there. Like all of his children, he supposed . . . except for Sean, that is. His lips went flat. No, Sean had always been the peacemaker, not a fighter, the dutiful son Patrick depended on, obedient, compliant. *A model son.*

"No, when I got back from helping Martin to the door, Sean was gone, back to work I assume since he said he had budgets to trim."

Marcy shifted to stare at Patrick, her eyes spanning wide. "Should we call him at the store? See if he's all right?"

"He's a grown man, Marcy," Patrick said with a pat of her arm. "Whatever is eating on him, he'll talk to us when he's ready."

"And if he doesn't?" Alarm seeped into her tone. "This isn't like him, Patrick."

"I know, darlin', and if this passes without a word, I'll get to the bottom of it when the time is right."

With a heavy sigh, she slowly nodded before sinking back against his chest.

"Well, I'm off." Steven stood to his feet. "You two want anything from Robinson's?"

Patrick eyed his son. "No, thanks, but I'd like to know why you're home tonight in the first place. It's Saturday night, for pity's sake, and the Fourth of July—I expected you to be out with Joe and your buddies, or at the very least helping Sean coach his baseball team tonight."

Steven cuffed the back of his neck, suddenly looking more exhausted at twenty-four years of age than Patrick felt at fifty-three. "Yeah, I know, but Joe and the guys are going to Revere Beach for a dance marathon tonight, and I just wasn't up to it. It's been a pretty grueling week at work, so I figured I'd just turn in early."

"You think you're going to like it—the Prohibition Bureau?" Patrick glanced up, feeling an edge of concern that the son who had burned the candle at both ends during college was now a nose-to-the-grindstone prohibition agent in bed by nine.

"Yeah, I think so. It's great, Joe and I being partners and all, although I don't think he's as enamored with the job as I am. I guess I like the idea of working for the Department of Justice, you know?" His lips quirked. "Like maybe it exonerates me from my questionable past."

Patrick felt a twinge in his chest. "Steven, you've already been long exonerated. Your exemplary behavior since my heart incident two years ago more than proves that. You're a hardworking and honest man, son, and I'm proud of you." He hesitated. "But you need to enjoy life too. Why don't you go with Joe and the others to Revere Beach tonight and have fun. Who knows? Maybe you'll meet a nice young woman."

A wry smile hovered on Steven's lips. "Nice young woman? Hanging out with Joe and the others? I don't think so, Pop. You didn't take a shine to the women I met hanging out with Joe and the gang before. What makes you think you will now?"

"I'm not talking about women like Maggie. Surely there must be some decent young girls you can meet and get to know?"

"Young?" Steven leaned to kiss his mother's cheek. "Yep, plenty of those. But decent?" He slapped Patrick on the shoulder. "Trust me, Pop, they're few and far between. See you later."

A thunderous clomping rattled down the staircase, followed by a slam of the front screen door, indicating Gabe was more than ready. "Steeeeeeeeeven!! Meet you on the porch swing."

"One Nehi only, Steven," Marcy warned. "And don't let her talk you into chocolate—heaven knows she already has enough sugar to keep her up for days."

"Yes, ma'am," Steven said with a wave. "Enjoy the solitude."

The screen door slammed again, and Patrick eased into the love seat with a sigh. He drew Marcy close. "Solitude," he whispered. "Heaven help me, I almost don't recognize it anymore."

He felt Marcy's chuckle against his chest. "Don't get too used to it, Patrick. We have two sons and a very active foster daughter who still call this home." Her sigh seemed one of pure contentment. "Besides, raising someone as young and vital as Gabe will help keep us young."

His fingers caressed the back of her neck before tilting her face to meet his. One brow edged high as he studied her with a slant of a smile. "I can think of better ways to stay young, Marceline," he whispered, allowing his eyes to linger on the fullness of her lips.

She pressed a hand to the scruff of his jaw and smiled while a faint blush colored her cheeks. "And better ways to spend your sweet solitude, I suppose."

"Mmm . . . ," he whispered, taking her lips with his own. His mouth trailed to caress the lobe of her ear. "Sweet solitude, indeed."

Emma unlatched the spiked wrought-iron gate and skittered up the red-cobblestoned steps of Mrs. Tunny's stately, brick row house to see Alli, her adrenaline still coursing from the excitement of the day. She pressed her finger to the ornate buzzer beside the carved wooden door impressively flanked by graceful Greek columns and whispered her usual prayer of gratitude. *Thank you, God, for helping me find such a wonderful home for one of my dearest friends.* And on Beacon Hill, no less.

The door swung wide, and she was met by a tiny slip of a woman with warm brown eyes and snow-white hair perched atop her head in a tight little bun. "Emma—come in, come in! How was the wedding? Oh, I bet Katie was a beautiful bride, wasn't she?" She steered her inside with a strength that belied the tiny, blue-veined wrist clamped to Emma's arm like a vise.

"Oh, you should have seen her, Mrs. Tunny!" Emma breathed. "She was stunning—a sleek satin dress handmade by her mother, all studded with pearls at the neckline. Trust me, Luke couldn't keep his eyes off her." Emma grinned and wagged a sack in her hand, her tone playfully singsong. "And I have wedding cake . . ."

Mrs. Tunny giggled like a schoolgirl as she closed the front door. "Oh, I'm so sorry Alli had to miss it, but the good news is I think the worst of her flu is over. And your timing is perfect because she just finished her dinner." The elderly woman snatched the bag from Emma's hand and shooed her down the hall. "Now, you go on and see her, and I'll serve up the cake. How about a cup of tea or coffee to go with it?"

"Oh, tea would be lovely, Mrs. Tunny, thank you." Emma

hurried to the end of the hall and peeked into the sunroom Mrs. Tunny had converted into a bedroom for Alli. Her lips lifted into a soft curve at the sight of the frail young woman asleep in the bed, barely a bump under the covers at the age of almost twenty. The last remnants of sunlight filtered into the room, casting an iridescent glow on the pale cheeks of one of Emma's most cherished friends who slept propped up against the headboard with a Bible in her lap. Alli Moser was both an employee and a friend whose many trials in life had not diminished her innate joy one fraction of an inch. In fact, Alli's faith seemed to grow daily, providing a constant source of delight and comfort for Emma herself. The young woman's shoulder-length brown curls fanned across the pillow as she rested, an angel with porcelain skin and the innocence of a child.

"Alli . . . are you asleep?"

At Emma's soft whisper, her friend's eyelids flickered open to reveal large brown eyes brimming with a dozy welcome.

"Emma—how beautiful you look! Tell me, was the wedding wonderful?" Scooting over in the bed, Alli patted the mattress in joyous expectation, indicating for Emma to sit.

"More than wonderful. How are you feeling?" Emma asked, concern crinkling her brow.

A sleepy smile inched across Alli's lips. "Much better, I think. No more fever, at least."

"The saints be praised!" Emma sat on the edge and adjusted her friend's pillow. "Oh, Alli, I have never seen a more glowing bride than Katie. I just know they're going to be happy."

Alli shimmied down into the bed with a dreamy sigh, resting her folded arms against the sheet on her chest. "Oh, I agree—they're perfect for each other." She hesitated, her gaze wandering into a faraway stare before she finally blinked up with a shimmer of hope in her eyes. "Emma . . . do you, you know . . . think something like that could ever happen for me?"

Emma smiled as she studied Alli Moser, a young woman

who'd spent her life as an orphan at the Boston Society for the Care of Girls. Polio had left her with braces on her legs while epilepsy had given her an occasional stutter when she got nervous, a habit that made most assume she was slow. And Alli was anything but, possessing a mathematical ability Emma had seldom seen. Since Katie had asked her to give Alli a job two years ago, this gentle girl had not only become invaluable at the store, but a godsend to Mrs. Tunny as well, both as a bookkeeper and a companion. And now, Emma thought with a catch in her throat, a very dear friend.

Her heart softened at the look of hope on the young woman's face. "I'm not sure what God has in store for you, Alli, but I do know one thing—it will be good. I've learned he doesn't skimp with those who have a heart for him. After all, his Word says he honors those who honor him, and that's certainly you, young lady. Besides, Katie and I prayed for a wonderful home for you, and lo and behold, I find out Mrs. Tunny was looking for a companion." Emma hiked a brow while a smile tugged at her lips. "Do you know, Alli Moser, how many young women would love to be in your shoes, leg braces or no, living in the lap of luxury on Beacon Hill? With one of the kindest, godliest women no less, who provides for your every need?"

A soft giggle escaped Alli's lips, and for the hundredth time, Emma thought that she had never seen a more transforming smile. There was nothing particularly beautiful about Alli Moser with her small, puggish nose set in a pale face, but no one noticed that when she smiled. Like shafts of sunlight bursting through an overcast sky, Alli had a smile that lit up the room as well as her face, making you glad to be alive.

"I do," Alli whispered. "I will be forever grateful to both you and Katie. Mrs. Tunny is the mother I never had, and the family I've always wanted." A sigh drifted from her lips.

Emma tugged one of Mrs. Tunny's small boudoir chairs to the side of Alli's bed and sank into its plump pillows, the satisfaction of Alli being taken care of as comfortable as the plush cushions beneath her. "I'm so glad you're feeling better," Emma said with a gentle stroke to her cheek.

"After my fever broke, I've been feeling much better. I plan to be at work on Monday."

"Good." Emma squeezed her hand. "Think you're up to some wedding cake?"

The twinkle in Alli's eyes made Emma laugh. "Oooo . . . I love wedding cake!" She hunkered down even farther in the bed and folded her hands in expectation. "Tell me all about the wedding."

Emma kicked off her shoes and happily chatted about the day—from flower girl Gabe blowing bubbles with Dubble Bubble while walking the aisle, to Charity being buzzed by a bee during the vows. Much to Alli's delight, Emma divulged every glorious detail of both the church ceremony at St. Stephen's and the reception at Kearney's Café, her smile dimming somewhat at the memory of Sean's altercation with Martin. Halfway through, Mrs. Tunny brought in cake on china plates and her silver tea service, capping off the telling of a near-perfect day.

When the grandfather clock in the parlor chimed six, Emma rose with a stretch. "Well, I have plenty of paperwork waiting at home, so I better scoot. See you on Monday, I hope?"

"I'll be there." Alli sat straight up in the bed, a hand to Emma's arm. "Wait—I know how you won the bouquet by accident, but you forgot to tell me who caught the garter?"

Emma blinked, the thought of Sean's rage coming to mind. Her smile faltered. "Uh, Sean did—also by accident. You see, Luke rather tricked him by calling his name and tossing the garter before Sean realized what it was. But Sean insists he'll never marry." Emma quickly sniffed Katie's bouquet to ward off a shiver, closing her eyes at the memory of Sean's violent assault. A lump bobbed in her throat. *And perhaps for the better.*

"Emma?" Alli hesitated for a moment and then tilted her head. "Do you . . . do you ever get sad?" Her throat shifted as if she were embarrassed to even pose such a question. "You know . . . regret that your marriage wasn't like what Katie and Luke will have?"

Emma blinked as heat swarmed her cheeks. *Regret*. Yes, something she lived with every day of her life. But not over the loss of her marriage.

She looked away and caught her reflection in Alli's dressing-table mirror, wincing as always at the woman whose beauty had been stolen by grease as blistering as the man who'd thrown it. Red welts on the left side of her heart-shaped face had long since faded, but they'd left pale scars that slightly disfigured one side of her lip and had stolen most of her left brow. Insistent that her friend's scars were no longer noticeable, Charity often teased that Emma was a "trendsetter" with one bare brow in an era when eyebrows were now shaved and drawn on. In typical Charity mode, she had gently but firmly revamped Emma's entire look—with a Joan Crawford haircut, ivory makeup that hid what was left of her scars, and eyelids and penciled brows dressed with petroleum jelly for that stylish, shiny look.

Rory had thought her beautiful once, as did the men who often sought her attention before Rory had spoiled that beauty, and yet for all the bold stares and brazen compliments, Emma had never once believed it. Despite men fawning over her from an early age on, her father had made sure that such compliments never changed the low opinion she had of herself, insisting that "any whore can turn a man's head."

Emotion shifted in Emma's throat as she stared at her image in the mirror, noting the pain in green-gray eyes that Rory had once claimed a man could get lost in. Eyes that had once held so much promise, now filled with tragedy due to a man's admiring gaze. Charity insisted she was "beautiful," but mirrors didn't lie. Rory had called her "a monster" in one of his drunken fits, and no matter how her scars had faded over the years or how Charity tried to encourage her, Emma could only see that he was right. She absently fingered the gold band on her left hand, grateful for the haven it offered from further rejection. It protected her from the humiliation of ever having to catch a man's eye.

The thought flushed her cheeks with painful color. As if she could! *What man would ever find me beautiful now?* The only beauty she possessed was her love for God, and Emma knew that the human eye was often blind to such beauty. She inhaled deeply, infusing her lungs with the peace of acceptance. Fortunately for her, it was more than enough.

She cleared her throat and looked up, contemplating Alli's question. *Do I ever get sad?* She was suddenly aware that her hands were clammy as she smoothed the skirt of her dress. "No, Alli, not anymore. Oh, I did in the beginning, of course, because I couldn't understand how something that felt so right could turn out so wrong. But when God brought Charity and me from Dublin to Boston eleven years ago, well, I suddenly understood. I could have never had this in Ireland—dear friends who accept me for who I am, a wonderful store to manage, and a family like the O'Connors who love and support me. And most importantly, a faith in God that fulfills me more than any man ever could." Serenity settled on her like a sigh. "Regret? No, Alli. I am a woman blessed by God, and contentment is my constant companion." She leaned to give Alli a hug. "See you on Monday."

"Emma . . ." With a gentle stay of her hand, Alli's palm touched hers. "My heart rejoices to hear that, truly, but I hope you understand that I love you, and because of that, I can't help but feel regret. Because if ever a woman was, Emma Malloy, you were meant to be loved."

Against her will, hot tears sprang to her eyes, and she swallowed hard, managing a shaky smile. She squeezed Alli's hand and then released it, exhaling a cleansing breath that, for the moment, banished all regret. "And so I am, my dear friend, so I am. By God and by you."

"Steeeeeee-rike!" The umpire indicated an out with a hard punch of his fist.

Groans filled the muggy night air as soon as Bobby Dalton struck out, awarding the opposing St. Mary's team their first victory all summer. Across the way, St. Mary's shouts of joy rose while the ten-year-old's shoulders slumped. He dropped the bat and trudged to the bench with defeat in his eyes, his confidence appearing to descend as quickly as the fading rays of sunlight edging toward dusk.

Empathy squeezed in Sean's chest as he stared at Bobby, the only kid on the team who didn't have a dad. His mother was supposedly a widow new to the neighborhood, or so Father Mac had said when he'd given Sean the signup roster. Ignoring the cheers and jeers, Sean met him midway and squatted. He patted the boy's arm in a manner meant to assure him it was okay. "Hey, Bobby, you played a great game, but nobody wins 'em all, buddy. You had a lot of power in that swing, but sometimes we don't always connect." Sean's lip crooked up. "Especially when life—or a pitcher—throws us a curve." He slapped Bobby's shoulder, as if man-to-man. "Don't worry, bud—we'll get 'em next time."

Bobby nodded with a sigh and lumbered toward the bench. Sean's heart buckled. "Bobby . . ."

The boy turned, a hangdog expression on his face while Sean approached.

"This is between you and me, bud," Sean murmured, squatting to slip his Snickers candy bar into the boy's pocket. "You played a good game."

A grin curled on the boy's lips. "Gee, thanks, Coach." He turned and jogged to the bench where teammates rallied around with sympathetic slaps on the back.

Drawing in a deep breath, Sean rose to his feet and exhaled, remembering all the times his father had been there for him, dusting him off when he'd struck out or been clobbered by a ball. He may not have kids of his own—nor did he ever intend to—but there was no denying he enjoyed being part of these boys' lives here and now, even if it was only as a volunteer coach. Especially someone as needy as Bobby.

Sean huffed out another weary sigh. And *especially* tonight, when he needed to get his mind off one of the worst days he'd had in a long, long while. First with Mr. Kelly's threat of layoffs that morning and then later when he'd lost his temper and bloodied some poor unfortunate slob at Kearney's Café. A groan trapped in his throat. At his own sister's wedding no less, and in front of one of the people he respected most in the world—Emma Malloy. The memory soured both his stomach and the smile on his face. Their easy and comfortable friendship had been damaged today, he'd seen it in her eyes, and for some reason he couldn't ascertain, the realization throbbed inside like an open wound. A wound that had bled when he'd returned to the store and then followed him all the way to the game tonight.

But as always, boys' laughter and parents' cheers had lifted his mood considerably, and once again, he was grateful for his love of sports. It'd been his savior over the years, a normal and acceptable outlet for all the roiling emotions he kept hidden beneath the surface. And tonight's game, win or lose, had taken his mind off the awful look on Emma's face. All he needed now was to vent his frustration in a late-night basketball game with Pete and the guys, and he'd be back to normal.

Almost.

"Hey, O'Connor, you still want an early warm-up before the Monday night game?" Pete Murphy looked up from his clipboard, brown eyes squinted in question.

Sean retrieved the discarded bat and ambled over to the bench, giving his assistant coach and best friend a one-sided smile. "It's St. Joe's, Murph, what do you think?"

"Hey, Coach, we'll cream 'em, just like last time," one of the boys hollered, and the others hooted in agreement while they poked and wrestled each other on the bench.

Sean grinned and slipped several bats and balls into the equipment bag, then walked over to shake the other coach's hand. When he returned, the wrestling match had moved to the dirt in a free-for-all of grimy legs, arms, and dust. Sean put his fingers to his teeth and let loose with an ear-splitting whistle. All motion froze as sweaty faces caked with dirt stared back, along with a handful of parents who stood chatting by the wooden bleachers. Several toddlers and mothers sitting on blankets glanced up with curiosity as Sean flashed a smile. "Okay, guys, listen up—you played a stellar game out there today, despite the loss, so you should be proud of yourselves. But if we're going to protect our lead in the parish league, we'll have to step it up a notch because St. Joe is breathing down our neck." He cocked a hip, arms loose and thumbs latched in the pockets of dusty gray trousers. "The Monday night game's at six-thirty, but I want you here no later than five-thirty so we can get in a little extra practice and warm-up, okay?"

"You got it, Coach. We'll make 'em wish they'd never been born," Cliff Mullen said.

"Yeah, we'll annihilate them," Bobby Dalton agreed.

Sean stifled a smile with a fold of his arms. "Winning isn't everything, guys, but playing well is. Which means you go to bed early Sunday night and show up here on time on Monday, got it? See you then." He ruffled the sweaty heads of several of his boys while they shuffled off, muttering their goodbyes.

Pete tossed the clipboard to Sean with a hike of a thick, black brow. "Winning isn't everything?" he repeated slowly, sarcasm coating every word. His lips kinked to the right as he hefted the burlap bag of equipment over a brawny shoulder. "Either you're in dire need of a confessional right now, O'Connor, or you're not the guy who goes for the throat every time he trounces me in a game of basketball."

A slow grin creased Sean's lips as he swiped a hand through his own disheveled hair. "Winning in sports isn't everything, Murph, which should be a relief to you since you seldom do." He tucked the clipboard under his arm and fell into stride beside Pete as the two headed for the street. "Trust me, I know. Seems I can whip almost anybody with a ball in my hand, but give me a chessboard, and suddenly I look like you on the court." He slapped his friend on the back. "Downright pathetic."

"Mr. O'Connor?"

Sean spun on his heel, clipboard dangling in his hand.

A pretty woman stood before him with a tentative smile, slender hands resting on the shoulders of none other than Bobby Dalton.

"Hi, Coach, this is my mother—she wanted to meet both you and Mr. Murphy."

Sean extended a hand with a warm smile. "It's good to meet you, Mrs. Dalton," he said, his gaze shifting from her to Bobby and back. "Both Pete and I think Bobby's a real bright spot on the team. The other guys love him, and he's got a pretty mean swing with the bat."

"Most of the time," Bobby muttered with a lopsided grin.

"Yeah, most of the time." Sean tousled Bobby's dark hair.

"It's good to meet you too, Mr. O'Connor," Mrs. Dalton said. "Bobby can't seem to talk about anything else but how much fun he's having and what a great team you have. He told me you're—" A faint blush stole into her cheeks as she shot a quick glance at Pete. "Well, both of you, actually—are wonderful coaches."

"Number one in the parish league," Pete said with a proud roll of his heels. He offered his hand, and Mrs. Dalton shook it. "I'm Sean's assistant, Pete Murphy."

"Nice to meet you too, Mr. Murphy. I can assure you, Bobby speaks highly of both of you." Her eyes returned to Sean, appreciation glinting in their depths. "Especially you, Mr. O'Connor, because of all the extra help you've given him with his batting. His father passed away two years ago, you see, but he loved working with Bobby on his swing, so you've definitely helped to fill that void."

Heat lined the collar of Sean's rolled-up shirt at the compliment, but he just smiled, fingering the clipboard in his hand. "Well, he's a natural, Mrs. Dalton, and a great kid. You've done a wonderful job."

"Thank you, Mr. O'Connor," she said with a shy smile.

"Call me Sean, please."

She nodded and patted her son on the shoulders, her smile suddenly warmer than the summer night. "Sean," she said softly, as if tasting the sound of his name on her tongue.

His stomach tightened at the sudden tilt of her head and the faint blush in her cheeks.

"Yes, and call me Barbara, please . . . *Sean*. Well, we've kept you far too long, I think. But we'll see you on Monday at five-thirty sharp. Goodbye."

"See ya, Coach," Bobby said as she steered him away, both mother and son shooting friendly smiles over their shoulders.

Pete let loose with a low chuckle.

"What?" Sean asked, turning away with a thin press of his lips. He slapped the clipboard under his arm and kept walking, irritated at the insinuation in Pete's tone.

"*What?*" Pete mimicked. He laughed outright, matching Sean's long-legged stride down a sidewalk emblazoned with chalk hopscotch squares. "Are you blind? Anybody can see that the widow's interested." He shifted the bag on his shoulder and grinned. "You may ride roughshod over me in sports, O'Connor, but when it comes to steering clear of potential matrimony, you can't seem to win to save your soul."

A rare scowl invaded Sean's face. He sidestepped a kid on a bike and gave Murph a sideways glance. "What are ya talking about? The woman was interested in meeting the guys who coach her son, nothing more."

"Yeah, yeah, I'll go along with that, but something tells me you have another sticky situation looming on your horizon, my boy. Just like with Howie Devlin's older sister and then Ricky Klaus's unmarried aunt and then Fred Langston's maiden cousin, twice removed—all women who sniffed you out till you ignored them to death—"

Sean halted and turned. He folded his arms with a tight smile. "So, what's your point?"

Pete grinned and dropped the bag to the sidewalk with a grunt. "My point is, you may say you're a confirmed bachelor, but nothing's more irresistible to unmarried females than a nice single guy who plays hard to get."

A noisy exhale puffed from Sean's lips and he shook his head, smiling despite himself. "You're really something, you know that, Pete? I am not playing hard to get—I *am* hard to get, period. I'm a nice guy who has no intention whatsoever of getting involved with a woman." He flicked a clod of dirt off Pete's shoulder. "Because unlike you and the guys, my friend, I'm strong enough to resist."

"Nope. 'Strong' is what me, Harv, and Adam are—guys who have no intention of tying the knot while we revel in the wealth of women who cross our paths. That takes true dedication to avoid being snared. You? You're nothing but a chicken who avoids women like the plague, and all because you're scared spitless one of 'em's gonna rein you in." Pete paused to hike the bag over his shoulder, halting Sean with a cocky grin and a hand to his arm. "Now you tell me—who's 'stronger' and has more guts?" He jiggled his brows. "Not to mention fun?"

Sean started walking again, and Pete strode alongside. "Face it, Sean, you're a good-looking guy, but what a waste. If me and the guys had as many gals after us as you do, we'd be in bachelor heaven. But you—you're so busy avoiding 'em, you miss out on the best part of being single—the affections of women."

Sean shoved his hands in his pockets and smiled, stomach rumbling at the smell of grilled burgers at the pub they just passed. "I enjoy my life just fine, Murph."

Pete gave him a sideways glance. "Yeah? When's the last time you really kissed a gal?"

Heat steamed his cheeks as he picked up the pace. "What's that got to do with anything?"

"Plenty. I tell ya, you're missing out, O'Connor, and I for one think you're crazy. Why don't you just be a man about it and get out there and mingle a little?" He eyed him with a taunting grin. "Who knows? It might help avoid another nasty mood like this afternoon. Or are you afraid some sweet little thing is gonna pitch a fast one that'll leave you tied to home plate?"

Challenge rose up in Sean as they passed Tucker's Bakery, as palpable as the smell of fresh bread that watered his mouth. "A woman hasn't been born who can tie me to home plate, Murph."

Pete laughed and slapped him on the back, then shifted the bag to his other shoulder with another grunt. "Oh, she's been born, my friend, and you can bet on that." He cocked his head. "If you're brave enough to get in the game, that is." He hesitated, his grin raising the bar. "Unless you're afraid of losing? You know, a knuckle ball that throws you a curve? I'll bet you wouldn't even see it coming."

A wide grin slid across Sean's face as he wrested the bag from Pete's shoulder and tossed it over his own. "Oh, I'd see it coming, all right, and I'll knock it out of the park, make no mistake. And you and the boys can set your watches by that."

Pete laughed. "Maybe." He slapped Sean on the shoulder as they parted ways at the corner. "If some little gal doesn't fix your clock first. Either way," he said with a grin that was more of a dare, "gotta feeling that one of these days soon, you're gonna run out of time."

Home, sweet home. Emma turned the key in the lock and eased her apartment door open, quite certain she had never been this tired. Between a grueling week at work, evenings helping Marcy and her girls prepare for the wedding, and a wonderfully full but exhausting day, Emma was spent. She closed the door and flipped the bolt, slipping her pink Mary Jane pumps off her feet with one hand while she clutched Katie's bouquet with the other. The shoes dropped against the claw foot of her Victorian desk with a thump, and Emma felt a niggle of guilt. They splayed haphazardly across the polished mahogany floor, the only sign of disarray in her otherwise meticulous apartment.

Too tired to care, she breathed in the calming scent of Katie's roses and flipped the switch on her electric fan before perching on the edge of her curved mahogany sofa to shed her silk stockings. Blessed relief feathered her face as she put her feet up and sank into the plush velvet upholstery, its rich color the exact shade of claret. She tucked a pretty paisley pillow behind her head and burrowed in to stretch her aching limbs, soaking in the vibrancy of her colorful parlor. Awash in sunlight that only deepened its vivid hues, it almost seemed alive with energy, helping to chase her fatigue away.

Contentment seeped into her bones as she scanned the room for her kitties. A backward peek confirmed their favorite nooks in the tall, cherrywood bookcase were empty, leaving a conspicuous hole among shelves brimming with rich, leather-bound books. Her gaze roamed past twin striped wingback chairs that flanked two towering windows, each affording a pretty view of Mrs. Peep's front yard. White sheers fluttered against a massive fern atop a walnut piecrust table, provid-ing the perfect jungle cover for a nine-year-old tabby who fancied himself a tiger stalking moths on the screen. But empty marble sills framed by burgundy swag curtains meant that Lancelot and Guinevere were most likely still napping on Emma's bed, as tired as she.

Her gaze lighted on a messy clump of blue yarn as it trailed out of her wicker sewing basket to squiggle its way across her floral-patterned rug. She shook her head and lay back while her lips tipped in a smile, quite certain that Lancelot was the culprit. The tail of it lay bunched beneath an oak easel with a half-finished canvas of a fat bluebird squinting down at her as if he'd had a bad day, his squat neck hunched into his stout chest of brilliant azure feathers. Her smile broadened at the memory of the plump, little bird who'd lighted on her window weeks past, making her giggle with his almost sour demeanor. She had promptly christened him "Grumpy Bluebird," capturing him with her beloved oil paints to hang on the wall. She stared back at him now with a grin, not-ing the stark contrast between the vibrant blues, greens, and yellows of the painting and Mr. Grump's gray mood. She tilted her head and grinned. "Cheer up, little fluff," she whispered. "I'll be painting 'Happy Bluebird' soon to keep you company."

With a smile still warm on her lips, she closed her eyes and buried her nose in Katie's bouquet once again, drinking in the heady scent along with the memory of a wonderful day. Outside her window, she could hear the laughter of children as it floated in on the summer breeze, merging with the muted sound of jazz from Mr. Harvey's radio one story above. Her thoughts flitted to the O'Connors, and another gentle smile curved on her mouth. "Thank you for this family, Lord," she whispered. And not for the first time.

From the moment she and Charity had first lighted from that ship in Boston Harbor eleven years ago, the O'Connors had welcomed her into their family as if their very blood traveled her veins. Never in all of her fifteen years with her own estranged family had she felt such a bond, such acceptance . . . such love. Her mood turned bittersweet at the thought of Da and Mum, turning her out in the streets for the sin of marrying a Protestant. She had betrayed them for a "worthless sot," a sacrilege in a family where Catholic clergy ran strong. And so she'd been sacrificed on the altar of piety, a sinner destined to "burn in hell."

A shiver traveled her body that had nothing to do with the gust of the fan. *Burn in hell*, she thought to herself, and tears pricked her eyes. A painful prophecy brought to pass by a man who had incinerated her every hope, scalding her first with his words and then with his actions, leaving her life in ashes.

Wherefore I abhor myself, and repent in dust and ashes.

Water welled beneath her eyelids and she opened them, her gaze fixed on the gold band of her left hand as it rested against the bouquet on her chest. Job's lament had been her own at one time, but in the gift of a precious friendship with Charity, God had changed her grief to joy, her repentance to rejoicing.

To give unto them beauty for ashes, the oil of joy for mourning, the garment of praise for the spirit of heaviness . . .

She inhaled deeply, reveling in the sanctuary of her cozy apartment, a respite untainted by the horrors of her past. Rory's ring may still mar her finger, but in the sacred sanctuary of her life here in Boston, she was free—from the rejection that branded her soul as surely as Rory had branded her face. Free to be the woman that God intended her to be, unencumbered by a past . . . *or* the wishes of a husband.

Setting the bouquet aside, she stared at the gold band, her smile melancholy as she grazed it with her fingers. Charity saw it as a shackle of doom, condemning her to a life alone, and Emma had to admit, there were times the truth of that statement pierced her very soul. Not during the light of day, of course, when career obligations and commitments to friends kept the loneliness at bay, but sometimes in the dark of night, when sleep evaded and longings stirred. Longings buried so deep, she sometimes forgot they were even there. Simple human desires—to be held . . . to be touched . . . to be loved for the woman she used to be.

And still secretly was.

Her eyelids weighted closed as she idly caressed the ring on her finger, refusing to allow impossible stirrings to steer her off course. No, for her, the love of a man had proven fatal to her adolescent dreams of romance, indeed, shackling her to a vow she could never escape. And yet, those same shackles set her free as well . . . to become all that God had called her to be. Because to her, this ring was a symbol of hope as well, guaranteeing a life of faith as pure and precious as the gold on her hand. She did God's bidding now, not Rory's, and with the infinite depth of the Father's love—and that of friends and family he'd supplied—she would *never* be alone again.

Something soft tickled her arm and she smiled at Lancelot, apparently up from his nap and ready for attention. Emma feathered a hand across the tabby's arched back, eliciting a soft hum that vibrated against her palm. "Well, hello, sleepyhead. Did you enjoy your day?"

The red tabby purred and stretched in response, his orange stripes the color of marmalade on fresh cream. With a bored flick of his tail, he sashayed over to his "throne" to hold court on his favorite burgundy and cream striped wing chair, draping its arm like a limp doily. Slits of amber eyes stared back, and Emma grinned outright, nodding at the tangles of yarn.

"I suppose you're exhausted from all this redecorating. What, no moths to stalk today?"

A knock sounded at the door as Lancelot closed his eyes, obviously choosing to ignore the playful tease in her tone.

"Coming," Emma called and bounded up with a noisy sigh.

She opened the door to her eighteen-year-old neighbor from upstairs, dressed in a brand-new outfit, judging from the grin on her powdered face.

"Casey—you look beautiful!" Emma said with a quick sweep of the young woman's stylish polka-dot dress. "Where are you going?"

Casey whirled around, her petite size and little-girl action making her look all of thirteen despite voluptuous curves. "Oh, Emma—I'm going to a dance marathon at Revere Beach with the most wonderful man!" She spun one more time to give Emma the full effect of her pleated blue-and-white dress, snug at her hips in the style of the day before flaring just below her knees. Propping her hands to her slim waist, she gave Emma a generous smile, lips sporting the popular "Crawford smear" with rose lipstick rounded above to exaggerate their fullness. Meticulously drawn brows lifted in question. "So, what do you think? Will this new dress catch his eye?"

Emma reached to straighten the matching polka-dot sailor bow that complemented the sleeveless white bodice and leaned back with a chew of her lip. "Mmm . . . I'd say his eyes will be on you most of the night, young lady, instead of the marathon." Her lips squirmed in jest. "Are you sure that's wise?"

A gleam lit in the young woman's blue-gray eyes as she wiggled her brows. She twirled a blond strand of hair from her Marlene Dietrich hairstyle, modeled after her latest *Photoplay* magazine, no doubt. "Maybe not wise, but certainly fun."

"Casey Miranda Herringshaw!" Emma folded her arms in the pretense of shocked disapproval, doing her best to bite back a smile. "What would your mother say?"

Casey laughed and surprised her with a voracious hug. "She'd say, 'If Emma approves, I approve.'" She pulled back to give Emma an impish smile. "You know you're the only reason she lets me stay in Boston by myself, don't you? Because you keep an eye on her little girl?"

Emma studied her through affectionate eyes, well aware that Susan, her best friend from the store, would have never gone home to Kansas to care for her sick mother if her daughter were alone in the big city. So Emma had not only found Casey an apartment in her building, but an excellent job with one of her suppliers as well, giving Susan her word that she would look after her daughter. A rush of love welled in Emma's chest as she cupped a gentle hand to Casey's innocent face. "Yes, and to keep an eye on the young men who come courting."

Casey grinned and squeezed herself in a hug. "Oh, Emma, he's such a dream! Tall, dark, and handsome and the perfect gentleman."

"Is he now?" Emma said with a curious tilt of her head. She motioned a hand toward her sofa. "Care to come in and tell me all about it?"

"I wish I could, but I told him I would meet him outside the Ocean Pier Ballroom at eight, so I have to run." She glanced at her watch, then looked up at Emma with a nervous tug of her lip. "Do you think I can borrow that darling little cloche I saw you wearing the other day, you know, the blue one?"

"Mmm . . . I suppose. In exchange for some information, that is." Smiling, Emma closed the door with a lift of her brow. "Like his name, for instance?"

Casey made a beeline for Emma's bedroom, shooting a smile over her shoulder. "His name is Johnny McIntire, and he's as Irish as St. Patrick himself, with the most wonderful brogue. His family moved here from Killarney, and now he's one of the top salesmen at work."

A frown puckered the bridge of Emma's nose as she followed Casey down the hall. "A top salesman? Goodness, how old is he?"

"Got it," Casey said with a snatch of a blue cloche off the shelf in Emma's closet. She ruffled a hand across Guinevere's silky, white body as she snoozed on the bed quilt amidst a splash of bright flowers, then hurried over to the mirror to put it on, finally turning with a squeal. "Oh, Emma, it's perfect! I can always count on you to have the latest styles from Dennehy's. How do I look?"

"Beautiful, as always." Emma's eyes narrowed the slightest bit. "How old, Casey?"

Casey's smile faltered. "He's really nice, I promise, and he goes to church . . ."

Moving to where Casey stood picking her nails, Emma adjusted the cloche just an inch to the right. Her voice softened to a whisper. "How old?"

A blush tinted the young girl's cheeks as she peeked up through heavy lashes. "Gosh, Emma, I don't know. Thirty-two, thirty-three, maybe?"

Emma dropped her head with a groan, pressing a shaky hand to her eyes. *Sweet mother of Job, Susan will have my head!* She shrugged off the fatigue weighting her shoulders and looked up with a firm lift of her jaw. "Casey Herringshaw—what were you thinking? You're barely eighteen and you agreed to go out with a man older than me? Your mother would have a conniption, young lady, and you know it."

Casey grasped Emma's hands in her own. The plea in her tone tugged at Emma's heart. "Emma, please, he's waiting for me now, and I really, *really* like him. Can't we give him a chance? *Please?*"

Casey's eyes disarmed her, glowing with hope. Emma drew in a heavy dose of air and released it again. "All right, young lady, you win—*this time*. But for the record, a real gentleman picks a lady up for a date, so I want to meet him next time—*if* there is a next time. Is that clear?"

With another squeal, Casey launched herself into Emma's arms. "Oh, Emma, you're the best! I promise I'll tell you all about it on our way to church tomorrow, all right?"

A reluctant smile tugged at the corners of Emma's mouth. "See that you do. What time are you going to be home?"

"No later than midnight, as always." Casey flew down the hall and opened the door. She suddenly whirled around, eyes wide. "Wait, I almost forgot—how was the wedding?"

"Wonderful. I'll fill you in tomorrow. Now scoot."

Casey shot her a crooked smile, tempered with sympathy. "You look tired, Emma. Get some rest, okay? And don't wait up." She blew her a kiss and hurried out.

Emma poked her head out the door. "I *will* wait up, young lady, make no mistake," she called after her, hand to her mouth, "so you best be home on time, you hear?"

Casey waved at the door, and Emma shook her head, suddenly wide awake at the prospect of Susan's daughter going to Revere Beach to meet an older man. An older, *more experienced* man. Rubbing her eyes, she trudged to the sofa and plopped down, eyeing Lancelot with more than a little jealousy as he snoozed on the arm of the chair. Her lips twisted. *Well, at least someone's getting some sleep.*

"Get some rest," Casey had said, conjuring up thoughts of Emma's promise to Susan. She pulled her Bible off the coffee table and settled into the couch, realizing for the first time what it must feel like to be a mother. She groaned and flipped a page, sympathy rising for mothers compelled to safeguard their children.

"Sleep," she said with a quirk of her lips. "As if that's even an option."

❦

God, help me . . . this is harder than I thought. Katie stared in the mirror and swallowed the lump in her throat, wondering if other brides were this nervous on their honeymoons. Anxious blue eyes stared back while the girl in the mirror gnawed on her lip, surveying the filmy negligee she wore—the one Charity had given her at her bridal shower. It had burned her cheeks then, and continued to burn her cheeks now, and she was pretty certain the heat wouldn't end there once her husband got a glimpse.

Husband. Her lips tilted into a wobbly smile. *Mrs. Luke McGee.* Who would have thought she would have fallen in love with a pest from her past, a man she'd butted heads with since the age of ten? But love him she did, and just the thought of Luke McGee's long, muscled body stretched out on the bed in the next room—*waiting for her*—promptly produced another rush of heat to her cheeks that quickly traveled her body.

With shaky fingers, she picked up her hairbrush and jerked it through her blond Dutch boy bob with a shudder, quite certain the task before her would not be an easy one. *Task? To make love with Luke McGee?* A sweet shiver slithered down her spine like warm butter. Hardly. Never had she met a man who wreaked havoc with her internal thermostat more than her new husband, reducing her to mere mush at the touch of his lips. Oh no, the real "task" would come in postponing the house full of children he longed for with every fiber of his being. She gulped. At least long enough for her to realize her dream of finishing law school—a dream Luke had no idea she still had.

"Katie? You've been in there awhile . . . are you okay?"

No, she thought, sucking in a deep breath, *I'm not.* "Yes, Luke, of course. Just a minute or two more, and I'll be right out."

She continued brushing her hair with a heavy sigh. Although that wasn't her biggest problem at the moment. She clenched the hairbrush in hand, wishing she had been brave enough to tell Luke about her plan to quit the BCAS for law school this fall. But could she help it if he'd taken his sweet time proposing in the first place? And the last thing she'd wanted was to rock the boat before she got him to say "I do." No, with somebody as stubborn and strong-willed as Luke McGee, Katie felt sure it was better to divulge her plan *after* the honeymoon, not before. She sighed. After all, it was better to batten the hatches on stormy seas than not set sail at all. Wasn't it?

"Katie . . . are you sure you're all right?" Luke's voice was edged with concern.

"Yes, I promise. Just thirty seconds more." She tossed the brush on the vanity and dabbed a hint of perfume just above the lacy neckline of her lavender negligee, just as Charity had instructed. With a deep ingest of air, she pressed a quivering hand to her abdomen and exhaled slowly. *Thank God we're safe through the honeymoon*, she thought with relief, but then closed her eyes to whisper a prayer nonetheless.

"Lord, thank you for my husband—I love him so much. And I truly want to give him the family he deserves, honestly I do. But if it's okay with you, I'd like to delay it just a bit . . . let's say . . . three years? Just till I can fulfill my dream to become a lawyer and work for women's rights somewhere down the road? I know several women lawyers who are mothers too, Lord, so I know it can be done. Please help Luke to understand how important this is to me and *please* help him not to be angry when I finally tell him." She swallowed hard and made a quick sign of the cross. "*After* the honeymoon. Amen."

Releasing a cleansing breath, she opened her eyes, suddenly feeling considerably calmer. Luke loved her and would understand, she was sure of it. After all, hadn't he agreed to let her continue working at the BCAS three days a week while Lizzie watched Kit? And going to law school five days a week wasn't much more than that, she reasoned. All it would take was for Luke to agree to refrain from lovemaking at inopportune times. Was that so difficult?

And if he refuses? Katie blinked in the mirror as her jaw pressed tight. Well, then, she'd just have to be the strong one, the one with the willpower. When the time wasn't right, she would just tell Luke McGee no, case closed. After all, how hard could it be?

With her mind firmly made up, she opened the bathroom door.

A gasp quivered from her lips when Luke met her with a possessive grip and a dangerous gleam in his eyes. "Sweet saints, Katie, if you're trying to build anticipation, you win, because I'm about ready to crawl out of my skin."

He cupped her face in his hands and pressed her to the wall, taking her mouth with such gentle force that a moan escaped her lips. When he pulled away, the blood in her cheeks warmed at the sight of his bare, muscled chest tapering into low-slung pajama bottoms. The heady scent of Bay Rum from his clean-shaven jaw merged with the smell of soap from blond hair still wet from his shower. She looked up and gulped, completely disarmed by the glow of love in his eyes.

"Heaven help me, Katie, you're beautiful," he whispered, his gaze scanning her negligee as if he wanted to swallow her whole.

The blue eyes recaptured hers once again, and her heart tripped at the desire she saw in his face. His generous mouth tipped up in a smoldering tease as he leaned in to nuzzle her neck. "Pinch me, Katie Rose, because I can hardly believe I get to make love to you for the rest of my life."

In a sudden sweep of his arms, he cradled her to his chest and carried her to their bed with the utmost care, setting her down on the smooth, cool sheets as if she were the most fragile of gifts. He eased in beside her and drew her close, his voice husky with emotion as he stared into her eyes. "I love you, Katie," he said, fingers sifting into her hair while his palms caressed her face. "So much that sometimes I ache inside." He kissed her then, slow and languid as he laid her back on the bed, the chaotic rhythm of her breathing as ragged as his.

Hungry hands grazed warm against the smooth silk of her gown, and a breathless sigh shuddered from her lips. "I love you too," she whispered, skin tingling while his mouth fondled hers slow and easy before wandering to the hollow of her throat.

Her body quivered as gentle palms slowly slipped the straps of her gown from her shoulders, his words hoarse and hot against her skin. "And you have my word, Sass—I will do everything in my power to make you the happiest woman alive." She caught her breath when his lips trailed down, sending shudders of warmth rippling through her body.

The happiest woman alive. Her eyelids fluttered closed. Sweet angels in heaven—there was no doubt about that.

3

For the love of Job, can it get any worse? Sean hurled his pencil in an uncommon display of temper, glaring as it skittered across a desk littered with invoices for inventory that was, apparently, doing nothing but gathering dust on the shelves. His jaw ached from grinding his teeth, an unconscious habit that surfaced only when he balanced books at the end of each month. At least, lately. He kneaded the knot of tension at the ridge of his brow with the pad of his hand, knowing full well that Mr. Kelly would be looking for any reason whatsoever to save the bottom line. Sean had literally begged the man just three months ago not to lay off two of Sean's employees, even taking a pay cut himself to sweeten his plea. But after this month's disastrous figures, Sean wasn't sure how much longer Mr. Kelly could sustain two hardware stores in an economy where neither was showing a profit.

He released a weighty sigh, absently unwrapping the Snickers candy bar he'd saved from his lunch, but he knew even his favorite obsession couldn't lift his spirits today. Taking a bite, he barely tasted it as his gaze wandered aimlessly past tattered posters of tools on the wall, taking in the cramped office he'd occupied for the last ten years as manager of Mr. Kelly's second store. Sean had never given the man a moment's regret, tirelessly building "Kelly's 2" into one of the most profitable mercantiles in the city. Chewing slowly, he rotated his chair to stare out in the alley, ignoring the crooked arrangement of framed certificates that confirmed his success on the wall by the window. His lips twisted. *Former* success, that is.

The scent of gasoline fumes and fresh asphalt drifted through the screen on a hot summer breeze, fluttering an obstinate strand of hair that persisted in tumbling over his forehead. His heyday as Kelly's golden boy didn't amount to much now, he supposed, not in the throes of the most devastating depression the world had ever seen. Despite the fact that Sean's was the only one of Mr. Kelly's two hardware stores that had eked out a razor-thin profit over the last year, he knew it was barely enough to cover the overhead of one store, much less two. Not when Sean suspected Mr. Kelly's nephew—the laziest piece of humanity Sean had ever seen—tapped into store funds for his own personal use.

He rolled up the sleeves of his white, starched shirt and blasted out another sigh, this one fraught with frustration over the fact he'd have to tell Mr. Kelly the bad news today, and it wouldn't be pretty. Somewhere a jackhammer pulverized a concrete sidewalk down the alley, and the battering was as merciless as the headache grinding in his brain. His eyes trailed into a blank stare, gaze fixed on lopsided towers of boxes and crates stacked against an eight-foot chain-link fence that separated Kelly's from the back door of the Five and Ten.

His jaw tightened as he contemplated the possibilities, none of them good. He might have to cut staff at the very least, manning the front counter for more hours than he did now, which didn't bother him as much as telling Andy, Mort, or Ray they no longer had jobs. The thought squeezed his heart like a vise, and he closed his eyes, racking his brain for another solution. He'd already returned all overstock he'd had, allowing his inventory to dwindle almost in half, and he'd even worked long after he clocked out rather than cut store hours.

But the bottom line stared at him now, drowning in a pool of red ink, and figures didn't lie—drastic measures would need to be taken. At the very worst, his store could close, robbing his employees of much-needed income, not to mention demoting him to assistant manager of the store across town. His eyes peeled open, the thought trapping a groan in his throat. It would be like starting over again, second in line after Lester. Which meant that Sean would do all the work while Lester pocketed all the glory . . . *and* the salary.

"Goodness, business *must* be bad—I don't believe I've ever seen you so idle before."

Sean spun around in his chair with a sharp intake of sticky air, the headache in his brain compounded by the "headache" in the door. He quickly rose to his feet and adjusted his tie, forcing a smile he didn't feel. "Miss Kelly . . . It's good to see you again."

Something in her secret smile set him on edge as he watched Rose Kelly pluck off dainty lace gloves that matched the trim of her lavender dress. "Is it?" she asked softly, tucking them into her clutch while hopeful brown eyes caused a cramp in Sean's gut. One perfectly manicured hand made a nervous sweep along the scoop neck of her collar before pausing at a satin tie that fell just above her tiny belted waist. "It's good to see you too, Sean," she whispered, her innocent tone belying the warmth in her eyes. "And I do wish you'd call me Rose."

Warmth surged and he cleared his throat, bending slightly to brace palms to his desk. He glanced up beneath cautious lids, more than wary. "Is there something I can do for you, Rose?"

Her smile was suddenly shy, reminding him that the gangly girl who'd harbored a crush on him from the age of fifteen was now a woman who could quicken his pulse. The thought unsettled him, eliciting a strong appreciation for the massive oak desk that provided a barrier.

She carefully shut the door before he could object, and every muscle in his body tensed. Her gaze flitted to a wooden chair across the room, stacked high with papers, and then back to him with a gentle smile. "Do you mind if I sit down?"

Yes, he thought with a silent groan. He hesitated, suddenly aware he was grinding his teeth again. "If you're here to see your father, I'm not expecting him for another hour or so."

Her air of confidence seemed to dissipate before his eyes with a pinch of penciled brows and a nervous lick of her lips. "I know . . . ," she said quietly, staring at her hands while she picked at her nails. When her gaze finally rose to meet his, he saw water well in her eyes, and he blinked in surprise. *The indomitable Rose Kelly . . . crying?* Against his will, a twinge of sympathy wedged in his chest and he straightened, wrinkles puckering the bridge of his nose. "Miss Kelly . . . Rose . . . are you all right?"

A frail sob broke from her lips and she put a quivering hand to her face. "No . . . no I'm not. And I'm not here to see my father . . . I'm here to see you." She sniffed and made a valiant attempt to square her shoulders before she shoved at several tears trailing her cheeks. "Please forgive me, but may I . . . *we* . . . please sit?"

He blinked, her own emotional well-being suddenly more important than his. She was twenty-two, but despite the stylish cloche hugging brunette curls and a tailored dress that clearly molded to the curves of a woman, Rose Kelly might have been fifteen once again. As if tears had washed away her façade, she was no longer the bold, confident flapper who'd breached his defenses in the storeroom two summers past. Instead, she stood before him, a slip of a girl with doleful wet eyes and a plaintive smile that tugged at his heart. Years of experience soothing sisters rose within, compelling him to retrieve the chair against the wall. With a deep swallow of air, he cleared off a month's worth of time sheets and set the chair beside her, waiting for her to sit. When she didn't, he gently guided her down, fighting a brother's urge to comfort with a tender embrace and a gentle stroke of her hair.

Clearing his throat, he returned to his seat and sat back, forearms flat on the armrests and eyes fixed on her tearstained face. "So . . . how can I help you, Rose?"

She fished a handkerchief from her purse and dabbed at her face. "You must think I'm crazy," she whispered, avoiding his eyes. "Coming to see you like this, your employer's daughter, engaged to another." She drew in a shaky breath and looked up, a mix of fear and pain in her face. "But I had to, Sean. You see, I'll be a married woman in less than two months and I . . ." A lump shifted in her throat. "I needed to know . . . something."

A hint of alarm curled in his stomach, and he eased farther back in his chair, desperate to distance himself. "What?" he asked, his voice little more than a croak.

She chewed on the edge of her lip, drawing his eyes to the fullness of her mouth, and heat tracked up the back of his neck. He forced his gaze back to hers and shifted, uneasy with the conversation.

"I guess it's no secret that I've had . . . eyes for you since I was a young girl—"

Jolting up in the chair, he pressed his palms to his desk. "Rose—"

"No, Sean, please . . . hear me out?"

He swallowed hard and sat back, sucking in a deep breath that stalled in his throat.

"I know I've made a fool of myself, especially when I kissed you in the storeroom that time." She looked away, a rise of color in her cheeks. "So I'm here to apologize for that."

A reedy breath slowly seeped from his lips. "Apology accepted."

"And to find something out . . ."

His stomach clutched.

"You see, I've done my best to love Chester, really I have. Father's crazy about him, you know . . . or at least crazy about his money, but I . . ." A faint shiver emanated from her petite frame as she glanced up, her eyes naked with longing before she quickly looked away. "Father's forcing me to marry him, but I don't love him, hard as I've tried." Her shoulders sagged and she slumped in the chair, her gaze pinned to the front of his desk and lost in a vacant stare. "Mother says I will eventually, that most marriages start out without love. She says true love is only a fairy tale, but I . . ." She gnawed at her lip again while twisting the diamond on her left hand. "I don't believe that . . . not when I still may have feelings for someone else." Her eyelids flicked up then, revealing the heart of her statement. "Feelings for you . . ."

She rose from her chair before he could open his mouth to speak, and when she rounded his desk, he shot to his feet. "Rose—no! You don't have feelings for me."

"But how will I know, Sean, I mean really know?" She placed a trembling hand on the edge of his desk and moved forward, a quiver lacing her voice. "Soon I'll be walking down the aisle to spend my life with a man I don't love, and I need to put these feelings to rest."

He stood his ground, resisting the urge to step back. "I agree, and the best way to do that is to go home—*now*—to your fiancé."

"No! I'm sorry, Sean, but I can't." The frantic volume of her words underscored the trembling lift of her chin. "Not until I know if these feelings are gone. I was willing to marry Chester, truly I was . . . until last month. You see, I had a dream about you. You kissed me in that dream, and I haven't been able to think of anything else."

"It was only a dream, Rose, a figment of your imagination."

She bent forward, a thread of challenge in her tone despite the wounded look in her face. "Was it a figment of my imagination when you kissed me in the storeroom?"

His jaw dropped. "You kissed me, as I recall, although ambush might be a better word."

"But you responded!" Moisture welled in her eyes as desperation strangled her tone. "Can you deny it?"

Heat crawled up his face, tapping into a well-hidden temper. He leaned in, hands low on his hips. "I'm a man, Miss Kelly—that's liable to happen when a woman throws herself at me."

Two doleful brown eyes blinked back, dribbling more tears. "I don't believe that. A man doesn't just return a woman's

70

kiss unless he wants to . . ." A lump bobbed in her throat. "Unless he has some kind of feelings for her."

"Rose, I *don't* have feelings for you—"

"You said that in my dream too, Sean, but it wasn't true. I kissed you and you responded just like in the storeroom that time, and suddenly I knew—knew that underneath all your denial, you actually care. Don't you see? I *have* to do this! I have to find out for sure, before I walk down that aisle." Her gaze flitted to his lips and held, skyrocketing his pulse.

He stepped back as shock coursed through his veins. "For pity's sake, Rose, you're engaged to another man—what kind of woman are you?"

She stepped close and poked a finger to his chest despite tears brimming her eyes. "A woman who wants to make good and sure she's not attracted to one man before she marries another. And there's only one way to find out. So you may as well kiss me, Sean O'Connor, because I'm not leaving till you do."

He crossed his arms, certain he'd never met a more stubborn woman—outside of Charity, that is. His jaw shifted as he steeled his voice. "Go home, Rose, there'll be no—"

Her lunge took him by complete surprise, causing a gasp to choke in his throat. She was maybe five foot three, but the force of her petite frame sent him sprawling back in the chair so hard that she rendered him speechless. A condition that suited Miss Kelly just fine, apparently, as she clung to his neck while parked in his lap, lips fused to his. He could smell the rose scent of her hair and feel the press of her hands as she clutched him close, and for several paralyzing seconds, heat infused his body like a blast from the wood-burning stove at the back of the store. All reason fled, and with a slam of his heart, he found himself responding with a fervor that stunned him so much, he jerked back in the chair.

"No!" he said, chest heaving as he tried to shove her away.

"I knew it!" she cried, water welling once again. "You care for me—you do!"

Shame stung his cheeks as he attempted to rise. "Not in that way . . ."

She clutched him tightly. "Yes, you do—I knew it!"

"Rose!" He pushed her back, fingers pinched hard on her arms and no recourse but the truth. "I may be attracted to you, but I don't want you—ever!"

The brutal impact of his words appeared to deplete her completely, and with a painful shudder, she crumpled in his hold, body quivering with sobs.

The sight of his own sisters' tears had always unnerved him, and it was no different now. Fraternal instinct kicked in, and he pulled her to his chest, stroking her hair to calm her down. "Rose—you're only twenty-two and I'm thirty-four, almost thirty-five. That's twelve years difference, and the truth is, I have no plans to marry anyone—*ever*—not just you." His words set off another round of weeping, and his heart constricted. "Trust me, Chester is perfect for you—he's young, wealthy, and he's in love with you, I'm sure—"

"B-but I don't love him . . ."

Her pitiful wail increased in volume, and Sean closed his eyes, his lips sporting the seeds of a smile. "You will in time, if you just give it a—"

"For the love of Jezebel, what in tarnation is going on here?"

Sean's eyes flipped open, glazed in shock as Mr. Kelly loomed in the door, slack-jawed over the sight of Rose in his lap. With a harsh gasp of air, Sean bolted to his feet in a knee-jerk reaction, plunking Rose to the wood floor in a noisy flail of arms.

"Dash it, man, are you crazed?" Mr. Kelly plucked her up in mere seconds, clasping her to his chest as she sobbed in his arms. "What the devil is going on here?"

"Mr. Kelly—I was just consoling her, I swear—"

"*In your lap?*" The man's voice cracked on a high note, and Sean felt the blood drain from his face.

"Sir, it's not as it appears . . ."

"Oh, really?" His eyes were slits of rage as he patted the

back of his wailing daughter. "For the love of all that's good and decent, O'Connor, the woman's engaged. So help me, if you took advantage of her—"

"No, sir, I swear—"

Mr. Kelly shook his daughter with a white-knuckled grip. "Did he, Rose? Tell me now—did he kiss you?"

Rose quivered as she stared, first at her father, and then at Sean. She turned away and gave a shaky nod, eyes rimmed raw with weeping.

"Rose—no, tell him the truth, please!"

"Are you calling my daughter a liar on top of everything else?"

"No, sir, I swear, but things are not as they seem. Rose, please—"

She seemed to sway on her feet as she closed her eyes with a shift in her throat. "I can't marry Chester," she whispered.

Sean's body went numb.

"What?" Her father rattled her small frame until the silk tie bobbed on her chest. "What do you mean you can't marry Chester?"

"I mean," she whispered, lips parted to draw in a shaky breath, "that I refuse. I don't love Chester. I'm in love with . . ."

The air seized in Sean's lungs.

Rose jerked free of her father's hold. Pained eyes flicked toward Sean for a brief moment before returning to her father's scarlet face with a rigid rise of her shoulders. Her arm rose like a guillotine before her quivering finger condemned him to death. ". . . *him*."

Sean stared, unable to blink, the whites of his eyes as dry as the tongue pasted to the roof of his mouth.

Mr. Kelly gasped, followed by a series of wheezes that suggested he was choking.

"You need water." Sean was midstride when his employer's glare singed him to the spot.

"No, Mr. O'Connor," Mr. Kelly rasped, the twitch of his bulbous nose a deadly sign. "I need vindication." He turned to his daughter, foul temper oozing from every pore. "You . . . ,"

73

he said with an ominous stab of a meaty finger, "I will deal with at home."

"But, Father—"

His grip drew a faint cry from her lips, leaving no room for rebuttal. "Leave now or I will truly embarrass you in front of the man that you 'love.'"

Sean winced.

Casting a watery look at Sean, Rose fled, weeping. The door slammed behind her.

"Mr. Kelly, I'm sorry about this, but I can explain—"

"Sorry doesn't even begin to cover what you will be, Mr. O'Connor, when I'm done with you. Do you have any idea what you've done?" He stepped forward, beady eyes as hard as the knot in Sean's chest. "I trusted you with my store, my money, my livelihood. And how do you repay me? By seducing my daughter—"

"No! That's not true—" Sean clenched his fists at his sides, fighting to contain his anger.

"And a woman engaged to another man, for pity's sake—"

"Let me explain—"

One bushy gray brow lifted in scorn. "Explain? Yes, I'm sure that would be rich, your tale as to how my daughter suddenly found herself in your lap." He crossed burly arms and blistered Sean with a glare. "But spare me the details, please. The only explanation I want is why you would stab me in the back after I've supported you all these years?"

"Mr. Kelly, my loyalty to you has been unquestioned."

"Yes, until now." He gave a sharp nod at the ledger on Sean's desk. "Tell me, Mr. O'Connor, have we made our numbers this month?"

Icy prickles nicked at his skin. He looked away. "No."

"I see. Or in the last six months?"

He closed his eyes while the truth bled the air from his lungs. "No."

"And you speak to me of loyalty?"

Sean's head jerked up, eyes burning his sockets. "For the love of God, there's a depression—"

"Yes . . . there is. A terrible time that can squeeze the loyalty out of any man." He drew in a deep breath and leveled a hard gaze. A nerve flickered in the heavy flesh of his cheek. "Are you skimming the coffers?"

"What?" Blood leeched from Sean's face.

"You know—stealing. Cooking the books. Robbing me blind. You get my drift."

Fury swelled in his chest till he thought he would choke. "How dare you accuse me of that!" he said, fists clenched at his sides. "I have done nothing but give you my all these last seventeen years, earning you a profit by the sweat of my brow."

"Your all? You mean like you were trying to give my daughter just now, stealing her heart like you've stolen my money?" A sneer lifted the corner of his employer's mouth. "Lester's had his suspicions of you for a long time, and now I see it's all true. A profit, indeed—no doubt by marrying Rose to secure your job at this store. *And* her money."

Shock paralyzed him for several seconds before white-hot anger seared through him like a high-voltage wire. "No, Mr. Kelly," he said, his breathing lethal with rage. He slammed the chair into the desk with such violence, his cold cup of coffee teetered on his desk, sloshing liquid all over the books. A spasm leapt in his neck as he seized the ledger and hurled it across the room. "That would be your nephew, and I'm not Lester."

His employer's eyes glittered as if he had won. "No, you're not," he said, his voice as slick as the sweat on his brow. "You see, *he* has a job. You have one week's notice beginning today, and so help me, if you don't honor it, neither you nor your staff will receive this month's pay."

Sean's rage siphoned out with the slam of the door, leaving only the sound of his own ragged breathing as he stared, unable to move. His eyelids flickered shut, heavy with the realization that his life as he knew it was over. He had been one of the lucky ones—a man who stood in authority while others stood in soup lines. Happy, carefree, unfettered by poverty or the need for a woman. But in the blink of an eye—or the brand of a stolen kiss—everything had changed, leaving him with a future as bleak and cheerless as the front page of the *Herald*.

As if in a stupor, he moved to his chair and slumped in the seat, his mind weighted with thoughts of impending doom. His body felt limp and lifeless, not unlike his future at the moment, and with an involuntary shudder, he lay his head on the back of the chair. Out of nowhere, the memory of Rose's kiss assailed his brain, unleashing a roll of heat that stunned him to the core. His harsh gasp hung in the air, prompted by a realization so sinister, it shivered his spine. Not only had he been stripped of his job today, but apparently his immunity to women as well. And with the combination of the two, Sean suddenly knew—as sure as the endless breadlines that trailed past Mr. Kelly's door—that when it came to bad news, the *Herald* had nothing on him.

"I just bet you have a bed in that supply room, don't you, made up all neat and proper?"

Surprise lifted the edges of Emma's mouth as she blinked up at Charity, who stood at the door, hip slanted.

"Go ahead—I dare you to deny it," Charity said strolling in with her clutch in one hand and a bulging shopping bag in the other. With a quick scan of Emma's spacious office, her blue eyes went wide, lids and penciled brows shiny with petroleum jelly in the style of the day. "Oh! You finally redid your office—I love it!" She nudged the rounded toe of her blue Mary Jane heel against a maroon geometric-patterned rug with clean, straight lines—except for one frayed edge—then hiked an appreciative brow. "No fringe—very art deco. *And* very expensive. So unlike you."

Emma smiled. "Clearance, Boss, damaged in shipping. Couldn't sell it to save my soul."

Charity nodded and eyed the rest of the office that Emma had worked so hard to make cozy. With as many hours as she spent here, Emma had finally relented to Charity's badgering to decorate her "home away from home." The result was a wonderful oasis where she'd transformed a cold, sterile section at the back of the second story into a warm and inviting office space that felt almost like home. A tall arched window boasted several lush plants as well as a view of a tiny city park where children now played before dusk chased them home. Pale pink light from the waning summer sun spilled into the room, casting a warm glow over cream-colored walls splashed with color from vibrant framed prints. Sleek, modernistic images of flappers and garden parties stared back, a haunting reminder of an avant-garde era that boasted better times. Charity deposited her shopping bag next to the phonograph machine on a cherrywood buffet against the wall, then leaned to inspect her lipstick in an art deco mirror with fanned edges of matching wood.

"Mmm . . . very nice," she said with a pucker of her lips.

Emma chuckled. "The furniture . . . or your face?"

Charity wheeled on her heels and grinned. "Both," she said with a smirk. She lifted a record from the phonograph and quirked a brow. "Spending your evenings with Rudy Vallee, are we? Why, Mrs. Malloy, you little vixen, you . . . and all this time I thought you were working."

A low chuckle parted from Emma's lips as she propped chin in hand to give Charity a sultry look, tone husky. "What can I say, the man and I work well together."

"Ha! 'Work' being the operative word." Charity strolled over to trail a hand along the cherrywood finish of Emma's desk. Her mouth sagged open. "A dining room set?"

Emma shrugged her shoulders and smiled. "A total dining room return—Mrs. Wellington III claims there was a gouge on the table when Horace delivered it."

"Was there?" Charity asked, plopping into one of the matching cherrywood padded chairs in front of Emma's "desk."

"Not anymore," Emma said with a proud smile. She scooted her antiquated typewriter back several inches to reveal a nasty scratch that was filled in with stain. "Horace says it wasn't there when he delivered it, but it's the store's word against hers, so I decided to make good use of it for both me and my trusty Remington."

Charity crossed her legs with a lift of her brow, and Emma caught a whiff of Chanel No. 5. "Very ingenious, but what are you doing with a typewriter? I thought that was Bert's job."

Emma grinned and laid her pen aside. "God bless her, Bertolina Adriani is crabby enough these days, so I'm just trying to lighten the load."

"Humph . . . God has already blessed her with a supervisor who does half of her work." Almond-shaped eyes thinned into a scowl, but Charity's voice held a hint of humor. "You are such a pushover, Emma Malloy, you know that?"

Emma spiked a brow. "Oh, and you're not, Mrs. Bleeding Heart? The woman who insists on giving bonuses for both Thanksgiving *and* Christmas, with her husband none the wiser?"

"Yes, but I'm a pushover nobody knows about, while you"— Charity flailed a hand at her best friend before nodding at Emma's prized carpet—"are as blatant as this unraveled rug and, I might add," a slight crimp of her brow offset the tease in her eyes, "probably walked on just as much."

"You know better than that," Emma said with a weary smile. "Bert's been going through a rough time right now with her son, so I'm just helping out. Heaven knows I can't afford to see her quit." She leaned back, allowing her hands to rest on the arms of the chair while she eyed the cherry-wood clock on the far wall. "Goodness, seven-fifteen? To what do I owe this honor and how on earth did you talk Mitch into leaving him this late at night? Did I miss a blue moon?"

Charity's lips veered into a wry smile. "I needed a new dress for a function at the *Herald*, so Mitch volunteered to watch the kids." She inclined her head toward the shopping bags with a mischievous smile. "Trust me, he'll be sorry I didn't stay home." Crossing her silk-stockinged legs, Charity eased back into the chair to contemplate her friend, arms folded and blue eyes pensive. She nodded toward the stacks of invoices and bills of lading on Emma's desk. "Speaking of 'home,' are you going to see yours anytime soon?"

The question brought a smile to Emma's lips. *Charity, the caretaker.* To some, a bulldozer, to others a tad bossy, but to Emma, the epitome of a God-given friend—honest, caring, and true. An enigma, her great-grandmother had once called her—someone who begrudges fiercely and loves fiercely, which Emma knew to be true. Although, she thought with affection, Charity had certainly mellowed with time. Emma studied her friend now, amazed that Charity's striking beauty never made her feel less. A deep sense of fondness warmed her heart. Perhaps because Charity's fierce devotion had always made her feel as if she were so much "more."

Forever fashionable, Charity wore the pale yellow Elsa Schiaparelli dress well, its daring shoulder pads, bias cut, and belted waist showing off her shapely body to best advantage. Her shallow-brimmed blue straw hat matched both the piping on her dress and her eyes perfectly, swooping low on one side where golden curls peeked out. Born the same year as Emma, Charity was as stunning at thirty-one as when Emma had met her at eighteen. They'd bonded instantly, two penniless clerks who shared an innate loneliness at Shaw's Emporium in Dublin, forging a friendship that saved Emma's life—literally and figuratively. It was Charity who'd bound her wounds after Rory had scarred her, and Charity who threatened to quit if Mrs. Shaw fired Emma for those same offensive scars. Without question she was a bold and daring friend who'd convinced her to leave Rory, sparing her a life of degradation and abuse, or worse.

Emma's thoughts traveled a million miles from the pain of Rory to where she was today—the manager of Charity's prestigious store, surrounded by people she loved—and wetness stung her eyes. Charity was the sister Emma had never had, the friend with whom she shared and prayed for all the secrets of her soul. Guilt instantly pricked, forcing a lump to Emma's throat. *Well, almost all.* Swallowing hard, she pushed the thought from her mind to focus on her best friend. When some had only seen a cool veneer on a pretty face, Emma had seen the vivacious little girl that Charity would always be—desperate to be beautiful and longed for and loved. Emotion thickened in Emma's throat as her lips tilted into a tender smile. *The friend of my heart.*

"You haven't answered me," Charity said with a cock of her head, bringing Emma back to the moment. "When are you heading home? And keep in mind, Emma Malloy, as owner of this store, I *can* order you to go."

Emma sighed and gave Charity a tired smile. "Soon. Although I remember many a night you burned the midnight oil at Shaw's, ignoring my pleas for you to go home."

Charity took on a faraway look, a faint smile tugging at her rose-colored lips. "Oh, how I used to love running that store! Which is why I miss my two days a week here so much now that the kids are home for the summer. I guess retail is in our blood, Emma, starting way back in Dublin." A hint of melancholy laced her tone as she trailed into a stare. "I was happy working at Shaw's, as I recall, despite all the heartbreak Mitch put me through back then." A heavy sigh shivered from her lips. "Goodness, that all seems so long ago, doesn't it?"

"A lifetime, my friend," Emma said wistfully. She picked up her pen. "And speaking of Mitch, you better get home. He can't be in a good mood these days with his workload at the *Herald*. And you've said yourself that Henry has a talent for trying one's patience."

The edge of Charity's lips crooked up. "Only mine, it seems. For Mitch he's a perfect angel, apparently." She scowled. "Must be my track record with Irish men. All I can say is thank heavens for my sweet twin, Hope Marceline. Can you imagine twins with two of Henry?"

"'Tis the grace of God, for sure, sparing you such a fate," Emma said with a chuckle. She scrawled her signature to a letter from the stack that Bert had typed today. "Although if anyone could handle it, it would be you."

"That's what Mitch always says." Charity flicked at some

lint on her dress and gave her a saucy smile. "Now if I can just learn to handle *him*."

Emma grinned. "I thought you had."

A sigh floated from Charity's lips. "In my dreams. The man is more bullheaded than me, if that's even possible." She eyed Emma as she tugged on her gloves. "I have to go, but before I do, I need to ask you something."

"What?" Emma signed her name to the next letter and looked up.

Charity swiped her teeth with a glide of her tongue, a nervous habit that told Emma the news wouldn't be good. She angled to give Charity her full attention.

"What is it? What's wrong?"

The tongue made another pass as Charity sat up straight, fiddling with her gloves. She drew in a deep breath, then dropped her hands in her lap and looked up. "Sean was fired yesterday."

The pen slipped from Emma's hand. "What? Why?"

"A misunderstanding involving Rose Kelly, apparently."

"No . . ." Emma sagged back in her chair with a silent groan. She closed her eyes, remembering their conversation the day of Katie's wedding. "What happened?" she whispered.

Charity vented a heavy breath, and Emma looked up, the slump of her friend's shoulders a telling sign. "Well, it seems Mr. Kelly found his daughter conversing with my brother . . ." Charity's sooty lashes flipped up while her gaze locked with Emma's. Her lips twisted in a painful smile. "In his lap."

Heat flooded Emma's cheeks. "The saints preserve us . . ."

"Yes, well, the saints are going to have to preserve something, because Mother says she's never seen Sean like this—moody, depressed, quiet." Charity sighed. "It breaks my heart."

Emma leaned forward. "I don't understand—how did it happen? And when? Because I know for a fact Sean had no interest in Rose whatsoever—he told me so at Katie's wedding."

"Yesterday. Sean's not saying a lot, but Mother did manage to pull out that Rose came by to see him, claiming she didn't love her fiancé. Apparently she kissed him, and when he tried to back away, he stumbled into his chair. The next thing Sean knew, she was in his lap, kissing him senseless." Charity shuddered. "Dear mother of Job, it sounds like something I would have done." She glanced up. "Way back when, of course."

"And Mr. Kelly found them like that? What did he say?"

"Fired Sean on the spot. Even went so far as to accuse him of stealing. Father thinks the whole thing is just a convenient excuse to lighten his payroll, the stingy ol' miser."

"Oh, poor Sean."

"Yes. And the worst part is that Sean has to go back there for two more weeks."

"What? I thought he was fired?"

"He is, but Mr. Kelly needs Sean to orientate Lester, Mr. Kelly's shiftless nephew who will take over the store, so he threatened to withhold everyone's pay if Sean didn't stay the two weeks. And although Sean would walk out in a heartbeat if it was just his salary at risk, he'd never do that to his employees." Charity sighed. "Mitch says with the unemployment rate edging 16 percent, it's going to be pretty rough to find a decent job in any field, much less retail."

With a faint groan, Emma sank back in her chair and put a hand to her eyes. "I just can't believe it—and after all Sean has done for that awful man, devoting his life to that store. I just wish there was something we could do."

"Well . . . actually . . . there is."

Emma glanced up. "What?"

Shifting in the chair, Charity leaned forward, the intensity in her manner as compelling as the excitement in her eyes. "How long have Mitch and I been after you to work decent hours?"

"I *do* work decent hours," Emma said with a ghost of a smile. "Given the work to be done."

"Always fighting us tooth and nail about adding more staff—"

"Charity, you know my budget can't afford it—"

"No," Charity said with a twinkle in her eye, pausing for effect. "But ours can."

Emma sat straight up, her heart beginning to race as

Charity's words sank in. Her lips parted with shallow breaths. "What are you saying?"

A smile tugged at the corner of Charity's full lips. "You need more help at the store, and Sean needs a job. You figure it out."

Emma's heart stalled in her chest. *Sean . . . here? At the store?* The memory of his rage at the wedding caused her smile to falter, and she swallowed hard. Sean had always been one of the people she'd enjoyed being around the most, but that had all changed when he'd thrown that first punch. She had never seen him like that before—crazed, out of control, violent. *So much like Rory.* The very thought caused her stomach to lurch, and she drew in a calming breath, forcing a bright smile. "Goodness, are you serious?"

"Absolutely. That is . . . if you're okay with the idea. Keep in mind that it would only be temporary until Sean finds another job and you would still be the manager in charge, of course. But he could do whatever you need him to—help Horace on the dock, make deliveries, or even fill in as a salesclerk." She bit her lip with a mischievous gleam in her eye. "Not to mention the dreaded inventory every month. Why, he can share Horace's office on the dock—"

"No!" Emma cried, the blood draining from her face. "I would never put Sean on the dock, not unless it was an emergency. For pity's sake, Charity, he was the manager of one of the top retail stores in Boston for over ten years now—we can't do that to him."

Charity chuckled and squeezed Emma's hand. "Calm down, Emma, whatever you say is fine. I just didn't want you to feel threatened, you know? Worried that Sean might be moving in on your territory . . . as manager, that is."

A shaky sigh wavered from Emma's mouth as she thought of the indignity to Sean's pride. From management to the docks, for goodness' sake! Her chin lifted as she shifted into managerial mode, working hard to dispel the uneasiness she felt inside. "I won't settle for him being here as anything less than assistant manager, and we'll create an office for him up here." An edge of her lip sloped up. "I'll just move my bed out of the storeroom and sleep at home. After all, I was planning on making it an office for Alli anyway, since it's so large and has a window. But she didn't want it—actually prefers to sit with Bert, if you can believe that."

Charity's leg ceased kicking as she stared at Emma. "Good heavens, she's a bigger saint than you. I hope she's rubbing off on Bert and not the other way around."

"She is, actually," Emma said with a smile. "Heard the two of them giggling and plotting like schoolgirls over Horace's nephew who's working on the dock this summer."

"Ah . . . women after my own heart!" Charity said with a grin. The stockinged leg resumed its bouncing as she honed in once again. "So, you're really okay with this? Because Mitch and I think it's the perfect way to kill two birds with one stone. Sean needs to stay busy in retail, and you're dying for help—talk about a match made in heaven!"

Not if it's like Rory and me. Warmth crept into her cheeks as she dispelled the thought. She focused her attention on studying her friend. "Do you think he'll do it?"

"Not if he thinks it's charity . . ." The blue eyes narrowed to the level of conspiracy.

Emma smiled. "No, only 'Charity' of another kind . . . a far more devious one."

Charity hiked her chin. "It's for his own good, Emma, and you know it. The man's confidence has been crushed and his pride is in flames. Heaven knows he doesn't really need the money right now, not with him living at home and hoarding his salary all these years rather than spending it on a woman. So we have no choice but to appeal to his chivalrous nature rather than his wallet, even though we'll supplement your budget for his salary." Charity pursed her lips, preening with pleasure. "And that's where *you* come in."

Emma blinked, well acquainted with Charity's talent for intrigue. "Me? How?"

Settling back, Charity cocked her elbow on the arm of the chair and propped a finger to her chin, eyes narrowed in thought as she mulled over the situation. "Well, you're no good at faking this sort of thing, so it's a godsend that you really are desperate for help. I suppose this is a clear case of 'all things working out for good for those that love God,' as you and Faith are so fond of quoting. Because somehow, we have to convince Sean that he—no matter how long he chooses to stay—is an answer to our prayers."

Emma swallowed her hesitation, determined that Charity would not sense her fear. She leaned forward, a palm to her chest. "Oh, but he is!" she breathed with as much enthusiasm as she could muster. "I can't imagine the joy of having someone with Sean's experience, no matter how long he stays. Why, I'm months behind on inventory alone because none of us can get to it."

"Good—that's the passion I'm looking for next Saturday night when you come to dinner."

"Dinner?" Emma whispered, suddenly losing her nerve.

"Yep, six o'clock sharp." Charity stood and tugged on her gloves, giving Emma the once-over. "Mmm . . . you look pretty tired now, but it'd certainly help if you went to bed late next Friday night and got up early Saturday morning. And wear that faded blue dress that washes you out."

"The one you told me to burn? Whatever for?"

"Because we need you to look the part, and that blue dress is perfect." Her lips slanted into a dry smile as she leaned to give Emma a hug. "I should have known you'd keep that old rag—you hate throwing anything away. And this is one time you can forgo the makeup. Although I suppose a dab of gray eye shadow would be nice—*under* your eyes, not on your lids, understood? I want you at your neediest best, Mrs. Malloy, or my brother will balk like a mule."

Emma shook her head, a soft chuckle parting from her lips. "I'd forgotten just how devious you can be when you really want something. Heaven help Mitch Dennehy . . . and, apparently, his brother-in-law."

Charity strolled over to the buffet to rifle through one of her bags. "Not devious," she said with a tinge of hurt in her tone, "I prefer to think of it as resourceful." She dug around until she found what she was looking for, then flourished a mottled green and gray silk scarf in the air with a decidedly devious smile. "Now *this*, Mrs. Malloy, is not only 'devious,' but downright dangerous as well. Because you see, not only have I found you a scarf that will make those remarkable eyes of yours an even deadlier weapon than they already are—" she positioned a striking teardrop earring against the sheen of the silk scarf, the twinkle in her blue eyes unmistakable—"*but* obsidian jewelry the exact shade of your eyes, which I have always said are rare gems all their own."

She hurried over to drape the scarf around Emma's neck while holding the jewelry to her friend's ear. A hushed sigh floated from Charity's lips. "I'll tell you what, Emma, your eyes alone could slay a thousand men with a single blink. You look stunning!"

Fingering the delicate silk of the scarf, Emma felt almost pretty. "Charity, why did you do this? You shouldn't be spending your money that way."

"Oh, fiddle-faddle. The scarf and earrings were made for you, and you and I both know it. Consider it an early Christmas gift if you will, but don't deny me the pleasure of bringing out the beauty of my dearest friend."

Throat tight with emotion, Emma squeezed Charity in a hug while tears pricked at her eyes. "They say beauty is in the eye of the beholder, my friend, and you are living proof. Thank you for always making me feel beautiful, Charity, despite the contrary . . . and for your remarkably bottomless heart."

Charity pulled back to caress Emma's face with her hand, her eyes intent. "That's because you *are* beautiful, Emma, you're just the only one who can't see it." Her fingers gently traced the faint scar by Emma's lip. "Because of these— wounds that no longer scar your beautiful face but still scar your soul. Would that I could take them from you, Emma," she whispered, a sheen of moisture in her eyes. "I would wear them as a badge of honor."

Tears pooled, and Emma closed her eyes, embracing Charity with such a wellspring of love, she found it difficult to speak. Swallowing hard, she quickly covered with a gruff tease. "Oh, go on with you now, Mrs. Dennehy, your bleeding heart is showing once again. As if you don't have scars of your own from tragedies you've borne. Maybe not on your face, my friend, but in your tender heart for sure, always pouring yourself out for your own, giving them your love, your support . . ." Affection bated her tone. "And in Sean's case . . . your conspiracy."

With a tight squeeze, Charity released her, a smile crowning the firm jut of her jaw. "I beg your pardon—I'm only thinking of everyone's best interest here, Emma. We both know how stubborn Irish men can be, and my easygoing brother is no exception." She chewed on the edge of her lip as she squinted in thought. "Except maybe he doesn't glare quite as much as Mitch, I suppose . . . Anyway, we all need to be on our game come Saturday night if my plan is going to work, and that means you, my friend."

"You mean if your 'plot' is going to work," Emma said, tease lacing her tone.

Charity made her way to the door with a swaggering stride and turned, one penciled brow arched in challenge. "Plan or plot, it's all the same to me, Emma Malloy. Either way, I need you engaged if this 'plot' is going to work. Unless, of course, you're partial to working long hours, cozying up with your Remington instead of your cats?"

"Don't worry, Mrs. Dennehy," Emma said with a tired smile and a token pat to her typewriter, "I'll be there—as pitiful a sight as you've ever seen. Although something tells me it won't be me convincing your brother to work at the store, dark circles notwithstanding." She propped elbows on her desk and rested her head in her hands, her smile crooking up. "We both know when it comes to getting something you want, you wield a lot more power than I do. Which means, my friend, the other guy usually doesn't have a prayer."

Charity's smile was dazzling. "I know," she said, and blew her a kiss. "I'll remind you before next Saturday, and don't be late. And go home, Emma, *now*—it's too late to be working." She turned to leave, shooting a final smile over her shoulder. "Oh, and one more thing. Since you mentioned prayer—you might engage in a little of that too." Her lips tilted into a coy smile. "After all, I'm not a complete heathen, you know. I know where the real power is."

Emma shook her head, her smile diminishing as the click of Charity's heels faded away, past Bert and Alli's work area into the store beyond. She pressed the cool of the silk scarf to her cheek, praying indeed—prayers of gratitude for the gift of Charity in her life. "Thank you for the love of such a dear friend," she whispered, quite certain Charity O'Connor Dennehy ranked as one of God's greatest blessings.

She laid the scarf on the desk and reached for the stack of letters awaiting her signature and then stopped, closing her eyes with a quiet sigh. Oh, she'd pray about it all right, there was no doubt about that. Because as much as she loved Sean O'Connor and needed him at the store, her comfort level with him had vanished since the day of the wedding, something that saddened her immensely. And yet now she had to work with him, day in and day out. "Still waters run deep," Charity had said once, and Emma had no doubt it was true. It had been true with Rory and something deep down inside told her it was true with Sean as well.

Shaking off her gloom, she proceeded to sign the rest of Bert's letters, hoping and praying it would all work out. She had no qualms about "still waters"—those she could handle. Her lips tightened as she signed the next letter with a flourish, attempting to diminish the anxiety inside. No, Rory had taught her well that it was the "deep" where danger lies, a place where one could easily find herself in over her head.

4

So, how did Sean survive his last day?" Charity broached the subject that nobody was eager to discuss. She glanced up from the plaid knickers she was mending, hoping to find some reassurance in her mother's face.

Marcy O'Connor paused, needle in hand. The summer heat was stifling, but nobody seemed to notice it or the shrieks of the children as they played a game of Red Rover in the backyard. Her mother's gaze flitted to the kitchen screen door before settling on her daughter. "Not good, I'm afraid," she said in a low tone, barely above a whisper. "Although I don't want to say too much because he could walk out here any moment."

"He did seem pretty glum when we arrived. Where is he now?" Faith asked quietly, her somber eyes a mirror reflection of her mother and sisters' as they convened around the back-porch picnic table for their weekly sewing fest.

Gliding tongue to teeth—a nervous trait Charity recognized all too well—Marcy bent to pick through the basket of sewing that afforded a bit of extra income during these trying economic times. "Upstairs, fixing that leaky faucet that Patrick's been hoping to get to." She released a heavy sigh as she pulled a pair of torn trousers into her lap. "I swear he's been like a machine this last week—cleaning, painting, repairing everything in sight." Her lips slanted. "So much so I'm tempted to break something else just to keep him busy."

"He's been looking for work, though, hasn't he?" Lizzie turned a hem, worry in her tone.

"Every morning like clockwork," Marcy said with a frown. "Scours the Classifieds and then bolts out the door, sometimes without breakfast." She fingered a jagged hole in the seat of the pants, face screwed in thought. "Now how do you suppose this got here?"

Charity chuckled. "I don't know, but I wish I'd been there to see it." She suddenly sat upright, her voice raised in warning as she glared into the backyard. "Henry! It's called Swing the Statue, for mercy's sake, not 'pillage' it. You best take it easy with those girls, or you'll be 'swinging' your legs in a chair, young man, bored silly."

"How are Sean's spirits?" Faith continued, Charity's threats against Henry as commonplace as air.

"Not great," Marcy said. "It seems as long as he stays busy, he's not too bad. But I'll tell you one thing—he hasn't been himself. No smiles, very little to say, and definitely none of his usual sparkle." She puffed out another sigh. "I think he's depressed."

"That's certainly understandable," Lizzie said. She hesitated, exchanging a quick glance with Faith before focusing on her mother with worried eyes. "Well, do you . . . you know . . . think he'd consider working at the print shop? I know Brady and Collin are swamped because they've had to let several pressmen go recently, but I think they'd consider hiring Sean to help out, at least part-time, don't you think, Faith? After all, he is family."

"Absolutely," Faith agreed. "I don't know about Lizzie, but I wouldn't mind seeing Collin come home a little earlier each evening. Heaven knows they can certainly use the help."

A pucker creased the bridge of Marcy's nose. "I'm not sure that would work. Brady and Collin already suggested it to Patrick last week, but when he broached it with Sean, he adamantly refused. Says he's a merchant, not a pressman.

Insists there's no way he'll take salary from his brothers-in-law when he knows they've had to buckle the belt themselves."

"That's ridiculous," Faith said with a glint of temper. "That's what families do—they reach out to each other in their time of need."

"Reach out, yes, but take?" Charity smirked. "Every man in this family would see that as charity, and we all know it. Face it, when it comes to stubborn male pride, we're lousy with it."

"Mama, it's Henry's turn in Mother, May I, and he won't do it." Hope skidded to a breathless stop. "Can you make him?" She shot a disgusted look at her twin, who was taking aim at a squirrel with a rock in his hand. "Says he won't do it 'cause he's a man, not a mother."

Charity's smile squirmed as she arched penciled brows at her mother and sisters. "I rest my case." She patted Hope's cheek. "Honey, just change it to Father, May I?, okay? And if he doesn't play nice, tell him he'll be playing 'Mother, may I please come out of my room?'"

Hope gave Charity a kiss before tearing down the steps. "Thanks, Mama—love you!"

"Love you too, princess," Charity called, craning her neck to watch the exchange between the twins. When she saw Henry stomp to one end of the yard for paternal duty, she sighed and turned to give her mother a grin. "Now I know why you had four girls and two boys. Didn't think it was possible, Mother, but I believe my respect for you has risen even higher."

Marcy smiled. "Oh, boys aren't so bad, right, Lizzie? Sean, Steven, and Teddy should be proof of that." Marcy stuck a needle in her mouth, assessing the trouser tear with a dubious eye.

"Spoken like a true grandmother," Lizzie said with a proud smile. "Teddy's a dream. I'd take ten more just like him."

In spite of the mugginess of the day, a cold chill shivered the butterfly-sleeve of Charity's pink wraparound blouse. "Ten more of Henry?" Another shudder followed. "Just shoot me now."

Marcy smiled. "Charity, he's just going through a stage—"

"Yes, Mother, I know—birth to college." She blew a limp strand of hair from her eyes as she snapped a piece of thread with her teeth. "I just hope I can tame him before he marries some poor, unsuspecting girl." She spit out a sliver of navy thread. "And while we're on the subject of 'unsuspecting,' I think I have a solution to our problem with Sean."

Three sets of eyes locked on Charity's face. "Oh, no, what are you cooking up now?" Faith said with a chuckle, her amusement somewhat tempered by a wary scrunch of brows.

Charity eyed the seam she'd just sewn, squinting to see if it was straight. "Oh, nothing. Just a surefire way to get our unsuspecting brother back on track until he finds a job."

Faith leaned in, elbows on the table and lips parted in doubt. "I don't believe it. How?"

With a lift of her chin, Charity folded the school jumper she'd just mended and placed it on the growing stack in another basket. "It just so happens that Emma needs help at the store—"

"Oh, that would be wonderful!" Lizzie said with a hopeful glow.

"What?" Faith's jaw dropped a full inch. "Are you crazy?" She shooed at a fly. "I can tell you right now he won't do it."

Charity stared her down, suddenly remembering all the times she and Faith butted heads growing up, sometimes resulting in a hair-pulling fight. The memory tugged a smile to her lips, filling her with gratitude for the closeness she now shared with her sisters. Her smile eased into a grin. "Oh, yes he will, you mark my words. And of course I'm crazy, as if that's any surprise." She winked. "Crazy enough to know it will work."

"But how?" Marcy asked, her tone as skeptical as Faith's. "Your father already offered to give his cousin Thomas a call. You know, the one who owns the freighter company? But Sean flat-out refused, just like he did with Collin and Brady's offer to work at the shop."

"Yeah, how?" Faith repeated, an edge of respect in her tone.

"Knowing you, sis, this ought to be good . . . and probably just devious enough to work."

"Well, surprisingly, it's not all that devious," Charity said with a hint of regret. She leaned to pluck a purple silk blouse from Marcy's basket, then settled back in her chair. "But I do believe it'll work. That is, if I can get Sean over to dinner on Saturday night. And trust me, when he sees Emma all ragged and worn from too much work for one person to do—"

"Emma?" Faith's mouth could have trapped flies. "Don't tell me you railroaded Emma?"

"Not railroaded exactly," Charity said slowly. "Think of it more like I engineered a plan and Emma's all aboard. Frankly, the woman's working herself to death at the store, and neither Mitch nor I can get her to cut back on her hours or hire more help. But," Charity said with a smug hike of a brow, "she *wants* to help Sean, so she's willing to hire him. And actually, she says with his retail experience, it's an answer to prayer. So you see, it's completely perfect—the dear friend I love gets the help that she needs, and my sweet, stubborn brother gets a job."

"But he's bound to suspect something," Lizzie said, violet eyes wide with concern. She chewed on the edge of her lip as she finished the hem. "He never goes to your house for dinner."

"I know, but I've got a plan—or as Emma calls it, a 'plot'— guaranteed to put Sean O'Connor's back to the wall, ensuring our success."

"*Our* success?" The corner of Faith's mouth tipped up. "So now we're accomplices?"

"You're not gonna force her to cry on demand, are you?" Lizzie asked, regard for Emma obviously foremost in her mind. "You know, like you did with me in our plot against Brady? Crackers in her eyes to make her cry and weaken his defenses?"

"Crackers?" Marcy gaped. "Charity, whose daughter are you? I swear you inherited your grandmother's creative flair for conspiracy as well as her beauty, God rest her soul." She sighed, a trace of tears in her eyes. "You're so very like her, you know."

"I know," she whispered, squeezing her mother's hand. "And therein is one of my greatest joys." She swiped at her eye and turned to grin at Lizzie. "And no, Lizzie, no saltines are involved, I promise. Only used them twice, you know—once with you to turn Brady's head and once with Mitch to turn his." Her nose wrinkled. "Or maybe it was twice with Mitch . . ." She waved her hand. "Oh, well, it's not important. All that matters is that it worked."

"Oh dear," Marcy said, her tongue making another quick swipe. "This isn't going to cost anyone anything, is it? Like someone's job or Emma's authority at the store or . . ." The faintest of smiles shadowed her lips. "Your brother's ire?"

Charity shook her head, her confidence unshaken. "Nope, only his pride. Not all of it, mind you, because heaven knows I can't perform miracles . . . but enough."

"So, Miss Mata Hari, Queen of Intrigue . . . how exactly are you planning to bait the trap? Barbecue ribs, perchance? Because Lizzie is right—Sean will sniff a mercy dinner a mile away."

"Just don't you worry, because I know—"

"Hey, Lizzie . . ." Sean pushed through the screen door, the sleeves of his old work shirt rolled up and splotched with telltale paint.

"—that as far as marriage is concerned," Charity continued seamlessly, as smooth as the silk blouse in her hand, "Katie will get the lay of the land soon enough, you'll see. I just wish poor, little Kit wasn't still under the weather, so Katie and she could be here. I, for one, would like a newly-wed update."

"I think I heard jabbering down the hall, so I suspect Molly may be up from her nap." Sean wiped his paintbrush with a wet rag obviously saturated in turpentine, prompting Charity to wrinkle her nose. His smile was lackluster at best. "Didn't want to peek in case she shouldn't be up yet, you know?"

"Uncle Sean!" Henry called, relief evident in his voice. "Wanna play catch?"

"Sorry, bud, I've got work to do, but maybe later, okay?"

Charity glanced up. "So, Mr. Handyman . . . I understand you fixed Mother's leak."

"Dry as dust in the desert," he quipped, his own tone equally so.

"Really . . . ," she said, giving him her full attention. She propped her chin in her hand and wiggled her brows. "So . . . what do you think you could do for my kitchen sink?"

"What's wrong with it?" he asked, slacking a hip as he swiped the sweat on his face.

She tilted her head. "Leaks like a sieve. Mitch has been meaning to look at it, but with the hours he's pulling at the *Herald*, I'm lucky to get a grunt and a kiss." She leaned forward and lowered her voice, chancing a peek at her twins in the backyard. "But between you and me, I'd just as soon he didn't get another chance, if you know what I mean. It's gone downhill since he fixed it the last time, and I'm tired of having water in my best pot."

A half smile flickered on Sean's mouth. "Sure, I'll look at it. Tomorrow okay?"

"Actually," she said, her smile dimming somewhat, "tomorrow probably won't work." Her nose crinkled in thought before she suddenly looked up, eyes as bright as the idea in her head. "Wait—how about Saturday after your game? We'll be home all evening."

His blue eyes squinted in thought. "That could work. My game should be over by six."

"Perfect! And you may as well stay for dinner."

He hesitated—prey stilled by the scent of the hunter. "I don't know, sis." One side of his mouth lifted a fraction of an inch. "I probably won't smell too good."

"But you're coaching, not playing, right? And you gotta eat anyway." Charity appeared hopeful as she cast her imaginary line.

Nobody breathed as the lure sailed through the air . . .

"Look, sis, I'm not the best company lately—"

"I don't mind if you eat and run, honest."

He cocked his head and gritted his teeth with a smile, his decision likely edging toward "no," given the apology in his eyes.

Uh-oh, fish or cut bait. Charity smiled and switched strategies. "That's okay, really—I understand." With a nonchalant air, she grabbed a spool of purple thread from the sewing box and gave him a wink. "Just more ribs for us." She held the thread against the silk blouse and looked up. "Hey, do these colors match?"

"Ribs?" Sean said weakly.

Charity fished in the sewing box again, ignoring his gaze as she fiddled with more spools. "Yes, sir . . . Mitch's applewood smoked variety, his secret sauce, candied carrots, my prize popovers, and—" she looked up, her face the picture of innocence—"potato salad."

"Potato salad?" He paused. His voice was the pained whisper of a man used to simpler fare prepared by a frugal mother victimized by the depression. He swallowed hard, as if drool were clogging his throat. "Mustard or mayonnaise?"

She plopped back into her chair and flashed him a bright smile. "Sorry, didn't catch that. What was the question again?"

"The potato salad—is it the mustard kind or the mayonnaise?" It came out as a croak.

Charity worked the edge of her lip, trying to remember Sean's favorite. "Uh . . . mayonnaise, I think."

The man groaned as if a sharp lure had just pierced the soft flesh of his lip.

Bingo!

She set the hook and reeled him in. "And, of course, my homemade deviled eggs, those barbecue butter beans you're so fond of, and last but not least . . ."

His mouth hung open like a large-mouth bass.

Victory coursed through her veins with a rush of adrenaline. "Warm peach cobbler in a pool of caramel sauce with cinnamon ice cream on the side—from Robinson's no less," she breathed, her tone hushed with respect.

"Oh, man . . ." His voice was a moan of defeat. He blasted

out a sigh that could have ruffled the leaves on the lilac bush at the edge of the porch. "What time again?"

"Six," she said with a flutter of lashes. "You can fix the drain, and then I'll feed you at six-thirty."

His lungs expanded and released, as if he'd given up the ghost. "Okay, sis." Shoulders slumped in surrender, he glanced at his mother. "Do you know where the mower is? I was hoping to mow the lawn, but it's not in the shed."

"I'm afraid your father lent it to Mr. Morris last week when his broke."

Another sigh that seemed to weigh as much as he did expelled from his lips. "Okay, I guess I'll pay him a visit." He turned to go, his heart clearly not in hobnobbing with neighbors.

"See you Saturday," Charity called after him.

He waved a hand in the air, not even sparing a glance. "Yeah, sure—Saturday." The screen door squealed open before he turned halfway, a touch of contrition in his eyes. "Sorry, sis, I forgot to ask if there was anything I could bring, like maybe the ice cream?"

"Nope, just your appetite . . . and your tools." Her smile was beaming.

He nodded, and the screen slammed behind him.

"Soooo . . . ," Charity said with a smug lift of her chin. She smiled at her mother and sisters, then cocked a brow in Faith's direction. "He won't do it, eh? You think you would have learned by now not to underestimate me."

"He hasn't shown up yet, nor agreed to take the job." Faith bit off the end of the thread from a shirt she'd just sewn and tied it into a knot. "Besides, you did have to pull the 'ribs' card, you know. For a moment there, I thought you were dead in the water."

"I know," Charity said, her tone humbling considerably. A sigh of relief wavered from her lips. "But the hard part's done. Now, all we need is for Emma to come through."

"You think she can do it?" Lizzie asked.

Charity tilted her head, thinking of the soft spot her brother harbored for Emma Malloy. "I think so. I mean the woman is as honest as the day is long, and I know Sean trusts her." Her lips twisted. "At least more than he trusts me. So if Emma tells him she needs his help, I think he'll do it. Because let's face it, he may be a man, stubborn to a fault, but he's also a sucker for anyone who needs his help. Which, as we all know, makes him the perfect knight in shining armor to rescue our damsel in distress." Charity eased a strand of thread through the eye of the needle, then grinned. "See? The perfect plan."

"No plan is perfect without prayer," Faith said in a wry tone. She tilted her head, giving Charity a mysterious smile. "We are going to pray about this, right?"

"Of course," Charity said, clearly aghast. "Do you think I'm crazy?"

Faith opened her mouth.

"Don't answer that," Charity warned. She slithered the needle into the silk as she prepared to patch a hole, then slid Faith a half-lidded smile. "Give me a little credit, will you? I may be crazy . . . but I'm not stupid."

⋙ ⋘

Meow.

Emma pooled cool water in her hands to wash the soap from her face, then carefully patted herself dry. She eyed Guinevere who perched on the back of the commode with all the regality of a queen on her throne as she groomed snow-white fur with dainty, ladylike strokes. "I'm moving as quickly as I can, Your Grace," Emma said with a quirk of a smile, "but one must never rush hygiene, as you surely must know."

The fluffy Persian stretched and purred when Emma grazed beneath her chin with a finger. Pale eyelids closed in contentment, concealing the fact that "Her Majesty" was missing an eye, a fate befallen her as a stray kitten abused by a cruel boy with a stick. A neighbor had rescued her and Emma had begged to keep her, feeling a kinship with this helpless creature with whom she shared a bond. Whether the loss of sight had sharpened her sense of smell or Guinevere was just a true female who loved the smell of chocolate, Emma wasn't quite sure. But the fact remained that Emma's night-time ritual of bathing and cocoa butter applied to her scars was truly a highlight of Guinevere's day.

Coaxing the cat into her arms, Emma carried her into the bedroom where Lancelot presided over Emma's floral bed-spread like a regent over a jungle of tropical blooms. Having no interest whatsoever in female primping, he ignored them both, happily snoring away. With the utmost care, she placed Guinevere on the marred Victorian vanity she'd salvaged from the store and then padded to the parlor to turn on her phonograph, the soothing sounds of Duke Ellington trailing her down the hall. With a gentle stroke of Guinevere's fur, she took her seat before the vanity mirror, thinking for the thousandth time what an oxymoron it was for her to pos-sess anything that bore the name "vanity." Nonetheless, she couldn't help but admire the lacy white nightgown she wore, one of the few luxuries she allowed because it helped her to feel so feminine, something she desperately needed in a world void of romantic love. Her lips tipped into a smile. Although never would she have chosen something so daring if Charity hadn't been along. But she had to admit that the soft swell of her breasts against the scalloped neckline did make her feel pretty, a rare accomplishment indeed. Leaning forward, she pushed chestnut waves behind her ears to examine her face in the glass, noting that the cocoa butter Charity had hounded her to apply had actually paid off, fading her once-blatant scars until they almost appeared not to exist.

But Emma knew better. Eyes in a squint, she saw herself as she'd been years ago—a child of inordinate beauty with the gift of song that had put a gleam of pride in her father's eyes. A father who'd flaunted that same beauty on nightly treks to the pub, toting his eight-year-old daughter along to sing for his friends. Against her mother's wishes. That is . . . until the song was silenced . . . and the beauty tainted forever. Emma's eyes fluttered closed, a familiar stab of pain at the memory of her father's revulsion, his fury, when his thirteen-year-old prodigy had been defiled by one of the same young men he'd taunted with his daughter's beauty.

Damaged goods. Just like the vanity.

And a father's love.

"*Meow . . .*"

She opened her eyes to Guinevere, grateful for the distraction. Shaking off the unwelcome memories, she started to reach for the jar of cocoa butter while humming along with the Duke, when her gaze lighted on the silk scarf from Charity. Unbidden, her fingers glided to where it lay, neatly folded next to the obsidian earrings, and with a deep draw of air, she picked it up. The silk was sensual to the touch, catching her pulse while she slowly grazed it against her cheek, a perfect caress against imperfect skin. Swirls of pale green and the softest of grays blended to create a hue that seemed to illuminate her eyes, pools from a mossy mountain stream as deep as the secrets she could never share. From scars to silk, and suddenly she felt beautiful again like so long ago when men's fingers, instead of silk, had grazed her skin . . . and hungry kisses replaced the love a father could no longer give.

"I love you, Emmy," Rory had whispered the first time he'd kissed her, setting her skin aflame with the tingle of his touch, the nuzzle of his mouth. His body had molded to hers in a way that assured her he wanted to love her, possess her, make her his own. Even now, her body warmed at the memory of his touch, and for one brief, blinding moment, she was a woman again, alive with passion and desire and the need to give of herself in every possible way.

Heart pounding, she twirled the scarf around her neck and closed her eyes, swaying to the music while its easy rhythm flowed through her veins, melting away the sins of her past. Instead, she saw herself as she might have been if temptation hadn't led her astray—clean, pure, and free—to be the woman she so longed to be.

The soft wisp of fur tickled her arm and she opened her eyes to Guinevere's delicate paw, poking for attention. A soft chuckle bubbled in her chest and she bowed at the waist.

"Why, yes, Your Majesty, I would be honored to give you this dance." Swooping the cat up into her arms, she cuddled her close while they twirled to the music, drifting off to places she could only go in her mind.

Swish . . . swish . . . The music stopped while the turntable continued to spin, a melancholy reminder that she was no longer in the arms of a fairy-tale prince but alone in her cozy bedroom with a cat in her arms. Holding Guinevere aloft, she deposited a gentle kiss to her pet's nose and then tucked her into bed next to Lancelot.

"Don't worry, girl, I'll slather up with cocoa butter and follow you soon."

She ruffled Lancelot's marmalade coat before heading to the parlor to turn off the phonograph, double-check the door, and turn out the lights. Returning to the vanity, she carefully folded the scarf and set it aside before smoothing a dab of the creamy, yellow butter onto her face until her skin glowed, breathing in the rich, heavenly scent of chocolate. A smile tugged at her lips. No wonder Guinevere snuggled close throughout the night. Dousing the small Tiffany lamp on her vanity, Emma quietly moved to the window to open the sheers, allowing both a ribbon of moonlight and a sweet, honeysuckle breeze to stream into the room. Locusts trilled and Lancelot snored, creating a peaceful symphony that lulled her to the bed where she slipped beneath the cool sheets and whispered her prayers.

Guinevere immediately curled into a ball on her pillow while Lancelot shored up the other side, the rhythm of their breathing warming her inside and out. Inhaling, Emma breathed in the sweet smell of cocoa butter along with the scent of a fragrant summer night, and her chest expanded with thanksgiving for the blessing of her home. True, as a woman, she would never again know the comforts of a man, but somewhere along the way, solitude had become her friend, as snug and sweet as the two precious kitties now cuddling against her sides. Burrowing in, Guinevere draped a protective paw across Emma's neck while Lancelot butted close, emitting nasal noises that made Emma smile. Closing her eyes, all loneliness slowly faded away as she succumbed to the magic of slumber, allowing contentment to seep into her bones. A contentment that, despite her solitary lifestyle, convinced her she would never be alone.

Because as a woman, yes, her marriage may be empty . . . but her heart and bed were full.

Please, Mrs. Clary, answer the door . . .

Standing on the kitchen stoop of St. Stephen's rectory, Sean reached to straighten his tie out of sheer habit, then stopped, blood warming his cheeks at the reality that there was no tie to adjust. His hand suddenly went clammy against the frayed open collar of his most presentable work shirt. In the catch of his breath, sweat beaded the back of his neck as the realization struck all over again: he was unemployed.

The thought never failed to jolt him, not once in the two weeks since Rose Kelly had ruined his life, and each and every time it only served to deepen this vile depression that had him by the throat. He hadn't felt this way in a long, long time—like someone had died or as if every step he took was weighted with grief, a cloying quicksand intent on sucking him in. For thirty-four years, other than during the war, the incident at Kearney's, and that one awful night of his father's near heart attack, all he'd known was a sense of peace and contentment with his life, a man who needed nothing more than the love of family, the fellowship of friends, and the satisfaction of a job well done. A nerve pulsed in his jaw. Yeah, a job well "done," he thought with a stab of bitterness. As in over . . . finished . . . kaput.

Just like my confidence.

He shook off the malaise and jabbed a firm finger to the button-size doorbell, hoping and praying that Father Mac would be out on afternoon hospital visits and Mrs. Clary would answer the door. It'd be so much easier asking the rectory housekeeper for odd jobs around the church and rectory, or even Father McCovey, rather than Father Mac. No, to Sean the parish associate pastor had become too good of a friend rather than a priest, an able teammate with Mitch and him in Saturday morning basketball against Collin, Brady, and Luke. Sure, he knew about Sean's layoff from Kelly's, but asking a friend for work was something else altogether. Originally a close friend of Brady's, Father Matthew McHugh had quickly become a friend to Sean as well, insisting he call him "Father Mac" or even "Mac" throughout the course of the summer. To ask Mac for work, well, it would be too difficult, too awkward . . . Sean sucked in a fortifying breath and punched the doorbell again. Too humiliating.

Not that he needed the money. No, that wasn't the issue. He had no intention of taking one red cent for any odd jobs. If managing his own store had taught him anything, it was to be an astute businessman, steady and sure with his capital. Over the years, while his friends had frittered their paychecks on women and other frivolous things, Sean had quietly squirreled his away, investing in long-term Treasury bonds rather than the stock market like his father and so many others. The result was a tidy savings that few enjoyed in this dismal economy. It was the one saving grace that separated him from the ranks of the almost eight million unemployed, and a sense of gratitude flooded his soul for the first time in weeks. *At least I can still help Father with much-needed rent.*

Sturdy footsteps jolted his thoughts and he winced. Uh-oh . . . either Mrs. Clary had put on weight or . . .

"Sean—come in, come in!" Father Mac stepped back and waved him inside the cozy black-and-white kitchen that was Mrs. Clary's domain, his thick dark brows ascending in jest. "It's not Saturday morning already, is it?"

Forcing a chuckle, Sean stepped in and was instantly assailed by the aroma of apples and cinnamon that watered his mouth. "Nope," he said with a smile, his glance darting to a fresh-baked apple pie sitting next to a basketball on the counter. "I promise this visit is far friendlier."

"Too bad," Father Mac said, his gaze following Sean's

to the golden, thick-crusted pastry. Strolling over to palm the basketball, he bobbled it while his stocky six-foot frame leaned against the white wooden counter. "Because Brady was supposed to take me on with a game of one-on-one during his lunch hour, but apparently a rush job came in." His gaze slid sideways to the pie and back. A smile flickered on his lips that matched the gleam in his brown eyes. The clean smell of fresh-mown grass drifted in on a summer breeze, feathering dark hair sifted with gray as Father Mac nodded toward the basketball hoop outside. "Care to work off a piece of pie with a game? Exercise is vital, you know, if I'm going to keep up with you young whelps on Saturday mornings."

Sean's smile was genuine as he ruffled a hand through hair void of Brilliantine, one eye still on the pie. "Sure, why not?" he said, taking in Mac's brawny arms beneath his rolled sleeves. At fifty-four, Father Mac defied age with enough muscle and stamina to put most men to shame, not to mention his diabolical determination to whip Brady and Luke at their own sport. *Must be all that clean living*, Sean thought with a hook of the chair as he eased into the heavy oak seat. *And his lifeline to God.* He stretched out an arm and absently flexed his hand on the table, taking note of his own forearm, heavily corded with veins and muscles. Each and every one had been earned from an endless array of sports despite his ripe age of thirty-four. His smile skewed to the right. *Well, I have clean living going for me anyway.*

"So, what brings you to my door on this rather pleasant summer day?" Father Mac asked, fishing a knife and two forks from the drawer. He reached for plates out of the cabinet overhead and proceeded to cut them each a healthy slab of pie. He deposited one in front of Sean, then shoved the other across the table, brows lifted in question. "Milk or iced tea?" he asked, gaze shifting to the empty coffeepot on the counter. "I'm afraid the coffee has expired for the day."

"Milk is great," Sean said with an easy smile that felt almost normal again. He descended on the pie with more of an appetite than he'd had in days. Father Mac set a tall glass of milk before him, which Sean half emptied in two thirsty gulps. He shoveled in another bite, then motioned to the pie with his fork, swallowing before emitting a low groan. "Wow, this is great stuff—my compliments to Mrs. Clary."

"I'll be sure to tell her. There's plenty more when you're done."

Sean wolfed down the final bite and shoved his plate away, shaking his head as he eyed Father Mac over the rim of his milk. He upended the glass to finish it, then slapped it on the table. "Man, that hit the spot, thanks. Especially since I didn't have lunch."

Father Mac carved out a piece of pie with his fork and looked up, his smile fading into concern. "No appetite?" he asked quietly.

The gloom of Sean's situation returned, roiling the pie in his gut. He sagged back in the chair, painfully aware of the heat crawling up the back of his neck. "Not much," he said as he slapped calloused hands to his belly and attempted a grin. "Which is fine by me. Since I moved back home last year, I've packed on extra pounds that are slowing me down on the court."

"Hardly." Father Mac took a quick swallow of milk. "You're a machine, my friend, the best athlete in the parish, bar none."

The grin came easier this time. "Mind putting that in writing? I'd like to give it to McGee."

Mac smiled, chewing while he studied him, then finished his pie with a final slug of milk. "Well, Luke's a married man now, and a wife and child take priority over workouts with the boys, so he's got a lot on his mind." He paused, shoving the empty plate away before folding thick arms on the table to assess through troubled eyes. "I'd say you do too. Care to get anything off your chest?"

Heat swarmed his cheeks as if he'd just wolfed down a bucket of chili peppers. He shifted in the chair, pretty sure the seat was as hot as any peppers. "No . . . no, Mac, I'm fine, really." He lowered his voice to the calm and confident level he'd perfected for family tragedies, irate customers, and little boys who had just swung out. "As a matter of fact, I expect to land another job any day now." He steeled his jaw, completely uncomfortable discussing his failure with the parish priest, good friend or no. "I'm looking for work every day, of course, but I can't just sit around with extra time on my hands." He sucked in a jagged breath and released it with a tight smile. "So if you have any odd jobs—here, the church, the school—I'm your man. You know, building cabinets, leaky faucets, whatever. I'm pretty handy and can do whatever you need."

Placing his fork on his empty plate, Father Mac leaned back and draped one arm over the back of another chair. "Well, I'd say that's perfect timing, then. Sister Bernice just badgered me for new choir risers last week. Claims we'll have a slew of broken arms and legs if the children are forced to stand on the old ones another season. When can you start?"

Sean slowly expelled the breath he'd been holding. "Today, if you want. I can give you most afternoons till the right job comes along. Mornings, of course, are reserved for pounding the pavement, but just give me a list of your maintenance needs, and it's as good as done."

A hint of a smile returned to Father Mac's eyes. "With occasional bouts of one-on-one thrown in for good measure, I trust?"

Sean grinned outright for the first time in weeks. "If you think you can keep up, *Father*."

Father Mac laughed. "I'd be careful, Sean—you're starting to sound every bit as cocky as Brady. I swear the man's in league with the devil the minute he steps foot on the court."

Sean's smile swagged to the right. "Hey look, I just lost my job—how about a little mercy? Trust me, there's not a whole lot I can feel cocky about these days."

"If it's mercy you want, it's mercy you'll get—out on the court. *After* we discuss terms, that is." Father Mac rose and stacked Sean's dirty plate and utensil on top of his. He dumped them in the sink and snatched the ball off the counter. "All expenses—lumber, hardware, paint, whatever—reimbursed with receipts. As far as hours, give me a rundown every Friday, and I'll see you get a check the following week." He started for the door. "We'll pay what you made at Kelly's—"

"No."

Father Mac turned, hand on the knob. "You want more?"

"No, Mac, I don't want anything. I'm volunteering my time. You know, so I don't feel like a bum while looking for a job?" Sean carried the empty glasses to the sink, then followed Father Mac to the door.

Tucking the ball under his arm, Father Mac held the screen open, his brow buckled. "Sorry, Sean, I can't agree to those terms—the laborer is worthy of his wages. It's the law."

Sean plucked the ball from Father Mac's hand with a jag of his brow. He paused to sail a shot into the side of the hoop. "Says who?"

"The Good Book."

Father Mac took swift possession, gaze pinned to the basket. He rose up on the balls of well-worn Keds to sail a long shot that clipped the back of the board. Sean winced at the sound of a neat, clean swish.

Mac grinned. "Arguing with the Ref, are you?"

Stifling a groan, Sean slacked a leg, hands perched low on his hips. "Look, Mac, I'm just looking to stay busy and maybe help somebody in the process. I don't need your money."

"Those are the terms, take it or leave it." Father Mac squinted and took aim, launching the basketball into the basket with an annoying whoosh. He retrieved the ball to score again with a hook shot, obviously indifferent to Sean's searing gaze. "But keep in mind that you'll be answering to Sister Bernice if you back out now." He wiped the sweat from his face with the sleeve of his cassock, then threatened with a pastoral gaze. "And it'd be a real shame if the boys on your team found out that their coach was a welsher."

Sean slapped the ball from the priest's grip and bounded in the air, his jump shot skimming the net with nary a sound. Fetching the ball, he tucked it under his arm and rolled the sleeves of his work shirt, his grin positively predatory. "I thought priests dealt in mercy, not blackmail. No more than a quarter of my former salary or I'm walking."

"Half," Father Mac shot back, dislodging the ball with a hard swipe. With a quick flick of his wrist, the ball glided through the air with angelic precision. "If you don't want to keep it, you can always donate it to Sister Cecilia. The Holy Childhood Association can use it, you know." He trailed a finger along the inside of his collar in an apparent attempt to tug it loose, then flashed an impressive gleam of white teeth. "I can hear it now. Pagan babies singing your praises."

"You're on." Sean snatched the ball and hurtled it toward the basket, his laughter winging along. "Thank God somebody'll be 'singing my praises,'" he said, enjoying the rush of adrenaline that pumped through his veins. "The silence has been deafening."

He jerked his shirttail out to wipe the sweat off his brow, feeling like a human being for the first time in weeks. "Because like you, *Father*, in this game we're about to have?" He grinned, his confidence rebounding once again. "I'll just take what I can get."

<hr />

"*Mama!*"

Charity's screen door squealed open and slammed with a bang. A streak of a blond moppet flew toward her mother with misty blue eyes and quivering lips. "Henry's at it again—and this time he threatened to put a can of worms down my back!"

Emma turned at the sink, heart softening at the look of distress on Hope's face. Charity stooped to pull her nine-year-old daughter into her arms and planted a kiss on her cheek. "He's only bluffing, Hope. He wouldn't dare risk the wrath of his mother with a stunt like that."

The little girl shuddered, clinging to her mother's neck. "He would, Mama—he said so! Said it'd be worth it—anything you or Daddy dished out. Can you make him stop, *please*?"

"How 'bout I send your father out there to put the fear of God in him?"

Hope shook her head from side to side, ringlets bobbing. "No, you! He's afraid of you."

Charity's lips skewed into a droll smile as she glanced up at Emma. She stood to her feet and patted her daughter's shoulder. "No, honey, this is a job for Daddy. Animals are involved."

Emma giggled, biting her lip to stifle her laughter. "Earthworms . . . animals?" She forced a serious demeanor, but her mouth twitched with tease. "Maybe for a sissy."

Charity's eyes narrowed, scathing her with a mock glare. "For your information, Emma Malloy, I am simply following the first rule of parenting Mitch and I established when the twins were born—he handles all animal-related incidents." She shivered and made her way to the door. "Besides," she said, scrunching her nose over her shoulder, "I can't abide those slimy, little things." She stood at the hallway and cupped a hand to her mouth. "*Miiiitttttch!* Your daughter needs you!" Calmly returning to give Hope a kiss on her nose, Charity shot Emma a smile. "It's time for him to check the ribs anyway—Sean will be here at six."

Emma turned back to peeling the carrots, her nerves suddenly as squirmy as a can of Henry's worms. Beads of moisture glazed her brow and she absently flapped the front of her blouse in an effort to cool off a sudden flush of nervous heat. She'd seen Charity plan and plot many a harebrained scheme, but never had she actually been a part of one before, and suddenly the prospect made her more than a little queasy. "Are you sure we're doing the right thing? You know, plotting this all out? Maybe you should just come out and ask him."

The deviled egg in Charity's mouth wedged still, her lips circling the egg to form a white O of shock. She quickly chewed and gulped it down. "Are you crazy? You know my brother. He may be the easygoing one of the lot, but don't let that fool you. If we even hinted we wanted to give him a job at the store, the man would disappear faster than Henry at bath time."

"I know, but—"

"So . . . what seems to be the problem here?" Mitch blew in with unruly blond hair that matched the moppet's. The scowl on his chiseled face softened when he saw Emma. "Hey, Emma, didn't know you were here yet. Did you sneak around back?"

Emma nodded, her smile warming at the sight of the only man she'd ever seen keep Charity in line. "Lured by the smell of your world-famous ribs, I assure you. When it comes to smoked ribs, you could teach the rest of the family a thing or two."

He grinned, obviously pleased with Emma's assessment given the barbecue wars that raged in the O'Connor clan. "Yeah, the secret's in the sauce *and* the apple-wood smoke, but don't tell that to Collin. Rumor has it he plans to usurp my authority come Labor Day." Mitch's blue eyes met those of his daughter. "Hey, what's the matter, honey? Did you get hurt?" He picked her up and bundled her in his arms, scanning her from head to toe.

"No, she's not hurt," Charity said with a kiss to her cheek, "but Henry's at it again. Threatened her with worms."

Mitch blinked. "Worms?" His jaw shifted while the blue eyes narrowed. He adjusted his daughter in his arms and slacked a hip, measuring the air with his finger and thumb. "The Red Sox are this close to humiliating the Yankees, and you call me away from the radio for *worms*?"

Emma couldn't help it—she snickered.

Charity engaged her chin to match his. "Last time I checked, worms were part of the animal kingdom, Mitch Dennehy, so don't give me any grief."

He bussed his daughter's cheek, then propped a firm finger beneath his wife's chin. "Wouldn't consider it, little girl," he said with a hasty kiss to her mouth. "That talent belongs to you and you alone." He turned and headed to the back door with Hope snug in his arms. "Come on, princess, let's go talk to your mother's son." The door slammed behind them.

"So you see, Emma, we don't have a choice," Charity

continued without missing a beat. She tucked the deviled eggs into the icebox. "You need help at the store, and Sean needs a job, and this is the only way that bullheaded brother of mine will even consider it." Absently chewing her thumbnail, she wandered off into a pensive stare, obviously lost in thought for several seconds. She suddenly glanced up in a squint. "Hey . . . can you cry on demand?"

Emma chuckled, Charity's talent for manipulation never ceasing to amaze her. She shook her head as she rinsed the carrots. "Sorry, I don't have much experience with crying."

"Humph . . . at least not anymore, thank heavens," Charity said with a grunt. She peeked into the oven to check on the barbecue butter beans. "Well, I know you're not as devious as me—what can I say? It's a gift. But that's exactly why you're the perfect person to convince Sean to take the job. My brother respects you, Emma, admires you and loves you like a sister."

With a heavy exhale, Emma cut off the carrot tops and pulled out a pot from the cabinet, wondering if that still held true, given her shock and dismay over the scene he'd made at the wedding. She filled it with water and put it on to boil. "Well, there's certainly a need for Sean at the store, no question about that. And, he's got some time on his hands until he finds another job." She reached for a knife and sighed. "I just hope I don't let you down."

"Don't worry, you won't." Charity looked up from the rolls she was placing on a cookie sheet and cocked her head. "Turn around."

Emma glanced over her shoulder with a pucker between her brows. "What?"

"Turn around, please . . . all the way."

Knife in hand, Emma reluctantly faced her friend, quite sure that Charity's expression, now kinked in thought, did not bode well.

"Mmm . . . you don't look as tired as I hoped, although that faded blue dress certainly washes you out—good job." She studied Emma intently, arms crossed and finger tapping her chin. "I'm afraid that lipstick has to go. It brings out the soft hint of green in those amazing gray eyes of yours, and we don't want that—too serene." She handed her a handkerchief. "Here, wipe the lipstick off, and then I have the perfect touch."

"Uh-oh, I don't like the sound of that," Emma said, wide-eyed as she cut a carrot into pennies and tossed them into the pot. She took Charity's handkerchief and blotted her lips, more than a little skittish over what her friend had in mind. "I've heard that tone before, and it's trouble."

"Oh, hush," Charity said, sliding a manicured finger along the dark edge of her own eyelid to smear her fingertip with eyeliner. "You're my best friend, Emma—you're supposed to trust me."

Emma's mouth tipped up. "Why should I when your own brother won't?"

"Exactly," Charity said, as if Emma had just proven her point. She leaned to dab her finger beneath both of Emma's eyes, smudging the dark makeup until a grin lit her face. "There—perfect!" She reached into her cabinet for a shiny stainless steel frying pan. "Here, see for yourself. You look like a zombie who hasn't slept in days."

"Oh, joy," Emma said, her enthusiasm as flat as the pan in her hand. She angled it just so and gaped. "For pity's sake, Charity, I look like a raccoon!"

Charity chuckled. "That's good, because pity is exactly what we're going for. Everybody knows Sean is a sucker for kids, animals, and a good cause. And you, Emma Malloy, whether you know it or not, are a very worthy cause." She paused, head tilted to listen before she shot a glance at the clock. "Oh, good—he's here, and he's early."

Emma froze, pan in hand. The sound of Sean laughing outside with Mitch threatened to upheave the butterflies in her stomach, worthy cause or no. Apparently "plotting" did not agree with her. Her lips slanted into a wry smile as she focused on cutting another carrot. *Maybe I should throw up . . . then "sick" and "tired" wouldn't be stretching the truth at all.*

"Emma! I didn't know you were going to be here." Sean stood at the screen door, muscled arm braced to keep it from slamming behind.

All of Emma's butterflies nosedived in her stomach as she stared at the man who had toppled her trust. She attempted a welcome smile to cover her nervousness, completely forgetting Charity's instructions to mope. "Sean, hello! Yes, your sister twisted my arm—dangling the promise of her husband's smoked ribs, no less."

He strolled in to give Charity a hug, then grinned, his white teeth a stark contrast to the deep tan obscuring his freckles. "Yep, the ribs got me too. That and the warm peach cobbler."

"Well, I had to do something to get Emma away from the store," Charity said, worry threading her tone. "The woman's worn herself to a frazzle working day and night."

"Now, Charity, you know that's not—" Emma began, forgetting her role.

"Day and night?" Sean's smile dimmed as he set his toolbox on the table. "That can't be good." He wandered over to give her a hug while ridges lined his brow, calling attention to errant strands of blond hair that tumbled into his eyes. "You look tired."

She peeked up at him, catching the scent of Snickers, soap, and the barest hint of sweat. His wilted shirt was dusty and open at the collar, revealing both a glimpse of sandy hair against a bronzed chest and muscled forearms taut with veins beneath rolled sleeves. Her smile felt strained as she pulled away, uncomfortable in his hold. "Well, I didn't sleep well last night."

"Don't believe her," Charity said, "it's sheer exhaustion. She clocked in over eighty hours at the store last week alone and still refuses to hire any help."

Heat dusted Emma's cheeks. "It wasn't eighty hours."

Charity jutted her chin. "Oh, all right—seventy-six—same difference. Either way, you're killing yourself, and I, for one, am worried."

Sean's mouth slacked open. "Seventy-six hours? In one week?" He sent his sister an accusing stare. "And you let her?"

"That's just it—I can't stop her." Charity slid the rolls in the oven, then cranked the egg timer with a huff. "And you think *I'm* stubborn."

Emma shook her head, a smile edging her lips at Charity's gift for drama.

Sean slanted against the counter with a fold of his arms and a hint of a smile. "Who would have thought? Sweet Emma Malloy, as pigheaded as my sister."

"More," Charity confirmed.

"Oh, now there's a trip to confession if ever there was," Emma said with a grin.

Sean's smile faded. "Seriously, Emma, working those kinds of hours is deadly. If you wear down and get sick, then who's going to run the store?"

"Yes, Emma, who?" Charity demanded. She flipped a flaxen strand of hair from her eyes and slapped her hands on her hips. "You know Mitch only allows me to work two days a week while the kids are in school and not at all in the summer. What if something happens to you?"

Emma blinked, caught off-guard by the truth of Charity's point. "Well, I . . . I guess I never thought of that."

"You should, you know," Sean said. "I had an assistant at Kelly's, and it's only half the size of Dennehy's. Trust me, Andy saved my hide more than once when I was out with the flu."

"But my budget can't afford an assistant manager," Emma said, sincerity softening the plea of her tone. "Sales are down 25 percent, and I've had to make staff cuts as it is." She chanced a peek at Charity, who winked, then spun around to check on the boiling pot. Steam misted the warmth of her cheeks as she turned the flame down, grateful that every word she spoke was truth. She drew in a deep breath and turned to face him once again. "Besides, where would I find someone trained in retail who would be willing to work from now through Christmas, our busiest season, for practically nothing? Goodness, we're talking merchandising, buying and selling, inventory, advertising, promotion, personnel, accounting, scheduling—the list is endless."

"Yes, where is she supposed to find somebody like that?" Charity piped in. "Even if she would allow us to increase her budget, which she won't." She shot Emma a pointed look.

Emma sighed, a tired smile lining her lips, both from Charity's pretend badgering and the reality of a budget already strained to its limit. "A good merchant works within a budget, Charity, and never more so than during difficult times." She glanced over her shoulder. "Right, Sean?"

Blue eyes the exact shade of Charity's studied her intently. "True, but not at the expense of your health, Emma. If you're drowning at the store, you need to hire someone to assist."

"Exactly," Charity said with a noisy sigh. She bent to retrieve a large pot from under the sink and tipped it toward Sean to reveal the dirty water inside. "And speaking of drowning . . ."

Peeking into the pot, Emma wrinkled her nose at an odor that made her nauseous. "Oh, that doesn't smell so good."

Sean looked in the pot, blond brows dipped low as he drew air through clenched teeth. He waved off a fly buzzing the stagnant brew. "No, it doesn't." He hiked the toolbox from the table and set it on the floor, then squatted to assess the damage beneath the sink.

"Here, give me that." Emma held her breath as she retrieved the pot from Charity and tossed the contents out the back door onto the grass.

"So, what's the verdict?" Charity asked, bent over to follow her brother's line of vision. "Think you can fix it?"

"Yep. Got an old rag?"

"Sure." Charity pulled a man's dress shirt with bold blue stripes from a bottom drawer and handed it to Sean.

Emma squinted, unable to believe her eyes. "Wait, is that Mitch's favorite shirt? The one he was looking for the last time I came to dinner?"

"Hush, Emma, he'll hear you!" Charity's gaze flicked to the screen door and back. "The sleeves are frayed and the collar's worn." Her chin nudged up. "Besides, it makes him look old and I hate it."

"Charity!" Emma feigned shock despite the smile on her lips.

She blinked, eyes wide. "What? The man has dozens of new shirts in his closet, but what does he always wear? The one that makes him look like he should be standing in a breadline, for mercy's sake." She tossed the shirt under the sink. "Please, do me a favor, Sean—finish it off."

A low chuckle rose from below. "I feel like a traitor to my sex," he quipped as he dried off the pipes. "Will somebody plug the sink and fill it halfway?"

"I'll do it," Emma said, anxious to help. She quickly inserted the stopper and turned on the tap.

Sean stretched out on the floor, face up beneath the sink. "Hmm . . . looks like a new sink trap. Did Mitch put this in?"

One edge of Charity's mouth crooked up. "Unfortunately. Obviously the man belongs in a newsroom, not under a sink."

"Emma? Mind pulling the plug now?" Sean shifted, long legs cocked at the knees.

"Sure. Here goes . . ." Emma tugged, silently praying while water glugged down the sink.

"Thanks." Long pause. "Okay, found the answer."

"Ban Mitch from the kitchen?" Charity asked, innocence dripping from every syllable.

Sean laughed. "Nope, the trap looks good. Just a loose slip nut. Happens all the time. Hand me the wrench, will you, Emma?" Mitch's shirt flapped, appearing to get quite a workout.

Charity peeked under the sink. "You're a lifesaver, Sean— bless you!"

"Yes, you are," Emma said, handing him the wrench. "Goodness—wish I had ten more just like you down at the store."

A faint squeak sounded below as the wrench tightened the nut, merging with a low chuckle. "Well, how 'bout just one?"

Emma's face went slack as she rose to her full height, gaze locking with Charity's. "W-what did you say?" She gulped, not trusting her ears while Charity pressed palms skyward, mouthing her thanks.

Sean rolled out and lumbered to his feet with a crooked smile. He tossed the wrench back and rolled his shoulders, blue eyes twinkling as they took in Emma's gaping stare. With a boyish grin, he tucked a finger beneath Emma's chin and lifted. "I'd close your mouth if I were you, Emma. You might catch that fly."

Her mouth snapped shut and she swallowed hard. She couldn't believe that Charity's ploy had actually worked. "Y-you'd consider helping me out?"

The grin eased its way across his handsome face as he wiped his hands with Mitch's shirt, butting back to lounge against the counter with legs crossed. "Sure, that was your plan all along, wasn't it? Yours and my sister's?"

Her eyes drifted closed as a flash of heat moistened her face and neck. *Oh, Lord, I'm going to faint* . . . She started coughing, and Charity patted her back while Sean quickly filled a glass with water.

"Plan?" Charity said with a convincing crimp of her brows. "What plan?"

Sean handed Emma the glass, and she gulped it down. "Thank you," she whispered, her voice a raspy squeak.

He slung Mitch's shirt over his shoulder and replaced the stopper, then shot them a smile while refilling the sink. "You know, the one to get your poor, unemployed brother a job?"

A fine mist of water sprayed from Emma's mouth. Sean offered her Mitch's shirt with a grin that made her wish she could claim his spot under the sink. Grabbing it, she wiped her mouth and then handed it back.

"You? A job?" Charity looped an arm around Emma's waist. "Don't flatter yourself. It's poor Emma I'm worried about here—"

Me too! Emma started hacking again and immediately upended the glass, draining it dry.

Dipping the clean sleeve of Mitch's shirt under the faucet, Sean squeezed out the excess water and eased the tap off. He turned and gave Charity a patient smile. "Oh, there's no doubt about that, sis, which is the only reason I'd consider it in the first place. Emma is clearly tired and needs the help." He angled a brow. "Although the dark circles are definitely overkill."

Emma wanted to die. Her fingers flew to the shadow Charity had smudged beneath her eyes. "You know?" she whispered, her voice a mere croak.

He chuckled. "Oh, yeah, I know—my sister, that is. The woman who hates to cook. I mean, come on—ribs, peach cobbler, and deviled eggs? You forget I lived with her for almost twenty years." He nodded at Emma. "Although I have to admit—I haven't seen this trick since the eighth grade."

Emma bit her lip, desperate to rub the dark circles away. *Oh, Charity!*

"What do you mean, 'trick'?" Charity demanded, hands propped on her hips.

"I mean," he said with a gentle stroke of Mitch's wet sleeve beneath Emma's eyes, "the ploy you used on Mother when you didn't want to go to school *before* you perfected the routine of throwing up." He looked at the sleeve, now stained black, then gave it a quick sniff. "Although I'm guessing this is eye makeup rather than ashes from the wood-burning stove, right? There you go, Emma."

"Thank you," Emma whispered, appropriately humiliated.

"Oh, bother." Charity snatched Mitch's shirt. "I forgot it was you who ratted on me."

He patted her cheek. "For your own good, sis. Just like now." He pulled the plug and squatted in front of the sink, squinting at the pipes beneath. "Well, that should do it. As dry as Mitch's shirt used to be."

"So, you'll do it, then?" Charity asked, her voice hushed with hope as she pulled a bowl of the neighbors beets from the icebox.

Sean rose, the affection in his gaze warming Emma's cheeks. "For Emma? You bet. *And* for you too—with or without plotting. Although the ribs and cobbler sure didn't hurt."

Charity beamed. "I knew it!" She thumped the bowl of beets on the table.

"On one condition."

Emma's eyelids fluttered close. *Lord, help me, please . . .*

"Uh-oh." Charity paused, her gaze thinning. "What?"

Eyelids edging up, Emma chanced a peek.

Sean folded brawny arms across his chest. The press of his jaw tightened the smile on his face. "All volunteer, no salary. And mornings free to look for work and help out at church."

Emma's eyelids popped all the way open. "Absolutely not."

The sharp clip of her tone dropped several jaws in the room, but she didn't care. She may allow Charity to mastermind the plot to employ Sean at the store, but when it came to running it, it was Emma who called the shots, and it was best that Mr. Sean O'Connor learned that right out the gate. Surprise flickered in his eyes, but Emma forged on before he could lodge a protest.

"I am not a charity case, Sean O'Connor, and if you work for me, you will do so under my conditions."

He blinked, the lift of his brows tempered by a measured response that held both humor and respect. "Yes, ma'am. And those conditions would be . . ."

Emma ignored Charity's open-mouthed stare with a heft of her chin, well aware that neither Sean nor his sister had ever seen her in extreme "management" mode. "You will draw a salary or you won't work. Mornings off are fine. However, there will be evenings you will be expected to work as late as I do, unless, of course, you have a scheduled game. Understood?"

Sean nodded, the humor in his eyes fading into approval. "Anything else?"

"Yes," she said with a square of her shoulders, steeling herself for a fight—a fight she *would* win, no argument. "Your title will be assistant manager—"

"No—I can work on the dock—"

Her brows arched high. "Are you challenging my authority already, Mr. O'Connor?"

Sean stared, the shock on his lips easing into a grin. "No, ma'am." He swallowed and buried his hands in the pockets of his dusty trousers. "Being your assistant would be an honor."

"Good. When can you start?"

"When do you need me?"

Emma's mouth quirked. "Last month."

He grinned and swept a calloused hand across tousled hair. "Earliest I can do is Monday afternoon. I'll have to bump Father Mac's risers to Saturdays after our basketball game, but I can do it." A gleam lit his blue eyes. "Might cost you some penance."

Emma pursed her lips, a tad peeved at Charity for masterminding this charade. "You mean over and above working for your sister?"

"Emma!" Charity flicked her with the tail of Mitch's shirt.

He laughed. "Oh, yeah. You may have to feed me part of your dinner on nights we work late, but I'll do it."

"Do what? Tackle the ribs? Because they're ready." Mitch hefted a mountain of ribs on the kitchen table with a thud, infusing the kitchen with the mouthwatering aroma of smoked meat. A telltale blotch of barbecue sauce edged the side of his mouth. His gaze honed in on the shirt in Charity's hand, which promptly disappeared behind her back. He squinted at his wife. "Is that my favorite shirt? The one I've been looking everywhere for?"

"Yes!" Emma and Sean's confirmation rang in unison, and Emma's stomach fluttered when Sean gave her a wink.

"Mitch, guess what?" Charity asked, ignoring his question with a little-girl glow.

His mouth skewed into a thin smile as he snatched the shirt from behind her back, holding it in the air where it dangled with all the dignity of a scrubwoman's mop. "What? You're going to wash and iron my lucky shirt?"

"No! And you mean your 'lucky you're not in a breadline' shirt," Charity said, lifting on her toes to distract him with a kiss. Her tongue swiped the remains of the sauce from the side of his mouth while tugging the shirt from his grip. "Mmm . . . your best so far, which is more than I can say for this shirt." She lifted her chin with an air of pride. "No, I meant Sean has agreed to help Emma out at the store."

"I know," Mitch said, casually strolling to the icebox to retrieve a pitcher of lemonade. He pulled several glasses from the cabinet and glanced over his shoulder. "Anybody care for lemonade? Emma, Sean . . . Mata Hari?"

He knows?? Emma blinked, another haze of heat crawling up her neck . . . for the *umpteenth* time.

"You *know?*" Charity stared, hands propped on her hips. "How can you know? He just agreed to it a few minutes ago."

"No, I agreed to it two days ago when Mitch asked me." Sean winked at Emma, and her cheeks went head-to-head with the neighbor's beets. "Thanks, Mitch, lemonade sounds good."

"Same here, Mitch," Emma said, her throat as dry as Sean's tone.

Charity gawked at her husband. "*You* asked him? Without telling me? So Emma and I debased ourselves for nothing . . . and I had to cook in the process?"

"Not for nothing, sis," Sean said in a hurt tone. "Feeding your poor, unemployed brother has to count for something."

Emma shook her head, hand to her mouth to hide a seed of a smile. *Goodness, I don't know who's worse—Charity or her brother.*

"Mitch Dennehy!" Charity stamped her foot.

He handed glasses of lemonade to Sean and Emma, then poured two more. He paused to take a drink, eyes smiling over the rim of his glass. "I did it for Emma. You're not the only one who worries about her, you know." He set Charity's lemonade on the table and bussed her cheek with a quick kiss. "I would have told you, little girl, but you're so darn cute when you're plotting up a storm that I just couldn't resist."

"I think 'cute' may depend on one's perspective," Emma said with a dry grin, her cheeks still warm from Charity's ploy.

Charity whirled to confront Sean. "And you agreed? Just like that? After turning Father, Collin, and Brady down flat?"

Sean shrugged, a grin tipping the corners of his mouth. He winked at Emma, effectively flaming her cheeks once again.

"I'd do anything for Emma, you know that, sis. Besides, she's a whole lot cuter than they are."

"Come on, Sean, we'll catch the tail end of the game while the ladies put the food on the table." Mitch cupped a hand to Charity's waist and drew her close for a kiss, then headed toward the door. He turned to shoot her a sultry grin, wagging his shirt in the air. "And this, Mrs. Dennehy," he said with a superior lift of his brow, "will find its way to Mr. Chu, someone who knows how to give a man's shirt the respect that is due."

With a jaunty salute of his glass in the air, Sean followed Mitch into the parlor, leaving both Charity and Emma agape.

A giggle bubbled from Emma's throat, her embarrassment all but forgotten. Hand to her lips, she peeked at Charity with penitent eyes. "Are you mad?"

Charity snagged a piece of barbecue from the platter and popped it into her mouth. "Mad?" she asked, lips curved into a definite smile. "Nope. More like proud that I have a husband who knows how to get me what I want. Because that, my friend," she said with a sparkle of tease in her eyes, "is the mark of a well-trained man."

5

Finally home! Luke waved a bouquet at the board member who'd dropped him off and glanced at his watch. After ten—another late night with Carmichael and the Boston Children's Aid Society board, hammering out a strategy to bolster dwindling funds. A tired groan rumbled in his chest as he mounted the steps to his four-story brownstone on Commonwealth Avenue. Tucking the roses for Katie under his arm, he reached for the tarnished brass handle of the etched glass door, almost oblivious to the thrumming of tree frogs and locusts crooning in the towering oaks overhead. Apparently philanthropy had taken a hike when prosperity had, disappearing faster than that weak, watered-down broth doled out at soup kitchens down the road. Unfortunately, like those haunted faces in breadlines that wound around the block, the BCAS needed far more sustenance to survive.

As do I, Luke thought with a twist of his lips, missing Kit and Katie so much it hurt. He sighed. *Especially Katie.* His body suddenly grew warm, but not from the summer night. He took the stairs two at a time, and his pace quickened along with his pulse as he shed his suit jacket and loosened his tie. Tonight was their one-month anniversary. He'd seen precious little of his new wife this week, and he missed her.

A lot. He honed in on their second-story apartment down the hall like a bullet bearing down on a bull's-eye, craving the soft, solid feel of his wife in his arms. She hadn't been able to work at the BCAS once this week because Kit had a cold, and the tension of her absence was evident in the edginess of his nerves. To make matters worse, he'd spent the last week getting home long after Katie was asleep, and now all he wanted to do was hold her, cherish her. *Love her.*

He eased the key in the lock and quietly opened the door, eyes scanning past the darkened parlor to the kitchen light at the back of the flat. Exhaling his relief, he bolted the door and tossed the suit coat on a chair, then rolled his sleeves as he strode down the hall. He paused at the door, bouquet in hand, and a rush of love swelled at the sight of her. She stood on a chair, bare feet perched on tiptoe as she tucked a bag of Pillsbury flour on a top shelf. His eyes roved the length of her, drinking her in, still in awe that Katie O'Connor belonged to him.

She jumped down, and her blue floral-print dress breezed up as she did, belted at the waist before hugging the gentle curve of her hips. It flared midcalf to shapely legs bereft of silk stockings, and his mouth went dry at the thoughts filling his head. A petite five foot two to his six foot three, she was just a slip of a thing whose strong-willed nature towered as tall as his own. But, sweet chorus of angels, when she needed him, depended on him . . . this woman could make him feel over ten feet tall. His pulse kicked up a notch. And she was all his. His "Little Miss Sass"—a nickname she'd certainly earned . . . and then some.

She was singing to herself, strains of "Five Foot Two, Eyes of Blue" filling the kitchen as she swayed to her own off-key beat. With a soft Charleston kick, she pulled a chicken from the refrigerator, and Luke couldn't help but grin. In two pulse-pounding strides, he stood behind her, intoxicated by her scent of rosewater and Pears soap. He took her by surprise when he hooked hungry arms around her waist and nuzzled the nape of her neck. With a tiny squeal and a jolt, she dropped the chicken on the counter and twisted in his arms. Her blue eyes spanned wide. "Luke McGee—you scared the living daylights out of—"

He pressed her to the counter and effectively silenced her complaint, kissing her until his blood heated several degrees. With uneven breathing, he feathered her earlobe with his mouth. "How 'bout I kiss the daylights out of you instead?" he whispered, voice husky with intent.

A soft moan of consent left her lips and he kissed her again, tossing the bouquet aside to thread fingers into the soft, blond hair at the side of her head. He cupped her face in his hands, thumbs grazing her cheeks as he stared into her eyes, convinced he was the luckiest man alive. "Katie," he said, voice thick with emotion, "you have no idea how I've missed you."

With a stroke of his stubbled jaw, she gave him a shy smile. "Oh, I think I do," she whispered. Her brows dipped. "Wait— are you hungry? 'Cause I can warm up that meat loaf . . ."

His gaze strayed to her lips. "Oh, I'm hungry all right, Sass, but not for meat loaf." Kissing the tip of her nose, he tugged her to the table and prodded her into a chair. "But first things first—how's Kit? Then tell me about your day while I finish off the last of the chocolate cream pie." Zeroing in on the icebox, he shot a grin over his shoulder. "That is, if there's any left."

"Hey, McGee, I'll have you know I saved the last piece for you, despite the fact it's my favorite." Katie popped up from her chair and butted him aside with a smirk. "Which wasn't easy, considering I've been alone the last few nights with nothing to do but stare at it after Kit goes to bed. Go on and sit—you look exhausted." She dished the last piece onto a saucer while he plopped into a chair, then placed it before him with a fork in the middle. "Kit's better today—the fever's gone, but the runny nose definitely kicked in, along with her appetite." She poured milk and handed it to him before sliding into her chair, chin in hand. "She actually tried to eat everything that wasn't nailed down today," she said with a wry smile. "Including the pie."

Luke grinned and shoveled a forkful into his mouth, practically gulping it whole. "Thanks, Katie." He swallowed another few bites, then took a quick swig of milk. "I'm relieved Kit's on the mend—she had me worried." He polished off the dessert, then pushed the plate away while he upended the milk. "Of course, some of my worry stems from the fact that Bobbie Sue and Gladys threatened to quit if you don't come back soon."

"Oh, so you need a buffer, do you, Mr. Priss?"

A wayward smile eased across his lips as he tugged her onto his lap. "I think that's fair to say, Mrs. McGee," he said, his breath warm in her ear. He dipped her back to explore her throat with his mouth, then pulled her upright again with a groan. Cuddling her to his chest, he planted a kiss on her head. "So help me, Katie, I'm so crazy in love with you, you've got me sidetracked." He sighed and kneaded her shoulders. "Tell me what you've been doing the last three days."

Never would there be a better time and Katie knew it. She sucked in a deep swallow of air as if it contained the courage she desperately needed. The beat of his heart pulsed in her ear as she lay against his chest, its rapid throb in rhythm with her own as she thought about what she had to do. Law school loomed a mere three weeks away, and her husband needed to know. She swallowed hard, knowing full well that what she had to say would jolt Luke McGee's world. *And mine*, she thought with a shiver. He buffed her arms, and she pressed in closer, breathing in the clean scent of his starched shirt, a hint of Bay Rum, and the faint trace of a man too long in a suit.

She forged on, expelling tentative words along with shaky air. "Well, Kit mostly napped the first day while I caught up on mending. We listened to *Little Orphan Annie* on the radio and read lots of books. Then we made cookies yesterday and picked up the laundry from Mr. Chu's, and Kit fell asleep on the couch while I cleaned house and ironed. Today she was feeling a lot better, so it was our busiest day." She twisted a lock of her hair, which correlated nicely with the knot in her stomach. "We shopped at Dennehy's and Woolworth's, bought stamps at the post office, splurged on a soda at Robinson's, went to the bank—" the air hitched in her lungs— "bought groceries at Miller's, fixed dinner, put Kit to bed, did the dishes, and now I'm putting groceries away." She finished in a rush, unable to ignore the sudden stiffness in his chest.

He shifted to study her face, thick blond brows raised in question. "The bank? But I left money for groceries in the drawer. Did you run out?"

"No, there was plenty for groceries," she said, avoiding his eyes.

"Katie?" He tucked a finger to her chin. "Then why did you go to the bank?"

She wriggled off his lap and stood to her feet, her breathing compromised considerably. "Because . . . I . . . well, I needed the money."

He blinked. "Money? For what?"

She hefted her chin, steeling her nerve, but a lump still caught in her throat. She swallowed it and met his gaze head-on, her body as tense as the sudden tic in his temple. "For law school," she whispered. "First-semester payment was due today."

He stared, mouth slacking open. The deep tan in his face faded several shades, highlighting the spray of freckles across his sculpted nose. "Law school?" he repeated, his voice as raspy and thick as if chocolate pie were lodged in his throat. He rose to his feet while a muscle twittered in a rock-hard jaw. "Tell me you're joking."

Katie took a step back, one hand braced to the chair for support as her eyes pleaded with his. "You knew from the very beginning that law school was my dream."

He slammed his chair in, his voice hard. "That was before I made you my wife, Katie, the mother to my child. Not once since I put that ring on your finger have you mentioned anything about law school."

"Luke, I know this is a shock—"

"A shock?" He jerked his plate and fork from the table and

practically hurled them into the dishwater, sloshing water all over the sink. He turned and ripped the tie from his neck, singeing her with a glare. "No, Katie, this is more like getting slammed with a blunt object."

His temper ignited hers. "You're being ridiculous—this is not a big deal."

"Not a big deal?" His brows lifted to a dangerous level. "You take money we don't have, then lie to me about law school—"

"I didn't lie!"

He fisted the tie and took a step closer. "You deceived me, Katie—it's the same thing. You're my wife, for pity's sake—we're supposed to make these decisions together."

"Would you have said yes?" Her chin jerked up.

"Are you crazy? No, I wouldn't have said yes. You have no business in law school. You have a daughter to care for, a part-time job at the BCAS, and we *don't* have the money."

She sucked in a deep breath, willing herself to be calm. "Lizzie's agreed to watch Kit five days a week, and you know yourself Carmichael plans to trim the payroll."

"And the money?" he asked, his voice as cool as the chicken bleeding on the counter. He braced hands on his hips, forearms strained with muscles.

The words on her tongue thickened, hesitant to part from her lips. "It's Parker's," she whispered, feeling the heat swarm in her cheeks at the mention of Luke's best friend whom she almost married. "From the account he set up for me when he broke our engagement."

His eyes flickered in hurt, as if she'd just swung that blunt object he mentioned right at his head. And then in a slow blink of his lids, his gaze hardened to ice and his jaw went rigid, shadowed with bristle that made him all the more ominous. "I see. Well, you sure know how to kill a mood, Katie Rose."

"Luke, this can work, I promise."

"No, it can't . . . because I won't allow it."

A harsh breath heaved still in her throat. "Excuse me? You won't *allow* it?" She slapped hands on her hips and leaned in. "In case you forgot, this isn't the BCAS and you're *not* my boss."

He moved close, hovering over her like impending doom. "I'm your husband, Katie Rose," he said in a tone as tight as the muscles in his face. "What I say goes."

"Over-my-dead-body," she enunciated, incensed at the crick in her neck as she seared him with a look.

"*If* . . . necessary." He ground out the words between clenched teeth.

She spun on her heel and stomped to the counter, snatching a knife and cutting board from the drawer to hack at the chicken. *Heaven help me, I married a Neanderthal.* She stabbed the poultry with the blade, sawing it into pieces with her husband in mind. Down the hall she heard the bathroom door slam and the shower turn on, and she was sorely tempted to steal his water pressure by turning on the kitchen spigot full force.

He's just tired. Guilt slithered in, as slick as the chicken grease now coating her hand. She sagged over the sink with a weary sigh. Of course he was. The poor man worked sixteen hours a day for the last week—who wouldn't be testy? After all, Luke McGee was a reasonable man. Her lips shifted to the side. *Most of the time.* Her gaze fell to the bouquet on the counter. And he *had* brought her flowers and cuddled her with that lovesick gleam in his eye. She thought of his lips on her neck, and a warm shiver tingled through her. And she'd certainly missed him as well—probably more than he'd missed her.

A thought flitted through her mind, and her knife stilled on the chicken, embedded deep in a thigh while a smile tugged at her lips. "Of course! I'll tease him out of it like I do when he's a grump." She glanced down the hall at the sliver of light beneath the bathroom door and grinned. Yes, a cool shower would calm him down, but hopefully not enough to cool the passion she'd seen in his eyes.

Rinsing her hands, she quickly dried them off and reached for the tube of Barbasol shaving cream she'd bought him from Woolworth's. A grin tipped her lips as she placed it in the middle of the hall floor rather than waiting to put it away in the bathroom, almost giddy at the prospect of his response over her little "tease." He would see it and smile, she was certain, then tickle her until she picked it up, no doubt, calling her Miss Sass and sealing it with a kiss.

As always.

Humming to herself, she finished cutting the chicken and sealed it into two butcher-wrapped packets. She paused, noting the shower had stopped, then smiled and hefted a package of chicken into the icebox. Singing her favorite song, she reached for the second packet. "Five foot two, eyes of blue, but oh, what those five foot could do. Has anybody seen my—"

A massive hand clamped on her wrist, and she gasped. The chicken in her hand plummeted to the floor in a dull splat as she broke free and spun around. He stood barefoot, striped pajama bottoms with muscled chest bare, blond hair dark and spiked from his shower.

"Pick it up," he breathed. A spasm twittered in the hard line of his jaw. "Now, please." With a heated gaze fused to hers, he jabbed a stiff finger toward the Barbasol in the middle of the hall floor. The deadly voice held a note of pleading, although his features could have been solid rock. "Pick it up, Katie."

"No, you pick it up," she quipped, her smile suddenly fading at the fury in his eyes. "Luke, I was just teas—"

"I *said*, pick it up—*now*," he repeated, his face as white as the paper-wrapped chicken lying on the floor.

Body quivering, she did as he asked, and when she rose, he snatched the tube from her hand. Without another word, he stormed down the hall and entered their room, then left once again with pillow and sheet in hand.

She followed him to the parlor, her heart in her throat. "Luke, it was just a joke, the shaving cream in the hall, I promise. Can't we talk this out, please?"

He hurled the bedding on the sofa before striding to the window to jerk up the sash, muscled arms bulging with the motion. "The time for talking is long past, Katie," he said in a harsh tone. "Go to bed."

"But, Luke—"

"*I said . . . go to bed.*" He stilled her with a look.

She blinked, fighting the sting of tears in her eyes. She'd only seen him like this one other time—the night Parker had walked out on them both. Hard, cold, angry . . . and hurt. She shivered and backed away, well aware that nothing she could say would soften him tonight. "I love you, Luke," she whispered. "Good night."

He ignored her and rolled on his side, his broad back stiff and knotted with muscles.

Katie returned to the kitchen, the heave of a sob in her chest as she put the groceries away. Her lips quivered as she spied the package of chicken on the floor, and she closed her eyes, hand to her mouth. *What have I done?* She sagged against the counter and began to pray, not sure when Luke would forgive her or even when he would speak to her again. And at the moment, she had no earthly idea if she would even see law school in the fall.

But . . . there was one thing of which she was absolutely certain. She swiped the tears from her eyes and bent to put the chicken away, a cold realization shaking her to the core.

The honeymoon was definitely over.

"You know, Bert, I do believe we've worn the boy out." Emma peeked in the supply room, now Sean's makeshift office, a smile squirming on her lips at the sight of her new assistant manager sprawled in his chair with eyes closed, sleeves rolled, and arms propped behind his neck.

One of Sean's eyelids slitted up while he rested at his battered desk during one of the rare moments he'd been able to slow down all week.

Bertolina Adriani cocked a hip to the door and folded thick arms across an ample chest. Legs crossed at the ankle, she eyed him through piercing hazel eyes, a perfect match for the tailored brown suit jacket and skirt that pulled tightly across generous hips. "You did tell him he has to do his sleeping at home, didn't you?" Dark brows scrunched in question, but the twinkle in her eye betrayed the gruff edge of her tone.

Alli giggled while Emma pursed her lips, studying Sean with a squint. She folded her arms across a moss-colored cardigan Charity claimed brought out the "dangerous green" in her eyes and then tucked a finger to her chin, as if deep in thought. "Mmm . . . I failed to mention that, I guess, but then maybe the cot in the corner gave him the wrong idea."

A slow grin eased across Sean's lips. "Keep it down, will ya, ladies? I need quiet if I'm going to save your hides here, brainstorming ways to counter that 25 percent dip in sales."

"Likely story," Bert said with a grunt.

"Come on now, Bert," Emma said, enjoying the first real banter she'd allowed herself with Sean since he'd started. "He did spend several days on the dock getting Horace organized and inventorying all deliveries, as well as building those displays for Michelle and drafting the ads for our Labor Day Sale."

"And he did rectify all the registers and balance the books the day I left early," Alli said.

"Not to mention his willingness to take over all monthly inventories, which is a huge plus." Emma crossed her arms and tapped a finger against her lips. "So what do you think— should we keep him on—despite his propensity to nap at the end of the day?"

"End of the day?" Sean eyed the watch on his wrist, then jagged a brow, obviously attempting to mask his smile with a frown. "Maybe for you slackers, but not for me. Because after you people mosey on home to your comfy-cozy apartments and homes, my workday will just be starting."

Bert cocked her head. "Well, he is kind of cute, I suppose, especially with that nasty scowl bunching up all those freckles." An evil glint shone in her gaze. "That is if we can keep him away from Michelle."

He flashed some teeth, but Emma couldn't help but grin at the ruddy color inching up his neck.

"Come on, Bert, just give me the word, and I'll dump Michelle Tuller to build you those shelves you've been whining about." His smile broadened when Bert's cheeks hazed to pink, a rare occurrence for the crotchety Italian who was as much a mother to Emma as secretary.

Emma shook her head, feeling a sense of satisfaction that warmed her more than the teasing about Michelle. It meant Bert actually liked Sean, a great accomplishment for anyone at Dennehy's, much less a man. But then, what was there not to like? The memory of his behavior at Kearney's suddenly niggled, but she quickly dismissed it, shaking off her unease.

He paused, giving Bert a slow wink. "Or maybe I should see if Horace wants to build them for you . . ."

Bert's pink cheeks fused to scarlet, and Sean laughed outright.

"Humph. I say give him his walking papers right now, Miss Emma. The boy's a little too big for his britches, if you ask me." Bert's tone was as tart as one of those lemon drops she kept in a bowl on her desk. She tugged a stylish new cloche over her dark finger-waved bob and waggled scarlet fingernails in the air. "My feet hurt—I'm going home. Toodle-oo."

"G'night, Bert," Sean called. "Thanks for the meat loaf sandwich."

Emma hiked a brow, her whisper laced with awe. "She brought you a meat loaf sandwich?"

"And her famous pound cake," Alli said with a giggle.

He slanted back in his chair with a lazy grin. "What can I say? The woman likes me."

Emma folded her arms with a new respect in her eyes. "Bert doesn't give anybody anything unless it's a hard time, except for Alli and me. That alone makes you worth your weight in gold."

He grinned. "Well, we'll have to talk to Charity about that, now won't we?"

Emma chuckled. "Yes, we will." She glanced at her watch and gave Alli's shoulder an affectionate squeeze. "Scoot, Alli. Mrs. Tunny's taking you to the theatre tonight, remember?"

"Oh, no!" The brown eyes widened. "I haven't done register totals yet."

"Go home, Alli," Sean said. "I'm staying late, so I'll be happy to log 'em in."

Her smile lit up the room. "Bless you! And for the record, I don't think you're too big for your britches." She waved and hobbled back to her desk to collect her purse. "Good night."

"G'night, Alli," they chimed in unison.

With Alli's departure, Emma's chest suddenly tightened. Clearing her throat, she shot Sean an awkward smile before turning to go. "I'll let you get back to work—"

"Wait—" His voice halted her at the door and she turned. "No reason to rush off, is there?" he said with a tentative smile. "I was kind of hoping we could talk since it's the end of my first week at work. You know, get comfortable as co-workers?"

He must have detected the hesitation in her manner, because when she opened her mouth to speak, he interrupted before she could say no. "Come on, Mrs. Malloy—don't turn me down, please? Even though we're almost family and have been friends for years, somehow it seems like we're strangers in this office." He shot her an endearing smile, brows arched in appeal. "Please?"

She paused, painfully aware that her comfort with Sean had been shattered the day of the wedding. And yet . . . how could she allow one awful moment to prevail over all the wonderful ones they'd shared over the years? She longed to let it go—this edgy feeling that his temper had unleashed, reminding her so much of Rory. But it wasn't easy. Like Sean, Rory had had the same ready smile and easygoing manner, lulling her into a sense of peace and security until his rage had taken it all away.

Emma drew in a thick breath and glanced up, noting the strain of Sean's smile, the plea in his eyes, and something inside wanted to believe he was different. That deep down, he was nothing like Rory. She slowly exhaled before finally moving forward to sit down, albeit stiffly, in one of the chairs in front of his desk. She clasped her hands in her lap. "So . . . why aren't *you* going home?" she asked with a polite smile. "The whole reason you're here is so all of us work less hours, remember? Besides, I thought you had a game tonight."

He glanced over his shoulder out the two-story window where ominous rain clouds pelted the empty park across the street. Windblown spray misted the marble sill, infusing the room with the fresh fragrance of rain. "Nope, rained out. So I figured I'd stay and work on some promotion ideas that have been rolling around in my head."

Emma blinked, noticing the weather for the first time. "Oh, my, I've had my head so buried in payroll today that I haven't even noticed the weather." Heat dusted her cheeks. *Behind closed doors—avoiding you.* She closed her eyes and inhaled deeply, helping to chase the stiffness away. She needed to do this—for herself, for Sean, and for the store—get comfortable with him again, at least as a co-worker. She could be warm and professional here and keep her distance whenever she saw him at O'Connor family functions. *I can do this,* she thought with resolve, the clean scent of rain washing some of her doubts away. She slowly released a cleansing sigh, allowing her head to rest on the back of her chair. "Oh, I love the smell of rain," she whispered.

"Me too," he said quietly, suddenly aware he'd been holding his breath. Easing back in his chair, his chest slowly contracted as the air left his lungs in one long, silent release.

Eyes closed, Emma seemed content to rest, head cushioned on the padded back of a gold velour dining room chair that matched the furniture in her office. The scent and sound of the rain seemed to tranquilize her, dispelling the anxiety he'd sensed after Alli had left, allowing him to study this woman who aroused his curiosity like no other. She was the reason his gloomy mood had lifted in the last week, the reason he'd enjoyed working at Dennehy's so much, despite the fact that her interaction with him had been painfully professional. He thought he had known her, but she had surprised him more than anyone ever had, slipping out from the shadows of ambiguity to become a strong and steady force in a world where men reigned supreme. He'd watched her dicker with a salesman over surcharges on a foreign shipment, battle a shipping agent over late delivery, and soothe a disgruntled customer, all in one day. She was calm and kind to her staff without leaving any room for lax behavior from any employee whose paycheck she signed. And yet through it all, she was Emma, a woman who preferred to fade into the background, and yet wielded a power that was serene, gentle, and strong. And somehow—in the intimacy of this setting—sensual. His neck warmed.

The fawn-colored eyes opened, revealing a hint of pale green hue, and he suddenly saw her as she must have been years ago, perfect features, hypnotic eyes, and a magnetic innocence so strong, it aroused both a strange longing within and an ache in his chest. He observed the faint scars on the left side of her face—and realized that for him, they had never hindered her beauty. "You're different here," he whispered, "secure, resolute, invincible."

She smiled, and weariness weighted her delicate features. "That's because too much rests on the success of this store— my debt to Mitch and Charity, the livelihood of every employee here . . ." She drew in a frail breath and buffed her arms. "My own peace of mind."

"You're a special woman, Emma Malloy. I'm honored to be working with you."

A wash of color ebbed in her cheeks and she quickly rose to her feet, avoiding his eyes. "Well, if I can't convince you to go home, then the least I can do is give you half of my supper." She peeked up, her manner tentative despite a shy smile that quickened his pulse. "It's not Bert's meat loaf by a long shot, but it should be enough to tame your hunger pangs for a while."

His lips parted in a grin. "Sounds good. And while we're dining, I'll share some of the ideas I have for increasing market share."

She paused, her hesitation halting the breath in his lungs. "Sorry, I'm . . . afraid I have a lot of work I need to finish before I go . . ."

"Ten minutes," he said quietly. "That's all it'll take to bolt some food and hear my ideas." He studied her profile, stomach cramping at the reluctance he saw in the downcast eyes, the shift of her throat, the hand on the knob. She was no longer comfortable being alone with him, and the very thought twisted his insides into a knot. Her lips parted in slow motion, and he held his breath, unwilling to hear the wrong answer. He rushed on, his voice quiet but firm. "Emma, we need to talk. To clear the air. Please . . . if only for my peace of mind?"

His words stilled her for a moment before she finally nodded, rib cage slowly deflating. Without another word, she slipped from the room, leaving him alone with his regret.

He released a weary breath and dropped his head on the back of the chair, a bittersweet smile edging his lips at the thought of dining with Emma and clearing the air. Whatever it took, he *would* regain her trust. Her friendship was too important. And so was the harmony they'd need to work side by side.

With a heavy inhale, he propped his hands behind his neck and surveyed the once-cluttered storeroom that now served as his office. Anxious to transform the large storage area into usable business space, Emma had taken advantage of Sean's carpentry skills by insisting he build floor-to-ceiling cabinets to partition off the supply area on the other side. The result was a cozy, rectangular office boasting a tall, arched window that flooded the room with sunlight during the day and lamplight during the night. Despite the close proximity of quarters, Sean felt at home here, and the view of the city park was certainly more pleasant than the littered alley outside of Kelly's.

"I assume being a full-blooded Irishman, you like corned beef and cabbage?" she asked upon her return, gaze averted despite a faint smile on her lips.

She deposited a small basket on the edge of his desk and popped the lid to unearth slices of corned beef swaddled in wax paper and a small bowl of cabbage sealed with aluminum foil. Smoothing out the foil, she carefully placed a sliver of corned beef on top and then scooped a child's portion of cabbage alongside. She produced two forks, obviously from the makeshift kitchen at the back of Bert and Alli's office, then placed the rest of the corned beef into the bowl with the cabbage. With an almost childlike focus that made him smile, she carefully slid it across the desk, keeping the smaller portion for herself.

He pushed it away. "Oh, no you don't—you take more than that."

"Don't make me pull rank on you, Mr. O'Connor. This is all I want." She nudged it back.

His tone was gentle. "You haven't called me Sean once since I started, Emma. Why?"

She fumbled with her foil, suddenly preoccupied with positioning the corned beef just so. "I just thought you'd appreciate more formality in the workplace, you know, in front of the employees."

"Emma," he said quietly. "Will you look at me?"

Her gaze lifted slowly, and his heart squeezed at the caution in her eyes. "We're alone now, but even if we weren't, I'd prefer you call me Sean."

She nodded and looked away, apparently reluctant to maintain his gaze.

"Emma," he said again, his voice as serious as it had ever been, and this time her eyes met and held his. "I hurt you deeply, I know, losing my temper at Kearney's that day, and I want you to understand that it will never happen again." He swallowed hard, emotion thickening the walls of his throat. "That degree of anger . . . well, it's only happened twice in my life, and I regret one of those times was with you." He paused, seconds ticking away like minutes. "Will you forgive me? Please?"

"I've forgiven you," she whispered, but it didn't ease the wariness in her face.

"No, I don't think you have. We're friends—good friends. But somehow I feel that friendship has been cut off—"

"That's not true . . . ," she said too softly, a twinge of pain in her eyes.

"Isn't it? You're not comfortable with me anymore, and you avoid me like the plague."

The timidity of her manner broke his heart as her gaze lowered once again. "You scared me, Sean," she whispered. "I thought I knew you."

"You *do* know me, Emma. We've known each other through thick and thin, weathered crises together, partnered in Pinochle and dominoes and horseshoes in the summer. I've told you things I've never told my sisters, and we've given each other advice and support during rough times. Please don't let one stupid mistake on my part take that all away."

Her fingers shook as she picked at her food, gaze fused to the beef on the foil. When she finally spoke, her words were frail and low. "Forgive me, Sean, please, but I'm afraid that when one has lived with a violent man, fear can become a constant companion." A muscle jerked beneath the creamy skin of her throat as she continued, the waver in her voice piercing him as her eyes trailed into a cold stare. "The first time Rory lost his temper in a fit of rage, he broke my jaw. Until then, I never knew he was even capable of such anger because he was always so gentle and kind, so devoted while we courted, and even after." The faintest of shivers skittered over her like a ripple on a mirror lake. "I remember feeling so safe with him because he was nothing like my father, nothing like the man who would rage and roar over the slightest little thing." A sad smile curved on her lips. "I was so grateful . . . grateful for a man without a temper who could protect me from my father's."

"Emma, I'm sorry . . . ," he whispered, the pain in his heart bleeding into his voice.

"I know you are, Sean, and I'm sorry too." Her gaze rose to meet his. "But the truth is, once that happens to a human heart, 'sorry' is never quite enough again."

He swallowed the ache in his throat. "What can I do, Emma, to win back your trust?"

The barest of smiles tempered some of the wariness in her eyes. "You can give me time and patience until this uneasiness fades. You can understand that although I value your friendship immensely, a part of me is not only struggling over trusting you again, but also a little angry that I even have to."

He leaned forward, eyes intense. "I *will* win your trust, Emma, you have my word."

"I know," she said quietly. "But it will take time."

Exhaling deeply, he slowly rose and extended his hand across the desk. "Well, there's no time like the present." His manner was easy despite the vise crushing his chest. "Shall we start over?"

She looked up, staring at him for several moments, as if torn between her fear and her willingness to give him another chance. He watched the muscles in her face slowly relax and felt the knot in his chest unravel like a clenched fist unfolding into an open palm. She gave him a gentle nod, and carefully shook his hand, releasing it almost immediately.

"Thank you," he whispered, his stomach beginning to rumble. He quickly reached for his fork and speared the beef, grinning like a little boy with a big crush on a little girl. "This looks incredible. When do you have time to cook like this?"

Some of the stiffness left her body as she eased back in the chair. "On Sundays. It's the only day I really get to rest and forget about the store. I enjoy fixing dinner for my eighteen-year-old neighbor, Casey, and my elderly landlady, Mrs. Peep. We have a lot of fun together—the three of us generations apart, yet giggling and playing dominoes like schoolgirls at a party. Casey's mother, Susan, used to work here at Dennehy's, but she returned to Kansas to care for her sick mother. She asked me to watch out for her daughter, so Casey and I have become very close."

"Let me see," Sean said with an exaggerated drawl, "you single-handedly manage one of the most popular stores in Boston, you make time for my family, Alli, and Mrs. Tunny, you befriend my sister, which is a full-time job in itself, and now you also play nursemaid to a teenage girl and cook for your neighbors?" He took a bite of the corned beef and chewed, his eyes warm with approval. "You're amazing."

A soft blush dotted her cheeks. "As far as managing the store, you forget I don't do that alone anymore," she said with a shy smile. She bit off a tiny corner of the beef. "You've only been here a week, and I honestly don't know how we managed without you." She hefted her chin in an uncustomary show of pluck. "It appears Mr. Kelly is not only a moron, but a fool."

He laughed, something he did a lot in her presence, and it felt good. He snatched some meat and took a bite while he leaned back in his chair, more relaxed than he'd felt in a long time. "I do believe that's the harshest thing I've ever heard out of those soft-spoken lips, Mrs. Malloy," he said, teasing her with his eyes. "Obviously my sister's a bad influence."

A low laugh rippled from her lips. "Don't be too sure about that. With Charity, at least one knows where they stand, which in some ways, is the height of honesty, being a woman so forthcoming. While I on the other hand, remain a mystery— even to myself."

"A mystery," he whispered, the very word intriguing him— like the woman herself. He chewed slowly, his blood warming at the prospect of exploring the inner recesses of this woman who drew him. For the first time, he understood fully the true treasure she was in his life, and his heart began to thud at the prospect of slowly unwrapping the gift that was Emma Malloy. Drawing in a calming breath, he studied her through curious eyes before exhaling and lightening his tone. "So solve it for me, Mrs. Malloy. I've often wondered what puts that glow in your cheeks, that peace in your countenance. Why is it I have never heard an ill word or complaint from your mouth until tonight and yet . . ." His gaze sharpened. "Your life has been anything but easy."

The green-gray eyes blinked, their depths as clear and mesmerizing as pale green beryl. "I'm . . . happy with my life, Sean."

"That's obvious, Emma, but I can't help but be curious. Most of the women I know, including my sisters, have been bent on falling in love, getting married—"

Color stained her cheeks. "I'm . . . already . . . married," she whispered, eyes focused hard on the food in her hands as she picked at it with shaky fingers.

Sean sat up, a sharp pain in his throat. "Emma—I'm sorry. I didn't mean to dredge up painful memories. I know you have a husband back in Ireland, but that's my point. I'd expect you to be lonely or bitter or at least angry with men like so many women I know, but you're not. You're different—calm, serene, joyful in your singular life. In fact you're the only woman I know who seems to be a lot like me—content to be alone." He drew in a deep breath and released it again while he sank back in his chair with a boyish smile. "Blame it on the fact that I've always enjoyed a good mystery, Mrs. Malloy, but I can't help but wonder why."

Her lips lifted in a gentle curve, and the tautness in his throat dissipated, easing his tight smile into a grin.

"Of course, I realize you could fire me on the spot for being so nosy . . ."

Her chuckle lilted in the air, and the sound expanded the warmth in his chest. "It would take a lot more than idle curiosity for me to fire you, Sean O'Connor," she said with a twinkle in her eye. "I would have to answer to Bert and Michelle if I did, and I don't relish the thought."

"Good point." He rested his head on the back of his chair and watched her through lidded eyes, his grin fading. "So do you? Ever get lonely?"

She tilted her head and peered out the window, as if contemplating the question. He hadn't realized he'd stopped breathing until she answered seconds later, and when she did, her voice held that peaceful assurance he'd come to expect. "Oh, here and there, I suppose, like most human beings, but mostly not. Your family, my friends, and the store have filled my life with a lot of joy and satisfaction. And then, of course, there's Lancelot and Guinevere."

"Excuse me?"

"My cats," she said with a soft smile. She paused to poke at the cabbage with her fork while her eyes trailed into a dreamy stare. "But if I were to be completely honest, I would have to say my greatest joy and contentment come from . . ." The dark lashes lifted, revealing greenish-gray eyes as serene and shimmering as Silver Lake at dusk. "My faith in God."

His mouth went dry, and he shifted in the chair, not really sure what to say. He knew she was a spiritual person, but he'd never really thought of her as intensely religious, and certainly not as devout as his sister, Faith. "Oh," he said, swallowing hard. "I . . . didn't realize that." His smile felt stiff. "Thus the mystery, I suppose."

She laughed, and the sound was bolder somehow, freer, as if she had lifted a veil for him to peek inside. The muscles relaxed in his face and he grinned freely. "What?"

There was a beautiful mischief about her—a sparkle in her eyes, a twitch in her smile—that he'd never seen before, somehow intimate in these cozy confines where the scent of rain filled the air. Her body seemed to melt against the velour and cherrywood back, relaxed as if reclining on overstuffed cushions rather than a stiff, hardwood dining-room chair.

She rested her head back and gave him a languid smile, hands limp on the arms. "You're not comfortable talking about God, are you?"

A flash of heat scalded his face and he cleared his throat. "Sure I am," he lied, moisture beading the back of his neck. "I'm just a very private person when it comes to . . . things."

She grinned. "I'm sorry for putting you on the spot, but I have to admit it does surprise me a wee bit." She scrunched her nose. "But come to think of it, Charity didn't have much use for God when I met her either."

"I have use for God," he said sharply, her words barbing more than he liked.

She sat up, palm raised in apology. "Of course you do, and I didn't mean to imply otherwise. But I can't help but notice you seem to have the same aversion to the mention of God as—" she chewed on the edge of her lip, eyes sparkling while a touch of the imp teased in her tone—"you do to women."

He stared before his lips eased into a slow smile. All tension seeped away as he lounged back in his chair. "Well, I guess you could say both subjects scare the tar out of me."

She laughed. "I thought so. And I certainly understand your hesitation with women." The twinkle in her eyes dimmed. "But why God?"

Sean cocked his foot against an open drawer and scrutinized the nail beds of his fingers, not really sure how to answer. "I don't know, Emma, I'm a man. Men fend for themselves."

"Not your father or Brady . . . or Mitch, Collin, or Luke for that matter. They all seem to be men who pray."

"I pray," he defended, "at meals and at church. Besides, doesn't the Bible say that God helps those who help themselves?"

She nibbled a piece of meat as she studied him. "Actually . . . no. That's a quote from Ben Franklin's *Poor Richard's Almanac*. The Bible says things like, God is strength to the needy in his distress and a refuge from the storm."

"Well, I can certainly attest to that. I don't think I've ever been as low as I was the week I lost my job, and the only place I felt any peace at all was at church." He pinched the bridge of his nose, the memory causing a dull ache before his lips tipped into a wry smile. "Trust me, in that one miserable week I made up for all the prayers I never said."

"Did they work?" She cocked her head, observing him beneath heavy lashes.

Arms folded, he propped a fist to his chin, eyes narrowed in thought. "Yeah, I think so."

"Then why does it scare you?" Her gaze was clear and light, probing with an intensity that made him pause.

He rubbed the length of his jaw, feeling the bristle of his late-day beard. "I don't know. I guess it's just habit, not asking for his help. I suppose it makes me feel weak."

"God told St. Paul in the Bible that 'my strength is made perfect in weakness.'"

His gaze thinned. "It says that? Really?"

She nodded.

"Huh," he said absently, the notion somewhat unsettling that his own weakness could empower God. He peered up. "So was it for you? His strength made perfect in weakness?"

Moments passed before she spoke, and when she did, something squeezed in his chest at the pain that flickered across her features. Her gaze trailed beyond him, out the window as if the rain were grace soaking into her very soul. "Yes."

His jaw tightened. "I have to be honest, Emma—I have trouble understanding that. I have never gone through what you have, to be sure, but to me, it almost seems as if it was God who turned his back on you, causing that pain."

A ghost of a smile shadowed her lips. "Not caused, Sean— allowed. As a loving Father, God allows us to suffer the consequences of our misguided actions . . ." She looked away, but not before he saw the depth of sorrow in her eyes. "Our wrong decisions, our sins . . ."

Sean snatched up a fountain pen from his desk and roughly rubbed the rounded cap, his fingers suddenly as taut as the press of his lips. "I don't know what sins you think you've committed in your past, Emma, but I do know the caliber of woman you are today. And at the risk of sounding blasphemous, I have to tell you—I have a problem with a 'loving Father' who would cause—or allow—a woman like you to experience the hurt that you have."

Leaning forward, Emma laid a small and tapered hand on his desk, her fingers slender and her nails bare of all polish. The intensity in her eyes captured him so completely that his heart thudded to a slow stop while he awaited her response. His breath stilled in his lungs at the faintest of smiles that curved on her full lips, another reminder that for him, neither scars nor pain would ever mar her beauty.

"No one escapes being hurt in this life, Sean, because unfortunately, we live in a fallen world. But please believe me when I say . . ." Her voice gentled, soothing and peaceful as the patter of rain on the marble sill. "There's a great gift in pain."

He stared, the air in his lungs slowly seeping out along with his frustration at God.

With a gentle sigh, she settled back in her chair, her gaze calming him as much as the steady thrum on the roof overhead. "It was the pain of my own sin and Rory's that allowed me to see a great truth that set my heart free. And that is that no matter how much joy or pain we have in this world—and I have experienced both—nothing satisfies the human heart like the love of God."

His thumb paused against the tip of the pen, strained in its grip. He drew in a halting breath and expelled it, then tossed the pen on the desk. "It would be nice to have that much faith, Emma, really, but I guess I'm just a little too practical."

She chuckled. "Peace is one of the most practical things one can have." Smiling, she drew in a deep breath and released it again, a fragile exhale of air that imparted a tranquility he'd come to identify with the woman before him.

In natural reflex, he felt his own rib cage expand and release as well, and suddenly he realized hers was a tranquility she never failed to pass on to him. A tranquility similar to the one he prided himself on presenting to the world. Only his was often a façade while Emma's was real. He studied her now, noting the peaceful smile that lighted on her lips.

"Because you see, Sean, my pain taught me that no one—not those abundantly blessed or those who are not—can ever truly be happy apart from him."

"I was happy . . . before I lost my job." He tried to temper the edge in his tone.

The gray eyes softened, her gaze as gentle as a caress. "Were you?"

The question caught him unaware, and his lips parted in surprise. *Wasn't I?* He thought of the endless hours he'd devoted to Kelly's to prove his worth, both to his employer and himself, and then the countless sports to which he committed all his energy and free time. Diversions all, diligently adhered

146

to because they filled his mind and days with a tentative sense of peace, purpose, and contentment.

But happy? He closed his eyes and in a catch of his breath it struck—that hollow, hopeless feeling that sometimes haunted in the still of the night between his head hitting the pillow and the weary slumber that followed. The same malaise that had disarmed him during the war when death and carnage had stolen his peace and his hope, leaving his heart vulnerable and exposed. Not only to the ravages of battle . . . but to a love more lethal than the German artillery shells that had assaulted their rat-infested trenches.

Clare. His heart skidded to a stop. Until the incident at Kearney's, he hadn't thought of her in years, but suddenly he could see her as clearly as if she stood before him—long raven hair, eyes as warm and inviting as melted chocolate, and a smile so innocent, she had captured his heart. She had given him months of joy, hope, and passion like he'd never experienced before. His jaw tightened. And a wound that had scarred him more than the war.

His first love. And his last.

"Sean?"

His head jolted up. "What?"

"Forgive me, please. I didn't mean to pry."

He blinked. A weighty sigh drifted from his mouth before he finally smiled, relieving the strain in his face. "No forgiveness necessary, Emma. And compared to my mother and sisters—Charity, in particular—you don't know the meaning of 'pry.' Besides, it's my fault for bringing the whole awkward subject up." He gave her a wink. "Trying to solve the mystery, you know."

She blushed and quickly retrieved his bowl and fork, eyes averted as she cleaned up from their dinner. "I'd rather you solve the mystery of increasing our sales, Mr. O'Connor. I assure you that's a far more profitable use of your time."

"But not as much fun." He rose to stretch, hands clasped to his neck and muscles taut as he pivoted elbows side to side. "But I'll tell you what, Mrs. Malloy. If you make us a pot of fresh coffee, I just may be persuaded to let you pry. You know, pick my brain? To strengthen your bottom line with ideas like redemption coupons and early-bird specials?" He hooked his thumbs in his pockets and grinned, gaze lidded and hands braced low on his hips. "Interested?"

More color washed into her cheeks despite a twinkle in her eyes. "In picking your brain?" She turned and sauntered to the door, shooting him a playful smirk over her shoulder. "Goodness, yes." She winked, the action so out of character that it heated the back of his neck. "One can only imagine the secrets I'll find."

6

*F*ace pinched in a scowl, Luke followed his brothers-in-law into Father Mac's kitchen, annoyed that even their Saturday morning basketball game hadn't improved his bad mood. His lips thinned. Correction: not "bad" mood . . . "vile" mood. The one Katie had detonated three days ago when she'd tossed a grenade into his life.

"We could have won if you'd carried your weight, McGee," Collin groused. "What's your problem anyway—you looked like a girl on the court today. For once I was on my game, but you—you played like you're half asleep."

Brady cuffed an arm to Luke's shoulder. "Yeah, bud, you got us worried—you're starting to look like Collin."

"Thanks, Brady," Collin said with a smirk. He plopped into a chair at the kitchen table with a mock scowl. "Nice to know I can always count on the defense of my partner and best friend."

"Anytime," Brady said with a grin before he zeroed in on Luke. His smile dimmed. "What gives, Luke? When Collin's game is better than yours, bud, something's not right."

Luke glanced up, a frown tainting his face. "What do you mean, 'what gives'? I'm off my game for once, so get off my back." His voice came out harsher than intended and the room fell silent as Father Mac delivered glasses of iced tea

149

to the table. An uncomfortable heat inched up the back of Luke's neck and he huffed out a sigh, mauling his face with his hand. "Look, I'm sorry, Brady, it has nothing to do with you." He slumped in his chair. "Sweet saints, is it really that obvious?"

"Only to someone who's married," Mitch said with a wry smile.

Concern sharpened Brady's features. "What's going on, Luke?"

Snatching a glass of tea, Luke chugged half and then slammed the glass back down, avoiding Brady's probing stare. His jaw shifted. "I thought marriage was about communication and compromise."

"So did I," Mitch said, taking a swig of his tea.

"That usually takes awhile to perfect." Father Mac placed a piece of pie in front of Luke, then patted his shoulder. "Give it time."

"Thanks, Father." Luke shoved a forkful of pie into his mouth and swallowed it whole, his eyes lost in a hard stare. "That's exactly what I'm doing—giving it time so I don't blow. Haven't talked to her in days."

"Not exactly what I meant," Father Mac said with a hint of humor in his tone. "The Bible warns not to let the sun go down on your wrath."

Luke grunted, bolting more pie. "A little late for that. Been on the couch three days."

"Well, we've all been there, Luke," Collin said between bites.

"Many, *many* times," Mitch agreed. He pushed his empty plate away.

"What happened?" Brady asked quietly.

Luke sighed and poked at his pie, a sour bent to his lips. "Oh, nothing much—just enrolling in law school without telling me."

"What?" Brady gaped, his fork halted midair.

"Yep. And she's already arranged with Lizzie to watch Kit five days a week."

"Lizzie knows?" Brady's shock was evident in the rasp of his voice.

"Apparently." Luke felt his blood begin to boil all over again. He'd been working hard to get his anger under control, but Katie's little stunt had tripped his temper like no one had in years, and the hurt festered so much he couldn't seem to get past it. The last time someone had wounded him like this, it was during a gang fight on the streets of New York where blood had been drawn. Back then when someone made him this mad, he'd simply lay 'em out flat with his fists, but this was his wife, a woman he thought he could trust. His jaw hardened to stone. "So not only has she gone behind my back and spent money I don't have, but she's imposed on Lizzie two extra days a week and left me high and dry at the BCAS." He gulped the rest of his tea, then banged the glass back down. "So much for love, honor, and obey."

"Maybe it was a spur-of-the-moment decision," Father Mac suggested slowly, "one made quickly before she had the opportunity to discuss it with you."

A grunt escaped Sean's mouth before he ducked his head, quickly scooping in more pie.

Luke honed in, noting Sean's face was as red as the cherries he shoveled in his mouth. His eyes narrowed. "What was that for?" he whispered. "What do you know?"

The clump of pie seemed lodged in Sean's throat as he blinked, obviously uncomfortable with the line of questioning. Hesitating, he finally swallowed hard. "Uh . . . nothing much." He looked around the table, then glanced at Luke before exhaling loudly. "Okay, all right. Apparently Steven saw a letter addressed to Katie from Portia Law School this summer."

The blood leeched from Luke's face. "*Before* we were married?"

Sympathy radiated from Sean's eyes. "I think so."

"Maybe it was just a letter from the college to renew her interest," Brady said.

Sean paused. "Not according to Gabe."

Luke stared, his anger mounting by the moment. "Oh, yeah? And what did Gabe say?"

"That she saw the letter on Katie's dresser early this summer, welcoming her to Portia Law School this fall. Katie made her promise not to tell you because it was a surprise."

A harsh laugh erupted from Luke's throat. "Oh, it was a surprise, all right. Enough to bring the honeymoon to an abrupt halt and put the marriage on hold."

"Luke, talk to her, clear the air," Brady said. "This is no way to start a marriage."

"Yeah? Well, tell that to Katie."

"No, Luke, you tell that to Katie." Father Mac's voice held a quiet authority that helped to diffuse the angst in Luke's chest.

He sucked in a shaky breath and blew out a blast of air. "I know I need to, Father, but it's hard. I'm so angry because I feel betrayed, duped. I haven't lost my temper in a long, long time, but I . . . well, I lost it with Katie." He looked up, shame evident in his tone. "That scares me."

"Marriage can be a very scary thing," Father Mac said with a curve of his lips.

Sean hiked his shoe on the rung of the chair, lips cocked in a grim slant. "Which would make you and me the smart ones here, Matt."

Father Mac silenced Sean with a tight smile. "Just ask Mitch, Collin, and Brady. But it's even scarier if you don't start out with open lines of communication. Lay the groundwork by telling Katie how she made you feel when she left you out of this decision. Tell her what you expect as far as communication in a marriage."

Luke pinched the bridge of his nose. "Yeah, well, I would think it's understood that lies and deception are not acceptable behavior."

"Uh . . . not always." Mitch plowed thick fingers through damp, unruly hair.

"Luke, she didn't lie . . . exactly," Brady said quietly.

Luke singed him with a glare. "She didn't tell the truth!

And that's easy for you to say—Lizzie is a normal wife who wants to stay home and raise your babies, not some modern woman who plots and deceives to get her own way."

Mitch cleared his throat. "As a man who knows a little something about a woman who plots and deceives, I suspect you've gotten Katie's attention by now. So don't waste any more time. Forgive her and then sit her down and spell it out like Father says. Make no bones about it that stunts like this only undermine your love and trust for her. That seems to work with Charity." One side of his mouth crooked up. "Most of the time."

"Spoken like a man with true experience," Father Mac said with a lift of his glass.

Luke huffed out a sigh. "Tell me this gets easier—*please*."

"It sure did for me," Collin said with pride in his eyes. "Faith tells me everything."

"Lizzie too," Brady said. His lips flattened into a thin line. "Or at least I thought she did."

Sean poked Mitch, an evil grin curling his lips. "What about Charity, Mitch? She tell you everything?"

Mitch gave him a narrow look. "Your time is coming, O'Connor, mark my words." His gaze shifted to Luke. "As far as Charity goes, what can I say—she's a late bloomer. But we have pretty solid communication now, although I'm guessing it took longer than with Faith and Lizzie. You might keep that in mind when it comes to Katie. After all, everybody knows her personality is more in league with Charity's than Faith or Lizzie's."

Luke groaned and put a hand to his eyes.

"You'll get there, bud," Brady said. "Just give it time and lots of prayer." He downed his tea and set the glass on the counter. "Before you know it, you'll have a marriage like Marcy and Patrick's, which is what we're all shooting for."

Collin lounged back in his chair and folded his arms. "Shooting for, yes, but let's face it—*nobody* has a marriage like Marcy and Patrick's. I mean, how could we? Theirs has been tested by time, trial, and—" he slid Luke a slow grin—"the tenacity of Katie Rose."

A second groan rumbled from Luke's lips. "Don't remind me."

Sean bolted down his final bite, then jumped up to deposit his dishes in the sink. He snatched the basketball from the counter and flipped it back and forth in his hands, taunting Luke with a lazy grin. "Come on, Luke, cheer up. We'll give you a chance to redeem your pride on the court. It'll be good practice for redeeming the pride in your marriage." He winked. "Not to mention a great opportunity to work off your hostility toward my kid sister."

Luke gave him a grudging grin. "It'll take more than grinding you in the dust to work off my hostility, O'Connor, but it's a start. And she may be your kid sister, but she's Marcy's daughter, so I'm hoping she'll end up like her mother—the epitome of love, honor, and obey."

Sean chuckled and headed for the door. "I wouldn't hold my breath on that one, McGee. You're likely to turn blue."

He laughed. "Okay, I'll settle for 'love, honor, and no secrets.'"

"Or plotting," Mitch said with a stretch of his arms.

"Yeah," Luke agreed, "just open, honest communication like their saint of a mother."

Ball tucked under his arm, Sean butted the screen door open with his hip and held it while the others ambled through. "Yep, my father's one lucky man."

Luke plucked the ball from Sean's grip and strode to the court, his gait cocky and his smile even worse. "Yeah, he is," he said, arms extended midair. His soles lifted off the pavement as he let the ball fly, allowing it to spin into the net with a satisfying swoosh. His teeth gleamed white against bronze skin. "With a *very* unlucky son."

───◆───

Marcy chewed the edge of her lip as she cut the coconut cream pie—Patrick's favorite. *Please, God, let tonight be my lucky night,* she prayed, the awful scent of coconut wrinkling her nose along with the thought. Sweet heavens, she hated coconut . . . almost as much as she hated keeping secrets from Patrick, but what choice did she have? Sweat beaded her brow—from the heat of the oven, the dog days of summer, and the monumental task of winning her husband's consent. Her anxiety was as oppressive as the August heat, and Marcy longed for a breeze to flutter the limp kitchen curtains. The sound of male laughter filtered in from the dining room, laced with the joyous giggles of a little girl. Marcy positioned the slice just right on the plate and peeked at the kitchen door that stood between her and her dream—the dream to become the mother of a ten-year-old street orphan. That is, if novenas held any sway.

"Don't gargle your milk, young lady!"

Marcy winced at the edge in Patrick's tone and knew that tonight wasn't the opportune time. Not when Sister Mary Veronica had called Patrick at work to complain that Gabe was bullying the boys in her Wednesday evening catechism class. A weary sigh drifted from Marcy's lips. Apparently Marcy's discipline didn't suit the good sister, so she went straight to the top, completely oblivious that she was jeopardizing Marcy's peace of mind.

Rolling her tongue to her teeth, Marcy sprinkled extra coconut on Patrick's pie, taking great care to position a luscious strawberry—partially cut to the stem and fanned just so—on top of the whipped cream. Opportune time, indeed. Unfortunately, with Gabe, there never seemed to be an "opportune" time, which is why Marcy now found herself sick with worry that tonight wasn't the right time to broach the subject of adoption with her husband. And yet, the new school year loomed mere weeks away, and Marcy would give anything to send Gabe to school as Gabriella Dawn O'Connor instead of Smith. *Even* if it meant pulling a "Charity" and "plotting" the right time to win him over. She divvied up pieces for Gabe, Steven, and Sean and then swiped a strand of blond hair from her eyes. The folded letter in her pocket all but burned a hole in her pale blue summer dress—*also* Patrick's favorite.

She should have eased him into it, she knew, laid the

groundwork better than she had. But something always managed to stand in the way. Whether it was Gabe in a fight with the neighborhood boys, Patrick's longer hours at the *Herald* for reduced pay, or his incessant worry over finances during a dismal economy, the moment had never been right. And now, with the new school year less than a month away, Marcy was running out of time. If Gabriella Dawn Smith was going to have a "fresh start" with a new name, she needed to be registered by the end of the month. Which meant that the petition for adoption in Marcy's pocket needed her husband's signature . . . *tonight*.

The rich rumble of Sean's baritone laughter reached her ears, and she smiled, grateful he was home for dinner rather than working late at the store. Their eldest son always had such a positive effect on Patrick, and right now, Marcy needed all the help she could get. *Thank you, God, that Sean is awful at chess*, she thought with a wry smile—a definite plus in upping Patrick's mood with a win. Drawing in a deep swell of air, she toted the tray to the door and butted her hip against the worn wood. A prayer and a smile hovered on her lips—in that order.

"Sweet saints, Steven, a ninety-six-year-old great-grandmother with a still in her basement?" Patrick's eyes crinkled at the corners as he took a sip of his coffee.

Lounging back in his chair, Steven ruffled a hand through dark chestnut hair as Marcy distributed dessert. "Yep. Claimed it was for medicinal purposes. And would you believe she even packaged it in medicine bottles?" He glanced up. "Thanks, Mother."

Sean chuckled and dove into the pie Marcy placed in front of him, giving her a grateful smile. "The tonic of choice for what ails, eh?"

"Apparently." Steven poured cream in his coffee with a wry smile. "Seems the neighbors call her Dr. Maude, but I'll tell you what—the good doctor's out of practice now."

"You didn't arrest her, did you?" Marcy froze, coffee pot poised over her empty cup.

"No, ma'am," he said with a sheepish grin as he stabbed at his pie. "The little dickens reminded me so much of Great-grandmother that I'm afraid I went soft. She's a little bit of a thing that you want to swallow up in a hug because she's so blasted cute, so Joe and I just dismantled the still and gave her a warning." He downed the rest of his coffee and then held his cup while Marcy replenished it, giving her a swerve of a smile. "*Before* she served us cookies and tea."

Patrick laughed. "Marcy, the pie is wonderful," he said, effectively wolfing it down. He winked and sipped his coffee. "Pot roast and coconut cream pie. What's on your mind, darlin'?"

A rush of warmth invaded her cheeks as she choked down a bite of her pie.

"Why's your face so red?" Gabe wanted to know, freckles in a scrunch.

The heat in Marcy's face climbed clear up to her feathered bangs. She snatched her napkin from the table to fan herself, giving Gabe a pointed look. "It was 95 degrees today, if you must know, not to mention I've been cooking over a hot stove all afternoon."

"You know, Marcy, an occasional sandwich on unusually hot days would not be a crime. I don't need a big meal every night of the week." Patrick patted his vest. "Although Steven will certainly need the sustenance if he plans to beat me at chess."

"No!" A second blast of heat braised Marcy's cheeks at her family's startled looks. She quickly rose to collect the empty plates from the table, avoiding Patrick's eyes. "I mean, I . . . uh, just assumed you'd play Sean tonight since he's so seldom home these days."

"Oh sure, throw *me* to the wolves, why don't you?" Sean rose to his feet and slapped his brother on the back with a smirk. "No, I think Steven should be the victim tonight. After all, if he can disarm a ninety-six-year-old bootlegger, he can certainly handle Father, right?"

"Oh, I can handle him all right," Steven said with a cocky

grin. He pushed his chair in and swaggered into the parlor behind Patrick, shooting his mother a wink over his shoulder. "The question is, will Mother be able to 'handle' Father when I obliterate him?"

Marcy groaned inwardly, latching onto Gabe's arm when she tried to slip away. "Oh, no you don't, young lady. You and I need to do dishes pronto so I can finish my sewing. Plus you have catechism homework."

Gabe's elfin features screwed into a mask of pain. She sagged against the table as if Marcy had banned her from her beloved Dubble Bubble for life rather than the one-week punishment Patrick had doled out before dinner. "But I'm no good at catechism," she moaned. "And besides, Sister Mary Vomit hates me."

"Gabriella Dawn Smith!" Marcy gaped, hand to her chest. "If I ever hear you refer to your teacher in such a crude manner again, you will be banned from Dubble Bubble for a year, is that clear? Now, apologize this instant!"

"Sorry," Gabe mumbled. Her lips hardened. "But she does. Picks on me all the time."

"Only because you probably make her life miserable, squirt." Sean pinched the nape of Gabe's neck with his fingers, eliciting a giggle and a squirm from the little girl. "Come on, kiddo, I'll help you do your homework, okay?" He glanced up at Marcy. "And, Mother, you go finish your sewing. Gabe and I'll do the dishes."

Marcy adjusted the stack of dirty plates in her hands. "Oh no, Sean, you worked all da—"

He tugged them from her grip and attempted a scowl, the effort unsuccessful given the twinkle in his eyes. "Hardly work. I spent the day building a sports display, which was a labor of love. Go on now, get busy in the parlor while Gabe and I polish off the pie."

"Gosh, Sean, really?" Gabe's face glowed as if Sister Mary Vomit had just choked on Dubble Bubble.

"No!" Marcy and Sean's voices rang as one.

"Okay, okay, you don't have to bite my head off," Gabe said

with a pout. She collected utensils on a plate, then glanced up at Marcy with hope brimming in her eyes. "If I finish my homework early, can I stay up and play checkers with Sean?"

Marcy studied the delicate heart-shaped face framed by loose curls and felt her heart swell with love. Almond-shaped eyes, as deep brown as the girl's rich mahogany hair, stared back in innocent question, confirming to Marcy once again that Gabriella Smith was nothing more than a battered little soul who needed to be loved.

"Can I, Mrs. O'Connor, *please*?"

Mrs. O'Connor . . . , she thought with a twinge in her chest, *when it should be Mother.*

The childlike plea of Gabe's tone, the innocence of her freckled face, disarmed Marcy completely. She thought how a game of checkers could disrupt Gabe's nine o'clock bed-time, which in turn would disrupt her husband's rigid code of discipline, and knew she dare not risk it. She glanced at the clock in the hall and sighed. "Gabe, it's almost seven-thirty, darling, I don't think you'll have time tonight." Her heart squeezed at the look of disappointment on Gabe's face, but it couldn't be helped. Not if Marcy wanted this waif as her daughter. She stroked the girl's cheek with a gentle hand. "How about I let you stay up to play the very next time Sean is home for dinner? I'll even do the dishes by myself so you can get an early start."

Gabe flung herself into Marcy's arms, and Marcy thought her heart would melt. She closed her eyes and squeezed tightly, certain that this little girl was a gift from God for the daughter she'd lost so many years ago. Tears pricked at the thought of Faith's twin, Hope, lost to polio at a young age, leaving her twin sister and her family devastated. No, there was no doubt in Marcy's mind that Gabriella Smith was not only an answer to prayer . . . she was Marcy's last chance at mother-hood as well.

"Wow, thanks, Mrs. O'Connor, you're the best! I wish I had a mom like you."

Oh, Gabe . . .

"Come on, squirt, if we fly through dishes and homework, there just may be a few extra minutes for a game of catch in the backyard." Sean hoisted the plates in his hands and headed for the kitchen with Gabe on his heels, bubbling like it was Christmas.

Marcy drew in a deep breath of air and put a shaky hand to her chest. *Please, Lord . . .*

The pinch of Patrick's lips immediately told her that Steven was winning, a revolting development that caused Marcy's tongue to glide across her teeth several times. She glanced at the board and uttered a silent groan. Steven had won the advantage of white while Patrick was black. *Black, indeed, like his mood is prone to be.* The parlor windows were wide open, but they may as well have been closed. Nothing stirred in the steamy summer night but heat—not children, not locusts, and not air, for that matter. Marcy dabbed her handkerchief to the V of her summer dress and glanced at her husband. He had dispensed both vest and tie, unbuttoned the top two buttons of his shirt, and rolled up his sleeves—not a good sign for a man prone to be neat. Sweat gleamed on his tan face, neck, and just above the dark hairs of his chest. His forearms corded with strain as he assessed the board before him.

Marcy chewed on her lip. Patrick hated the heat almost as much as losing at chess, a thought that iced Marcy's skin despite the warmth of the room. She reached for her sewing basket and settled in her chair, only to startle at the sound of glass shattering in the kitchen.

Sean popped his head into the parlor with an awkward smile, an apology evident in the sheepish look on his face. "Sorry, Mother, but I'm afraid 'we' had a little mishap—the coconut cream pie took a dive along with your glass pie pan, but we'll clean it up."

Patrick groaned. "Not my pie . . ."

"Check!" Steven said with a deft move of his rook, and the very sound shattered Marcy's calm as thoroughly as Gabe had shattered the pie plate.

She tried to focus on threading the needle, but her hands

refused to comply, shaking while Patrick's fingers drummed incessantly on the table. *Please, God, let him win . . .*

Twenty minutes passed before the muscles in Marcy's stomach began to relax. The jangle of the phone jarred her in her seat and she flinched, stifling a cry when she pricked her finger. *Sweet heavens, what else can go wrong?*

"Father, it's Mr. Hennessey."

A dangerous groan garbled in Patrick's throat as he stood, eyes fixed on his son in a veiled threat. "As if you need more time to strategize my demise," he said with a thin smile. He adjusted his trousers with a sharp tug and strode for the kitchen, leaving Marcy in panic mode.

"Steven!" Her voice was hoarse. "I need your help."

He turned, forehead crimped. "What's wrong?"

Sucking the blood from her finger, she rose and hurried to her son's side with a nervous peek over her shoulder. "Steven, I beg you—you've got to let your father win tonight."

His mouth parted in surprise. "But I've got him just where I—"

"I don't care!" she rasped, her whisper a harsh plea. "Please, do this for me . . . for Gabe."

"What do you mean, do it for Gabe?"

She rattled his shoulder, fingers as pinched as her voice. "I don't have time to explain, but just trust me on this—*please*."

Steven blinked. "All right, Mother, if it's that important to y—"

The kitchen door blasted open. "You may as well put me out of my misery now, because when Mitch hears what Hennessey wants me to do, he's going to be sorely tempted to do the same." Patrick stormed back into the room with a deep ridge in his brow. His eyes narrowed as he took his place across from Steven. "That is, if my son doesn't finish me off first."

Marcy hurried to her chair, grateful Patrick hadn't noticed her collusion with Steven. "What does Hennessey want you to do?" she asked, settling in with less composure than she felt.

"It's not what he wants *me* to do—it's what he wants *Mitch* to do. Marjorie needs a cochair for the Fogg Museum auction, and apparently, Arthur has handpicked Mitch for the job."

"Who's Marjorie?" Steven asked.

"Hennessey's spoiled niece," Patrick said with a press of his jaw. "Who will make Mitch's life miserable. Which," he said with a press of fingers to his temple, "will in turn, make my life miserable. The man is so overworked now, he's like a sleep-deprived grizzly without a cave."

"Can't he decline . . . or at least get some help?" Marcy asked.

Patrick's brows shot up a half inch. "In this economy? At an understaffed newspaper that's just itching to lay somebody off? It would be sheer suicide." His lips flattened as he studied the chessboard. "Which may not be a bad option at the moment, come to think of it."

Steven made a move, and Marcy noted the subtle lift of Patrick's mouth, easing the tension in her chest. *Bless you, son.* She exhaled slowly while knots untangled in her stomach.

It was almost nine when she finished mending several school uniforms—Gabe's bedtime. With a weary sigh, she folded each of the mended items in a neat little pile and rose from her chair, her only thought to get that girl safely in bed and out of harm's way.

The kitchen door squeaked open and Marcy froze, fingers stiff on the plaid material of Kelly O'Connell's school uniform. Sean steered Gabe through the door, hand gripped at the back of her neck while he ushered her into the parlor with a somber look in his eyes. "Uh, Father—Mr. Lambert would like to speak to you outside."

Patrick looked up, forehead rippling. "What about?"

One glance at Gabe—sullen gaze glued to her feet, lips compressed—told Marcy that no win at chess would save her tonight.

Sean hiked a brow. "Well, it seems our Gabe has developed a fondness for tomatoes. Mr. Lambert claims she stripped his vines bare."

"What?" Patrick was on his feet faster than Marcy could

gasp. He strode to within an inch of the little girl and jerked her chin up. "Did you steal Mr. Lambert's tomatoes?"

The tiny jaw quivered against his thumb as she nodded.

"For the love of all that is decent, why? You don't even like tomatoes."

"I needed 'em . . . ," she whispered, eyes downcast. "For Civil War."

Patrick jerked his rolled sleeves down and rebuttoned the cuffs while a tic pulsed in his cheek. "What are you talking about?"

Gabe's gaze flicked to Marcy and glazed with tears before she faced Patrick once again with the barest lift of her chin. "We play Civil War in the neighborhood, girls against boys," she said with all the dignity of a soldier caught behind enemy lines. "And I'm the general."

Patrick folded his arms. "And the tomatoes?"

"Cannon fire," she muttered.

A cough that sounded suspiciously like a strangled laugh hacked from Sean's throat. Pursing his lips, Patrick shot his son a narrow gaze before returning his attention to Gabe with folded arms. "I see. Well, General Smith, the battle is lost. Not only will you pay for your thievery with Dubble Bubble, you are now Mr. Lambert's prisoner for an entire week."

"What?" she sputtered.

"You heard me," Patrick said. "Which means your troops will have to do without you for the next seven days while you complete every mission Mr. Lambert or I assign, is that understood? Tending to his garden, hoeing, sweeping, plant-ing—whatever the man needs."

"But that's not fair!" Gabe cried.

"Neither is war, young lady, nor pilfering vegetables for that matter. Now, I'm going out to apologize to Mr. Lam-bert, and I suggest you go to bed—you're going to need all the sleep you can get."

Gabe groaned.

Patrick strode toward the kitchen. "And, Marcy, after you've tucked the prisoner in, I'll need her shoebox of Dubble Bubble please. Compensation for Mr. Lambert's tomato supply."

"No!" The blood drained from Gabe's face as if she had just been shot.

Hand on the swinging door, Patrick turned, eyeing his foster daughter through pencil-thin lids. "Yes, General Smith, something needs to convince you that stealing is wrong. Just think of it as an opportunity to give yourself to the great and glorious cause . . ." He gave her a mock salute. "Preservation of your backside from the blistering you so richly deserve."

The kitchen door whooshed closed and Marcy wasted no time steering Gabe upstairs. "Did she finish her catechism?" she asked Sean with a worried glance over her shoulder.

"In record time." He winked at Gabe before plopping onto the sofa with Patrick's discarded newspaper. "She's a quick study when she wants to be. G'night, squirt."

"Sleep well, Gabe . . . hear tell Gus Lambert can be a real slave driver." Steven's grin deepened the little girl's scowl as she shuffled out with shoulders slumped.

Marcy's eyes flitted to the swinging kitchen door and back. "Pssst . . . Steven," she whispered. "I'll make double-fudge brownies for you if you let the man win and win fast. Sean, tell your father I went up to tuck Gabe in and I'll see him upstairs, okay? Good night, boys."

Steven grinned and Sean chuckled. "Good night, Mother."

Marcy bundled Gabe close and trudged up the stairs, quite certain that tonight her foster daughter would sleep more soundly than she. Her heart softened as she ushered the sleepy girl through the process of brushing her teeth, washing her face, changing her clothes, and saying her prayers. Curling into a ball under the cover, she yawned sweetly and told Marcy she loved her, and the moment the words parted from the little girl's lips, Marcy knew she was doing the right thing. She placed a gentle kiss on Gabe's freckled nose and turned out the light with a quiet sigh.

Now to convince my husband.

Getting ready for bed, Marcy tried to ignore the guilt

that needled her mind, but it bothered her all the same as she slipped into the satin nightgown that Patrick loved. She dabbed the barest hint of perfume on her throat, telling herself that her cause was just—Gabe was way too important. A halting breath wavered from her lips as she stared in the mirror. *And my husband way too stubborn,* she thought with a glide of her teeth. She drew in a fortifying breath, grateful that she didn't make a habit of coercing her husband, but the fate of some things—and some people—just couldn't be left to chance.

It was almost an hour later when Patrick finally entered their room with a yawn that told her he was as tired as Gabe. Marcy lowered the book in her hands and smiled, watching as he unbuttoned his shirt and tossed it toward the hamper. "Did you beat him?" she asked.

He glanced up with a secret smile, and her stomach fluttered for the first time in a very long while, taking her by surprise. His dark hair was sifted with gray at the temples and badly in need of a trim, and the clean line of his jaw was shadowed with dark stubble, but to Marcy, Patrick O'Connor had never been more handsome. He stepped out of his trousers and tossed them over the trouser press, his grin gleaming white in a tan face etched with the rugged lines of a man who was aging well. "Humiliated might be a better word."

She studied his tall frame as he slipped into his pajama bottoms and felt her pulse catch when he stripped off his T-shirt and sailed it toward the hamper, revealing a broad chest matted with hair. "It's too blasted hot to wear clothes tonight," he muttered, flipping the switch on the fan before dropping down beside her, eyes closed and hands folded on his stomach. She traced the curve of his bicep with her palm, suddenly aware she'd been so focused on Gabe, she'd forgotten just what a gift her husband truly was. "I love you, Patrick," she whispered.

One eyelid edged up. The breeze ruffled a stray curl on his forehead. "Don't toy with me, Marceline, I'm way too tired."

She laid her book aside and grinned, snuggling into his

embrace while she feathered her fingers through the dark and silver hair on his chest. She thought of Gabe, still a little girl while her own daughters now had children of their own, and wistfulness laced her tone. "Do you ever feel like time is passing us by, Patrick? You know . . . moving too quickly?"

His chuckle sounded more like a grunt. "Every day, darlin', especially when Steven now holds his own at chess." He kissed the top of her head. "Makes me feel old."

The edges of her lips tilted as she breathed in the scent of musk soap and the hint of maple and vanilla pipe tobacco. "No, my love, 'old' will be when you lose to Sean."

His chuckle was warm against her ear. "Heaven help me if it comes to that."

She paused. "Patrick . . . can we talk?"

"I thought we were, darlin'." Gliding his palm the length of her satin gown, he suddenly shifted to face her, tugging her close to bury his lips in the crook of her neck. "Although with the way you feel and smell tonight, darlin', I could be coerced into communication of a more intimate nature."

Coerced. Heat fanned through her body, but not for the right reasons. The usual flutters from Patrick's touch gave way to skitters instead as she gulped, grateful for the drone of the fan that helped to diffuse the waver in her voice. "I mean . . . about Gabe."

Her stomach kinked at the sudden press of his lips. His hand dropped to the bed, leaving her feeling exposed. "If you're trying to kill a mood, Marceline, you've succeeded. Heaven help us, if ever a child needed a firm hand, it's that one. I thought Katie was bad, but saints almighty, Gabe is the queen."

Her breathing shallowed. "Really, Patrick, she's not that bad . . ."

He flopped back on the bed, fingers tightly laced as they rested on his chest. The ridges in his brow deepened as he closed his eyes. "No, she's worse. Tell me, Marceline, don't you find it a wee bit ironic that my heart problems began the month *after* Gabe came to live with us?"

Marcy gasped. "Patrick! That's an awful thing to say."

His eyelids nudged up halfway, contrition in his gaze. "I'm sorry, darlin', but the thought has crossed my mind more than once in the last year." He closed his eyes again, tone tired and lips flat. "I know you're attached to her, Marcy, but I'd be lying if I said there aren't times when I wonder if we've made a mistake."

The air seized in her lungs. *God, no, please!* "How can you even think that, Patrick," she whispered, the rasp in her voice betraying her fear. "Gabe is like family, and you love her, I know you do!"

He glanced up, brows dipped in concern. Reaching for her hand, he squeezed and gave her a tired smile. "Of course I'm fond of the girl, Marcy, and yes, she is *like* family. But the fact remains that she is *not*, and quite frankly, I'm grateful. I've always prided myself on my firm discipline of our children, something that Gabe has made increasingly difficult. For pity's sake, she's the age of our grandchildren, Marcy, and I no longer have the energy of a young man to stay the course in raising any child, much less a difficult one." He sighed, settling in on the pillow once again. "I suppose I should be grateful we're only foster parents or I couldn't live with myself for my failure to rein the girl in."

"Oh, Patrick . . ." Tears stung Marcy's eyes.

He looked up and sighed. Drawing her close with a tug of her hand, he kneaded her shoulder and released another weighty breath, his whisper tinged with regret. "Aw, darlin', I'm not wanting to make you cry, really I'm not, but after that rift we had over Sam years ago, you and I pledged to be totally honest with each other." He kissed the top of her head. "Did we not?"

She nodded, more moisture lining her eyes as guilt nicked at her heart.

He patted her arm. "So, I need to be honest and let you know my true feelings. But . . . that said, let's just take it one day at a time and see where God leads us with Gabe, all right? Who knows—maybe one of these days she'll surprise us all by becoming the perfect foster daughter."

Marcy nodded again, the breath she'd been holding slowly seeping from her lips. *No, my love—the perfect "daughter."*

She snuggled in close, her grip tightening along with her resolve. *And oh yes . . . one of these days . . .*

"Now," he said, slipping his hand to her waist. He pressed a second kiss to her head. "What was it you wanted to talk about?"

"Nothing," she whispered, anxious to deflect his attention from a subject that would have to wait for the right time. She reached up to deposit a kiss on the edge of his bristled jaw. "I don't want to talk anymore."

His low chuckle tickled her ear as he slowly rolled her back on the bed, hovering with a dangerous gleam in his eye. "Good," he whispered, easing in to trail his mouth along the curve of her neck. "Neither do I."

7

I guarantee you, young woman, Filene's wouldn't treat a valuable customer this way."

Mustering all her strength and patience after a particularly trying day, Emma slowly counted to five before addressing Mrs. Arthur Bennett III with a kind smile. "I assure you, Mrs. Bennett," she said, shooting a comforting glance at Livvie, the ashen-faced salesgirl to whom Mrs. Bennett had given a rather pointed piece of her mind, "if we could take this cookware back, we certainly would, as we pride ourselves on customer service here at Dennehy's—"

"Customer service, my foot," the woman said, her voice rising in volume. "Why this young snip of a clerk—" Mrs. Bennett glared at the girl's name tag with a huff, "this *Livvie Allman*, here—as much as called me a liar!"

Livvie's eyes expanded. Her startled gaze skittered to Emma's and back. "Ma'am, I meant no offense, just that this cookware was not purchased at Dennehy's."

"You see?" Mrs. Bennett's silver brows arched in threat. "I distinctly remember purchasing this pot at this very counter, not two months ago, and it's an absolute travesty what it does to my whipped potatoes."

God, help me . . . With a silent sigh, Emma calmly reached

169

for the pot in question and turned it over. "You see, Mrs. Bennett," she said with a trace of her finger across the insignia on the back, "this is a Revere Copper and Brass product, most likely sold by Filene's. As of the first of January, Dennehy's only handles West Bend cookware."

The woman snatched the pot from Emma's hand, her face as flushed as its copper bottom. "Yes, I see—you're calling me a liar too! You sell me an inferior product and now you won't do anything about it. Well, this will certainly be the last time I shop here."

Emma countered the quiver in her stomach with a firm lift of her chin. "I sincerely apologize, Mrs. Bennett, for this unfortunate situation—"

"I'll show you unfortunate," Mrs. Bennett snapped, wagging the cookware at Emma as if it were a call to battle. "Once I tell my friends how shabbily I've been treated, over an inferior product no less, you will rue the day you ever butted heads with Mrs. Arthur Bennett III."

"You're absolutely right, Mrs. Bennett," Sean said.

Emma turned as he strode forward, his manner as easy and relaxed as if he and Mrs. B. were the best of friends. It was a contest whose mouth gaped wider—hers or Mrs. Bennett's.

Disarming the irate woman with a kind smile that soothed the ridges in her brow, Sean nodded toward the pot clutched in her hands. "May I?"

As if mesmerized, Mrs. Bennett relinquished it to Sean's possession, never blinking as he circled a palm to the inside surface. "See this chrome plating?"

Mrs. B. nodded, her eyes fixed on Sean rather than the pot.

"Revere Copper and Brass product is a quality company, to be sure, but this particular product was not one of their best efforts. You see, Mrs. Malloy here . . ." Sean inclined his head toward Emma, giving her an encouraging smile, "received complaints just like yours when we carried this product, because apparently the chrome flakes off into the food—"

"Oh my goodness, exactly!" Mrs. Bennett said. "Ruined my potatoes with silver flecks."

Sean nodded in sympathy, and Emma tried to hide the smile that pulled at her lips. He handed the pot back. "The Revere salesman asked us to reconsider, but when Mrs. Malloy tested the pot herself, the same thing happened. It seems that when potatoes are cooked in saltwater in a chrome-plated pot, it causes a chemical reaction that peels the chrome right off."

"My word," Mrs. Bennett said, mouth slack and a bejeweled hand to her pearl-clad neck.

"So you see, Mrs. Bennett, in the best interest of our customers, Mrs. Malloy wisely made the decision to discontinue this cookware immediately at the first of the year, well ahead of Revere themselves pulling the product." Sean gave the fry pan a conciliatory pat, his demeanor one of complete empathy. "Regretfully, the store where you bought this did not."

The woman's sagging mouth snapped shut, and Emma took a step forward. "Mrs. Bennett, we are truly sorry and wish there was something more we could do—"

"Actually . . . ," Sean began, his gaze locking with Emma's, "there may be, Mrs. Malloy. You were kind enough to approve the Customer Alliance Affiliation program last week, and I was thinking that perhaps Mrs. Bennett might serve as our first member. What do you think?"

Emma blinked, her lips curving at the little-boy twinkle in his eyes that belied the efficiency of his query. "Why, what an excellent idea, Mr. O'Connor!"

"And what, pray tell, is the Customer Alliance Affiliation?" Mrs. Bennett asked.

A knot of nerves untangled in Emma's stomach as she swept her hand in Sean's direction, bestowing a grateful smile on her assistant manager. "Mr. O'Connor will be happy to explain, Mrs. Bennett, but I think you'll like what you hear. The Customer Alliance Affiliation or CAA is only one of many exciting programs that Mr. O'Connor has proposed to serve our customers better." She stepped aside with a tilt of her head. "Mr. O'Connor?"

Sean handed the pot back to Mrs. Bennett. "Unfortunately, Mrs. Bennett, although we can't reimburse you for this cookware, we can make sure your visit to Dennehy's today ends on a positive note. You see, we're implementing the CAA program to reward loyal customers with favored status. As a result, we'd like to issue you a special Dennehy's shopper's plate—the very first one, mind you—that will entitle you to special benefits such as early-bird specials, two-for-one sales, and a point system where you'll receive awards for every $50 you spend in the store."

"Oh my," Mrs. Bennett whispered, apparently rendered near speechless.

"Not to mention," Emma added with a proud lift of her chin, "that your shopper's plate will also afford you the opportunity to purchase on credit rather than with check or cash."

The woman's jaw dropped.

"And," Sean added, relaxed efficiency at its best, "your name will be announced in a future circular as our very first 'VIP' —very important patron."

A gasp sputtered from Mrs. Bennett's mouth as she put a hand to her chest. "I am . . . honored, to be sure! When do I receive my card?"

"Within weeks," he said. "And we can complete the paperwork now if you have time."

"Absolutely! Lead away, young man."

Relieving her of the errant pot, he tucked it under one arm and extended the other to usher her to the stairs where she turned to shoot Emma a narrow gaze edged with a smile. "I suspect this young man may be the best bargain in this store, Mrs. Malloy."

"That's kind of you to say, Mrs. Bennett," Sean said with a genuine smile. "But I suspect your shopper's plate will change that opinion in a hurry."

"Balderdash, young man. I'm a crusty old woman who knows a skilled merchant when I meet one." She turned to give Emma a final searing look. "And you, Mrs. Malloy, best take heed—this is one man to be paid what he's worth."

Sean shot Emma a wink that caused her to chuckle. Mrs. Bennett's laughter faded as the unlikely pair disappeared around the corner arm in arm, and Emma couldn't help but marvel at how Sean O'Connor had changed her life for the better. *A man to be paid what he's worth, indeed.* She shook her head, enjoying a secret smile. "Heaven knows I wish I could, Mrs. Bennett," she whispered with a wistful sigh, "but no one has that kind of money."

"Da-da?"

Katie sighed. *Good question.* She tucked a teddy bear in the crib next to the little girl and wondered the very same thing. "No, darlin', Daddy's still at work," she said with a taut smile, suddenly feeling the need to scoop the toddler back up in her arms to nuzzle a kiss against Kit's silky skin. The clean scent of baby powder and Pears soap soothed Katie's senses, and for surely the twentieth time that week, Katie's heart swelled with gratitude for the little bundle in her arms.

It hadn't taken long for Katie to fall in love with Luke's adopted daughter, and now, after a little over a month of being married, Katie had difficulty even remembering her life without Kit. As stubborn and independent as Katie herself, Kit reminded her of what she might have been like at the age of fifteen months, and the very thought forged a bond between them that she never expected. Big Sass and Little Sass, Luke would call them, and the fact that she and Kit shared both temperaments and the love of the man they both adored only drew them closer. Katie burrowed her nose into the neck of the curly-haired moppet who called herself "Kit" instead of "Kat" or "Kitty," and the little dickens' giggle brought a smile to Katie's face.

"What do you say we rock awhile to see if Daddy comes home?" she whispered in the crook of Kit's neck, and the little girl laughed and wiggled away with hope in her eyes.

"Da-da?" she said with a dance of her fat legs, and Katie's heart squeezed at how much Kit missed her daddy. She ruffled her fingers through Kit's wild auburn curls. "Join the club, sweetie," she whispered. "I miss Daddy too."

The clock in the parlor chimed eight-thirty as Katie sank into the white oak slatted rocking chair handcrafted by Sean. Nestling Kit against her shoulder, she crooned a lullaby against the baby's soft curls in time with the steady rhythm of the thick rockers that groaned and squeaked against the polished hardwood floor. In almost no time, Kit's chunky body molded to her own in the blessed state of sleep, and Katie closed her eyes, awed by the sense of closeness she felt with this child not of her own blood. To Luke and her family, she was Kit's new mama, and yet Katie had worried that working at the BCAS three days a week and eventually law school might rob her of ever really connecting with Luke's daughter, a worry she now knew to be unfounded. Kit not only filled the hole left by Luke's absence during the day—and now the nights—but loving her came as naturally as breathing, it seemed. Katie sighed. Maybe motherhood wouldn't interfere with her dreams of law school after all, she thought with a sense of peace. One eyelid edged up as she stared at the ceiling. "But if it's all the same to you, Lord, can we wait awhile for the others?"

The chimes heralded the nine o'clock hour, and Katie wished just once Luke would get home before Kit went to bed. Between board meetings with headquarter brass from the New York Children's Aid Society and Luke's obvious avoidance of Katie, neither Kit nor she had seen more than a glimpse of him the entire week. And the strain was beginning to show—on a daughter who couldn't stop chattering about him all day . . . and a wife who couldn't stop thinking about him all night. Tucking a sheet around Kit and her bear, Katie startled at the sudden click of a lock. Her head shot up when the front door opened and closed.

"Da-da?" Kit sat straight up, wide-eyed, both teddy bear and sleep suddenly forgotten.

Ignoring the surge of her pulse, Katie forgot to breathe as she and Kit waited to greet the man they both loved. She sucked in a deep breath. *And* the man whose anger toward Katie was still as cold and sharp as the few curt responses he'd sent her way.

"Da-da!" Kit's chubby legs thumped against Katie's side as the toddler did a jig in her arms.

Her squeals bounced off the walls of their tiny parlor, and Luke glanced up with a broad smile that eased the fatigue in his handsome face. Jerking the tie loose from his neck, he closed the door and strode forward to whisk Kit into the air, swooping her high amidst shrieks and giggles. "How's my little peanut?" he said, burying his lips in the crook of her neck until she squealed again. "Are you feeling better?"

"Better!" Kit gurgled with glee, planting a slobbery kiss on his tan cheek.

"I'd say she's 99 percent, with just a tinge of a runny nose." Katie's smile was timid.

"Good." He tossed Kit over his shoulder and headed down the hall without giving Katie a second glance. "Come on, Peanut, I'll read you a story before I put you to bed."

"Are you hungry, Luke?" Katie called, praying he was finally ready to sit and talk.

The click of the door was his only answer, and Katie's temper heated her cheeks. With a tight press of lips, she plopped on her parents' old and faded flame-stitch sofa and folded her arms, her mood as belligerent as the groan of its springs. Usually she enjoyed sitting in their snug second-story flat with its arched window open to the stately oaks lining Commonwealth Avenue. Occasionally a breeze fluttered past the delicate sheers, rustling the lush fronds of Katie's Boston fern while infusing the room with the salty scent of the Charles River Basin.

But tonight she took no comfort in a cozy love nest that had become a silent war zone. She snatched her *Harper's Bazaar* from the coffee table and swiped at its pages with mounting fury, seeing nothing but a mule of a husband who'd given her the silent treatment all week. The man had barely spoken to her since their fight over law school, except for a grunt before he left in the morning and even less when he lumbered in each night to sleep on the couch. Katie's eyes narrowed as she eyed the pillow and a sheet neatly folded on the far side of the sofa, further indication that Luke McGee still harbored a grudge.

Her patience was as thin as the flimsy pages of her *Harper's Bazaar*, which she now flipped so hard that one tore in half. Drawing in a cumbersome breath, she dropped the magazine to her lap and closed her eyes, willing her own grudges to calm. After all, she loved the pigheaded lout even if he was being completely unreasonable. And she *had* sprung an awful shock on him, she supposed, but was that any reason to become a deaf-mute to his wife? Katie sighed. She'd been wrong in not telling him—she knew that now, but she really had had no choice. Luke never would have agreed had he known, perhaps even rethinking his engagement to Katie, and she couldn't risk that. So she'd laid low as the compliant fiancée until the band was on her finger, opting to deal with Luke's stubborn streak head-on . . . *after* they were married.

Her lips squirmed to the right. A tactical error, evidently, given her husband's reception, which closely resembled that of a rock wall. Katie had felt her own walls going up over Luke's refusal to even discuss it, but she'd worked hard to do the right thing—to say no to her anger and yes to God. To forgive Luke and give him time to forgive her. She drew in a fortifying breath and tossed the magazine aside, refolding her arms as her gaze burned into the door at the end of the hall. Well, the rock wall had had seven days to be chipped away, and Katie was running out of the strength—and patience—to chisel. The time for silence was over—they needed to talk. *Now.*

Kit's door opened, and Katie's stomach rolled when Luke carefully closed it to just a crack, disappearing into their own room. She counted to ten a number of times, attempting to calm her temper as well as give Luke a few moments to do the same. But when he exited their room a few moments later in a change of clothes and a small duffle in his hands, she felt the blood siphon from her face.

Her rib cage contracted, cutting off her air. "You're leaving again?" she asked, her voice strained despite her best efforts to remain calm. She glanced at the Victorian table clock that had been a wedding gift from Emma and swallowed hard. *Nine-thirty and he's leaving again?* "You just got home, Luke—where are you going?"

He glanced up with sullen eyes, his shadowed jaw sculpted in stone. "Clancy's," he said in a clipped tone, then turned away to rifle through the duffle while her mouth sagged in shock.

"The gym? At this hour?" She stood to her feet, vaguely aware of a wobble in her legs.

Snapping the duffle closed, he looked up, his temple flickering as he pierced her with a shuttered gaze. "Yeah. Don't wait up."

He turned to go, and her heart caught in her throat. It took every shred of her will to keep her voice humble. "Luke, wait, please—can't we talk before you go?"

A muscle tightened in his broad back while he stood at the door, head bowed and hand on the knob. "No. I'm not ready yet—I still have frustrations to vent." He opened it to leave, and her humility died an ugly death.

With a harsh gasp, she flew across the room and slammed the door, blocking his way. "No need to duke it out at the gym, McGee," she snapped. "I'll give you a good fight right here."

He jerked her aside. "Get out of my way, Katie, we'll talk when I'm good and ready."

"No," she said, shoving him back, "we're going to talk now."

He leaned in, eyes flashing. "Get this straight, Katie Rose, and get it good—you don't run this household and you don't run my life."

"Our life!" she hissed, tears pooling against her will. She battled the quiver of her lip with a thrust of her chin. "We're one, whether you like it or not. In God's eyes, if not in yours."

"One flesh, Katie, but two wills. What you did . . . ," he shook his head, eyes naked with pain and voice hard, "wounded me. You're my wife, my family, the one I should trust . . ."

Her throat constricted. "You can trust me, Luke, I promise. I won't ever do this again."

Fatigue shadowed his features as he tightened his grip on his bag. "No, Katie, you won't. Because if you do, you'll jeopardize our marriage more than you know." He opened the door. "We'll talk later, when my anger's under control, but for now, I'm leaving."

"Well, that makes two of us then," she whispered. "When you get back, Kit and I will be gone." A sob rose in her throat as she ran down the hall, tears streaming. She heard the front door slam, but ignored it, hauling her suitcase from the bedroom closet and thrusting it on their bed. Hands shaking, she opened her dresser drawer and snatched an armful of clothes.

"What the devil are you doing?" he asked from the doorway, his tone taut.

She continued to pack.

He strode forward and hurled his duffel onto the floor, the sting of a curse sizzling the air. "I said, what are you doing, Katie?"

Yanking more clothes from the drawer, she flung them into the bag, facing him with fire in her eyes. "You refuse to talk? Fine. I refuse to stay. I won't live in silence, Luke McGee, no matter how angry you are. We'll stay at my parents'." She turned away to retrieve her toiletries from her vanity.

"You're not going anywhere—"

She spun around. "No? Well, to borrow a phrase—you don't run my life."

Jaw ground tight, he seized her suitcase and dumped it out before pitching it on the floor.

She stared, mouth gaping. "You're a devil," she rasped, voice straining low to avoid waking Kit.

Muscled arms to his hips, he gave her a thin smile. "Yeah? Well, you wouldn't exactly make it past the pearly gates, you little brat." He scooped up a skirt and tossed it at her. "Put your clothes away."

He headed for the door, and she jerked the suitcase onto the bed once again to repack her clothes.

She singed him with a scathing look, her whisper harsh. "This isn't the BCAS, you brainless Neanderthal—you can't order me around."

In two powerful strides he had her suitcase upended again and clothes toppled in another unsightly heap. He launched the bag on the bed. His voice was a threat edged with a hard smile. "Sure I can, Katie—I'm bigger than you. I suggest you put the clothes away—*now*."

She reared up to kick him, but he was too fast and deflected her with an innocent parry that toppled her back on the bed. He slacked a leg, hands parked low on his hips. "You're a handful, Katie Rose, but so help me, I will wear the pants in this family or die trying."

Katie gritted her teeth, anger hissing through every syllable. "Now that's the best idea you've had yet, you overgrown ape—croak away!" Her lip curled in a sneer that belied the tears in her eyes. "And you were going to make me the 'happiest woman alive'—HA!"

Luke stared, his breathing as ragged as his wife's as she lay, chest heaving and tears trailing her cheeks. Shame crawled up his neck with a heat that scalded his pride. He exhaled a halting breath, painfully aware that as a man of God and the spiritual head of his home, he had set a poor example. Yes, Katie had been wrong initially, but he wasn't responsible for Katie's heart, only his. And he had failed—both God and his wife—miserably.

Easing down on the bed with a weary sigh, he reached for her hand, feathering her wrists with his thumbs. His words were halting, hoarse, and difficult to say. "Katie, I'm . . . sorry . . . for giving in to my anger."

"Sorry doesn't change the fact that you're a bully," she said, practically spitting the words in his face.

He could smell the rose scent of her hair and a faint whiff of baby powder on her clothes, and all at once he was keenly aware just how much he had missed her. His gaze wandered from blue eyes glinting with ire, to pink, full lips, angry and parted with every heave of her breasts, and in a wild thud of his pulse, all anger dissipated as quickly as the air in his lungs. He swallowed hard, suddenly craving her so much, he thought he would lose his mind. "Katie, please—let's not do this. I've missed you more than I can say." Her eyes flared as he bent close, and the groan that escaped his throat was no more than a rasp when his mouth tasted hers.

She bucked like a rodeo filly that'd never been ridden. "Oh, no you don't, McGee," she hissed, thrashing her head side to side. "You are not going to sweet-talk me now—"

He silenced her with a kiss that nearly consumed him, and his breathing was heavy when his mouth slid to suckle her ear. "Come on, Katie," he whispered, "let's kiss and make up . . ."

"Not on your li—"

Slipping his hands to her waist, he pulled her close with another kiss that reminded him just how much he needed her in his life . . . wanted her. His lips trailed her throat while blood pounded through his veins. "Look, Katie, I told you I was sorry . . . and I need you, Sass . . ."

Two petite palms slammed hard against his chest, holding him at bay with a voice that threatened despite the glaze in her eyes. "Hold your horses right there, buster! There'll be no needs 'met' until we talk." She wrenched free and shimmied to the far side of the bed, back butted hard against the headboard and palms splayed as if ready to bolt.

"Okay, Sass," he said with a tight smile, "you're the boss." He moved to sit beside her and rested a palm on her thigh, gaze focused on hers as his thumb slowly circled.

She smacked his hand. "Do we have to take this to the kitchen? Focus!"

"I am," he said, arm draped casually over the headboard. His gaze slid to her mouth.

Huffing out a sigh, she pinched finger and thumb to his jaw and thrust up, her brows arched in expectation. "On my *eyes*, McGee, not my mouth. We have serious issues to discuss."

Luke sucked in a deep breath and blew it out again. He folded his arms and fixed his gaze on Katie's, his manner suddenly serious. "Okay, you're right—we do have a lot of air to clear. So why don't you start by telling me why you would keep something this important to yourself?"

The sparks in her eyes tempered while she inched sideways to face him. Her chin elevated just a smidge before she glanced away, picking at the nubby rose motif of the quilt her mother had made. He studied her as she focused on the coverlet rather than his face, and although her voice carried the strength of recent fury, she chewed on her lip, betraying her guilt.

"I shouldn't have done it, Luke, I can see that now and I'm sorry." She glanced up, eyes holding a residue of anger. "But this week has certainly been proof as to how . . . unreasonable you can be."

He jagged a brow. "Unreasonable? That my wife excludes me from a life decision that affects us all?"

A lump shifted in her throat despite the further lift of her chin. "Yes, because when you are bent on a certain course of action, Luke McGee, you can be quite the brick wall, and I was afraid that if I told you . . . ," a faint shiver rippled her body, "well, that you might postpone the wedding or even . . . ," she peeked up, teeth tugging her lip, "not marry me at all."

His heart melted as always when Katie let her vulnerable side show, and he tugged her into his arms, closing his eyes as he pressed his lips to her hair. "I could never *not* marry you, Katie, don't you know that? You and Kit are the family I've waited for my whole life." He pulled away to lift her chin with his thumb, his voice husky with emotion. "Loving you, marrying you . . . has been like finally coming home."

Tears pooled in her eyes and she fell into his arms with a hoarse cry. "Oh, Luke, I love you too, and I am so sorry for not telling you, but I was afraid. Law school has been a dream of mine for so long and yet I know it interferes with your dream of a family."

Exhaling a heavy breath, he kneaded her back with a gentle palm. "It does present a dilemma, no question about that—Lizzie having Kit five days a week and then losing you at the BCAS." He held her away with a wry smile. "Nor am

I thrilled that Parker will be funding your dream instead of me. But . . . ," he cupped her face in his hands, "if this is important enough that you quake in your boots at the prospect of me saying no, then I guess it should be important enough for me to say yes." His lips skewed to the right. "And I did promise to make you the happiest woman alive, so I guess my goose is cooked."

"Oh, Luke!" She thrust herself back into his arms. "You won't regret it, I promise."

He held her at bay with a firm grip. "Not so fast, Sass—there are conditions."

A smile nudged the edge of her lips as she feathered his arms with her thumbs, giving him a lidded gaze that focused only on his mouth. "To make you the happiest man alive?"

His throat suddenly went dry, and he tightened his hold. "No, Katie, I want your promise that you'll never keep secrets from me again when it's something I should know."

She nodded, exhaling a slow breath.

"And that we will discuss and pray about *everything*," he said with a stroke of her hair.

"Of course, Luke, whatever you say."

"*And*," he said with finality in his tone, quite sure his last condition would not be to her liking. His eyes locked on hers. "If you get pregnant at any time during law school, you will quit and stay home, no questions asked."

"Forever?" Her eyes gaped as wide as her mouth.

He softened his hold, resorting to thumb feathering of his own. "Just until the kids are in school and Kit's old enough to watch them. Say sixteen? Then, we'll see what we can do."

She tilted her head. "You promise?"

He leaned in. "Absolutely," he said with a slow nibble of her ear. "That way we both keep our dreams, but it's God who makes the decision."

A moan trembled from her mouth and he smiled, descending on her lips to seal the deal. "So, what do you say? You ready to put both of our dreams in God's hands and let him decide?"

She nodded, a hazy look in her eyes.

"Good," he said, teasing her lips with a playful tug of his teeth. "Then I say we get busy." He lowered her to the bed, his breathing rapid and warm as he whispered against her skin. "Because as you know, I don't like to lose."

"I know, but you can't always win, McGee."

His chuckle rumbled against the hollow of her throat as his fingers toyed with the button of her blouse. "Sure I can, Katie," he whispered. His mouth explored her collarbone with deadly intent. "Because when it comes to winning," he said with a lingering kiss, "I seldom strike out."

"Da-da? Stor-wee?"

Luke froze, lips fused to Katie's throat while her chuckle vibrated beneath his mouth. She wiggled from his hold to sit up and grin at Kit, who stood in the door with a book in her hand.

Katie patted the bed. "Sure, Peanut, Daddy would love to read you another story, wouldn't you, Luke?" Her smile was innocent. "By the way, honey, did I mention Kit's learned to climb out of her crib?"

A groan trapped in his throat as their daughter scrambled into their bed with the same dexterity with which she obviously escaped her own. He scooped her up and settled her on his lap with a kiss to her neck, then took the book from her hand. His gaze thinned as he shot his wife a warning smile. "Don't get cocky, Katie Rose—this is only a rain delay, not a loss."

"Whatever you say, Luke," Katie said with a bored yawn. She jumped up to collect her clothes from the bed, then sauntered to the dresser, delivering a sassy smile over her shoulder. "Which only goes to prove my point, McGee, that if you think you're going to win *this* competition"—she angled a brow—"I'd have to say you're all wet."

"Gosh, Emma, I don't know who's the better cook—you or Mrs. Peep." Eighteen-year-old Casey ladled the last spoonful of strawberry trifle in her mouth with a moan, winking at their elderly landlady who sat across from her at Emma's kitchen table.

Emma tossed her young neighbor a smile, the aroma of stew and fresh-baked bread mingling with the smell of fresh-ground coffee beans that Emma had just prepared to brew. The happy sound of chatter merged with the chug of the coffee and the laughter of children playing stickball in the street outside Mrs. Peep's six-family flat. Lemon-yellow gingham curtains fluttered in the summer breeze, infusing the kitchen—and Emma—with the clean scent of new-mown grass, along with a cozy feeling that fit as snugly as the floral wallpaper hugging the walls.

"The better cook? Why, Emma, of course." Mrs. Peep spooned a bite of dessert into her mouth, savoring it with a dreamy roll of her eyes. Shadows from crystal candlesticks flickered and swayed across a lemon-yellow tablecloth bedecked with floral-patterned china cups and saucers salvaged from a return at the store. She patted a napkin to lips now pursed in a pout, then hiked one silver brow in a show of authority. "Although my Archie swore till the day he died that it was my cooking that got him to the altar." Her blue eyes suddenly twinkled. "Said it was better than a Big Bertha cannon at a shotgun wedding."

Emma glanced over her shoulder, smiling at her pert landlady and the young woman who'd become more like a daughter. "I'd put your money on Mrs. Peep, Casey. I can't compete with a woman who cooked for six strapping sons over the years and a hungry husband too. *Whom*," she said with a lift of her brows, "I guarantee didn't marry her just for the taste of her food." Emma dipped her head in tease, eyes warm with affection. "You forget I've seen your portrait on your mantel, Mrs. Peep, the one that's a dead ringer for Greta Garbo."

"Oh, pshaw!" Mrs. Peep tossed her head, but Emma could see her pleasure in the glow of her face, dewy and soft despite an abundance of wrinkles. Finger waves glimmered against her temple like white satin as she straightened in her chair, a tiny woman, petite and pretty in a perky housedress that brought out the blue of her eyes. Weathered lips crooked into a droll smile when she leaned in to return Casey's wink. "I can tell you right now that if I were a dead ringer for Garbo, Archie wouldn't have let me spend so much time in the kitchen."

"Mrs. Peep!" Even Casey's cheeks hazed pink, probably the exact shade of Emma's.

The tiny woman chuckled, sipping the cup Emma had just filled. "My Archie was a real Romeo, romantic to the core," she said, her exuberance edging into a touch of melancholy, "and I can't help but remember him that way. I was young once, you know." Her gaze trailed into a faraway look that tipped her lips with a soft smile. "Truth be told, I still am." She closed her eyes to sip her coffee before they popped open with a cheeky grin. "Now, if I can just convince my mirror."

Emma bent to give the old woman a hug. "Fifty-two years with the love of your life is a lot of blessing, Mrs. Peep, and more awaits when you see Archie in heaven."

Her smile trembled. "I know, my dear," she said with a sigh. She patted Emma's cheek, eyes brimming with fondness. "You're too good to waste, Emma Malloy, you know that?"

"I totally agree," Casey said. Sitting cross-legged on her chair, she swiped whipped cream from her lip with the tip of her tongue, as if she were eight instead of eighteen. "It's a real shame Emma doesn't have anyone to cook for."

"I do too," Emma said with a mock scowl. "I cook for you and Mrs. Peep every chance I get."

Casey licked her spoon with a glint of mischief in her blue-gray eyes. "Come on, Emma, you know what I mean. You should be making these wonderful concoctions for a grateful man who can shower you with praise . . ." She wriggled her brows. "Or kisses . . ."

"Casey Miranda Herringshaw!" Emma's cheeks flamed hot as she poured cream into her coffee. "You're as bad as Mrs. Peep, for goodness' sake. Must I remind you I have a ring on my finger?"

The imp chuckled. "Oh, that ring *claims* you have a husband, Mrs. Malloy, but I sure don't see one around. Which is a real shame, because Mrs. Peep isn't the only one who thinks you're too good to waste—Mama and I do too."

Emma stifled a smile with a stern jut of her brow. "So now my life is a waste, is it?"

"Now you know that's not what we mean, Emma," Mrs. Peep said.

"Of course not. We just wish you had a little romance in your life, that's all." Chin in hand, Casey drifted off into a dreamy stare. "Because every girl needs a little romance, right, Mrs. Peep? Someone tall, dark, and handsome to weaken her knees?"

Mrs. Peep giggled like a schoolgirl, leaning to give Emma's hand a quick press. "Or tall, blond, and handsome, such as my Archie. But yes, even though I know it can never be, Emma, nothing would give me more pleasure than seeing a little romance in your life."

Gulping her coffee too quickly, Emma scalded her tongue, a timely reminder of how "romance" could do the same. Memories assaulted her—of roses from Rory, candlelit dinners, the warmth of his lips, the stroke of his hands—and her heart cramped at the knowledge that she would never have that again. *Nor the pain*, she reminded herself for the thousandth time since she'd left Rory's bed.

Blowing on her coffee, she studied Casey and wondered if she'd made a mistake in convincing her mother to let her stay in Boston. For all of her independence, Casey seemed too naïve when it came to love, much like Emma at the same age. Too wide-eyed and unaware as to just how treacherous the wrong relationship could be.

She swallowed a sip of coffee and smiled. "Romance isn't always moonlight and roses, you know, especially if you fall in love with the wrong man."

The faraway look in Casey's eyes melted into sympathy. Her voice was gentle. "I know that happened to you, Emma, because my mother told me everything. And I can't express how sorry I am. But I hope—and I certainly pray—that my Johnny is nothing like your Rory."

Guinevere meowed and grazed against her legs, and Emma picked her up, choosing her words carefully as she absently stroked the white bundle of fur now balled in her lap. Sadness tainted her smile. "I'm afraid the man I fell in love with was nothing like my Rory either, Casey . . . at least not in the beginning. Not all of us are as lucky as Mrs. Peep in finding our Archie."

"Unfortunately, Emma's right. Out of five girls in my family, my sister Margaret and I were the only two who weren't married to lying cheats and sots."

"Goodness, you're both starting to sound like Mama! She's always fretting some Lothario will break my heart. But I'm eighteen now, and I can sense when a man has feelings for me, truly. Like Johnny. He genuinely cares for me, Emma, I'm certain."

Emma's lips curled into a soft smile. "You are, are you?" she said, a teasing brogue slipping into her tone.

The sparkle returned to Casey's eyes as she folded arms on the table with a smile. "Well, almost certain. All I know is when I'm with Johnny, I feel beautiful . . . special."

"That's because you *are* beautiful and special," Emma said. "Not because of Johnny."

Mrs. Peep tipped the rest of her cup and set it in the saucer before pushing it away. She rose to carry her cup to the sink. "Dinner was lovely, Emma, as always. Thank you so much."

"You're not staying for dominoes?" Emma blinked up at her, coffee cup in hand.

"I don't think so, dear, not tonight."

A frown pinched Emma's brow as she rose. "Do you feel all right, Mrs. Peep?"

"Of course." She gave Emma's arm a gentle squeeze. "Just tired and thinking of Archie, that's all. I believe I'll boil some milk and head on to bed with a good book . . ." Melancholy settled in the crook of her smile. "Or maybe a few of the love letters he wrote me before we were married." Her gaze shifted to Casey. "Good night, dear, and good luck with your young man."

Casey jumped up to give her a hug. "Thanks, Mrs. Peep. Good night."

Ushering her landlady down the hall, Emma paused a moment to poke through the drawer of her Victorian desk before slipping ten dollars into Mrs. Peep's pocket.

"Oh, no, Emma, not again—I won't take it." Her landlady thrust it back.

Emma captured her in a tight hug. "Yes, Mrs. Peep, please? It's not much, and it's only fair for all you do for me."

"But it's a difficult time right now, and you can't afford it any more than anyone else."

"I can, Mrs. Peep, truly." She ducked to smile into her eyes. "Now, honestly, what else do I have to spend my money on? You know I work six days a week, which leaves no time to spend anything. Besides, I'm not the one who has two empty apartments to rent, remember?" She clasped the old woman's hand, her eyes pleading. "Let me do this . . . please?"

Water welled in Mrs. Peep's eyes. "You already pay too much, then feed me dinner too."

"Yes, just like you insist on sneaking into my apartment and doing my laundry, so hush. You would do the same for me, and you know it. Now, you get yourself into bed, all right?" Emma opened the door. "I'll check on you tomorrow to see how you're doing."

Mrs. Peep nodded, tears seeping into the tiny ridges that fanned from the side of her eyes. Her frail lips trembled as she squeezed Emma's hand. "Good night, Emma. You are truly something special—the kind of woman who brings a smile to God's face."

Heat braised Emma's cheeks. "I certainly hope so, Mrs. Peep," she said with a forced chuckle and then quietly shut the door. Hand still on the knob, she slumped back with head bowed. A woman who brings a smile to God's face? She sighed. *Maybe now . . . but definitely not before . . .* Exhaling quietly, she made her way to the kitchen where Casey washed dishes at the sink.

Arms folded, Emma tried to look stern. "How many times have I told you that you're my guest, Casey—I don't invite you to work."

Casey shot a grin over her shoulder, a blonde curl obscuring one eye. "Just say 'thank you,' Emma, because we both know Mama would tan my hide if I didn't."

Emma sighed. "Thank you, Casey, I appreciate it, and your mother would be proud."

The young girl paused, her smile pensive as she dried her hands. "So, why do you do it?"

"Do what?" Emma gathered the soiled tablecloth and placed it on the counter before retrieving the domino set from the bottom drawer of her cupboard.

Casey studied her, gaze narrowed in thought. "Give extra money to Mrs. Peep."

Emma rose and turned, the wooden box clutched to her chest. "What do you mean?"

Tossing the towel over a rack, Casey ambled to her seat and settled in, arms folded on the table and lips twisted in a wry smile. "Come on, Emma, I know you give money to Mrs. Peep, just like you give money to me and heaven knows how many others. And as if that isn't enough, you insist on fixing us dinners and lending me clothes. You keep Mama posted on my progress and you watch me like a hawk—" One side of her mouth crooked up. "A 'mother' hawk, to be exact, hovering over me, taking care of me. I've seen you bake brownies for people at work, kids in the neighborhood, and just yesterday, Margaret Latham told me you've been tutoring her in math." She cocked her head. "So, tell me, because I really want to know—why do you do it?"

Emma blinked, Casey's question catching her off-guard. She laid the box on the table and thought about all the dinners they'd shared, all the conversations about movies or fashion or love. Sure, Emma had given advice here and there, even referring to prayer or her deep faith occasionally on their

189

strolls to church. Her pulse quickened. But for Casey to ask such a question outright meant the door was open for more. More of Emma's heart.

And more of God's?

She swallowed her hesitation and sat down, scooting close to the table to upend the box. Dominoes spilled across the lemon-polished wood with a clatter while Emma peered up, her heart spilling with love. "Because I have to, Casey, I can't help it." She cocked her head and gave her a mischievous smile. "You know how you feel when you're with Johnny, as if you're going to bubble over for the love he brings into your life?"

Casey nodded, a blush blooming on her face as she released a lovesick sigh.

"Well, it's the same with me," Emma said in a matter-of-fact tone, fingers flitting across the sea of tiles to turn each of them face down.

Ridges formed in Casey's brow. "I don't understand. Rory hurt you and now you're alone." She squinted, as if trying to comprehend. "Do you mean love for friends?"

"Yes, affection for you, Mrs. Peep, and others, certainly, but that's not the love I mean."

"What, then?" Casey asked, the innocence in her face plucking at Emma's heart.

Emma paused, fingers lingering on a tile. She glanced up with a tentative smile. "The kind of love that has the passion of a lover and the faithfulness of a friend, Casey—God's love."

Casey's eyelids lowered as she shifted in her seat. "But we can't see or feel God, Emma, so how can you feel his love? I need more than prayers to a God I can't touch, see, or hear—I want to hear words of love, see kind actions, feel hugs and kisses . . ."

"We all do, because yes, we're human beings. But we were made in *God's* image." Drawing in a deep breath, Emma leaned back in her chair, her eyes tender. "Which means, Casey, like Father, like daughter. You want to be loved? So does he. You want to be touched? So does he. You want to feel the rush of a kiss or the warmth of a hug?" Tears pricked Emma's eyes. "So does he, Casey. Which is why I rushed to him when Rory hurt me and my family betrayed me. And you know what? I found a God whose arms were open wide and whose heart leapt with joy when I called his name. As protective as a mother and as jealous as a lover, this was a God who wanted me for his very own. *Me*—Emma Malloy! To touch, to bless, to fill with his pleasure." She swallowed hard, her gaze locked on Casey's. "Until I overflow, spilling his love on all those around me—treasured possessions of a passionate God."

Casey stared, wide-eyed. "But I don't feel that way about God, Emma, and I don't know how to change that."

"No, but he does." Emma squeezed her hand. "Pray, Casey, for him to be the center and source of your life, for a passion for him that's so strong, you feel him, touch him, hear him, just like he wants you to. And when you do, the love he pours in your heart will wash over everything in your life, making it the very best it can be." Emma smiled. "Especially romantic love with someone who weakens your knees."

The glow returned to Casey's eyes. "Oh, Emma, I hope so, because I really do think Johnny may be the one." She hugged her arms to her waist with a whimsical smile as if she were hugging Johnny himself, and then in a soft huff of another sigh, a bit of trepidation clouded the stars in her eyes. She chewed on her lip. "I just wish there was a way I could know for sure."

With a sweep of her palm, Emma shuffled the dominoes and peered up. "There is."

"How?" Casey asked with a kink of her brows.

Emma commenced selecting her dominoes, the smile on her lips at odds with the concern in her heart. She leaned forward, her voice tender and low. "Emotions are a powerful force, Casey. They can cloud our judgment and lead us into things that can hurt us, especially when we think we're in love. But . . . not if you do it God's way. It's the only way to remain unscathed in a relationship." Emma straightened and drew in a deep breath, determined to protect Casey like she wished someone had protected her. Absently brushing the scars on her face, she released a weary sigh. "Trust me, Casey—my life would be very different if I'd heeded what I'm telling you." Emma reached to graze Casey's hand. "Which means a good-night kiss at the door is fine, but anything more will only muddy the waters." She drew in a deep breath and withdrew her hand, her gaze fused to Casey's. "And never, and I repeat—*never*—allow Johnny into your apartment alone. It's too dangerous."

A hint of rose crept into the girl's cheeks as she quickly selected her tiles. "But I don't understand, Emma—how will that help to make sure that he's the man for me?"

Emma picked her own tiles slowly, carefully, as if their import were as critical as what she was about to say. "Because the right man will love and respect you more for your strength of commitment, while the wrong man will only push to have his own way, all the while professing a love to sweep you away."

Her thoughts trailed back to Rory as her voice faded to a whisper. She stared blankly at her tiles, sick with regret that it had been Rory's "love," rather than God's, that had shaped her future. She shivered, suddenly aware of Casey's probing stare. Drawing in a cleansing breath, she lifted her chin, never surer of the truth of her words. "Trust me, Casey, if I had followed God's will and remained pure, I wouldn't be bound to Rory today. Because when it comes to true love, there's no better safety net than God's precepts to protect you from hurt and heartbreak. When the wrong men come face-to-face with a woman who follows God's laws, they *will* leave. But the right one?" She smiled, her words infused with the same sense of peace and certainty she felt in God's presence every day of her life. "Now *he*, my friend, will stay."

8

With a nostalgic caress of Alli's adding machine, Sean punched in register totals with rapid-fire precision, unleashing a forgotten rush of adrenaline with every jerk of the lever. Saints almighty, how he loved numbers and totals and healthy bottom lines, a shocking realization that made him miss Kelly's for the first time in months. He held his breath as he entered the final sales for the quarter, heart pounding while he pulled the lever one last time . . .

"The saints be praised!" he shouted, borrowing Emma's pet phrase as he ripped the tape from Alli's machine and bounded to his feet. He kissed the ink-splotched total and glanced up at the doorway of Emma's office, where the woman herself stood wide-eyed, mouth gaping. "We did it!" he said with a broad grin, rendering her speechless when he plucked her up in his arms and whirled her in a spin. He plopped her back down and grinned. "Sales are up 6 percent."

Emma swayed on her feet, the color in her cheeks fading to pale. "Six percent?" she whispered. "Are you sure?"

"See for yourself, Mrs. Malloy," Sean said with a wink. "Numbers do not lie."

She took the tape and slowly lowered into Alli's chair, dazed. "But how can this be?"

He shot a quick glance at the clock to make sure it was past closing, then stripped off his suit coat and loosened his tie with a gleam of white teeth. "Our plan, remember? Reducing overhead with shorter store hours, scaling down inventory, early-bird specials, two-for-one sales, store credit, and a shopper's rewards system that Filene's can only dream about." He rolled up the sleeves of his pinstripe shirt and shot her an easy smile. "And last but not least, the only Coca-Cola vending machine to be found in a department store in the entire city."

"B-but you've only been here a short time," she whispered.

He grinned, hands hooked low on his hips. "I know. Makes me kind of dangerous to Filene's, don't ya think?" Reaching into his pocket, he pulled out a dime and flipped it in the air. "This calls for a celebration, Mrs. Malloy. Coca-Cola on me."

Emma jumped up, her shock apparently wearing off as she squealed and threw her arms around him so hard, it prompted both a chuckle in his throat and an erratic beat in his heart. He grinned, euphoric not only over the numbers, but at Emma's apparent comfort level now that their friendship was restored. He held her at arm's length. "Whoa—a simple thank you would suffice, although I admit, this is much better."

His words sent a pretty blush to her cheeks despite the sparkle that danced in her eyes. "We have to celebrate, and I just happen to have two fudge brownies to go with that Coca-Cola."

Masking his grin with a playful scowl, Sean patted his stomach as he moved toward the door. "You're no good for me, Emma Malloy, tempting me daily with cookies and cakes. I need to be lean and fit if I'm going to stay ahead of Luke and Brady on the court, you know."

Hands resting on her hips, she assessed him through squinted eyes. "Oh, go on with you now, you look fit as a fiddle from where I'm standing," she said, a definite Irish lilt to her scold.

"From you running me ragged, no doubt," he called and

whistled as he made his way to the prized soda machine on the first floor.

When he returned, Emma had draped the small conference table in Bert and Alli's cozy work area with a lacy tablecloth. A candle flickered in a dented silver candlestick dead center between two white china plates sporting brownies dusted with confectioner's sugar. Crystal goblets gleamed in the light of the candle, as if in anticipation of the fizz and bubble of cold Coca-Cola.

He whistled, filling the goblets with soda. "Very pretty. If I'd known I'd get this kind of treatment, I'd have shot for 10 percent." He hoisted a goblet in the air. "To the success of Dennehy's . . . and the woman at its helm."

"Oh, no—this is about you, not me," Emma said, clinking her glass to his. "Sales were down by 25 percent before you came, and I couldn't staunch the flow. There's no question that you're a force to be reckoned with, Sean O'Connor—smart, creative, devoted, and not afraid of hard work. Completely at home whether unloading furniture on the dock, tallying inventory with Bert, or charming a disgruntled customer, and all with a smile." Her eyes softened, conveying a love and respect that thickened the walls of his throat. "The truth is, Sean, you are one of the most humble and generous men I know, and I count it a privilege to call you my friend." Her lips curved into a soft smile. "I honestly don't know how I can ever thank you."

"Brownies might work," he said, grinning to diffuse the heat inching up the back of his neck. He pulled a chair out for Emma, then settled in to tackle dessert.

She chuckled, and the sound warmed him as he studied her over the rim of his glass. "What?" he asked with a faint smile.

Chewing slowly, she tilted her head, humor aglow in her eyes while she washed the cake down with a sip of her pop. "Although truth be told, it may well be Mrs. Bennett to whom we owe our thanks. I do believe her word of mouth could rival the promotional skills of your sister when it comes to uncovering a well-kept secret."

"Who, Charity?" He polished the brownie off and pushed the empty plate away. Stretching back in his chair, he propped arms behind his head and legs on a ledge beneath the table. "I wouldn't be surprised if Charity's the whole reason for the surge in the first place, given her talent for scuttlebutt. After all, she did attend that *Herald* dinner with all the society bigwigs."

With a final bite of brownie, Emma nudged her plate aside and leaned in, elbows on the table and a smug smile on her face. "What d'ya wanna bet Kelly's profits didn't go up?"

Her smirk was so against the grain, he laughed out loud. "Emma Malloy—I do believe that's a gloat in your eyes, and all I can say is it's about time." He cuffed the back of his neck and all at once his humor veered into a blank stare as thoughts of his old store shadowed his mood. "I swear I'd give anything to know how ol' Lester did with the books this month."

A dainty cough sounded from the hallway. "I believe it was the worst month in the history of the store," Rose Kelly said shyly, a small purse clutched in her hands while she chewed on her lip at the door. Her pastel floral dress cinched her waist and followed the curve of her hips before falling into gentle pleats midcalf. Dainty cap sleeves and a V-neck tie made her appear younger than she was, despite a stylish short-brimmed hat slanted over chestnut curls.

Sean's legs dropped from the ledge with a clunk, right before his knees banged on the table when he shot to his feet. Blood leeched from his face while he stared, his eyes dry sockets of shock. "Rose . . ." Her name came out raspy and thick, as if adhered to his tongue, which seemed likely given no other words could eke past.

Her step forward was timid for someone so prone to barging ahead, and her furtive glance at Emma revealed a hint of hesitation in doleful brown eyes. "Excuse me for interrupting," she whispered, contrition heavy in her tone, "but I wondered if I might speak with Sean." Her gaze returned to his, begging consent. She swallowed hard, causing the pearl choker she wore to bobble on her neck. "Alone . . . if I may."

"*No.*" It came out hard, clipped, and so uncommon for him that he heard Emma catch her breath. Ridges cut into his brow as he glared, his voice riddled with blame. "What do you want?"

Her fingers pinched white on the purse. "To apologize . . . and to say how sorry I am."

He pushed his chair in, the gesture more of a slam than a courtesy, then faced her with a cold stare, muscles tight and arms locked to his chest. "All right, you did. Now leave."

"Sean!" Emma jumped to her feet. "That's not like you," she whispered. "For goodness' sake, she came to apologize."

A tic pulsed in his jaw. "So she says, Emma, but you can't trust anything she does." He burned Rose with a look. "The store is closed. How did you get in?"

She lifted her chin, but he could see the hurt in her eyes. "I hid in the restroom . . . until they locked the doors and everyone went home."

"See?" His mouth sagged as he extended his hand. "She has no ethics whatsoever."

"That's not true!" Rose cried. "I'm a bit unconventional at times, but I do have ethics."

"Yeah, too bad you don't use them. Go home, Miss Kelly . . . or Mrs. Connealy . . . or whoever you are, and leave me alone."

"Sean, stop, please!" Emma's tone rang with an authority she seldom employed, causing heat to crawl up the back of his neck.

With a grind of his jaw, he pinched the bridge of his nose and sucked in a deep breath, suddenly ashamed of his boorish behavior. "Rose, Emma . . . I'm sorry. Please forgive me. I had no right to treat you disrespectfully."

Emma slowly sat back down while Rose nodded with tears in her eyes. "I forgive you, Sean, as I hope you'll forgive me." She faced him with a square of her shoulders despite a slight quiver in her voice. "And for your information, it's still Miss Kelly and likely to remain so, at least for the foreseeable future. You see, I hoped we could . . . well, go somewhere and talk. Over coffee, maybe, because I . . . ," pearls shifted on alabaster skin, ". . . need you to forgive me."

Something twisted in his chest, but he ignored it. She'd cost him his job, his dignity, and seventeen years of his life, and his anger ran deep. She stood before him, a beautiful woman whose heart was breaking. Even now he felt the attraction, and that was the thing for which he blamed her the most. His cheek pulsed as he stared her down, his cool manner masking the seething inside. "After what you did to me, Miss Kelly," he said in a rigid tone, "and I suspect to both Chester and your father, it appears you're in the market for a good deal of forgiveness. Which," he said with a thrust of his jaw, "in my case, is going to take some time." He reached for his jacket. "I'll see you out—we don't want to add stealing to your list of infractions."

Rose paled as if she'd been slapped.

"Sean! That's quite enough." Emma rose and took a step forward, her voice as soft as Sean's was hard. She indicated a small chaise in front of Alli's and Bert's desks where a comfortable sitting area had been arranged, complete with coffee table and magazines. "Miss Kelly, may I ask you to wait while I speak to Mr. O'Connor privately?" Emma studied the young woman whose eyes brimmed with tears and spoke again, her voice barely a whisper. "Please?"

Rose nodded and sat on the chaise, her gaze focused on fishing a handkerchief from the purse in her lap.

"Emma—" Apology laced his tone, but Emma only moved to her office and stood at the door, her gaze avoiding his. He blasted out a sigh and strode in, wheeling around when he heard the click of the lock. "Look, Emma, I apologize for this, but the woman had it coming," he began gruffly, his tone void of remorse. "It's just an unfortunate situation, and I'm sorry you had to see it."

She stood at the door, her back to him for several seconds and hand still on the knob, and when she turned, his heart sank in his chest.

"It's not me who needs your apology, Sean," she said quietly. Her voice was as gentle as he'd ever heard, and her face as ashen as when he'd shocked her with the good news. But this time, no smile softened her lips and no light danced in her eyes. Only grief, etched deeply in the ridge of her brow.

And disappointment.

His anger slithered into shame, forcing him to look away.

A gentle hand lighted on his arm. "This is an unfortunate situation, Sean, it's true, but the thing that grieves me the most is that one of my dearest friends and the kindest, most caring man I know has been so hardened by anger." She lowered herself into one of two chairs in front of her desk and released a fragile sigh. "Will you sit for a moment . . . please?"

He complied against his will, back bent and elbows stiff on his knees. His chin felt like rock pressed to tightly clasped hands. A nerve quivered in his jaw as he stared straight ahead, fully aware of her gaze. He steeled himself for her reprimand.

"Did you know, Sean, that I was supposed to be a boy?"

He blinked. Whatever he had expected her to say, this wasn't it, and his head swiveled toward her, chin still propped on his hands. "What?"

A faint smile shadowed her lips and she clasped arms tightly to her waist like a little girl, as if it were the dead of winter rather than a balmy day in September. "You see," she continued, sounding like they were chatting over a leisurely lunch, "Mrs. Doyle swore to my father that he would have a strapping boy." A wry smile crooked a corner of her mouth. "She had quite a reputation, you know, as somewhat of a seer in County Kildare where I grew up. It seems every time she swung a woman's gold band on the end of a thread, the ring would circle for a girl and go back and forth for a boy, and apparently the woman was seldom wrong. So you can certainly understand that when Mrs. Doyle's tea leaves confirmed it and my mother carried low, well, naturally my father was certain he had sired the next archbishop in the county."

Her easy manner faltered as her gaze trailed into a vacant stare, dulled by a melancholy that seemed to take her far, far away. "He was devastated, of course," she whispered, "but not as devastated as his only child, who bore the brunt of the blame with the back of his hand." She blinked and suddenly the hurt little girl disappeared and she was Emma once again—beautiful in her calm and at peace with the world. Her eyes gentled as they searched his. "It was my bitterness and unforgiveness that forced me into the arms of Rory against their wishes, Sean, the hardness of my heart that led me down a path of pain. I wanted to wound them, make them pay for the hurt they caused me. And when God finally healed my heart toward them, it was too late." Tears brimmed as she stared, her gaze pleading with his. "Suddenly they were gone . . . snuffed out in a fire that scarred my life as surely as Rory had scarred my face."

Her sorrow stabbed like his own, tightening his chest until he couldn't breathe. A fierce protectiveness rose within, and he stood and tugged her up in his arms, embracing her with the same tenderness she'd always shown him. "Oh, Emma," he whispered, "that breaks my heart . . ."

She hesitated, and he felt her sigh against his chest. "Then you know how I feel when I see someone I care about make the same mistake." She pulled away and clasped his hands. "Please, Sean, don't let bitterness change who you are, because it will. It'll harden and rob you of the joy in your life as surely as sin snuffs out the light in our souls. Please—have that cup of coffee with Rose, talk to her, forgive her. It's the only way you'll be free from the hurt that she caused."

He eased his hands from hers, his body stiff. "I can't, Emma. She doesn't deserve it."

Her smile was sad. "Neither did I, but God is a God of mercy, and he requires the same of us." She patted his hand. "You can do this."

If it were any other person on the face of the earth, he'd rise and make light of it, teasing his way out of an uncomfortable situation. But the woman beside him was no ordinary person, at least not anymore. She was Mrs. Emma Malloy, the only one he'd ever allowed a glimpse of his soul, and the one he respected more than any woman alive, outside of his family. He glanced up, and suddenly those mesmerizing green-gray eyes—the hue of pale jade or onyx—tripped his pulse, an unsettling awareness that hers, for whatever reason, was the opinion that mattered the most.

Exhaling loudly, he allowed a hint of annoyance in his tone. "I suppose you mean now?"

Her gentle chuckle brought a quirk to his lips and he sighed. "I'd rather you just docked my pay," he muttered and then blasted out another sigh. Lumbering to his feet, he unrolled his shirtsleeves while studying her through narrow eyes. "Okay, Mrs. Malloy, you win." His lips twisted as he straightened his tie. "I'll do it, but out of pure principle, I oughta make you pay for the coffee *and* my time."

Her soft laughter was a tonic that never failed to ease the agitation in his soul. "Oh, you'll get paid all right, Mr. O'Connor," she said with a smile that reminded him of a little girl with a secret to share. She rose and rounded the desk to sit in front of her Remington, casually inserting a piece of paper that defied the sassy wink of her eye. "Just not on your paycheck."

This was a mistake. The thought plagued Steven O'Connor from the moment they left the Blackthorn where they'd had dinner, all the way to Joe's girlfriend's apartment, leaving a queasy feeling in his stomach along with the two burgers he'd just consumed. Not that the girl Nellie had fixed him up with wasn't pretty—no, she had a face and a body that put Steven on edge, stirring desires he'd worked so hard to suppress. The last thing he needed was to get involved with another girl like Maggie, taking him down the same path that had almost destroyed his life. He slid a sideways glance at Joe nuzzling Nellie's neck, then at Nellie's roommate, Pauline, who clung to Steven's arm as if permanently attached, and stared straight ahead, lips clamped tight. He could smell her perfume in the cool breeze that ruffled her platinum curls, and something in his gut told him that this would be a very early night.

"So, what do you do for fun?" Pauline asked with an innocence that was anything but.

"Steven doesn't know how to have fun," Joe chided with a wink. "Which is where you come in, Pauline. I'm counting on you to save my best friend from dying of piety and resurrect the Steven O'Connor I know and love."

Steven's lips skewed to one side. "I've grown into a mature, responsible human being, Agent Walsh, if you even know what that is."

Hand splayed on his chest, Joe feigned offense. "Hey, I'm responsible, O'Connor, just ask Nellie, right, hon?" He cupped her close to plant a kiss on her neck, making her giggle. "I'm responsible for keeping my girl happy. Besides, responsible doesn't have to mean boring."

"Boring?" Pauline breathed with a half-lidded gaze that focused on Steven's mouth. "Somehow, I find that *very* hard to believe."

A once-familiar heat rolled through Steven's body at the huskiness of her tone, and he gave her a stiff smile. "Believe it. When it comes to having fun, Joe leaves me in the dust."

"Mmm . . . we'll have to see what we can do about that," Pauline teased.

"Attagirl," Joe said, tugging Nellie up the cracked steps of her four-story apartment building. He opened a paned-glass door and grinned while Nellie and Pauline hurried through, giving Steven's shoulder an affectionate squeeze. "The man is in dire need of a good time."

Steven shook his head while a faint smile edged his lips. *Maybe I am.* Although Joe's tone was thick with humor, Steven knew his best friend worried about him, at least ever since his breakup with Maggie, which seemed to affect Joe as much as it had Steven. And, why not? Their tight college group had disbanded, ending life as they'd known it—parties and drinking and women as free and easy as the bathtub gin they poured down their throats. Steven absently licked his dry lips, guilt souring his tongue as if it were the hard-grain alcohol he'd once been so partial to.

But overnight, everything had changed. His reckless ways had driven a wedge between him and his father until they'd jeopardized the very life of the man he loved. Patrick O'Connor's brush with a near heart attack after their fight two years prior had finally stripped Steven of all rebellion, neatly replacing it with a gnawing guilt instead. A guilt that compelled him to uphold a law he'd once flaunted, becoming a tight-lipped prohibition agent bent on righting his wrongs. He felt the stroke of Pauline's finger against the rough skin of his palm, and his jaw tightened. *And* a guilt that kept him at arm's length from women like Maggie.

Nellie opened the door of her apartment with a twist of her key and flicked on the light.

"Relax," Joe whispered in his ear, while Steven reluctantly followed Pauline in, annoyed that his eyes strayed to the gentle sway of her hips. He quickly diverted his gaze to their apartment, taking in the gold brocade sofa and love seat with its abundance of colorful pillows and fringed floral rug. The coziness of the room seemed to relax him somewhat, and he silently exhaled, watching as Pauline turned on a Tiffany lamp that sheathed the room in a warm glow.

"What's your pleasure?" Nellie asked from the kitchen, giggling again when Joe stole a kiss. "Not that, Walsh," she said with a playful swat, "I meant drinks."

"I'll take a Coca-Cola if you have it," Steven called, grabbing a magazine from the coffee table as he sat on the couch. Pauline kicked her shoes off and joined him, snuggling a little too close for comfort while he absently flipped through the pages.

"Here you go." Nellie delivered Coca-Colas before settling on the love seat next to Joe, her glass in hand. "So, anyone up for poker?" she asked with a wriggle of brows. "I feel lucky, and we sure could use some help with the rent."

It was actually just what he needed, Steven realized after they'd played several hands, relaxing on pillows Nellie had tossed on the floor. Between Joe's corny jokes, Nellie's lively personality, and Pauline's doting attention, Steven enjoyed himself more than he'd thought possible, laughing and trading insults with Joe like old times. Even Pauline didn't seem like such a threat anymore, cheering him on as he arm-wrestled with Joe.

When Steven had won all of their money, Joe jumped to his feet and extended Nellie a hand. "What do you say I take a look at the curtain rod you wanted me to fix in your bedroom?"

"Sure," she said with a broad smile, following him down the hall with a wink over her shoulder. "Be good, you two."

Feeling awkward, Steven reached for the cards. "Know how to play gin rummy?"

"I do," Pauline said with a tentative smile, "but if it's okay with you, I'd rather just talk."

"Sure." Steven stood and offered his hand to help her up from the floor. "So how did you and Nellie come to be room-mates anyway?" he asked, tossing the cards on the coffee table. He upended his Coca-Cola and eased back onto the couch.

"We were best friends in high school," she said, offering him a peppermint candy. Lowering to the sofa, she tucked her legs beneath her skirt. "I understand you and Joe go way back as well—kindergarten, right?"

Steven placed his empty glass on the table and shifted to face her. "Yeah. We've been good friends all of our lives, and now that we work as partners day in and day out, we're more like brothers who occasionally get on each other's nerves."

Her hand idly caressed the couch next to his leg, her eyes following the stroke of her fingers. "He worries about you, you know. Thinks you're still bleeding over Maggie."

He puffed out a sigh. "Maggie is over and done, and Joe knows that better than anyone."

Her lashes lifted slightly as she watched him through veiled eyes. "He claims you've had no interest in women since," she said quietly. "Is that true?"

Heat cuffed the back of his neck. "Joe talks too much," he said in a rough voice.

Gentle fingers lighted upon his leg. "Or cares too much," she whispered.

Warmth generated from her touch, and he studied her for

several seconds, drawn to the pull of green eyes soft with concern and full lips parted in invitation.

As if sensing the attraction, she leaned in, her palm warm on his thigh as she brushed soft lips against his. His breathing quickened, awakening urges dormant since Maggie. He hesitated for the briefest of moments and then clutched her close, deepening the kiss as he eased her against the couch. Pulse skyrocketing, his mouth took hers with an intensity that had once been second nature. And then in a ragged heave of his breath, he pushed her away, the heat of passion burning away in the heat of his anger. "You're drinking?" he rasped.

"Steven, no, I promise . . ."

But he saw the lie on her face, and he tasted it in her mouth, not quite masked by the peppermint candy she'd offered him earlier. He shot up and sniffed her half-empty glass before striding to the kitchen to jerk cabinets open. He found what he was looking for on a top shelf—an innocuous bottle of witch hazel, tucked behind a package of Quaker Oats. He screwed off the lid, and the scent of oil of juniper assaulted his senses. Fury surged through his veins as quickly as this home-brew gin could travel the bloodstream, and with tic in his jaw, he dumped it down the drain with violent force. Hurling the bottle into the sink, he turned on Pauline, eyes itching hot. "Oh, this is rich! Entertaining prohibition agents with a stash in your pantry. I oughta haul you in." He pushed her aside and stormed toward the door.

"Steven, wait—"

He spun around. "No, you wait, Pauline. Joe may be starry-eyed enough to overlook this, but I'm not. I'm sworn to uphold the law, and that's what I intend to do." He leveled a finger, warning twitching in every muscle in his face. "You best tread lightly, Miss O'Shea, because if I catch you or Nellie with alcohol again, I guarantee you'll be doing your entertaining behind bars."

He slammed the door and charged down the stairs, flinging the front door open so hard, it ricocheted off the brick wall. He was met with a blast of cool air that did little to temper the heat in his cheeks. "They're all the same," he muttered, thoughts of Pauline's kiss burning as much as the taste of the alcohol. He plunged his fists in his pockets and headed home, wondering if he'd ever find a woman untainted by an era where pleasure came before morals. Sarcasm curled his lip as he rounded the corner. *Maybe in a church or a convent.* Unfortunately, that pious kind of woman didn't appeal either. Because deep down he still craved a woman like Maggie—vibrant, alive, with a dangerous gleam in her eye. He scowled and kicked a rock, pinging it at a streetlamp with no little force. His jaw hardened. Too bad guilt had ruined him forever.

Arriving home, he unlatched the front gate and glanced at his watch, grateful the parlor window was blessedly dark. It was almost eleven, which meant his parents were in bed. Steven exhaled his relief. The last thing he needed was an inquisition from his mother.

Did you have a good time?

Why are you home early?

Was the young lady nice?

He grunted. *Yeah . . . nice and loose.* He slipped his key in the lock with a wry slant of his lips, thinking of his father's persistent concern over Steven's departure from women. He shook his head and opened the door. One moment they're coming to blows over his lust for Maggie and life, and the next, his father's worried he's not living enough. He sighed. A *no-win situation.*

Squinting at the sliver of light beneath the kitchen door, Steven ambled through the dining room to investigate.

"What are you doing home?" he asked with a palm to the door. "I thought you shot hoops on Friday night with Murph and the guys." He strolled in and snatched a piece of the brownie from Sean's plate and popped it in his mouth. "Wow, is there any more?"

"Nope." Sean chewed with cheeks full. "Emma made it, and this is all she sent." He pushed the plate toward Steven. "Want the last bite?"

Pouring himself some milk, Steven sat down and gave Sean a sour smile. "No thanks, I'm afraid one more taste is going to make me want more."

"Yeah, I know the feeling," Sean said with a scowl. He pushed the plate away, stretching back in his chair with legs propped up. "I wasn't up to a game tonight. Too tired."

Steven stared, glass midway to his lips. "Too tired for basketball? You sick?"

"Yeah, a terminal case of stupidity." Sean scrubbed his face with the palms of his hands.

"Nothing stupid about you, not when you steer clear of women like you do."

Sean rested his head on the back of the chair and folded his arms, eyes closed. "Sure, a real intelligent guy. That's why I invited Rose Kelly to my playoff game tomorrow night."

Milk spewed from Steven's lips. "What? The dame who lost you your job? You crazy?"

"Apparently," Sean said. "Crazy and stupid. You may as well lock me up now."

"But why?" Steven sputtered, wiping the milk from his mouth and shirt. "I thought you hated her."

"Nope, hate is a luxury I don't have, evidently, according to Emma." Sean opened his eyes and kneaded the bridge of his nose. "Rose came by the office tonight to apologize. Said she wanted to talk, ask my forgiveness, get a cup of coffee. I lost my temper and screamed. Practically threw her out, and Emma took me to task."

"No joke? Emma called you on the carpet?" Steven could hardly believe his ears. First his easygoing brother loses his temper a second time and now sweet Emma pulls rank?

"No, nothing that drastic. Just a heart of gold that has a way of making mine look pretty black." He sighed. "She shamed me into forgiving Rose, clearing the air over coffee."

Sean would have been comical if not so depressed. Steven bit back a smile. "And?"

His brother glanced up beneath lidded eyes. "I let it slip I coach St. Stephen's team on Saturday nights and told her she could come sometime. 'How about tomorrow night?' she says like the spider to the fly." He spiked shaky fingers through his hair, wreaking havoc with the Brilliantine. "So I told her yes." He sighed. "What else could I say?"

"Oh, I don't know—*no*, maybe?" Steven shot a pointed look, then shook his head. "For crying out loud, Sean, you can't say no to a woman? Not to mention the one who lost you your job?"

Blond brows slashed low over narrowed eyes as Sean shifted in his chair. "I don't remember you being so all-fired good at saying no to Maggie, as I recall. Besides, you know what it's like with women today—they practically throw themselves at you."

"Tell me about it. Joe fixed me up tonight with his girl-friend's roommate, and I had to pour a bottle of booze down their drain."

Laugh lines fanned the edge of Sean's eyes as humor lit his gaze. "You're kidding."

"Nope." Steven's lips zagged into a droll smile. "Tasted it on her breath *after* she hauled off and kissed me." He shook his head. "Do you honestly think there are any women out there who are really decent? You know, not in a fever to get friendly with every other guy? Some sweet, nice gal with morals who's actually willing to let the guy wear the pants?"

Sean rose to carry dirty dishes to the sink. "So help me, I hope not. I'm having enough trouble staying away from the pushy ones who annoy me." He washed his plate and utensils and stacked them in the dish rack, then turned to give Steven a tired smile. "Of course, there are our sisters, although Charity could be a stretch." He paused, his gaze wistful. "And Emma, of course." He folded his arms and leaned back against the counter, eyes trailing into a pensive stare. "I'll tell you what—when it comes to marriage, I'd be long gone if there were more women like Emma out there. She's truly one of a kind." He blinked, suddenly breaking his reverie. "But, who knows? I'll bet the perfect girl's out there to put the fever in your eye."

Steven snorted. "What a dreamer—I plan to stay on my guard more than you."

A chuckle rumbled from Sean's throat as he stretched. "Well, if I am going to stay on mine, I need sleep." He gave his brother's shoulder a sympathetic slap on his way to the door. "Looks to be a long, ugly day tomorrow, and I'm going to need all the energy I can get."

A devilish grin eased across Steven's face. "To fend the lady off?"

Sean laughed. "Trust me—there'll be no fending, no friendship, and definitely no fever."

"Never know . . . you may like it," Steven said, a sly look in his eye.

The kitchen door squealed open as Sean paused, hand splayed against the wood. He hung his head and glanced up, eyes twinkling as they peered beneath weighty lids. He shook his head and laughed. "And you call *me* a dreamer."

9

Bang! Slam! Groan . . .

Emma and Bert exchanged glances. "How long has he been like this?" Emma whispered, leaning over Bert's desk with a nervous peek into Sean's office.

"Since he came in this morning." Bert's mouth flattened. "I'm thinking of going home to yank the tail of my neighbor's Doberman—more fun and way less risky."

"Oh, my . . . ," Emma said with a grate of her lip, wishing she hadn't spent the morning catching up on paperwork behind closed doors. "Any idea what's wrong?"

Bert grunted, shuttered eyes betraying her concern. "Says he's fine and dandy. 'Course, the nasty scowl says he's a liar, but he's a man after all, so enough said."

The creases at the bridge of Emma's nose eased as she patted Bert's hand with a tentative smile. "Well, I brought in the last of the brownies, so maybe that will cheer him up." She glanced at her watch and caught her breath, a hand to her cheek. "Oh, Bert, you need to go! It's bad enough I drag you in on a Saturday, but now it's past two, and the day's almost gone."

"I'm going, I'm going," Bert said with a glower that made Sean's mood appear almost tame. She dragged herself up with another caustic squint. "He's startin' to get on my nerves. Can't stand anybody grouchier than me. Puts a real damper on my sunny mood, you know?"

"I know," Emma said with a squeeze of Bert's arm. "Enjoy the rest of your weekend—what's left of it, anyway. And thanks so much for coming in today. You're a lifesaver."

"Yeah, yeah, yeah." She wrestled a pretty straw cloche over wavy black tresses, then slapped a matching purse under her arm, giving Emma a thin-lipped smile that was more of a threat. "Tell him to cheer up or I'll really give him something to moan about."

"Yes, ma'am," Emma said with affection. "Goodbye, Bert, see you on Monday."

Bert's grunt followed her out the door as she flopped a hand in the air.

Emma grinned and turned, her smile fading into a sigh at the slam of another drawer. She tiptoed over, absently chewing her lip as she peeked in his office.

Despite the vibrancy of a sunny September day, Sean O'Connor lay sprawled in his chair, eyes closed and looking as spent as if he'd tossed and turned all night in his bed. *In his clothes.* Clean-shaven when he'd arrived, a shadow of beard was beginning to emerge as he reposed, head back and legs crossed on his desk. His eyes were shaded with fatigue, nicely complemented by facial muscles that drooped as if in dire need of sleep. Even the shirt that he wore, usually so starched and so neat, seemed to sag along with the man, sleeves rolled and tie tugged loose. Wayward hair, the exact color of autumn wheat, fluttered against his tan forehead while a breeze rustled the paper held limp in his hand. Generous lips that usually sported a smile now bent in a frown, ratcheting Emma's pulse along with her concern. With a deep draw of air, she inched into the room, arms hugged to her waist as she inhaled the scent of freshly mown grass from the park across the way.

"Sean, are you . . . okay?"

His eyes lumbered open and he gave her a smile that fell flat. "Yeah, I'm fine. Why?"

"You just don't seem yourself today. No energy, a bit worn, and maybe . . . a bit edgy?" She hesitated, noting the lack of humor in his eyes. "Even Bert noticed . . . and we're worried."

He scrubbed his face with his hand and slid his feet to the floor, tossing the paper he held onto his desk. "Well, don't be, I'm fine. Didn't sleep great last night, that's all."

She eased in, confused by the bite in his tone. "I have brownies . . . ," she whispered.

He yanked a drawer open, then slammed it after finding what he wanted. "No, thanks."

"Well, if there's anything I can do—"

"You've already done enough, thank you."

The sharpness of his tone heated her cheeks. She took a step back, lips parted in hurt.

He huffed out a noisy sigh and looked up, eyes softening and voice contrite. "Look, I'm sorry, Emma, you don't deserve my nasty mood." His mouth slanted. "Or maybe you do."

She cocked her head. "This wouldn't have anything to do with Rose, would it?"

He angled a leg against a drawer and peered up. "No, Emma," he said dryly. "It has *everything* to do with Rose." His gaze sharpened. "You forced me to have coffee with her."

She blinked. "Forced?" She bit back a smile but somehow it escaped to her eyes. "I don't remember firearms being involved, Mr. O'Connor."

His piercing gaze glinted with a hint of his trademark humor. "Oh, they were, Mrs. Malloy, trust me on that, and I have the insomnia to prove it." His smile was stiff. "Shot clean through the heart with both barrels, taking me down with a double blast of guilt and shame."

"Sean, I—"

He raised a hand. "And now," he emphasized, enunciating each word, "because of your expert marksmanship, Rose Kelly has finagled her way into coming to my game tonight."

She what? Emma's heart stalled in her chest, mouth agape. "You mean she came out and asked you?"

"Oh no, Mrs. Malloy, she's far more devious than that.

Gets me talking about myself, how I coach the St. Stephen's team and then cries me a river about she's an only child and never had a chance to experience things like that. Next thing I know, I mutter something about how she should come sometime and *bam!* 'How about tomorrow night?' she says with a bat of her eyes."

Emma pressed a hand to mask a smile. "Oh, Sean, I'm so sorry." Her eyes widened in a calculated innocence that would have made Charity proud. "But maybe she just likes baseball."

His gaze narrowed. "This is *not* funny, Emma." He leveled muscled arms on the desk, accusation thick in his tone. "Because of you, I have to deal with this headache one more time."

With a gentle sigh, she slipped into the chair in front of his desk and gave him a sympathetic smile, affection warm in her voice. "It was the right thing to do, and you know it. And if there's one thing I've learned about you, my friend, it's that you're a man who always does the right thing . . ." Her teeth tugged at the edge of her lip. "Sooner or later."

He grunted. "You can put the gun away, Emma, I've already gone down in flames."

A chuckle bubbled in her throat. "I was only aiming at the unforgiveness, Sean, not your bachelorhood. After the game, just make it clear to Miss Kelly that you're not interested . . ."

One blond brow shot high. "Clear? To Rose Kelly?" He grunted again. "The only thing that would be clear to that woman is a gold band on my hand . . . *and* in my nose."

"I'm sure if you just tell her in no uncertain terms—"

His mouth sagged open. "Don't you think I have? I must have told her in three or four different ways, but the woman just blinked at me like I was speaking Chinese. I practically painted a picture for her in living color, but she's obviously color-blind too."

"Well, it *was* you who asked, you know . . ."

His words ground out between clenched teeth. "As-a-blasted-courtesy, not-an-invitation."

Emma squinted in thought. "Why not tell her what you

told her before? You know, after she cornered you in the storeroom that time—that you're 'seeing' someone." Mirth laced her tone at his contrived defense at the time, claiming it wouldn't be a lie, because he *was,* after all, "seeing" Emma at every family function, wasn't he?

"Yes, but that was when she had Chester. Now she's free as a bird—a vulture, to be exact—and she's circling, I can feel it."

Mischief tugged at Emma's lips. "Then just tell her the truth, that it's nothing personal, but you're contemplating the priesthood."

A harsh laugh erupted from his throat. "Oh, yeah, like that's going to stop her." He gouged his temples with the span of his hand. "I tell you, the woman is diabolical." Dropping back into his chair, he blew out a ragged sigh. "I think she apprenticed under Charity."

Emma couldn't help it. She laughed and shook her head. Rising to her feet, she straightened her skirt and challenged him with a devious glint of her own. "Well then, Sean O'Connor, I suggest you get on the phone this instant to give Charity a call." She strolled to the door and turned, a crooked grin on her lips. "Because if I'm not mistaken," she said with a twinkle in her eye, "I suspect other than prayer, your only hope is to call in a professional."

"For pity's sake, Mitch, would you *please* sit down?"

Mitch Dennehy halted midstride to stare at his father-in-law, a sharp retort weighting his tongue. He swallowed it hard, unwilling to break his vow to curb his temper, especially with his editor. His frustration pulsed in his cheek as he plopped into the chair at the front of Patrick's burnished wood desk. He forced a tight smile. "Sorry, Patrick, but I'm having trouble understanding why Hennessey hauled us in on a Saturday and then makes us wait two blasted hours. Hours that could have been spent far more productively, I might add."

Patrick glanced up from some galleys to give his assistant

editor a sympathetic smile. "Both of us have had a chance to catch up on a few things while waiting, Mitch, and you could use the extra time to go over last year's donor list, you know. That would be time well spent." His lips shifted in irony. "Although not nearly as cathartic as pacing the floor, I'm sure."

Mitch huffed. "You know I can't concentrate when I'm riled. And nothing riles me more than Hennessey foisting some high-society soiree on us when he knows how swamped we are." His mouth gummed in a tight line. "Especially when it keeps me from fishing with my son."

With a slash of his pen, Patrick redlined a galley before sailing it into a bin on the corner of his desk. He laid the pen down and massaged his eyes. "I certainly understand—not to mention incurring the wrath of our wives. If Charity is anything like her mother—" he lowered his reading specs to deliver a wry look over the square rims, "and we both know she is—she's probably still stewing. Marcy actually gave me the silent treatment this morning for working another Saturday. Which," he said with a trace of humor in his tone, "given the highs and lows I've experienced during her change of life, is actually preferable at times. Silence is golden . . . at least when the alternative is a mood swing that unleashes anything from a rant to a crying jag."

A smile wheedled its way to the corners of Mitch's lips. "Yeah, mood swings—I remember them well with the twins— nine months of biting my tongue till I thought it would bleed. I'll tell you right now I'm not looking forward to more of those if we have another child." His smile faded into a grimace. "*Or* when Charity reaches the change, whichever comes first."

Patrick chuckled. "Well, judging from Marcy, you have another twenty years before the notorious change of life—a remarkably accurate term, I might add. Plenty of time to fill that house up with babies like Charity always wanted, if the good Lord is so inclined."

Mitch fanned fingers through his hair, his discomfort

evident in the press of his jaw. "Yeah, well, I've shown up for my part in giving Charity the family she wants, but the good Lord seems to be lagging behind." He scowled at the door. "Not unlike Hennessey and his niece."

Glancing at his watch, Patrick rose from his chair. "Well, he said they would be here at one-thirty and it's three-thirty now, but he did mention that they might be running late. Something about a luncheon Marjorie needed to attend."

Mitch exhaled a gust of frustration. "And why aren't we doing this on Monday, again?"

"Marjorie was busy—she's the chairperson for a number of committees, not the least of which is the Fogg Art Museum, for which you will be spearheading this auction."

Mitch couldn't contain his groan. "When is the blasted event anyway? I'd like to know how long I'll be shackled to this ball and chain."

"The day after Christmas—it's a joyful holiday event they hope will complete the renovations for Harvard's most prestigious museum." Patrick calmly adjusted the sleeves of his suit coat with a tug of his fingers, but the flat press of his lips indicated he agreed with his son-in-law. "It's Hennessey's alma mater, naturally, and Marjorie went to Radcliffe."

"Yeah, well, bully for Marjorie and Merry Christmas to us."

"Don't move—I'll make fresh coffee." Patrick rose and headed to his door.

"You're not leaving, I hope?" Arthur Hennessey met Patrick with a smile and a handshake. Neatly combed dark hair, white at the temples and only lightly salted with gray, made him appear far younger than his sixty-five years. "Please forgive our tardiness, Patrick, but Marjorie had some errands to run. Hello, Mitch, good to see you again."

Mitch reached for his pad and pen before rising in a slow turn, hands and teeth a matched set—both tightly clenched. His smile was strained. "Good to see you again too, sir." *Finally.*

He pocketed the pen and moved toward the door to extend

a hand. Arthur pumped it with enthusiasm and then steered in a Jean Harlow look-alike, complete with platinum blond hair and sultry mouth. Upon entry, the scent of gardenias filled the room. Cool green eyes assessed Mitch from head to foot in a sweep of sooty lashes before dismissing him with a bored shift of her gaze. She directed a smile in Patrick's direction and held out a hand heavy with diamonds. "Hello, Patrick, it's lovely to see you again. I missed you and Marcy at the spring benefit."

Patrick shook her hand with a warm smile. "Marjorie, always a pleasure. And my apologies—Marcy came down with the flu the day before, but she's looking forward to the auction in December." He released her hand and directed her attention to Mitch. "And you remember my assistant editor, Mitch Dennehy, I trust—your cochair for this year's auction?"

Arthur Hennessey's niece swept him with another cool gaze, finally lingering on his face with a faint smile and a handshake. "Thank you for volunteering, Mitch. Arthur assures me that you are more than capable of ramrodding this important event so dear to my heart."

Volunteering? His eyes flicked to Patrick's in a barely concealed glare before returning to Marjorie, the smile stiff on his face as he took her hand. "Yes, well, it's Patrick who deserves the thanks, Mrs. Hennessey—he's fully aware of my fondness for charitable causes."

Patrick cleared his throat. "Shall we convene in the boardroom? I think we may be more comfortable there. Coffee anyone? I'll make a fresh pot while Mitch sees you to the room."

"Perfect," Arthur said. "And coffee sounds wonderful. Black for me, please, and cream for Marjorie." He cupped a hand to Marjorie's elbow and ushered her out the door while Mitch followed. Suddenly he turned, his brow buckled in thought. "Oh, blast, Patrick—I left the circulation figures I wanted to discuss upstairs in my office."

Patrick turned. "Are they on your desk, Arthur? I'll be happy to get them for you."

"No, you'd never find them. Why don't we head up that way and they can get started?"

Patrick glanced at Mitch, his voice contrite as he walked with Arthur to the stairwell. "You mind making the coffee, Mitch? We won't be long."

"Not at all," Mitch said. He led Marjorie into the *Herald*'s boardroom, which was bathed in sunshine from a wall of windows overlooking the city below. He tossed his pad on the table and moved to open several more sashes, heaving each up with a hard thrust of his arms. A warm breeze fluttered in, bringing with it the smell of the sea mingled with exhaust fumes. He returned to the table and pulled out a leather padded chair. "Please make yourself comfortable, Mrs. Hennessey. It won't take me a moment to make the coffee." He started for the door.

"Marjorie," she said, stopping him in his tracks.

Mitch turned. "Excuse me?"

"Since we're going to be working so closely together, Mitch, I think it would be more comfortable to be on a first-name basis, don't you?" Her eyes fused to his as she lowered herself into the chair, slowly crossing long, shapely legs. She reached into her purse and pulled out several sheets of expensive-looking stationery that he swore were scented with perfume. "I look forward to working with you . . . and to the coffee. You're obviously a man of many talents."

Alarm curled in his stomach as he recognized the look in her eyes from years past, before Charity, when he was attracted to women like her. "You haven't tasted my coffee," he muttered.

Great, he thought as he fumbled with the coffeepot in the *Herald*'s makeshift kitchen, *Hennessey's infamous niece is a beautiful woman with a roving eye. What else could go wrong?*

She was still alone when he returned, her slender back to him as she stood at the window. Manicured hands rested lightly on the marble sill while a single finger idly circled in slow motion. Old habits returned to haunt him, and he found his gaze raking her from head to toe. He frowned and looked away, suddenly missing Charity so much, it was a physical ache. He set the tray of coffees down, then dropped into a chair with a groan of the leather cushion. He plucked a pen from his pocket and tossed it on the table with a soft clunk before distributing the coffees.

She turned, arms folded. "How old are you?" she asked, her tone matter-of-fact.

He tried to smile, but it came off more as a scowl. "I wasn't aware age was a prerequisite, Mrs. Hennessey."

Her brows lifted noticeably. "You're rather forthright, aren't you?"

"Only when necessary. Shall we get started?" He placed her coffee in front of her chair.

Her movements were fluid as she slipped into her seat, hands lighting on the stationery in front of her. "Thirty-five," she said in a silky whisper.

Mitch glanced up from his notes. "Pardon me?"

"I'm thirty-five and divorced. I thought you might be curious."

He laid the pen on the table with a smile as strained as the nerves in his neck. With a casual air, he placed his left hand on the pad before him and leaned in, sunlight glinting off the gold of his wedding band. The look he gave her was cool, but polite. "Mrs. Hennessey, forgive me, please, but the only thing I'm curious about is how you and I are going to pull off the best fundraiser Harvard has ever had. In the interest of time, I suggest we get started and you tell me exactly what you expect of me."

He saw a blink of surprise in the green eyes before they narrowed. She scribbled something on the sheet in front of her, and then with a regal lift of her chin, she handed it to him, her voice considerably cooler. "I expect weekly meetings here at the *Herald*, preferably early evening—my days are too full to fit another thing in. Thursdays work best for me as I'm already in the city. Shall we say six o'clock? Call me at this number if an emergency arises and you can't make it. Otherwise, I suggest you be here."

Mitch ground his jaw to obliterate a sharp retort on his tongue. Heat fused up his neck and into his cheeks, a nice complement to the tic in his temple. He shoved the paper in his pocket.

Her full lips eased into a controlling smile. "I believe Patrick has given you the donor list from last year. I need it cross-checked against the invitee list so I know exactly who the heavy hitters are. You'll be arranging a special reception for them prior. If you've any skills as an investigative reporter, use them. I want the invitee list increased by at least 20 percent, and 30 would be lovely. I expect a final list by our meeting next Thursday, understood?"

Mitch swallowed his pride and nodded, lips pressed so tight, his teeth ached.

"I'd also like to at least double prize donations from last year," she continued with a lift of a meticulously thin brow. "Mitzi Wellington is as atrocious at soliciting donations as she is at tennis. Which is why I told Uncle Arthur we needed someone with grit who wouldn't take no for an answer." She gave him a pointed look. "Like me."

She sipped the cup of coffee that Mitch had prepared and put it back down with a wrinkle of her perfectly sculptured nose. "Goodness, let's hope your fundraising skills are better than your coffee." She sighed and brushed a platinum curl out of her eyes and gave him a look that assured him he was working for her. "Now, we'll discuss the theme. But first, any questions?"

He gripped the hot cup of coffee and gulped it, wincing when it seared the back of his throat. Questions? Yeah, he thought with a grind of his jaw. *How badly do I want my job?*

Come on, Bobby, bring it on home . . . Sean held his breath until the winning run slid into home plate in a cloud of dust, wrenching the air from his lungs with one ragged exhale of relief. Shrieks of joy split the night, merging with groans and catcalls and a cacophony of tree frogs celebrating the win.

Scrambling to his feet, the grinning boy loped to the bench and was immediately swarmed by dirty, sweaty teammates. *From team joke to MVP in one season.* Sean shook his head with a proud grin. *You're my hero, Bobby.*

"Hey Dalton!" Sean made his way through the horde of jubilant kids to lock an arm around the ten-year-old's neck, knuckling his head with a Dutch rub that made him laugh. He gave Bobby's neck an affectionate squeeze, then extended a hand with a mist of pride in his eyes. "Put it there, bud, looks like you're our new MVP. You worked real hard, Bobby. I couldn't be prouder if you were my own kid."

Bobby grinned, ear to dirty ear. "Thanks, Coach. Couldn't have done it without you."

"Hey, what about me?" Pete asked, tickling the boy's neck from behind.

"You too, Coach," Bobby said with a squeal, twisting away from Pete's fingers.

"Okay, guys, listen up." Sean swiped his forehead with the side of his arm, then latched thumbs in the pockets low on his hips. "You guys played a great game tonight, and Pete and I couldn't be prouder if you'd won the pennant. You not only deserve this championship win, but . . . ," he paused, a grin splitting his face at the grimy faces blinking back at him, "you deserve ice cream at Robinson's as well—our treat."

Sean winced at the exuberant shrieks that pierced the air. He grinned at Pete, then glanced at his watch. "Okay, everybody, Robinson's in fifteen or you buy your own, got it?"

Pete ground a finger in his ear with a grin, teeth gleaming white against olive skin. "I may not be able to hear for a week," he said with a chuckle. "I hope the parents don't expect free ice cream too," he said, tossing bats, balls, and gloves into the equipment bag. "I still have rent to pay this month."

Sean hefted the bag over his shoulder. "Forget it, Murph, my tab. I could have never done this without you, so it's the least I can do."

"Oh, no, buddy boy, we're in this together. Nobody can

accuse Pete Murphy of not pulling his weight, no matter how many times I gotta eat beans in a week."

"Man, that can't be good for the love life," Sean said with a sideways grin. "Nope, I'm the intelligent one who hoards his money instead of blowing it on women, so I can afford it."

"Uh, not for long," Pete muttered, nodding his head toward the far side of the bleachers.

A groan trapped in Sean's throat at Bobby Dalton heading his way with his mother in tow.

Pete hooked the clipboard under his arm and nudged Sean's shoulder, his voice low. "Hate to tell ya, but I heard Bobby bragging his mother was gonna invite you to dinner this week."

This time the groan slipped past his lips, and heat crawled into his cheeks as he planned a quick escape. "Murph, I'll meet you at Robinson's after I drop this stuff at the rectory, okay?" Shooting a glance over his shoulder, Sean hurried toward the side street opposite the bleachers.

"Sure thing," Pete called before heading toward Bobby and his mother, obviously in a valiant effort to ward them off. Unfortunately, Bobby sidestepped Pete to jog after Sean.

"Hey, Coach O'Connor—wait up!"

Sean froze midstride, eyelids drooping closed as if they were weighted with lead. He released a weary sigh and rotated slowly, his smile as stiff as the brand-new catcher's mitt peeking out of his bag. "Hey, Bobby, you're supposed to be heading over to Robinson's."

Bobby screeched to a stop, spindly chest heaving. His mother hustled twenty feet behind, obviously hot on his heels. "We are, Coach, but first my mother wants to ask you something." He bent over with hands on his legs, huffing like he'd just run the bases.

"Sure thing, Bobby." Despite the coolness of the night, Sean could feel the sweat beading at the back of his neck. He shifted the bag on his shoulder and smiled at Mrs. Dalton, who was breathing almost as hard as her son when she finally caught up. Sean sucked in a deep breath, his smile polite. "This boy was a star tonight, Mrs. Dalton—you should be very proud."

"Oh, I am, Sean," she said, looping an arm around Bobby's shoulders and giving her son a squeeze. She tilted her head shyly. "And I thought we agreed you would call me Barbara."

"Uh . . . yes, we did . . . Barbara." He swallowed hard. "Well, you two better head on over to Robinson's—I'll see you there—"

"Coach, wait—we have something to ask first, don't we, Mom?"

Pink tinged Barbara's cheeks as she took a deep breath. "Why, yes, Bobby, we do. You see, Coach O'Connor . . . *Sean* . . . we were wondering . . ."

Sean's breath petrified in his throat.

". . . if perhaps next Saturday . . ."

His body tensed, all air suspended.

". . . you could—"

An arm hooked to his waist, forcing a gasp from his lips. "The game was wonderful, darling—you and your team certainly deserve the championship." Rose Kelly lifted on tiptoe to press a kiss to his cheek and then awarded Bobby with a luminous smile. She extended one hand to the open-mouthed boy while the other fused snugly to Sean's hip. "Congratulations, young man. I suspect the talent scouts will be looking for you before long."

Bobby completely ignored her hand, mouth gaping. Not unlike Sean, who stood rooted to the ground like the hundred-year oak just beyond.

Barbara prodded her son's shoulder, color rising. "Bobby! Say thank you to the lady."

"Thanks," Bobby muttered, his gaze dropping to his shoes as he kicked at a clump of dirt.

"Yes, thank you, Miss . . ." Barbara offered her hand.

Rose shook it with indisputable warmth. "Kelly, Rose Kelly—Sean's girlfriend."

The oak had nothing on Sean—his body went as stiff as hardwood lumber.

Barbara's eyes widened. "Oh, I . . . I didn't realize . . ."

Sean started to cough.

"Goodness, are you all right, Sugar Bear?" Rose commenced slapping him on the back.

He kept hacking, but shock lodged in his throat as tightly as the sour ball that choked him in the fifth grade when Pete put candy corn in his nose. *Sugar Bear???*

Barbara turned Bobby toward the street. "Well, I guess Bobby and I need to head over to Robinson's . . . Nice to meet you, Miss Kelly."

"But, what about Coach coming for dinner?" Bobby said, a plea in his tone.

Barbara's blush deepened. "Well, I . . . that is, *we* . . . thought maybe you . . ." She gulped, eyes flitting to Rose. "Both of you, of course . . . uh, might come for dinner Saturday night."

All the blood in Sean's body seemed to converge in his face as the coughing spell ramped into humiliation. "Uh, Mrs. Dalton . . . *Barbara*—"

Rose latched her arm through Sean's. "Oh, I really wish we could, Barbara," Rose said with a pucker in her brow. "But Sean and I have plans on Saturday night." She glanced up with warm brown eyes that seemed surprisingly sincere. "Right, darling?"

Thud. Sean's bag hit the ground. He nodded dumbly, tongue too thick for words to pass.

Relief washed into Barbara's face along with another painful blush, giving she and Sean matching sunburns. "Yes, well, another time, then. Come along, Bobby, we don't want to be late. See you at Robinson's, Coach O'Connor . . . Rose."

Sean blinked, mouth ajar as Barbara made a dash for the street that could rival a sprint for home plate. He wheeled on Rose. "Just what in the devil do you think you're doing?"

Hurt crimped her brows. "Why, saving your hide. You didn't *want* to go, did you?"

"No, of course not!" he said, his voice little more than a hiss.

She eyed him with a tilt of her head. "Oh, I see. And you would have been able to look into those big brown eyes of that adorable little boy and his mother and tell them both no?"

He swallowed hard, the truth swelling his throat as tightly as the clench of his fists.

"I thought so," she said with a purse of her lips. "So, the way I look at it, you owe me."

His jaw dropped. "For what—lying? Making a fool of me with your . . . your—" he waved his hand in the air, words stuttering off his tongue like buckshot—"your fairy-tale notions that I could *ever* be romantically linked with a woman who lies, manipulates, and throws herself at a man like some . . . some . . ." He groped for the right words, his face feverish with fury. "Some desperate floozy hawking her wares on Ann Street?"

The air stilled. Wet shock welled in her eyes, and he knew his words had pierced her like a well-aimed bullet. Two tortuous tears trailed down her pale cheeks, and his heart ripped in two as thoroughly as he had ripped hers. Chin trembling, she turned away.

"Rose, wait—" He gripped her arm. "I didn't mean that, I swear. I was just angry . . ."

Her small frame convulsed with sobs, and the bullet ricocheted to nail him right in the heart. With a low groan, he tugged her into his arms, his voice hoarse with repentance. "Forgive me, Rose, please—that was cruel and utterly untrue." He closed his eyes and massaged her back, completely indifferent that he stood on a field at dusk with a woman in his arms. He held her away, his thumbs slowly grazing the sleeves of a cashmere sweater that fit her body a little too well. Ducking his head, he gave her a sheepish smile. "Will you forgive me? Please?"

She sniffed, and he handed her a handkerchief, then tucked a finger to her chin. "Come on, Miss Kelly," he said with tease in his tone, desperate to make amends. "You owe me."

"I owe you?" she cried with a thrust of her jaw.

He grinned. "Yes, ma'am—fired, remember? So you have to forgive because I did."

She chewed on her lip. "Oh, that's right—drat!" The sparks in her eyes tempered to a tiny sparkle as she tilted her head. "On one condition."

Every nerve in his body tensed as the smile faded from his lips. "What?"

"You buy me ice cream at Robinson's—tonight."

"Oh, man, Robinson's!" He sucked in a sharp breath and glanced at his watch, emitting a low groan. "Sweet saints, I'm going to be late."

She adjusted her shapely sweater over a slender tweed skirt that boasted just as many curves and offered her arm. "*We're* going to be late, so we best be going."

He froze. "We?" Hands parked low on his hips, he dug his heels in for another fight.

"Yes, *we*," she said with a lift of a penciled brow. She gave him a thin smile. "You know, you and the woman who lies, manipulates, and throws herself at a man like some—"

"All right, all right!" He swabbed his face with his hand, certain he'd never met a more exasperating female. His mouth slanted as thoughts of Charity came to mind, giving him a true appreciation for Mitch Dennehy. He aimed a thick finger at Rose, determined to make it crystal clear he had no room for a woman in his life. "I'll take you to Robinson's, but after that, it's done. I am not interested in having a relationship with you or any other woman. Is that clear?"

She nodded, lips pursed in consent.

He peered at her through narrowed eyes. "You're sure? You promise to leave me alone?"

Flinching, her nod was weaker this time. "I promise . . ."

The breath he'd been holding slowly seeped through his lips in one arduous exhale.

She drew in some air. "After our date on Saturday night, you will *never* see me again."

He choked, his hoarse gasp triggering yet another coughing fit.

"You really should see a doctor about that." She patted his back. "It could be allergies."

He slapped her hand away with fire in his eyes. "We are *not* going on a date on Saturday night, Miss Kelly, or any other night."

"Oh," she said with an innocent blink. "Well, Mrs. Dalton will certainly be glad to hear that. What time should I tell her you'll call?"

The tic in his eye slowed to a crawl. "You wouldn't . . . ," he whispered, teeth clenched.

"Well, I certainly wouldn't want to, Sean," she said with a show of sincerity, "but I know you're adverse to women who lie, so naturally I'll need to set the record straight." She patted his hand. "She's a lovely woman, really. I think you'll like her." She turned to go.

He clutched her arm and spun her around so hard, she let out a soft gasp. Jerking her close, he loomed over her, his face pure granite and mere inches from hers. "You're just brazen enough to do it, aren't you, you little brat? You're *that* crazy!"

She seemed to melt in his arms while the faintest of smiles tipped her pretty pink pout. He was so close he felt the warmth of her breath as that deadly cashmere sweater rose and fell. The scent of Chanel No. 5 taunted him, a scent Emma often wore—sensual, stirring, and as bold as Rose Kelly herself. Her brown eyes softened, and he could feel his defenses crumbling to his feet.

"No, Sean," she whispered in a husky tone that heated his skin, "I'm that crazy about *you*."

His fingers flinched away like the woman was on fire. And heaven help him, apparently she was—enflamed with the insatiable desire to have *him*. His gut constricted. Every fiber of his being railed at the thought of any woman forcing his hand—least of all Rose Kelly—but that didn't stop his body from thrumming at the invitation in her eyes. He took a step back, jaw hard and eyes slits of warning. His lips went flat as he pumped the front of his shirt to cool off his skin. He sucked in some air before blasting it out again. "Are you a God-fearing woman, Rose?"

Her lips parted while a hand fluttered to her throat. "Why, yes, of course." Her brow puckered. "My father's cochair for the Cardinal's Appeal this year, as a matter of fact. Why?"

He folded his arms and forced a cold tone. "Because, Miss

Kelly, I want you to swear right here and now—before me and before God—that once our 'date,' as you call it, is over, you will never, *ever* darken my door again." He ignored the hurt in her eyes and forged on. "Swear to me, Rose—right now—that you will leave me alone after Saturday night. Or so help me, I will march up to that fancy house of yours on Beacon Hill and ask your father to do it for you."

The creamy skin of her throat shifted. Seconds felt like years before she finally nodded.

He leaned in, enunciating every syllable. "Out-loud, Rose, in-plain-words—swear-it."

Her body quivered as she drew in a deep breath, and he wondered how in the blink of an eye, a woman could go from being a vamp who stirred his blood to a little girl who tugged at his heart. She bit on her lip with tented brows, as if this were the most important decision she would ever make. Inhaling again, she uttered the words he was desperate to hear. "Yes, Sean, I swear to you now, before God and man, that after Saturday night, you will never see me again."

The air drained from his lungs, allowing his muscles to finally relax.

"Unless, of course, you want to," she finished with a hopeful flutter of lashes.

He grunted and hoisted the equipment bag to his shoulders, eyeing her as if she'd just said she could fly. "We're both too old for fairy tales, Miss Kelly." He turned on his heel to head for the street, and she followed along, chattering as if she were one of the kids on the team.

"I've been dying to try that Italian restaurant, you know, the one at Washington and Summer? We wouldn't want Father to know, so let's just meet there, say seven o'clock?"

Sean ignored her and shifted the bag on his shoulder, but it didn't seem to matter to Rose, who carried on as if he weren't even there.

"Perfect! Oh, and now ice cream too! I just love ice cream, don't you?" she said with a giggle, running to keep up with his long-legged stride. "One taste and I think I've died and gone to heaven." Her sigh was pure contentment as she tagged along, motor still running at the next light. "I do believe that nothing tingles my tongue quite like butter pecan. How about you?"

He slid her a sideways glance, and she looked up with a smile on those soft, pink lips. His mouth went dry. What tingled his tongue? His gaze jerked straight ahead, and his pulse pounded as if the bag over his shoulder was loaded with lead. *None of your business*, he thought with a grind of his jaw. But heaven help his sorry soul—it sure wasn't ice cream.

10

oodness, it's hard to believe Gabe's been a part of your family for two years now." Emma breathed in the lingering scent of apple pie in Marcy's homey kitchen, content as always to partake of the love and laughter that thrived within these warm and welcoming walls. She dried the wet dish that Faith handed her and sighed. "All I can say is, Gabe is one lucky little girl to have a foster family like yours." A chestnut curl fell into Emma's eye as she tipped her head to give Marcy a teasing smile. "I don't suppose Mr. O'Connor would consider taking on another?"

"Oh, please, Emma, you're already as much a part of this family as I am," Charity said as she wiped off the table, absently flicking a few crumbs on the floor. "The only thing you don't have is the name, and now, neither do we."

"Hey, I already swept over there," Lizzie said with tented brows, looking as if she wanted to pop Charity with the broom in her hand.

"Oops, sorry, sis—wasn't thinking."

"A common occurrence, no doubt," Katie said with a grin. She covered the leftover ham with a generous sheet of aluminum foil and carried it to the icebox. "If Father won't claim you as a foster child, Emma, I'm pretty sure Luke will." Her lips swerved into an off-center smile. "The man is just itching for a large family, by hook or by crook."

"I'll go along with that," Faith said. "Luke's a glutton for punishment when it comes to kids." She shook the rinse water off of the bowl and handed it to Emma with a smile. "I can't seem to convince the girls that he's not their own personal jungle gym." Faith glanced at her mother, her green eyes squinted in question. "By the way, Mother, since tonight *is* a celebration of Gabe's two-year anniversary with our family, when do you plan to pop the question to Father about adopting her? I mean, she's already a little sister we all adore, so don't you think it's high time we make it legal?"

"It certainly seems the logical step," Emma said with a sip of her tea, wishing she were as lucky as Gabe, soon to be officially and legally a part of this family she loved.

A blush crept into Marcy's cheeks as she hurried to the pantry to jot a needed grocery item on the list inside the door. "In time, Faith, in time. Once he gets over the shock of paying for Katie's wedding and settles in, I hope to ease in to the subject by Christmas." A heavy sigh drifted from lips pursed in a dry smile. "That is, if Gabriella Dawn Smith's antics don't sink my efforts first. It seems every other week the little dickens is getting into some scrape or another with the boys at school, not to mention the growing stacks of warning notes I've received from Sister Mary Veronica on Gabe's rather—" Marcy cleared her throat, a rise of color staining her cheeks—"shall we say, colorful vocabulary? But I'm hoping in time Gabe will settle down along with Patrick and I can introduce the subject without the man going into shock."

"Yeah, well, good luck with that, Mother. When I broke it to Luke that I'd enrolled in law school, you would have thought I'd committed first-degree murder." Katie poked a finger beneath the foil to pilfer one last piece of ham before closing the icebox door.

"Uh, you did, sis . . . on his pride." Charity smirked while she wiped down the counter.

Katie shot her an evil grin. "Oh, please! As if you haven't taken potshots at Mitch like a sideshow sharpshooter. He's got so many holes in his pride, he probably thinks he's part Swiss."

Charity's gaze thinned as her mother, Emma, and sisters chuckled. "Yeah? Well, he's a very proud man, Katie Rose—he could use a little thinning out. He's the most stubborn person you'll ever meet."

Rising to reheat the teakettle, Emma gave Charity's shoulder an affectionate squeeze. "Or one of them, anyway."

Charity's blue eyes narrowed in a mock scowl. "Excuse me, Emma, but I don't need my best friend taking shots at me, if it's all the same to you—I have Henry for that." She honed in on Katie with a slant of a smile. "And sisters, apparently."

Katie grinned. "Just doing my job, sis, both as a sibling and a woman who hopes to be a defense attorney someday."

"I don't know, Charity," Lizzie said with a sigh, "I think Brady could give Mitch a run for his money. It was the man's pride that almost derailed our life together, as you recall." She swept Charity's crumbs into the dustpan and glanced up. "You can't believe how upset he was that I didn't tell him Katie asked me to watch Kit five days a week. Said he was totally embarrassed in front of Father Mac and the guys at their weekly basketball game." She tossed the crumbs in the waste can and glanced at Katie with a sympathetic smile. "He claims Luke's frustration over Katie enrolling in law school triggered a heated conversation about wives keeping secrets from their husband. Says one minute he and Collin are bragging their wives don't keep secrets, and then the next—"

"Wait . . . Collin was bragging too?" Faith said.

Lizzie hung the dustpan on the pantry door and blew a strand of dark hair from her eyes. "Yes, but my saintly status has been jeopardized, while yours, apparently, is still very much intact."

Charity rolled her tongue in her cheek. "But not for long, eh, sis? When Collin finds out you're to be published in *Lady's Companion* magazine when he had *no* clue you were even writing again, I'm going to look like the good sister," she said with a thump of her chest.

Emma returned to her seat with a low chuckle. "Oh, I'm pretty sure there's no danger of that."

With a playful pinch of Emma's waist, Charity honed in on Lizzie. "I don't suppose Mitch did any bragging, did he?" She released a heavy sigh and tossed the dishrag into the sink. "Oh, well, the man's on pride overload as it is."

Faith chuckled, giving Charity a wink. "See how perfect you are for him?" Faith said with a flutter of lashes. "The sweet thorn in his side that keeps him humble."

"Thorn?" Emma said, eyes wide and hand splayed to her chest, enjoying the ribbing of her best friend, who could certainly dish it out too. She winked. "We're talking a rose trellis rivaling those in the James P. Kelleher Rose Garden, I suspect."

"Gee, thanks, Emma, I feel so loved."

Lizzie grinned. "Well, anyway, I had to laugh, Mother, when Brady said I should be more like you." Her eyes twinkled. "An open book who *never* keeps anything from her husband."

"An open book, am I? Mmm . . . that's very true, Lizzie." Despite the sudden flush in her cheeks, Marcy smiled on her way out of the kitchen, hand pressed to the swinging door. "Just remember, it's best to bide your time in turning the page." Shooting a grin over her shoulder, she looked a lot like a little girl with trouble up her sleeve. She inclined her head toward the parlor. "Like now, when your father is at his fullest and happiest, surrounded by men he can demoralize in chess?" Her lips twitched. "What better time to divulge that his foster daughter has blackened the eye of the class bully?" She sighed. "Heaven help Jeffrey Kincaid."

"Brian Kincaid's little brother?" Lizzie said with a gape of her mouth. "Sweet saints, is everyone in that family a bully?"

Faith drained the dishwater. "Probably. Have you seen Mr. Kincaid? A perpetual scowl worse than Mitch's when Charity pulls one of her stunts."

"Due to the fact his wife keeps secrets, no doubt," Charity said with a grunt.

"You're right—Stanley Kincaid's a bully too," Marcy said. "Obviously the entire family could do with some chastening."

"Or more time with Gabriella Dawn Smith," Katie said in a droll tone.

"Ahem . . . hopefully Gabriella Dawn O'Connor in the not-too-distant future." Marcy sucked in a deep breath and forged through the door. "Say a prayer."

Faith tossed her apron on the counter. "Wouldn't it be nice to be *totally* forthright with our husbands *all* of the time? But honestly, sometimes reticence is for their own good."

"And ours," Charity said with a wiggle of brows, rising when the whistle of the kettle pierced the air. "Anybody feel like another cup of Earl Gray?"

"Oooo, me, me!" Lizzie slid into a kitchen chair with a moan. "I just need a few more quiet moments while Brady is in charge of the kids."

"Sounds wonderful," Emma said, treasuring every moment she spent with these women she loved. She closed her eyes and breathed in the wonder of family with its hint of cinnamon from the pie or the citrus scent of Earl Gray, all laced with easy banter and good-natured teasing. How she relished this time with dear friends! *No*, she thought with a contented sigh, *sisters, really, much more than friends*.

"Yeah, I could use more downtime with Earl right about now too." Faith blew out another sigh and slumped into a chair. "A man who can calm my nerves instead of frazzle them. I mean, let's face it—you remember how Collin always pouted when I worked for the *Herald*? You would have thought that my job and my writing were a personal assault on his manhood."

"Tell me about it," Charity said. "Up till two years ago, Mitch was the same about me working at my own store, no matter how much Emma needed the help." Her smile slanted while she poured more tea for each of them. "Just the mere mention of it would put the man's nose so far out of joint, he looked like a blind prizefighter." She plopped the kettle back on to boil and slid into her seat, steeping her tea with a vengeance. "Remember, Emma?"

"Oh, yes," Emma said with a grin, remembering all too well the heated discussions in the Dennehy household over Charity working at the store. "And to be honest, he's *still* not fond of you working the two days a week during the school year, either, even though he agreed to it." She swirled her tea with her spoon and hiked a brow. "Ten to one says he'll try to talk you out of coming back once the kids go back to school next week."

Charity's brow pinched in thought. "You're probably right. Maybe I just won't bring it up at all, you know? Just go ahead and do it to spare him his grumpy mood—and me. Heaven knows the mere mention of my working makes the man down-right belligerent, agreement or no."

"My point, exactly," Faith said. "So really, you not telling Mitch and me not telling Collin about my writing is in their best interest, right? I mean, how did I know that one of my stories would sell?"

"Well, you're going to have to tell him sooner or later, just like I had to tell Luke." Katie leaned in, elbow on the table and head in her hand. "Trust me, the longer you wait, the worse it will be."

Faith vented with a loud puff of air, then plopped crossed arms on the table to cradle her chin. "I know." Her gaze flitted to Emma. "Was it this hard for you, Emma, with you and Rory?"

Emma blinked, not used to being consulted regarding her role as a wife. Heat burnished her cheeks as memories flooded back. "Well, that was eleven years ago, Faith, and I was only with Rory for six." Her eyes glazed into the past to when Rory would slap her for hiding bills to spare his foul mood. Or rant if she used sewing profits to secretly chip away at their debts. Her smile strained. "Yes. So hard, in fact, I lied and deceived enough to make Charity look like a saint."

Even Charity had trouble swallowing that one. "Come again?"

Emma chuckled, helping to release some of the tension inside. "You don't own the title of vixen, Charity Dennehy, no matter how much you think that you do."

A muscle shifted in Charity's throat. "I don't believe it," she whispered. "You—Emma Malloy? I swear I hear the flutter of angel wings whenever you enter a room."

Laughing outright, Emma squeezed Charity's hand. "I suspect you've confused it with that of bat wings in the belfry, my friend."

"Emma—you busy?" Sean popped his head in the door.

Charity cleared her throat. "Yes, Sean, she *is*, as a matter of fact. In case you haven't noticed, we are having a very important discussion here. Besides," she said with a pout, "she's my friend and I don't get to see her all that much while *you* get to see her six days a week. So, don't be a pig." She swished him away with her fingers. "Go . . . lose at chess or something."

He grinned. "Sorry, sis, but it seems Gabriella Dawn has a hankering for ice cream, and since it *is* her party, Mother asked me to run to Robinson's and get a few pints. I just thought Emma might want to ride along so we could discuss the Christmas promotion."

"Well, she doesn't, do you, Emma? So, shoo . . ."

"Hey, it's your store we're trying to keep afloat, you little brat, so go bully your husband instead." A playful smirk lifted a corner of his mouth. "Or *try*."

Emma squeezed Charity's hand and rose to her feet. "We'll be right back, I promise."

"It's Wednesday night, so Robinson's shouldn't be too busy." Sean glanced at his watch. "It's 6:00 now, so we should be back by 7:00 or so, okay, if not before?"

"Oh, pooh!" Charity said. "Well, don't dawdle—I need both Emma *and* ice cream."

A sparkle lit Faith's eyes as she took a sip of her tea. "And not necessarily in that order."

Sean steered Emma to the door, his words suddenly low while a ridge dimpled his brow. "Thanks, Emma, I was hoping we could talk. And not just about the Christmas promotion."

Reaching for her purse from the coatrack, she cocked her head as he opened the front door. "Looks pretty serious. You're not giving me your notice, I hope?"

"Nope." He closed the door behind them, bobbling car keys in his hand while he sauntered toward the street where his father's Model T was parked at the curb. "You're stuck with me, Mrs. Malloy, at least until some other employer snaps me up." He gave her a skewed smile. "Which doesn't appear to be anytime soon."

"Well, then what is it . . . Oh!" Emma went flying, the heel of her ankle-strapped shoe caught on a raised crack in the sidewalk.

In the catch of her breath, Sean broke her fall, bracing her to his side with an iron grip. "Whoa! You okay?"

She blinked up with her heart in her throat, his shadowed jaw mere inches from her face as she stood, welded to a chest as hard and unmovable as the concrete that just tripped her up. The clean smell of Ivory soap mingled with the spicy tang of Barbasol shaving cream to flood her senses with his familiar scent, more potent now as she stood pressed to his muscled body.

Her stomach did an odd little flip, and she jerked back, cheeks aflame. "Goodness, I can be so clumsy."

He cleared his throat and opened the passenger door. "My money's on that nasty crack in the sidewalk, Emma, in the dark, no less. 'Clumsy' is the last thing I'd call a woman like you—you're the epitome of grace." He slammed her door and glanced at the crack. "I really need to fix that."

Adjusting her skirt, she drew in a deep breath, unsettled at the way she'd felt in his arms. "So, what's on your mind?" she asked too quickly, grateful the dark hid the blush in her cheeks as he slid behind the wheel.

He turned the ignition and glanced behind to make sure traffic was clear, then shifted into gear before easing down Donovan Street. His tone was suddenly strained, so foreign for the man who always seemed to smile with his voice. "This is a very uncomfortable subject for me, Emma, but I swear I'll go crazy if I don't talk to somebody." He shot her a sideways look encased in a frown. "I can't talk to my mother or sisters because I'd never hear the end of it. Nor can I bring it up with Pete and the guys because they think I'm crazy." He shifted to maneuver the corner, jaw set in stone as he stared straight ahead. "And maybe I am."

A tiny stab of jealousy took her by surprise as she angled to face him. "This wouldn't be about Rose Kelly, would it?" she asked quietly.

Another blast of air parted from his lips. "Unfortunately, yes. I mean, come on, Emma—have you seen anything else put me into ill humor like Rose?"

A smile tickled the corners of her mouth. "Well, yes, as a matter of fact. I did notice you got a wee bit testy the day Bert ate the last fudge brownie."

His face relaxed into a smile. "Yeah, that did sour my mood. But I only have you to blame. Your brownies are downright sinful."

She grinned. "Goodness, I'm not sure if that's a compliment or not."

His smile was halfhearted at best before he returned his attention to the street ahead. Arms resting on the steering wheel, he drove with torso hunched forward in apparent malaise. Quiet for several blocks before he finally spoke, he shifted gears with a low grunt, his voice just above a whisper. "What am I going to do, Emma?"

"About what?"

Turning the corner, he slowed to a stop down the street from Robinson's, then turned the ignition off and pocketed the keys. He heaved a heavy sigh and finally turned to face her. "I mean what am I going to do about Rose? We have a date tomorrow night."

Emma opened her mouth to speak, but no words came out.

A tungsten streetlamp crackled overhead, highlighting the tension in his face with flickering shadows. "Yeah, that's how I feel too—kind of numb and jaw sagging in shock."

She swallowed a knot. "But how . . . I mean, when? I thought you despised the woman."

"I do . . . or I did. Before she tricked me into seeing her again."

On a date? For some reason Emma felt herself bristle and folded her arms. "Now how can a woman 'trick' you into seeing her a second time, Sean? For heaven's sake, did she put a gun to your head?"

His forehead crimped, as if he'd expected more sympathy. "No, but she's devious, like I said." His thick blond brows dipped low over slatted blue eyes. "I'd appreciate some understanding here, Emma, instead of more grief. Rose already gives me enough of that."

It was her turn to sigh. "I'm sorry, but I honestly don't know how a self-proclaimed bachelor of thirty-four, *almost* thirty-five—and a stubborn one at that—can allow an innocent girl of nineteen—"

"Twenty-two," he said, grinding the words, "and as innocent as a time bomb."

"Even so," she said with a frown, "a man of your age should have more control."

He blinked, his gaping mouth a mirror image of hers moments before. His usual good humor went as flat as his lips. "I don't know why you're acting so huffy, Emma, I'm the one with the problem. Forget I even brought it up." He opened his door.

A merge of guilt and hurt squeezed in her chest. *I am acting huffy*, she thought with surprise, and a chill slithered through her because she didn't know why. She reached for his arm before he could exit the car. "Sean, I'm sorry—forgive me, please?"

He dropped back against the leather seat, one hand rising to pinch the bridge of his nose. "No, I'm the one who should be sorry. I'm just touchy because Rose makes me so crazy."

"How did this happen?" Emma asked gently, trying hard to focus on the problem at hand.

He expelled a weighty sigh and closed the door once again. "She showed up at my game and warded off a dinner invite from a widowed mother." He peered at Emma out of the corner of his eye. "Actually had the nerve to say she was my girlfriend. And I'll tell you what, you never saw a widow hightail it so fast."

Hand to mouth, Emma stifled a gasp. "No . . ."

"Yep, afraid so. I told you she was devious. So when Bobby begged his mother to invite me to dinner, Mrs. Dalton—or Barbara, as she suggested I call her—was mortified, but went ahead and extended an invitation for Saturday night." His mouth twisted. "For me *and* Rose."

"Oh, dear!"

"Rose apologized, saying we already had plans, and all I could do was nod my head like some woodenheaded bobble toy. So when Barbara dragged Bobby away, I turned on Rose, faster than a blind slugger on the third strike. Called her a liar, a manipulator, and a floozy . . ."

Emma's hand dropped from her mouth as if wrapped in a fifty-pound cast. "You didn't . . ."

"I did. Felt like a heel the minute the words were out of my mouth."

"So what did you do?" Emma whispered, unable to imagine Sean saying such hurtful words, even to Rose Kelly, despite the disastrous effect she obviously had on him.

He closed his eyes, head resting on the back of the seat. "What could I do—I apologized. That's when she finagled going to Robinson's." He massaged his temple with the ball of his hand. "Right before she insisted we keep our 'date' so it wouldn't be a lie."

"Oh, my."

"So, now I'm stuck having dinner with her tomorrow night."

Emma worried her lip. "Well, it's just one night. How bad can it be?"

His eyelids nudged up to give her a dubious stare. "Uh, I

don't think you understand, Emma—this is Rose Kelly. You know, the woman who not only cornered me in the storeroom with a lip-lock but got me fired by giving me mouth-to-mouth while perched in my lap?"

A tiny gasp popped from her lips as heat steamed her cheeks.

"Yeah, now that's more the reaction I was going for." He shifted to face her, arm draped over the seat and his manner serious. "Look, Emma, I know it sounds like I'm making light of this, but trust me, that's only a cover. Deep down inside, the woman scares me silly."

She tucked a leg beneath her skirt and slanted against the seat to study him, an unsettled thought churning in her brain. "That's more than obvious, Sean, but I can't help but wonder why."

He glanced up, eyes expanding and brows jagged high. "Why? I already told you why! The woman's as loose as a pocket of change."

She hesitated, a difficult question poised on her tongue. "Which would only be a problem if . . . ," she swallowed the sour taste in her mouth, "you were attracted to her, right?"

It was his turn to blush, and he complied nicely with a swoosh of ruddy color bleeding into his cheeks. He gouged the back of his neck. "For pity's sake, Emma, I'm a man, not one of those blasted mannequins down at the store. Of course I'm attracted to her."

For some reason his words stung, but she ignored their effect and tilted her head, brow wrinkled in concern. "Well, for the first time, I guess I find myself wondering just why that would be such a bad thing? You know, why you fight this attraction to a woman who is obviously crazy about you?" She paused to draw in a deep breath, then laid a calming hand to his arm. "But most of all I can't help but wonder why you have an aversion to falling in love when it might be exactly what God has in mind?"

He blinked, her frank question obviously catching him off-guard. She noted the sharp shift of his Adam's apple and immediately knew she'd struck a nerve buried deep. Averting his gaze, he stared out the windshield, lips compressed.

She removed her hand from his arm to rest it on the purse in her lap, her palm idly smoothing the cool leather while her voice carried low. "Actually, it's been a curiosity of mine for a while now—why someone with such a capacity to love would be so deathly afraid of giving that love to a woman. Charity's always been convinced that some woman broke your heart during the war, but I've never given much credence to that theory." She studied his chiseled profile, his face as serious as she'd ever seen, and slowly released a tenuous breath. "Until now."

He remained silent, but the muscle flickering in his jaw told her she was treading on ground where no one had ever gone. And in the slow rise and fall of his chest, she suddenly knew. Knew without a word uttered, that the man beside her—the friend she loved—had been fatally wounded during the war. A protective instinct rose up in her so strong, that she reached for his hand, clutching it as tears stung her eyes. "Talk to me, Sean," she whispered. "Please . . . so I know how to pray. Because I love you too much to watch you suffer this way."

He slowly withdrew his hand, gaze glued to the dash. "Don't do this, Emma. It doesn't make for pleasant conversation."

The hackles rose on the back of her neck, lending an uncustomary sharpness to her tone. "I'm not interested in 'pleasant' conversation, Sean, I'm interested in seeing old wounds healed for one of my dearest friends."

He turned. Thick, blond lashes lifted, revealing hooded eyes dark with pain. "I've never talked about it before."

"I know," she whispered, "but if it still hurts, then it's time."

Still, he didn't answer, his gaze lost in a hard stare into the cobblestone street where couples strolled in the hazy lamplight. It seemed a surreal contradiction—the muted strains of laughter and music from a pub down the way while his breathing tumbled out shallow and harsh, filling the silence with his torment. He finally straightened and draped sturdy arms across the top of the thick, black steering wheel to rest his chin on massive hands. "It's been so long," he whispered, his voice laced with melancholy, "since I've allowed myself to even think about it . . ." A muscle worked in his throat as he stared, his profile little more than a shadowed silhouette. "So long since I've even whispered her name."

She had sensed it was a woman, and yet his words shocked her anew, plumbing the depth of their friendship in a way no other words had. Air stilled in her lungs while she waited.

"Clare." His mouth seemed to caress the word as it breathed from his lips, and Emma's heart stopped at the tenderness emanating from that single name. A silent heave shivered the broad expanse of his shoulders before he sagged back against the leather seat, lamplight glinting off the sheen in his eyes.

"Did you . . . love her?" Her whisper wavered, all breath suspended.

"Love her?" he repeated. The barest of smiles hovered at the edges of his mouth. He nodded, and the words from his lips, though barely a whisper, pierced her heart with his sorrow and regret. "How could I not? She was the mother of my child."

His statement drifted in her brain, its impact silent, slow, and deep, like a knick she didn't know she had until she saw the blood on her hand. And then in a harsh catch of her breath, her heart constricted, and a low moan died in her throat. She reached for his palm. "Oh, Sean . . ."

He gripped her hand until the pain in her heart throbbed like her fingers, and then as a chasm yawning wide, the man before her quietly unburdened his soul, allowing a glimpse into Sean O'Connor she suspected few had been privileged to see.

He'd met Clare in November 1917, he said, while stationed in Château-Thierry, and they'd fallen desperately in love. His eyes took on a faraway look that made Emma feel alone in the car despite the lifeless drone of his voice.

"I'd never felt like that before, Emma, nor since—consumed

by a love that made me almost grateful for the war that brought us together." He told her how General "Black Jack" Pershing mandated months of extensive training before the American Expeditionary Force faced combat in the spring, which allowed the soldiers frequent leaves that he and Clare always spent together. He looked away, more wetness shimmering in his eyes. "I wanted to marry her, Emma, I swear—more than anything in this world. But her parents wanted nothing to do with me."

"Did she love you?" Emma asked, her pulse slowing to hear his answer.

The strain on his face eased as a faint smile curved on his lips. "Yeah, she did. Enough to want a lifetime together . . . and enough to give herself to me." He looked up then, as if to measure the assessment in her eyes. "What we did was wrong, I know, and I was certainly raised to know better." He drew in a deep breath and then exhaled slowly, his sorrow appearing to be more from his loss than his actions. "But the world was at war and men were dying, and at the time it seemed as if our lives might be snuffed out too. We'd both waited a lifetime for this and didn't dare squander it because in the next moment we knew . . . it might all be gone. All we had were fleeting moments where we could see inside of each other's souls, two people who might never speak a word and yet somehow knew . . . knew what the other was thinking." He exhaled again, and the tenor of his tone went as flat as the press of his mouth. "When she told me she was pregnant, I vowed to marry her, only her father refused." His eyes were glazed and fixed straight ahead. "I found out from one of her friends that he hated Yanks, so he beat her in a rage and she . . . ," he lowered his head, shoulders slumped as if weighted with memories that crushed not only his heart, but his spirit, ". . . lost the baby."

"Oh, Sean . . ." Emma's voice was barely a whisper.

"I tried to see her, of course, but her father refused, threatening me with the authorities if I came around again. So I laid low for a few weeks, hoping to reason with him when he cooled down, only"—a nerve flickered in the hollow of his cheek as his jaw hardened along with his words—"when I went back, she was conveniently married to someone else, handpicked by her father."

Emma caught her breath. "Sean, I'm so sorry . . ."

"No, I'm sorry for burdening you with this, Emma, but I guess I've never really gotten over it." He attempted a smile that failed miserably. "And I did warn you it wasn't pleasant."

"Yes you did," she whispered. She squeezed his hand as she studied him, her gaze bonded to his. "Now let me warn *you*, Sean O'Connor. There is no way I can allow someone as dear to me as you to carry such a heavy load."

A muscle quivered in his jaw. "Trust me, Emma, if I could lay this down, go back and change the past, I would. Because as surely as I draw breath, I know it was my weakness, my desires . . . that ultimately cost my child's life. And as if that isn't horrible enough, I have to live with this seething anger inside, not just toward Clare's parents, but Clare herself— the woman I would have loved and protected for the rest of my life . . . if only she'd stood up to them and given me a chance."

"Oh, Sean . . ."

His voice was lifeless as he stared straight ahead, obviously mired in thoughts as dark as the hate with which he wrestled. "They say confession is good for the soul, Emma, but all it does for me is dredge up painful things I'd rather forget." His voice broke and he put a hand to his eyes, his silence thick with shame and regret. "Like the kind of man I am deep down inside."

"Sean . . . we're all sinners . . ."

The torment in his eyes chilled her. "Yes, Emma, we are . . . but we're not all murderers."

Her breath caught in her throat. "No! You didn't murder your baby, Sean—Clare's father did!"

"Not the baby," he whispered, "a man, Emma. A man I killed during the war."

Her brows knit together. "A lot of men were killed during

the war. It's the nature of the beast, defending one's country. That's not murder."

He sank back against the seat, closing his eyes as if he dreaded seeing the shock on her face. "It wasn't my country I was defending, Emma, it was Clare."

"What do you mean?" she whispered.

"I mean I lost my temper." He gouged his forehead and then opened his eyes, chest expanding as he drew in air. She saw the hard press of his lips as he finally locked eyes with hers. "Like the night at Kearney's when I assaulted your friend. I told you later that it's only happened twice in my life—once with you, and once during the war." Unleashing a weary sigh, he sifted hands through his hair to clasp the back of his head, eyes trailing into nothingness. "I've always known I had a temper, but I kept it under wraps because it's not something I'm proud of. And then on one of my weekend leaves, I was supposed to meet Clare at a new pub, but when I walked in, some guy was manhandling her and I just lost it. Slammed him against the wall just like I did Martin, only this guy fought back, and the next thing I know, my buddies are pulling me off, afraid I'm going to kill him." A lump shifted in Sean's throat and he closed his eyes again, his face a mask of pain. "And I would have, Emma, because the rage was like nothing I've ever felt before . . . so dark, so evil, like I wanted to kill him for even touching Clare. I turned away, and then Clare screamed. I swear I never even felt the knife, only something warm and wet on my arm as this guy came at me again. When I realized it was my blood on his blade, I snapped. Picked up a heavy wooden chair like it weighed nothing at all and swung it, catching him on the side of the head so hard I swear I heard his neck crack."

Emma watched as Sean put a hand to his eyes, his voice choked with emotion. "I can still see it, even after all these years—that look of total shock in his eyes before he slumped to the floor, knife still in hand. The pub was crowded that night, and my buddies dragged me out of there so fast that nobody really knew what happened. I didn't find out until later that he was dead, nothing more to the locals than a knife fight gone awry." His throat shifted. "But I know better."

The horror of the situation sickened Emma until she thought she would faint. Forcing herself to breathe, she struggled to reassure him. "It was self-defense, Sean," she whispered.

He looked up then, and never had she seen a more broken human being. Tears glistened in his eyes, and she fought the urge to pull him into her arms. "So everyone said," he whispered, his voice thick with shame, "but in my heart, Emma, I have to live with the truth—that it was my rage, my temper, that were ultimately responsible for a man's death that night, and nothing anyone could ever say or do will free me from that prison in my mind."

"You're wrong," she whispered, knowing full well that Someone already had done *and* said something that could set Sean free.

He hath sent me to bind up the brokenhearted, to proclaim liberty to the captives, and the opening of the prison to them that are bound.

She reached for his hand. "God can."

He stared at her a long time, the tic in his jaw confirming his doubts. "Maybe," he muttered, "but even God can't convince me that falling in love again is a risk I should take. Not only because I don't deserve a second chance after botching the first, but I don't trust myself either." His smile was hard. "Nor any woman."

"Not even me?" she asked softly.

He cupped her face and smiled, the hardness fading in his eyes. "Ah, but you're not just 'any' woman, Mrs. Malloy. No, you're one in a million. Not only are you the only woman I love, respect, and admire outside of my family, but the only woman alive I trust with the deep, dark, and dangerous secrets of my soul."

"Just your secrets . . . or your soul too?"

He cocked his head, eyes narrowed in tease. "Why do I get the feeling I should say no?"

Her eyes gentled. "Do you trust me, Sean? To help set you free from the past?"

He leaned back against the seat, eyes fixed on hers as the smile sobered on his face. "I'd give anything to be free of my past, Emma, but I don't think that's possible."

"Anything?"

Folding his arms across his chest, he peered at her, eyes squinted in thought. "Anything."

"How about forgiveness?" Her voice was a whisper, but it seemed to echo in the car.

An edge crept in his tone. "I've already forgiven Rose, Emma, what more do you need?"

"It's not what I need, Sean, it's what you need to live the kind of life God wants you to have. The heart of the matter, literally—your anger toward Clare, her parents, and even yourself." She breathed in deeply. "And forgiveness from God for your rage that played a part in taking a man's life."

He stared at her, his gaze unblinking. "I don't know if I can."

"Oh, you can, trust me. I believe in you because I know the caliber of man that you are. And I believe in God because I know the caliber of God that *he* is . . . and how much he loves you."

He glanced up, moisture in his eyes. "I can pray to forgive Clare because I loved her and I can even pray to forgive myself because I was just a stupid kid who fell in love. But I have no stomach to forgive her father, Emma, because he ruined my life, taking the life of my child and the girl I would have made my wife. If anything, I pray for God to curse him."

Chards of ice pricked Emma's skin, a painful reminder of her own battle with hate. She drew in a cleansing breath and released it slowly, along with silent prayers for God's help. "'And ye shall know the truth, and the truth shall make you free.' And the 'truth' is, Sean, that it's sin that ruins people's lives, and no one is immune. Sin ruined my life with Rory and it was sin—yours and Clare's—that ruined yours."

He looked away, and she sensed a battle waging. He had

become a master at hiding his feelings and hurts, presenting an image to the world that was carefree and calm. Everyone's brother, everyone's friend, and yet deep down, he had buried his grief so well, he was a stranger to even himself. A stranger to any love that God intended him to have. She watched the rise and fall of his chest as he exhaled, as if finally relinquishing the fight, and with an almost imperceptible quiver in his temple, he lowered his head. "Okay, Mrs. Malloy," he whispered. "I'll work on it."

Air seeped through her lips as she slowly released the breath she'd been holding. *Thank you, God.*

He glanced at his watch, his mood sober as he reopened his door. "If we're going to be back by seven-thirty, I better go get the ice cream. You want to go in with me or wait here?"

"I'll wait here if you don't mind," she said, as unsettled as he appeared to be by the secrets he'd shared. She gave him a gentle smile. "But I'd make it fast if I were you—she's liable to create a ruckus if we take too long."

He grinned, the tension in his face easing considerably. "I don't think so—Father can handle Gabe."

Her lips tilted in a mischievous smile. "I was talking about Charity."

He paused, one leg braced on the street while he studied her for several seconds, the grin on his face fading into a soft smile. And then all at once, he leaned in, pulled her into his arms, and rested his head against hers, his words warm and fervent in her ear. "Rory Malloy must be the sorriest moron alive, because I have never met another woman like you." Pulling back, he pressed his lips to her cheek, and her heart stopped as his thumb slowly kneaded the small of her back. He tucked a finger to her chin with a smile that caused her stomach to flutter. "I'll tell you what, Emma Malloy, if you didn't have that ring on your finger, you'd be in trouble right about now. But since it's there, then I'll just thank you for being the best friend a man could ever have." And with a final stroke of her cheek, he climbed from the car before hunching to give her a smile. "You sit tight, Mrs. Malloy, I'll be right back."

He closed the car door and she swallowed hard, watching the easy sway of his broad shoulders as he strode toward Robinson's, hands in his pockets.

Sit tight? She closed her eyes and put a palm to her face where his lips had been. "Tight" certainly wasn't a problem at the moment, she thought with a rush of heat to her cheeks. His hug had knotted her stomach and nettled her nerves, making her rib cage feel two sizes too small. She sucked in a deep breath and exhaled slowly, desperate to return to a semblance of calm. But all she could feel was the touch of his hand stroking her back, the warmth of his lips as they'd caressed her cheek, and the scent of a man who had held her close and quickened her pulse.

She blinked. *What on earth is wrong with me?*

Maybe the intimate nature of their conversation had set her on edge. She inhaled and put a shaky hand to her chest. Yes, that was it—discussing personal things that drew them closer than ever before. Releasing a shaky sigh, she closed her eyes. And in one ragged beat of her heart, she was back in his arms again, only this time his lips nuzzled her mouth instead of her cheek, clutching her close as he deepened the kiss.

No! Her eyelids shot up as she caught her breath, a forbidden warmth purling through her body like an opiate, drugging her conscience. Her breathing came in halting breaths as her mind raced. *No, God, please—this can't be happening!*

The evening was warm, but the sweat on her brow was not from the weather. Her uneven breathing stilled as her paralyzed lungs refused to comply. *God help me, I'm falling in love . . .* The very thought sent her heart thudding against her rib cage so hard she was gasping for air.

"I'll tell you what, Mrs. Malloy, if you didn't have that ring on your finger, you'd be in trouble right about now."

Too late. She was in trouble *now* and knew it—her body humming from the touch of his hand, the feel of his lips, the smile that turned her world upside down. *No—this couldn't be!* She had to do something—*anything*—to keep these feelings away. Water welled in her eyes as she stared at the band that Rory had placed on her hand.

Till death do us part.

She squeezed her eyes shut, desperate to remain true to her vows.

If a man vow a vow unto the Lord or swear an oath to bind his soul with a bond; he shall not break his word, he shall do according to all that proceedeth out of his mouth.

Her eyelids flipped open while her breathing shallowed in her chest. Whatever it took, she would spare Sean the indignity of falling in love with a woman like her. A woman who deserved both the scars on her face and the man that put them there.

"*Come back to me, Em . . .*" Rory had written, the first letter she'd received in eleven years. Two thin sheets of paper buried deep in her bureau drawer, postmarked last month by a man in Dublin who now wanted her back. Painful words that revealed a painful truth.

"*I need you, love, and we'll renew our vows in front of a priest this time . . .*"

Hot tears streamed her face. No! She would never return, but she *would* keep her vow . . .

And ye shall know the truth, and the truth shall make you free.

She'd quoted it to Sean, but some truths were never meant to be revealed. Her hands shook as she fingered the ring. Just like some people were never meant to be free . . .

But Sean was. With quivering hands, she pulled her handkerchief out of her purse and quickly blotted her face. If ever a man was meant to be free to love a woman, it was Sean O'Connor. Never had she met a kinder, stronger human being, one whose teasing humor and big heart were a balm to her soul. He needed someone to love and return that love with all the happiness he truly deserved, and Emma had every intention of seeing it done. Inhaling deeply, she squared her shoulders and patted her hair, the seeds of a plan already forming in her mind.

Moments later, she glanced up to see him strolling back down the sidewalk, two buckets of ice cream swinging in his arms while wheat-colored hair fluttered in the breeze. Moisture stung in her eyes. *Oh, God, bring him a good woman who will love him to the depths of his wounded soul! And if it's Rose, please help her to be the woman you want her to be.*

A quarter block away, he flashed her a grin, and her heart swooped in her chest. She waved, then put a palm to her waist to calm her nerves, her thoughts tumbling as fast as her stomach. *And make it quick too, Lord, will you, please?*

He opened the door and slid in, his eyes twinkling like a little boy with mischief on his mind. "Now that didn't take too long, did it, Mrs. Malloy?" he said, giving her a smile that made her stomach dip. "And knowing you, I'll bet you spent the time wisely, telling the Almighty exactly what's on your mind."

She swallowed hard, quite sure the Almighty already knew, even if she had just realized it herself. Drawing in a deep swallow of air, she extended her hand to take the ice cream, then averted her gaze, one thought foremost in her mind.

Thank you, God, for Rose Kelly.

11

*H*eaven help him, could he be any more drained? Mitch's first Thursday night meeting with Marjorie Hennessey and he was so edgy and tired he was sorely tempted to take up drinking again. Not only had the vamp kept him until almost midnight, but she'd forced him to come to her Beacon Hill mansion instead of the *Herald* as agreed, making him both sick *and* tired of Marjorie Hennessey. He entered the dark foyer of his home and eased the front door closed with a silent prayer no one was awake. He had neither the fortitude nor energy to deal with any more women tonight, least of all his wife, whose talent for exercising his patience was second to none. Although, he thought with a press of his jaw, Marjorie Hennessey certainly came close.

He clicked the dead bolt and winced, the sound constricting his gut. "Please, God, let Charity be asleep." A faint jingle sounded behind him, and his thirteen-year-old golden retriever, Runt, pressed his snow-white snout into Mitch's hand, earning a scrub of Mitch's fingers. "Thanks for the welcoming committee, big guy, but I hope you're the only one."

With a wide yawn, he mounted the steps along with Runt, taking great pains to avoid every squeak and groan of the curved mahogany staircase, stealth of the utmost importance.

Noiselessly, he slipped into the bathroom to brush his teeth, stripping down to his customary pajama bottoms before entering the room where Charity lay buried beneath the covers. Gritting his teeth, he lifted the top sheet and eased into the bed as slowly as humanly possible, coaxing the springs into total submission with nary a squeak. His air suspended until every aching muscle became one with the mattress, and only then did he release it in one long and silent breath.

Charity twitched, and his heart seized in his chest, but she only rolled over with a soft little snort. Eons passed before he allowed himself to even begin to relax, and when he did, thoughts of Marjorie Hennessey attacked without mercy. He shut his eyes, wishing he could shut out Hennessey's spoiled niece as easily. Although he'd couched his refusal of her charms in every way possible short of quitting his job, she was a woman who didn't take no for an answer. He'd made it perfectly clear—from polite coolness to point-blank rudeness—that he had no interest in dallying with a wealthy socialite. But Mrs. Hennessey was not a woman to be put off.

Not unlike his wife, he thought as Charity shifted beside him in her sleep. He released a silent sigh. She was worried about Marjorie—he knew it. From the moment he'd told her he would be working Thursday nights with the socialite, he could sense it in the way Charity looked at him, clung to him at night, subtle things like cooking more, fixing his favorite meals, pouting when he worked late. *Especially* tonight, his first meeting with the "Queen," as Charity had dubbed her. Every word out of her mouth seemed to probe, dissecting his day, curious about where he went, every woman he talked to. One edge of his mouth crooked up. Except for his secretary, that is. Thank God Dorothy was twenty years his senior and happily married, or his wife would be fretting about her too.

Mitch released a silent sigh. He hadn't seen Charity like this in years. She was nervous, tense, needy for his love like before they were married, suspicious, crazy, with that dangerous gleam in her eye. Years ago, it had pushed him away because, yes, as a man, he wanted to be needed, but he didn't want a needy woman. And God help her, whatever the reason, Charity was needy right now, demanding his love at a time when work sapped him of both the time and energy to give it.

She rustled in the bed beside him and he froze, waiting for her to settle in once again before her soft breathing brought a faint smile to his lips. No matter how many ways he'd tried to tell her, she didn't understand that there was no woman alive who'd cast a spell on him like she did, and he craved to disrupt her sleep to tell her so with a passion that was long overdue. It seemed like forever since he'd made love to her, but there was no one to blame but himself. The depression had taken its toll at the *Herald* too, thinning the staff until Mitch felt as if he were carrying double his workload, too exhausted from fourteen-hour days to do anything but collapse in his bed at night and sleep. And for a man with a voracious appetite for making love to his wife, he could feel the absence of it in the tension of his body and the edginess of his mind. He wondered if Marjorie could feel it too, and the thought unsettled him even more. Her flirtations, her demands on his time had escalated all evening, and for Mitch, his tenure as auction cochair couldn't end soon enough. Only three months to go, he thought with a weary sigh, and a pariah with provocative dress and seductive ways would be history. The thought eased the tension from his mind, and he rolled over, more than ready to succumb to exhaustion.

He didn't know how long he hovered on the edge of consciousness before sinking into the slumber of the dead, but he did know the exact moment his life flashed before his eyes. It was when a sharp slash of pain gouged his back, erupting him from the bed like a horde of hornets had impaled his flesh. And when his wife hurtled forward with a guttural cry, he stumbled back in a daze, shock and stupor thwarting his defenses. For one paralyzing moment, he saw the fury in her eyes before she pounced again, and in a knee-jerk reaction, he warded her off, apparently stealing her balance as she toppled back on the bed.

"Are you out of your mind?"

She sprang to her feet, fists clenched at her sides while her chest heaved with rage. Pale moonlight distorted the anger in her face. "Out of my mind? No, but you're out of my bed until I get a straight answer. Where were you tonight?"

He stared, too numb to move. "I was working, I told you that."

"Liar! Angus said you left hours ago." She leaned in, eyes on fire and fists balled at her sides. "Do you have any idea how humiliating it is to be told your husband's gone 'home'—only to some other woman's instead of his?"

"Charity, I'm sorry—I called and left a message with Henry. Didn't he tell you? Marjorie wasn't feeling well and asked if I'd come there for our Thursday night meeting. And why does it matter anyway—you know I'll be working late every Thursday for the auction."

"*Work?* Is that what you call it?"

Her words detonated his temper and he stared her down, eyes itching with anger and his humor as spent as his patience. He ground his teeth. "No, I call it pure torture having to work all night with an obnoxious, spoiled socialite and then have to defend myself to a wife who acts like a shrew."

"You want shrew? I'll show you shrew!" She lunged.

Deflecting her hand midair, Mitch blistered her with a glare. "I don't have to take this," he said. He snatched his pillow from the bed and strode to the door. "I'll sleep in the study."

"Don't you dare walk out on me!" Her hiss edged toward panic. With a broken sob, she ran and pummeled his back.

He spun and disarmed her with an iron grip, her nails nicking before he could clamp her to his chest. "Charity, stop it!" he said, his breathing harsh. "I'm not letting you go till you calm down."

She thrashed in his arms for several seconds before finally collapsing in a fit of weeping so painful, it wounded his soul. *Heaven, help me, I'm an idiot*, he thought with a low groan, his heart sick with regret over the first fight they'd had in years. Holding her close, he swept her up and laid her back on the bed, cradling her as she wept in his arms. "God forgive me, Charity—I never meant to hurt you, I swear. I lost my temper and I—" He swallowed hard, his sorrow thick in his throat. "Please forgive me, I love you."

Her sobs softened to frail whimpers as she wept, tears soaking his chest. He held her tightly until her breathing was calm and still, then pulled back to cup her face in his hands. "Charity, as God is my witness, nothing happened. Nothing ever could. I despise the woman, and I'm desperately in love with my wife."

She sniffed, body shuddering with pitiful heaves. Moments passed before her final shiver, and when it came, he clung to her with everything in him. "You have to believe me, little girl—I love you, only you!"

He felt the warm breath of her lips against his skin, and longing pulsed in his veins. Her voice was a hoarse whisper. "I love you too . . . so much that the thought of another woman . . ." She shivered in his arms. "Oh, Mitch, I would die if you ever left me!"

A grin tugged. "No, little girl, I'd be the one who would die, because I'm pretty sure you'd claw me to death."

She sat up, her face glistening with grief as she caressed his jaw with her fingers. The whites of her eyes expanded at a scratch on his neck. "Oh, no . . . did I do that?"

"And this . . ." With a tight smile, he palmed her hand to stroke the bulge of a bicep, scarred by her vengeance.

A hand flew to her mouth. "Oh, Mitch, I'm so sorry—can you ever forgive me?"

In slow motion he rose up and gently nudged her back on the pillow, his eyes burning with intent and his blood pulsing with need. A dangerous smile curved his lips as he pinned her to the pillow. "I might," he said in husky warning, "if you tend to my wounds." He grazed the curve of her jaw with his lips, his breathing as shallow as hers. "Trust me, they're pretty raw."

Her voice brimmed with regret. "Oh, Mitch, I feel awful—"

He silenced her mouth with his own, his love for this

woman so deep, every fiber of his being ached. "Charity, when are you going to learn that you possess me body and soul . . ." His voice was a heated rasp as his hands wandered and his lips trailed her shoulder. "And I want *you* . . . only you."

His mouth took hers with a low groan, having its way until she melted in his arms. Molding her body to his, he feathered her throat with kisses before nuzzling the lobe of her ear. "So don't feel awful, Mrs. Dennehy, because when I'm through making love to you," he whispered, reveling in the silky touch of her body, "you have my word—*neither* of us will feel 'awful' anymore."

<hr />

"How someone as little as you can eat that much is beyond me." Sean held the carved wooden door of Nicoletti's Steak and Pasta while Rose sauntered out with a smug smile, her fur-trimmed coat wrapped tightly around her slim body. The intoxicating scent of Chanel No. 5 collided with the hearty aroma of oregano and garlic, embedding a sensory memory into his mind he wouldn't forget anytime soon.

"I'm like a shark—I never stop moving," she said with a sassy smile. Her playful chuckle floated in the cool night air, merging with the blare of car horns and the sultry sound of jazz from the nightclub across the way. She sashayed to her father's red Cadillac roadster parked at the curb and pivoted to face him, one manicured hand trailing the sleek fender as she gave him a teasing smile. "Of course, that also means I have a very sharp bite."

He strolled to just short of where she stood and slacked a hip, arms folded while studying her through hooded eyes. A bit of the devil twitched at the corners of his mouth. "Which is exactly why I stay out of the water, young lady. No matter how good a swimmer, a man could get eaten alive by a woman like you."

Her laughter had the ring of confidence, but he knew the pink in her cheeks stemmed from more than the autumn chill. He glanced at his watch, then gave her a patient smile. "I best be going. Gotta walk off this meal before my basketball game tonight." The crestfallen look on her face tugged at his heart. He cleared his throat. "Uh, I had a good time, Rose—thanks."

She took a step forward, a hand fluttering to her throat. "Can I . . . give you a lift home?"

The hope in her eyes almost undid him. "No, no, I need to walk, really. Thanks anyway."

"Please?"

A lump jerked in her throat, and his stomach twisted at the fragile plea in her tone. He groaned inwardly, hating himself for being such a sucker for a vulnerable woman, especially since Rose Kelly was anything but. And yet there she stood, shivering in the night, appearing to be just that. His jaw tightened in an effort to remain strong, but she reached out to squeeze his hand.

"Please? It seems so cold to just end our evening like this." Her body stilled, as if she were holding her breath, teetering on just the right words from his lips.

With another silent groan, he inhaled deeply, resignation rising from the pit of his stomach and into his throat. He expelled it in a harsh cloud of air that swirled up in a fog. He was just too blasted nice for his own good, he thought with a clamp of his lips, something Pete ribbed him about all the time. "If you would just treat them a little more rudely, women wouldn't hound you like they do," he'd say, giving Sean that smirk that told him loud and clear it was his own blasted fault. He stared at Rose now and knew if he didn't say something soon, the woman would turn blue from lack of air.

Gouging his temples with the tips of his fingers, he sighed again. "All right, Rose, you can give me a lift home. No harm in that, I suppose."

Yeah, right.

He reached to open the passenger door, and Rose slid in before him, peeking up through sooty lashes while she handed over her keys with a shy tilt of her head. "Would you mind driving? I tend to get distracted when I drive and talk at the same time."

His lips quirked as he snatched the keys from her hand. "And we wouldn't want that, now would we?" He closed her door and strolled around the Cadillac Victoria, a twinge in his chest at the beauty of the vehicle before him. His pulse accelerated as he glided a hand along the glossy serpentine fender where massive bullet-type headlights were mounted to a gleaming chrome crossbar. He couldn't help it—a low whistle escaped his lips as he stared in awe, quite sure that driving this baby would be well worth any time he had to spend with a woman like Rose.

"Was that whistle for me, I hope?" she asked when he opened his door and eased in, his palm skimming across the leather seat like it was made of satin. With a tingle of awe, he inserted the key, and the engine purred to life with a rumble that sent warm goose bumps across his flesh. He caressed the steering wheel with as much reverence as he would a brand-new Louisville Slugger signed by the "Babe" himself, then awarded Rose a boyish smile. "No, ma'am, but a few minutes behind the wheel of this baby, and I'll whistle all you want."

"Or anything else?" she asked with an innocent lift of brows.

Adrenaline pumped through his veins as the caddy cruised down the street, infusing him with a reckless air. He shot her a half-lidded smile out of the corner of his eyes. "Maybe."

A pretty shade of rose crept into her cheeks, and she hiked her chin as if to steel her nerve, shooting a flirty look. "Why, I didn't know you were such a tease, Sean O'Connor."

He grinned, enjoying the thrill of control—both with the powerful vehicle beneath his grip and with the woman sitting in it. "Only when I'm behind the wheel of a beauty like this, Miss Kelly. You're a very lucky woman, you know, driving an automobile like this."

"I could be luckier," she whispered, her look of longing crashing him back to earth.

He cleared his throat and took a corner with the same

skill and focus as if swinging a bat, his manner considerably sobered. The last thing he wanted to do was lead this girl on. "Look, Rose, I had a nice time tonight, but—"

"You did?" The hope in her tone gnawed at his gut.

"Yes, I did," he said quickly, "but please don't misconstrue what I'm saying. We had an agreement—" He slid her a sideways glance tempered with a smile. "Or an extortion, I should say, and a deal's a deal. You swore that after tonight, I'd never see you again, remember?"

With a dejected nod, she picked at her nails, looking more like a sad-eyed little girl than a twenty-two-year-old vamp whose open coat revealed a neckline that had taunted him all night. Raking perfect teeth over a flawless lip, she looked up. "Not unless you want to see me again."

See her again? Not likely. He shifted gears at a traffic light, and the engine vibrated beneath the chassis like the nervous tic in his cheek. He shot her a quick glance, noting the slump of her shoulders, then steeled his gaze straight ahead to stare at the red light. No way, he thought with a set of his jaw, although he'd enjoyed the evening, no doubt about that. Maybe because after tonight he'd never have to see her again, allowing him to relax without worry of more.

The light turned green and he gunned through the intersection like the devil was on his tail, and maybe he was. He'd enjoyed the dinner with Rose more than he'd expected. His favorite pasta—Chef Louie's tortellini—had tasted particularly good tonight, and he wasn't sure if it was because Rose doted on his every word, or the intimate ambiance of the candlelit booth, or even the laughter and ease of stimulating conversation. Whatever the reason, she'd surprised him, engaged him, warmed him with a glow that had rivaled that blasted candle in the middle of that blasted linen table. She was an unpredictable mix of sensuous woman and sassy flirt, and yet he sensed the real Rose was no more than a wide-eyed girl in love with the idea of being in love.

With him.

He swallowed hard as he maneuvered a corner. But the

thing that really bothered him right now—besides Rose, that is—was this unsettling feeling inside that a woman's affection, someone caring for him deeply, actually held some appeal. He hated to admit it, but Rose made him feel strong and needed and more like a man than he'd felt in a very long time. *Since Clare,* he thought with a press of his lips. The way Rose's eyes sparkled with invitation whenever she smiled, the tilt of her head as she twisted a curl around her finger . . . the way her silk blouse listed to the side to reveal a creamy white shoulder. All of it had stirred something inside that quickened his pulse and slowed his breath until he thought he couldn't breathe. He already knew he was attracted to Rose Kelly. He just hadn't known that he liked her. Until now. Which proved once and for all that if he was that much in the dark about his feelings for a woman, he had no business being involved with one. He sucked in a harsh breath. Because judging from the way her company had triggered his pulse tonight, he was already in way over his head.

See her again? Not on your life.

With a firm swipe of the wheel, he turned the corner and glided to a stop in front of his house, silence thick in the air as he switched off the ignition. "I had fun tonight, Rose, but we both know that this was a onetime thing." He drew in a deep breath and held out his hand, his chest tightening at the sheen of tears in her eyes. He cleared his throat. "I wish you well, I really do."

He had never been comfortable with tears—not his sisters', not his own, not even those shed in joy by his mother at Christmas. It had something to do with that sucker mentality that Pete always razzed him about, some genetic defect that nailed his heart to the wall and made it impossible for him to walk away from a woman in tears.

Like now.

He huffed out a weary sigh, eyeing her with the same wary feeling as if he were up against a shut-out pitcher during a championship game. He took her small hand in his, shocked at how icy it felt, then kneaded it to generate some warmth.

"Rose," he whispered, his palm swallowing hers as his thumb massaged back and forth. "We've been over this before—I'm too old and the last guy your father would allow you to see."

"He'd allow it if I begged him," she said with a pitiful heave. Her brown eyes glistened like melted chocolate as water pooled at the edge.

With a wild thump of his heart, he watched two crocodile tears slither down her face, causing his stomach to cramp. *Noooooo!*

Desperate words rushed from a tongue as thick as the air in his throat. "Listen, Rose, you think you like me, but you don't know me. I constantly whistle off-key, which drives my sisters crazy, and I drum my fingers when I'm thinking—an annoying habit that even gets on *my* nerves." He leaned in. "And my eyebrows? See how the left is thicker than the right?" He nodded with satisfaction as if his next words would have her recoiling in disgust. "Nervous habit—don't even know I'm doing it. But if I get too stressed? Look out—they could go bald."

Another tear rolled down her cheek and snagged in the corner of her half smile, easing the tension in his shoulders as he patted her hand. "Trust me, you can do much better than a man with bad sinuses who clears his throat all the time or one who's so consumed with sports even his mother doesn't know if he's coming or going. If I were you, I'd consider yourself lucky, Miss Kelly. You don't want a man who has no time for a woman, even one that he likes."

Her lips quivered, dislodging a tear. "You like me?" she whispered.

Lie, O'Connor, and get out of this car . . . now!

He dropped her fingers like a Lefty Grove fastball just stung his bare hand. "Yes, but not that way." He gripped the door handle so hard, it gouged the calluses on his palm. "I gotta go."

The heaving whimper that rose in the air fused his trousers to the seat as surely as if they were hand-stitched to the red leather. She began to sob, hands to her mouth, and the whites of his eyes expanded in shock. "Rose, please—"

A wailing moan finished him off, and his blood froze as she wept against the back of her father's Moroccan leather seat. Heaven help him, he had *way* too much compassion for his own good, a trait he could obviously blame on his parents. With an agonizing sigh, he dropped his head in his hands and gave up the ghost, finally pulling her to his chest and patting her on the back. "Rose, don't cry, *please*! It's like fingernails on a chalkboard—I can't handle it." Her body continued to heave, and he stroked her hair, rocking her with a gentle motion as he whispered in her ear. "It's okay, Rose, you're going to be fine, I promise." The waterworks continued, and her sobs grew, obliterating any thoughts but those for her welfare. "Rose, Rose," he said, kissing her hair. He closed his eyes, and her scent aroused his senses, a heady meld of Breck shampoo and Chanel No. 5, warming his blood while he warmed her arms with the buff of his hands.

Her travail rose in volume and he panicked, weaving fingers into her hair to cup her face in his hands. "Rose, shhh . . . it's okay . . . it's okay . . ." Like he'd done a million times with Gabe or Katie or any of his nieces, he pressed his lips to her cheek, and her moist lashes lifted, spiky with tears and swollen eyes awash with surprise. His breath caught at the tremble of her lips, parted and wet, the innocence of her face, mottled with weeping, and a once-familiar heat singed his body like an electric shock. Her breathing was husky and shallow like his, filling the silence between them with something other than grief. His gaze settled on her lips and his mouth went dry, confirming that *this* kiss on the cheek was far more dangerous and far more compelling.

He jerked away. "Rose, I need to go."

"Sean, no, please . . ." Her voice was nasal and husky, drawing him back like the hands now clasped to his neck. Before he could retreat, she captured his mouth with her own, paralyzing him to the spot.

It was a brisk autumn night, but the taste of her lips made

it feel like a blistering day in June, melting his resolve and fogging the windows as much as his mind. The woman may as well have been made of magnetite—her lips drew his with a pull he hadn't felt since Clare. His eyelids weighted closed, heavy with need as his mouth devoured hers, and he wrenched her close while their breathing merged into one. Glazed with desire, he gripped the nape of her neck and kissed her hard, a groan trapped in his mouth as he pressed her to the seat.

What am I doing?

But his body didn't seem to care. She was putty in his hands, warm and willing, and heaven help him, he hadn't felt like this in such a very long time. A moan left her lips, and he groaned, lost in the taste of her mouth, the scent of her skin, the feel of her body clinging to his.

"Sean, I love you," she whispered, and his body froze, colder than October frost on her daddy's steel bumper.

He jerked away, mind in a stupor. "Rose, no . . . you can't . . ." Shame surged within, cooling the heat of her kiss. "Forgive me, please, I was wrong—"

"No, Sean, you weren't! We're attracted to each other— why do you fight it?"

He stared, chest rising and falling with tortuous breaths and his body still humming from the heat of their kiss. *Why?* Because he'd only felt like this one time before, and that had ended in the most excruciating pain of his life. A fatal attraction, pulsing with passion and little else, starting fast and finishing faster . . .

Like this . . . tonight.

He put his hand to the latch of the door. "Rose, I need to go . . ."

Need and want were two different things, apparently, at least to Rose Kelly. She sidled close, sending his pulse into overdrive faster than her daddy's Cadillac Vic. Reaching up to nuzzle his neck, she feathered his ear with her whisper, her words warm and husky. "Stay with me, Sean, please? Just for a while?"

He was a responsible man, moral to a fault and loath to

hurt anyone's feelings. He needed to end this before he got in too deep and someone got hurt. And he would. He closed his eyes and drew her close as the blood throbbed in his veins.

Right after the next kiss.

———❦———

"Okay, somebody's in trouble because I *just* picked up those toys." Katie stared, arms folded and mouth flat as she assessed a parlor that looked as if it had been gutted by a pack of wild children rather than just two.

Luke and Kit looked up at the same time, sitting in a sea of Tinkertoys and wooden blocks that sprawled from window to wall.

"Mama!" Kit's little legs pumped in joy beneath her nightgown. "Da-da . . . fun!"

Rubbing her temple to alleviate yet another headache, Katie shot Luke a narrow gaze. "Yeah, well, there won't be a lot of 'fun' for Da-da if he doesn't get those toys picked up, pronto." She squatted and held her arms out to Kit. "Come on, big girl, it's time for bed."

Before Katie could steal Kit away, Luke swooped the little girl up and blew raspberries on her belly, sending baby giggles bouncing off the fleur-de-lis papered walls. His blue eyes sparkled as he winked, flashing Katie a sultry smile. "Admit it, Katie, you're just sore because I'm playing with Kit instead of you." He tossed Kit over his shoulder and rose to his feet, sending Katie a smoky look that never failed to quiver her stomach.

Except for tonight.

Luke leaned to give Katie a quick kiss on the lips. "Don't be so grumpy, Mrs. McGee. I'll put your daughter to bed and pick up the toys." He lifted her chin with his finger, teasing her with his eyes. "And if you're a good girl, Katie Rose," he whispered, "I'll play with you too."

She returned his warm gaze with a cool one. "No thanks, McGee, I've had enough playtime with you as it is." She kissed Kit's cheek as the little girl giggled and squirmed over Luke's shoulder. "Good night, Kitty Kat. I'll come tuck you in after Daddy reads you a story."

Brow kinked in concern, he palmed Katie's cheek while Kit's chubby legs flailed his back. "What's wrong, Katie? You've been edgy all night. Don't you feel well?"

Tears stung her eyes and she turned away. "I'm fine, just need to finish the dishes."

He grabbed her arm, tone tinged with worry. "Has something happened? What's wrong?"

Steeling her chin, she blinked to dispel her tears. "Nothing. I'm just crabby, that's all."

A blond brow jagged high. "Yeah? Well, I'd say that's an understatement. Why don't you take a hot bath, and I'll finish the dishes?"

She jerked free from his hold and hurried toward the kitchen, unwilling for him to see the tears streaming her face. "No, I'll do them," she called. "You just put Kit to bed, okay?"

Slipping into the kitchen, she closed her eyes and put a hand to her mouth. Her shoulders heaved with silent sobs as she pressed against the wall. *Oh, Lord . . .*

Giggles escaped down the hall to taunt her, first Kit's high-pitched squeal and then Luke's low, husky laughter, an untimely reminder of just how much joy they brought to her life.

With a shaky swipe, she pushed tears from her eyes and sucked in a deep swallow of air, willing it to calm her, settle her, before Luke came back in the room. She needed to be tough, efficient, a pillar of strength. And as cool and calm as the lawyer she'd always dreamed she'd be.

Even if those dreams were dead in the water.

Exhaling her grief, she moved to the sink to finish the dishes, plunging her hands into dirty dishwater as cold and slimy as the fear snaking its way through the pit of her stomach. She'd always seen herself in a courtroom with high heels and a tailored suit, giving birth to her dreams of fighting for women's rights, first as a lawyer and then finally a judge. She sagged against the sink and hung her head, dispelling more tears as she placed a wet palm to her abdomen. Well, she'd give birth, all right . . . but not to her dreams. No, she'd spend the rest of her life changing diapers instead of the world. The thought terrorized her, and she slumped over the sink, nausea curdling her stomach. *Oh, Lord, I don't know how to be a mother . . .*

"Katie?"

She spun around, no longer concerned about the tears coating her cheeks. Her lips quivered while a sob broke from her throat. "Oh, Luke . . ."

In three urgent strides he had her in his arms, stroking her face with the pads of his thumbs. A fierce protectiveness girded his tone. "Katie, what's wrong?"

She collapsed against his chest, body convulsing in tears. "Oh, Luke . . . I'm so scared."

"Of what?" He bundled her close, kissing her hair, kneading her neck.

A raspy heave wrenched from her lips. "Of b-being a m-mother. I'm s-so s-scared."

Luke stilled, hand paralyzed against her back. He opened his mouth to speak, but nothing came out. Jerking away, he grasped her at arm's length. "What are you talking about, Katie?"

She continued to weep, swollen eyes meeting his as she splayed a quivering hand to her stomach, and in that instant, everything—his heart, his blood, his air—slowed to a crawl. His mind raced, reflecting on all the headaches lately, irritable moods, being weepy at the drop of a hat and snapping at him.

He swallowed hard, his voice no more than a croak. "Are you . . . late?"

A dribble of tears spilled when she nodded, and he worked hard to hide the joy that pumped in his chest. Without another word, he picked her up and carried her to the parlor, dodging blocks and Tinkertoys on his way to the sofa. Tucking her head against his, he sat and snuggled her in his lap. He kissed the top of her head and buffed the side of her arm, his voice cautious and low.

"How late?" he asked, every muscle taut as he awaited her answer.

She sniffed, and he fished his handkerchief from his pocket. With the utmost tenderness, he wiped the tears from her face and then pressed it to her nose. "Blow."

She did, rather loudly, and his lips tipped into a smile.

"Almost two months," she whispered, and her wavering sigh vibrated against his chest.

"It could be a false alarm," he said carefully, caressing her hair with gentle, calming strokes. "Have you ever been late before?"

She shook her head, and the motion caused her hair to tickle his jaw. She sniffed. "Always twenty-eight days, just like clockwork."

He drew in a deep breath of hope and strove for calm. "Law school has been pretty stressful, Katie," he said in a tone meant to ease her fears. "And I've heard that stress or any number of things can throw a woman's cycle off."

She sat up and blew her nose. "Maybe . . . but what if I am pregnant? What if I have to give up law school and stay home and be a mother?" Tears welled as she searched his face. "I don't know anything about having a baby, Luke, or being a mother, for that matter. Faith and Lizzie were born to it, just like Mother, but Charity and I . . ." Two giant tears trickled her cheeks before her voice trailed off into a pitiful wail. "We don't seem to have the mother gene."

His heart swelled with love. "Katie," he whispered, "you'll be an incredible mother to my children. You're smart, funny, and a disciplinarian like nobody I've seen. I've watched Lizzie spoil and pet Kit until she was rotten, and then when I married you, you whipped her into shape and fawned over her at the same time in that wonderful, quirky way that I love. Studying with her in your lap while you feed her ice cream or teaching her to Charleston when she couldn't even walk." He held her face in his hands, more grateful for Katie O'Connor than he'd ever been in his life. "Mothers come in all shapes and sizes, Katie, and every one with their own personal weaknesses and strengths, but don't underestimate the wisdom of God in matching a child with a mother. By God's decision alone, you become the perfect fit for any child God chooses to send. Trust me, Katie—you *are* an amazing woman who will make an amazing mother."

Her chin wobbled. "But how can you be sure?"

The grin finally broke free. "I just am." He grazed the tip of her jaw with his finger, his grin softening into a smile. "As sure as I am that I want to spend the rest of my life loving you, Mrs. McGee." He kissed her softly on the lips, in awe of the God who'd blessed him with this woman. "I love you, Katie, and if we do have a baby right now, I give you my solemn vow—I will see to it you go to law school when the time is right, I promise."

His words were meant to soothe, but they only prompted more tears in her eyes. With a feeble sob, she laid her head to his chest and wept. And in the frail tremble of her body, his euphoria over a child leaked away along with the tears that now dampened his shirt. Closing his eyes, he shared her grief over law school, holding and stroking her until her weeping finally ebbed. The scent of rosewater filled his senses as he gave her a kiss, her skin wet and cool against his lips. "Tomorrow's Saturday, Sass," he whispered, "and we can finish the dishes then. I'll pick up toys and you get ready for bed. Then I want to hold you till you fall asleep, okay?"

She nodded and he gently scooted her off his lap, squeezing her hand before she made her way down the hall, shoulders slumped and handkerchief to her eyes.

"God, help her, please," he whispered. An uneasy mix of gratitude and sadness bled the joy from his heart as she disappeared into Kit's room. It certainly appeared as if he were on his way to the family he'd always longed for. A child of his own—his blood, his genes, and possibly a son to carry on his name. And yet the moment was bittersweet because the woman he loved had to sacrifice her dream for his.

Releasing a weary sigh, Luke lumbered up from the sofa and proceeded to pick up the toys in the room, his mind wandering to the prospect of another mouth to feed. It would be tight, but they could do it. And the depression couldn't last forever.

Could it?

He tossed Tinkertoys into the wooden toy chest that Sean had made for Kit, and his heart suddenly leapt at a thought. *A son. A daughter. A child of my own.* His pulse began to race. Which meant once this baby primed the pump, that family of four he and Katie agreed upon could be here before they knew it. And who knows? Katie might like being a mother so much, he could talk her into six kids or eight. He grinned. Or maybe his own basketball team . . .

He thought of Katie's passion for law school, and his grin flattened into a frown. He exhaled loudly and glanced around the room to make sure it was picked up, then turned out the lights and trudged down the hall. Flipping the bathroom light, he closed the door and stripped off his clothes, hurling them into the hamper. He reached for his toothbrush, then sagged against the sink to stare at the man in the mirror. The one who had just obliterated all of his wife's hopes. He huffed a sigh and brushed his teeth with a vengeance, determined to get Katie through this.

The room was dark when he finally entered, but he could hear her muffled weeping from the door, inflicting a sharp stab of regret. He padded to their bed and climbed in, silently tugging her into his arms. With a hoarse heave, she clutched tightly, and he eased back on the pillow, caressing her head as she wept against his skin.

"I love you, Katie," he whispered. "You and Kit are my life, and more important than anything in this world . . . including having a baby."

Her weeping slowed and she sniffed, moments passing before she finally spoke. "Luke," she whispered, her voice nasal and thick, "do you . . . think I'll ever be a lawyer?"

He closed his eyes, swallowing hard at the fragility of such a question. He drew in a deep breath and released it again, feeling the weight of his wife's fears heavy against his chest.

"I don't know, Katie, but I do know we serve a God who delights in giving us the desires of our hearts, especially when those desires are one with his."

A frail whimper rose as she slowly sat up. She swiped at her eyes with a handkerchief now as sodden as the skin on his chest. With a final sniff, she averted her gaze, head bowed in apparent concession. "Will you . . ." The muscles shifted in her neck as she stared, a dark profile stark against a moonlit window. "Will you pray I can accept his will?"

His heart squeezed at the familiar lift of her chin, the glint of silver trailing translucent cheeks, and his throat tightened. He swallowed hard, loving Katie O'Connor more with every breath he took. With a slow nod, he drew her back, aching to seal her in the warmth and protection of his embrace. He felt the rise and fall of her chest, the steady beat of her pulse in rhythm with his as she lay silent and still in his arms, and in one fragile breath of air, he knew they were one. Not just in God's eyes or in their lovemaking or even in the family he one day hoped to have. No, they were one flesh, just as God's Word proclaimed—if her heart broke, he ached, if her dreams died, he mourned. Expelling a shaky breath, he closed his eyes and gripped her close, willing the hope in his heart to seep into hers. He knew a thing or two about dreams and the God who instilled them, especially for those with one knee bent at the throne. A quiet peace settled as his body slowly relaxed against hers, and faith girded his prayer until it was steady and strong.

Because he knew, as surely as his love for this gift of God in his arms, that when it came to heart's desires and the wishes of a loving Father . . . more often than not, they were one and the same.

12

"What's this?" Emma stooped to pick up a rose petal from the floor, marveling at its softness as she grazed it against her cheek. "Roses? In October? Where did this come from?"

With a wry slant of her lips, Bert swiped a clean sheet of paper off her desk and shoved it into her typewriter. She nodded toward the far corner of Alli's desk and then shot Emma a sideways glance as thin as her patience. "A secret admirer," she said with a snort of disdain. "As if we aren't busy enough without this inane distraction."

"Come on, Bert, you're just jealous." Sean strolled from his office with a boyish grin. "A secret admirer would probably leave roses for you too, if you didn't scare him half to death."

Her hazel eyes narrowed to slits. "'Death' being the operative word, because if any joker pulled that stunt on me, he'd be spitting roses for a week—thorns and all."

"I think it's sweet," Emma said with a smile at Alli, whose face was as pink as the roses on the edge of her desk. "Who do you think it is, Alli?" she asked, lifting the vase to take a sniff.

"Fly Boy," Bert said with a scowl, spinning her paper into the platen with a noisy grind. "He's up here all the time, delivering shipping statements now instead of Horace, thank God."

More color whooshed into Alli's complexion, making the roses pale by comparison.

"James?" Emma put the vase back, thinking of Horace's assistant who'd lost a leg in the war as a bomber pilot. He was a hard worker who was always courteous and kind, attributes Emma valued in an employee. Although James was attractive in a quiet, unpretentious way, she'd just assumed that at almost thirty-eight, he was a confirmed bachelor devoted to the care of his elderly mother. Folding her arms, Emma positioned a hand to her cheek, absently chewing on the nail of her pinky. Thirty-eight to Alli's twenty? "Goodness, isn't he a little old?"

"Hey, watch it, Mrs. Malloy," Sean said. "You're trampling on feelings here, you know."

Emma chuckled. "I meant for Alli, *Grandpa*." She tilted her head and studied the mortified girl who was now fanning her face.

"S-stop it, you th-three," Alli said, a blush bleeding into her bangs, "I'm dying h-here!"

Rounding Alli's desk, Emma looped her arm around the petite girl's shoulders to give her a motherly squeeze. "Come on, Alli, somebody here thinks you're special enough to leave you flowers. And this *is* kind of fun, isn't it? Speculating who it might be?"

"No," Bert said with a grunt.

Alli peeked up beneath thick lashes while she picked at her nails. "It's probably just Mr. Wilkins in the shoe department, trying to be nice. He says I remind him of his granddaughter."

"I don't think so," Sean said with a squint, as if pondering the question at hand. "Take it from another guy—men only give flowers when they're trying to win a girl's heart."

Emma shot him a mischievous smile. "Uh . . . experienced at this, are we?"

He grinned. "Nope, just smart."

She shook her head and returned her attention to Alli, head

cocked in thought. "Well, it could be Eddie, you know. Our mail delivery has never been this good . . . or this frequent."

"You got that right." Sean parked himself on the corner of Bert's desk. "We better be careful or the postal service will steal him away."

"Wish they'd steal Horace," Bert mumbled.

"Bert, hush!" Emma peeked out the door, expecting sweet, gentle Horace to be standing right outside, wounded by Bert's constant rejection. "Horace is a dear man who's just lonely since he lost his wife years ago. You can't blame him for harboring a little crush, you know."

"Yeah, Miss Adriani," Sean said with a grin, "a doll like you? After all, the man's only human."

"*Mrs.* Adriani," Bert said with the hint of a smile, obviously disarmed by Sean's lavish praise. Her lips twisted into a mock scowl, emblazoned with a deep shade of red that complemented lustrous black hair tipped with silver. "Believe me, I *earned* that title the hard way after living with a bum like Alphonso Adriani." She made the sign of the cross. "God rest his soul."

Emma peered at Bert. "So, why do you think it's James carrying the torch?"

"M-miss E-emma!" Alli actually stuttered Emma's name, a sure sign she was mortified. "I assure you, nobody is 'carrying a torch' for me!"

Sean gave Alli a wink. "Sure they are, Miss Moser, starting with me."

Alli slunk low in her chair, her pale face whooshing past pink, straight to scarlet.

Bert peered up to answer Emma's question, the staccato tapping of her fingers halted on the keys. "Because his mother used to work at the Boston Flower Exchange and grows roses in her kitchen window."

"How do you know that?" Sean asked in disbelief. "I can't get two words out of James."

Bert lifted her chin, attempting a hard stance, but the quirk of her lips indicated her true affection for Sean O'Connor.

"Well, it looks like your boyish charm has its limits, then, doesn't it? Besides, we had coffee one night after Miss Emma hired him on."

Sean gaped, a grin tugging at his lips. "You? Had coffee with James? Why?"

Her gaze narrowed. "Because he lost his leg in the war, and I felt sorry for him, okay?" She put a hand to her eyes. "If you must know, I had a brother who lost both legs in the war."

All the color leeched from Sean's face, making the spray of freckles across his nose all the more prominent. "Oh, Bert, I'm so sorry—are you serious?"

She went back to her typing, fingers flying and a satisfied smile lining her lips. "Nope, but it sure wiped that smart-aleck smirk off your face in a hurry."

"Why, you little . . ."

He dove for her neck, and she batted him away with a low, husky laugh that echoed in perfect harmony with Alli's giggles, both of which brought a grin to Emma's face. She shook her head, glowing with affection for this work family God had given her . . . *especially* Sean O'Connor. Somehow the man had single-handedly infused more life and excitement into Dennehy's than she'd seen in ten years. She sighed. *Thank you, Charity.*

"Well, it sounds like it may be James, then, doesn't it?" Emma handed her purse to Sean, then plucked her coat off the rack to slip it on with his help. "Do you like him, Alli?"

With a shy nod, Alli toyed with the tip of her brown bob, the soft glow in her eyes making her seem almost beautiful. "But I can't imagine why he'd ever be interested in me."

"Okay, Alli, knock it off," Sean said with a hike of his brow. "You're as cute as a bug's ear and everybody knows it." His smile tipped. "Why, I have to wrestle myself most nights just to keep from taking you home in my pocket."

"Sean!"

The blush was back full force, and Sean laughed. "Sorry, but it's true. You're just flat-out adorable. That heart-stopping smile of yours, your gentle nature, your pure heart—all of it.

James is a very smart man." He reached for his coat. "Has he made a move yet?"

Alli blinked. "A move?"

"You know, flirted," Sean said. "Compliments, small talk, presents—a *move*."

Emma snatched her purse. "And how, exactly, would *you* know about moves?"

"Hearsay," he said with a grin, then honed in on Alli. "So, has he?"

Alli gave it some thought. "He did buy me a Coca-Cola from the vending machine several times, and then joined me that one warm day last week when I ate my lunch in the park."

"Sounds like a move to me," Sean said with a grin. "What do you think, Mrs. Malloy?"

"Mmm . . . could be," Emma said with a secret smile.

Alli chewed on the nail of her thumb. "But how will I know if he makes a move?" She glanced up, a bit of the imp slipping into her smile. "And if he doesn't, how do I get him to?"

"Humph . . . sounds like a job for Mrs. Dennehy," Bert said with a wry smile.

"Now, there's a thought . . . ," Emma said, finger to chin.

"Oh, no you don't." Sean cupped Emma's elbow on the way to the door. "You two are not going to sic my sister on this sweet, innocent girl. Come on, Mrs. Malloy, I'm anxious to try this restaurant you're always bragging about. I'm starved."

Emma halted at the door. "Bert, if the Brooks Brothers rep calls, will you tell him I'll call him back? And Alli, would you mind pulling the numbers from the Brooks Brothers promotion last month?" She slipped the strap to her clutch over her shoulder. "Either of you want anything? A coffee, bagel . . . Mario's homemade cannoli?"

A slow smile eased across Bert's scarlet lips. "Yeah, Mario . . . on a bun."

"I thought you weren't interested in men," Sean said with a crooked grin.

"I can look, you know—I'm not dead, after all." She reached

for a stack of Emma's handwritten letters piled in her in-basket. "But just for the record . . . I'm *not* the one he ogles."

Ignoring Bert's remark, Emma dragged Sean through the door. "We'll be back by one."

"What's that supposed to mean, she's not the one he ogles?" Sean asked, wrestling into his coat as they descended the stairs. "Does this Mario character ogle you or something?"

She gave him a sideways glance, surprised at the edge in his tone as they dodged clusters of customers on their way to the front doors. "For your information, Sean O'Connor, Mario Gattucio is a sweet, older gentleman still grieving his dead wife, of whom," she said with emphasis, "I apparently remind him. He's as harmless as dear Mr. Wilkins, I assure you."

Sean held the glass door open, one brow jagged high. "Yeah? Well, for your information, Mr. Wilkins doesn't ogle—he's pushing sixty and near blind."

Shaking her head with a smile, she slipped past him onto the busy sidewalk, wrapping her unbuttoned coat tightly around her. Palm pressed firmly to the small of her back, Sean steered her through the lunch-hour traffic where three-piece suits, pink-cheeked women in woolen coats, and various uniforms bustled about, intent upon food, fortune, or the next delivery to be made. The shrill sound of traffic-cop whistles and the blare of horns could be heard while the aroma of fried fish and vendor hot dogs competed with the briny smell of the sea and bus fumes.

Emma started to speak when something caught her eye over Sean's shoulder. With a hand to his arm, she halted him while people streamed past. "Casey? Casey!"

A distinctive purple cloche turned, revealing wide eyes in a porcelain face. "Emma?"

Tugging Sean along, Emma wove her way to where her young neighbor stood pressed against a store window, hand to her chest.

Emma squeezed the girl in a tight hug. "Goodness, I've missed you—haven't seen you all week!" She pulled away, and the smile faded at the sight of a nasty bump above Casey's brow. "Good heavens, what happened?"

The color waned in Casey's face, making the purplish bruise more apparent. "I slipped in the bathroom and hit the tub." Her smile seemed forced. "Mama always said I was a klutz."

With gentle fingers, Emma touched a hand to Casey's brow. "When did this happen?"

"A few days ago. You know what a slob I can be, Emma, so when I washed some clothes in the bathroom, I got water all over and—*boom!* Found myself on the floor, cheek to the tub."

"Honey, why didn't you knock on my door?" Emma said, stroking Casey's hair.

"I get tired of bothering you for every little thing. Besides, it's not a big deal, really."

Releasing a heavy sigh, Emma braced Casey's shoulders. "Next time something like this happens, I will be irate if you don't come and get me, understood?"

Casey nodded.

"Good girl." Emma hooked an arm around her shoulder and gave her a squeeze, peering up at Sean with a proud smile. "Sean, this is my neighbor and dear friend, Casey Herringshaw. Casey, this is Sean O'Connor, my assistant manager."

A genuine smile bloomed on Casey's face. "So you're the infamous Sean O'Connor!"

Sean shook her hand with a grin, one brow cocked as he shot Emma a sideways glance. "Infamous? What horror stories are you spinning about me, Mrs. Malloy?"

"Oh, nothing more than your dangerous notoriety with women at the store—Mrs. Bennett, Michelle Tuller . . ." Her lips curved into a smile. "*Rose* . . ."

"I know everybody thinks this woman is a saint, but don't believe everything she says." Sean tugged on one of Emma's curls. "Any notoriety I have is because she tends to be bossy."

"I am not!" Emma swatted at him.

"I ask you, Casey—did she or did she not just use a threatening tone with you?"

Casey giggled and nodded.

"I rest my case." He glanced at his watch. "Bossy. Which means she'll make me bolt down my food if we don't get a move on."

Emma gave Casey a final hug and pulled away, one finger raised in warning. "I want you to come to dinner tonight, no argument, understood? Seven o'clock. We need to catch up."

"See?" Sean rolled his eyes. "Bossy," he mouthed to Casey, making her laugh.

"I will, I promise. Nice to meet you, Sean."

"Seems like a nice kid," Sean said after Casey departed, hand loosely latched to the nape of Emma's neck as he guided her through the crowd.

"She is, but I can't help but worry. I talked her mother into letting her stay in Boston, but sometimes I wonder if that was a mistake. She's so young and vulnerable."

"We're all young and vulnerable at first, Emma, and then life forces us to grow up."

"I suppose . . ."

By the time they reached Mario's glass-front deli two blocks down, Emma was laughing again, her concern over Casey forgotten as Sean entertained her with the details of his encounter with Mrs. Bennett that morning. Grinning, he opened the glass-paned door emblazoned with the colors of the Italian flag to unleash the mouthwatering aroma of Sicilian meatballs simmering in Mario's special sauce. Her senses were met with pleasure at every turn—smells, sights, sounds that somehow eased the aches in her shoulders and the tightness between her eyes. Red-and-white-checked tables and booths crowded with chattering patrons, and the buzz and hum of the lunch crowd warmed her inside as much as the fire in the cozy brick oven where Mario baked meat pies. She breathed in deeply, closing her eyes to savor the smell of garlic, oregano, and spices for which Mario was famous, wondering why she had stayed away so long.

"Ah . . . Emma Malloy—my day is complete!"

Her eyes flipped open to see an apron-clad Mario hurrying

280

around the counter to greet her, pleasure written across his face as if he had just sampled a meatball. He made a scolding sound with his tongue. "Why do you torture me with your absence?"

Sean gripped her arm and bent low to her ear. "Harmless, eh?"

Emma smiled and extended her palm, suddenly viewing the man now kissing her hand through Sean's skeptical eyes. As a full-blood Sicilian, Mario was certainly a credit to his nationality. Tall of stature with wavy dark hair that gleamed silver at the temples, his olive skin was already shadowed with a swarthy growth of afternoon beard. Eyes as rich and warm as his famous melted dark chocolate cake, he scanned her head to foot, so innocently that she'd never noticed before. But now, for the very first time, she was painfully aware of the approval in his dark eyes, now lidded and warm. He pulled her close in an affectionate embrace as always, and the aroma of oregano caused her stomach to growl. He kissed her on both cheeks and stepped away, hands grasped tightly to hers.

"Em-ma, Em-ma," he bellowed, as if savoring a decadent piece of tiramisu, "you are cruel to stay away when your smile brings me so much joy."

She'd been to Mario's dozens of times over the course of the year, and his overt affection never bothered her before. But now, with Sean by her side, she could feel the heat rising in her cheeks as she stared, eyes wide at the warmth of Mario's greeting. She swallowed hard to clear the shock from her throat and took a step back. *Heaven, help me . . . could Bert's teasing be true?* Did Mario actually see her as more than a customer? The notion was so foreign to her senses that she had never even entertained it, but there was no denying it now as the man scooped a brawny arm to her waist and swept her away to a booth by the window. Helping her off with her coat, he seated her with the utmost care and then snapped his fingers in the air. "Guiseppe, *acqua*!"

Mario bowed and took her hand once again. "Whatever you want, Miss Malloy, it will be my pleasure to provide—on the house, of course. Just give Guiseppe your order for both you and your friend." He winked, sending another flash of heat into her cheeks. "You see? I have not forgotten my promise to buy you lunch." He kissed her hand once again, the warmth in his eyes contrasting sharply with the coolness in Sean's. "Although I'd much prefer to buy you dinner . . ." Squeezing her fingers, he left her to Guiseppe, who delivered two glasses of water. He handed them both a menu and then departed to give them a moment to decide.

Sean leaned forward, elbows flat on the table and brows slanted high. "You can't be serious—*harmless*? That guy was drooling so much, he could be related to Pavlov."

Emma gulped and picked up her menu, desperate to avoid Sean's probing eyes. "I honestly don't know what's gotten into him. He never acts like thi—" She stopped, her fingers clammy against the cardboard menu while her pulse slowed to a crawl. The air hitched in her throat as she suddenly saw through Sean's eyes what she'd been too blind to see through her own—this man was attracted to her! *Her* . . . Emma Malloy . . . the "monster" Rory had deemed too scarred to be loved. At the thought, heat scorched her cheeks and the menu slipped from her hands. She covered her eyes, the embarrassment of such a possibility too painful to ponder. "He . . . he just feels sorry for me, I'm certain." *Nothing more than kindness to a disfigured woman—*

"Stop it, Emma—now!" Sean's voice held an edge she'd seldom heard. He gripped her hand in his. "I don't want to hear any talk of pity or any of those types of lies you believe in your head." He shot a hard glance at the counter where Mario was keeping a close eye, then returned his gaze to hers. His tone softened. "Emma, when are you going to see yourself for who you are? Yes, you have scars from your past, but not for a moment do they detract from your beauty." The press of his fingers, the gentle look in his eyes seemed to bond her to the seat of the booth. "At least not for me," he said quietly. He nodded toward the counter, lips clamped tight. "And apparently not for Romeo, either."

She tugged free from his grip, fingers trembling as she placed them on the menu, eyes fixed on her hands. "I never dreamed he thought of me in any way other than a friend. I just assumed he was an overly affectionate man, hugging me, hugging Bert. He said I reminded him of his wife, so naturally I was kind to him." She shivered. "This is . . . such a shock."

"For pity's sake, doesn't he know what that ring on your finger means?"

Heat broiled her cheeks as she twisted the ring and looked away, afraid that Sean would see the shame and guilt in her eyes. *Apparently not. But then it didn't mean what I thought either.* Fingering the menu, she glanced up, relieved to see Guiseppe making his way to their booth. "Of course, although I wouldn't put it past Bert to tell him I'm a widow— she tells that to everybody."

Guiseppe arrived with pad in hand, and the knot in her stomach began to unravel.

"Oh, good—I'm starved."

Once the waiter had taken his leave, she forced a bright smile and perked up her tone, determined to steer the conversation in another direction. "So . . . what's it been now . . . four dates, going on five? Sounds as if Miss Kelly may be on her way to taming the bachelor in you yet."

Sean scowled and downed half his water in one nervous tilt. "Five, going on six, and this is why I've avoided women all of my life, Emma. They seep into your system like alcohol, skewing the way that you feel, think . . . changing you." He gulped another swig of water and put the glass back down with a clunk, grinding his jaw. "Just like this guy I used to work with at Kelly's who was an alcoholic—the poor man did everything in his power to quit, but the alcohol had a hold on him that wouldn't let go." He gouged a hand through his hair. "Like Rose."

She took a sip of water, then cupped the glass in her hands, thumbs grazing its sides as she studied him through teasing eyes. "So you're a Rose-aholic now, are you?"

He exhaled again and sagged back against the booth,

peering at her with a sheepish smile. "I guess, because I sure can't seem to say no. What is it with women, anyway, Emma? How do they manage to get under our skin? It seems like the more I—" he paused, eyelids heavy as color stole up his neck—"*see* her, the more I *need* to see her."

"That's just how it is when people fall in love," Emma said with a half smile, unsettled by a sudden stab of jealousy. She took another drink. *God, please—help me to be happy for him.*

He grunted. "Nobody's falling in love here, Emma, trust me. Unless it's Rose."

Relief flooded, followed by guilt. She frowned. "Well, you must care for her, don't you?"

"Of course, but I'm not ready for anything more, and that's the problem—Rose is."

"Do you . . . think you could love her? I mean, eventually?" She held her breath, achingly aware of just how much this could change the closeness they shared.

He studied her, forehead wrinkled as if the question were giving him a headache.

"Ah . . . here we are—ravioli for the lady, and a spicy meatball sandwich for the gentleman." Guiseppe set both of their plates down with a flourish, and the heavenly aroma watered Emma's mouth. He clicked his heels. "Will there be anything else?"

"Not for me, Guiseppe, thank you," Emma said with a polite smile, positioning her napkin. She glanced up at Sean. "You?"

"No thanks, this looks wonderful." Sean slapped his own napkin across his lap before taking a bite of the sandwich with a low moan. He quickly chewed and swallowed, washing it down with a drink of water. "Sweet saints, this is one of the best things I've ever eaten! Too bad you're already married, Mrs. Malloy, because this guy sure can cook."

Another sling of shame heated her cheeks as she quickly picked up her fork. She stabbed a fat ravioli while regret did the same to her, and nibbling on the edge, she studied Sean from across the table, hoping to deflect her thoughts. "So . . . you never did answer my question."

He looked up and swiped sauce from his mouth with the tip of his tongue. "What?"

She took a deep breath and suddenly the ravioli wasn't as good as she remembered . . . but then, maybe the question soured the taste. "Do you think you could love her? Rose, that is? In time?"

His blue eyes were pensive as he chewed, watching her as the idea apparently rolled around in his head. He swallowed his food, took a quick drink, then released a quiet sigh, one hand splayed to the table. He hesitated. "Maybe."

Her heart dipped, but she countered it with a bright smile before reaching to cover his hand with her own. "Sean, that would be wonderful!" she said, her heart clearly not as euphoric as her tone. "Because if ever God intended a man to be a husband and father, it's you."

His gaze settled on her hand as it straddled his before slowly rising to meet her eyes, causing her stomach to swoop. "Not all of us are meant to marry, Emma," he whispered, the intensity of his look racing her heart. "You should know that."

Yes, I do . . . Cheeks burning, she awkwardly slipped her hand from his, well aware of the truth of his statement. She hadn't been meant to marry, certainly, but somehow she suspected it wasn't the same for him. She studied him now, this man with a heart more tender and caring than any she knew, and prayed he would never have to be alone. Poking at another ravioli, she vowed to do everything in her power to make it so. "Yes, I agree, not all of us are meant to marry, Sean." She took another bite and chewed slowly before swallowing her food, eyeing him while she sipped at her water. "But I happen to think you are."

"And why is that, Mrs. Malloy?" he asked, a slow grin chasing all solemnity away.

"Because you fight it too hard," she said, a twinkle warming her gaze. "That's a dead giveaway. You see, you're a man blessed with an abundance of love—" she patted her mouth with her napkin, unable to obscure a smile—"matched only by his fear to avoid it."

"Maybe it's just intelligence—ever think about that?"

"Or obstinance," Emma said with a hike of her jaw.

He laughed and pushed his empty plate away. "Well, I'll admit I'm attracted to Rose, but I'm not sure that's enough for a lifetime of bliss."

"Well, as Charity would say, 'it's a start.'"

He paused, scrutinizing her through lidded eyes. "And what would Emma say?"

She blinked, the subject as uncomfortable as Mario's unwanted attention. She coughed into her napkin. "Well, I'm hardly the one to ask."

"On the contrary," he said with renewed interest, "you're the perfect one to ask—a woman who's experienced the worst in a marriage." His gaze softened. "So, tell me, Mrs. Malloy, if you could start all over again—would attraction be enough?"

Her eyelids weighted closed as she remembered the desire in Rory's eyes before she'd said yes, the tingle of his touch before they'd become one. "No," she whispered, ". . . never."

"What, then?" he asked, curiosity lacing his tone.

Her eyelids lifted, and she stared into the blue of his eyes, eyes that were open and honest and true, a constant caress to those he loved. Tender eyes that offered a glimpse into the soul of a tender man—one who elicited trust, respect, and love. A smile lighted upon her lips. "Someone like you, Sean O'Connor, who puts others before himself."

His smile faded. "Don't canonize me just yet, Emma, especially when it comes to Rose." He exhaled loudly and pinched the bridge of his nose. "I'm not exactly a knight in shining armor who puts her needs before mine, you know."

"I don't believe that—I know you."

He glanced up, the blue of his eyes suddenly dark with challenge. "You know me with you, Emma, not with Rose. Which is what scares me. You have this unique talent of bringing out the best in people. I've seen it with everyone you touch—Charity, Katie, Bert, Alli, even Casey from what I saw today. So when I'm with you, I . . . ," his jaw shifted while a muscle twitched in his cheek, "I like who I am. I'm decent and hardworking, a man you can trust."

"Because that's who you are!"

"No!" His voice was sharp. "Not with Rose. Never with Rose." He looked away, head bent. "She loves me, Emma . . . and I . . ." He drew in a deep breath. "Well, I take advantage of that."

Her breathing slowed. "What do you mean, you take advantage of that? Just because she wants to get serious and you don't is no reason to think—"

His head jerked up. "Yes . . . it is. Because I know better." He exhaled a breath that seemed to drain the usual life from his eyes. A knot jerked in his throat as he averted his gaze. "I'm not proud of myself because I feel like I'm . . . leading her on." His fist suddenly slammed on the table, causing her to jolt. "But blast it all, Emma, the woman makes it so blamed easy! Which I resent because I'm a decent man . . . or I used to be. Which is why I never wanted to get involved in the first place—I knew this would happen." He put a hand to his eyes, voice trailing off into a pained whisper. "So help me, Emma, it's so hard to say no. To do the right thing. To keep a clear head." He released a sigh fraught with frustration, then looked up, a lock of sandy hair tumbling over his forehead. The half smile on his lips was at odds with the regret in his face. "So much so I'm almost willing to consider marriage to ward off the guilt."

The impact of his meaning struck, warming her cheeks and stabbing her chest. She swallowed hard. "Then maybe you should."

Sharp furrows bit into his brow. "Consider marriage?"

She nodded, feeling the pound of her pulse in her ears. "You like her, you have fun with her, and something tells me that underneath all that fear of marriage, you also care for her."

"I do, but—"

She leaned in, fervor burning in her eyes. "Then pray about it, Sean, and see where your heart goes—*please*. Because sometimes fear can deter us from happiness meant to be."

"But—"

She gripped his hand, her desire for this man's happiness as intense as the chaotic thudding of her heart. "Listen to me—you're a man with a conscience whose needs have been awakened by a woman who loves him. Don't let the pain of your past rob you of your future." Drawing in a harsh breath, she slowly released it again, desperate to secure God's best for this friend that she loved. She forced a smile. "Besides, haven't you heard 'it's not good for man to be alone'?"

He paused too long. "You are," he whispered, his quiet tone pricking her eyes.

She nodded, her smile melancholy as she patted his arm. "Well, we're not talking about me, now are we? Please— promise me you'll pray long and hard about Rose."

The muscles in his face relaxed, as if her touch had somehow left him with peace. He cradled his palm over hers, and his smile warmed her as much as the heat of his hand. "I will, Emma, I promise." His smile veered to the side. "Heaven knows I could use some divine intervention right about now. Rose is too attractive for her own good—and mine."

She withdrew her hand. "That would be wise. She's a beautiful woman."

The humor in his eyes melted into affection. "So are you, Emma, inside and out."

No. His words were meant in kindness, she knew, but they only lanced her heart. She'd once been adept at accepting compliments for her beauty, but that talent had long since come and gone. Her eyelids weighted closed and she absently touched a hand to her cheek. No, hers was a scarred face and a scarred soul, where the only beauty to be found was in her obedience to a vow she'd sworn to keep.

She jolted at his touch on the hand she now held to her face, her eyes opening wide.

"They still bother you, don't they?" he whispered. His voice was gentle as he caressed, both her hand and the scars beneath, before slowly pulling away.

Her breath caught in her throat as shame seared her cheeks

as thoroughly as hot grease had once seared her face. Hands shaking, she clasped them in her lap, eyes fixed on the knot of tangled fingers. Bother her? Her scars? Her vision honed in on the ring on her left hand, and she knew he would never understand that both her scars and the ring on her finger were just punishment for a woman who'd more than earned it.

Pushing a strand of hair from her face, she looked up, her piercing gaze begging him to understand a secret she could never share. "Bother me?" Her smile was sad. "No, not anymore," she said, hoping to alleviate the concern she read in his eyes. "'Beauty is in the eye of the beholder,' as they say. So, unlucky to most, I suppose, my scars have taught me that true beauty comes when we see ourselves through the eyes of *him* whose image we bear." Reaching for her purse, she scooted to the edge of the seat, then rose, her chin edging up with the strength of her convictions. "So no matter my scars or failings, inside or out," her lips trembled into a smile, "—and God knows they are many—he is the lover of my soul, and to him, I will always be beautiful."

Their gazes bonded as he rose, and the tender look in his eyes warmed her more than the woolen coat he now slipped over her shoulders.

"Well, then," he said with a firm hand braced to the small of her back. "It appears that for once, God and I are in sound agreement." His fingers rose to playfully tweak the nape of her neck as he guided her to the register. "Because you're not just beautiful to God, Emma Malloy," he said with a wink that sent a blush to her cheeks. "But to me and Mario as well."

Mitch scanned the list of donors and emitted a deep growl that rivaled the rumbling in his stomach. At least ten high-rolling donors from last year had failed to respond, which meant more blasted phone calls he didn't have time for. His fingers made another pass through his already tousled hair to rub at the back of his neck, easing muscles that were as tight as the clamp of his jaw. He glanced at his watch and groaned, noting that Marjorie was late—*again*—then exhaled his frustration and returned to his notes.

He bent over the conference-room table and focused hard, unwilling to allow the woman to unnerve him. A little over two months—that's all he had left—of her seductive ways, her provocative dress, her not-so-subtle suggestions that were wearing him thin. Not to mention what it was doing to his marriage. Thursdays were sheer torture—from the tension in Charity's manner in the morning, to the stiffness of her body when he came home at night. And to make matters worse, he'd forgotten the sandwich she'd packed for his dinner, causing his stomach to churn along with his mood. Heaven help him, he was literally starving—for food, for Charity, and for this fiasco to be over. He pressed a hand to his eyes and wished he were home, where the touch of his wife always soothed him, calmed him. The taste of her lips—warm, soft, inviting . . .

The press of someone's mouth—also warm, soft, and inviting—suddenly grazed the back of his neck, and he jerked up in the chair and spun around. "What the devil are you doing?" he rasped, staring at Marjorie as if she were the devil himself.

Her face was a mask of innocence. "Just making sure you're awake, Mr. Dennehy. It quite appeared as if you'd fallen asleep."

He scoured the back of his neck with his handkerchief, cheeks burning with fury. "I thought I told you to keep your hands off me."

"You distinctly said 'hands,' not lips." She pushed his chair out of her way and moved in close, trailing a finger down his arm. "Or fingers, for that matter."

He fisted her hand, fury pumping as he raked her with a hard gaze—from her shadowed eyes and scarlet lips to the satin blouse that draped a suggestive swell of breasts. "Then let me be perfectly clear, Mrs. Hennessey," he said through clenched teeth. "Keep your hands, your lips, your fingers, *and* your body to yourself—I couldn't be less interested."

"Why, Mr. Dennehy, you're blushing! And I do believe your

breathing has accelerated." Gripping his waist, she molded herself close. "Methinks the gentleman doth protest too much."

He distanced her with two iron fists that gouged into her arms. The scent of her expensive perfume rose to taunt him, exhausting his control. His voice could have bruised if his grip didn't. "Get yourself another boy, Marjorie, this one's going home to his wife." He turned to collect his things.

Heels clicked as she moved to the head of the conference table and smoothly slid into her seat. Her manner cooled as she studied him through narrowed eyes. "Leave now, Mitch, and don't bother coming back."

He rammed his papers into his briefcase and snapped it shut. "Don't worry, I won't." He stormed for the door.

"I mean *ever*, Mr. Dennehy."

He stopped to give her a withering stare that had no effect. "I'm fired? For refusing your advances? I doubt even you can accomplish that."

She eased back in her chair and slowly crossed her legs, affording him a generous view of her very short skirt. "Try me," she whispered.

"No, thanks, I'll take my chances." He opened the door.

"I own 50 percent of the stock, and I chair the board. Unless you want to cause serious problems for yourself *and* Patrick . . . I suggest you close that door and sit down. *Now*."

A tic vibrated in his cheek and he ground his jaw hard, teetering on the edge of slamming the door in her face. He wheeled around and strode to the table, flinging his briefcase down with a sharp slap of leather. He turned and barreled for the exit.

"Where are you going?" she demanded, her manner as impervious as a queen.

"To the men's room," he said with a heave of the door, suddenly feeling dirty. "May take awhile, Mrs. Hennessey, so why don't you just start without me. I have a sudden urge to scrub my hands raw." Mitch slammed the door with a deafening bang, rattling both the wall and the door, not to mention his nerves.

And it wasn't nearly hard enough.

"I am *not* going to dance." In a rare show of the mule, Sean's jaw hardened as he peered up at Emma in the doorway of his office. He jerked the Snickers candy bar from his shirt pocket, unwrapped the paper, and bit down hard, the taste of his favorite candy powerless to chase the sour taste from his mouth.

Emma appeared rooted in place, arms folded to her waist as if to protect herself from his wrath. With the slightest lift of her chin, she gave him the same tight-lipped look Bert always did whenever he pilfered the last lemon drop from the crystal dish on her desk. "It's a wedding, Sean, you have to dance—it's an unwritten rule."

He shot up, muscles twitching beneath tightly rolled sleeves as he stood, palms and candy bar propped hard to his wooden desk. A silent growl vibrated in his throat, giving his voice the same grinding tension he'd noticed in Mitch when Charity pushed too far. "So-un-write-it, Em-ma," he said in a clipped tone as foreign to him as the notion of dancing. "Rose is lucky I'm going at all as much as I hate weddings. Heaven knows the garter will find me, even in the restroom, so the woman needs to count her blessings and let it go."

The steely look in Emma's eyes softened, which meant she was obviously rethinking her approach. Two little puckers formed above her nose as she slowly entered his office, and her brows sloped up in that sad-eyed stare that always signaled his doom. Because unlike Charity who often employed the same little-girl-lost technique with Mitch, this was pure, unadulterated Emma Malloy, heart bleeding over someone else's misfortune.

Sean blew out a heavy breath and put a hand to his eyes. "Please don't look at me like that, Emma, you know I can't handle it."

She moved to his side, her light touch trapping a groan in his throat. Her voice was the whisper of an angel—gentle and caring and wringing the starch from his conscience. "That's because you hate it as much as I do when you disappoint someone, Sean," she said quietly, "and you've already told me how much it would mean to Rose if you danced."

He didn't answer, hoping she'd go away.

"Please?" She ducked to smile into his eyes, and his groan escaped into a full-fledged growl. She chewed on her lip, apparently in an effort to bite back a grin. "I can teach you the fox trot and the lindy hop right in my office," she said softly, "which would help a lot in getting you through the night." Without waiting for his answer, she carefully disarmed him of his candy bar and tucked it back into his shirt pocket before tugging his hand. "Come on, you big baby, just thirty minutes. That's all I need to make Rose the happiest woman alive. Please?"

He huffed out a sigh as she dragged him toward the door, lips leveled in a tight line. "No, it'd take a rock the size on Charity's finger to make Rose the happiest woman alive." Jerking free, he strode into Emma's office ahead of her, turning with hands locked on his hips and a scowl on his face. "What? Is she paying you or something, for you to badger me like this? Well, I'll tell you what—you're lucky everybody's gone, or I wouldn't be doing this."

"I know," she said meekly, the twinkle in her eyes belying her solemn manner. "But if you could have seen the look on Rose's face when she said how she wished you could dance . . ."

"I've seen it," he said in a terse tone, "and apparently it had a greater effect on you than it did on me." He huffed out a sigh. "Close the door, Emma," he ordered, rather enjoying making her pay for forcing his hand. She had way too much influence on him as it was and sometimes it ruffled his Irish. He folded his arms and perched on the edge of her desk, experiencing a sudden twinge of sympathy for both Mitch and Luke in dealing with women like his sisters—strong-willed, stubborn, and bent on getting their way. Emma Malloy certainly hadn't fit into that category until recently, he thought. His lips slanted. Until he'd started dating Rose.

With barely the sound of a click, she closed the door and

turned, hands tight on the knob while she stared at him with those soft, gray eyes that always reminded him of a deer about to bolt.

His jaw set. To the devil with the deer—*he* wanted to bolt, but the shy, hopeful look in her eyes had him by the throat, a talent that Emma Malloy seemed to master without even trying.

He blew out his frustration on a wave of noisy air. "You've got thirty minutes, Malloy, but I'm gonna warn you right now—Fred Astaire I'm not."

Her lips curved into that innocent way that always melted his heart, and he found himself relenting—*as usual*—with a reluctant smile. He lumbered to his feet with a groan. "Okay, Ginger, let's put your foot where your mouth is."

"I promise this will be fun," she said in a rush, hurrying to the cherrywood buffet against the wall where an RCA Victor phonograph stood ready and waiting. His mouth went flat. Further evidence of her plot to goad him into making Rose happy.

He shook his head and watched her while she bent over the phonograph, his gaze traveling the length of her before he realized what he was doing. Heat ringed his collar and his pulse notched up a degree when he suddenly realized Emma Malloy had a beautiful body. How had he never noticed before—those long, willowy legs that slid up to gentle hips and a small waist? Fire scorched his cheeks as he admired generous breasts all the more obvious in a new pale yellow sweater that brought out a touch of green in her eyes. He cleared his throat and looked away while she carefully lifted the needle into place with a scratchy sound before it glided into the record's groove. The mellow sounds of Duke Ellington's "Three Little Words" suddenly floated through the air, and oddly enough, his muscles began to relax. He closed his eyes to enjoy the magic of one of his favorite songs, by an artist Emma *knew* he loved.

"I know what you're doing, I see it all too clear . . ."

He inhaled deeply, and all of his resistance fled, because

he knew exactly what Emma was doing and why. Her mission in life seemed to be to make those she loved happy, and for whatever reason, Emma desperately wanted to see him happy, to make a go of it with Rose, to walk down that aisle into a life she believed would bring him much joy. The air in his lungs released in a slow, tranquil sigh at the gift of Emma in his life. He had never felt this close to a friend, much less a woman, and he marveled at the fact that when he was with her, contentment seemed to purl through his body as languidly as the Duke's music now oozed through his mind.

His eyelids opened, and there she stood, arms outstretched and an impish grin on her face.

"I knew the Duke would work his magic," she said, taking his left hand in hers and clasping it at eye level. "Which I must admit, has me feeling a wee bit like Charity." Absently nibbling her lip, she placed his right hand on her shoulder blade and rested her arm on his. "Now relax, because you'll find the fox trot to be a smooth, easy dance very similar to the waltz."

His mouth angled up. "Oh, that helps a lot, since I know how to waltz too."

She lifted her chin, apparently striving to be professional, but the twitch of her lips gave her dead away. "First, left foot forward, one-two, then right foot forward, three-four . . ."

Without a word, he followed her effortlessly, as if he had Astaire blood in his veins. It should have felt strange, holding her this way, but somehow it didn't and Sean wondered why. Maybe because he was from an affectionate family that hugged all the time, he reasoned, so naturally closeness and hugs had already become a part of their friendship.

"Left foot to the side, five-six . . . ," she said, gaze intent on their feet.

Their proximity allowed him to study her close up . . . the way one side of her mouth tilted when she scraped her teeth against her lip, like now, indicating she was focusing hard on the lesson. For the first time he noticed an almost invisible sprinkling of tiny freckles across her nose, subtle and shy like Emma herself. He caught a faint whiff of the perfume Charity had given her—Shalimar—with its hint of lemon and vanilla, and he breathed it in, the scent teasing his senses with the same innocence and beauty of the woman he held in his arms.

"Then left foot forward, one-two . . ." She glanced up with a smile. "Good . . . good, you've got it, now. Then turn your right foot one-quarter angle, three-four . . ."

He wasn't surprised that he picked it up quickly—athletics had always come easily for him, and apparently dancing was no different, but to say he was shocked he enjoyed it was an understatement. The music seemed to flow in his limbs and in no time, he was whirling her in his arms, hand firm against her back as he drew her close with confident ease. He gave her a crooked smile. "Look out, Fred Astaire!"

A breathless giggle escaped her lips as the music stopped, and she put a hand to her chest. "Goodness, you're a natural, although I should have expected that with your affinity for sports." She dashed back to the phonograph to reset the needle, shooting a grin over her shoulder. "Once more, and you'll be giving me lessons, I promise. And then it's the lindy, and your life will be complete." She returned, clasping his hand.

Maybe it was the door being closed . . . or Emma near breathless . . . or even the velvet voice of the Duke that created an intimacy he found he rather enjoyed. He smiled, his voice husky with affection. "So, Mrs. Malloy, tell me how you've become so light on your feet—have you been frequenting the dance marathons at Revere Beach?"

The pink of her cheeks deepened as she cocked a brow. "Why, yes, Mr. O'Connor, I find it a great release for the little energy I have left after twelve-hour days, six days a week."

He laughed and tightened his hold for a spin. "Then it's a wonder we haven't bumped into each other, because heaven knows that's how I spend my free time."

Her eyes warmed with approval. "This will make Rose very happy," she whispered.

His chest expanded as he studied her with a wry smile,

reveling in her praise. "I know, but isn't it about time you start thinking about *my* happiness? Dancing and marriage—two things that give me indigestion, and yet you seem intent on prodding me into both."

It was her turn to laugh, the gray of her eyes sparkling like polished silver. "I *am* thinking of your happiness, bound and determined that your fears will not keep you from all God has."

The music stopped, but he retained his hold, assessing her through pensive eyes. He nudged a finger to her chin and smiled. "So that's how you spend your free time, then—as a guardian angel to the people you love?" His thumb grazed the curve of her jaw, marveling at its silky touch. "Tell me, Mrs. Malloy, just how did I rate you as a friend?"

"Why, as a favor to Charity, of course," she said with a wink, the action so uncharacteristic that it made him laugh outright. "She asked me to keep an eye out for her big brother, because . . . well, apparently he has a few flaws . . ."

"Flaws?" He released her and crossed his arms, eyes in a squint. "Such as?"

She scrunched her nose. "Well, she says you're a late bloomer for one."

"Late bloomer," he repeated, head cocked. "And what exactly does *that* mean?"

She peeked up, lips curved in a tease. "Oh, you know, a mature man on the outside, but inside, nothing more than a little boy who refuses to grow up and fall in love." She worked her lip as if to suppress a grin. "Which, Charity claims, is simply because you're a little . . . ," there was no mistaking the sass in her eyes now, ". . . dense."

His jaw dropped, along with his arms. "I'll show you dense," he said with a tickle, the plane of his hand to the side of her neck causing her to squeal and tuck in a knee-jerk reaction.

"I didn't mean it, I promise," she shrieked with a giggle, twisting to escape.

Laughing, he pinned her arms to her sides, eyes narrowed in a mock glare. "Say it, Emma—'Sean O'Connor is not dense, he's one of the most brilliant men I know.'"

Cheeks flushed with fun, she masked her humor with a serious sweep of lashes followed by a show of humility that softened the gray of her eyes. "Sean O'Connor is not dense," she repeated slowly. "He's one of the most . . . ," she gave him an innocent blink, ". . . brilliant men I know."

A grin broke free as she plucked the half-eaten Snickers out of his pocket and lurched away. "I mean little boys!" she shouted, her giggles bouncing off the walls as she skittered for protection on the other side of the room. She faced him at the window, chest heaving and palms braced on the ledge, the candy bar smashed in her hand. Behind her, a tangerine moon rose ripe in a starry sky, its hazy glow encircling her like a halo despite the mischief in her eyes.

The thrill of the hunt broadened his grin as he took his time, his gait slow and easy while he rounded her desk, gaze hungry and locked with hers. "Give it back, Mrs. Malloy," he whispered, feeling the adrenaline of horseplay that pumped in his veins.

"No!" she cried, more giggles bubbling over. She jerked her chair to block his way, then eased around the desk, waving the Snickers like a taunt, her impish smile reminding him of Gabe. "Not until you learn the lindy *and* promise to leave the candy at home when you go to this wedding. You may be a late bloomer, but at least you won't smell like a little boy."

That did it. Slamming the chair in, he lunged, surprising her with a firm clasp of her arm. He dove for the Snickers, but she fought him with shrieks of wild laughter, the candy bar clutched tightly behind her back. He reeled her in and grinned, challenge coursing his veins as he gripped her to his chest.

"Give it up, Emma," he breathed, "you won't win."

Locking her with one arm, his other circled her waist while his hand wrestled with hers to recapture the candy.

Her body stilled . . . and in a catch of his breath, everything changed. One moment she was laughing, and in the next, her laughter faded away, leaving her lips parted with shallow breaths while gentle eyes slowly spanned wide. The effect totally disarmed him, causing his heart to thud to a stop. Silence pounded in his ears as he became aware of her body pressed to his, her warmth, her scent engaging his pulse to a degree that jolted him. He swallowed hard, feeling the rise and fall of her chest, the burn of her hand embedded in his, and a flash of heat traveled his body until it scorched in his cheeks. He flinched away.

"Emma, I'm sorry—I didn't mean to manhandle you." He stepped back and plunged his hands in his pockets, desperate to deflect the embarrassment he felt. His smile was awkward. "Keep the candy then, I have more in my bottom drawer."

God, help me . . . Cheeks aflame, Emma wavered on her feet, mangled candy bar clutched to her chest as it rose and fell with every ragged breath she took. Her body quivered with the same heady feeling she'd felt the night in the car outside Robinson's, only this was far worse. As if she'd just ridden the Cyclone roller coaster at Revere Beach, skin tingling and every muscle reverberating with the danger and excitement of soaring through the air. Except tonight the danger was very real, evident in the flush of her body and the hammering of her heart. Even now, blood coursed from his touch, converging in her face and throbbing in her brain, hands clammy from the desire to be in his arms again, to feel the press of his body warm against hers.

God, forgive me . . .

Hands shaking uncontrollably, her eyes avoided his as she held out the candy. "No, really—it was my fault, and I'm sorry." He didn't take it, and her gaze darted to the clock while her words rushed out, shallow and hoarse. "Goodness, it's late, and we need to go home." She whirled around, candy still in hand, rushing to where the phonograph circled soundlessly like the guilt in her mind.

"Emma . . ." His voice echoed with pain, remorse . . .

No! Please—just leave me alone. She didn't respond, fingers fumbling to turn the machine off. The whirring stopped and she put a hand to her eyes, her pulse finally slowing to a rational pace. *God, help me to face him, please. To get past this and back to what we had.*

Drawing in a deep breath, she turned with a square of her shoulders, determined to put this embarrassment behind. Meeting his gaze, she forced a stiff smile. "Goodness, that was certainly awkward, wasn't it? But . . . we both learned something very valuable today, didn't we?" she said, infusing a lilt into her voice as she marched to his side. She extended the candy bar once again, but this time her eyes held a tease she labored to convey. "You learned to dance the lindy and fox trot . . . and *I* learned not to steal your candy."

She heard his slow exhale before the strained look slowly disappeared from his eyes, and when his lips eased into that familiar smile, she found herself exhaling too.

He took the candy and shoved it in his pocket, his tone taking on its usual playful banter. "I think you learned something else, Mrs. Malloy, that should serve you well in the future."

"And what might that be, Mr. O'Connor," she said, sensing their camaraderie was well on the mend.

He tapped her on the nose. "I may be a late bloomer, but I don't think I need to worry about you ever calling me dense again." Stretching with a groan, he eyed the clock. "You haven't taught me the lindy yet, so what do you say we give it a whirl?"

Her smile faded just a hair. "I don't think so, Sean, it's getting late—" She took a step toward the door and he stilled her with a hand to her arm.

"Please?" he whispered, his eyes strangely serious. A muscle shifted in his throat. "I don't want to go home, Emma, not yet." He released her then and shoved his hands in his pockets, color hazing his cheeks as he gave her a smile that quickened her pulse. "Besides, you said it yourself—I need to learn the lindy for my life to be complete."

She folded her arms to ward off the mix of feelings whirling inside. "I'd say your life is more than com—"

"Emma—" His voice held intensity she'd never heard before. "Please? For Rose?"

Rose.

300

The woman who could save her from herself . . . and Sean.

She drew in a deep breath and exhaled. "All right. One dance, and then we go home."

He glanced at the clock. "No, one dance, and then I take you to dinner. It's the least I can do for keeping you so late."

She tilted her head to study him. "That's not necessary."

"I know, but humor me." He strolled to the phonograph and turned it on, flashing a smile over his shoulder. "Like I humored you." He held up one of the records stacked on the buffet. "Lucky Lindy, I presume?" She nodded, and he set the needle and strode to where she stood, arms raised. "Let's get this lesson over with, Mrs. Malloy, I'm hungry, and I have a dinner to buy."

She shook her head. "That's very nice, but it's late and we're both tired. Besides, teaching you to dance has been fun." A twinkle returned to her eyes. "I enjoy broadening your social horizons."

"Dining out is part of the social landscape you know. And you can teach me which fork to use so I don't embarrass Rose."

She gave him a quirk of a smile. "I'm quite sure that if you ate soup with a fork, Mr. O'Connor, Rose Kelly would still revere you more than the Pope." She took his left hand in her right and then positioned his other against her shoulder blade. "The answer is still no."

"Come on, Emma," he coaxed with a boyish smile, "it's the least you can do. First you shame me into dancing, insult my intelligence, and then steal my candy. And now, since dinner is long over at home, you're forcing me to eat alone as well." Palms clasped in dancing position, he offered a crooked grin. "Please? For me?"

She studied him, swayed by the hopeful look in his eyes and the tease of his smile, and all at once his friendship made her feel safe and whole once again. Just like always, working together, laughing together, sharing lunches and dinners more times than she could count. Just like tonight. No difference at all, she told herself with a press of her lips.

As long as there was Rose.

Releasing a gentle sigh, she gave him a ghost of a smile. "I'll say one thing, Sean O'Connor, you certainly have your sister fooled with that silver tongue of yours, I can tell you that. A late bloomer, indeed." She shook her head. "All right, I'll have dinner with you," she said with a lift of her chin, "but I warn you, I expect fancy footwork prior to." She angled a slim brow. "And I don't mean just with your mouth."

13

"Mama, Henry's smoking Grandpa's pipe again."
Hope burst into Marcy's kitchen in her stock-inged feet and skidded to a stop, blond hair flying and the swinging door swaying behind.

Katie looked up from the trousers she was patching and actually grinned at the frantic look on her niece's face, real-izing more every day what it meant to be a mother. There was a time when she'd spent her Saturdays studying rather than joining her sisters to help their mother sew, but today, for some reason, she found the air in her lungs expanding at the pleasure of it all.

Some reason? Children's shrieks and laughter could be heard from the parlor, a sound that usually set Katie on edge, but not today. For the first time since she'd missed her period over two months ago, she was easing into the reality that her calling was—at least for the present—to raise children instead of awareness for women's rights. All the tears, all the anger, all the hurt over the loss of her dream had ebbed and slowed, and she was finally ready to let it go.

Your will—not mine—be done.

She tugged on her final stitch and broke the thread with

her teeth, hoping with everything in her that Faith's words were true: *His* will . . . the path to our highest pleasure.

"Where's Grandpa?" Charity asked, never missing a beat while mending a pair of corduroy knickers bunched in her lap.

"Asleep with Kit," Hope said, her look indicating that Grandpa was no threat to Henry.

"With all the commotion in there?" Katie glanced at her mother. "Is Father going deaf?"

One side of Marcy's smile curved up. "Not deaf, Katie Rose, just experienced. Seven babies, and the man never heard one of you cry in the middle of the night." Her features softened. "But in his defense, he didn't sleep well last night because of a cold, so it's no wonder he nodded off."

"Sounds like selective hearing to me," Charity said, sucking her finger where the needle had poked her. "Or a male-chromosome thing." She patted Hope's arm. "Tell Henry if he touches Grandpa's pipe again, I'll have Gabe tutor him in math instead of his father."

"Oh, that's good, Mama, he'll hate that!" She gave Charity a quick hug and bolted for the door, halting midswing with a scrunch of her freckled nose. "Wait, how do you put out a pipe?"

Charity shot to her feet. "Sweet saints, it's *lit*?"

Hope nodded, two delicate brows sloped in concern. "You know how much he likes fire."

"Mercy." Charity tossed the knickers on the table and barreled for the door, eyes smoldering as much as Grandpa's pipe, no doubt. "I'll show him fire. *Henry!*"

The door creaked closed, and Katie shot a grin at Faith and Lizzie. "I'll tell you what—if it wasn't for you two, with four sweet girls and one fairly reasonable boy, I'd be real worried."

"Come on, Katie, Kit's a dream and you know it," Lizzie said with a chuckle.

"It's not Kit I'm worried about," Katie responded, fighting the urge to confide in her mother and sisters. "It's the prospect of having another Henry that puts the fear of God in me."

Faith squinted to thread her needle, the tip of her tongue

tucked at the edge of her mouth. She peered up, giving Katie a pesky smile. "Why worry about that now, Sis . . . *unless*—" she wiggled her brows—"our Luke is getting pushy about the size of his family . . ."

Katie drew in a deep breath, lashes lifting to reveal a sheepish look that matched the blush in her cheeks. "I'm afraid that 'our' Luke has done a little bit more than push."

The pinafore Marcy held dropped to her lap. "Katie Rose, you're not saying you're—"

"With child?" Katie's lips squirmed to the right. "It would appear that Luke McGee's infamous luck extends well beyond sports and cards, because yes, I think so."

"Oh, Katie!" Lizzie's smile dimmed after she gave her a hug. "But, wait—are you okay with this?"

I don't know . . . am I? Katie closed her eyes and grazed a gentle palm across her swollen stomach, feeling the familiar nausea bubbling inside. She sighed and opened her eyes, squeezing Lizzie's hand with a peaceful smile born of resignation. "Not at first, Lizzie, but God has helped me to accept what is obviously his—" her smile slanted, "and Luke's—will."

"But are you sure? I mean, have you seen a doctor?" Lizzie asked.

"Doctor? Sweet saints, who's sick now?" Charity sighed. "Besides Henry, that is."

"Katie thinks she's pregnant," Lizzie said, her gaze hesitant.

"Really? Katie, that's great!" Charity sank in her chair, eyes in a squint. "But you're not sure?"

Katie offered a tentative smile. "Well, I haven't seen a doctor yet, but I am late."

"How many periods have you missed?" Marcy asked, the torn pinafore all but forgotten.

Katie sucked in a deep swallow of air and exhaled slowly. "Two."

Marcy leaned forward, her maternal instincts as sharp as the look in her eyes. "Any other symptoms? Tender breasts, nausea, vomiting, fatigue, backaches, headaches, food cravings . . ."

"Mmm . . . now there's incentive for a religious vocation if ever there was . . ." Charity jabbed her needle into the bulky corduroy with a grimace. "That and Henry . . ."

Katie nodded. "All of the above. Not to mention tears and tirades." She grated her lower lip before she slid them a guilty smile. "Luke says it's like living in a minefield."

"Ah, the barbed-wire no-man's-land beyond the trenches . . . yes, Mitch knows it well."

Faith chuckled. "I suspect all fathers-to-be know it well."

"Not Brady," Charity said. "Everybody knows Lizzie's a saint."

A nervous giggle erupted from the "saintly" sister in the bunch. "Uh, you might ask Brady to show you his scar."

All talking and sewing ceased. Four sets of eyes converged on Lizzie, pinking her cheeks.

"His scar?" Faith whispered. Her jaw sagged along with her sisters'.

The blush on Lizzie's face deepened as she nodded. "It happened in my seventh month when I got upset over something—can't even remember what, now. But Brady tried to pacify me with that exasperating calm of his, and I tried to flick him away. Unfortunately, I was threading a needle at the time and I . . . ," she hesitated, gnawing her lip while her color continued to rise, "accidentally gouged him."

"*Gouged* him?" Charity asked, her respect effectively engaged. "As in draw blood?"

Lizzie nodded, her lavender-hued eyes soft with remorse. "He calls it his 'war wound.'" Her lips tilted into an awkward smile. "Claims I gave him shell shock."

Charity's tone was tinged with awe. "Yeah, Mitch has a few of those battle scars too, only I don't think shock was ever a factor."

Faith leaned across the table to grip Katie's hand in hers. "Oh, Katie, you are going to love having a baby—"

"Come again?" Charity's tone clearly indicated shell shock of her own.

"*After* the delivery," Faith emphasized with a crooked grin.

"Trust me, when you hold that tiny little replica of you and the man you love in your hands, it's as if nothing else in the world will ever seem as important again . . . not even law school. Right, guys?" She looked to Charity and Lizzie for support, and both sisters nodded.

"Even for me, kiddo," Charity said, misting up. "I complain about Henry a lot, but truly, most of it is just a front. Because honestly other than God, nothing—" she hiked her chin, belying the faint tremble of a tight-lipped smile, "and I repeat—*nothing* has brought me more joy or made me feel more special and whole as a woman than the birth of my twins."

Katie couldn't help it—moisture welled in her eyes. *Special. Whole as a woman.* The very desire of her heart that compelled her to be a lawyer, that secret longing buried all these years beneath a mountain of hurt and rejection—could it be? Would motherhood with its innate love and nurturing ease the hidden ache of a lonely little girl? Closing her eyes, she placed a palm to her stomach and breathed in the possibility of such a transformation. She thought of Kit, and a bubble of joy rose in her throat over the little girl she now loved like her own. A solitary tear plunked on her hand, filling her heart with a gratitude that swelled warm in her chest. Because suddenly she knew—*yes*, it could. Kit was living proof. And she knew why—because with God, all things were possible. She swatted another tear from her face. "Thanks, sis—I needed to hear that."

"Sure, kid, anytime." Charity sniffed, exchanging grins with Faith and Lizzie, both of whom were blotting at tears of their own. "God help us, we're a weepy lot, aren't we though?"

Marcy laughed. "God help our husbands, you mean."

"Exactly." Faith paused. "So if you *are* pregnant . . . what about law school?"

Katie's rib cage expanded and contracted with a quiet sigh. "Well, it just means I'll lay it aside for now to raise my family. That's the deal that Luke and I made."

"Lay it aside for now?" Marcy asked. "Does that mean you intend to go back someday?"

Mental calculations flitted through Katie's brain—she was twenty now, and Luke promised she could return to law school when Kit was sixteen. Which meant if things worked out, she'd be thirty-six—tempered and seasoned enough to make a difference. Or so she hoped. Her gaze met her mother's. "Yes, Mother, that's the agreement, when Kit turns sixteen."

The kitchen door squealed open to reveal a groggy grandpa toting a sleepy-eyed Kit. "We're up from our nap," Patrick said with a yawn, bobbling the little girl in the crook of his arm. His lips zagged into a droll smile. "And I'm giving fair warning—we're wet."

Marcy jumped up, squeezing Katie's shoulder before rescuing Kit. "I'll take her, Katie, while you finish talking to your sisters. You and I can chat later." Depositing a kiss on Kit's auburn curls, Marcy patted Patrick's cheek. "And you, my love, can change yourself."

"Very funny, darlin'." Patrick shot his wife and daughters a smirk while they chuckled. "You better hope I'm a long ways from that state of affairs, Marceline, or God help us both." He prodded her through the door. "Get a move on, woman. Gabe and Hope are upstairs, which means Henry's alone and we're all at risk."

Charity sighed. "Explain why I get the boy terror while you three get off scot-free?"

"Poetic justice, maybe?" Faith offered a lazy smile.

Charity's eyes narrowed. "There's nothing poetic about it, nor any rhyme or reason why you all get Pollyanna, and I have to butt heads with Huck Finn."

"Teddy can be a handful too, you know," Lizzie piped up, obviously hoping to cheer her sister up. She jumped up to retrieve a plate of oatmeal cookies Marcy had waiting on the counter. "Here, have a cookie—it'll lift your spirits."

"Thanks, Lizzie." Charity snatched one and popped half in her mouth. "I'll take a 'handful' of Teddy over a mouthful of Henry any day." She scowled with chipmunk cheeks, tugging on a needle stuck in a corduroy seam. "I swear he's in cahoots with Mitch."

Faith reached for a cookie. "So, Katie, do you think Luke means it? About law school?"

Katie paused, remembering Luke's tenderness the night she told him. She drew in a deep breath, as pregnant with certainty as she was with his child. "I do. Luke knows how much this means to me, and as I'm learning very slowly, I need to trust my husband."

Charity shoved the rest in her mouth, cheek bulging. "Yeah, well, good luck with that."

"Come on, Charity, you trust Mitch, I know you do." Lizzie's tone held a tease.

"Well, I thought I did . . . till last month."

Faith halted mid-chew, jaws stiff with oatmeal. "What happened last month?"

Charity slumped back in the chair with a second cookie in hand while her eyes trailed into a hard stare. "We had a fight—an awful one. Worse than ever before."

"But, why?" Lizzie asked.

"Because he was working late, and I called the *Herald* and he . . . well, he wasn't there."

"What? Where was he?" Faith said, leaning in.

Charity's almond-shaped eyes thinned as she took another bite. "At Mrs. Hennessey's."

"Who's Mrs. Hennessey?" Lizzie wanted to know.

Faith's lips tightened. "Only one of the richest women in Boston and a high-society flapper. *And* key stockholder." She brushed a crumb from her lips. "Why was Mitch there?"

Charity puffed out a sigh. "Because Mr. Hennessey assigned him to cochair the auction with her. They meet Thursday evenings at the *Herald*, which is why Mitch works late. But that Thursday she wasn't feeling well, so she had him come to her house. Which would be fine, except . . ."

"Except what?" Faith's eyes fixed on her sister's face.

Charity chewed on her lip instead of her cookie. "Except I sent one of his suits to the cleaners the other day, and I found a folded paper in the pocket." She swallowed hard. "It reeked of perfume and had her name and phone number on it. So

when I called work and Angus told me he was at her house
. . . I . . . I was crazy with jealousy."

Katie placed a hand on Charity's arm. "Mitch loves you,
Charity, and he's a good man. Nothing would ever happen."

"I know," Charity whispered, her gaze fastened to the half
cookie she held in her hand. Her lower lip protruded into
the faintest of pouts. "But lately, well . . . it just seems as if
he's lost interest in me—always too tired to . . . ," her lower
lip quivered the slightest bit, "you know . . ."

Faith exchanged glances with Lizzie and Katie, then leaned
in, her eyes intent. "Charity, you and I both know that in this
economy, the *Herald* is operating on a skeletal staff. Mother
says Father has been going in earlier and coming home later
than ever before, even working some Saturdays, which he
knows how much she hates. And Mitch is such a workhorse,
anal to a fault, so of course he's exhausted."

She shook her head, a sheen of tears glimmering in her
eyes. "No, you don't understand—Mitch is an amorous man
and exhaustion has never stopped him before. He's always
been the type who seems to need my love all the more when
he's stressed and overworked." Her jaw tightened. "But that
all changed when Marjorie Hennessey came into the picture.
I've seen her once or twice from afar at *Herald* functions,
and she's more of a vamp than I could ever hope to be." She
took a sip of tea and swallowed hard. "And even good men
fall if they have a reason."

"Oh, fiddle! What reason could Mitch possibly have?"
Katie demanded.

Charity's eyes brimmed with tears.

"Charity?" Katie paused, brows knit.

"What's wrong?" Faith asked quickly, gripping Charity's
arm.

Charity put a hand to her mouth as if to stifle a sob. "I'm
so scared I . . . worry that I'll push him away." A heave shivered through her, and she looked away for several seconds
and then sniffed, suddenly straightening her shoulders as if
desperately trying to compose herself. "I haven't felt like this

since before we were married, when Mitch was engaged to Kathleen—frantic inside, you know? Worried sick that I'll lose him." Her throat worked hard as she looked up. "And Mitch can sense it too, I just know it. It pushed him away before when I got possessive, needy, and I'm worried it will push him away now too . . . " Her lip began to quiver and she put a hand to her mouth, her voice trailing into a wail. "Right into the arms of Marjorie Hennessey . . ."

Faith jumped up and embraced her sister while Lizzie and Katie hovered close. "Charity, listen to me. Mitch is crazy about you, and he would never cheat on you, so you need to get your fear under control."

Charity shook her head, her face twisted in anguish. "No, you don't understand—I can't! I've tried, but it rises up and consumes me the longer he works with that woman. And Thursdays?" She shivered with a nervous buff of her arms. "God, help me—he may as well lock me up because I pace all day like a crazy woman as it is."

"You can fight this, Charity," Faith said with a firm squeeze, "I just know it. You can't let fear cut you off from Mitch's love and respect. If you do, Marjorie wins and you lose. Is that what you want?"

Charity shook her head, forcing rivulets of tears to stream down her face.

"Well, then, fight it!" Faith yanked her to her feet and gripped her shoulders, giving her a sound shake. Anger burned in her eyes. "Rebuke the fear in Jesus' name and put Mitch and your marriage into God's hands. Where's that annoying stubbornness of yours? And since when do you lie down and let anyone ride roughshod over you? Because that's what you're doing—letting fear rob you of your peace, your joy, and your marriage." Faith finally released her and stood up straight, arms crossed and fury sparking in her eyes. "Are you going to fight it, Charity Dennehy, or lay down and die?"

Charity blinked, apparently too stunned to utter a word.

Katie's eyes widened. Her oldest sister, usually so calm and so rational, seared each of them with a look before squaring her shoulders. "Don't you dare stare at me like I'm crazy; it's the truth, and it's high time you know it. The Bible says that the devil came to steal, kill, and destroy, but Jesus came that we might have abundant life. So, what's it going to be, Charity—you going to live your life cowering in fear, or are you going to give the devil some of the same grief you always give Mitch?"

Charity's mouth quivered before it parted into a wobbly smile. "Have you always been this volatile or have I been deluded into thinking you're the sweet, sane one?"

Faith flushed, a bit of tease slinking into her tone. "Well, you do have a history with delusion, you know. Both in your own mind in thinking Father and I hated you all those years, and in your prior tendency to delude others." Her lips sloped. "Especially Mitch."

"Hey, I got my man, didn't I?" she said with a pout.

Faith plunked her hands on her hips and leaned forward. "Yeah, but now you want to keep him, right?" Stuffing the rest of the cookie in her mouth, she chewed hard, grilling Charity with another heated look. "Which means we're going to pray about everything—your jealousy and your fear of losing your husband." She gave Charity a gentle shove back into her chair and then eased into hers with a lift of her brow. "Where's that passion you used to have, that fight to the death?"

Charity scowled. "Trust me, the passion is still there—it's just cowering behind the fear."

The smile tempered on Faith's lips as she reached for Charity's hand and gave it a gentle press, her eyes moist with understanding. "I know, sis," she whispered, "but there are ways to send the fear packing, I promise."

"How?" Katie sat up, her interest piqued.

"By applying some biblical principles. You can figure God's pretty adamant about fighting fear head-on when the Bible commands us to 'fear not' hundreds of times."

"Yeah, but that's easier said than done," Katie said, rubbing her stomach.

Faith leaned forward. "Yes, but doable, trust me. The Bible

makes it crystal clear we wrestle not against flesh and blood, but against spiritual wickedness in high places."

"A spiritual battle?" Katie peered at Faith, then glanced at Lizzie who nodded her head.

"Brady calls it spiritual warfare," Lizzie confirmed.

Charity buffed her arms. "Hate to tell ya, but it all sounds a bit scary to me."

"Not with God on our side. The Bible says 'greater is he that is in you, than he that is in the world.'" Faith sucked in a deep breath and softened her gaze. "Look, when fear, jealousy, bitterness, or any other sin tries to take me down, I've learned you can defeat it with a few simple steps. And believe me, I've been doing this for years, so I know that it works."

Katie propped her chin in her hand, challenging Faith with a squint. "Yeah? What are they?"

Lifting her hand, Faith ticked each point off with a finger. "Well, first you repent. Two, you bind and loose."

"Come again?" Charity said, face in a scrunch.

"The Bible says whatever we bind or loose on earth will be bound or loosed in heaven, so if you're battling bitterness, for example, bind it in Jesus' name and loose the opposite, such as love, or for fear, loose peace, et cetera. Three, you counter it with Scripture. For instance, whenever I'm afraid, I pray 2 Timothy 1:7—'Thank you, God, that you have not given me the spirit of fear; but of power, love, and a sound mind.' Next, I praise God for the situation and pray for the person who provoked it. And finally?" One edge of Faith's lip curled as she angled a brow. "Repeat as often as necessary."

Katie scrunched her nose. "And it really works?"

"Every single time," Faith said with a grin. "Give or take a few hundred repetitions."

The blue of Charity's eyes narrowed to slits. "Wait a second. This doesn't mean I have to pray for Marjorie Hennessey, does it?"

Faith exchanged smiles with Katie and Lizzie. "Afraid so."

She squinted. "I don't suppose I can 'pray' for a wart? Say, on the tip of her nose?"

"Uh, not if you want God on your side."

Charity shoved another cookie in her mouth and swiped the crumbs with a roll of her eyes. Her lips flattened as she slumped back in her chair. "Yeah, I didn't think so."

"Please Rory, no! Nothing happened, I promise. And he's just a boy . . ."

He raised his arm, and she winced. The force of his hand flung her against the wall with a loud crack, buckling her knees as she slid to the floor.

"With a whore like you, that hardly matters, now does it?" He staggered toward her, and the metallic taste of blood in her mouth merged with the bile to cause her breakfast to rise. She cowered in the corner and curled into a ball while fear released itself in a puddle at her feet. A gasp broke in her throat at the impact of his boot to her side, and pain sliced through her, wrenching a scream from her throat.

"Shut up, you whore," he rasped.

She twisted toward the wall to protect the babe in her womb. Anguish dimmed the light in her eyes. No, please, no . . .

"Get up!" The disgust in his voice was as cold as the sweat beading her body. He shook her with a fury that rattled her brain . . .

"Get up now!"

Emma lurched up, eyes glazed and breathing harsh.

"Forgive me for waking you, Emma, but I knocked and knocked, and you didn't answer." Mrs. Peep stroked her hair, her voice fraught with concern. "I came to your door to talk about Casey, but I heard you scream, and I was worried sick, my dear, so I let myself in. I hope you don't mind. You were having a nightmare."

Emma blinked, the horror of Rory's attack still thick in her throat. She swallowed hard and looked up, pushing the hair from her eyes. "No, no, that's fine . . . is something wrong?"

The worried slope of her landlady's eyes was enough to

put Emma on guard. She jolted up in the bed and braced a hand to Mrs. Peep's arm. "Tell me what's wrong."

The old woman patted her shoulder, her touch shaky. "Now, now . . . nothing specific, my dear, it's just that . . ." Her throat shifted. "Well, I've been uneasy all night, you see . . ."

"Why?" Emma's gaze locked with hers as she slipped from the covers. She swung her legs to the floor, the cool wood chilling her as much as the hesitation in her landlady's tone.

The old woman exhaled, two silver brows converging with the wrinkles in her brow. "I heard noises last night . . . from Casey's apartment."

"What kind of noises?" Emma's breath slowed in her lungs.

"Bumping noises, like something had fallen. And she had her radio on louder than usual."

Emma reached for her robe. "Casey loves to dance, maybe she was just practicing."

"Maybe, and that's what I thought too." Mrs. Peep shook her head, lips clamped tight. "But when I checked on her last night, she seemed strange, almost a glazed look in her eyes."

"Was she sick?"

Mrs. Peep nodded. "She said she was, as a matter of fact, thought she might be coming down with the flu. She even asked me to tell you not to come by because she wanted to sleep in this morning. Said she'd talk to you later."

"Poor thing." Emma exhaled. "I'll let her sleep and then check on her later."

A frail hand lighted on Emma's shoulder. "I don't know how to explain it, Emma, but something's not right. I've been tossing and turning all night, and yet I have no idea why. I thought that . . . well, maybe that . . . you know, you might—"

Emma shot to her feet. "I'll get dressed and go check on her right now."

Mrs. Peep puffed out a sigh, wrinkled hands clasped to her chest. "Oh, thank you, Emma, that would make me feel so much better." She handed her the spare key. "I tend to worry."

"Not at all, Mrs. Peep," Emma said with a hug. "You're a

dear friend who cares about those she loves. Now, go back to your apartment, and I'll stop by after I check on Casey, okay?"

"Bless you, my dear." Mrs. Peep toddled toward the door and turned. "And then you'll stay for breakfast, you hear? And I won't have an argument about it, either."

Emma smiled. "Sounds lovely, Mrs. Peep, thank you." She drew in a deep breath and released it when she heard the click of her front door. Goose bumps that had nothing to do with the cool of the room prickled her arms and legs. Dressing quickly, she ran a brush through her hair and hurried to the door, shutting it quietly before she tiptoed up the steps.

Ear to Casey's door, she slipped the key quietly into the lock, intending only to check on her and not wake her up. She eased the door open without a sound and then closed it again. Her eyes scanned the room, taking in the burgundy velvet love seat she'd given to Casey when she'd decluttered her own apartment. A small vase of roses from Johnny, no doubt, stood on a makeshift coffee table of stained wood blocks Emma had asked Sean to make, along with two similar end tables graced with secondhand lamps. Everything seemed in order, and Emma sighed, relief parting from her lips in one slow, steady breath.

Drawing in air, she started for Casey's bedroom and stopped, her pulse slowing at the scent of something amiss. She closed her eyes, and she could smell it, the memory of Rory—as vile and vicious as the stench now hovering in the room. *God, no, please . . .* Her blood froze at two empty glasses toppled beneath the love seat. Heart in her throat, she stooped to pick up a glass and sniff. A raw moan left her throat as it tumbled from her fingers onto Casey's rug.

Alcohol. A coward's courage, the devil's poison . . .

A lover's curse.

Heart hammering, Emma flew down the hall and jolted to a stop at the sight of Casey alone in her bed. She exhaled her relief and bent to shake her. "Casey—wake up!"

"Emma?" Her voice was groggy as she pushed blond strands from her eyes. Clarity sharpened her gaze and she clutched the covers to her nightgown. "What are you doing here?"

A muscle twittered in Emma's cheek. "Mrs. Peep said you were sick, and now I know why. You've been drinking, haven't you?"

The whites of her eyes expanded. "Just this once, I promise. We were celebrating because Johnny proposed. Let me get dressed, please, and I'll come right down."

Emma's eyes hardened as she glanced at Casey's left hand. "Where's the ring?"

A knot hitched in Casey's throat. "Please, Emma, go—I'll come right down."

The toilet flushed, and Emma's blood froze.

Casey sprang from the bed with panic in her eyes. She grasped Emma's arm just as the bathroom door opened. Her whisper shuddered with fear. "Emma—go! He'll hurt you, he will!"

"That's no idle threat, darlin'." Johnny stood, arms propped in the doorway and blue eyes as cold as slate. He wore a bath towel draped low on his hips and nothing else, forcing a blast of heat to Emma's cheeks. He strolled in, dark curly hair as unruly as that which matted his muscled chest. His voice was hard despite the charm of an Irish brogue. "Just who in the devil do ya think you are, barging in like this?"

Casey eased in front of Emma. "Leave her alone, Johnny, please. Emma's my mother's friend. She watches out for me."

"Not anymore, doll, you got me for that now." He strolled in and jerked Casey to his side, fondling the straps of her silky gown with a lurid smile. "So why don't you crawl back in your hole, *Emma*, because Casey and I are real busy."

Emma's legs wavered, her bones dissolving into limp muscle as memories of Rory paralyzed her to the floor. The chill of his arrogance, the stench of his liquor, the lust in his eyes—it was all there. Her breath came in ragged heaves as she stared, years flashing by until it was Rory who stood before her instead of Johnny, mocking her, debasing her, sucking the life from her soul. Terror nipped at her, icing her skin with a glaze of fear. *Oh, God, where are you?*

Within, Beloved. A spasm jerked in her body, and she

gasped, stunned at the silent fury seeping into her limbs. Clenching her fingers, she steeled her shoulders and stepped forward, wrenching Casey from his grasp. She shoved her to the door. "Casey, go to Mrs. Peep's—now!"

"Emma, no, he'll hurt you—"

"Casey, if you leave, you'll regret it . . ." Johnny's threat shivered the air.

"Now!" The force of Emma's words propelled the girl down the hall like a shot.

"Casey!" Johnny turned, but Emma launched against the door, blocking his way.

Her stomach quivered, but her voice was steady with a cold rage that matched his, word for word. "You will leave this instant," she whispered, "and you will never come back."

He rammed her hard against the door, rattling her jaw. "Get this and get this good, you scar-faced witch. I'm not going anywhere, and if you so much as breathe a word to Casey's mother, I'll pretty up the other side of your face, make no mistake."

She didn't blink despite the sweat beading her brow. "I'll have you arrested."

He leaned in, his breath foul. "I don't think so, darlin'. Unless you want Casey to look like you." His lip curled, making his handsome face almost ugly. He stroked a finger down the length of her scar. "She's too pretty for that." His grin was demonic. "Like you used to be—"

"Get your filthy hands off me."

He laughed, his finger trailing to the neckline of her blouse. "Or what?"

"Or I'll have you arrested for assault." She hurled his hand away. "That is, as soon as the police arrive." She had no talent for lying, but the words rolled off her tongue with the ease of a politician selling used cars. "I asked Mrs. Peep to call before I came up."

The scowl died on his face. "You're lyin'."

"No, I assure you I'm not. Because unlike you, I'm rather partial to the truth."

He cursed and shoved her away. "You'll pay for this." His gaze darted, an animal caught in the sight of a hunter. Another profanity hissed in the air. "Where's my clothes?"

It was a moment graced by God, and Emma knew it. A soiled heap of clothes that littered the bathroom floor, along with his shoes. He turned toward the bed, and she fled, scooping them up on her way to the door. She spotted his coat on the rack and snatched it as well. A bubble of laughter tickled her throat until Casey's door slammed behind her, and then it tumbled from her lips as she scrambled down the steps. Her breathing was labored when she pounded on Mrs. Peep's door, but never had she felt so alive . . . so free . . . *SO* vindicated!

"Are you okay?" Casey's voice was shrill as the door swung open.

Emma rushed in, chest heaving. "Lock it, now. And call the police."

"Already did," Mrs. Peep said, eyeing the pile of clothing in Emma's arms. One silver brow jutted high. "His clothes? You stole his clothes?"

With a quick perusal of Casey's tiny frame, Emma plunked the pile onto Mrs. Peep's couch with a grin. "Let's hope nothing in Casey's closet fits . . . at least until the police get here."

Casey put a hand to her mouth. "Oh, Emma!" Her lips trembled into a smile before a sob broke from her throat. With a halting groan, she threw herself into Emma's embrace and wept, her body heaving in Emma's arms.

Emma held her close, soothing her with gentle strokes of her hair. "Shhh . . . it's over now, Casey, it's over. We won't let him hurt you anymore."

"Oh, Emma, can you ever forgive me?" Casey pulled away, her cheeks sodden with tears. "H-he was s-so attentive and loving in the b-beginning, and then he started to p-push."

Emma cupped her chin. "Of course I forgive you, because I know how that can be, a man who puts stars in your eyes and makes you feel so special and so loved." She pushed a blond strand away from Casey's face, her eyes somber. "But you know what this means, Casey." A fragile sigh drifted from Emma's lips. "You have to go home."

Casey stared, a trickle of tears streaming her cheeks as she nodded.

A door slammed upstairs, and a cry of terror whimpered from Casey's lips as she lunged to clutch Emma with a racking heave.

Heavy footsteps thudded down the steps, and Emma held her breath. They thundered past Mrs. Peep's apartment and out the front, jiggling Mrs. Peep's pictures when the door bashed against the wall. Emma's stomach clenched before she ran to the window, Casey giggling over her shoulder and Mrs. Peep chuckling at her side. But it was a barefoot six-foot-plus man charging down the street that brought a true smile to Emma's face. Ablaze with lemon-yellow flowers, Casey's tiny housecoat barely covered his hairy body, although it did show off his legs to nice advantage.

Emma sighed and turned, her smile easing into a grin. "Mmm . . . I'm not sure, but I think that may just be his color." She cocked an innocent brow. "Don't you?"

14

irty laundry. The perfect activity for a Thursday night when the kids were in bed and she was all alone. Charity scowled as she heaved her wooden laundry basket from the floor of her closet, wondering again why she always saved her least favorite chore for her least favorite day. Her lips kinked. Maybe because she put it off . . . like she did with thoughts of Mitch working with that woman. And then, *boom!* Suddenly it was Thursday again, and her hampers were full of grimy clothes, and her mind, grimy thoughts.

She sighed and wished it were easier—what Faith had taught her to do. Taking every thought captive—her wild imagination, the jealousy, the fear—and keeping her thoughts pure. And for the most part she had, reining in her doubts and her temper to stay squeaky clean. But come Thursday, it seemed she was always in need of a wash, and then her clothes and her guilt would be scrubbed within an inch of their lives.

Basket on hip, she moved to her bed to strip off the sheets, reflecting on the Scripture Faith insisted she memorize.

For the weapons of our warfare are not carnal, but mighty through God to the pulling down of strongholds; casting down imaginations . . . and bringing into captivity every thought to the obedience of Christ.

She chewed on her lip. Easier said than done . . . especially for a wife whose "weapons" tended toward "carnal"—that is, except in the bedroom of late, where her husband's desire seemed as exhausted as his body at the end of a grueling day, compliments of the *Herald*. Heaving a sigh, she dropped the sheets into her basket and proceeded to flip the mattress, a habit she'd acquired during pregnancy when she'd been afflicted with constant backaches. Apparently it was a sure-fire way to keep the lumps out for the best support, at least according to her mother. Charity grunted as she heaved the mattress in place. *How about a surefire remedy for keeping the lumps out of my marriage?* she thought with a wry bent of her lips, wishing application of Faith's Scripture was as easy and simple as turning a bed.

Especially on Thursday nights.

She remade the bed with fresh sheets and carried the basket to the hamper in her bedroom closet, quoting Faith's Scripture in her mind.

For the weapons of our warfare are not carnal . . . She tossed three pairs of Mitch's underwear into the basket.

But mighty through God to the pulling down of strongholds . . . Several pajama bottoms and socks followed.

Casting down imaginations . . . She stopped, noting something peeking from behind the hamper, items that Mitch had obviously carelessly flung. *So that's where his pin-striped shirt went,* she thought with a shake of her head, retrieving the shirt that she loved along with a pair of wrinkled trousers. She dropped the trousers into the basket and then with a rush of longing, she crushed the shirt to her face and breathed in his scent, craving his touch. She closed her eyes and dwelled on him—her gruff and practical husband, tall and strong and dangerously handsome. A man who exuded a quiet strength and passion in everything he touched—whether in his faith, in his family . . . or in his bed.

Fingering the soft, smooth material in her hand, she

wondered how late he would be tonight. It seemed every week "the queen" demanded more and more of his time. She sighed and tossed the shirt into the basket, the fabric fluttering in slow motion as her arm froze in the air. Paralysis claimed her mid-blink, and she stared, all breath lost in her throat. With trembling fingers, she bent to retrieve the shirt and gasped.

A streak of scarlet lipstick edged the collar like a bloody gash, bleeding all rational thoughts from her mind. Her body jerked, and she dropped it again, slumping to her knees with a choked sob. *No, God—please!*

Vile thoughts pelted her mind—perfumed notes, a woman's scent on his clothes, late nights at the office, and then at her house. Charity shivered. And scarlet lipstick on his collar. *The color of sin.*

No! She put a hand to her eyes, desperate to fight it. *Casting down imaginations, casting down imaginations . . .* She drew in more air. Mitch loved her, he did, and he was a good man. But all she saw in her mind was Marjorie Hennessey, the darling of Beacon Hill—wealthy, beautiful . . . and notorious for indiscretions. Temptation in the flesh.

Especially for a man whose wife's jealousy and neediness pushed him away.

Charity shot to her feet, fear warring with fury. Bolting from the room, she rushed downstairs, fingers shaking as she dialed the phone. She waited, ring after ring till finally—

"Hello?"

She collapsed against the wall. "Emma, I need you. Can you come over, please—now?"

"Charity? What's wrong?"

She started to heave. "I . . . I need to see Mitch, but I c-can't leave H-henry and H-hope."

"I'm on my way."

With a hand to her chest, she clicked the receiver several times and rang for the operator to call for a cab. She sucked in a calming breath, determined to regain control. She could do this, she could! This was *her* territory, *her* husband, and *her* fight, and by God, she'd make sure that Marjorie Hennessey knew that Mitch Dennehy was hands-off.

She was ready in record time, armed in Mitch's favorite dress—the blue satin with a neckline that drew his eye—and the perfume that drove him crazy. She surveyed herself in the mirror with a grim smile, confident in the fashionable lay of her finger-waved bob and the deep rose of her lips. The doorbell rang, and she grabbed Mitch's shirt and her purse and flew down the stairs, never more grateful that her children were in bed.

Emma rushed in as she opened the door, fear etched in her face. "What's wrong?"

"I have to see Mitch." Tears welled in her eyes, and she fought them off.

With a slow scan of her attire, Emma paled. "No, Charity, please—you can't do this . . ."

"She's after my husband, Emma, I know it."

Emma grabbed her arm. "You're letting your imagination run away with you. She's a woman he chairs a committee with and nothing more."

"No, it's more than that, I can feel it. For months I've been fighting this uneasy feeling inside, you know that, Emma. And now I know why—she's making advances to Mitch."

"You don't know that—"

"I do know it!" she rasped. She shoved the stained shirt into Emma's hand, noting the flare of alarm in her friend's eyes. "There's perfume on his clothes and lipstick too, her phone number on a scented note, and meetings at her house. How much proof do I need?"

She jerked her coat off the rack by the door, and Emma clutched her shoulders. "Charity—no, I beg you! Confront Mitch when he gets home, if you must, but don't go down there. You'll only make a fool of yourself and embarrass him."

A horn sounded, and Charity snatched the shirt from Emma's hand. "Hope and Henry are in bed, and I won't be long." She kissed Emma's cheek. "I love you, Emma. Pray for me?"

Emma squeezed her in a tight hug, then pulled away, hands

still gripping Charity's arms. "I will pray for you, but *here*, please! Charity, don't go—I'm begging you. This isn't like you, at least not anymore. That woman will think you're crazy, and Mitch will be furious."

Her lips cemented in a hard line. "He'll get over it, Emma, but hopefully she won't. Let her think I'm crazy because I am—about my husband—and I refuse to let her get close. I want that woman a little bit scared of just what I might do." She gave Emma a tight smile. "Insanity can be a wonderful deterrent, you know. Especially to those who step on your toes."

The horn sounded again, and Charity blew her a kiss, bounding out the door with confidence surging in her veins. Twenty minutes later, the cabbie pulled up to the *Herald*, and she felt her dinner rise in her chest. *God, forgive me . . . what am I doing?* She was a thirty-one-year-old mother acting like a brainless sixteen-year-old girl, and for one quaking moment, her feet were glued to the floor of the taxi. And then in a painful beat of her heart, she felt Mitch's shirt clenched tight in her hand, and her fury rebounded. With resolve in her bones, she paid the driver and hurried into the *Herald*, greeting the night watchman with her brightest smile.

"Good evening, Angus, how have you been?"

The old man blinked in surprise and then gave her a toothless grin. "Miz Dennehy—what a sight for sore eyes. It's a pleasure to see you again, ma'am. And I've been just fine, thank ye. Would you like me to let your husband know you're here?"

"No, Angus, it's a surprise. Is he in his office, do you know?"

"No, ma'am, he's in the boardroom with Miz Hennessey. You know where that is?"

She hurried toward the staircase with a wave and a smile. "Yes, Angus, I do, thank you." She put a finger to her lips. "Remember, it's a surprise."

Heart hammering in her chest, she quickly shed her coat and ascended the landing, then pushed through the windowed double doors that led to the newsroom. She smiled at several workers as she honed in on the boardroom at the end of the hall. Much to her relief, activity was subdued this time of night, although a handful of reporters and second-shift copywriters offered curious stares as she peered into Mitch's empty office.

With a lift of her shoulders, she made her way to the boardroom, then paused to suck in a deep breath before she laid her hand to the knob. She turned it slowly, quietly, inching the door open just enough to peek in. She was met with the staccato punch and click of an adding machine as Mitch pounded numbers in at a dizzying pace, his broad back bent over the task with great focus while Marjorie Hennessey looked on. It was almost hypnotic, the rapid-fire movement of his fingers combined with the powerful jerk of his arm on the lever, his sleeves rolled to reveal tight muscles bent on the task at hand.

The noise and distraction allowed her to study the woman whose lips had obviously strayed to her husband's neck, and one glance told her all she needed to know. Marjorie Hennessey perched on the table, silky legs crossed and torso bent forward with chin in hand. She leaned close to Mitch, barely a breath away, skirt edging her thigh and blouse gaping to reveal a deep cleft of breasts. Darkly smudged eyes fixed on the ticker-tape tally spitting out of his machine while blood-red nails clicked on the table, almost grazing his arm.

Suddenly the machine stopped, and with a snatch of the tape, Mitch launched to his feet. "Sweet saints, we did it! Do you realize what this means?"

Marjorie slid off the table with a husky laugh and eased her body close to his. "I believe it means you're amazing, Mr. Dennehy." She gazed up with seduction in her eyes while one scarlet nail slowly trailed his arm. "What do you say we celebrate?"

Charity heaved the door open. It banged against the wall with a deafening slam. "What do you say we don't, and you get your hands off my husband?"

The element of surprise had always served her well, but never more so than now. Mitch jerked around, almost stumbling against his chair while Marjorie went stiff as a corpse. He was not a man prone to blushing, but he did so now, profusely, the blood in his cheeks a telling contrast to the lack of it in Marjorie's, whose face was as pale as death. With shock glazing their eyes, both appeared to be struck dumb until Mitch finally spoke, his voice little more than a croak. "Charity . . . what are you doing here?"

Mitch wasn't the enemy, but suddenly it didn't seem to matter. Months of fear, anger, and jealousy had boiled inside until it had nowhere to go but over the top, scalding anyone in its path. Sauntering in with hands on her hips, all rational thought fled as she singed him with a look, her voice as sharp as the click of her heels. "No, Mitch, why don't you tell me what *you're* doing here . . . with *her*."

In a grind of his jaw, all shock appeared to evaporate as he shoved the chair out of his way and charged toward the door, hurling it closed. He wheeled on her with fire in his eyes and a tic in his cheek, his voice tight with tension. "You will leave this instant, and we will discuss this at home. Is that clear?"

She leaned in, defying him with an angry thrust of her chin. "The only thing clear to me is that woman's intent and . . . *obviously* . . . your willingness to comply."

The grinding accelerated as he gripped an iron fist to her arm. "Don't you dare accus—"

"Mitch . . . I assume this is your lovely wife?" Marjorie had found her voice, apparently, as well as her composure. She eased back on the table and crossed her legs once again as she studied Charity through cool eyes. "Please accept my apologies for taking so much of your husband's time, Mrs. Dennehy, but I'm sure you can understand that as cochair for one of the most important charities in all of Boston, Mitch has been invaluable to the *Herald*."

Charity jerked her arm free and strode forward, her fingers itching for a handful of hair. "It's not my husband's value to the *Herald* that has me concerned, Mrs. Hennessey."

"Charity, I want you to leave—*now*! This is a place of business—"

Her eyes bore into Marjorie. "Monkey business, if my assessment is correct."

He grabbed her from behind and spun her around, fusing his hands to her shoulders. His voice, dangerously low, held a note of warning she had never heard before. "I'm asking you for the last time—please leave now, and we will discuss this at home."

"Mrs. Dennehy, I assure you that the relationship between your husband and me is strictly professional, a working relationship and nothing more."

Charity glanced back to rake the woman with her eyes—from the haughty, scarlet lips and platinum hair, to the revealing satin blouse that glided over slim hips to a shockingly short skirt. Her mouth edged into a thin smile. "That's quite clear, Mrs. Hennessey," she said with ice in her tone. She broke from Mitch's grasp to hurl his soiled shirt on the table. "And obvious to me from the lipstick on my husband's collar, that *you've* been working particularly hard."

Mitch clamped a hard arm to her waist and literally lifted her toward the door.

"Good night, Mrs. Dennehy," Marjorie said in a superior tone. "Thank you for letting me . . . *have* . . . your husband on Thursday nights. I can't tell you what a pleasure it's been."

Charity lunged around, wild-eyed in Mitch's hold. All at once, something snapped inside at the smug look of victory on Marjorie's face, and fresh rage pumped through her veins like adrenaline. With a hiss of air, she twisted free and flew toward the woman.

"Charity!" Mitch's voice was no more than a distant roar as her fingers dove into that artificial hair, yanking with all her might like she used to with Faith.

"Mitch, get her off me!" Marjorie was flat on the table with Charity on top, the terror in her voice reverberating through the room.

She heard Mitch's grunt before he wrenched her free, ignoring her kicking and screaming as he carried her to the door. His arms were like a vise locked to her waist while his voice threatened in her ear, harsh and hot. "You will walk out of this office like a civilized human being if I have to drag you every step of the way. And I suggest you keep your mouth shut, or I will gladly shut it for you." He seized the knob and opened the door, glaring over his shoulder. "Marjorie, I apologize for my wife and this unfortunate disruption. I will be happy to meet with you tomorrow evening to finish our meeting or any evening of your choosing. Good night."

He dropped Charity to her feet without the least bit of care, seizing her arm in his as he opened the door and hauled her through.

"Mitch, I—"

His eyes cauterized her, burning the words to her tongue. "Not-a-word," he said, teeth clenched and his voice brutal in its coldness. "Or so help me . . ."

She swallowed hard and closed her mouth, almost running to keep up with his angry stride. Never in their ten years of marriage had Mitch ever treated her like this. She bit her lip and fought the sting of tears. But then again, she had never acted like this before, at least not since they'd been married, and suddenly she felt ashamed of her behavior.

"Good night, Mr. and Miz Dennehy—you have a good evening, you hear?"

"Good night, Angus," Charity managed in a frail voice as they hurried out the front door.

She peeked up at her husband who remained silent, his face like rock except for the angry twitter of a nerve in his cheek. He dragged her down the street where his car was parked and opened her door. With a hard palm to her back, he shoved her in and slammed the door, rounding the car to get in on the other side.

"Mitch—"

His eyes burned like coals, singeing her to the seat. "One more word, and I will throw you out of this car and let you walk. Is that clear?"

She nodded, the hurt thick in her throat. She clutched her arms to her waist and stared out the window, tears trailing her cheeks. She had never seen him like this, so cold, so hard. Something skittered in her stomach, and she realized it was fear.

Dear God, what have I done?

The vehicle growled to life with a grind. He slapped the headlights on, and the car lurched from the curb with his hard swipe of the wheel. His profile, chiseled in stone, was that of a stranger as he gunned the accelerator and sped down the road. Silence had never been so painful.

When they arrived at the house, she followed him in the door, her heart sick in her chest.

"You're home," Emma said, hurrying in from the parlor. Her eyes flicked to Mitch and then Charity. "Is everything all right?"

"Fine, Emma." Mitch's tone was clipped. "I'll drive you home."

"No, that's not necessary—"

He walked out the door without another word, and Emma grabbed Charity's hand. "Good heavens, what happened?"

Tears welled once again, and she threw herself into Emma's arms, heaves shuddering her body. "Oh, Emma, I did the most awful thing, and now Mitch hates me."

"What did you do?" Emma breathed, her voice laced with fear.

"I-I said awful things to her and to h-him, and then I . . . I knocked her on the t-table and started p-pulling her hair."

Emma groaned as she hugged Charity tightly. "Oh, no . . ." She pulled away, her eyes gentle with concern. "But he'll get over it, I'm sure he will. And I'll try and talk to him—"

"Emma!" Mitch's tone rang with impatience.

"Oh, Emma, will you please? Mitch loves you like a sister, and he would listen to you."

Emma squeezed her hand. "Stop worrying and start praying, do you hear?"

Charity nodded.

She raced out, and Charity closed the door, fingers trembling from the strain of the evening. With a deep swallow of air, she squared her shoulders and closed her eyes, face lifted to heaven. "Lord, I'm a fool, I know, and I'm so sorry for what I did tonight, and for hurting Mitch. Forgive me for my anger toward Marjorie and please—" the muscles in her throat convulsed—"please bless her and help her to forgive me too. I'm so scared because I've . . . I've never seen my husband act this way, never been cut off from his love before . . . and I'm frightened. But your Word says you have not given us the spirit of fear, but of power, love, and a sound mind. So, I'm asking, Lord—please deliver me from this fear and give me a sound mind and the love to face Mitch's anger. And please, God, heal this rift in our marriage."

She took another deep breath, and with a semblance of peace in her soul, she hurried to their bathroom to get ready for bed. Her body was shaking as she washed her face and brushed her teeth. She undressed, then unhooked Mitch's favorite nightgown from the back of the door and put it on, the satin cool as it shimmered down her body. She stared in a daze at the woman in the mirror—golden hair and swollen eyes, and full breasts mounded in the V of her gown. With a hand pressed tightly to her stomach, she swallowed hard, knowing full well there would be no lovemaking tonight. There had been nights when she was so desperate for his physical love—the assurance that he was still attracted to her, loved her—that his exhaustion had angered her. But for once it didn't matter. Not tonight . . . maybe not ever again. Nothing mattered if she didn't have all of Mitch's love.

Her heart quaked as the door downstairs opened and closed, and she slipped into the bed to wait, and hope, and pray. Her blood pounded in her ears as his footsteps rose on the staircase, and when he entered their room, her stomach cramped at the fury in his face.

"Mitch, I'm so sorry—"

His silence was a blow as he entered the bathroom and shut the door. Water ran as she uttered silent prayers, desperate for resolution. And then a shaft of light lit the room and went dark. She watched his shadow move toward the bed and her heart leapt in her breast. But when he reached for his pillow, her breath caught in her throat. "Mitch, no, please—"

He moved toward the door in silence, and she wanted to scream to shatter the deafening quiet. *No more silence, please, anything but that.* She jumped up and ran to the door, her heart breaking. "Mitch, don't shut me out, please—talk to me!" Her voice broke on a sob.

He turned then, his face as hard and cold in the moonlight as a marble sculpture. His eyes were slivers of blue ice. "All right, Charity, I'll talk." He faced her point-blank, his voice a cold blade with deadly intent. "I want you to leave me alone. I want you to stay far away from me. Until I'm ready to talk. And quite frankly, I'm not sure when that will be. What you did tonight was not just a whim, a pretty tantrum that I'll forget about tomorrow. It was the destruction of a piece of our marriage, my trust and my love. And I pray to God I can get over it, but I'm not sure about that either. In the meantime, I'll be sleeping in the study for the foreseeable future."

She clutched his arm. "Please, Mitch—don't leave me. We can work this out."

He stared at her face, streaming with tears, and she shivered at the lack of love in his eyes. No warmth, no caring, as if his heart had been sealed off, an invisible barrier shutting her out. "Maybe," he said, his tone as lifeless as his love. "But not without a lot of pain, little girl . . . and definitely not tonight." He closed the door and she stared, her heart strangling in her chest.

With a wild pumping of her pulse, she flung the door wide and chased after him, following him down the stairs as she pleaded her case. "Mitch, please, don't do this," she cried.

But he did. And when he slammed the study door and bolted her out, she felt as if she were suffocating, the air bleeding from her lungs in the rawest of pain. She staggered back to their room, barely able to catch her breath. Cold comprehension stabbed anew, wounding her with painful revelation. She was alone and despised by her husband, a woman whose very existence depended on his love. Like oxygen to her body and hope to her soul. And now it was gone. Pain slashed through her like jagged pieces of glass, and she collapsed on their bed in unfathomable grief. His words droned in her brain, piercing anew and haunting her mind. She had feared his silence, thinking nothing could be worse.

But she had been wrong.

His words had gashed into the soft and tender flesh of all that she was, all she had been—a little girl, rejected and abused, fearing the absence of a man's love. And now it was here—as cold and empty as the look in Mitch's eyes—she was alone. A chill shivered through her and she keened on the bed with hurt so stabbing, she thought she would die. His love had been shut off, and a gaping hole had opened wide, leaving her empty and exposed to the whisperings of death.

He will never love you again.

Your marriage is a lie.

Your life is over.

"Nooooooo!" Her hoarse whisper echoed in the room, drowning out the lies. And then in a violent beat of her heart, she jerked her knees to her chest and cocooned into the safety of God, her arms clinging to his love with head bent and heart sheltered. "Oh, God, forgive me and save me . . . from myself and from my sin. I need you—and only you—to be the lover of my soul. Fill my emptiness with your Spirit and love so I may be all you've called me to be."

And with a final shiver of her body, she let it all go—Mitch's anger, his silence, and the loss of his love, placing it where she knew it belonged—at the foot of God's throne. And in that one simple transfer of will, sorrow seeped from her eyes as a wellspring of hope, weighting her pillow, but lifting her soul. Moonlight streamed across her bed like the grace of God, and finally she closed her eyes to take her rest.

Yes, a woman broken in a bed of sorrow . . . but whole in the hand of God.

Sean glanced at the clock and frowned. Noon. At this rate, he wouldn't get to Emma's till one. He peered at Bert as he slipped his coat on. "Did she say what she thought it was? Fever, cold . . . ?" His smile tipped. "Exhaustion? Heaven knows the woman works herself to death."

Bert spun a sheet of paper into the platen of her typewriter. "Nope, just said she felt achy and tired. Says her throat is sore and her head hurts so much, she can barely keep her eyes open." Worry lines creased the bridge of her nose. "Which is a first, so she must *really* feel rotten."

"I don't understand—she seemed fine yesterday." Alli chewed on the tip of her pen, her brow buckled in worry.

"Yeah . . . she was." Sean buttoned his coat with a pensive smile. "Spunky, almost. *And* pushy." One corner of his mouth inched up. "She made me help her clean out the store closet."

Bert shook her head, her smile flat. "The woman is a fanatic about being neat. She's been harping about that closet as long as I can remember."

"It does look nice, though," Alli said. "Will you just tell her we miss her, Sean?"

Sean tugged on his gloves. "Sure. After I ply her with chicken soup and my secret remedy, guaranteed to cure all ills."

Bert slid him a sideways smile. "Your 'remedy' wouldn't contain anything illegal, now would it, Mr. Straight and Narrow?"

Sean winked on his way out the door. "Well, you'll just have to get sick to find out, won't you, Mrs. Adriani?" He stopped and turned, hands braced in the door. "If any problems pop up, just put 'em on ice till I get back, okay? And, Alli, those inventory figures Emma wanted are finished and ready to type up when you get a chance. Sorry, I left them sitting on my desk."

"No problem, Sean. Just take care of Miss Emma. It feels strange here without her."

"Yeah, I know." Sean angled a salute and bounded down the steps, thoughts of Emma in pain doing funny things to his stomach. Someone as special as Emma Malloy shouldn't be by herself when she was sick, he thought with a pinch of his lips, fending for herself when she probably couldn't even get out of bed. He nodded at several employees on his way out the door, then winced at the sting of icy wind upon exiting the front entrance. Turning up his collar, he forged into the Saturday crowd, eyes focused on the red-and-gold Woolworth's sign at the end of the block. His stomach rumbled as he quickened his pace. *First stop—the best soup in town.*

Maintaining a brisk walk most of the way, he was out of breath by the time he reached Emma's apartment, loaded down with soup, ginger ale, tea, and other select items he hoped would help. Balancing the carton with his knee, he knocked on the door and waited. When there was no answer, he butted the box to the door to try again, knuckled fist poised in the air.

"She's asleep."

Sean spun around, almost upending the soup. A tiny old woman in a gray nubby sweater that all but swallowed her up peeked out the door, blue eyes glaring as if she'd just caught him breaking in.

"I have soup," he said stupidly, feeling the warmth crawl up the back of his neck. He lifted the cardboard carton loaded with bags. "To help her feel better."

One silver brow spiked up. "Feel better? Little late for that now," she muttered, opening the door more than a crack to reveal a rolling pin in her hand. She squinted up at him, making the paper-thin wrinkles that fanned from her eyes all the more pronounced. "Who are you?"

"Sean O'Connor—Emma's assistant manager from the store."

Her scowl softened into a smile. "So you're the one she's always gabbing about."

His mouth tipped up. "That depends—is it good or bad?"

She grinned, evolving from a pint-sized threat into a huggable grandma. "Good. Anybody that can bring a little joy to Emma Malloy is okay by me."

"Couldn't agree more." He lifted the carton. "Think she'd mind if you let me in, Mrs. . . ."

"Peep, Elvira Peep, Emma's landlady and good friend. Most people call me Vi 'cept for Emma and Casey, that is. They call me Mrs. Peep, but that's only 'cause Emma worries about teaching Casey respect for her elders." Bustling past, she tucked the rolling pin under her arm and reached into her pocket for a key. She inserted it into the lock, then paused to look up, eyes pensive. "Emma thinks mighty highly of you, Sean O'Connor. Claims you're friends."

"We are, Mrs. Peep—good friends." He bobbled the carton, his fingers suddenly clammy. "You might say she's my closest friend and I . . ." Emotion shifted in his throat. "I love her a lot."

"Call me Vi. And you can bet those freckles on that handsome face of yours that she feels the same." The blue eyes narrowed, locked on him with uncomfortable precision. "You know, call me senile, but it seems to me there's a spark of something more than just friends."

He blinked, her statement cutting off his air. "Pardon me?"

With barely a sound, she turned the key in the lock, then dismissed his surprise with a wave of her hand. "Oh, I don't mean you, of course," she said with a shake of her head, "but her. Talks about you a lot, if you ask me. Seems to respect you, admires you."

"Well, like I said, Vi, we're close friends."

She exhaled a burdensome sigh. "I know. And more's the pity."

His breathing thinned as he shifted the box in his hands. "Why's that?" he asked, not all that sure he wanted to know.

She exhaled, eyelids weighted with regret. "Because she's in love with you, you know, just doesn't know it herself."

He blinked. She may as well have slammed him across the head with that rolling pin—no difference. His body went numb. He tried to speak, but the words seemed tied to his tongue.

A sigh drifted from her weathered lips. "And it's a rotten shame too, because the woman is bound and determined to honor her vows to that pathetic excuse for a man, and him an ocean away, no less. Of course, her faith doesn't allow divorce, so there you have it. One of the finest people on God's green earth remains shackled to one of the worst. A travesty if you ask me, especially at a time like this, when she could use the protection of a man she loves."

Her words sliced through his shock. "What do you mean, 'at a time like this'?"

She peered up, gumming her lips as if deciding how much to divulge. She shook her head. "No, I refuse to keep her secret. She'll be angry, I know, but then Emma Malloy's wrath is akin to most people's good mood." She sucked in a deep breath and turned to face him dead-on, pain etched into every wrinkle. "She was beat up, Sean, by Casey's no-good boyfriend."

His heart slammed to a stop. Needles of shock prickled his skin as her words stole the air from his throat. Their meaning burned in his mind, and hot blood whooshed into his face on a floodtide of fury. Seldom had he known such rage. Oh, he'd had an inkling of it the day that he'd been fired, and more so at Kearney's and then during the war, but never like this, blood coursing through his veins like boiling lava, ready to spew. He gripped the box tightly, fingers gouging the sides. His voice was a whisper, but the brutal bite of it made the old woman wince. "When? How?"

"Last night, when she got home from work. He was waiting and slapped her around real good." Her tone matched his, sharp and bitter. "Apparently the scum is prone to hitting women, so Emma shipped Casey home to Kansas, and Mr. Scum of the Earth didn't like that one bit." Her lips trembled into a smile as tears welled in her eyes. "But you would have been so proud of her, Sean. Despite her past with that bully she married, she had the courage to stand up to that lowlife last week when he forced himself on Casey and spent the night in her apartment." Mrs. Peep hiked her chin, lips settling into a grim smile. "Got the best of him, she did, stealing his clothes and shoes while I called the police. It was a pretty sight, I can tell you that, watching him slink down the street in nothing more than Casey's floral robe."

"Is she—" the words stuck in his throat, making it difficult to breathe—"badly hurt?"

She shook her head. "I don't think so, more scared than anything, but I gave her some sleeping pills I had because of the nightmares she's been having lately. All I could see was a nasty bruise on her face and neck, so nothing appears to be broken, but I wouldn't be surprised if she's black and blue under her clothes. I heard her screams and called the police, but he roughed her up plenty before I was able to get my rolling pin."

His gaze dropped to the unlikely weapon she held and he tried to smile, but his jaw was as stiff as the piece of wood in her hands. A muscle pulsed in his cheek. "Who is he?" he whispered. "Where can I find him?"

"Johnny something or other. I wish I could tell you more, Sean, but I don't even know his last name. And Emma knows where he works, but I doubt she'll say." She put a veined hand to his arm, a wisp of fear in her tone. "He threatened to come back and finish her off, and I know she's scared to death. Frankly, I am too—for her—and if there's any way you can convince her to stay somewhere else for a while, I'd be happy to take care of her cats."

He closed his eyes, willing his temper to calm. The last thing Emma needed was more rage. Not now. Better to save it until he could get his hands on the lowlife who hurt her. And he would, if he had to look under every rock to do it. His eyelids lifted, the heat in his gaze in stark contrast to the coolness of his manner. "Open the door, Mrs. Peep."

Nodding, she eased it wide and motioned him in, halting him halfway with a stay of her hand. "I'm glad you're here, Sean. If you need anything, I'll be across the hall."

He turned. "You're not coming in?"

"No," she said, a sad smile lining her lips. "I have a feeling you're all she needs."

The door shut quietly behind her, and he drew in a deep breath. Emma's scent filled his senses with grief as he looked around, seeing her beauty and tranquility in everything she touched. A graceful fern, green and lush with care, boasted splashes of color with carved green and yellow lovebirds perched on a tall wooden stick. Gleaming wood bookcases, resplendent with leather-bound books, showcased the Kewpie doll he'd won for her the night they'd strolled Revere Beach. He noted an easel with a half-finished painting depicting children at play, then smiled at another on the wall behind it, where two fat bluebirds perched on a sill. One happy and one sad, they reminded him so much of Bert and Alli that his heart squeezed in his chest. *Oh, Emma, I didn't even know you could paint . . .* His gaze trailed to a half-crocheted afghan of bright blues, reds, and golds, depicting a passion and vibrancy in the woman he'd only just begun to see. He could smell the clean scent of lemon oil from the cherrywood coffee table where a Bible with jeweled bookmark lay, its ribboned page displayed like an exquisite piece of art. Not unlike the woman whose fingers caressed it. *Oh, Emma.* Hand to his eyes, he felt a lump shift in his throat.

So much faith . . . so much love. *The kindest person I know.*

Steeling his emotions, he moved toward the kitchen and set the box on the table, feeling oddly at home in this room where everything reminded him of her. Sunny yellow curtains, graceful crystal candlesticks, and the inviting smell of ground coffee beans still potent in the air. Sparkling counters and sink explained the hint of bleach he smelled, and the gleam of the black-and-white tile floor indicated it was spotless and clean. *Just like Emma.*

He braced himself, the shaft of light at the end of the hall drawing him like a spell he couldn't break. He should have felt like an intruder, but he didn't. This was Emma, the woman with whom he shared everything. His lunch, his laughter, his thoughts.

He paused to press a shaky hand to his eyes. And his heart? *She's in love with you, you know.*

The air stilled in his lungs. *No . . . I didn't.*

He moved to stand in her door, and his heart plunged in his chest. He should have been prepared, but somehow he wasn't, and he knew at once that nothing would calm the fury that now pulsed in his brain. She lay limp on her back with her face to the side, dark lashes sweeping against porcelain skin. Her cheeks were pale ivory except for a swell of purple, temple to jaw, and her full lips were the color of death, bloodless and white. Mottled marks trailed her long, slender neck, sinking well past bruised shoulders into the folds of a satin gown. She shivered in her sleep, and he held his breath as tears stung his eyes.

"Oh, Emma . . ." He hadn't meant to speak it out loud, but his grief couldn't contain the words, and at the sound of his whisper, her eyelids fluttered.

———

Another dream? Her drowsy eyelids lumbered up and she stared, vision and thoughts woozy from the Luminal Mrs. Peep had given her to help her sleep. A valiant—but futile— effort at keeping the nightmares at bay. But this dream seemed so real and so welcome—Sean at the door, sober, vigilant, an angel of mercy with grief welling in his eyes. She blinked, still unsure if he was real or just part of the hallucinatory dreams in which she'd been floating in and out of all night.

"Emma . . ." The apparition spoke again, broken and hoarse, and a violent longing stabbed within. Her eyes immediately filled with tears at the fierce protectiveness emanating from the sheen of sorrow in his own, his lips pale and pinched. In two powerful strides, he was beside her, squatting by her bed with a stiff smile while his fingers gently grazed the unbruised side of her face. "How do you feel?" he whispered, his voice rough with emotion.

She stared at him through haunted eyes, suddenly scared, timid, void of the peace that had always prevailed. Peace that had always comforted her in the past, steadied her, healed her . . . until now.

All shattered by a slap of a hand.

She swallowed hard and silently grimaced at the soreness the action produced, then attempted a smile that felt no better. But at the moment, pain didn't matter, only smiles. Because he must never know, never suspect the horror that had claimed her once again. The corners of her mouth trembled into a pitiful excuse for a grin. "How do I feel? Like I just went ten rounds with Mrs. Bennett and lost."

He smiled, tempering the pain she saw in his face. "She's not a tenth as tough as you are, Mrs. Malloy . . ." Brushing a strand of hair from her eyes, he rose to his feet. "Nor as kind."

With a soft grunt, she scooted up to sit against the headboard, too foggy to remember the silk nightgown she wore. Sean cleared his throat, then awkwardly averted his gaze. She peered down and gasped, jerking the covers up to cover the swell of her breasts against the lace of her gown. Heat singed her face that rivaled the crimson tide crawling up the back of his neck. "Forgive me, Sean, I . . . I'm still half asleep."

He thrust his hands in his pockets. "Nothing to forgive, Emma." Tender eyes locked with hers. "You're a beautiful woman, Mrs. Malloy," he whispered, and then exhaling loudly, he glanced over his shoulder to the closet. "Is there a robe or something I can get you?"

She nodded quickly, a healthy dose of heat warming her cheeks. "On a hook behind the closet door, thank you."

Fetching a silk robe that matched her gown, he handed it to her along with her slippers, then turned around while she put them both on. He slacked a hip, thumbs latched to his trouser pockets and arms loose at his sides. "So . . . you hungry? I brought soup."

Her stomach instantly rumbled, reminding her she'd had no appetite since Johnny had—

She swallowed the bile that rose in her throat. "Oh, that sounds good. What kind?"

"Your favorite—Woolworth's chicken noodle." She heard a smile in his voice. He shifted a hip, hesitation thick in his words. "Uh, you're not too sick to eat, are you? Because if you have a fever, you probably shouldn't. You know, feed a cold, starve a fever? What is it you have, exactly, do you know?"

Silence hung in the air while she fumbled with the tie of her robe, reluctant to answer.

"Emma?"

"Uh, not sure, just achy all over and the remains of a headache, but no fever."

He paused. "And the bruises?"

She worried her lip, straining to come up with an excuse. When she didn't answer right away, he did a slow about-face, eyes hard and a nerve twitching along the steel line of his jaw. The whites of her eyes expanded and she stood to her feet, fingers pinched at the top of her wraparound robe. "I . . . tripped on the steps." Her lips wavered into a smile that bore no joy. "I can be pretty clumsy, as you know."

"Don't lie to me, Emma," he said, his whisper harsh. "Where is he, the man who did this to you? I want his name and address—*now*."

Tears brimmed in her eyes. She shook her head, spilling them down her face. *No, Mrs. Peep, why?* Her voice broke on a heave. "She sh-shouldn't have told y-you, she promised."

He strode forward and gripped her arms as gently as possible given the fury sparking in his eyes. "Yes, she should! She loves you, and I love you." Color shot up his neck. "We all do," he stuttered, "and you shouldn't close us out when you need us the most."

All at once her body began to quiver and she put a shaky hand to her mouth, eyes brimming with tears. "Oh, Sean . . . I'm s-so s-scared . . ."

She couldn't help it. All resolve to stay strong slithered away and in one painful heave, she collapsed against him, no longer willing to bear this trauma alone. He swept her up and carried her down the hall, his voice crooning gentle comfort as she wept in his arms. Lowering to the couch, he tucked her close, stroking her back as he whispered in her hair. "Shh, Emma . . . it's all right . . . it's all right. I'm not going to let him hurt you anymore, I promise."

"It w-was j-just like it w-was with Rory, and I w-wanted t-to die . . ." Her body shuddered against his chest as she clung to him, the scent of soap and Snickers as soothing as the warm palm that kneaded the nape of her neck.

"Shh . . . shh . . . it's okay, Emma . . ." He fanned his fingers through her hair, then cupped her face in his palms, his gaze a tender caress. "I'm here now," he whispered, kissing her forehead, her temple, her cheek . . .

Her pulse quickened while her weeping stilled to soft, little heaves, and as her eyelids drifted closed, her heart stuttered when he brushed them with his lips.

"I'll keep you safe, I promise," he whispered, and a silent moan faded in her throat as his mouth trailed to her temple. "I swear no one will ever hurt you again . . ."

Heat throbbed within as she lost herself in the caress of his hand, her mind dazed while his mouth explored. The soft flesh of her ear, the curve of her throat, her body humming with need as never before. She felt his shallow breaths, warm against her skin, and with a low groan, he cradled her neck to capture her mouth with his own. "Oh, Emma," he whispered, his voice hoarse against her lips, "I want to be there always, to protect you, cherish you . . ." He deepened his kiss, and she tasted the salt of her tears.

All reason fled and she was lost, the air hitching in her throat a mere heartbeat before she returned his passion, her mouth warm beneath his. She knew it had never been like this with anyone—not with Rory or others or even in her wildest dreams. A merging of souls as well as bodies, where hope soared and love swelled in her chest until she thought she would burst.

Sean—*her Sean*—tasting her like this, loving her like this, felt so right, so natural, the missing piece of her soul. Kisses both tender and hungry, uniting them, changing them, molding friends into lovers for the rest of their lives . . .

"God, forgive me," she whispered, her body shivering from the caress of his mouth to her throat. Her words vibrated beneath his lips, fragile and tinged with awe. "I never knew . . . never dreamed . . . it could be like this . . ."

He clutched her close, his uneven breathing in rhythm with hers. "Emma, I'm so stupid—I never saw this coming, but may God help me . . . I'm in love with you."

No! She jolted away, his words searing her conscience with a pain more awful than any Johnny had inflicted. Fear clawed in her throat, forcing her back against the wood arms of the couch. "No, Sean, please—you can't!"

He stared, his face filled with grief. "It's too late," he whispered. "I can't not love you—not now, not after this."

"But it's wrong!" She put a hand to her neck, her chest heaving and her mind convulsing with guilt. *God, how could I have done this?* Tears stung her eyes as self-loathing rose in her throat like bile. She was everything Rory had branded her—a liar and a whore, scarred and hideous, not fit for any man's bed. She looked away, nauseous at the thought that Sean might see her for the vile woman she was. Her voice shuddered with shame. "We can't do this, Sean, ever—do you hear? I gave my vow to Rory, and you need to marry Rose. You belong with her."

Tragedy welled in his eyes as he shook his head. "No, Emma, I belong with you . . ."

Her head jerked up, eyes crazed and fear burning inside as if a scarlet letter singed her very soul. She stared, voice bordering on hysteria and hands clenched. "No, don't say that—"

He reached to feather her knuckles with his thumb. "It's the truth, Emma, no matter how uncomfortable it makes you feel. I suspect I've been in love with you for a long time—I just didn't know how much." His voice held the barest trace of a tease, obviously intended to lighten the moment. "A late bloomer, remember?"

She found no humor in his jest. "Sean, no. You can't love me that way—it's wrong."

"No, Emma," he whispered, "the only thing wrong is that I can't show you how much." He quietly folded her into his arms and eased her head to his chest. The warmth from his body seeped into hers as his hand slowly fondled the back of her neck. "Heaven knows I've tried to fall in love with Rose, for you more than for me, but it was never really there, and now I know why. Charity was right—I am dense. I can see now I've been in love with you for a long time."

She squeezed her eyes shut, fists clenched on his chest. "Stop saying that, it's not right."

"That may be true, Emma, but nothing has ever felt more right in my life."

She wrenched away, shame suffocating until she thought she couldn't breathe. "No—I'm . . . ," she paused, the very words on her tongue proof that Sean deserved better, "another man's wife."

His eyes were gentle as he twined his fingers with hers. "That may be, Emma . . . but you belong to me, not him."

She yanked her hand from his and shot to her feet. Out of desperation, she forced a hard tone. "To me, it's adultery, Sean, and I won't do that—not to someone I love and not to God."

His eyes never strayed from hers as he rose. "I know that," he said quietly, feathering her arms with his palms, "but it doesn't change the fact that I love you . . . and you love me."

"No, I don't love you! Not like that." A sob broke from her throat.

Against her resistance, he slowly gathered her into his arms to rest his head against hers. His voice was soft and low and so full of love that it made her tremble. "Yes, you do," he whispered, "but I love you too much to ever hurt you with that love." He lifted her chin, his gaze tender. "You are the best thing that has ever happened to me, Emma Malloy, and I want you in every way a man could ever want a woman." He stroked her jaw with the pad of his thumbs. "But if you don't want me to act on it, then I give you my word that I won't."

Chin quivering, she flung herself in his arms, clutching him so tightly that the buttons of his cotton shirt ached against the bruise in her cheek. She could hear the pounding of his heart and she closed her eyes, her heart spilling over with gratitude for this man whose love made her feel almost whole. Almost worthy.

Almost human.

Pain shifted in her throat. "Oh, Sean, what are we going to do?" she whispered. His scent enveloped her, soothing her senses with the clean smell of soap and Barbasol and a hint of Snickers.

"Well, for starters," he said with a stroke of her hair, "we're going to eat soup."

She glanced up, acutely aware of tiny blond bristles that shadowed his chiseled jaw and lips that had kissed hers, now curved in a smile. "You know what I mean. What are we going to do about us . . . at the store?" Her voice faltered. "I . . . don't think we can do this . . . day in and day out. One of us will have to leave—"

"No." His voice was firm, leaving no room for debate. He palmed the side of her face, his touch gentle, but his mouth as rigid as the set of his jaw. "*Nothing* has changed. We loved each other as friends . . . and now we're simply friends who love each other. And we'll go on as before." His fingers grazed her chin, lifting to emphasize his intent. "Because if I am to be denied loving you as my wife, Emma, then by God, I will love you as a friend. I promise you, we can do this." A nerve pulsed in his cheek. "We *will* do this."

With a stiff smile, he gently buffed her arms and then strode toward the kitchen, his tone taut with authority. "You go change while I warm up the soup, and then pack a bag with whatever you'll need for a week. We'll come back for the rest."

"What?" She wrung the top of her robe together, fingers cinched at her throat. "What do you mean?" she whispered.

He turned, hands loose on his hips and gaze slatted enough to know she had a fight on her hands. "I mean I'm not leaving you here so that lowlife can hurt you again. You'll stay with us for the foreseeable future, until I feel it's safe to come back."

"With you? At *your* house?" Her voice edged toward shrill.

His lips cemented into a hard line. "There or at Charity's, take your pick. But either way, Emma, you're not staying here, and that's final."

"But I can't! Mrs. Peep needs me . . . and my cats."

"Mrs. Peep loves you and wants you to be safe. She'll watch your cats, she already told me so." The blue of his eyes steeled to gray as he peered at her, the flicker of a dormant temper glinting in his eyes. "I won't stand here and argue with you, Emma. I'm not usually a volatile man, and you know that, but this is too important. Trust me on this—I will take you by force if I have to. So I suggest you pack your bags while I warm up the soup." He turned away, disappearing down the hall where sunlight streamed into her kitchen.

A heave shuddered from her throat and she put a hand to her eyes, numb over how her life had changed in just a few short hours. Yesterday she had been content to be alone, fear as foreign to her now as Rory's violent scorn. And yet, with one vile slap, her yesterday had shifted into a present steeped in fear, shame, and guilt, all neatly laced with denial and despair.

"We *will* do this," Sean had said.

The memory of his mouth caressing hers burned in her thoughts, unleashing a flood of shame and guilt that caused her to quiver. Her hand trembled to her lips as tears slipped from her eyes.

No, God, we won't . . .

15

Charity worried her lip as she paced in her elegant Victorian parlor, wringing the damp handkerchief in her hands with every step she took. Autumn sun streamed through her rich, velvet-swagged windows onto a pastel Oriental rug—where Runt snoozed unaware—infusing the room with hazy ribbons of light that provided sharp contrast to her weepy mood. She stopped at the front window for the twentieth time and parted the sheers to peek out, swollen eyes scanning the street for any sign of Emma. All she saw was Mitch's Ford Model A Roadster parked at the curb, newly washed as always. Its midnight blue paint gleamed in the sun in front of their lush, manicured lawn now dappled with russet and gold leaves from towering oaks overhead. Moisture pricked at her eyes. Her husband's automobile and his lawn—two things he considered his pride and joy. A sad smile lined her lips as she dabbed at her tears. *Like I used to be.*

She glanced over her shoulder at the closed door of his study across their spacious foyer, his constant refuge since she'd made a fool of herself at the *Herald*. Day or night, the door was always closed, as tightly as his heart, while he refused to speak to her, look at her, be with her. He'd barely uttered a single sentence, at least to her, other than a grunt here and there in response to questions he chose to answer. His pretense with the children was flawless, easy banter and laughter while avoiding interaction with her at all cost. And the cost was high—almost forty-eight hours of intermittent weeping over the fact that her marriage appeared to be over.

And now this—*dear Emma*—the friend she loved like a sister, had been brutalized once again. Charity peered out the window, moist eyes trailing into a vacant stare. Her mind traveled far from the giggles of children as they launched into a colorful mountain of leaves across the street or the pungent smell of wood smoke curling into the air. No, instead she saw memories—the freshly scalded flesh of her dearest friend, oozing blisters the length of her face, once tender tissue, now scarlet and wet. Charity's eyelids shuddered closed, desperate to shut out the image of battered skin, bruised and broken, forever scarring not only a beautiful face, but a beautiful soul.

The chug of her father's Model T pulled her back to the present, and her eyelids popped open as it eased against the curb behind Mitch's roadster. Sean rose from the driver's side, and Charity bolted across the hall to quickly tap on Mitch's door before thrusting it open. "They're here," she cried, complying with his request to let him know as soon as Sean and Emma arrived. Without awaiting his answer, she rushed to the etched-glass-and-wood front door and flung it wide, grateful that Henry and Hope were at Faith's on an overnight with their cousins. She darted past the stately white columns of their large brick portico, completely oblivious to the cold bite in the air as she bounded down the brick walkway lined with boxwoods and mums.

Charity rushed to where Sean was helping Emma from the car, and bile rose at the sight of pulpy bruises on her dear friend's face. "Oh, Emma," she whispered. Her voice cracked with emotion as she embraced her as gingerly as possible, powerless to staunch the flow of tears to her eyes. She cupped the smooth side of Emma's face and forced a smile, determined to fight the quiver in her voice. "Let's get you inside with a cup of hot tea, all right?" She glanced up at

Sean, her concern a mirror of his own. "Everything's taken care of—her bags, her cats?"

He nodded, gently kneading Emma's shoulder before retrieving her valises from the car. "Mrs. Peep is keeping her cats, and we packed all essentials and a week's worth of clothes." He hiked two hefty suitcases from the car and gave Charity a stiff smile. "I'll bring the rest of her things over later, but I'll warn you right now, she insists she's only staying a few weeks."

"She'll stay as long as it takes to guarantee her safety, and that will be that." Mitch grabbed a suitcase, his eyes softening as they lighted on Emma. "Is that understood?"

"Mitch, that isn't necess—" Emma began.

"Oh, yes, it is, Emma," Charity gently circled her waist to lead her to the door, "and it's best not to argue, given the mood he's been in." She peeked at her husband, her tone cautiously playful as she tilted her head against Emma's. "He's liable to give you the silent treatment."

Mitch inclined his arm, indicating for them to go ahead. "Don't worry, Emma, I only reserve that for the most extreme cases." He glanced back at Sean. "Who did this to her and where can we find him?" His harsh tone carried despite his obvious attempt at a whisper.

Emma turned at the door, dislodging Charity's arm with the motion. "My neighbor's boyfriend, but I won't tell you his name or where he works because I don't want you involved."

Mitch's jaw ground tight in a manner all too familiar. "We're already involved, Emma. You mean the world to us, and neither Sean nor I are about to let this spineless vermin get away with this. *Or* do it again."

"Trust me, Mitch—I sent Casey back to her mother in Kansas last week, so I don't expect him to come around anymore."

Sean moved to her side, eyes tender as he gently rubbed her arm. "That's not what Mrs. Peep told me, Emma, and you know it." His gaze flicked to Mitch's and hardened, along with his tone. "The lowlife threatened to come back and finish her off."

A shiver trembled through Emma's body while tears welled in her eyes. The suitcase plunked to the porch as Sean pulled her into his arms. He held her close, head tucked against hers. "Emma, I'm sorry to frighten you, but you need to understand how serious this is. I . . . *we* . . . love you, and we'll do everything we can to make sure you are safe."

Releasing a frail sigh, Emma nodded against his chest, and Charity's heart stilled when Sean kissed her hair. She held her breath while her brother palmed a gentle hand to her best friend's cheek, the love in his eyes as thick as the air in Charity's throat. "Now let's go inside and get you settled in, okay? Then you need to get into bed—you look exhausted." His mouth tipped up as he opened the front door. "Which is no great surprise with the hours you work."

Mitch followed them in, humor masking the threat of his tone. "Am I going to have to get tough with you like I do with Charity, Emma, and badger you into working less hours?"

"Better do what he says," Charity whispered loudly. "He's the biggest bully I know."

Sidling past, Mitch took the other suitcase from Sean and hoisted both in his hands, shooting Charity a thin smile as he mounted the steps. "Only when warranted, little girl."

Charity's heart skittered at the use of his nickname for her, praying it signaled that his anger was on the thaw. She turned back to Emma, unlooping her friend's purse strap from her shoulder as she studied her weary eyes. "I think Sean's right—you look tired. How about you go up and settle in to the guest room, and I'll bring tea up shortly?"

"That sounds nice." A smile wavered on Emma's lips as she fumbled with her coat.

Sean whisked it from her shoulders and handed it to Charity before shifting Emma to face him, hands clasped to her arms. "Look, I have to get back to the store to finish up a few things, but I'll drop by this evening, just to see how you're feeling, okay?"

"Sean, I'm fine, really, you don't have to do that—"

He silenced her with a splayed palm to the back of her

head while his thumb grazed the curve of her jaw. "Yes, I do, Emma—I love you and want to make sure you're all right." He glanced at Charity. "She insisted on bringing budget reports along, but don't let her have them because she needs to rest." His mouth crooked up. "She comes across all sweetness and light, but trust me, she's got a mulish streak that rivals yours, so you may have to crack the whip."

Emma's lips trembled into a smile. "Stop that, Sean O'Connor, nobody's that stubborn."

Charity folded her arms, relief whirling over Emma's playful jibe. She singed her friend with a mock glare. "Emma Malloy—you're supposed to be my friend!"

The old Emma surfaced with a bit of the imp. "I am, Mrs. Dennehy, which is why I love you in spite of your pigheaded obstinance. Because when it comes to being bullheaded, everyone knows you're the undisputed queen."

"I'll second that," Mitch said as he strode down the steps. "But don't worry, Sean, between your pigheaded sister and me, we'll make sure Mrs. Malloy toes the line."

"Good." Sean turned back to Emma, his grin fading into a soft smile. Holding her gaze, he moved in close and pressed a lingering kiss to her cheek, eyes closed and fingers caressing her arm. "You're precious to me, Emma, and I don't want you ever to forget that."

She nodded while tears pooled in her eyes.

Sean exhaled and moved toward the door, casting a final glance at Charity and Mitch. "Thanks for taking her in. She needs to be around people she loves, and she didn't feel comfortable going home with me." He hesitated. "You didn't have plans tonight, I hope—"

"Absolutely not," Charity said. "In fact, since you're coming by later anyway, why don't you just plan on dinner here, say around six?"

His eyes flicked to Emma and back. "I would love that, but you're sure you don't mind?"

Charity stood on tiptoe to buss his cheek. "Not if you help with the dishes."

He tugged on her hair. "Deal—you wash, I'll dry. See you at six." With a wink at Emma, he turned to go.

"Sean!" Emma's panicked cry echoed in the foyer as she shot into his arms, and he scooped her up in an instant, clutching her close as moisture glazed his eyes. And then in a blink of Charity's wide-eyed stare, Emma pulled quickly away, her motion almost abrupt. "Thank you, Sean—for everything. Please know—your friendship means the world to me."

His throat shifted and he nodded. "I know," he whispered, and without another word, he opened the door and left, closing it quietly behind him.

Emma's shoulders rose and fell before she turned around, her gaze almost skittish. "I . . . am tired, so I think I'll head up now." She squeezed Charity's hand. "If you don't mind, I'll pass on that tea right now, but promise you'll wake me in time to help with dinner and we can talk then, all right?" She started past Charity, and then in a catch of her breath, she whirled to embrace her with the same ferocity with which she'd just hugged Sean, clutching her so tightly that moisture stung Charity's eyes. Emma's voice faltered, frayed with emotion. "I love you, Charity, and I would be lost without you. You have been a gift from God, my friend, and there isn't a day passes that I don't get on my knees and thank him for you in my life."

With a wobbly smile, she embraced Mitch too, her eyes tired but tender. "Thank you for the refuge of your home, Mitch. I feel safe here. You have that effect, you know. From the first moment we met, your kindness and strength has always felt like the hand of God."

His voice was gruff. "Our home is your home, Emma, you know that. As long as you need it."

She patted his arm and moved toward the stairs, stopping only to tease Charity with an unexpected jag of her brow. "Well, the only way I'll stay for even a while is if I can carry my weight, so you best wake me to help you with dinner . . . or else."

Charity saluted. "Yes, ma'am. I hate peeling potatoes, so

that suits me just fine." Her smile dimmed as she watched Emma climb the stairs, and then Mitch broke her reverie when he edged past on his return to the den. Heart in her throat, she halted him with a stay of his arm, her stomach twitching faster than the nerve in his jaw. "Thank you . . . for allowing Emma to stay."

He paused, his manner aloof. "I love her too, you know."

She nodded, feeling her palms begin to sweat. Chewing her lip, she clasped her hands together. "I know. Can I . . . fix you some tea, coffee, or maybe something cool to drink?" A muscle shifted in her throat as she implored with her eyes. "I thought maybe . . . well, you know . . . maybe we could talk?"

Her pulse stalled as he studied her, his shuttered gaze unable to hide the cool anger in his eyes. "This doesn't change anything, Charity, Emma being here. I'll keep up appearances for her sake and the children's, but for now, I have nothing to say."

She flinched as if he had struck her, followed by a swell of anger so fierce, she thought she would faint. Inhaling deeply, she fought it off, determined to offer the love and forgiveness she so craved herself. He turned away, and she clutched his arm once again, her voice a painful plea. "Mitch, talk to me, please—I can't bear this silence."

Blue eyes that had once devoured her in a single glance now lanced her heart with a cold stare. "You should have thought of that before you made a fool of yourself—and me—at the *Herald*, little girl." His hand removed hers as casually as if flicking away unwanted lint. Strong, capable hands that had once held her, stroked her, made her feel so safe and so loved. She caught her breath as those same hands now slammed the door in her face.

Her eyelids fluttered closed.

Charity suffereth long, and is kind . . . beareth all things . . . hopeth all things . . . endureth all things.

Sucking in a harsh breath, her body shuddered as she relinquished her anger in one halting expulsion of air. With a lift of her chin, she drew in another deep breath and opened eyes wet with pain, shaking off her hurt with a square of her shoulders. *Charity suffereth long.* The taut press of her mouth crooked up. "As long as it takes, Mitch Dennehy," she vowed, ignoring the ache of once gentle hands that now pushed her away.

Just like the hand of God, Emma had said. "Hardly," Charity muttered with a swipe of her eyes, sweeping into her kitchen with all the command of a woman bent on getting her own way. "But I believe 'the hand of God' is about to change all that." She tugged a clean apron from her drawer and moved to the window, eyes scanning the heavens with a holy resolve. Exhaling softly, she released Mitch's rejection to the God who loved her more than her husband ever could, allowing his peace to ready her soul. "All it takes is a little faith, my love . . . ," she whispered. Her lips curved as she tied the apron with a flourish. "In a God more bullheaded than you."

God, forgive me.

Emma lay on the bed, gaze fused to the ceiling in a glazed stare, her throat as raw as her eyes from weeping for more than an hour. Weeping . . . praying . . . repenting. She blinked and a stray tear trickled her cheek, slithering cold and damp against her neck—like the guilt in her soul—chilling her skin. As if she wasn't tarnished enough, now she had lured Sean into her ugly web of sin. Dear, sweet, kind Sean—in love with a woman bound to another through sins only an oath could forgive. A scarred and worthless woman who didn't deserve God's forgiveness, much less the love of a man like him.

God, forgive me, please . . . I never meant for it to happen.

And yet it had, and Emma knew deep in the mired recesses of her soul that she was to blame. She'd allowed them to get too close despite the seeds of attraction burgeoning beneath the soil of a friendship so deep, she would give her life for the man. Another tear trailed, causing her to shiver. And now God had given her the chance—to sacrifice her life for his.

He deserved so much more than to love a woman like her, someone who could now add adultery to her long list of sins. Grief heaved in her chest. More than a human being whose soul was as marred as her face, undeserving of all marital love except that of a forgiving God.

The Bride of Christ—perfect and spotless in God's eyes. Imperfect and ugly in her own.

If the Son therefore shall make you free, ye shall be free indeed.

Yes, she had believed that, and through the kindness of the O'Connors, God had given her a measure of freedom she never dreamed possible. A life devoted to him, where peace and forgiveness and joy flowed instead of tears from her eyes. Where love and acceptance as a woman was not tied to a gold band but to a God who loved her despite all of her sins. And God knows they were many. A silent groan stabbed in her throat. *And now there are more.*

She flinched, her palm burning hot against the cool sheets of paper beneath her hand, tear-blotched and scattered across Charity's quilt like the thoughts in her head. Letters she had read over and over, only to dismiss them each and every time she packed them away . . . out of sight and out of heart . . . like she'd done with her life as Mrs. Rory Malloy.

A knock at the door jolted her, and before she could answer, Charity peeked in. "Emma, the potatoes are call—" She stopped. Her gaze traveled from Emma's tearstained face to the scattering of papers strewn across her bed. Shadows darkened her face, and without another word, she stepped in and closed the door while Emma fumbled letters into the nightstand drawer.

Jumping up, Emma adjusted her skirt and sweater, avoiding Charity's eyes as her friend approached. "Goodness, I hope you didn't let me sleep too long."

"It doesn't appear much sleeping was involved," Charity said quietly, her face etched with worry as she squeezed Emma's hand. She paused, her eyes a naked plea. "Talk to me, Emma."

Emma attempted a smile. "We can talk while we make dinner, all right? I don't know about you, but I don't want to incur the wrath of Mitch Dennehy's stomach."

Charity sat down on the bed and tugged Emma alongside, her tone light but her countenance heavy. "A few loud and growling hunger pangs might do the man good. At least that way, he'll be talking to me . . . even if it's only with his stomach."

Emma's heart lurched. "He's not still mad about the incident at the *Herald*, is he?" She studied her friend's face and for the first time, noticed faint shadows beneath her eyes, as telling as the redness rimming her lids. "But I don't understand—he seemed fine when we arrived."

"Yes, well, apparently that's one of the man's many hidden talents—putting on a show when his pride is at stake. And, yes, you might say he's still angry about what I did at the *Herald*." She sighed. "He's slept in the study the last two nights."

Emma folded Charity in a tight hug. "I am so sorry, but he'll come around."

"I hope so," Charity said with a trace of humor. "At least while I'm young enough to enjoy it." She pulled away, hands locked on Emma's arms. "But it's not Mitch I'm worried about right now, Emma, it's you." Her smile diminished. "Something's desperately wrong, and I have a gut feeling there's more to it than Casey's no-good boyfriend."

Emma glanced away, focusing on mauve curtains looped over a double window where sheers fluttered from a radiator below. She swallowed to clear the emotion in her throat while her gaze wandered to pictures of pastoral scenes gracing pale green walls. "Please," she whispered, striving for assurance she didn't feel, "it's nothing to concern yourself with. I'm fine, really."

Charity cradled the side of Emma's face. "Nothing to concern myself with?" she whispered sadly. "Even when the friend of my heart has fallen in love?"

Emma froze. "What . . . do you mean?" she said, her words as slow and thick as the bile rising in her throat.

Compassion glimmered in Charity's eyes. Her voice was gentle, like the touch of her hand. "Emma . . . this is me, the friend who loves you like a sister, and the sister who knows you better than you know yourself." She exhaled softly, gaze tender. "You're in love with my brother . . . and he's in love with you."

Emma jerked away as heat scalded her cheeks. "No, don't say that—ever! It's not . . ." The weight of a near lie forced hot tears from her eyes.

"Not . . . true?" Charity finished, her tone barely audible.

Every fiber of Emma's being wanted to deny it, but she was loath to add to her sins. She lowered her head, gaze glued to her hands now limp in her lap. "No . . . it's not . . . right." Her voice shuddered as she closed her eyes, reluctant to witness her best friend's shock. "It's against my vow to both Rory and God, Charity," she whispered, "and a grievous sin before God."

Charity clasped Emma's hands, her voice intense. "Only if it's acted upon in the flesh, Emma, which is something I know you would never do."

Emma shot to her feet, the weight of her guilt suffocating her. "God, forgive me . . . I'm nothing more than an infidel, a harlot who bewitched your brother." She gasped for air, a hand to her throat. "Rory was right—a worthless whore."

Charity bolted up from the bed, shaking Emma hard. "Stop it, Emma—now! Rory was never right a day in his life, and you know it. I thought after all this time, you finally understood that—that everything he ever said to you was a lie."

Emma collapsed into a sob, and Charity folded her in her arms, stroking her hair.

"I love you, Emma, and you are the dearest human being I have ever met. If my brother is in love with you, and he would be a fool not to be, then it's because of who you are—a woman gentle and kind and so full of God's love that you helped to save my very soul." She pulled away to study Emma through tortured eyes. "You haven't . . . acted on it, have you? You and Sean?"

Emma shook her head, lips quivering with every word she spoke. "No, not that w-way. And h-he's only kissed me once, I swear." She looked up, eyes haunted by the secrets of her soul. "But God help me, Charity, the m-moment his lips touched mine, I craved to b-belong to him in every possible way . . ."

"It was only one kiss, Emma," Charity said quietly. "A simple mistake that doesn't have to happen again." She pushed Emma's hair back with gentle hands. "You're good friends, you and Sean—there's no sin in loving him, you know."

Emma closed her eyes, the memory of Sean's kiss searing her conscience. "No, not in loving him," she whispered, her throat shifting with grief, ". . . just in wanting him." She put a shaky hand to her eyes as another heave rose in her throat. "I . . . don't think I can do this . . . face the temptation day after day . . ."

With a heavy sigh, Charity hooked an arm to Emma's waist and tugged her back to the bed, resting her head against hers as the two sat, shoulder to shoulder. "Well, my faith has come a long way from our days in Dublin, Mrs. Malloy, so I say we just put your friendship with Sean in God's capable hands, and let him worry about it."

Emma slid her a sideways glance. "You mean like you did with Mitch before you got married?"

Charity wrinkled her nose. "Oh, yeah, I forgot about that. That was pretty difficult, as I recall." She chewed on her lip, then sighed and patted Emma's leg. "No matter, you're much stronger than I could ever hope to be, so I'm sure you can do this—with God's help, of course."

"You are, are you?" Emma said with a tug of a smile, her gloom dissipating somewhat.

"Absolutely," Charity said with a straight face, right before she gave Emma a mischievous wink. "At least until Rory kicks the bucket."

"Charity!" Emma's shock echoed in the room, earning a broad grin from her friend.

"Come on, Emma, with Rory's drinking, womanizing, and

propensity for brawls, the man can't be long for this world. Who knows? Maybe he's already gone on to his great reward."

Guilt pricked over Emma's lack of shock at Charity's remark. She sighed, shoulders slumping against her friend's. "Not unless they post letters from wherever that is."

Charity squinted, head cocked. "What do you mean?" All at once she sat straight up, eyes gaping along with her mouth. "You mean those letters I saw on the bed, they're from Rory?"

Emma nodded, the gravity of her situation prompting more tears.

Charity fished two clean handkerchiefs from her pocket and handed one to Emma. "Here—Mitch hoards them, so you may as well keep it. I've cleaned out half his stash already, but the way I see it, if the man is going to make me cry, at least he can provide the handkerchiefs." She blew her nose and sniffed, blue eyes narrowing to slits. "So that no-good louse has been writing you letters? For how long?"

"Almost two months now," Emma said, dabbing her eyes.

"And you didn't tell me?"

Emma squeezed her friend's hand with a gentle slope of brows. "I didn't want to upset you since I had no intention of responding." She looked away, avoiding Charity's eyes. "But that was before . . ." Her throat shifted. "Before I became a liability to your brother."

"So help me, Emma Malloy, if I hear you tear yourself down one more time . . ." A loud exhale puffed from Charity's lips as she shifted on the bed, staring Emma down. The heated glint in her eye issued fair warning. "So what does the browbeater want now? Your paycheck? Your peace of mind? Or just another pretty face to slap when he's down in the bottle?"

Emma looked away, fighting the sting of tears.

"Emma?" Charity's voice jumped an octave.

Taking in shaky air, Emma's chest expanded as if drawing in strength to face Charity head-on. "He wants . . . ," she swallowed hard, unable to stem the moisture in her eyes, ". . . me."

"No!" Charity bounded to her feet, her shriek bouncing

off the walls like a battle cry. "He can't have you . . . you don't belong to him anymore!"

Emma looked away, the sound of Charity's shallow breathing filling the silence of the room. Her shoulders bent as she bowed her head, weighted by the whisper that wavered from her lips. "I gave him my vow, Charity . . . and he needs me."

"No!"

Tears welled as she stared up at her friend. "He was injured, at the factory where he worked, and now he's all alone—"

"Good!" Charity said with a fold of her arms.

Emma rose, her heart heavy. "He says the accident and other things have changed him, opened his eyes to God and the truth . . ." Her tongue stalled at words she was reluctant to say. "He . . . wants me to forgive him . . . ," emotion clogged in her throat, ". . . and to come home."

Charity shook Emma's shoulders, her gaze gouging as deep as the grip of her fingers. "You can't do this, Emma. You can't leave those who love you for someone who doesn't. A monster who abused you, might have killed you had you stayed."

"It's the right thing to do," Emma whispered. "Especially now." Her chin quivered despite the rise of her shoulders. "I will not add adultery to my sins by breaking a vow to God."

"Your sins? Listen to yourself! The only sin you're guilty of is marrying Rory Malloy, and I refuse to let you throw all your happiness away because of some misguided vow."

Emma dabbed at her eyes. *Misguided, yes, but a vow, nonetheless.*

Charity's mournful sigh broke the tension between them. She pulled Emma into a tight hug, head tucked close while a tear dampened Emma's neck. All anger and challenge faded from her voice, leaving only the wounded little girl that Emma was privileged to love. "Don't do this, Emma, please, I beg you. I love you and I need you . . . and so does Sean. Don't do this to us."

"Charity, I—"

"No, listen to me." Charity gently kneaded Emma's shoulders, tears of hope brimming in her eyes. "We can put you on different shifts if we have to, Sean and you—"

"Charity, no—"

"I'll talk to him, warn him that anything more than friendship will drive you away—"

"It's not Sean I'm worried about, Charity, it's me." Emma tried to smile through the blur of tears. "I'm not strong enough . . ."

"You are!" Charity rattled Emma's shoulder, a lioness with a cub once again. "If you're strong enough to bear the drunken beatings of a monster for six years, then by the grace of God, you're strong enough to love my brother as a friend and only a friend, do you hear?"

Emma blinked, a tiny smile wobbling on her lips. "No wonder Mitch won't talk to you. Do you manhandle him too?"

A twinkle lit Charity's eye, defying the press of her jaw. "This isn't funny, Emma," she whispered. Her gaze sobered considerably. "You can do this."

Could she? Emma closed her eyes, considering the possibility for the very first time. *Maybe . . . if Sean married Rose . . . and he and she became only friends once again.*

"Well? I'm right, aren't I?"

Emma looked up, squinting at Charity as she pondered the question. "Maybe."

"No 'maybe' about it. Anybody who can put up with me, Mitch Dennehy, and Rory Malloy can certainly put up with a little attraction to my brother." Charity pressed a kiss to Emma's forehead. "Now promise you'll stay right here with those of us who love you, and I promise to wage prayer on your behalf like the heavens have never seen. Deal?"

Emma sighed, patting the hands still gripped to her shoulders. "I promise to *try* . . ."

Charity exhaled loudly as she pulled away, her face easing into a relaxed smile once again. "Good." She linked arms with Emma on the way to the door. One perfectly manicured brow angled high as her lips cocked to the right. "Now if we can just get Mitch Dennehy to promise the same thing . . . ," she gave Emma a wink, "I'll be one happy woman."

"You do have a way about you, Luke McGee, I'll give you that." Katie's contented sigh drifted in the air as she snuggled close, pressing a kiss to her husband's bare chest. The clean scent of soap from his shower filled her senses as they lay in the dark, their bedroom lit only by the silver glow of moonlight as it skimmed across Luke's muscled body.

"You give me more than that, Katie Rose," he whispered, his husky chuckle rumbling warm against her ear as his hand glided the curve of her satin nightgown. "Now, admit it, being pregnant eliminates all the worry of getting pregnant, doesn't it?"

Katie shifted up on her elbow. "Oh, now there's logic for you."

He laughed and tugged her back into his arms. "Come on, Katie, now that you don't have to worry about getting pregnant, you're more relaxed when we make love, more content"—she could almost hear the grin in his voice—"more lovesick than ever before."

She tried to pop him, and he wrestled her to the bed, straddling her with a glint of trouble in his eyes. She fought her laughter with a thrust of her chin. "You're awfully sure of yourself, McGee. If you ask me, you're the one who's lovesick—over becoming a father again."

His grin softened in the moonlight, melting into the same look of love she always saw in his eyes. "I am sure of myself, Katie," he whispered, stroking her cheek as he studied her face. "Sure that my life has never been more complete." He bent to kiss her softly on the mouth before easing down to bury his lips in the crook of her neck. "I'm crazy about you, Sass, pregnant or not, and if we never had another child, I'd still consider myself a lucky man." Rolling on his back, he brought her along and tucked her close. He paused, his words weighted and slow. "You seem . . . happier these days," he said quietly, fingers grazing her arm. "About the pregnancy, I mean . . ."

She drew in a deep breath and exhaled, molding herself to the sculpted curve of his chest. "I am. Once God got it through my head that this was the way it was going to be, I actually let it all go—my hurt, my anger, my will." Her lips tilted into an off-kilter smile. "For a while there, I felt a lot like Kit when I pry candy out of her hands before dinner— kicking and screaming because I want what I want. But the thing is, I love her so much I only want what's best for her." Katie sighed at the touch of Luke's gentle hand on her hair. "Just like God does for me."

His chest rose and fell beneath her cheek. "I love you, Katie Rose."

"I love you too, Luke, and I can honestly say that nothing gives me more joy right now than carrying your baby."

He kissed her head, and then reached for the covers, tugging them up to her chin. "Me too, Sass." Releasing a tired sigh, he bundled her close. "Good night, Katie, sleep well."

"You too, Luke." She burrowed into his hold and closed her eyes, enjoying this precious time when she could sink into his arms and sleep. She'd never been this tired before, drained at the end of every day. But then she supposed that was to be expected. She was grateful that the constant bubbling in her stomach didn't produce the morning sickness that her sisters had warned her about. Katie pressed a hand to her abdomen, even now feeling the rumbling that seemed to occur every day, not unlike mild cramps she'd experienced in the past. She was three months late today, and she was looking forward to her appointment with the doctor next week. It wouldn't be long now before she was showing, her mother had said, and her sisters had already washed and ironed every maternity item they owned, packed away into boxes now stored in Kit's closet.

With a garbled snort, Luke rolled on his side, bringing a smile to her lips when he butted hard against her as he snored in his sleep. That was one of the side effects of carrying Luke McGee's child, she supposed—the man always touching her and hovering over her as if she were some priceless treasure he longed to protect. She grinned in the dark. *And he calls me lovesick!*

Katie tried to get comfortable, but knew it was no use. With a silent groan, she slipped from their bed and padded to the bathroom, her lips twisting at yet another one of the side effects of carrying Luke's baby—an overactive bladder. Flipping on the bathroom light, she quietly closed the door, glancing in the full-length mirror behind as she turned toward the commode.

Air seized in her throat.

Blood on my nightgown?

Her knees buckled, and she braced herself against the sink, her breathing ragged as she stared in the mirror. With shaky fingers, she clutched the back of the gown, and her stomach cramped at the scarlet stains that she saw.

God, please, no . . .

Sinking to the floor, a low groan wrenched from her lips. Crimson blots blurred while sobs rose in her throat. "My baby . . . ," she whispered. "Please not my baby . . ."

Thoughts swam in her brain of things that might not be—a sleeping infant tucked warm and safe in its bed or the sweet sound of baby chuckles as Luke swooped his son or daughter over his head. No scent of baby powder or freshly laundered rompers and dresses stowed away in drawers, nor ribbons or booties or a lacy christening gown to be worn. Katie closed her eyes while her heart plunged in her chest. Nothing but cool, calculated ambition that didn't require the warmth of a mother's arms. Keening against the wall, Katie grieved for the baby who'd become more precious than the dream that had once fueled her hope, causing her spirit to bleed along with her body. All at once, she thought of Luke, and grief stabbed anew, choking until she couldn't breathe. *Oh, Luke, I'm so sorry . . .*

With a frail heave, she reached for the toilet paper and wept for a long while, legs to her chest as she slumped against the wall. She jerked at a knock on the door.

"Katie?"

"W-what?"

"Are you okay?"

"N-no . . ."

"Can I come in?"

"N-no . . ."

"Please?"

She wadded more tissue paper and blew her nose. "I'm all right, Luke, go back to bed."

"You're not all right—you're sobbing in the bathroom, for pity's sake. Open the door."

"You have work tomorrow—go back to bed, please."

"I'm coming in, Katie."

"No, I don't need—"

The door opened, and the sight of Luke—hair tousled, pajama bottoms rumpled, and eyes bleary from sleep—made Katie tear up all over again. In a catch of her breath, he scanned her face and then the bathroom before his gaze froze at the sight of blood on her gown. He knelt by her side. "Katie, what happened?" he whispered, voice taut as he kneaded her arm.

Heaving with sobs, she lunged into his arms with a broken cry. "Oh, Luke, the baby . . . something's w-wrong . . ."

He slid to the floor and pulled her close, soothing her with gentle strokes to her hair. "Shh . . . it's okay, Katie, it's okay. Tell me what happened."

"I g-got up to g-go to the b-bathroom, and then I s-saw the blood . . ."

"Have you been having any pain . . . with the bleeding . . . or when we made love?"

"N-no."

"Any cramping, clotting?"

"My stomach's been churning for months, you know that, but no, no cramping really, except maybe a little tonight, and certainly no bleeding till now."

His heavy sigh feathered her face. "Katie, this might be a miscarriage, but maybe not." He pulled back, thumbs caressing her skin as he held her at arm's length. His eyes locked on hers, gentle with understanding. "You might just be late, you know, given all the stress of law school, and maybe never pregnant at all. And I'm no expert, but it seems that with a miscarriage, there would be a lot of cramping and pain, but you haven't had any of that, nor any morning sickness either. Which leads me to suspect this may be a delayed period and not a pregnancy gone awry." He buffed her arms and kissed her cheek. "Think about it, Katie—a false alarm," he whispered, "a chance to get back on track with your dream."

Tears welled in her eyes. "But I don't w-want a dream," she said with a hitch, "I w-want a b-baby . . ." Her voice trailed off into another painful sob.

He smoothed the hair from her eyes, lips curved in a smile. "Me too, Sass, me too." He lifted her chin with a finger, his tone husky as he nuzzled her mouth. "But just think how much fun we'll have making one, huh?"

"Luke?"

"Mmm?"

"Do you think it will happen—me having a baby?"

He jumped to his feet, and tugged her up. "You bet, Sass, sooner or later."

"But when?" she whispered, her mournful sigh rustling the scant hairs on his chest.

His chuckle vibrated against her temple, lifting her spirits. "When God says it's time."

She glanced up, grating her lip while a wrinkle puckered her brow. "But how do you know he will?" she asked in a timid voice, sounding a lot like Kit when she was scared.

Luke paused to gently tuck her hair behind her ear. "How do I know?" he asked softly, grazing her chin with his thumb. "Because look at you, Katie Rose, crying on the floor of the bathroom because you're not pregnant, when months ago you were crying because you thought you were." He tapped her nose. "It's not like God to put a deep desire in our hearts unless he's got plans to fulfill it."

She sniffed, twining her arms around his waist. "I guess. But how do we know I'll be any good, Luke . . . you know, at being a mother?"

"I just know," he whispered, fanning her hair from her face as he kissed her softly on the lips. His smile all but melted her heart as he tucked a finger to her chin. "You're already a wonderful mother to Kit and I know it will be the same with each of our children. Besides, something tells me that deep down in that legally logical, incredibly practical, do-or-die heart of yours, counselor—" he paused to plant a soft kiss on the very tip of her nose—"is one starry-eyed mother just aching to be born."

16

One minute life is normal . . . the next minute it's not.
Sean stood stiff at his office window, shirtsleeves rolled and hands in his pockets, sucking a lemon drop that was as sour as his mood. Lost in a cold stare, his eyes trained on the game of tag in the park below where children skittered to and fro, bundled to the throat in colorful jackets and caps. He could feel a cold draft and smell the exhaust fumes from autos and busses despite the sealed window, which was now fogged at the bottom from the heater below. The click-clicking of Bert's rapid-fire typing drifted in from the outer reception area where Sean could hear Emma discussing a report with Alli. Everything seemed normal—the smell of burnt coffee too long on the burner, Bert's gravelly gibes followed by Emma and Alli's occasional laughter, the chug and hum of the radiator as its warmth rustled the hairs on his arms. Yep, just another day . . . as normal and natural as the scent and taste of lemon drops mingled with Snickers.

And yet, not.

Sean sucked in a harsh breath and slowly blew it back out, pinching the bridge of his nose with fingers that no longer felt "normal." No, these fingers had touched Emma's face, her lips, swept the contour of her back, her waist, her hips.

Fingers that had twined in the silk of her hair and caressed cheeks as soft and fragrant as rose petals. Unexpected explorations all, now haunting his mind and tormenting his body. Each touch, each memory . . . convincing his heart with brutal clarity that "normal" would never be normal again.

"Headache?"

Sean spun around, the air stalled in his chest. He slowly released it and scoured his forehead with the ball of his hand, attempting a smile at Bert, whose usual gruff tone actually held a note of sympathy. "No, no, just lost in thought, that's all." He glanced at his watch. "Hey, it's almost six on a Friday and you're still here? Alli left ages ago, and you should be gone too."

She strolled in and tossed a stack of papers on his desk, dark brows pinched in a frown as she parked a hand tipped with scarlet nails on ample hips. "I'm going, I'm going. And trust me, I'd be a distant memory if it wasn't for this report you've been yapping about all day. Heaven knows as crabby as you've been, Monday would be a nightmare if I didn't finish it for you."

Chuckling, Sean reached for the report and flipped through it, spiking a brow. "Crabby? Nightmare? Tell me, Mrs. Adriani, as the Mistress of Grump, can you actually sleep at night after pointing the finger at me?"

She buffed her nails against a navy wool suit that actually slenderized her voluptuous frame while a lazy grin stretched across ruby-red lips. "Like a baby feeding on a bottle of warm cream, *sir*," she said with a wink, ". . . laced with rum, of course."

He grinned. "You know what, Bert? This place would be mighty dull without you."

She surprised him by fishing bars of Snickers from her suit pocket and plopping them on his desk, dark eyes suddenly somber. "You mean like this week . . . with you in the dumps?"

He caught his breath and slowly exhaled, folding his arms with a slack of his hip. "I've been busy, Mrs. Adriani, or haven't you noticed?"

"Oh, I've noticed, all right," she said, countering with her own cross of arms while she studied him with a squint. "But that's never made you crabby before . . ."

A huff of frustration leaked out as he reached for a Snickers. "I'm not crabby, Bert, trust me. My mood is just fine."

"Mmm-huh . . . and I'm Pollyanna's sweet maiden aunt." She eyed the Snickers as he ripped it open. "How many is that today?"

"Pardon me?" He paused, the candy halfway to his mouth.

She hiked her chin. "Candy bars, Mr. Sweet Tooth. You usually limit yourself to one a day except this week when you tore through 'em like Horace through Milk of Magnesia." She blinked. "Usually means you're stressed or . . . ," the smile slid into a smirk, "crabby."

Sean bit off the candy with a vengeance, figuring it was better than biting off Bert's head. She meant well, he knew, but it annoyed him all the same that she'd seen through his façade.

She eased into one of the wooden chairs in front of his desk, allowing no chance for rebuttal. "And seeing that Miss Emma's been holed up in that office of hers all week and the two of you have barely said 'boo' to one another, well, it just gets me thinkin', you know?" She cocked her head, elbows propped on the arms of the chair and hands folded. "Kind of makes a body wonder if your 'crabby' isn't connected to her 'solitude' somehow."

Heat crawled up the back of his neck, and it was moments like this that he wished he had Pete's knack for bluffing. Never had he seen a better poker face on anyone—unreadable, cryptic, downright mysterious when he wanted to be. Sean's lips flattened. *Unlike me at the moment.*

He opened his mouth, ready to defend his so-called crabbiness with anything other than the truth, when Bert rose to her feet and smoothed out her skirt. For one of the first times he could remember, there wasn't a hint of guile to be found in her face. Instead, dark eyes stared back while her gruff voice lowered to a whisper. "You and Miss Emma mean the world to us, Sean—especially to Alli, and God knows that sweet, little thing is about as tenderhearted as they come. So this . . . this distance . . . between you and Miss Emma, well, it has her pretty worried." She shifted, and her chin jutted with the motion. "But me? I'm gonna tell you right now that I'm not a woman prone to sentimentality, and nobody knows that better than you." She leaned in then, one fist flat on his desk, and he could have sworn he saw a glint of moisture in those hazel eyes. Leveling a finger, she stared him down. "But if you and that woman don't come to terms and smooth out whatever's going on right now, I don't mind saying that the two of you will be responsible for making this tough old bird break right down and cry." Without another word, she wheeled around and barreled for the door, stopping only to intimidate with a glare over her shoulder. "And leave your crabby mood at home next week, will ya? There's only room for one of us, and I was here first." She scowled and flailed a hand in the air. "I'm going home."

The outer door slammed, and he blinked. "G'night, Bert." He cut loose a weighty sigh and gouged his fingers through his hair, painfully aware of the awful silence throughout the office. Which meant only one thing. Emma had her door closed *again*, preferring to hide away rather than face the problem at hand. Him. Her.

Them.

Retrieving Bert's report, Sean dropped into his chair and forced himself to read it before delivering it to *Mrs. Malloy*. Truth be told, that was the primary reason he rushed Bert in the first place, because he needed an ironclad excuse to actually sit down and talk to Emma. He wasn't sure how or when she'd done it, but somehow the woman had conveniently arranged her workload so that their interaction was scarce, choosing to deal primarily with Alli since Monday while Bert had been allocated to him. He thought about Bert's crusty mood all week, which had obviously been exacerbated by his, and his lips twisted. *Thanks a lot, Emma.*

Twenty minutes later he finished the report and blew out another sigh, running a thick finger along the inside of his collar. Heat over the task ahead stifled him despite the cool of the day, and he rose and straightened his tie. He tucked the papers under his arm and headed for her office, his steel jaw as formidable as Emma's closed door. *Not leaving till we talk, Mrs. Malloy, whether you like it or not.*

Resisting the urge to pound on the door, he knocked, waiting on her response before he twisted the knob. Upon entering, he flashed his usual easy smile, carefully calculated to put most people at ease, but somehow it had little effect on the pale woman behind the desk. Seldom had he seen Emma less in control than now—jumpy, jittery, and throat shifting while she fiddled with an ink pen in her hand. The bruises were mostly gone, but the fear was not, deeply etched into the tented slope of her brows and the tiny lines above her nose. Her chin lifted the slightest degree, and somehow it drew his gaze to the curve of her regal neck, the delicate lines of her heart-shaped face, the pale pink blush of parted lips. He swallowed hard as his eyes met hers.

Looking away, she quickly signed the sheet before her, hand trembling and voice too. "H-heading out?" she asked, offering a cautious smile before she signed the next sheet.

"Soon, but first I have that report you wanted to see." He started to close the door.

"No!" She jumped to her feet, hands knuckle-white on the desk. Her chest rose as she drew in a harsh breath and slowly released it with a nervous smile. "I mean, I prefer you left it open . . ."

His temper flared along with the heat in his face, and he closed the door anyway, venting with a hard slam. He took a step forward. "For pity's sake, Emma, I'm not going to attack you—I'm a man of my word."

He could hear her shallow breathing as she put a quivering hand to her eyes. She sank back into her chair, visibly shaken. "Forgive me, Sean, I'm just . . ."

"Scared, I know." He took another step forward, his voice

wounded. "You have nothing to be afraid of, Emma, because I won't let anything happen—I promised, remember?"

She nodded and pushed the hair from her face, finally meeting his gaze with a guarded one of her own. "You're right—I'm being silly." She straightened her shoulders and managed a stiff smile. "Your breakdown on product lines?" she asked, extending her hand.

"Yes, ma'am." With a silent exhale, he turned the report over while an attempt at a smile tipped his lips. "Bert will probably deny me all lemon drops in the foreseeable future, but I hounded her to get it done since I know we have decisions to make on inventory."

"Thank you." She flipped through the pages as he had, eyes scanning each sheet. "This looks good, Sean, and I don't have to tell you how much it will help with trimming the waste." She laid the sheets on the side of her desk and looked up, giving him that shy smile that always warmed his heart . . . and now his body too.

He looked away, drumming his palms on the arms of the chair before returning his gaze to hers, brows arched in question. "So, ready to discuss this?"

She swallowed hard while a hint of rose crept into her face.

His smile was tender. "I meant the report, Emma. You told me to put it together and we would discuss it, remember? Last month?"

A deeper blush stained her cheeks, and he grinned, feeling a little guilty that she was more uncomfortable than he. But not too guilty, he realized, because when she looked at him like that, with that soft, skittish gaze, she made him feel like he could bring the world to its knees. He was a man with plenty of flaws, but somehow when he was with Emma, all he noticed were his strengths, and he wasn't quite sure how she did that. All he did know was that she was the only woman who ever had, and suddenly, the limitations to their love dampened his mood.

He sighed and stood to his feet, palms pressed to the front of her desk. "Look, Emma, can't we put all this discomfort behind us? Yes, I kissed you, and yes, I'm in love with you, but we're also friends who have to work together, peers who need each other's help and support." He rose to his full height and exhaled, feeling a lot like a little boy as he tunneled his hands in his pockets. "Besides," he whispered, "I miss you."

Tears filled her eyes, and he couldn't handle it. He rounded her desk before she could object, lifting her to her feet with hands latched to her arms. "Emma, please—let's get past this awkwardness." He wove his hands into her hair, clasping her head in his palms. "I need you—as my friend, my companion, the woman I work with, talk with, bare my soul to. I need to be able to touch you, hug you, comfort you if you're sad or swing you in my arms if you're overjoyed." He gripped her face in his hands, his eyes pleading with hers. "Like before, when we were friends—" a knot shifted in his throat—"and the heat of attraction didn't get in the way. I swear I'll never go over the line, no matter how much I want to, so you don't have to worry. You can relax and be the woman I need you to be. Because I love you, Emma, and I need you in my life."

"Sean . . ." Tears streamed her cheeks, and he pulled her into his arms, rocking her, soothing her, heartsick that he couldn't love her as a woman, but terrified to lose her as a friend.

"Promise me, Emma, that we can go back to where we were, before our desire for each other got in the way."

She shook her head. "I don't know if we can . . ."

"We can, Emma—I swear."

Her body shuddered as she sighed against his chest. All at once, she jerked away, arms clutched to her waist. Seconds passed like hours before she finally answered. "All right . . . I promise I will try. If . . . ," she looked up, her gaze firm, "you promise me something."

Relief flooded as he released the breath he'd been holding. "You have my word, Emma, I will never kiss you . . . or touch you . . . in an intimate manner, I swear."

Her eyes sought his, gentle gray orbs that steadied his pulse. "Not just that," she whispered. "I need you to promise something else."

"Anything."

She drew in a deep breath, as if gathering her strength. "I need you to promise . . . that you will continue to see Rose."

"No!" He stepped back, his tone sharp. "You can't ask that of me. I don't want to see her anymore. I can't be with her when I'm in love with you."

A calm lighted upon her as soft as the haze around the moon, reminding him of just why he had fallen in love with her. The barest of smiles edged her lips, sad and peaceful at the same time. "It's the only way I'll agree to this, Sean."

The temper he so rarely displayed nipped at him, stiffening his jaw. "But why? You're pushing me at a woman I don't want—a woman who tempts me in all the wrong ways."

The implication of his words made her flinch, and he hated the satisfaction that welled within. But she needed to know—know that Rose would be offering something that she never could. He stared at her, a nerve pulsing in his cheek. He could deny his passion with Emma because he was in love with her. He could never deny his passion with Rose because it was lust.

She distanced herself and squared her shoulders. "Then you need to marry her, because she's in love with you and we both know it. I have a feeling you'll grow to love her, have children with her, and then we can spend the rest of our lives as God intended—as friends."

He shook his head in defeat. "Why are you making me do this?"

She stepped forward, as if this final condition had given her the strength she needed. "Because I refuse to stand in the way of all that God has for you. You're a man, Sean, and you need a woman to love, to have children with, a family. You were created for that, I know that as surely as I know that I love you. Do this for me, please. Because when I see you happy with a woman who can love you as I cannot, my joy will be complete." She placed a gentle hand on his arm, her voice a hushed appeal. "Promise me—please."

Moisture filled his eyes, and he looked away. "I promise to

try, Emma," he whispered, unwilling to commit to something he wasn't sure he could do. "But I don't love her."

"But you're fond of her, I know."

He looked up, all energy depleted. "Yes, I am fond of her."

"Then try, Sean, please—that's all that I ask."

He nodded and turned away, moving toward the door with a heavy heart. He fisted the knob and glanced to the side. "You know, I don't know whether to hate Rory Malloy or to thank him. Because without him, you wouldn't be here." He hung his head, lost in a hard stare. "But then again with him . . . you're out of my reach." He opened the door, never once looking back. "Good night, Emma."

———

Her courage crumpled in her chest, convincing her that no pain had ever equaled this. Not Rory's vile slaps, not his cutting words or his heartless philandering. Not the death of parents who didn't care, or the loss of her beauty at the hands of a monster, transforming her into a monster herself. No, this was deep, touching the core of everything she'd ever hoped to be, everything she'd ever hope to have . . . everything she'd ever dreamed or prayed.

She slumped into her chair and closed her eyes, wondering why the God she depended on, the God who loved her, had brought her down to this—a pain so sharp that she could barely breathe. *Why, God?* Giving her contentment in living for him and only him, and then taking it all away with a taste of what might have been. A taste of something good that she could never have.

The Lord giveth, and the Lord taketh away; blessed be the name of the Lord.

Emma laid her head on the desk as Job's words pierced, prayers streaming from her lips as quickly as tears streamed from her eyes. "I do bless you, God, because I know that all things work together for good to them that love you." A heave shuddered through her as she begged God to give her the grace, the strength to praise him in this situation that tormented her soul, and when she finally spoke, her voice was no more than a rasp of pain. "No matter how hard, no matter how difficult, God, I will always say, 'blessed be the name of the Lord.'"

"Emma?"

Head jerking up, she quickly swiped at her eyes. "Rose?" She glanced at the cherrywood clock on the wall. "It's after seven, how on earth—"

"I hid . . . in the ladies' bathroom . . . just like the last time." The young woman hesitated at the door, a contrite look on her face and a beaded clutch in her hands.

"Oh." Emma swallowed hard and rose to her feet. "I'm sorry, you just missed Sean."

"I know," she whispered. "I didn't want to see him. I wanted to see you."

"Me?" Emma sagged into her chair, ridges lining her brow. "Why?"

Rose indicated the chair where Sean sat earlier. "May I?" Emma nodded, and Rose perched on the edge of the seat, still fingering the beaded clutch in her hands. "I . . . know this may seem odd, Emma, but Sean respects your opinion so much that I thought . . ." She hesitated, as if the words pained her. "I mean he loves you a lot, so your word carries a lot of weight . . ."

"Rose, what are you trying to say?"

She breathed in deeply, gaze glued to Emma's. "I . . . need your help."

Emma shifted in the chair. "What kind of help?"

Her hands trembled as she folded them on top of her purse, all the while studying Emma through wary eyes as if deciding how much to reveal. "Emma, you already know that I'm desperately in love with Sean, have been since the age of fifteen, and there isn't anything I wouldn't do—" she swallowed hard before forging on—"to convince him to marry me."

"I know Sean's fond of you too, Rose, because he's told me so."

Her eyes honed in on the purse in her lap. "Yes, yes, he is

fond of me, I do know that." She glanced up, and Emma's heart clenched at the longing in the young woman's eyes. "But I'm not stupid, Emma, I know he doesn't love me." She paused, fingers fondling the beads on her clutch. "Not like he loves you . . ."

Emma jolted up in her seat, heat scorching her cheeks. "Rose, I assure you that Sean and I are nothing more than friends."

"I know that, Emma, truly I do. And to be honest, if you weren't married, I'd probably be pretty worried because he talks about you all the time, and I can tell that he . . . well, that he cares about you very much."

"Sean cares about all of his friends."

"Yes, he does . . . but you're the one he listens to."

Emma nodded, not sure what to say.

"So . . . I thought I would come here tonight to appeal to you, woman to woman."

"How can I help?" Emma whispered.

"I've convinced my father that I intend to marry Sean one way or the other, and he has finally agreed." A smile flickered on her lips. "Of course, it doesn't hurt that the sales for the second store have plummeted since Sean left, and my father would do anything to lure him back." Rose leaned forward in her chair, fingers pinched on Emma's desk. "Father has offered to not only give Sean his store back, but a substantial raise and—if we get married—full partnership in the stores."

Emma's pulse picked up. "That's . . . a very generous offer, Rose."

"It is, Emma, and if we got married, Sean would become a very wealthy man doing the thing that he loves the most—running his own store. And I would be"—her eyes glowed at the prospect—"needless to say, a *very* happy woman."

Reaching for her pen, Emma absently doodled on Sean's report, her pen stilling at the memory of his words before he'd left. *"You're pushing me at a woman I don't want, Emma—a woman who tempts me in all the wrong ways."* She swallowed hard, desperate to do everything in her power to protect both

Sean and Rose from temptation. Glancing up at the young woman before her, she knew that if given the chance, Rose would be a good wife. The hopeful glow and youthful vulnerability she saw in her face softened her heart, and she drew in a deep breath. "Rose, would you mind terribly if I gave you some advice regarding Sean?"

Rose's eyes spanned wide and she clasped the front of Emma's desk like a little girl. "Oh, Emma, please! I need all the advice I can get if I'm going to convince that man to propose."

Emma tried to smile, but her attempt faltered as she idly fingered her pen. "Sean is . . . a very old-fashioned man, very moral, very drawn to a godly type of a woman. He and I have had many a conversation about this, and I feel certain when I say that the woman who gets Sean to the altar will be the one who offers him the purity and self-discipline he's looking for in a wife." She hesitated, giving Rose a gentle smile. "Do you . . . understand what I mean?"

Dark stains of red bled into Rose's cheeks until her face was as pink as the coral scarf strewn around her neck. She nodded, gaze dropping to the purse in her hands. "Yes," she said quietly, "and I appreciate your candor, Emma, really I do. I . . . well, I've been feeling a bit guilty anyway, over how close we've become . . ." She looked up, her eyes wide. "Oh, nothing drastic, understand, it's just that when we kiss lately, things tend to get a bit out of hand . . ."

A bit out of hand . . . Emma closed her eyes, each word a knife through the heart.

"Emma?"

"Oh!" She dropped the pen and looked up. "Forgive me, Rose, what did you say?"

"I asked if you would help me convince Sean to take the job at my father's store."

Lose Sean? Not only to Rose, but to Kelly's as well? She swallowed the lump in her throat. "Absolutely, I think that's just what he needs. After all, neither of us expected his stay at Dennehy's to be permanent."

"Oh, Emma!" Rose giggled and bounded to her feet, heels clicking as she circled the desk. Swiping tears of joy from her eyes, she scooped Emma up in a hug, her voice breathless. "You are everything that Sean says you are—kind, generous, and completely selfless. I don't know how to thank you."

Emma hugged her back, fighting the moisture in her own eyes, which was anything but tears of joy. "Well, I do, Rose," she said quietly. She drew in a deep breath and patted the young woman's arm, brow angled to indicate a demand rather than a request. "Just make him happy."

"Here are the menus, Mr. Dennehy—three selections from each of the ten restaurants you asked me to call, all typed up for Mrs. Hennessey. Do you need anything else before I go?"

Mitch glanced up from the sea of papers scattered across his desk—donor lists, donation inventory, pledges, and patron ads ad nauseam—and reached to take the sheets from his secretary's hand. He gave her a grateful smile. "Thanks, Dorothy, you're a lifesaver. Just my luck that Mrs. Hennessey had a falling out with the caterer who's been booked since July. She's been clamoring for these for weeks now, but I've been too busy to tackle it."

Dorothy gave him a sympathetic smile. "I honestly don't know how you're doing everything on the auction and your job too. I wish there was more you'd let me do."

He shuffled papers into neat, little piles before tucking them into his briefcase. "Yeah, well, I wish there was more you could do too, but Mrs. Hennessey is bent on my handling every detail myself." His lips twisted. "I suspect it's her way of keeping me under her thumb."

She smiled and headed for the door. "Well, it will all be over soon. Good night, Mr. Dennehy. See you tomorrow."

"Good night, Dorothy." He slipped the menus into the briefcase and exhaled, glancing at his watch to check the time. Not that it mattered—Marjorie was usually late, another one of her ways of keeping him in line, he supposed.

Women. There were days when he wished he could do without them—at least the blond variety. He scrubbed his face with his hands and yawned, leaning back in his chair to close his eyes in a rare moment of rest. He could use a little peace and quiet, especially after the horrendous day they'd all had. The market had taken another nosedive today—just another blow in its steady slide since April. Two years had passed since Black Thursday, the day that sent Wall Street reeling when panicked sellers unloaded nearly 13 million shares on the New York Stock Exchange. It had been unprecedented—trading three times the normal volume, culminating in losses over five billion dollars for investors around the world. Anxiety tightened his throat. Investors like Patrick, who'd sunk his savings into the market. Mitch's sigh was laden with worry, thinking how hard Patrick and Marcy had been hit and still struggled today, pinching pennies in these tremulous times. Patrick had encouraged him to invest as well, but he'd put it off, never being much of a gambler with his money. *Only with love*, he thought with a press of his lips, reminded once again that loving Charity, apparently, was the biggest gamble of all.

Exhausted, he drew in a deep breath to clear his mind of his worries, determined to take advantage of Marjorie being late and indulge in a quick nap. He couldn't remember when he'd been this tired. Sleep had been almost nonexistent lately, at least since two weeks ago. His jaw hardened. Two weeks ago that his wife had not only made a fool out of herself, but out of him. Never had he been so furious with Charity, not even in the two years prior to their marriage when such harebrained stunts had been as natural to her as breathing . . . and lying. But this time she'd gone too far, humiliating him in his place of business, not only in front of his co-workers—for whom it was front-page news—but in front of a superior as well. A superior who, obviously as mortified as him, hadn't shown up for their meeting last week. He grunted. Superior. Yeah, right. The only thing Marjorie Hennessey was superior at was getting under his skin.

A trait she obviously shares with my wife.

Mitch sighed and pinched the bridge of his nose, thoughts of Charity inflaming his senses as they had every waking hour for the past two weeks. And during some fitful hours of sleep as well, if "sleep" was even accurate for a six-foot-four frame on a five-foot-ten sofa.

In a fit of jealous rage, she'd lost his respect overnight, something he hadn't believed possible, at least not for a woman who possessed his soul. And although she'd rebounded with calm humility and even tender love in the face of his anger, the humiliation and fury of that night still scalded the back of his neck. Fury that she had invaded his work life, exposed him to ridicule, and then thwarted his authority in front of God and man. He ground his jaw. Fury that she had the audacity to accuse him of infidelity with any woman, much less Marjorie Hennessey. Nothing churned the anger in his gut more than that, lipstick on his collar or no. Not when he had fought Marjorie tooth and nail for months now.

And for what? So that the woman he actually lusted for— his own wife—could accuse him of dallying with another woman. The unfairness of it stung his pride something fierce, and he found his anger stoked white-hot once again. If ever there'd been a time he'd needed Charity's understanding, her love, it had been the last four months, when another woman seemed hell-bent on giving him hers.

Hell-bent. An apt description for Marjorie Hennessey, and yet Mitch couldn't deny the pull she provoked. Less frequency of making love to his wife had a dangerous effect, he soon discovered, making him more vulnerable to Marjorie than he liked. Drawing his glance to the swell of her breasts, warming his body with a slow cross of her legs. He licked his lips as his mouth went dry, remembering the trigger of his pulse whenever her body eased against his.

Purely physical. And purely wrong.

And yet, you can have her.

The thought sucked the air from his lungs as his heart rate accelerated. He jolted up in the chair. "God, help me," he whispered and dropped his head in his hands.

"Go home to your wife, Mitch, Marjorie isn't coming."

For the second time in mere seconds, all air abandoned him as he startled, paralyzed at the sight of Patrick in his door. He blinked, still in a daze. "What?"

"I said, go home to your wife, Marjorie isn't coming."

His prior thoughts and Patrick's untimely words suddenly merged, forcing a blast of fire into his face.

Patrick studied him for a moment, then slowly walked in and shut the door, his gaze never leaving Mitch's as he moved into the office. Without a word, he sat down at the front of Mitch's desk, his body looking tired and worn and battered from the day. He rested his hands on the arms of the chair with fingers limp over the edge. Releasing a weary sigh, he peered up with a cloudy look that registered concern. "You want to tell me what's going on?"

Mitch ignored the roar of heat in his cheeks and steeled his jaw, leaning forward with palms on his desk. He ground his words out. "Maybe you need to tell me, Patrick, since Marjorie has obviously chosen to inform you rather than her cochair. Why isn't she coming?"

Patrick stared for several seconds, then propped his elbows on the arms of the chair and steepled his hands. "You're off the auction, Mitch."

He blinked, eyebrows raised and jaw going slack. "What?"

"You're to turn all your notes over to O'Reilly, first thing in the morning."

"You're joking . . ."

Patrick idly tapped two tented fingers against his lips, his steady gaze fused to that of his son-in-law. "No, I'm not."

"But, why?"

Patrick drew in a quiet breath. "It would seem my daughter has put the fear of God into Marjorie Hennessey, which," he said with the trace of a smile, "is not necessarily a bad thing."

Mitch gaped. "She told you that?"

"No, not in so many words, but I'm not deaf, Mitch, and I'm not blind, either."

Mitch blinked, his sagging jaw apparently a permanent

condition tonight. "You knew? Knew how Marjorie has been after me, and yet you did nothing?"

"No, I didn't know at first, of course, other than knowing her reputation with men. But frankly, there was nothing I could do. Arthur specifically requested you, and to be honest, I trust you and respect you more than I can say."

Mitch looked away, shame adding to the heat crawling up the back of his neck.

Patrick paused, his tone measured. "Mitch, being tempted by a woman and giving in are two entirely different things."

Mitch swallowed hard and closed his eyes.

"Besides," Patrick said with a hint of levity in his tone, "I know my daughter and had every confidence that Marjorie had met her match."

Mitch's eyes popped back open, his anger rekindled. "Your daughter humiliated me, Patrick, made laughingstocks of both of us—you and me, not to mention herself."

"Yes . . . yes she did, no question about that. But you know, Mitch, in her own misguided way, she also proved just how much she loves you. She took a stand with Marjorie to make sure that woman wouldn't get too close. A she-cat with her mate, if you will. And," he said with a slant of his lips, "she managed to accomplish something neither you nor I could do—cut you loose from a project you disdain . . . and deliver you out of the clutches of Marjorie Hennessey." He smiled. "If I were you, I'd go home and thank her."

Mitch didn't share his sentiments. His lips flattened. "No, thanks, Patrick, I think I'll nurse this grudge awhile longer. At least long enough for my pride to heal and Charity to learn that she can't go off half-cocked whenever she gets a whim."

Patrick sighed and slowly rose to his feet. "I'm sorry to hear that. It seems I remember being in a similar situation when Sam O'Rourke came to call a number of years back. I wasn't ready to forgive Marcy then, either, and I believe it was you who told me not to take too long to forgive. That my time for healing might be Marcy's demise . . . and mine."

Patrick walked to the door, then turned halfway with his

hand on the knob. "I wish I had listened then, Mitch . . . just like I wish you would listen now." He sighed. "But I can't make you, any more than you could make me. But I can pray . . . pray that you will put that hurt pride of yours aside long enough to realize that life is too short and love is too precious to waste even a single moment. Go home to your wife. Forgive her and tell her you love her." His lips skewed into a bittersweet smile. "Trust me, I have painful experience."

Without another word, he opened the door and left, leaving Mitch to stare after him with the sour taste of pride in his mouth. The thought came to him to pray, but he put it aside for the moment, knowing full well that the time would come when he would.

He would pray. And he would forgive. And he would even love his wife once again.

But . . . not until he was ready.

◦◦◦

"For mercy's sake, Sean . . . it's a basketball game, not a duel to the death." Father Mac gasped, hands on his knees and scarlet face lined with sweat despite heaving breaths that billowed like smoke into the chilly November night. "At this pace, I'll need Last Rites."

Sean grinned, swiping the sweat from his own face with the sleeve of his gray rolled-up sweatshirt, his breathing not near as raspy as that of the fifty-four-year-old priest, but definitely strained. "Come on, Mac, given your age, you're in better shape on the court than Collin, Mitch, and probably Brady too, even though all of them work out at the gym religiously."

"Yes, well, I work out religiously too, but one does not get a lot of exercise in a three-by-three confessional." He straightened with a groan and stretched brawny arms in the air, a glimmer of a smile twitching at the corner of his mouth. "Although I confess I've been sorely tempted to hide a set of dumbbells when Miss Ramona rambles on about her latest dance recital." He fished a handkerchief from his cassock pocket and mopped his face with a wry smile. "Probably

386

should anyway, to beef up for moments like this when certain members of the flock have a mind to clip me on the court."

"Sorry, Mac," Sean said with a smile. "Had some frustrations I needed to vent." He draped a loose arm over the winded priest's shoulder on their way to the rectory kitchen.

Father Mac held the door while Sean ambled through, then headed straight for the icebox. "Figured as much. Haven't experienced that much humiliation on the court since Brady's struggle over Lizzie before they got married." He waggled a milk bottle in the air, brown eyes pinched in a squint. "Milk, coffee, or tea? My nose tells me that Mrs. Clary just baked a fresh batch of snickerdoodles, so make your decision accordingly."

"Milk sounds great, thanks." Sean placed the basketball on the counter and scrubbed his hands at the sink, his mouth watering from the smell of cinnamon still hovering in the air. His stomach rumbled while he dried his hands on the towel, suddenly nervous about the real reason he was here tonight, other than to vent his frustrations on the court. He sucked in a bolstering breath and straddled a chair, watching Father Mac as he poured two tumblers of milk. He cocked his head, eyes trained on his friend. "You ever get tired of it, Mac? People venting?"

Father Mac turned at the counter where he was raiding Mrs. Clary's pink pig cookie jar. He dumped a mountain of cookies on a plate and smiled, replacing the lid before returning to the table. "Never. I thrive on it, Sean. Just like you thrive on helping others, whether it's coaching the baseball team, building risers for Sister Bernice"—his mouth inched into a grin—"or raising funds for Sister Cecilia's pagan babies." He dropped into a chair with a grunt and nudged a glass of milk forward, along with the plate of cookies. He took a healthy glug while eyeing Sean over the rim, then wiped his mouth with his sleeve. "*Or* helping Emma out at the store for less pay when we both know you've been offered a job making far more."

Sean glanced up, his half-eaten cookie wedged in his mouth. "What? Who told you that?"

Father Mac chewed slowly, studying Sean with a pensive air. "You forget my weekly meetings with the parish council. Seems Ted Russo was quite put out you refused his magnanimous offer to manage his new Woolworth's. I actually had to calm the man down."

Sean sighed and pushed the plate of cookies away, his appetite suddenly diminished. "Yeah, well, I couldn't leave Emma in the lurch, Mac, nor Mitch and Charity for that matter."

"Ah, yes . . . your propensity to help others in play once again, neatly timed with my propensity to let people vent." He brushed cookie crumbs from his lap and leaned back in the chair, assessing Sean with a patient gaze. "Anything you'd like to 'vent' verbally rather than on the court?"

The cookies churned in Sean's stomach like cookie dough in Mrs. Clary's mixer. Suddenly this didn't seem like such a great idea, talking to Mac about Emma. What had he been thinking, anyway? *That I could use some divine assistance*, he thought with a clench of his jaw. *Preferably before I lose my mind*. He ground the ball of his hand along the socket of his eye, trying to alleviate the onset of another headache . . . the same one that seemed to throb whenever he thought about his problem with Emma. He blasted out his frustration with a noisy exhale and peered up at Mac, eyes shuttered to keep him at bay. "What makes you think I need to vent?"

The priest responded with a low chuckle, propping his legs up on the seat of another chair. He locked his hands behind his neck. "Well, I suppose I could convince you that it's my keen sense of intuition, but that would be dangerously close to a lie. So, let's just say as a priest, one's skills of observation tend to become finely tuned."

Sean leaned back in the chair and folded his arms, a trace of a smile shadowing his face. "Yeah? How so?"

"Well, for instance, when a typically easygoing and unusually kind parishioner annihilates his pastor on the court like Beelzebub himself, one begins to take notice that something is amiss."

Sean's smile crooked higher.

"And then of course, when said parishioner chooses an

evening with the parish priest over decadent desserts baked by his mother and sisters, one gets a wee bit suspicious."

Sean grinned, shaking his head.

"But the true tip-off, my boy, is something so remarkable that, indeed, the Vatican itself might classify it as a miracle . . ." Father Mac inhaled deeply, obviously enjoying his ruse.

"Yes?" Sean hiked a brow.

A smile eased across Father Mac's face. "Sean O'Connor, stopping at one cookie—indeed, rarer than canonization for sainthood." The priest leaned in to fold his arms on the table, his smile subsiding, along with the jest in his tone. "So, tell me, Sean, why are you really here tonight?"

His pulse stilled. This was it. The moment he could finally unload all the grief and acute disappointment strangling him inside. To confess it to another human being. Someone who could comfort him, counsel him, and yes, even pray for him. Sean looked up at the man who had not only offered his friendship, but could offer his absolution as well, and his eyelids weighted closed. He didn't want to reveal his pain, his weakness, his sins to anyone, but he needed peace and God knows he needed absolution. Absolution for what he had done . . . Shame burned in his throat. And absolution for what he feared he would continue to do—at least, in his mind.

He sucked in a shaky breath and put a hand to his eyes. "For the first time in my life, Mac, I've run into a situation where I don't know what to do." He exhaled loudly, his gaze glued to the table while his voice trailed to a whisper. "I'm in love with a married woman."

His statement was met with silence, and when he glanced up, he saw the shock on Father Mac's face before sympathy edged in. Sean looked away, wishing he had never come.

"Emma Malloy?" Father Mac asked quietly.

Sean nodded and leaned on the table, his face in his hands. "I never meant for it to happen, Father . . . and neither did she."

"So she's in love with you as well?"

"Yes."

"Have you . . . acted on it?"

Sean shook his head. "Not adultery, but the seeds of it—in a kiss."

Father Mac paused. "A single kiss . . . and no other intimacies?"

Heat gorged Sean's face. "Yes, a pretty intense kiss, to be sure, but no, no other intimacies." He shielded a hand to his eyes. "Except for those in my mind."

"I see." Father Mac shifted. "When did this begin?"

Sean closed his eyes and exhaled. "A little over a week ago. Emma was bruised up pretty badly by a neighbor's boyfriend, and I . . . I was just trying to comfort her, I swear."

Sean felt the solid touch of Father Mac's hand on his arm. "I believe you, Sean. But what do you intend to do about it now?" he asked, his voice measured and low.

"I don't know, I guess I was hoping you could tell me."

"Her husband is still alive in Dublin?"

"Yes."

Father Mac withdrew his hand and released a heavy sigh, elbows tented on the table. "Well, the only choice you have is to stay away from each other, which will be difficult with you working side by side, day in and day out."

Flexing his fingers, Sean stared up at the ceiling, his mind traveling back through the last week. "You have no idea, Mac, what a nightmare it's been at work. Emma avoiding me, stilted and scared when she does talk to me, and then me trying to work and smile like nothing is wrong." He glanced back at Father Mac, his eyes wandering off into another hard stare beyond the priest's shoulder. "And the whole time I feel as if my insides have been shredded . . . like I'm going to bleed to death if I don't get rid of this shame and guilt, not to mention the agony of loving a woman I can never have."

He heard Father Mac's plaintive sigh before the priest spoke, his voice laced with compassion. "I know it's not what you want to hear, Sean, but you have to leave the store."

He hung his head. "I know, but the truth is I don't want

390

to." He jumped up and started to pace, chafing the back of his neck with his hand. "I keep thinking we can do this, maintain our friendship just like before." He stopped, pleading his case with his eyes. "And I believe that, Mac, honestly I do, because I promised her I would never cross that line again, and I mean it."

Father Mac peered up, as if contemplating the possibility of such a plan. "We're fallible human beings, Sean, and we say a lot of things we mean, but as the Bible so painfully points out, the spirit is willing, but the flesh is weak." The corner of his mouth tipped up. "This is a classic example of avoiding the occasion of sin if ever there was." He paused, as if to arm himself for the next words he would say. "You mentioned . . . intimacies . . . in your mind. Now that your love for Emma has been awakened, does being around her prompt . . . impure thoughts?"

Heat snaked up the back of his neck, and he looked away. "No, of course not, not if you mean thoughts of . . . making love to her." He returned his gaze to Father Mac's, his eyes intense. "Believe me, Mac, I love Emma and respect her far too much to let my thoughts go in that direction. But I'd be lying if I told you I didn't think about her, about what it would be like to be married to her, hold her, kiss her, touch her at will." Dropping back in his chair, he suddenly felt drained, elbow cocked on the table and head in his hand. He stared aimlessly at the floor, his whisper flat and monotone, as if all emotion had siphoned out. "The truth is I want her in every possible way—as my friend, as my wife, as my lover." Wetness stung in his eyes and he shielded his face. "But I know I can't have her that way, and every day, it eats at me a little bit more." A heaving breath left his lips. "And to be honest with you, Mac . . . I'm not sure I can live with that."

Father Mac rose to refill their glasses, gripping Sean's shoulder in a show of support before sitting back down. Leaning forward, he locked gazes with him, elbows on his knees and hands clasped. His voice was low and resonated with a strength that Sean needed to hear. "Yes . . . yes, you can. There's a very handy Scripture that tells us we can do all things through Christ who strengthens us." He patted Sean's hand and eased back in his chair. "Even this."

"How?" Sean whispered.

"Do you love her?"

A wave of emotion surged in his throat. "More than my own life, Mac."

Father Mac stared, sorrow etched in the lines of his face. "Then you have to go," he said, the very utterance of those words depleting all air from Sean's lungs . . . all hope from his heart. "Because if you stay, something as pure and beautiful as your love for Emma could be used against her in the battle for her soul . . . and yours."

Sean hung his head, the truth weighing him down . . . and yet, somehow setting him free at the same time. He nodded and exhaled slowly, relinquishing in that one excruciating moment, all hope of a love affair with Emma. Not a love affair of the flesh, no. He'd known from the start that his love for her would never allow him to hurt her that way. But a love affair of the spirit, where he'd hoped to be lovers emotionally, if not physically . . . through friendship.

Friends who longed for each other. His eyes drifted closed. Adultery, all the same.

"Nothing satisfies the human heart like the love of God."

Her words lighted on his mind, driving home a painful truth. His desire for a love affair with Emma in spirit, if not body, could very well jeopardize her love affair with God . . . jeopardize her peace, her contentment, placing his needs above her own. Needs and desires forever unfulfilled, all neatly cloaked in friendship. Tears stung his eyes. *God, forgive me.*

"Is there . . . anything else?" Father Mac's voice held a note of caution.

Sean looked up, a crook in his brow. "What do you mean? Isn't this enough?"

"Yes, this is certainly a start, but . . ." Father Mac hesitated, finally peering up beneath salt and pepper brows. "I was just wondering because Patrick mentioned something awhile back that's been bothering me."

"Yeah? What?" Sean squinted, no earthly idea what was on Mac's mind.

Father Mac exhaled. "Well, it seems he's worried about you."

Sean sat straight up, face pinched in a frown. "About what?"

The priest studied him with that somewhat professional air that Sean noticed whenever he went to him for confession, something he usually avoided due to their friendship. A counseling mode that said for the moment, Father Mac wasn't just his friend, but his pastor as well. "He said that you lost your temper after Katie and Luke's wedding, something about pulverizing a friend of Emma's for no apparent reason."

Heat blasted his face, and he glanced away, unable to face the look of concern in his friend's eyes. "So what, Mac? Can't a man lose his temper without it being a federal crime?"

"Not a man like you, my friend—one of the most even-tempered, disciplined men I've had the pleasure to know." His exhale carried the weight of his concern. "Patrick's not the only one who's worried, Sean, Steven is too. As am I."

Sean looked up, lips parting at the seriousness of his tone. He forced a tight smile. "Well, don't, Mac—I'm fine, I assure you. It was a one-time thing."

Father Mac paused, the gravity in his voice slowing Sean's pulse. "Well, tell me, my friend—are the nightmares a one-time thing as well?"

Sean stared, the air in his throat thick with shock. "What are you talking about?"

"Steven says they're frequent, that you wake him up more often than he likes, thrashing, yelling, cries for help. Apparently it's been going on since you moved back home, he says. Claims that when it first happened, he came to your room and found you weeping in your sleep, begging for forgiveness. He tried to talk to you, but when he realized you weren't awake, he let you be." Father Mac shifted, elbow flat on the table and hand to his head. His eyes were pensive as he studied him, one finger to his temple and a thumb to his jaw. "He let it go, Sean, figuring it was just memories from the war, but when he had to pull you off Emma's friend at the wedding, he felt he needed to tell someone." Father Mac huffed out a sigh. "So he told me."

Sean kneaded his temple, his mind dazed. "I . . . didn't know. I don't remember having many nightmares. One or two, maybe, but no more." He glanced up. "Did he say how often?"

"Weekly . . . but you have no recall?"

He slowly shook his head, stunned by the revelation.

"So you can certainly understand our concern, especially after the incident at Kearney's." Father Mac hesitated, as if weighing the effect of his next words. "Did . . . something happen, Sean . . . you know, during the war? Something you need to get off your chest?"

Sean's breathing shallowed as he bent forward, elbows on his knees and head in his hands, mind whirling at how the war had come back to haunt . . . first with Emma, and now with Mac. He sucked in a deep breath and closed his eyes, gouging his fingers through his hair. "I've . . . ," he swallowed hard, finding it difficult to expel the words, "had a rage problem, Mac, but only twice in my life, I swear. Once at Kearney's after Katie and Luke's wedding . . . and then . . ." His Adam's apple bobbed in his throat. "Once during the war."

"What happened at Kearney's, Sean?" Father Mac said quietly, his tone patient.

Sean huffed out a sigh and leaned back, gaze focused on the ceiling. His upper arm strained flat on the table while his fist clenched tight in the air. He absently flexed his hand. "I thought Emma's friend was a drunk who was bothering her. I wasn't in the best of moods that day because Mr. Kelly threatened layoffs, so I guess my temper got the best of me."

A semblance of a smile flitted across Father Mac's face. "I didn't even know you had a temper."

A harsh laugh erupted from Sean's throat. "Yeah, well, nobody does." His gaze lowered to meet his friend's, resignation steeling the line of his jaw. "Nobody but Emma's friend, that is . . . and some unfortunate man during the war." Sean averted his gaze, a knot jerking in his throat. His voice was hard. "But only one of them is alive to talk about it."

Pause. "You . . . killed a man?" Father Mac whispered.

Sean closed his eyes, lips tight at the shock in his friend's voice. His fist tightened till he thought the tendons in his arm might snap. "Yeah, Mac, I did . . ."

"Talk to me," Father Mac said quietly, and all at once Sean knew that it was finally time. The moment he'd dreaded—and yet hoped for—was finally at hand. *Deliverance.* He thought he'd safely buried his past, kept it hidden all these years from the people he loved, but apparently not. It would seem that sins, like vermin, had a way of infesting one's life. He had begun the process of letting go of his pain with Emma, and now he would finish it with Mac. And maybe . . . just maybe, he would find absolution at last.

He began at the beginning, with Clare, and walked Mac through the dark corridors of his mind—a mind whose torment he had borne alone. Until now. When his voice finally died away and his face bore the ravage of tears, he waited, body bent and elbows on his knees with head in his hands. He felt the warmth of Father Mac's palm on his shoulder and he closed his eyes, the touch of absolution a balm to his soul. "As far as the east is from the west, so far hath he removed our transgressions from us," Father Mac whispered with an intensity that brought more moisture to Sean's eyes. He paused. "But there's more to this, Sean."

Sean's head shot up, lips parted and eyes wide. "What are you talking about? I've told you everything, I swear."

Father Mac eased back in his chair and folded his arms, eyes squinted and lips pursed as if contemplating a move in chess. "You're not a violent man, my friend, but somewhere along the way, violence found *you*, and I think we need to get to the bottom of what that is."

Sean blinked, his heart beginning to race at the notion that his rage could be related to anything other than his own sin. "What do you mean, Mac? Like when I was a kid?"

"More than likely. These bouts of rage have only happened twice as an adult, correct?"

Sean nodded.

"Did you lose your temper any other time? As a boy, maybe, on the schoolyard, with your family, or in a tussle with anyone at all?"

Brows pinched, Sean closed his eyes, trying hard to remember. "Only once that I recall . . . in the eighth grade when Herman Finkel threw a snowball and made Becky Landers cry. I was sweet on her, I remember, and when I saw Herman hurt her, I . . ." The words froze on his tongue, the memory suddenly as sharp and painful as the fingernails now embedded in his palm from the clench of his fist. He looked up then, his face screwed in a frown. "I remember I beat him up so badly that my father punished me for a year, taking the profits from my paper route."

"Did that deter you from future bouts of temper?"

Sean grunted. "Oh, you bet it did. I never did anything like that ever again."

"To win your father's approval?"

Sean nodded, his smile stiff as his gaze wandered beyond Mac's shoulder. "I was always the good boy," he whispered . . . almost wincing because somehow, the admission caused him great pain.

"So, you never lost your temper as a boy except in the eighth grade? Never got angry over anything else—your parents' discipline, squabbles with siblings, not getting your own way?"

Sean's eyelids weighted closed, his breathing suddenly erratic as he traveled back in time. "No . . . no, nothing. I was the perfect son—compliant, nonconfrontational, the peacemaker in a family of Irish tempers. I was the oldest, you know, the big brother who was expected to set an example and take care of his sisters . . ." His voice suddenly trailed off, and in one heave of shallow air, his heart cramped in his chest. He squeezed his eyes even tighter, as if to ward off the shock of unwelcome thoughts, while his pulse throbbed in his brain. "Only . . . I . . . didn't," he rasped, his voice hoarse with emotion as tears stung his eyes. "Oh, dear God . . . I didn't . . ."

Father Mac leaned in. "You didn't what, Sean?"

He saw it in his mind's eye, then, and bile instantly rose in his throat, forcing his eyes to open in shock. "Protect her," he said, his voice half dead. "I couldn't protect her."

"Who?" Father Mac asked.

His breathing accelerated as he stared straight ahead. "Charity," he whispered, seeing his beautiful six-year-old sister in the lap of Uncle Paul. "I didn't protect her . . . from him." And suddenly he was all of nine years old again, the summer his sister, Hope, died of polio while Faith, her twin, lay sick in a hospital far away. "You're in charge of your sister," his father had said before his parents left, "to make sure you both do everything that Uncle Paul says."

And he had. Obedient to a fault.

Sean closed his eyes in a futile attempt to block out the memory of Charity's cries every time Uncle Paul had shut him out with a door in his face. "Your sister needs to be disciplined," his uncle would say, and each and every time, fear and nausea had roiled in Sean's gut, telling him something wasn't right. But he was a good boy, who always did what he was told, and so he let it go. Against his will. And Charity paid the price.

"Protect her from whom?" Father Mac asked quietly.

"From the devil," Sean said, his voice edged with hate. "Uncle Paul." His chest wavered as he drew in a heaving gulp of air. He opened his eyes to a sheen of tears. "He molested her, Mac, and even at the age of nine, I sensed something wasn't right the summer my parents left us in his care. I should have done something, *anything*, but I didn't."

"You were a boy, Sean, and your parents had no idea . . . how could you?"

He put his head in his hands, the anguish of guilt eating him raw. "I don't know, Mac, but I had an uncomfortable feeling inside and I just let it go. I didn't even tell my parents when they came home because they had so much on their minds,

a Heart Revealed

you know? With Faith in the hospital and losing Hope? So I did what I did best, what a good boy always does—I kept the peace and I kept quiet." A knot of guilt heaved in his throat as his voice trailed into a harsh whisper. "Shoving it so far down that I didn't even remember it until now."

A weary sigh escaped Father Mac's lips as he sat back in the chair, one palm splayed on the table while the other kneaded the bridge of his nose. "And you've been trying to make up for it ever since . . . safeguarding your sisters, coming to their defense, vindicating Clare . . . and protecting Emma . . ."

Sean looked up, the truth of Father Mac's statement sagging his jaw. "I have, haven't I? Assuaging the guilt of a little boy who only wanted to be good."

"No, Sean . . . a man desperate to right the wrongs that a little boy couldn't."

Releasing a shaky sigh, Sean nodded his head, his heart sick over the injustice to his sister. "I need to talk to Charity, Mac . . . to ask her to forgive me, and I will." He looked up, his vision a blur for the moisture in his eyes. "But in the meantime, how do I forgive myself?"

A faint smile lined the priest's lips. "We take it to the cross, Sean, where the shed blood of Jesus Christ will make it whiter than snow."

Sean peered up, his lukewarm faith making it difficult to believe. "Really? Just like that, and I'm off scot-free? I mess up and he pays the price while I do nothing?"

Father Mac's smile eased into a half grin. "Well, you have to lay it down, of course . . . and repent."

"What if I can't?" Sean asked, squinting up. "Lay it down, I mean? Because I am more than ready to repent—for pity's sake, I've been repenting most of my life. But to let the guilt go?" He plowed a hand through disheveled hair. "Not sure I'm strong enough to do that. For all of my physical strength from workouts at the gym and sports, this rage has taught me that inside, I'm a very weak man."

A chuckle parted from Father Mac's lips. "Then, this is

your lucky day, my friend, because when St. Paul asked God to take away a thorn in his flesh, God said, 'My grace is sufficient for thee: for my strength is made perfect in weakness.'"

Sean's smile was melancholy. "That's exactly what Emma said to me once."

Father Mac shifted forward in the chair, hands clasped on his knees. "A very wise woman, your Emma."

The smile faded on Sean's face. "She's not my Emma," he whispered.

Sobriety settled on Father Mac's features. "No, Sean, she's not. You can't have her, but you can have God's forgiveness, his peace, and his blessing for the path ahead, the path that he has specifically ordained for you. And therein . . . joy, from a God who loves you more than any human being ever could."

Sean's eyelids drifted closed, Emma's words whispering soft in his mind. *"He is the lover of my soul, and to him, I will always be beautiful."*

The lover of my soul. God, not Emma.

He drew in a cleansing breath and for the first time in his life, he surrendered all to a God, who up till now, he'd only given lip service at mass and mealtime grace. Surrender all—the sin, the guilt, the rage—*and* the love of his life. He released a sigh that expelled all the ugliness he'd carried inside for most of his life. "Thanks, Mac, I needed to hear that."

"Ready to take it to the cross?"

Sean nodded and bowed his head, heart fervent as Father Mac led him to total surrender, repentance, and the clean heart for which he'd waited a lifetime.

When they finished, Sean rose to his feet, a different man than when he sat down. He extended his hand. "Thanks, Mac, for saving my life."

Father Mac stood, respect and affection warm in his eyes. He shook Sean's hand, then slapped him on the back. "I didn't save your life, Sean, the Savior did. I just reminded you."

Sean nodded. He paused, glancing up beneath leaden lids. "Pray for me, will you, Mac? I'm going to need all the strength I can get."

Father Mac smiled. "You have it, my friend. Keep in mind that the Bible says God will strengthen you to break a bow of steel."

Sean's lips pulled into a faint smile. "Steel, huh? Well, that could definitely come in handy." He pushed his chair in and carried his glass to the sink, painfully aware he was about to embark on a new life. A life without Dennehy's . . . without Emma . . . and without the only true love he had ever really known. He bent over the sink, the reality stabbing so hard, that he gripped the counter. *God, help me to do what I have to do*. Sucking in a harsh breath, he finally turned to face Mac, desperate to reclaim that casual humor that always carried him through. He eased his hands in his pockets and attempted a pitiful smile. "Destined to a life of pain as a bachelor after all," he said, exhaling slowly as he arched a brow. "Oh, well . . . so much for happiness."

No one—not those abundantly blessed or those who are not—can ever truly be happy apart from him. The memory of Emma's words imparted a sudden sense of peace like nothing Sean had ever felt or seen—except in her. A faint smile edged his lips at the irony that the woman who'd uttered that thought would be the very one who would teach him its lesson.

Father Mac rose, anchoring Sean's shoulder with a steady hand. "You gonna be all right?"

Sean exhaled, giving his friend a firm handshake. "Yeah, Mac, I think so." He walked to the door and opened it to the chill of the night. Cool air blew in, infusing him with a tranquility he didn't quite understand, and he turned, eyes moist with surprise and more than a little hope.

"Yeah, I'm going to be okay," he whispered, feeling the presence of God like he had never felt it before. He smiled. "And probably for the first time in my life."

17

"... happy birthday, dear Charity, happy birthday to you!"

Squeezing her eyes shut, Charity made a wish and blew out the thirty-two candles on her cake with all the bluster of a nor'easter, determined that not a flame would be left burning. She opened her eyes to see smoke curling in the air, and a smug smile eased across her lips. *Take that, Mitch Dennehy*, she thought with a lift of her chin.

"Hey!" Gabe said with a swipe of her face. "Blow it out, not spray it out."

Collin chuckled and tickled Gabe's neck, causing the ten-year-old to scrunch her shoulders with a giggle. "Come on, Gabe, plain old wind wouldn't have done it on that cake, and you know it. It had so many candles blazing I thought I was going to have heatstroke."

"Yeah, you're right—look at me!" She held out a skinny arm marred with scrapes and smudges from arm wrestling with Henry in the dirt. "Pert near fried the hair clean off!"

Charity peered, first at Collin and then at Gabe, her smile as thin as her gaze. "You two are a regular Laurel and Hardy, you know that?" She aimed a smirk in Collin's direction. "But don't give up your day job, Ollie. And you," she said with a tweak of Gabe's hair, "aren't you supposed to be in charge of cupcakes in the kitchen? So scoot, and remember it's chocolate, so Henry's limit is two. If he gives you any trouble, you have my permission to use force."

"Wow, really?" Gabe whooped, disappearing faster than the flames on Charity's candles.

"If it helps, sis, you don't look a day over twenty-two," Sean offered with a grin.

"Mmm . . . doesn't the Bible say a day is as a thousand years?" Faith asked with an innocent blink of her eyes.

Charity shot her a narrow look. "Et tu, Brute?"

"You know, I think you may be right," Katie agreed, her flutter of lashes equally angelic. "But there's no way Charity looks anywhere near over a thousand years." Her lips squirmed. "Although I do believe there were enough candles blazing to rival the second coming."

Chuckles rounded the table as Marcy hooked Charity in a hug. "Ignore them, darling, you're more lovely at thirty-two than you were at twenty-two, if that's even possible. Right, Mitch?"

Charity's smile stiffened as she glanced up at her husband who sat at the other end of the table next to her father with a glass of ginger ale in his hand. The only way he could get any farther away was to sit with the babies in the kitchen. Her mouth crooked up. *Where he belongs.*

His gaze met hers with a smile as starched as her own. "If we're talking physical beauty, Marcy, then yes." He held his ginger ale aloft while his lips veered into a one-sided smile. "If we're talking inner beauty—common sense, wisdom, *maturity*—then I plead the fifth."

"Uh-oh, you been giving your husband grief again?" Collin asked, handing Charity the knife.

Luke tweaked Katie's bob. "Hope so. Hate to be the only husband on the receiving end."

"I beg your pardon, McGee, and just where are you planning on sleeping tonight?" Katie asked with a hike of her brow.

He grinned and nuzzled her neck before she had time to wiggle away. "Right next to you, Katie Rose, and there's not a thing you can do about it."

Tongue in cheek, Charity sliced into the chocolate cake, head cocked in Mitch's direction with a smile as sweet as fudge frosting, her dry wit getting the best of her. "Yes, and where will you be sleeping this evening, darling? Rumor has it that the sofa in the study is quite comfortable."

She regretted it the moment it left her tongue, guilt pricking when Mitch's jaw began to grind, a perfect complement to the ruddy haze creeping up his neck. Covering with a stiff smile, his eyes all but singed her—*and*, unfortunately, her temper as well. Fresh hurt stabbed as sharp as the knife in her hand. *It's my birthday, Dennehy—you can't let your anger go for one night?*

"Ah, conjugal bliss," Patrick intervened, leveling a kiss of his own to Marcy's cheek. "Nothing quite like it, eh, Marceline . . . unless it's your chocolate cake." He nodded toward the two 9 x 13 cake pans sitting in front of Charity. "Faith, I suggest you help your sister cut the cake before conjugal bliss is severely threatened."

Masking her hurt, Charity flashed a stubborn smile and plopped a pitiful piece on a plate with a splat, icing down. "No need, Father," she said, her embarrassment over Mitch's rejection in front of her family taking its toll, "I'm perfectly capable of cutting both my cake—*and my husband*—down to size." She speared a fork into the broken piece of cake and handed it to Faith to pass down, then arched a manicured brow, stomach roiling. "This one's for you, darling."

"So, what did Mitch give you for your birthday?" Lizzie asked, her face all aglow.

"A hard time, apparently," Charity said, sucking a glob of stray frosting from her finger, Mitch's obvious lack of a gift heaping more salt on a wound that was already pretty raw. She drew in a cleansing breath, determined to do this God's way, not hers, no matter how hateful Mitch treated her. With a silent prayer for forgiveness, she handed off pieces to everyone, then nodded at Emma in an effort to steer the conversation clear of Mitch's snub of her birthday. "But Emma stitched me the most beautiful friendship sampler you ever saw, and Hope wrote me a poem that made me cry."

"And what did Henry give you?" Steven wanted to know, a lazy smile spanning his lips.

Charity lifted her chin, two palms crossed to her chest and eyes closed in ecstasy. "Oh, Henry's gift made me cry too—a beautiful card pledging not to sass for a week."

"Sounds like that could cause the boy some pain." Brady smiled as he tackled his cake."

Luke grinned. "Yeah, pain as in watching Collin with a basketball in his hand."

Collin chuckled. "Or you vowing to rein Katie in," he said with a flash of teeth.

Katie spun around. "You said that?"

Tucking an arm to her waist, Luke attempted to disarm her with a kiss. "Come on, Katie, that's just Collin shooting his mouth off."

Collin bolted down the last of his cake and cut another piece. "After you shot yours off, you mean." He dropped a hefty piece on his plate. "I'd get the couch made up, Luke my boy, if I were you—I think you're going to need it. More cake, anybody?"

"More over here, unless the birthday girl wants it first," Sean said, deferring to Charity.

"Nope, I'm done. How about you, Emma?"

Emma shook her head. "Couldn't eat another bite, but I concur with your husband, Mrs. O'Connor, the cake is wonderful."

"Why, thank you, Emma," Marcy said, hopping up to pour more coffee. "I take that as the ultimate compliment since Sean says you're one of the best cooks around."

A blush tinted Emma's face as she rose with her dirty plate. "Yes, well your son *is* Irish, Mrs. O'Connor, so he's not above spinning tales, I'm afraid."

"Oh, so Irish men are not to be believed, is that what you're saying, Mrs. Malloy?" Sean sent her a smile that launched another tinge of rose to her cheeks.

"I think Emma is just stating the obvious," Charity said with an angled smile, "so if I were you, I wouldn't ask for a show of hands."

Faith popped up. "All right, enough of this chitchat—it's time to get serious. Who's up for a game of Blitz or Rummy? Charity's choice."

"Oh, I wish I could," Charity said with a yawn, "but I didn't sleep well last night, so I'm afraid I'm going to call it a night."

"But it's your birthday," Faith said with a scrunch of brows. "It won't be any fun without the birthday girl."

"Sure it will," Steven said with a wink.

Charity rubbed her temple with a conciliatory smile. "I'm sorry, but I actually don't feel all that well, either—must be a headache coming on." She reached for the cake pans to carry them to the kitchen. "Mother, dinner was wonderful—thank you for having everyone over."

Marcy huffed and snatched the cake pans from Charity's hands. "You are not helping to clear the table or do dishes on your birthday, for heaven's sake. And I'd hardly call chili dinner, Charity, but you're very welcome. I just wish it could be more."

"Chili's one of my favorites, and you know it. Especially with corn bread and honey butter. Besides, you keeping Henry and Hope overnight is a godsend in itself because I'm exhausted." She bent to give her mother a kiss. "Love you."

"Love you too, dear, and we're thrilled to have the cousins tonight, aren't we, Patrick?"

"'Thrilled' might be a tad over the top, darlin', but yes, we're more than happy to host a pajama party for the children. *Especially* since Steven promised to join them in the fort he plans to build on the sunporch. We *are* thrilled, however, to give our children and their spouses a night alone." Patrick stood and gave Mitch a pat on the back. "May they utilize it wisely."

Charity's smile faded as she assessed color rising up her husband's throat once again. *A night alone.* Her heart twisted. "Alone" being the operative word.

"I'm sorry I won't be able to help with the dishes, Mrs. O'Connor," Emma said as she rose to her feet, "or play cards with the rest of you."

"Oh no you don't," Charity said, "you're staying. Sean'll bring you home, won't you, Sean?" She bit back a smile at the sight of Sean and Emma, a matched set with pink hazing their cheeks.

"Uh, sure, I'll be happy to drive her home," Sean said, recovering quickly.

"No, really—I don't want to be a bother." Emma appeared flustered.

"You could never be a bother, Emma," Sean whispered. "I insist."

"Then it's settled." Charity glanced up at Mitch, fully aware of the firm set of his jaw. "You don't mind taking me home, do you, Mitch? You can always come back if you like."

His eyes bore into hers as he pushed his chair in. "No, little girl, I'm pretty tired myself." He headed toward the kitchen to say good night to the kids, and Charity silently followed, her mood in stark contrast to the busy chatter of sisters clearing the table and cousins painting pictures with chocolate frosting. When they returned to the foyer, Mitch shook hands with Patrick and gave Marcy a kiss on the cheek. "Thanks for taking the kids tonight. I can't remember the last time I slept in on a Saturday morning."

"You're welcome, Mitch," Marcy said. "Just take care of our girl on her birthday."

"Yes, ma'am." Red blotches bled up his neck as he quickly retrieved Charity's wrap. He placed it around her shoulders while sisters hugged all around. He opened the door. "Ready?"

She glanced up at his rugged and angular jaw, shadowed with heavy evening bristle as always, and her heart broke all over again at the coolness in those piercing blue eyes.

Was she ready? For more hurt and rejection? No, but apparently she had little choice in the matter. Other than to forgive . . . to love . . . and to pray.

"Yes, I'm ready," she whispered. And through the grace of God . . . she was.

"Honestly, Sean, this wasn't necessary. I could have just as easily gone home with Charity and Mitch." Pulse erratic, Emma kept her eyes focused on the walkway while Sean ushered her to his father's Model T, the protective touch of his palm against her back making her feel anything but safe. She stumbled slightly on a catcher's mitt strewn across the dark sidewalk, and his sturdy arm immediately hooked her to his side, causing her heart to climb into her throat.

"You okay?" He scooped the wayward mitt up and tucked it under his free arm while the other remained snugly latched to Emma's waist. "Wait till I get my hands on Henry," he said with a shake of his head. "I'll tell you what, Charity's got her comeuppance with that boy."

A weak chuckle left Emma's lips, the sound strained and nervous as she attempted to slip from his embrace. "She always tells me Henry is her penance for all the times she tormented Faith."

A low laugh feathered the side of her head as he tightened his hold. The clean scent of soap, shaving cream, and Snickers coaxed an extra beat out of her heart while his husky whisper baited her. "Hold on there now, Emma, I'm not going to bite, you know. I just want to see you safely to the car. As I recall, this sidewalk's sent you flying before."

The heat coursing into her cheeks defied the cool of the night. She quickly ducked into Patrick's car as soon as Sean opened the passenger door, hands shaking as she tucked them into the pockets of her coat. Before the door closed, she caught a glimpse of his easy smile in the glow of the lamplight overhead, and her heart took a tumble. She closed her eyes. *God, please . . . give me the grace that I need.*

"So . . . you sure played a pretty mean game of Rummy tonight, Mrs. Malloy." Sean scooted in on his side and slammed the door, tossing the stray baseball mitt onto the seat before jiggling his key in the ignition. The car roared to life, and he flipped on the headlights, casting a quick glance in the rearview mirror before shifting into gear. Shooting Emma a quick grin, he slowly maneuvered the vehicle down the dark street.

She could tell he was trying to put her at ease, but the kindness of his intent only endeared him all the more. She drew in a cold breath of air and slid him a shy smile. "Charity and I used to play Rummy a lot during our lunch breaks at Shaw's in Dublin. We both got to be pretty good, but I guarantee that your sister would have walked away with the win had she played tonight. She's a lot like Luke at Pinochle, you know—almost unbeatable."

Sean's chuckle seemed to warm the car despite the chill of the air. "Yeah, Luke's pretty unbeatable at most games, I'd say." He cut her another grin. "Except the game of marriage."

Emma tilted her head, studying him with a faint smile while her brows dipped in surprise. "You see marriage as a game?"

He downshifted at an intersection, looking both ways before continuing on, then sent her a sideways look. "Yeah, don't you?"

She laughed, the motion easing some of the tightness in her chest. "No, of course not. What makes you think it's a game to be won or lost?"

"Well, take Katie and Luke, for instance," he began, right arm relaxed on the back of the seat while he steered with the other. "Luke's brand new to the game, so he's like a bull in a china shop when it comes to dealing with Katie's independent nature. He approaches his role of husband a lot like he approaches a basketball game—he's fast on his feet, drives hard, and likes to control the ball. Problem is, Katie's the same way, so they end up with a lot of fouls and more than a little temper."

"What about Charity and Mitch?" she asked, fascinated by his thinking on the subject.

He shifted to make a turn, his profile crimped in thought. "Well, Mitch is like a long-distance runner, mind focused on the road ahead, easy pace, lots of endurance. While Charity, on the other hand, is a sprinter—nips at his heels, spurts of emotional energy that kicks dust in his face, and sometimes even attempts to steer him off course, all to get his attention, of course. But he's like a machine, legs pumping steady on one path and one path only—his—either running Charity down in the process or carrying her across the finish line tied to his back."

She shook her head, dumbfounded at the amount of thought he'd spent on the subject. "The saints be praised, Sean O'Connor—and to think all this time I believed you were this naïve bachelor who never gave marriage a passing thought." She shifted to face him, head cocked in question. "So tell me, Mr. I-never-saw-a-sport-I-didn't-like, if you see marriage as a game, then why on earth are you so deathly afraid of it? I would think your competitive nature would be challenged, exhilarated by the prospect of winning at a game that few men have mastered."

Taking the next corner with relative ease, Sean veered the vehicle several blocks down at a steady pace, finally shifting to maneuver the turn onto Charity and Mitch's street. He smiled, offering a sideways glimpse shadowed with mischief. "It's simple, really—I don't like to play sports—or games— where my opponents have an unfair advantage."

"You see a wife as an opponent?"

His grin broadened in the glow of the streetlamp as he eased to a stop. He shifted into park, turned off the ignition, and turned to face her. "I see *women* as the opponent."

"And what's the unfair advantage, pray tell?"

Leaning his head back against the window, he draped an arm over the steering wheel and studied her through hooded eyes, his veiled look unable to hide a glimmer of tease. "Why, moods, tears, and manipulation, Mrs. Malloy, all powerfully compounded by the deadly pull of sexual attraction."

An onslaught of blood assaulted her cheeks, and she looked away. "Oh," she whispered, palm taut on the handle of the door. She swallowed hard and gripped it tightly, ready to flee.

"Emma."

Her fingers stilled on the latch when he touched her arm.

The sound of her name had parted from his tongue as a mere whisper, yet the depth of its passion buoyed her heart with a joy she had no right to feel. Her pulse pounded in her ears as she stared at the strong hand now caressing her own and her eyes drifted closed, unwilling to face the man to whom it belonged.

"Look at me," he said quietly, and her breathing shallowed as she slowly raised her eyes to his. The intensity of his gaze caused her stomach to quiver.

"You are like no woman I have ever met, and if God would allow it, I would get down on my knees right now and commit to cherish and love you all the days of my life."

"Sean—"

"No, please—hear me out. I need to say these things, at least once. Before I go."

Her breath hitched in her throat. "Before you go?"

He distanced himself, and she felt the loss of his touch. Settling back again, he picked up the baseball mitt to finger the binding, absently staring at the glove as he toyed with its laces.

"I've given a lot of prayer and thought to us, Emma, and I think the best course of action would be for me to leave."

"Leave?" she whispered, the very word cleaving to her tongue.

His eyelids lifted halfway, revealing his sorrow. "Denne-hy's—for good."

Her heart stuttered in her chest, stealing her air.

"I know this comes as a shock, especially after what I said to you, both in the office last week and that day in your apartment when I"—his throat shifted—"when *we* . . . discovered our true feelings for each other." He gently took her hand in his, and she was too stunned to resist, staring at his thumb as it feathered her fingers. "I thought we could continue on as friends, but every time I look at you, touch you, see your smile, hear your laugh . . . ," his large hand swallowed hers in a tender hold, squeezing gently before letting go with a deep draw of air, ". . . I only crave you more. To hold you, to love you . . . to make you my wife."

Paralysis claimed her tongue as tears stung her eyes.

With a heavy exhale, he rested his head on the back of the seat, eyes staring aimlessly out the window. "I thought I was strong enough—to be your friend and only your friend, but my thoughts tell me otherwise." His eyelids drifted closed as his voice lowered to a bare whisper. "I actually believed that if I laid aside my physical desire, that we would be free from sin. But I can no longer deny that deep in the recesses of my mind, I wrestle with wanting you so badly, that I fear adultery in my heart." He looked at her then, his eyes naked with regret. "I don't want to leave you, Emma, but I love you too much to stay."

Her eyelids fluttered closed, the loss of him almost unbearable. And yet, she'd known all along that this had been their destiny. This was the path she had chosen. The vow she had made, to God . . . and to Rory. A reedy sigh left her lips as she looked up, fingers quivering while she brushed a stray tear from her cheek. "Where will you go?"

His chest expanded and released. "I don't know . . . I don't really need the money right now, so maybe I'll just donate my time to the church till I find something I like. I was offered a job awhile back . . . maybe I'll look into that."

Her pulse quickened. "Your old store at Kelly's?" she asked, grateful he could return to a job he loved and the woman who loved him.

"No, I don't think so."

She blinked, ridges lining her brow. "But Rose said—"

He glanced up, his gaze suddenly sharp. "Rose and I are over, Emma."

Shock congealed in her throat. "Over?" she whispered. She felt her ribs constrict. "But why would you do that?" she asked, her voice cracking with strain. "She can offer you everything. Everything you should have—your own store, a woman who loves you, a family . . ."

His voice gentled. "I'm not in love with her."

"But you can learn!" she shouted, hysteria rising in her tone as tears welled in her eyes.

With a tender gaze, he slowly gathered her into his arms against her will, gentle strength locking her to his chest where his heart beat steady and sure. She closed her eyes at the touch of his hand stroking her hair, and she had no power over the sobs that rose in her throat.

"No, Emma, I can't . . . because I won't."

"But you're attracted to her, you told me so . . ." Her voice broke on a heave.

He kissed her hair, head resting against hers. "Yes, she stirs my body, but not my soul. When I kiss her, touch her . . . it's your lips I'm kissing . . . your body I touch. That's not fair to Rose, Emma, and it's not fair to me."

"But you're a man who deserves to love and be loved . . ."

"And so I will be," he whispered, grief threading his tone. "Because you and I will always love each other from afar."

She sagged against him then, fingers clutched white on his coat. "No . . . you're a man with needs, desires . . ." Her frail moan slowly ebbed away.

Like her dreams for him.

His chuckle held little mirth. "The way I see it, Emma, if Father Mac can do it, I can."

"But you deserve better," she whispered, her heart raw.

He pulled away to cup her face in his hands, and in his eyes she saw all the pain and regret she felt in her own. A sad smile shadowed his lips. "No," he said quietly, caressing her cheek with gentle fingers. "Because if I deserved better, I would have you." Pressing a lingering kiss to her forehead, he gave her arms a quick buff. "Come on, you need to go in." He opened his door and got out, ducking his head to flash his trademark smile. "The good news is, Mrs. Malloy . . . you get your storeroom back." He shut his door and rounded the car, offering his hand after opening her side. He braced her shoulder on the walk to the door.

"When will you leave?" she asked, leaning on him more than she should.

"As soon as Mitch can hire someone to replace me."

"No one can replace you," she whispered.

He turned her to face him on the portico, the pale lamp-light from brass sconces revealing his sorrow. A hint of the twinkle she loved returned to his eyes. "I know that, Emma, and you know that, but let's not let Mitch in on it, okay? You know how he loves control."

She attempted a smile that failed miserably.

Sean rubbed her arms, voice soft, jaw firm. "Come on, Mrs. Malloy, I know this seems pretty bleak right now, but underneath all the heartache, I suspect God's will for both of us contains blessings we've only dreamed about."

Her eyes lifted to his while her lips parted in surprise. "God's will?" she uttered, a wisp of a smile in her tone. "Just when has God's will become important to you, Sean O'Connor?"

His mouth quirked as he tapped a finger to her nose. "Since I fell in love with the boss. God knows I need something to hang my heart on since I can't hang it on her."

Fingers shaking, she cradled his cheek. "Well then, Mr. O'Connor, if our heartbreak has brought you closer to him, then I consider every tear a priceless treasure."

She felt the bristle of his beard beneath her palm when he pressed his hand over hers. "Priceless treasure," he said, his voice tinged with awe. "My thoughts exactly." He squeezed her hand and stepped away, drawing in air as he lifted his chin. "I'll let Charity and Mitch know, but I was thinking two weeks' notice might work." Several creases popped in his brow. "I know it's probably not enough time to train someone else, but I figure the sooner I leave, the better."

She nodded, a lump thick in her throat. "Two weeks should be fine, especially since I have no plans to replace you."

He tucked a finger to her chin. "Hate to tell you this, Mrs. Malloy, but it's not your call. When Mitch and Charity hear the hours you keep *with* help, there'll be no argument, trust me."

"I do," she whispered, suddenly realizing she trusted no-body more.

"Likewise," he said with that same boyish smile that had captured her heart. His fingers traced the curve of her jaw before he opened the door. "G'night, Emma. See you on Monday."

"Good night, Sean," she whispered, heart buckling at the sight of the man she loved walking away. Tears blurred her vision as his broad back slowly faded into the night, and with a broken cry, she flew down the brick walkway with her heart in her throat. "Sean!"

He turned at the street, and within mere seconds she launched into his arms, body heaving with the need to let him know just how much she loved him. With tears streaming her face, she kissed him with all the tenderness, all the passion, all the love that was his alone, and for one breathless moment in time, they belonged to each other. "I love you, Sean, and if I never reap another blessing from the hand of God, I will consider my life a joy because of you."

He clutched her so tightly, they stood as a solitary figure, two hearts beating as one. He gently smoothed the tears from her face. "I will love you forever, Emma," he whispered. "Through all the family gatherings where we chat and see each other in passing, I want you to always know—my heart belongs to you." He pressed a final kiss to her brow. "Get some rest. Next week looks to be a backbreaker."

Squeezing her arm, he rounded the car and opened the door, giving her a wink as he slipped inside. She watched him churn the ignition and shift before pulling away from the curb.

"A backbreaker," she whispered, her words lost in the rumble of the Model T as it disappeared down the road. "And a heartbreaker too." Clutching her coat, she made her way to the door as her weary sigh collided with the frigid air to become vapor, forever fading away.

Just like our friendship.

She stopped on the portico and turned, face elevated to the sky. "Thank you, God, for the touch of Sean's love in my life, no matter how brief and no matter how painful. And I beg you, *please*—if not Rose, bring him another woman he can love."

Turning the crystal knob of the carved oak door that Charity "just had to have," Emma's heart swelled with gratitude for the friend lying upstairs who would see her through. Charity O'Connor was one of the most resilient, loving, and misunderstood women she had ever had the privilege to meet, and the strength of their friendship was one of the few comforts that warmed Emma tonight. No stranger to heartbreak from a past that seemed a lifetime ago, Emma knew that with Charity by her side, she had an able ally in the difficult months ahead. With a silent bolt of the lock, Emma closed her eyes, forehead pressed to the cool of the etched glass door. *Please, Lord, heal the rift between Charity and Mitch.*

Releasing another heavy sigh, she slowly unbuttoned her wrap and slung it on the ornate pewter coatrack already laden with winter gear. Turning, her breath caught in her throat.

No, please, not on her birthday . . . Emma stared, her heart suddenly bleeding more than the sliver of light that bled beneath the study door. Her eyelids fluttered closed as she pressed a quivering hand to her chest, as if she could still the painful pounding within. *Oh, Mitch, open your eyes—your pride is robbing you of precious moments of time.*

It wasn't Emma's habit to interfere in Charity's marriage, not with unsolicited opinions nor advice, but something deep down rose within, compelling her to knock on the study door. She straightened her shoulders as she awaited Mitch's response, jaw inching up. What choice did she have? People she loved were at stake.

"What?" His tone, abrupt and cool, prickled with impatience.

Emma peeked in with a timid smile. "I'm not disturbing you, I hope?"

Mitch peered up from his desk, the scowl on his face diminishing considerably. "No, of course not, Emma—my door is always open to you." He removed the wire spectacles perched on the tip of his nose and leaned back in his cordovan leather chair, splayed finger and thumb kneading both his temples. "What can I do for you?"

She opened the door wider, taking in the sea of disheveled

galleys strewn across a desk where coffee cups and glasses hovered precariously close to the edge. Her eyes scanned the room that reflected the personality of the man she respected and admired—simple but warm. A massive cherrywood desk presided over a large oval rug of deep russet hue distinguished by a thin band of gold circling the edge. A set of barbells and weights rested on a table in the corner, underscoring the solid strength and resolve of the man before her. The quiet and calm of a library emanated from a formidable floor-to-ceiling bookcase beyond, where endless volumes of literature bespoke a love for the written word. Despite the elegance of the room, there was nothing ornate or complicated about Mitch Dennehy, a man who preferred his surroundings—like his life—simple, direct, and without the clutter of knick-knacks or formality. Dark, rich hardwood floors reflected the glow of a crackling hearth where cedar logs spit and popped in an angry fire, infusing the room with the fresh scent of cedar and . . .

The air stilled in Emma's throat as her pulse slowed to a crawl. Her gaze flicked to a half-empty glass of amber liquid she'd just assumed was iced tea, but the unmistakable scent of whiskey and an open bottle on the bookcase confirmed it was not. Her heart cramped in her chest. *Oh, Mitch, no . . . not after all this time . . .*

Stepping inside, Emma carefully closed the door. "I was hoping I might have a moment of your time . . ." She paused to draw in a deep swallow of air. "To talk about Charity."

The smile on his face compressed. "If she sent you to plead her cause—"

"No," Emma said quickly, "she didn't, I assure you. I come of my own accord because I'm concerned about Charity, yes . . ." Her gaze flitted to the whiskey on the shelf beyond before returning. "But more so about you."

His sideways glance followed hers to the bottle and back, and ruddy color worked its way up his neck. With a grinding of his jaw she recognized all too well, he cocked his head and picked up his glass. "Why? Because I choose the comfort of whiskey over that of my wife?" He held it aloft with a defiance she'd seen only one time before. In Dublin, before he and Charity were married—when he'd gone off the wagon following Charity's betrayal. He emptied the glass in one hard swallow before clinking it back down with a weighty expulsion of air. He closed his eyes and pinched the bridge of his nose, his voice fatigued. "Go to bed, Emma, this is not a habit I plan to continue, so there's no need for alarm. Just enjoying a gift from Marjorie Hennessey for a job well done." His eyelids lifted half-mast while his lips twisted in scorn. "Of course, that was *before* my wife humiliated me in front of my superiors, peers, and subordinates."

Emma silently moved to one of two leather club chairs that flanked the front of his desk, and studied the man that Marjorie Hennessey—and scores of other women from his past—had attempted to possess. But only one had succeeded, and Emma knew from the shadows beneath blue eyes spidered with red and a hard-sculpted face now marked by fatigue, that Charity possessed him still. Perching on the edge of her seat, Emma leaned forward, her eyes soft with compassion. "Mitch, Charity is sick about what she did—"

"Yeah? Well, that makes two of us. Only my nausea grows every day in the workplace where I'm branded a fool."

Emma's gaze met his over the fold of her hands, voice gentle. "Along with your pride?"

Blood gorged his cheeks and he shot up, slanting forward with a tic in his jaw. "Look, Emma, I respect you more than most, but if you think I'm going to let you walk in here and—"

"Tell you the truth?" she said quietly, her words halting him midair.

He jerked around and fisted the whiskey, sloshing more into his glass before he slammed the bottle back down. "What do you want from me, Emma? Blood?"

"No, Mitch," she whispered, "just sorrow over a sin that's robbing you blind."

He blinked, the glass of whiskey halfway to his mouth. His throat shifted and he looked away, slowly placing the glass on the desk. His fury seemed to dissipate as he lowered into his chair, sagging back with a hand to his eyes. "For a quiet and gentle soul, you sure pack a punch."

The semblance of a smile flickered at the corners of her mouth. "Only when I see someone I love make the same mistakes I did."

He huffed out a sigh and gouged blunt fingers through rogue blond curls already badly tousled, then looked away. "She scared me," he whispered. "Shades of the old Charity returning to haunt." He glanced up, tired eyes laden with regret. "I lost respect for her, and my fury took over. Fury over the fool she made me to be, over the disrespect she displayed, over her total lack of judgment." His eyes trailed into a hard stare. "Over destroying the love and trust I thought that we had." He inhaled deeply, gaze settling on the bottle of whiskey once again. "She's not a stupid woman, Emma, and yet what she did was the most harebrained stunt I have ever seen."

Her lips tilted into a gentle smile. "Oh, surely not . . ."

He looked up, and a grin slowly surfaced on his face. "No, I guess not. The old Charity pulled things that would curl one's hair." He huffed out another sigh, giving Emma a slatted look that held definite tease. "Mine used to be poker straight, you know."

It was Emma's turn to grin. "The curls are quite becoming, I think."

Hands propped to his neck, Mitch sloped back in the chair and studied Emma in a squint. "So, if Charity didn't put you up to this, why did you—take me to task, that is?"

Her palms smoothed the arms of the chair before she eased back and rested her head like his, assessing him through sober eyes. "Because sin robbed me of the one true love I was meant to have, Mitch, and I don't want that to happen to you."

Mitch's gaze softened. "You're speaking of Sean, aren't you?"

Heat rose in her cheeks and she looked away. "I see Charity told you."

"No," Mitch said quietly. "You did—just now." His tone turned dry. "One does not live with Charity and remain oblivious to the interplay between a man and a woman."

She nodded and smiled. "You and Charity have been given a gift, Mitch." Moisture pricked her eyes. "Do you have any idea how blessed you are?"

He stared, sadness shadowing his features. "Yes, but I'd forgotten . . . until now. I'm sorry for your pain, Emma, both yours and Sean's. I wish there was something I could do."

"You can," she said quietly. "Forgive my best friend."

He hesitated before releasing a quiet sigh. "I'll try."

"Good. Then my work here is done." She rose, trailing a hand on the polished surface of his desk. Her lashes lifted with the barest of smiles. "I haven't wasted my breath, I hope."

"No, ma'am," he said, lips slanting.

"Thank you." She headed for the door, turning only when her hand met the knob. "It's your wife's birthday, you know." She tilted her head, as if deep in thought. "I wonder . . . what does one give a woman who wants for nothing but the love of her husband?"

He shot her a hooded smile. "Good night, Emma."

"Good night, Mitch." She opened the door and slipped out, shutting it quietly behind her. Closing her eyes, she leaned back against the cherrywood door, the faintest of smiles warm on her lips.

"Happy birthday, Charity," she whispered, her heart swelling at the love of a God who taught how to forgive. "And may it be your best one yet."

Mitch stared long and hard at the study door, knowing full well that Emma was right. It was time. Time to forgive his wife, time to ask her to forgive him, and time to deal with this blatant sin in his life. He rubbed his eyes, feeling the effect of both the whiskey and weeks of poor sleep on a sofa that had served his pride but not his body.

His pride. The same pride that bucked like the devil every

time a woman had ever attempted to control him—whether it had been his negligent mother or his adulterous first wife or even Marjorie Hennessey with her lure of seduction. The image came to mind of Charity straddling Marjorie with a fistful of hair, and a semblance of a smile curved on his lips for the very first time. His wife . . . the woman upstairs who wielded the ultimate control.

Despite ten years of keeping a very tight rein on the woman who possessed him, shades of the brat she'd been before they'd married had suddenly surfaced again, scaring him silly. From her seduction years ago when he'd been engaged to Faith . . . to the outrageous shenanigans she'd pulled to become his wife, Mitch had known marrying Charity would be a challenge. But never in ten years of controlling the woman whose love controlled him, had he expected this, and his blindness in a situation that had obviously driven her over the edge shook him to the core.

Lumbering to his feet, he moved to the hearth to scatter the fire and narrow the flue, casting a final glance at the leather couch responsible for more pains in the neck in two weeks than his wife had given him in ten years. His mouth crooked. *Almost.*

He returned to the desk and turned off the lamp, tucking the bottle under his arm while he gathered dirty glasses and cups. Depositing the dishes on the kitchen counter, he poured the whiskey down the drain, the amber liquid swirling away along with the anger at his wife. He closed his eyes and for the first time in two weeks, remorse slashed like a physician's knife, bringing the healing of repentance. "Forgive me, God, for my stubborn pride. I'm called to cherish my wife, and yet I've failed miserably. Help me make it up to her."

Tossing the empty bottle into the trash, he turned out the light and checked the front door before scaling the steps with more energy than he'd felt in weeks. He paused on the landing, heart racing as he listened to the stillness of the house, marked only by the sound of clock chimes signaling the eleventh hour. His lips shifted. Appropriate timing for a thickheaded Irishman, he supposed. His pace quickened as he moved down the hall, eyes fixed on the room where his wife slept alone. Easing the door open, he stared in the dark, his own breathing suspended so he could listen for hers , but the only sound was the jingle of Runt's collar as he ambled over to lick Mitch's outstretched hand. Seconds passed before he broke the silence with a hoarse whisper.

"Charity?"

He heard her rustle in the bed before she flicked on the light and blinked, eyes foggy with sleep and rumpled hair grazing bare shoulders. He swallowed hard. Heaven help him, she looked more beautiful in the dead of night than any woman had a right, and his pulse accelerated as he moved into the room. Gaze welded to hers, he sat down on the bed and took her hand in his, ignoring the drop of her jaw.

"I'm ready to talk," he said quietly, circling her palm with the pad of his thumb. He sucked in a harsh breath and blew it out again. "Charity, I should be horsewhipped. I've treated you poorly these last few weeks, and I apologize."

She blinked, her beautiful features going from sleepy to stunned.

"What you did was outrageous, but my response was more so. Will you forgive me?"

Her lips parted, but no sound came forth.

A sheen of moisture shone in her eyes, and his throat ached with love. Yes, she was a handful and challenging and infused his life with more drama than any woman he'd ever known, but life with Charity was never boring, never dry, and always an adventure. She was the most passionate woman he'd ever met, loving her family, her friends—*him*—with an intensity that took his breath away. *She* took his breath away, and Mitch drew in a halting breath as gratitude swelled in his chest. He caressed her face with tender hands, grazing her jaw with his thumbs. "I love you, Charity, and I don't deserve you."

The whites of her eyes expanded, prompting a low chuckle from his throat. He grinned. "And then again, maybe I do. We're both stubborn to the bone, and I suspect God knew what he was doing in matching us up. You definitely keep me honest . . . and on my toes."

She placed her hands over his. "Like iron sharpening iron?"

His lips slanted. "That's an understatement, if ever a Scripture was." He tugged her into his arms, resting his head against hers. "Am I forgiven . . . for putting my pride before you?"

She pulled away, tears welling as she stroked his cheek. "Oh, Mitch, of course I forgive you." Her brows tented as she worried her lip. "And you forgive me? For what I did?"

He bundled her close and sighed. "What choice do I have, little girl—my life is totally empty without you . . . not to mention dull. I won't say you didn't make me crazy, because you did. You triggered my temper like never before, and I literally needed time to cool down."

She angled a brow. "But two weeks?"

He huffed out a sigh and took her hand in his. "You trampled my pride, Charity, and you threatened my trust in you. But as your father so wisely pointed out, in your own misguided way, you were proving how much you love me."

"Father said that?"

He lifted her chin with his hand. "Yes, but I'm warning you, little girl—don't ever do anything like that again if you value our marriage, do you hear?"

"Yes, sir," she whispered, leaning in to brush her lips against his.

He kissed her back with a hoarse groan. "Oh, and he said I should thank you too."

"Thank me?" She jerked away in surprise.

The barest of smiles lifted at the corners of his mouth as he studied her through lidded eyes. "For getting me pulled off the auction. Apparently you scared the daylights out of Mrs. Hennessey—a first, I believe, in the history of the *Herald*." He planted a soft kiss to her nose. "Thank you, little girl . . . but don't ever do it again. Talk to me first, okay?"

Her smile wavered. "So . . . was it my imagination or not?"

A weighty sigh expanded in his lungs before he exhaled. He looked her straight in the eye. "It wasn't your imagination, but I thought I could handle it." His mouth zagged up. "But apparently not as well as my wife."

She lowered her gaze as she picked at her nails. "So . . . nothing happened?"

His palm cupped her face, pulling her gaze to his. "No, Charity, nothing happened—ever. There's only one woman I love, one woman who turns my head, and one woman who drives me to distraction." He bent to nuzzle her mouth. "And I think we both know who that is."

"Mitch?"

"Mmmm?" He wandered to the lobe of her ear.

"There was more to it, you know . . . than just my imagination . . ."

He kissed her neck, intoxicated by the scent of her. "And what's that, little girl?"

She paused, her body shivering beneath his lips. Her voice was a whisper. "I was worried . . . and not just over Marjorie."

His lips froze to her skin. He pulled away, a crimp in his brow. "What do you mean?"

"I worried that you—" she glanced up, eyes skittish—"aren't as attracted to me as you used to be."

He blinked, the notion as foreign to him as affection for Marjorie Hennessey. A slow grin eased across his lips before he slowly prodded her back on the bed, devouring her with his mouth. The blood pumped in his veins as he nuzzled her throat, his breathing shallow and warm in her ear. "Now I ask you, little girl, does this feel like I'm not attracted to you anymore?"

He felt her shiver beneath him before she pushed him back, two palms to his chest. "No, not at this precise moment," she whispered, her breathing as ragged as his, "but in the last six months, your interest in me—" a lump dipped in her beautiful throat as she gave him a frail smile—"in *this*, seems to have waned. And to be honest, Mitch, that's never happened before. So I just thought that . . . well, that maybe you didn't want me as much."

He sat up with a noisy sigh, pulling her up to level firm

hands on her shoulders. "Charity, let's get something straight right now. I want you *all* the time, but the reality is that in this dismal economy, not only is work getting more demanding, but you forget that I'm getting older too, not able to keep up with both it and you like I used to." He grazed her jaw with the pad of his thumb. "Trust me, little girl, there are times during the day when all I have to do is think about you, and I want you so badly that I can taste it, but I have to force myself to focus on work instead, driving myself all the harder."

"So . . . ," she said, her tone suddenly light. "I actually help you at work, do I?" There was a tease in her eyes, her smile definitely smug.

He hooked the nape of her neck to pull her close, pulse pumping as he nibbled on the lobe of her ear. "Oh, yeah," he whispered with a low chuckle. "You're the carrot dangling at the end of my day, you little minx."

"Mitch?"

"Mmm?" He worked his way down the side of her throat, the taste of her driving him crazy.

"Can we . . . make a deal?"

He paused, lips hovering over the crease of her collarbone. "What kind of deal?" he said, suspicion edging his tone as he lifted his head.

She leaned in to feather his jaw with soft, little kisses before he groaned and forced her back to the bed. Her giggle tickled his mouth. "I agree to be more understanding when you're too tired to . . . well, you know . . ."

"Make love to you?" he whispered, the very sound of the words chasing his pulse.

She nodded. "If you promise to love me, want me a little more so I don't jump to stupid conclusions like I did with Marjorie. You see, I prayed with Faith and Lizzie about it—"

He groaned. "For pity's sake, Charity, do you have to drag our bedroom through the mill?"

She squeezed his hand. "I had to, Mitch, because you know how I've always measured your love by how much you want me, so when you're too exhausted, I tend to get crazy, needy.

Besides, the prayer worked in keeping me calm and rational while you shunned me these last two weeks."

His lips flattened as he thought about it. The respect he'd lost for her in the showdown with Marjorie had been totally restored, hard-won by her patience and kindness during the weeks he'd turned her away. "Shunned you, huh?" he said with a one-sided smile.

"Yes," she whispered. "So if you're willing to love me more, I'm willing to be more patient."

"If I'm willing?" he asked, sarcasm coating his tone.

She looked up with the glow of love in her face. "Are you? Willing to love me again?"

He studied the woman he loved more than life, the body he craved more than sleep, and tugged the tie from his neck, giving her a heated look as his fingers slowly moved down the buttons of his shirt. Stripping it off, he hurled it away, eyes burning with an intensity that conveyed both his love and intent. He kicked his shoes onto the floor and gave her a dangerous smile. "I don't know, Charity. Give me a second to think about it."

With a toss of her honey hair, she gave him a saucy smile while she slowly slid the strap of her gown off of one creamy shoulder, revealing the deep cleft of her breasts.

His mouth went dry.

"As a birthday present, then?" she whispered, ever the vamp.

He reached for his belt, and then for the light, his laugh low as he kicked off his trousers and slipped in their bed. "You bet, little girl . . . ," he whispered, her skin warm against his mouth. With a slow caress of fingers, he fondled the other satin strap of her gown while trailing her shoulder with lingering kisses. "As long as *I* get to unwrap the presents . . ."

18

Sean opened the box jam-packed with candy bars and shot Bert a wide grin. "Are you in league with my dentist, Mrs. Adriani? This is more Snickers than I've seen in a lifetime."

"Liar," Bert said with a roll of her dark eyes. "It's just shy of a week's supply, and you know it." She folded her arms and perched on the edge of Sean's desk, shooting Emma a wink.

Sunset cast a pink glow as the laughter of his colleagues filled his cozy office, giving Sean a warm feeling that was truly bittersweet. He glanced up at the group of people he'd grown to love and wondered if he'd ever be as happy working anywhere else. Bert made a crack about his departure saving her money since he wouldn't pilfer lemon drops anymore, and more hilarity filled the room where he'd spent some of the happiest hours of his life. His eyes strayed to Emma. Wonderful hours with a woman who now claimed his job as well as his heart.

"So, Sean, any chance we can steal you away from St. Stephen's for odd jobs here and there?" Michelle tilted her head with a playful flutter of lashes she always reserved just for him. "Seems a shame to waste all those handyman skills on the nuns when we're in dire need here."

"Some of us more than others," Bert mumbled.

Michelle ignored her and smoothed her sleek blond tresses with a hopeful smile. "But I warn you—I have lots of ideas for the spring display."

"Yeah, I'll just bet you do," Bert said under her breath.

With a warning squeeze of Bert's shoulder, Emma placed a plate of fudge brownies and Bert's famous pound cake in the middle of Sean's desk. "No more talk about work, please," she said with a smile. "This is the man's last day—let's bury our sorrow in sweets."

Sean patted his stomach, firm from weeks of no appetite and muscles taut with stress. "That's one thing I won't miss—extra pounds from all the desserts you ladies forced me to eat."

"Forced?" Alli said with a giggle. Her innocent gaze flitted from Emma to Bert. "I don't recall seeing his arm in a sling from any arm-twisting, do you?"

"Very funny, Miss Moser." He took the knife from Emma and waggled it at Bert. "You're a bad influence on this young woman, Mrs. Adriani, you know that?"

Bert huffed out a sigh. "Heaven knows I try. Cut the cake," she snapped with a scowl.

"Any job prospects yet, Sean, besides helping out at the church?" Horace's smile was kind as he pushed his eyeglasses back up to the bridge of his nose. A soft-spoken man well into his forties, the dock manager was slight of stature but big in heart, garnering everyone's respect. Everyone but Bert's, that is, who tended to pick on Horace because of his size.

Slicing the pound cake into thick slices, Sean glanced up, offering Horace a half smile. "Nope, not yet, but I've got a few irons in the fire, so I expect to hear something any day now." He slapped a piece onto a salvaged china plate and handed it to the middle-aged man.

"I sure hope so," Mr. Wilkins said. Dennehy's longtime shoe manager reached for the plate Sean handed him with a crimp in his snow-white brows. "Even though everyone knows the job market's as flat as fallen arches on a 300-pound man." He squinted, weathered lips curved in a jest. "But that shouldn't keep a young whippersnapper like you down for long, I suspect."

"I don't understand, Mr. O'Connor," Livvie asked, nibbling on her cake. The salesclerk Sean had rescued from Mrs. Bennett on more than one occasion cocked her head with a squint. "If you don't have another job, then why are you leaving?"

Sean paused, plate frozen midair as his eyes unwittingly flicked to Emma and then away. His neck grew warm as he handed cake to another clerk. "Well, Livvie, my tenure at Dennehy's was to be temporary all along. I was only hired to help out during a particularly busy season."

The young woman blinked. "But our busiest season is Thanksgiving through New Year's, Mr. O'Connor. Why would you leave before that?"

"Because I'm kicking him out, Livvie," Emma responded with a tight smile. She quickly plopped brownies and pound cake on the rest of the plates and commenced handing them out. "I discovered that Mr. O'Connor turned down a very lucrative job because of us, and I'm not about to let that happen again." She brushed her hands with a lift of her chin, addressing the small group at large. "This man is too talented and too valuable not to be managing his own store." She pushed a plate of pound cake at Sean before taking one for herself. "*And* entirely too kindhearted to do anything about it." She took a bite and stared him down. "So we are."

"Well, I know I speak for the rest of us, Mr. O'Connor, when I say you will be sorely missed." James returned his empty plate to the desk and held out his hand. "You've been an inspiration to me, sir, with the number of hats you wear around this store."

Sean rose to his feet and shook his hand. "Thanks, James, but Mrs. Malloy is the real inspiration here, as you'll discover firsthand with the career path she has in mind for you."

James nodded, a spark of gratitude in serious brown eyes as he glanced from Sean to Emma. "Thank you, sir, and you too, ma'am, for your confidence in me."

"You've worked hard, James," Emma said with a kind smile, "and Horace can't sing your praises highly enough, so I'm happy to promote good people from within whenever I can."

Michelle laid her empty plate on the desk. "Well, break's over, I guess, and I've got a register to close out." She rounded the desk to give Sean a hug tight enough to make his collar feel three sizes too small. "Don't be a stranger, Sean O'Connor, you hear? Come by and see us when you can." Cupping his face in her hands, she shocked him with a wet kiss smack dab on his lips. Eyes sparkling, she pulled away and patted his arm. "Been wanting to do that for as long as I can remember." She bounded out the door with a wave of her hand.

Bert rose with a grunt, scowling as she fished a handkerchief from her pocket. She tossed it at Sean. "Here, wipe your mouth, will ya? Before you catch something."

"Good luck to you." With a shake of Sean's hand, Horace filed out along with James while Livvie and several other salesclerks lingered to wish him well. When everyone had left except Bert, Alli, and Emma, Sean dropped back into his chair with a groan, giving them a pathetic smile. "This is a little harder than I thought it would be."

"For you, maybe," Bert said with a bored pat of her hair. "For me, it's a piece of cake." Her lips shifted. "Pound cake, to be exact."

Sean gave her a wink. "Thanks for making this easier, Mrs. Adriani. Gotta feeling I'm gonna miss your mouth almost as much as your cake."

"Then you best drop in now and then," Bert said with a thin smile. She gave a curt nod at Alli and Emma. "Can't sharpen my tongue on these two, or it'll be dull as a butter knife."

With a latch of hands to his neck, Sean winked. "There's always Horace, you know."

A wicked smile lifted the corner of Bert's scarlet lips. "Mmm . . . that's right. Thank heavens for 'small' favors, and I use the term literally."

"Especially," Sean said with a grin, "now that you'll be doing inventory with him."

Her razor-sharp look could have cut a cast-iron cake. She moseyed to the door and shot a lidded gaze over her broad shoulder. "Don't let the door hit you on the way out."

She sauntered into the outer office with a sassy sway of hips, and Emma shook her head. "She's going to miss you more than anybody, mark my words."

"Not more than me," Alli said with a watery gaze. A smile trembled on her lips as she circled Sean's desk with a sharp heave, hugging him with all her might.

"Aw, Alli, I'm gonna miss you too," he said with a lump in his throat. He rose to tuck her against his chest in a fond embrace. "But I'll be back to visit soon, I promise. In the meantime, Emma can keep me informed at Thanksgiving on all the latest developments with a certain assistant dock manager." He pulled away, hands clutched to her arms. "In fact, why don't you come for Thanksgiving too? I know Katie would love to see you again, and so would I."

"I wish I could, Sean, but Mrs. Tunny already invited us— Emma and me."

Sean glanced at Emma, a knot wedged in his throat as tight as a turkey bone. "You won't be at Thanksgiving?" he whispered, never believing for a moment that his departure from Dennehy's also meant Emma's departure from his life.

She lowered her head, eyes focused on the task of cleaning up while a haze of rose tinted her cheeks. "When I found out Mrs. Tunny has six grandchildren to feed in addition to Alli, her daughter, and son-in-law, well, I just felt like I needed to help."

"Emma." He said it softly, but his inflection bore a hint of a scold.

"Yes?" Her eyes remained fixed, never wavering from the task at hand.

"Look at me, please," he whispered, waiting until her eyes met his. "The woman has a cook, and you've never missed a holiday with us in eleven years."

She hesitated, her gaze flitting to Alli and back. "Mrs. Tunny gave her cook Thanksgiving off, Sean, because she wants to fix the meal herself. And I just thought this might work best with all the extra mouths your mother has to feed."

"Are you going to do this every holiday?" he asked, his voice too sharp.

Her lips parted as if she intended to speak, but then a knock sounded at the door.

"Miss Emma, there's a gentleman to see you, so I took him to your office." Michelle hurried in, breathless, while Bert carefully closed the door.

Sean glanced at his watch with a scowl. "It's almost closing, for pity's sake—couldn't he come back tomorrow? Who is he and why'd you bring him up?"

"*She* brought him up," Bert said with a tight-lipped nod at Michelle, arms crossed to her chest. "Everybody knows she's a sucker for a pretty face, and apparently he sweet-talked her."

"He claims to owe Miss Emma an apology," Michelle explained before propping her hands on her hips to glare at Bert. "And as if you weren't salivating when I brought him in."

"Wipe your mouth, Michelle," Bert said with a sneer, "ya got drool all over your chin—"

"Okay, okay, wait a minute, you two." Emma ducked her head, brows arched in question. "Do either of you happen to know just *who* this person is? A customer, maybe? A salesman?"

Michelle sighed. "Didn't get his name, Miss Emma, but I'll tell you what, if that man's selling anything, I'm first in line."

Emma squinted at Bert. "You haven't seen him before either? He's not that salesman from Schiaparelli that you swore looked like Valentino last year, is he?"

"Nope," Bert said with the closest thing to a sultry look Sean had ever seen on the woman's face. "Trust me, if I'd ever laid eyes on this guy, I would have remembered."

Emma frowned. "Well, I guess I can't keep him waiting, so tell him I'll be right in."

"My pleasure," Bert said, her smug look obviously intended for Michelle.

"Wait . . ." Emma looked up, her face suddenly as pale

as the stack of china saucers in her hands. "What's he look like?" she whispered, voice quivering more than the dishes.

Michelle pressed a hand to her heart. "Well, let's put it this way, Miss Emma, if you look in the dictionary, you'd find him under tall, dark, and handsome. Nigh to six foot four, curly black hair, light blue eyes a girl could get lost in, and dimples so deep they go clear back to his jaw."

The dishes dropped to Sean's desk with a loud clatter. Emma's fingers trembled to her chest. "Johnny," she whispered.

The very name unleashed a flash of fury that scorched through Sean's body. He started for the door, his voice an angry hiss. "I'll take care of this."

"No!" Emma's shriek halted him with his hand on the knob. She rushed over, her voice as shaky as the palm gripped to his arm. "I will handle this, Sean, I don't want you involved."

"I'm already involved," he rasped, his fingers itching for revenge. "I'm not letting you face him alone, Emma, so don't argue."

"All right, but promise me . . ." Her voice trembled from bloodless lips. "Promise you won't touch him. Violence is not the answer and I . . . I couldn't bear to see that in you again."

He stared, drawing in a harsh breath before exhaling it slowly. He nodded, then dropped his hands to his sides and looked away, a muscle twitching in his jaw.

Emma turned. "Tell him I'll be right in, Bert, then go home. Michelle, tell James and Horace to come up because we may need them, then you head out as soon as you can. Alli, if you would be kind enough to clean up quickly, I'd be most grateful, then you need to go too. Understood?"

Alli nodded, eyes wide and face ashen while she, Bert, and Michelle filed out, leaving Emma to stare after them, her cheeks as pale as chalk. Sean braced an arm to her back, and her eyelids flickered closed for a moment while she wavered on her feet. He squeezed her shoulder. "Ready?"

She didn't move, simply stared straight ahead, feet rooted to the faded hardwood floor.

Apparently not, he thought with a grim press of his lips, wishing he'd never promised to leave the lowlife alone. With a weary exhale, he took her hand. "It'll be fine, I promise. Ready?"

Her gaze flicked to his, and his stomach clenched at the flash of fear in her eyes. But then just as quickly as it had come, it left with a firm lift of her chin. Arms to her waist, she nodded and followed behind as he walked into her office, his tall frame blocking her view. "What do you want?" he asked the man who stood to his feet, his tone none too kind.

"To speak with Mrs. Malloy." The voice was polite with the barest hint of a brogue.

Sean assessed him, noting the fedora in his hands and a scar over his lip. Pale blue eyes stared back from a chiseled face framed by an unruly crop of black curls, badly in need of a trim.

"Who are you?" Sean asked, a hand to Emma's elbow to bring her into view.

Dimples made way for a slow smile as the man nodded at Emma. "Mrs. Malloy . . ."

With a jagged catch of her breath, Emma stiffened, then slid to the floor in a dead faint.

"Emma!" Sean swept her limp body up in his arms and carried her to her chair, repeating her name while stroking her cheek. She stirred with a moan, and he spun around, turning on the man with a fury. "Who are you and what the devil do you want?"

Bowing slightly with hat to his chest, the man's troubled gaze lighted first on Emma, and then on Sean, his manner anything but coy. "Beggin' your pardon, sir," he said, his smile as tight as the line of Sean's jaw, "but the name would be Rory Malloy."

It was the strangest feeling—her body numb while she sat in the chair, hands politely folded on her desk as if interviewing just another supplier with a bill of goods she "couldn't do without." She stared at her estranged husband, her eyes no longer glazed with shock, but serene and cool, giving no evidence whatsoever that her heart was in her throat. He spoke in the same soft, lilting brogue that had once turned her head, fluttered her pulse, lured her into sin, but this time the words were laced with regret, repentance, and the promise of hope. She was painfully aware of Sean's presence behind her, perched on the windowsill, muscled arms braced to his chest like a silent threat. The wings of an angel sheltering her from evil.

Evil. Oddly enough, that was the last thing she felt as she studied the man before her, her face stiff in the professional mode reserved for salesmen she didn't trust. Suspicion, yes, and anxiety, certainly, but the evil that had destroyed her life and mutilated the very beauty that had drawn him in the first place was no longer present. In its stead she discovered a gentler man with a humility that was as foreign to the old Rory as a woman's refusal, with piercing blue eyes that begged her forgiveness. And perhaps that was the very reason the evil appeared to be gone—she had forgiven it a long, long time ago.

"You didn't answer my letters," he said softly. "That's not like you."

She licked her lips, pulse pounding. "It's not like you to write them," she whispered.

He drew in a deep breath, finally leaning back in the chair with an answering smile. "No, no it's not, Emma, and I don't blame you." His lips tilted in that crooked way she had fallen in love with, that endearing grin that had sealed her fate. "I wouldn't have answered me either," he said, reminding her of just how much she had loved him before the bottle had ruined their lives. The smile faded into the worn look of a man who'd been broken. "I don't deserve your kindness, Emma, but it's your kindness that brings me to see you today . . . to ask your forgiveness."

"I forgave you a long time ago, Rory, I told you that in the note that I left."

"Yes, you did, but I needed to tell you—in person—just how much I regret what I did."

She heard Sean's blast of frustration, and it re-steeled her guard. Her chin leveled up. "What exactly do you want?" she asked quietly, her nerves raw.

His gaze flicked up to Sean with the same hardness she'd known in the past and then softened when it returned to her once again. "That's an easy one, Emmy, I want you—"

A curse hissed as Sean lunged up from the sill. "Why, you sorry excuse for a man—"

"Sean!" Emma jolted to her feet, blocking his path with a trembling palm to his chest. Her eyes pleaded as her voice dropped to a whisper. "You promised."

"I promised I wouldn't touch the other lowlife, not this one." His eyes, usually so rational and calm, now burned with the same crazed look she'd seen that day at Kearney's. He gripped her arms. "You're not swallowing this, are you, Emma? The man's a God-forsaken liar!"

"He's right, of course," Rory countered, "on two scores, at least—I am a sorry excuse for a man and I was a liar . . ." He stood, his voice grew gruff with emotion. "But one thing has changed, Emmy—I'm no longer forsaken by God."

She peered over her shoulder, his words stilling the air in her throat.

"Get out—now!" Sean pushed her aside and rounded the desk with blood in his eyes.

"Stop!" Emma threw herself between the two men, hands clutched white on Sean's arms. "If you can't contain your anger, then I must ask you to leave."

He strained forward against her hold, his words clenched and spewing venom. "I'm not leaving you alone with this monster . . ."

Her quiet response might have been a slap, given his flinch. "Then don't force me to make you," she whispered. "His ring is on my finger, Sean," she said quietly, speaking words that stabbed at both of their souls. "And truth be told . . . he has as much right here as you."

His sharp intake of breath pierced her before he finally backed away, his temple throbbing with cool rage. Without another word he moved to stare out the window, his stance as stiff as the muscles ridging his back.

Emma released a fragile breath and turned, her stomach swooping at the nearness of a man who had once weakened her knees . . . and her nerve. Even after eleven years, the scent of him affected her still, swamping her emotions with memories of both love and hate. The faint whiff of licorice from the Sen-Sen he chewed merged with the clean, carbolic smell of Lifebouy soap, taking her back to both the best and the worst times of her life. She quickly backed away to distance herself behind her desk once again, wondering why she wanted to believe he'd changed after all this time.

Gaze locked with his, she slowly lowered into her seat, her voice calmer than she felt. "What do you mean," she repeated, "that you're no longer forsaken by God?"

He returned to his chair with a slow exhale, threading blunt fingers through a riot of black curls she'd always envisioned on a son. His gaze faltered, averting to the front of her desk with a faraway stare and a monotone voice. "I wrote you that I got hurt at the factory, Em, and it ruined me. Couldn't work for months and my lady friend and I . . . ," he glanced up, and she could see the shame pooling in his eyes, "well, we fought like the devil, we did. Sure, I always tipped the brew, but never like then with so much idle time on my hands and no money coming in. Never once did I dream things could get any worse, but they did." His Adam's apple bobbed as he absently twisted the brim of his hat. "We . . . we lost a child, you see . . . a three-year-old son . . ." With an abrupt swipe of his arm, he wiped the moisture from his eyes. "Sure, I could have spit 'im out of my mouth, so much was the little beggar like me—curls as black as night and blue eyes clearer than a Donegal morn."

He looked up then, a father in pain. "Except Aidan was good, Emmy, the only good thing I've ever done, and he loved me, wanted to be just like me, following in my steps every chance he could take." A harsh laugh erupted from his throat as more tears welled in his eyes. "And he did . . . right down to finishing my bottle the night I'd passed out." He steadied himself with a harsh intake of air, his gaze seeking Emma's once again. "I as good as killed 'im, Emmy, the one night his loving da was to watch 'im while his mam was out—poisoned by the same brew that poisoned the love between you and me."

"No! Oh, Rory . . . I'm so sorry . . ."

"As well I knew you'd be," he said, his voice tender, "because that's the kind of woman you are—kind, deep, and full of sorrow over the likes of a wretch like me." He drew in a harsh breath and closed his eyes. "After Aidan . . . I couldn't live with myself, you know . . ." A choked laugh broke from his throat. "Nor could Aidan's mam, for that matter. So I did the only thing I could do, the same thing you did when I hurt you—I turned to God."

Her breath caught in her throat, and he opened his eyes, both joy and fear fusing the words to her tongue.

His gaze slipped to the ring on her hand. "I've given up the drink, Emmy, and I want to make amends if you'll let me. It's my ring on your finger, Love, and my cruelty on your face—give me a chance to make it right, to give you the marriage God wants us to have."

Slamming his fist to the wall, Sean jumped up with a curse. "You beat her and cheat on her, then think you can waltz in here and pick up where you left off? After *eleven years?*"

"No . . . I don't think that!" Rory said, the tight strain in his voice indicating his struggle to remain calm. "No woman alive would even consider taking me back, and I know that all too well. But from your ardent defense, I suspect you already know—there's no woman alive like Emma."

Sean pulled her to her feet and gripped her arms, his tone frantic. "Emma, don't trust him—he's a devil, and he ruined your life. He doesn't deserve you."

"That's true," Rory said, the desperation in his voice battling with Sean's. "No more than I deserve the forgiveness of God . . . and yet, I have it."

She stared from the man who'd given her his name to the man who'd given her his heart, and felt the air bleed from her lungs as surely as the hope that now bled from her soul. Fingers numb, she caressed the hand still clutched to her arm while her gaze caressed his face. "Sean, would you mind . . . walking me home now? I need time to think . . . and to pray."

Without a word, he gently pulled her into his arms and rested his head on hers. She felt the warmth of his hand as he slowly rubbed her back, and when he spoke, his voice held the trace of a threat. "I'm not going to let him do this to you, Emma."

"I believe the choice is hers." Rory's quiet voice rose to the challenge.

"Get out of here!" Sean hissed, his body suddenly stiff.

Emma squeezed his hand and pulled away. "Rory, where are you staying?"

He rose to his feet, hat in hand. "A boardinghouse down by the pier, The Allen House. I dropped my bags off this afternoon when I arrived."

She nodded and raised her chin, assessing him through cool eyes. "Don't come to the store again, do you hear? I'll give it some thought and then contact you so we can talk. Agreed?"

"You can't be serious . . ." Sean's voice was an angry rasp.

"Agreed?" she repeated, her tone sharper this time.

Rory gave a short nod, his gaze crystallizing to ice as it shifted to Sean.

"You wanted to see us, Miss Emma?" Horace and James stood at the door, concern ridging their brows.

"Yes, thank you, Horace, James. Sorry to detain you, but would you please escort Mr.—" she paused, swallowing the embarrassment coating her throat—"this . . . gentleman out?"

"Yes, ma'am." Horace gave Rory a polite nod and extended his hand. "Sir?"

"Thank you," Rory said. Offering Emma a half bow, his eyes lingered as if he were reluctant to leave. "I appreciate your consideration of my proposal, Mrs. Malloy, and look forward to discussing it further." With a faint nod, he followed James and Horace out the door.

Emma didn't breathe until she heard the click of the outer lock, and when she did, she dropped her head in her hand.

"Tell me you're not considering this." Sean's voice was no more than a hiss.

A reedy sigh withered on her lips. "I don't know what I'm considering," she whispered.

He braced her arms firmly, his voice a hoarse plea. "Consider the truth, Emma—the man was a drunken monster who cheated on you, beat you, and scarred you for life. Do you really believe someone with that many sins can change overnight?"

She looked up then, heart writhing as tears blurred in her eyes. Her hand trembled when she stroked his face with her fingers, desperate to make him understand just how much God had changed her life for the better.

"Oh, Sean," she whispered, her own past searing her brain as it had every day since. "The truth is . . . if I didn't believe that, I would have had no hope at all."

"Sean!"

He turned to see Charity's silhouette in her open front door. The backlight of the parlor masked her face in shadows, but he could hear the alarm in her tone all the same. Wrestling on a coat, she shut the glass door behind her before skittering down the brick walkway, puffs of labored breathing drifting skyward with every step she took. She halted several houses away from where he stood, her chest pumping vigorously. He drew in a frigid breath, a headache now throbbing in his brain, and steeled himself for what he knew was about to come.

"What's wrong with Emma?" she sputtered, her breathing as ragged as his nerves.

"She's just tired."

"No, 'tired' is several yawns over a cup of chamomile tea and 'how was your day?' Not bolting up the stairs with 'good night, I'm going to bed.'" She squinted at her wristwatch in the dim light of the street lamp. "And at seven o'clock, no less." Arms folded, she stared him down. "Don't pull a lip-lock on me, Sean O'Connor, this is me you're dealing with here."

He huffed out a sigh that rolled into the cool night air with the same force that his sister was rolling over him, and he silently berated himself for not hightailing it the moment Emma had shut the door. "She's just upset, okay? And that's all I can say." He turned to go.

A hand clamped on his arm with all the force of a six-inch steel band. "Oh no you don't, you're not going anywhere until you tell me why my best friend just vaulted up my staircase faster than Henry when I need help with the dishes." She folded her arms, her tone suddenly softer. "Is it because this was your last day?"

He studied her with weary eyes, wondering if God would consider it a lie if he just said yes. After all, there *had* been a certain edginess, a malaise in Emma at his farewell party. Kneading the bridge of his nose, he wished he'd never promised his silence because when it came to the truth, Charity could sniff it out like a bloodhound, twitching until she was nose-to-nose.

Like now.

She tapped her foot on the leafy pavement. "Something's up, Sean, I can feel it in my bones, and so help me I will badger you all the way home if you don't spill it now."

His frustration blasted out in a cloud of smoke. "I can't tell you, Charity, I promised."

"Oh, fiddle, that's an easy fix. I'll just ask the questions, and you give me that stone-faced look of yours that will tell me everything I need to know."

"But that's not right."

"Sure it is," she said, dismissing his concern with a wave of her hand. "I do it with Mitch all the time." Head cocked, she chewed on her lip. "Okay, it's something that happened at work, but it has to be personal because Emma's steady as a rock in all business matters, right?"

He stared, trying not to blink.

"Okay, good, a personal situation at work that involves a person other than you."

His jaw dropped. "I never said that."

"Sure you did, when you did that pinching thing with your nose as a stall tactic."

He crossed his arms to his chest, emotional battlement to ward off the enemy.

"Now . . . let's see," she said, finger to her chin. "Somebody upset Emma pretty badly, which means it has to be someone who doesn't work at the store."

"Why?" he asked in exasperation, his patience as thin as his energy.

Charity blinked. "Why? Because the woman who bolted up my steps was as pale as death," she said, enunciating slowly as if explaining something to Henry. "Which means it has to be someone she feels threatened by, and that rules out everyone at Dennehy's."

His lips compressed.

She gave him a quick nod and started to pace, head down and arms folded. "Okay, so it has to be an outsider she's afraid of and probably a man." She halted midstride, eyes spanning wide. "Wait, it's not that bum who beat her up, is it? You know, her neighbor's boyfriend?"

Swallowing his discomfort, he gave her a blank stare, facial muscles relaxing.

She blew out a sigh of relief. "Oh, good. For a second there, I was worried."

"How the devil do you do that?" he said in a choke, lips parted in shock.

She tapped a finger to her head. "Stone face, remember?" Her mouth flattened. "It's a gift—honed to perfection by Mitch Dennehy."

"I gotta go—you're starting to scare me."

"Wait!" she latched onto his arm again, her manner sobering considerably. "You can't leave—I need to know. Emma's like a sister to me."

"Then you ask her."

"Don't you think I've tried? I could tell something was wrong the minute I heard her tell you goodbye, but she's even more tight-lipped than you. Said she's fine, but too tired to talk, then locks me out, just like Henry tried once."

He sighed. "Then you're just gonna have to catch her before she leaves for work in the morning, because I gave her my word." He squeezed her shoulder, suddenly feeling sapped of all energy. "Just pray for her, okay?" he whispered. "Good night, sis."

"No . . ." His sister's hoarse whisper halted him dead in his tracks, ten feet away.

He turned.

She looked straight through him, her face cast in stone. "Please . . . tell me it's not Rory."

The shiver of her body was apparent, even from a distance. He could only stare, his own grief telling her what she didn't want to hear. When she didn't respond, he slowly walked to where she stood and tugged her into his embrace, forgetting his own fatigue to comfort his sister. "Just pray, Charity, okay, and I will too. I can't say any more, so just see if she'll talk to you tomorrow."

"Tomorrow, nothing," Charity said with a bite in her tone. "She will talk—*and pray*—with me tonight."

He pulled back. "I thought you said she locked you out? Not literally, I guess, huh?"

She gave him a hug. "Yes, literally, as in an annoying click of a bolt. But this situation is far too serious and Emma is far too important to let a puny lock keep me out." Her chin notched up. "Trust me, you don't have a son like Henry without a spare key tucked away."

For the first time all evening, Sean felt a smile pull at his lips. He tweaked her hair. "Tell me, sis, does Mitch have any idea just what he has in you, because you're pretty special."

A twinkle lit in her eye. "Thanks, Sean, and yes, I think the man has been educated thoroughly enough, at least for now." Her smile softened. "Thanks for telling me about Emma."

He grinned. "I didn't."

She patted his cheek. "That's okay, honey, you keep thinking that. I'm married to you-know-who, remember? I know how important pride is to a man." Turning to go, she suddenly spun around, eyes narrowed in warning. "But just for future reference? Don't toy with me, Sean, just spit it right out next time—it will save both of us a lot of precious time. Now go home and get some sleep—you look whipped. And don't worry—we're not going to let her do this."

He nodded, suddenly feeling much lighter at the thought of this woman joining forces with him against Rory Malloy. "Thanks, Charity. You're a good friend to Emma."

Her lips quirked. "You may be the only one with that opinion tonight, but such is love."

"Yeah, I know," he said with a cuff of his neck. "But she's worth it.

"That she is," Charity whispered and gave him a quick kiss on the cheek. "Good night, Sean."

She spun to go and he caught her hand. "Charity, wait."

With a half turn, she peered up, eyes in a squint. "Yes?"

He stared at the sister who had captured the attention of men all of her life, and felt the muscles thicken in his throat. "Too beautiful for her own good," he'd once heard Mitch say, and for the first time Sean realized just how true those words had been for this sister, whose natural beauty had wrought so much pain in her life. Unbidden, moisture stung at the memory of a golden-haired, little girl, whose silent pleas screamed from blue eyes swimming with tears over Uncle Paul's shoulder. Sean's eyelids weighted closed while a thousand knife points stabbed in his gut. A six-year-old innocent carried upstairs "to be punished" for crimes she'd never committed. Crimes that belonged to her uncle . . . Sean winced as pain slashed within. *And the brother who didn't stop him . . .*

"Sean? Are you okay?" Charity lifted on tiptoe to press a kiss to his cheek. "Because Emma is going to be fine—I won't let anything happen to her, I promise."

No, you wouldn't—unlike me . . .

"Sean?"

She waggled the hand still clutched to her own, and he opened his eyes, sorrow a poor salve for the wounds in his soul. "Charity," he whispered, his voice no more than a rasp, "forgive me, please . . ."

A smile bloomed on her beautiful face. "For what? Loving my best friend, because that's—"

"No—" He stilled her words with a gentle squeeze of her hand. "For not . . . ," his voice cracked as his words cleaved to his tongue, "saving you from Uncle Paul."

She blinked several times while his statement billowed away into the frigid night air, and then its impact struck, prompting a harsh shift of her throat and a swift swell of tears. "You were only a boy," she whispered, her voice as hoarse as his. "How could you know?"

"I . . . sensed something, Charity, something not right, and yet I did nothing."

"You were *nine*, Sean," she emphasized, cupping his face with her palm. "Too young and noble to think such things could happen. You were the big brother I looked up to, the good boy I admired." Her lips crooked into a wry smile. "Unlike Faith who was the good girl that got on my nerves."

"But I should have done something, anything, followed my instincts . . ."

She cocked her head, blue eyes wide with surprise. "But you did, don't you remember?" Another sheen of tears invaded her eyes. "You offered to go in my place, to be punished instead of me, but Uncle Paul refused." She clasped his arms, her words clogging his throat with painful emotion. "You were always doing that, Sean—for all us—protecting us, taking up for us, binding our wounds whenever one of us got hurt. Don't you remember?"

He shook his head, his guilt obliterating all rational view.

"Well, you did," she said with a quick pat of his cheek. "The consummate big brother, always bleeding for the wounded." The smile faded on her face as sorrow welled in her eyes.

"Which is why you're so good for Emma. If ever a wounded soul walked the earth, it's Emma Malloy, and she needs you, Sean—both of us—now, more than ever."

"I know," he said quietly, the gloom of Emma's situation shrouding his soul. A nerve pulsed in his jaw while his fingers twitched for revenge. "I'd give anything to rid the world of vermin like Uncle Paul and Rory Malloy."

Drawing in a deep breath, she huffed it out again, clouds of vapor as thin and elusive as his quest for justice. "We both know that's not going to happen. But . . . we can rid ourselves of the pain of their memory, and it was Emma Malloy herself and Mitch, surprisingly enough, who taught me how."

He looked up, his liberty glimmering in the love he saw in her eyes.

"I've already forgiven you long ago, Sean, along with Father and Faith, although none of you bore any responsibility for what happened to me. Ironically, it was the pain of Uncle Paul's actions that taught me the most important lesson I have ever learned." Her lip quivered before she hiked her chin in that beautiful obstinance he'd come to know and love. The barest of smiles flickered at the edges of her mouth, reminding him so much of Emma. "And that, my dear brother, is that forgiveness is really just another word for freedom."

"No one escapes being hurt in this life, Sean, because unfortunately, we live in a fallen world. But please believe me when I say . . . there's a great gift in pain."

He blinked, Emma's words haunting his memory.

"So let it all go, Sean, all the bitterness for Rory and Uncle Paul and yes," she said with a slight curve of a smile, "even Herman Finkel. Do it—for me, for Emma, and especially for yourself." She gave him a playful tap on the cheek. "Because we love you, you big lug, you know that?"

He swallowed hard, thinking of Emma once again. "I know," he whispered.

Latching onto his arm, she prodded him around, bullying

him like she did with Henry. "Now, shoo—go home and get some rest because I can't handle this woman alone, and I need you in top form. She'll talk to me tonight or else, trust me. I'm as diabolical as Henry when it comes to getting my way."

He sucked in a crisp, clean draw of air, welcoming the energy it infused into his body before releasing it again in a purge of spirit that was long overdue. "I know," he said with a tug of his sister's hair. With a slant of a smile over his shoulder, he ambled away with a heart much lighter knowing Charity was involved. "Thanks, sis, for everything." His smile broke into a grin. "And all I can say is . . . God help Emma Malloy."

"That's the plan," Charity called, hand to her mouth. She watched and waited until her brother rounded the corner despite the fact that she was chilled to the bone. Turning, she finally headed for home, shoulders slumped and heart heavy at the cost love had extracted from her brother. He was such a good man . . . and Emma was such a good woman . . . and they loved each other. Couldn't God see that? She sighed. In the past, this would have been one of those times when she would have railed at the heavens, shaking her fist in the air at his obvious disregard for two people who loved him.

And we know that all things work together for good to them that love God, to them who are the called according to his purpose.

"Yes, God, I know," she whispered, thinking of her brother's weary form as it faded into the shadows. "I've certainly experienced it firsthand more times than I can count since I've given my heart to you, so I know you have good things in store for both of them." She bundled her coat with a shiver. "I just wish it was with each other and not—" Head down, she made her way down her brick walkway, plans forming with every step she took. A familiar resolve hardened in her bones as she opened the front door. "Not him, Lord, please," she whispered. "Alone for the rest of her life, maybe, but not a life with him . . . *please*."

"Where'd you go?" Mitch asked when she returned. He peered over the *Boston Herald* sprawled open before him. "Henry's in a sulk because I made him help Hope with the dishes."

She stared at her husband—wire rims perched on his nose and concern etched in his handsome face—and gratitude welled as tears pricked at her eyes.

"What's wrong?" he asked abruptly, the paper now relegated to his lap.

Fighting the trembling of her lip, Charity moved to where he sat every night, his cordovan easy chair shaped and molded to his large frame as comfortably as the two of them in ten years of marriage. She sat on the wide arm and leaned against him, craving the security of his hold as he tugged her close.

"What's wrong, little girl?" he repeated softly, pressing a kiss to her temple.

She closed her eyes, allowing his warmth and the familiar scent of Bay Rum to soothe and settle her nerves. "It's Emma," she whispered with a faint shiver. "Rory's back."

"What?" He shifted, his sharp tone matching the furrows in his brow. "Here? In Boston?"

"Apparently," she said with a wavering sigh. "Came to the store today, or so Sean said."

"But why?"

"Sean wouldn't say, but I think I know. Emma's been receiving letters from him for the last few months or so." Her tongue swiped her teeth in nervous habit. "He wants her back."

Stormy blue eyes pierced through her, accompanied by a grunt. "Well, he can't have her, and that's that." One blond brow shot up. "She's not actually considering it, is she?"

Her gaze trailed into a hard stare, well aware that allegiance was one of Emma's most honorable traits . . . and deadliest. At least when it came to Rory Malloy. "I think she is, Mitch, or at least that's what she indicated when I confronted her

about the letters. But I'd hoped I'd talked her out of it."
Charity's jaw tightened. "Until this."

"But why would she even entertain such a cockeyed notion?
The woman's more intelligent than most people I know, but
this is just plain stupid."

Charity exhaled her frustration. "I know, but when it comes
to Rory, Emma's thinking has always been a little skewed,
and I don't know why. It's like he has a hold on her. I swear,
Mitch, it's downright demonic."

"*He's* demonic," Mitch said with a grind of his jaw. "When
are you going to talk to her?"

"Now." Charity lumbered up, lips awry. "Despite the fact
she so rudely locked her door."

His mouth tipped. "Can't be too smart if she thinks she
can keep you out. Need help?"

She squeezed his hand. "Yes—say one that she listens to
reason."

"How can she not?" His lips swerved. "Coming from one
who so seldom resorts to it?"

"You're lucky you're so cute, you know that?" She bent
to give him a quick kiss. "Or I would have dumped you and
your biting wit a long time ago."

He gave her a droll smile. "Yeah, lucky me."

"Wish me luck," she said with a square of her shoulders,
then drew in a deep breath as she took the stairs two at a time.
Entering her bedroom, she made her way to the bureau where
she unearthed the spare key from beneath a mountain of
negligees, knowing full well Henry would have never looked
for it there. She tiptoed toward Emma's room and pressed
her ear to the door. Her stomach clenched at the sound of
muffled weeping, and with a clamp of her jaw, she inserted
the key in the lock and opened the door.

"Charity, what on earth . . . ?" Emma sat up on her bed,
face swollen and dress rumpled.

She strolled in and quietly closed the door, forcing a smile.
"Oh, just using one of my many God-given talents, Emma—
I'm prying."

Most people saw Emma Malloy as sweet and compliant, and they'd be right much of the time. But Charity knew better when it came to Rory Malloy, as evident in the slit of Emma's eyes and the square of her jaw. "I'm asking you politely, Charity—leave me alone."

"Or what?" Charity folded her arms, incensed that Emma was closing her out.

Dangerously calm, Emma rose to her feet, gray eyes as hard as granite and arms stiff at her sides. "I'll leave," she whispered, the threat borne out in the thrust of her chin.

"What? To run back to Rory?"

Her features flinched before she strode to the closet to pull out a valise. Hurling it on the bed, she turned, fists clenched. "Sean promised!" Her lips curled in a sneer Charity had never seen. "But, I just bet you twisted it out of him, didn't you? In your usual meddling way."

The barb hurt, but Charity let it pass. "Yes, I did, as a matter of fact. And don't blame it on Sean—the man never said a word about anything. I just asked questions, and his face gave him dead away." She hiked her chin, jaw to jaw with the woman more stubborn than most people knew. "If you must, take issue with God for giving me a sixth sense about people I love."

Emma looked away, a sheen of moisture in her eyes. "Don't, Charity, please. I will *not* talk about this right now."

With a soft exhale, Charity moved forward, tugging her to sit down on the bed. Bracing Emma's shoulders with one hand, she buffed her friend's arm with the other, resting her head against hers. "Okay, you win. No talking tonight—just prayer, all right?"

With an abrupt heave, Emma dropped her head in her hand and began to weep.

Hurt stabbed in Charity's chest as she bundled her in her arms, moisture welling beneath her own lids. "It's okay," she soothed. "God has never failed us before, Emma, and he won't fail us now."

Emma continued to weep, but with every wrenching heave,

faith rose in Charity's soul, instilling hope where there seemed to be none.

I will not leave you comfortless: I will come to you.

And in a steady voice that held the firm assurance of a faith tried and true, Charity began to pray. For Emma, for Sean . . . and for the miracle they so desperately needed.

19

o, how are . . . things?" Marcy looked up from her sewing, the same pinch in her face that Charity felt in her gut every time someone asked about Emma. She shivered despite the cozy warmth of her mother's kitchen where her sisters huddled at the mahogany table while beef stew bubbled on the stove. The aroma of meat and vegetables mingled with the mouthwatering smell of fresh-baked bread and hot apple pie, providing a cozy contrast to enormous snowflakes that fluttered outside of Marcy's ice-frosted windows. The shrieks and laughter of children building snowmen in the backyard seemed a surreal backdrop to the sober conversation about to ensue.

Charity bit her thread in two . . . just like she wished she could do with Rory. "Not good, Mother. Emma's making noises like she's actually considering going back after the first of the year."

"With him?" Katie asked, brows climbing clear to her bangs.

Charity's lip twisted. "Yeah, Happy New Year one and all. He's been 'courting' her, you know, pouring on the charm like nobody's business."

"She's been seeing him a lot, then?" Marcy frowned as she threaded a needle.

"Two to three times a week," Charity said with a scowl. "It's downright nauseating."

"They're not . . . intimate, are they?" Faith asked, worry lacing her tone.

"I don't think so," Charity said, "although I wouldn't put anything past Rory Malloy. Charm is his greatest asset, you know . . . right after manipulation."

Lizzie bit her lip. "Emma says he's changed," she whispered. "Maybe he has."

Charity blustered out a noisy sigh. "Yeah, maybe. All I know is that he's put on quite a show for Emma—going to church with her, helping Mrs. Peep with things around the apartments, cleaning Emma's flat, cooking her dinner . . ." Her mouth kinked to the side. "Sweet saints, if Mitch did that for me, I'd think he was seeing another woman."

"Not everybody is as suspicious as you," Faith said with a sliver of a smile.

Charity shot her a narrow gaze, a healthy touch of tease in her tone. "No, only you and me, apparently, judging from your reaction that time Collin hired Evelyn." Her mouth swagged into a droll smile. "Who would have thought—you and me, two peas in a pod?"

Faith chuckled as she basted a hem. "Yes, but I don't recall any hair pulling with me."

"No there wasn't," Charity said with a sigh. She sagged back in her chair, closing her eyes to massage her temple. "But there's plenty now with Emma—and it's all mine."

The teakettle began to squeal, and Katie jumped up. "Has this Rory found a job yet?" she asked, proceeding to pour more water into each of their cups.

"No, although he claims to be looking while he's living at Emma's, and Mrs. Peep says he's gone out every day. But times are hard for the most educated of men, and the only experience Rory has is at the Guinness Brewery in Dublin." She grunted in the grand fashion of her husband. "Although I suspect he drank more than he brewed."

"You really hate him, don't you?" Faith said quietly.

Charity glanced up, shocked at the fury that rose in her throat. "I hate anybody who would lay a cruel hand to someone I love." She drew in a jagged breath and released it again, hand to her eyes. "I'm sorry. I know that's wrong, and I try to pray for him, really I do, but if you could have seen what he did to her, over and over . . . Besides," she said with a sniff, "Emma says he's been talking a lot about Killarney, where Emma's family lived, and I can't help but worry . . ." She swallowed hard, reluctant to even utter the words. "You know, that he'll take her away."

"Would that be so bad," Faith whispered, gaze gentle, "if he made her happy for once?"

"If he made her happy, no," Charity said in a bitter tone, "but if he abuses her and lives off the sweat of her brow and drinks all of her profits again . . ."

"Emma says he doesn't drink anymore." Marcy's whisper was tentative.

A harsh laugh broke from Charity's lips. "If you can believe him."

"But wouldn't Emma know?" Lizzie asked, eyes wide as she restitched a felt flower to a burgundy cloche. "I mean, she's seeing him quite a bit, right? For dinner and visiting at her apartment? I would think if Rory were drinking, Emma would know."

"Yes, one would think that," Charity said in a huff. "But this is Emma—the woman who turns a blind eye to Rory Malloy. Besides, I'm sure in Emma's own misguided view, she believes she's doing the right thing for Se—" She stopped, realizing her near slip had earned curious looks from her mother and sisters.

"The right thing for whom?" Katie said, needle halted midair.

Charity quickly held up a blouse, blocking her sister's view to squint at the alignment of buttons she'd just sewn. "Herself, of course, and Rory."

The blouse buckled when Katie slapped it down in the middle. "The right thing for whom?" she repeated, eyes narrowing.

"You weren't talking about Emma or Rory, were you? Nor you and Mitch, for that matter, because why would Emma leaving be good for any of you?"

For once Charity was speechless, her heart stilled by the killer instinct in Katie's eyes.

Katie folded her arms, a prosecutor badgering a witness. "So . . . just whom exactly would Emma be doing the right thing for? And while we're at it, suppose you explain why Sean has left a job he loves so he can, quote, 'pursue other interests.' And at Christmas, no less, when Emma is likely to need him even more?" She pressed both palms on the table and leaned in, gaze locked on her sister's. "Tell me that, Charity, huh? Especially when he has no other job in sight?"

Charity blinked, taken aback by Katie's affront. Staring hard, she wondered for the first time if she should reveal Sean and Emma's secret, even though she'd never promised either of them that she wouldn't. But like her, they'd just assumed discretion, and yet perhaps her family had a right to know the heartache her brother and best friend had endured. Certainly Sean and Emma needed all the prayers they could get, and none were more diligent at prayer than the women at this table. She slumped back in her chair, eyes scanning the faces of her family. "All right, I'll tell you, but only if you promise not to let Sean or Emma know."

Katie's silent nod matched that of the others.

Charity sighed. "Neither Emma nor Sean meant for this to happen, but it seems they've . . . ," she paused, realizing once again the full extent of the tragedy at hand, "fallen in love."

Katie sank back in her chair, her voice stricken. "Oh, I just knew it," she whispered.

"Me too," Faith admitted quietly, her face pale with concern.

"Oh, no," Marcy whispered. "He's not been himself, but I just assumed he missed Dennehy's." She looked up, pain etched in her brow. "How are they? You know, emotionally?"

Charity hunched her shoulders. "Well, Sean's sick about it, of course, but he's Sean, the one with the perpetual smile and driving need to lift everyone else up—he fakes it. And

Emma?" She blew out a weary breath. "She's dying inside because she's afraid—afraid to work with Sean, afraid to see him out of a job, afraid that his love for her will cut him off from everything she wants him to have. Trust me, it's just like her to be thinking that if she left Boston with Rory, Sean could not only come back to Dennehy's, but he would be free to fall in love with Rose."

"What a heartbreak," Lizzie said with tears in her eyes.

"Yeah, well, if I'm going to betray their confidence, then I suppose the least we can do is pray about it, right?"

"Charity?"

She turned, surprised to see Steven in a suit and tie, arm propped to the kitchen door. "What are you doing here? I thought you were on special assignment this weekend."

He nodded, eyes flicking to his mother and sisters before focusing on Charity once again. "I am, but I needed to talk to you." He shifted uncomfortably in the door. "Got a minute?"

She blinked, the mended blouse poised in her hand. "Sure." Setting her sewing down, she glanced at her sisters and mother. "I'll be right back, and then we can pray."

Steven held the door while she strode through, and she nodded toward the parlor. "Father's taking a nap in the den, so will the parlor do?"

"Yeah."

Adjusting her skirt, she sat on the edge of the sofa, hands to her knees. "Okay, Steven, what's Henry done this time? And don't look so dire—he's only ten, so it can't be that bad."

He straddled the arm of the loveseat, the serious look in his eyes warranting far more than a prank by Henry. Palms to the sofa, she suddenly jerked upright, spine stiff. "What's wrong?"

"It's not Henry, Charity," he said with a shift in his throat. "It's Emma."

"Emma?" Her voice was a chilling echo. She shot to her feet, throat constricting. "What about Emma? Is she okay?"

He drew in a deep breath and released it, his gaze never leaving her face as he held up a hand. "Calm down, Emma's fine. I just thought you needed to know that I arrested Rory today . . . at a speakeasy on the north side."

She sat down once again, eyes drifting closed. *Dear God, please . . . not again.*

"I didn't know it was him," he continued quietly, "I thought he was just some blowhard who'd had too much to drink. He took a swing at Joe, and I cuffed him. Threw him in a private cell to sleep it off." He rubbed his head, palm spanning from one temple to the other. "That's when he started spouting off that he had money and we better treat him with respect. Said his wife inherited a fortune from an aunt that would keep him in clover for a long time to come."

Steven looked up then, his face laden with sorrow. "Claimed she had some fancy job running a big store, but that he planned to take her to Killarney to move into a mansion . . ." Steven paused, the words obviously as difficult for him to say as they were for Charity to hear. "Then he laughed . . . and said something I thought was pretty odd."

The blood in her body stilled to a crawl. "What?" she whispered.

He hesitated, eyelids heavy with reluctance. "He said, 'And this time I'll make it legal.'"

Cold seeped through her like ice water slithering in her veins. "He's lying," she rasped, the words near choking in her throat.

"Maybe," Steven said, "but if they were married, why would he say that?"

"Because Emma wouldn't lie!" Charity jolted up again and began to pace, arms clutched to her waist.

Steven exhaled. "Okay, maybe he is lying, but that doesn't change the fact he's drinking again . . . and broke the law." He peered up. "And maybe not just in Boston."

She turned, her body stiff as ice. "What do you mean?"

"I mean he's wanted in Dublin, for questioning in the death of a three-year-old boy."

She slowly lowered herself to the sofa, too dizzy to stand. "Oh Lord, have mercy."

"When I realized he was Emma's husband, I was so angry I threatened to deport him, and he changed his tune real fast. Begged me not to send him back. Said he'd be leaving for Killarney soon enough. And that's when I got suspicious. So I wired the authorities in Dublin and sure enough, they're looking for Rory Malloy." He huffed out a weary sigh. "Papers have been filed for a deportation hearing, but we can't hold him 'cause he posted bond."

Charity glanced up. "Who in their right mind would post bond for Rory Malloy?"

Steven's jaw hardened. "The woman he was with, apparently. Trust me, I wish I could lock the bum up and throw away the key." Glancing at his watch, he stood and retrieved his hat and coat from the rack in the hall while Charity followed him to the door. He turned, his manner somber. "I gotta get back, but I wanted to let you know. Somebody needs to tell Emma." Steven sighed and idly fingered the brim of his hat before leaning to give her a kiss on the cheek. He squeezed her shoulder. "I'm sorry to be the bearer of bad news, sis, but I'm not sorry about Rory."

She nodded, her mind numb. He opened the door.

"Steven!"

He turned, and she sucked in a fortifying breath, her desperate gaze locking with his. "Do you . . . do you think he's telling the truth . . . ?" Pain hitched in her throat. "About the marriage . . . ?"

He studied her for several seconds, and she held her breath, realizing how deeply his opinion mattered. This was the serious and introspective boy who'd once courted rebellion in college and was now a man bent on the law. Honesty and integrity fairly shimmered in his eyes. "I do," he whispered. His mouth crooked up, the effect less teasing than sad. "And probably for the first time in his life." He tipped his hat. "Tell Emma we love her, will you? She doesn't deserve this. And he definitely doesn't deserve her."

She found herself staring long after the click of Steven's departure. Emotional paralysis glazed both her eyes and her mind while a kaleidoscope of feelings swirled in her brain. Colorful pieces of jagged glass, capable of producing both beauty and blood in a quest for the truth.

Emma was free. But she chose to live a lie.

Charity closed her eyes, the revelation evoking great joy and great pain, leaving her bereft of all answers. Answers that now proved as elusive as the woman she thought she knew, the friend she thought she trusted.

Sean's image stirred in her mind—so in love and so in grief—and her heart cramped in her chest. Why would Emma do this? To him? To her? A shiver spanned the length of her spine and she opened her eyes, knowing full well she had no answers. She didn't know why Emma would deny the man that she loved, and she didn't know why she would deny herself. But there was one thing Charity did know, and it was as certain as the square of her shoulders on the way to the kitchen.

She sure in thunder was gonna find out.

--------⟅≈⟆--------

"Hey, what are you doing here?" Sean asked his brother, cheeks ruddy and a wet snow shovel under his arm. A few snowflakes still drifted in the air, dusting both his shoulders and the front walk he'd just shoveled that morning, blanketing it with a fine mist of snow that glittered in the sun. "I thought you were on special assignment this weekend."

Steven tugged on his gloves and shot his brother a somber smile as he met him at the front gate, his breath swirling up into the blindingly blue sky. "I am, but I ducked out to give Charity a message." He nodded toward the shovel, lips in a slant. "Giving snow jobs now?"

Stabbing the shovel into a snowdrift, Sean grinned and slacked a hip, gloved hand draped over the handle. "Sure. Not working Saturdays anymore gives me more time, so I figured I'd hedge my bets on the state of my soul by shoveling the church parking lot." The tips of his mouth inched higher. "And Father Mac was so thrilled I cleared the basketball court, I think he was sorely tempted to grant me a plenary indulgence."

Steven grinned. "Yeah, the way you trounce the clergy in basketball, I suspect you're gonna need *all* the help you can get." He slapped Sean on the back. "See you later."

"Hey, wait—must be a pretty important message if you brought it in person." Sean squinted. "Everything okay?"

Hand on the gate handle, Steven paused, a look of introspection in his gaze as if deciding how to respond. With a slump of his shoulders, he exhaled loudly. His blue eyes, already several shades deeper than his brother's, darkened even further. "No, not really, at least not for Emma."

Sean's skin iced as cold as the snow he'd shoveled all morning. "What do you mean?" he said, his voice almost harsh.

Lips compressed, Steven hesitated for several moments, then peered up at his brother. "Maybe you better talk to Charity, Sean. It's not my place to say."

The shovel slammed to the ground as Sean took a stride forward, his good humor crashing along with it. "You *better* say, Steven, because Emma is important to me, and I have a right to know."

"Look, Sean, she's Charity's friend—it's her decision to tell you, not mine."

Steven matched him in height and muscle, but that didn't stop Sean from fisting the front of his brother's wool coat and yanking him up, his tone as grinding as his jaw. "She's my friend too, Steven, so you best tell me now—what's wrong with Emma?"

Steven shoved him away, the fire in his eyes rivaling his brother's. "What's wrong with Emma? What's wrong with *you*! You're acting crazy again, like you did at Kearney's."

Sucking in a deep breath, Sean took a step back, desperate to control the fire in his gut. "Look, I'm sorry . . . but Emma means the world to me, and I have a right to know."

Venting with a sigh, Steven adjusted his coat while the taut muscles in his face eased into concern. "Look, Sean, I know you care about Emma—we all do. And I'll tell you, but only if you give me your word you won't go off half-cocked."

Sean felt his jaw stiffen, but he worked hard to keep his

expression cool. "Come on, Steven, since when do I go off half-cocked about anything?"

Assessing him through wary eyes, Steven offered a smile that went flat. "Since I had to pull you off some poor slob at Kearney's like a rabid dog." He sighed and cuffed the back of his neck. "All right. But keep it to yourself, will ya? This is Emma's business, but I didn't feel it was my place to tell her, so I asked Charity to."

"Tell her what?" Sean asked quietly, keeping his frustration at bay.

Steven's sigh billowed in the air. "I arrested Rory Malloy in a raid today in a speakeasy on the north side. He was pretty loaded and took a punch at Joe, so we threw him in the brig. He'll be released today, but if it were up to me, I'd lock him up forever."

A tic twittered in Sean's jaw. "Emma said he quit drinking."

"Yeah, well, I'm afraid you'd get some argument from us on that point." He hesitated, his eyelids heavy with regret. "That's not all, though. He was with a dame who was hanging all over him like a cheap suit." His lips skewed to the right. "And him, her."

Sean couldn't help the curse that hissed through his teeth, shocking Steven as much as it did him. "That no-good snake." He swore again. "Why does Emma even let him come around?"

"Well, if Charity has her way, she won't, not after she finds out for a second time what a bum he is. But he's a real con man, Sean, so I just hope she doesn't let him sweet-talk her again."

"Don't worry—she won't." He bit the words out, teeth clenched as tight as his fists. "And this time I'm going to make sure." With a harsh inhale, he snatched the shovel and unleashed a blast of fury that exploded into the air like storm clouds. "Trust me—that slime won't lie or cheat on her again."

Steven clutched his arm. "What are you going to do?"

"Nothing more than have a friendly chat with a wife beater."

"Sean, no! Although that wouldn't have bothered me a couple of months of ago, since Kearney's, I gotta admit—I'm a little worried what you might do."

Sean flung his brother's hand away. "Malloy's the one who needs to worry, not you."

"I want your word that you won't hurt him," Steven said, the authority of a prohibition agent steeling his tone. "Your fists are like weapons, Sean, just like Pop Clancy always said. Scare the slime if you have to, but don't rough him up. Besides, it may backfire and win Emma's sympathy." Steven stepped forward, the chiseled calm in his face making him appear as seasoned at twenty-four as Sean was at thirty-five. "Promise me."

Sean paused, his eyes itching hot as he stared at his brother. "I promise not to kill him," he whispered, the fury in his mind bleeding into his tone. His lips twisted as he strode to the front porch to prop the shovel against the wall. He shot a smile over his shoulder that was anything but. "But when I'm through? You mark my words—the scum will sure wish I had."

<hr />

From its cubbyhole in the bookcase, Emma's antique clock chimed three times, the tinkling sound almost deafening in the silent apartment where Sean sat in the shadows, lying in wait for a monster who had hurt Emma Malloy for the last time.

His body felt as stiff as the striped wingback chair in which he'd hunkered down over an hour ago after he'd convinced Mrs. Peep to unlock Emma's door.

"He didn't come home last night," Mrs. Peep had whispered. "And it's not the first time." An abundance of worry lines fanned from eyes that held a glimmer of moisture while two silver brows inched up in concern. "He fooled me at first, but lately he's been coming home all hours of the night, and I knew something wasn't right. I'm worried for her, Sean."

"Me too, Mrs. Peep," Sean muttered out loud, the sound earning a bored look from Lancelot as he groomed himself on the couch. Sean's muscles twitched under his skin as if he'd just downed a pot of Katie's day-old coffee, a quick scan of Emma's apartment revealing that Rory was not only a monster, but a slob as well. Newspapers littered the sofa where Lancelot lay, spilling onto the floor in disheveled heaps occasionally punctuated by discarded socks. Several coffee cups crowded the cherrywood coffee table that now sported a layer of dust and additional coffee-cup rings. The once clean scent of lemon oil gave way to the distinct smell of licorice mingling with the odor of stale cigarettes, now a mountain of butts ground into a floral china plate. An empty package of Lucky Strike cigarettes lay crumpled on top of Emma's Bible, prompting a tic in Sean's jaw. Yeah, Lucky Strike, for sure.

My fist, his face.

"Don't rough him up," Steven had warned. And yet Rory had never hesitated with Emma—hitting her, beating her, scarring her for life. The very thought kindled Sean's fury until it was white-hot, and he flexed his fingers, every nerve as taut as a wire trap begging to spring.

Like a hunter stalking his prey, Sean's body stilled at a key in the door, and when Rory lumbered in, he quietly rose to his feet. A hard smile curled on his lips, and his voice was deathly still. *Like Rory's about to be.* "Well, would you look at what the cat drug in."

Rory's body jerked at the door, wide eyes narrowing as they leveled on Sean. "How the devil did you get in?"

A spasm twitched in Sean's temple as he slowly moved forward, adrenaline fairly quivering in the sinews of his arms. "No, I think the question is, how the devil did you get in, Malloy? Back into Emma's life to lie and cheat on her again?"

The blue of Rory's eyes fused to black as he yanked the door wide. "Get out—*now!*"

"You took the words right out of my mouth, you blood-sucking leech." Striking like a rattler, Sean heaved the man up against the door, knotted fists buried into his half-buttoned peacoat like meat hooks, his bristled jaw just inches away.

"Get out, *now*—out of this apartment and out of Emma's life."

A slow smile slid across Rory's face as his eyes glinted like steel. "Well, well, what do you know—the boy's in love with my wife." With surprising strength, he thrust Sean away and laughed, his breath as foul as the intent in his eyes. "You want a piece of my Emmy, do you?" He fumbled with the buttons of his coat, peeling it off and tossing it on the floor, then egged Sean on with a wave of his fingers. "Or maybe you already have . . ."

Rage exploded in Sean's brain and he lunged, slamming him to the wall with brute force that put a glaze in Rory's eyes. "You aren't worthy of speaking her name, much less calling her your wife." With iron fists, he jerked him up hard, his voice a dangerous hiss. "I'm warning you now—walk out of her life, or so help me, you won't be able to."

Rory shoved him back, and then readied his stance with a heated look and a cold smile. "I don't think so, Yank. It's my ring on her finger, and it's my bed that she'll warm." His grin could have belonged to the devil. "And there's not a bloomin' thing you can do about it."

"No?" With unnatural speed, Sean drove an iron fist to his jaw, crashing him to the wall with a sickening thud. Blood splattered when his lip split like overripe fruit.

Swiping the side of his mouth, Rory's eyes narrowed to slits. "You wanna play rough, do you now?" A feral smile curved on his lips as he reached back in his waistband. He fumbled with something, and then with a faint click, a blade shot forth from the knife in his hand. "I won't kill ya for Emma's sake," he said with the touch of the brogue, and then he grinned. "But you're gonna bleed, Yank, make no mistake about that."

With a wild jab, he sliced the knife through the air and Sean jumped back, body taut and instincts ready. He saw the same crazed look in Rory's eyes he had seen before, in the eyes of the man who stabbed him during the war. His skin prickled as Rory circled, the blade gleaming in the sunlight that spilled through Emma's window. Blood pounding in his brain, Sean backed up slowly with a quick scan of the room. His gaze lighted upon Emma's coffee table.

Rory advanced, his confidence restored by the blade in his hand. "Afraid, are ya? Well, I would be too, Yank, if I were you. Because I'm gonna take my Emmy away, and you're gonna be left with naught but a bleedin' heart . . ." He awarded Sean with a handsome gleam of teeth. "Not to mention a bleedin' body." And in a catch of Sean's breath, he charged, the slash of his knife a mere whisper in the air as it nicked Sean's hand with a scarlet gash.

His blood pooled and slithered down his arm, and something sinister rose within, bringing him face-to-face with an evil he had courted before, suffocating him with the desire to kill. Gasping for air, he felt it swallow him up, a blackness in his brain that blotted out everything but the need to avenge, the urgency to right a wrong. *I promise not to kill him*, he'd said, but it was a promise he couldn't keep . . .

Pulse roaring in his ears, he bent to heave the coffee table high overhead, arms bulging from the effort and adrenaline surging through his veins. With a guttural groan, he heaved it at Rory's head, buckling him at the knees. His merciless kick sent the knife in Rory's hand clattering across the room while the Irishman clumped into a heap on the floor. Chest heaving, Sean launched a foot into Rory's gut, leveling him flat on his back with a garbled groan. But it wasn't near enough. Suddenly he saw Uncle Paul and Rory and men like them, preying on women, defiling them, abusing them, and a vehemence rose so strong that it stole the breath from his lungs.

With a mindless power that seemed to take control, he descended upon Rory with his fists, bludgeoning him until he lay limp on the floor, his groans dying to a whisper.

Kill him, he heard his mind say, and a surge of power shot through him, vile and cruel, luring him with a depraved pleasure that empowered his rage. A rage that had lain dormant until the war, a vile and ruthless time when he'd been trained to kill. A soldier who'd been nothing more than a machine, schooled to destroy. And yet, he'd survived it all, moments in hell that changed a man forever, haunting some with distant memories and nightmares. While for others—those with a demon inside—branding them as killers forever. Killers like him, bearing silent shame until someone unleashed the monster within.

Someone like Rory.

Whosoever hateth his brother is a murderer: and ye know that no murderer hath eternal life abiding in him.

Gasping for air, Sean froze, hands clenched and covered with blood.

Finish him . . . now . . . to vindicate Emma . . .

His fist hardened to rock, ready for vengeance . . .

Vengeance is mine, saith the Lord.

Rory's eyes fluttered open and spanned wide as Sean drew his fist back, ready to take a life that wasn't worth living.

Be not overcome of evil, but overcome evil with good.

He froze midair, muscles quivering with hate, no strength to halt his need to avenge.

He teacheth my hands to war . . . a bow of steel . . .

A spasm traveled his arm that felt like fire, and in a violent heave, his fist shuddered to his side, all air wrenching in his chest. Sweat trickled the back of his neck while harsh breaths rattled from a throat parched with the thirst to revenge. He slowly rose to his feet, Rory's blood and his coating his hands. Swiping his mouth with the side of his arm, he trudged down the hall to Emma's bedroom and retrieved a battered suitcase and men's clothing out of the closet and drawers. Returning to where Rory lay, he tossed the suitcase on the floor and threw the clothes in his face. "Get out now," he rasped, "and if you're here when I come back or you ever come near Emma Malloy again, I'll kill you with my bare hands."

With labored breathing, he retrieved the knife across the room and carefully closed it, the blade bearing his blood an eerie reminder of how close he had come. Not in the pain to his body, no, but in the pain to his soul in taking another man's life. Dropping the knife in his pocket, he moved to the door and slipped his coat from the rack, suddenly aware he had won.

My grace is sufficient for thee: for my strength is made perfect in weakness.

Without looking back, he quietly closed Emma's door, his arm as taut as a bow of steel. He drew in a cleansing breath and lumbered down the steps and out the front door, understanding for the first time in his life, that the strength to conquer one's sins had never been his.

No, he thought, oblivious to the bitter cold for the warmth flooding his soul.

It was God's.

20

ord, give me the grace to get through the holidays.
Emma sighed, peering out the window of the
crowded motorbus in an attempt to see past the flurry of
snowflakes that obscured her vision. Saturdays were supposed
to be her easiest days, but with the arrival of the holidays on
the heels of Sean's departure, nothing was "easy" at Dennehy's anymore.

A snort sounded, and she glanced at the sleeping man
beside her. She smiled at the jingle of bells on his red and
green sock hat while he snored with a bag of Christmas gifts
in his lap. *Now there's an idea for catching up on my rest,* she
thought with a twist of her lips. Between extra holiday hours
at Dennehy's and several evenings with Rory, there seemed
to be less and less time for sleep these days. Emma rested her
head on the back of the seat and closed her eyes, choosing
to follow the example of the holiday Rip Van Winkle in the
next seat.

Her thoughts immediately drifted to Rory, and a shiver
danced down her spine that she couldn't quite blame on the
cold. Rory Malloy had been nothing but kind, doting on her
every need and tempting her with his charm, and yet Emma
remained uneasy. He had no qualms about praying with her,

going to church with her, and she'd even found the Bible open several times on those rare occasions she'd visited him at her apartment. He seemed to be genuinely grieving the tragedy in Dublin, for he was noticeably reluctant to talk about it, and so Emma didn't pursue it, but she wasn't completely convinced the resultant conversion was real. No, that would take more than a few weeks of wooing as far as she was concerned, although Rory didn't seem inclined to give her more time.

He had begged her to start a new life with him in Killarney, and despite the grief over leaving those that she loved, she was actually mulling it over. *With conditions.* They both would find jobs and live separately while he courted her, until she was dead certain that he had changed. *And* never again would they become intimate until their vows were renewed . . . by a priest. He had readily agreed, and yet he quietly persisted in pursuing intimacies she wasn't ready for—the stroke of his thumb to her palm, the touch of his hand to her waist, a look in his eye, a stolen kiss. Intimacies that, in truth, she wasn't sure she would *ever* be ready for.

Except with Sean.

Her eyes popped open at the thought, and she felt a swell of heat in her cheeks. She peeked at the sleeping man beside her, grateful for the snores that grew in volume despite the bag jostling in his lap. She exhaled slowly and stared straight ahead, lips cemented like her will, which assured her she would do what she needed to do.

She would leave.

And Rory was the perfect excuse, the perfect reason . . . *the perfect sacrifice.*

A ragged breath wavered from her lips. Then Sean would finally have his store. And someday, God willing . . . a wife.

"Huntington and Tremont," the bus driver called, and the motorbus lurched to a halt, jolting the sleeping man awake.

Digging a dollar from her purse, Emma lumbered to her feet with a nod at the bleary-eyed man beside her. "Merry Christmas," she said before inching her way down the aisle. She waited for others to get off before slipping the dollar bill in the flap pocket of the bus driver's bomber jacket. "Merry Christmas, Mr. Tuttle, I haven't seen you on this route in a while."

The gray-haired gentleman grinned with a lift of his salt-and-pepper moustache. "Mrs. Malloy! Now you don't need to be spending your hard-earned money like this . . ." He attempted to fish the dollar from his pocket. "Seeing your pretty face is tip enough for an old man like me."

She blushed and plucked the bill from his hand, tucking it back in his pocket with a grin. "Then use it for the eyeglasses you so obviously need. When I board a bus, I want to make sure the driver can see."

A rich chuckle parted from weathered lips as he gave her a wink. "Yes, ma'am," he said, patting the bill in his pocket. His smile sobered. "You're one of those angels everybody sings about this time of year, Mrs. Malloy, and make no mistake about it. Merry Christmas."

She tossed a smile over her shoulder as she descended the steps. "Merry Christmas, Mr. Tuttle." She was still smiling when the bus pulled away, the bitter cold unable to dampen her spirits as she plodded her way to Charity's house. Giving was what Christmas was all about, she thought, gingerly sidestepping a sooty snowdrift. And *nothing* brought more joy than giving. *Especially to Sean* . . . A sweetness like nothing she had ever known ached in her chest, filling her up with the overwhelming need to give of herself to the one man who loved her just as she was.

And to Rory? Her smile faded as she reflected on the early years of her life. Yes, especially to Rory. To give of herself to a man who desperately needed to be loved for just who he was. A shard of fear pricked in her heart, as cold and biting as the snow now stinging her face. Yes, she was afraid, but God had not brought her full circle for nothing, and now she had the chance to be his instrument in Rory's life. God's grace had changed her, and she knew deep in her soul that it could change Rory as well. Had, in fact, already begun, if Rory's presence here was any indication. But only time and prayer would tell, she realized, a lesson she'd learned once when she'd had nothing to give. And yet, in the midst of her pain, God had not only sustained her with the gift of his Son . . . but with the habit of giving, saving her from a lifetime of bitterness over what she did *not* have. With a rush of joy, she closed her eyes, wishing with all of her heart that people knew. Giving of one's self—like Jesus had—was the only love that healed.

Unconditional love.

A sad smile touched her lips, along with the ice crystals that fell from the sky. *And the one gift I can give Sean this Christmas . . .*

Ribbons of lamplight spilled from Charity's windows onto a crystalline blanket of snow, welcoming her home. Stomping her boots on the brick porch that Mitch had obviously shoveled, Emma peeked through the etched-glass door into Charity's polished foyer, experiencing a twinge of grief over leaving these people she loved. She opened the front door to the sound of Charity's voice, and a gloom instantly settled despite the soft glow of a Tiffany lamp that graced a marble table. Emma bent to slip off her snow-crusted overboots and set them on the rug by the door, placed there for that very purpose. Rising to her full height, she stood for a brief moment, eyes closed to embed in her memory the sound of her best friend's laughter. A lump immediately formed in her throat. *Oh, Charity, I will miss you so . . .*

"There you are!" The object of her thoughts posed in the parlor door, peeking at the watch on her hand. "I thought you fell into a snowdrift, and we'd have to send out the St. Bernard."

Emma smiled and tugged off her gloves, shoving them in her pockets before she hung up her coat. "Without the brandy, I trust," she said with a crooked grin. She glanced around, head cocked as she listened for Mitch and the twins. "It's awfully quiet—where is everybody?"

Charity's voice faltered, but not her smile as she linked an arm through Emma's. "Mitch took Hope and Henry to spend the night at Faith's because Mitch and I have a special guest." She ushered Emma into her holiday-ready Victorian parlor where a ceiling-height Christmas tree dazzled with endless strings of lights and countless glass ornaments shimmering in their glow. The nostalgic scent of pine mingled happily with that of gingerbread men on the tree, while the hint of hickory lent coziness from a wood-burning fire that crackled in a brick hearth.

Emma halted at the edge of the pastel Oriental rug, eyes spanning wide at the sight of Father Mac reclining in one of Charity's gold wing chairs. "Father Mac!" she said with a welcome smile. Mischief tugged at her tone. "Uh-oh . . . what trouble has Henry gotten into now?" She shot Charity a sloe-eyed smile. "Or maybe it's his mother?"

Father Mac rose, his smile far dimmer than Emma's. "I'm happy to report that Henry's in the clear for the time being, Emma, and so is his mother." He glanced at Charity with a twinkle in his eye. "Although it's a close call as to which of the two garners more of my attention."

Charity jutted her chin. "I'll have you know, Father McHugh, that I have been incident-free for well over a month now."

"I'll vouch for that," Mitch said as he strolled in from the kitchen. He looped an arm around Charity's waist and planted a kiss on her head. "Although it hasn't been easy, I'm sure."

"Mitch Dennehy!" Charity elbowed him away. She squinted her eyes. "You did remember to tell Faith to restrict Henry on chocolate, I hope?"

"Yes, dear," he said with a droll smile, giving Emma's shoulder a squeeze. "Cold enough out there for you, Mrs. Malloy? I told you I would have been happy to pick you up."

"I know, Mitch, but I'm never sure these days just when I'll be heading home."

"Did you eat?" Charity asked, arms folded as if she were addressing Henry.

Emma smiled. "Yes, Mother. You packed both a lunch and a dinner, remember?"

"Good. Then how about coffee or tea? I have peach cobbler . . ." She wriggled her brows.

"Uh-oh, my favorite dessert," Emma teased, eyes narrowing. "What do you want?"

The bob in Charity's throat didn't mix well with the smile on her face. She spun on her heel to address Father Mac. "Father, warm cobbler with or without ice cream and coffee or tea?"

"Coffee, black sounds wonderful," he said with a wink. "And keep in mind it's a sin to serve cobbler without ice cream."

"Yes, sir." She offered a quick salute and turned to her husband. "Mitch, would you mind doing the honors while Emma and I visit with Father?"

"Absolutely." He squeezed Charity's arm before he left for the kitchen.

Emma's stomach did a flip. *Oh, no—what's she up to now?* More than a wee bit nervous, Emma seated herself on the couch, and Charity followed suit, her friend's chattiness definitely at odds with the stiff smile on her face.

Emma slid her a curious gaze. "So, what's on your mind," she said with a quick glance in Father Mac's direction, "that you need to call out the clergy?"

Charity exchanged looks with the priest before she turned to face her friend dead-on. Inching closer, she laid a gentle hand on Emma's arm. "Emma, we need to talk . . ."

Pinpricks nettled her skin. "I hope this isn't about Rory again, because I already told you it's time I move out of your home." Emma exhaled her frustration at the relentless meddling of her friend, then forced a light tone. "Although I suspect the real reason you don't want me to go is you like having an accomplice when you raid the kitchen at night."

Tears welled in Charity's eyes. "No, the real reason is that I love you . . ."

A knot formed in Emma's throat as she embraced Charity hard. "I love you too, more than I can say. But it's time to get on with my life . . . and that might mean with Rory."

"No . . . ," Charity whispered over her shoulder, her voice thick with sorrow. "It doesn't."

Emma pulled away, studying her friend's face. "What do you mean?" Her stomach clenched as tight as the fingers she now gripped to Charity's arms.

Charity squeezed her hand. "Emma, there's a good chance that Rory may be deported."

The lights on the tree blurred into one as Emma stared beyond Charity's shoulder, trying to process the words co-agulating in her brain. "What? Why?"

Charity averted her gaze while Father Mac cleared his throat. "Emma," he began quietly, drawing her eyes to his, "Steven arrested Rory at a speakeasy this afternoon."

White spots that weren't part of the tree danced before Emma's eyes. Her eyelids quivered. "Was he . . . drinking?" She swallowed hard on the word, praying that it wasn't true. *He promised me . . . promised me he had quit.* "Because an arrest at a speakeasy doesn't mean that he was drinking, you know . . ."

"He was very drunk, Emma," Father Mac said softly, his gaze more than gentle. "He tried to assault Steven's partner, so they locked him in a private cell."

She found herself struggling for air. "But . . . but raids happen all the time, Father, and they don't just ship people out of the country."

He drew in a breath and released it slowly. "No, no, that's true . . ." He paused before he spoke the words that stole the wind from her pipes. "Only immigrants wanted for questioning in the death of a child."

A gasp stung in her throat. "No! It isn't true . . . it was an accident, he told me so."

Father Mac leaned forward, hands clasped. "Be that as it may, Emma—Steven verified it with Dublin authorities. And the truth is, at some point soon, Rory will have to go back."

She closed her eyes and water stung beneath her lids. Her body was stiff, barely registering that Charity still held her hand. "It was an accident," she said numbly, refusing to believe the worst of a man so in dire need of mercy. "The guilt is eating him raw, I'm sure of it." She looked up then, her heart in her throat. "But he's been sober until now, Father, and he can be again, I know it. He just needs someone to help."

"Maybe," Father Mac whispered, pausing too long. "But there's also another woman."

She stared for several moments, the words paralyzing her pulse, and then with the gentle touch of her friend's hand, she crumpled into a heap. Clutching her close, Charity soothed with gentle words while Emma wept against her chest and agony ripped at her mind. Not over a man she hoped to love, but over a man she hoped to heal. And, she thought with a painful stab in her heart, a man who could have healed *her* of a lifetime of guilt.

Charity handed her a handkerchief, and she wiped the tears from her face like she wished she could wipe the scars from her soul.

"Are you okay?" Charity whispered, and Emma nodded, not sure that she was.

Stroking Emma's hair, Charity offered a sad smile before rising to her feet. Her gaze flitted to Father Mac and back. "If you both will excuse me, I'll just go check on dessert."

Emma blotted her face, eyes raw as she looked up at Father Mac. "Thank you, Father, for telling me. I . . . I know this wasn't easy for either you or Charity."

"Or you," he said, his tone kind.

A frail laugh broke from her throat. "No, not at all. I had hoped . . . prayed, really . . . that Rory had changed. That we could restore our . . . ," her cheeks warmed, ". . . what we had."

Father Mac sat forward again, chin resting on steepled hands as his sorrowful gaze flicked to her wedding band and back. "You mean your marriage, Emma?" he asked quietly. "So, you and Rory said your vows before a priest?"

Heat scorched her cheeks, and she looked away, almost stumbling over her words. "Really, Father, why would you even ask such a thing?"

The empathy in his tone all but embraced her. "Because in his drunken stupor, Rory revealed things to Steven that will be painful for you to hear, Emma, but the truth must come to light. For your sake . . . and for Sean's."

The breath hitched in her throat. "No," she whispered, her voice a rasp, "he wouldn't . . ."

Father Mac's tone remained steady. "He not only would, Emma . . . he did. Boasted to Steven that he was a wealthy man because his wife had inherited an estate from her aunt."

Her eyelids listed closed while the air seized in her lungs. *Killarney . . .*

"Said he intended to take you there to claim it . . . *after* he married you, nice and legal."

She slumped over, head in her hands, too mortified to face the man before her.

His tone gentled. "Emma, I need the truth. Were you legally married to Rory Malloy?"

It started in her stomach, an awful quivering that inched its way to the tip of each limb until she felt as if her brain would chatter along with her teeth.

"*. . . your lawful husband, to have and to hold, from this day forward, for better or for worse, richer or poorer, in sickness and in health, to love and cherish until death do you part?*"

"*I do.*"

"Emma . . ." His touch burned as he slowly pried her fingers from her face, but shame wouldn't let her open her eyes. "Look at me," he whispered.

She shook her head, and the motion unleashed a trickle of tears.

Father Mac carefully took her face in the palm of his hand. "Please."

There was no trace of judgment in his tone, and his kindness wrung a sob from her throat. Her eyelids fluttered open, and each word tasted of pain. "Oh, Father, not by a priest . . ."

"By a magistrate, then?" His whisper held a thread of hope.

Hot moisture scalded her eyes, forcing her lids closed once

again as shame choked the words from her throat. "No . . . not a magistrate . . . ," she whispered, the salt of her tears stinging her tongue. "A clerk in the magistrate's office, a friend of Rory's." She put a hand to her eyes, desperate to withhold the truth, but unwilling to lie to a priest. "Only . . . only he wasn't a clerk at all, it seems—he was a janitor in the magistrate's office who Rory paid to steal and forge the marriage certificate. Rory let it slip in a drunken fit years later, laughing that he'd gotten what he wanted without having to marry me at all." A harsh laugh spewed from her throat. "Years living in sin, Father, when all along I'd thought it'd only been the six months before he put the ring on my hand."

She looked up then, eyes swimming with pain. "I know it was sin, Father, sleeping with Rory before I took the vow, but once he placed that ring on my finger, I felt redeemed and whole. When he told me it was a lie, my world crumbled around me and I couldn't handle it—the guilt, the shame. So I clung to my vows, real or not, because in my heart we were man and wife, as surely as this ring on my finger. I said my vow before God, I swear, and I've honored it ever since."

"Why?" he asked quietly, and the word made her flinch, like a sudden shaft of light in a dark cellar where roaches and rats skittered. It was a question she didn't want to answer . . . a question she'd hoped no one would ever ask. And yet, it hung between them now, a deadly noose, quivering in the wind. Eons passed before she realized she hadn't answered, only stared at him like some crazed woman who was deaf, unable to comprehend his words.

"Why, Emma?" he repeated, and she closed her eyes, realizing her creditor had finally come to call.

Why had she chosen to live life as a lie? A violent spasm heaved in her throat. Because the truth was simply too awful to bear.

She felt his touch on her arm, warm and secure, countering the cold grip of sin that fisted her soul. "It's over, you know . . . ," he said, his words as tender as the stroke of a mother's hand. "Though your sins be as scarlet, they shall be as white as snow; though they be red like crimson, they shall be as wool."

Scarlet, crimson. *The color of blood.*

Barriers tumbled, and all at once agony bled from her pores while memories bled from her mind. Forbidden memories, pushed and hidden away . . . until now. A pool of blood, fetal tissue in the privy, bedsheets the color of bittersweet berries and just as lethal. A withering sigh quivered from her lips like a death-row confession, and when she began to speak, her words were no more than a wisp of shame, frail and feeble.

"Rebellion owned me once, Father, hard as it may be to believe. I defied my parents like I would have defied God . . . ," her watery gaze lifted to his, "had I believed in him." She looked past him then, her smile hollow while her eyes trailed into a dead stare. "And therein lies the greatest gift Rory Malloy ever gave to a lover—a flame of faith fiery enough to incinerate an infidel's sins." She rose, hands clenched at her waist, rambling through Charity's parlor like her thoughts rambled through her past. "My parents forbade me from seeing him, you know, but I was fifteen and had plans of my own." She turned, and tragedy pooled in her eyes. "A baby," she whispered, "to love me unconditionally . . . like my parents never would."

The mercy in Father Mac's eyes begged her to go on, and so she continued to walk, confronting ghosts in the corridors of a tormented mind. "Rory promised to love me forever, of course, and so I gave myself to him. And when I—" her eyelids twitched while muscles shuddered in her throat—"became pregnant, well, naturally he swore to marry me." She blinked, suddenly finding herself staring aimlessly out the window, her secrets drifting free like the snowflakes in the sky.

A raspy sigh shuddered forth, and she turned, arms still clutched at her waist as she resumed her stroll, an arduous journey to where Father Mac patiently waited. "To quote Dickens, Father, it was the best of times and the worst of times. The best because the seed of a child burgeoned in my womb, bringing me closer to being loved for just who I was.

But also the worst of times, because now disgrace threatened my very proper family. You see, in Ireland, a young girl pregnant outside of marriage was forced to leave home. I had little choice—The Magdalene Laundry or The Good Shepherd Convent. Either option would destroy a family and rob me of my baby."

She returned to the sofa, her manner suddenly still. Calm, she supposed—not unlike a gush of sewage that had slithered into a pool, stagnant at her feet. "So I coerced Rory Malloy to marry me against his will. I knew he loved me, although 'obsessed' might be a better word." Her words trickled into a whisper. "But he was traumatized by marriage, you see, by a deed that was done when he was a wee lad of only five. It seems he witnessed his mum take a butcher knife to his da during a row where his father had bloodied his mother." Tears stung, and Emma realized that even after all these years, she still grieved for the boy who was Rory Malloy. Her voice faltered. "H-his mother was hanged, of course, and Rory went to live with his uncle, whose marriage was almost as bad. So it became plain, Father, that Rory was afraid of marriage. But with a baby in my belly, I needed a ring on my finger, sanctioned by the Church or not. And so I talked him into a secret civil marriage, and because he wanted me so badly, he finally agreed." Her half smile was laced with pain. "So we said our vows to a clerk instead of a priest . . . ," her head bowed in shame, "who was really just a janitor instead of a clerk."

"What happened to the baby?" Father Mac whispered, and the question sliced through her, not unlike the cold blade with which Rory's mother had ended his father's life.

She squeezed her eyes shut, defying more tears to fall. "As I said, Father, Rory was obsessed with me, but once I had what I wanted—the promise of a baby to love me—my interest in his . . . affections . . . waned, and that wounded him. He started drinking more than usual, sometimes to the point of a jealous rage—first, over the baby, then over other men he feared I preferred." Her words slowed as the paralysis of pain did its work, dulling her tongue. "And then one night I told him no, and he was furious. Started drinking heavily, not coming to bed till hours later." Her voice began to shake, and water welled in her eyes against her will. "When he did, he became cruel, trying to force me, hurt me. And when I tried to fight him off, he . . . beat me . . . ," the tears she had fought finally spilled from her eyes, ". . . before he accosted me . . . cruelly." A spasm twitched in her jaw as her gaze lapsed into a vacant stare. "I was four months along, Father," she whispered. "I bled for days before I lost my baby." A heave shuddered in her throat as she closed her eyes. "Precious tissue swimming in a pool of blood."

She heard the crack of his knees as he rose, and in a quiver of her chin, he was beside her, gathering her in his arms. "Emma, my heart grieves for you and the loss of your baby."

Her pause seemed an eternity. "Babies . . . ," she whispered.

Father Mac pulled away. "I don't understand—do you mean twins?"

"No, Father, not twins," Emma said, dabbing her face with Charity's soggy handkerchief. Her stupor contrasted with the shock in his eyes. "A second child that I lost the same way."

"God, have mercy." His voice was a pained rasp. "When?"

"A few years later when Rory accused me of cheating. You see, he was so angry and jealous over my desire for a baby, he almost never . . . wanted me after that. That's when he started drinking more, seeing other women." Emma twisted the cloth in her hand. "But I still wanted a baby, Father, more than anything, so I . . ." Her cheeks heated. "I tricked him."

"Tricked him?"

She chewed on her lip. "Like Lot's daughters in the Bible."

Father Mac blinked. "You slept with him when he was drunk?"

Emma nodded. "Half the time he wouldn't even remember the next day, so when I became pregnant, he accused me of adultery." She forced the words from her mouth, bile tainting her tongue. "I kept it from him for months, but when I began to show, he went into a rage, slapping and kicking me until my baby was nothing more than a pool of blood on the floor."

"For the love of God, Emma, why didn't you leave? Tell your parents the truth?"

When her lips began to tremble, she clamped down to ward it off, blinking several times to clear the moisture from her eyes. "My parents disowned me when they first saw the ring, Father, furious I had married a Protestant. Even so, I might have tried to reason with them if . . ." She shivered, yesterday's despair revisiting once again. "If they hadn't died in a fire."

"Oh, Emma . . ."

Rising, she buffed her arms to stave off the shivering that threatened to take hold. She walked to the window and peered out at the ice and snow, realizing that when she'd lost her babies, her heart had grown as cold. "I couldn't live with myself, Father," she said quietly. "Not only did I feel responsible for the death of my parents—or at least the death of their dreams to have the son my father so desperately wanted—but also for the death of my children. Because I knew—as surely as the bruises on my face and the scars on my body—that it had been my sin, my rebellion, my will over God's, that not only robbed me of the love of my parents and my husband, but my babies as well. Babies conceived in sin because their mother wanted to be loved . . ." A heave stalled in her chest. "And babies murdered by that very mother when her sin put them in harm's way." She turned then, her face devoid of all emotion and her heart just as empty. "In my mind's eye, I killed my babies and wasn't fit to live, and so I decided if my babies had to die, then I should too . . ."

"No—" Shock pulsed in Father's Mac's whisper from across the room.

A sad smile edged her mouth. "Not to worry, Father. My da always said I was good for nothing and apparently he was right—I wasn't even good at ending my own life. My neighbor found me, and the next thing I knew, I was being tended by the good sisters of The Good Shepherd Convent." Emma drew in a cleansing breath, and for the first time since she'd begun unraveling her sordid tale, she felt the heaviness lift from her shoulders. "It was there that I learned about the love of God, about his forgiveness, his mercy . . ." Tears sprang to her eyes. "His salvation." She hugged herself, unable to suppress a shaky smile. "Dear, dear Sister Marguerite—all of four feet eleven and the stature of a giant, twinkling eyes and a formidable chin, who would have none of my self-pity, none of my self-loathing. Instead she showed me the kind of love I'd never seen before, the kind of love that bound my wounds, kindled my hope, and healed my soul." A sheen of tears glazed her eyes as she stared at the fire. "It wasn't until much later that I realized it was the love of Jesus I'd seen in her face."

Emma brushed her tears aside. "But I was ashamed, ashamed of the kind of life I had lived, and so I lied to Sister Marguerite too, allowing her to believe that Rory was my husband. Of course, she encouraged me to go home and be the kind of wife Jesus would want me to be." Emma exhaled, the motion all but draining her. Her gaze lifted to Father Mac's for the first time in a long while. "And so I did, Father. I went home and swore to God that I would remain faithful to Rory, not as his legal wife, perhaps, but as the wife I vowed to be before God until the day I would die. The Bible says 'two shall be one flesh, no longer two but one,' and in my mind's eye, when I entered Rory's bed, carried his babies, took my vow, I became his wife, sanctioned or not. I committed to him body and soul, and in my eyes—and God's—we are one. Man and wife."

"But not in the law's eyes or that of the Church," Father Mac said quietly, the tenderness of his gaze convicting her more than any pious accusation.

Her shoulders slumped, and the air depleted from her lungs. "No."

Father Mac rose with a loud exhale that told Emma he was ready to render judgment. He moved to where she stood and braced gentle hands to her arms. "Emma, dear, dear Emma—marriage is sanctioned by God. Entering Rory's bed was a sin, not a commitment to God or to Rory. Don't allow sin to be elevated to the will of God. It was not his will for you to give yourself to Rory illicitly; it was yours, and by refusing to see it as the sin that it is, you allow its hold to rule in your life, cutting you off from the blessings of God."

Warmth prickled her neck and cheeks, and she lowered her eyes. "I . . . can't . . . let myself believe that, Father."

He took her hand in his, his touch as gentle as his whisper. "You can, Emma, because it's the truth. You are not married now, nor have you ever been married, and deep down in your soul, you know it. Your shame tells you it's true. You lied to your parents, you lied to Sister Marguerite, and you've lied to yourself . . . and you've been lying ever since. To Charity, to Sean, and to everyone who loves you."

"No . . ." A sob choked in her throat and she bent over with a low moan, her body shuddering with heaves. "Please, Father, no! I'm married, I am . . . don't you see? I could never live with myself if it wasn't true."

Father Mac pulled her into the shelter of his arms. "It isn't true, Emma," he whispered. "And closing one's eyes, no matter how fervently, does not make the truth go away."

She crumpled in his arms then, her guilt and shame too much to bear. "I can't face it, Father, I can't." She gasped for air, her throat raw with pain as she fought to block out his words that struck at the very heart of her oath to God. An oath that enabled her to pay for her sins and earn God's favor, penance served for all that was due. And a prophecy sealed by her own father's words . . .

I pray to God you get what you deserve . . .

"You can," he said quietly, his grip shoring her up. "But only through the grace of God."

Her voice was nasal and broken as she went limp in his arms. "But I don't deserve it."

"Nobody does," he said, his words gruff with emotion, "and therein lies the mystery. 'For God so loved the world, that he gave his only begotten Son, that whosoever believeth in him should not perish, but have everlasting life.'" Father Mac held her at arm's length, compassion shining in his eyes. "Grace, Emma, pure and simple—the favor and blessing of

God to those who don't deserve it. And through his grace, you can be free—not only from a marriage that never existed, but free from the bondage of the guilt and shame that kept you there."

She squeezed her eyes shut, her sodden cheek pressed against the smooth cotton of Father Mac's cassock. *Free! Oh, Lord, how can it be true?*

If the Son therefore shall make you free, ye shall be free indeed.

All at once a heady warmth took residence within that had nothing to do with the heat of Father Mac's arms as they held her close. A tiny pinprick of realization seeped into her brain until it radiated through her body like rays of the sun. *Free!*

With a firm squeeze of her arms, Father Mac ushered her to the sofa and seated her there, squatting in front of her with her hands tightly in his. "Emma," he whispered, "the kind of love you were looking for in your parents, in Rory, in your precious babies, can only be found in Christ, and you know that now. But what you don't know is that in God's infinite love for you, he not only wants to heal your wounds and set you free, but restore what the locusts have eaten . . . ," he paused, his next words measured and slow, "with the love of a good man, Emma . . . a man who will love you on earth while God loves you in heaven."

Her eyes flared wide. "Oh, Father, no, I can't . . ."

His voice was gentle. "You can, Emma, because you're free. And Sean loves you."

She shook her head. "But I'm not worthy."

The edge of Father Mac's lips crooked up. "Not many of us are . . . and yet, God loves us still."

"But Sean is . . . ," wetness blurred in her eyes, "the most wonderful man I've ever known. He deserves the best there is."

Father Mac feathered a stray curl from her eyes. "And so he has it—in you."

"I wish I could believe that, Father, but I will never be good enough."

He tucked a finger to her chin with a slant of his lips. "Why don't you let the man decide for himself?"

Her breathing thickened, his words too good to be true. "But you heard me—I lied to him, to Charity, to everyone . . . and my life has been steeped in sin."

"You're in luck, then," he said with a jag of a smile. "I believe I'm just the man you need." He cradled her face. "Are you truly sorry, Emma, for everything you just confessed in this room?"

Emma pressed her hand over his with a tearful heave. "Oh, Father, with all of my heart!"

He raised his hand in the sign of the cross. "Then I absolve you, Emma, in the name of the Father, and of the Son, and of the Holy Spirit."

Barely believing it to be true, Emma breathed in the cleanest air she'd ever drawn, and with a heart weighted more with gratitude than guilt and shame, she closed her eyes, her voice quivering with intent. "O my God, I am heartily sorry . . ." Every syllable of her Act of Contrition carried all the awe and reverence of a soul set free from the darkest dungeon into the glorious light. With each word spoken, she tasted the sweetness of a forgiving God, and her heart felt lighter, freer than she'd ever felt before.

Head bowed, she reveled in the warmth of Father Mac's hand on her hair as he issued penance and then blessed her, and when he finished, her eyelids lifted, unleashing more tears.

"How can I ever thank you, Father, for all you have done?"

He chuckled and attempted to rise from his squatting position with a grunt. "Well, for starters, you can help me up, young lady, as my knees are not what they used to be."

She laughed and gripped his arms, tugging him to his feet.

"Secondly," he said, "you can embrace the truth and refuse to believe the lies of the devil—lies that you can't be forgiven or that you're unworthy to reap the blessings of God. Outright lies, each and every one. And finally," he said with a twinkle in his eye, "you can do me a favor and pay some attention to a very good friend of mine who, I don't mind saying, has been a bit of a grump lately." He winked. "I suspect he could use some cheering up."

She gave him a shaky smile. "I . . . will try, Father, I promise, but I think it may take me some time, you know, before I can face him again?"

He nodded. "Sure, sure, take all the time you need. I believe Charity invited him for dessert, if I'm not mistaken, so I'm sure he'll just wait in the next room."

Blood drained from her face as she put a hand to her throat. "No . . . he's here? But I'm not ready . . ."

"Not ready for dessert? Nonsense." Charity breezed through the door with a tray in her hand.

Emma's throat went dry as nausea rolled in her stomach. Rory had divulged Emma's awful secret to Steven, which meant that now Charity knew too. Emma stared at the floor, unable to look her friend in the eye. "I . . . I don't feel well, Charity, I think I need to go to my room."

"Emma . . ."

Father Mac's voice was gentle, but Emma ignored the plea in his tone with a stiff nod. "Thank you, Father, for all of your time. Good night." She moved toward the door, but not before Charity halted her with a hand to her arm.

"Emma," she said quietly, "stay—please. We need to talk."

Face aflame, Emma looked away. "We will, Charity, I promise. Just not tonight, please?" She paused, swallowing hard. "I . . . I'm just not ready. But I need you to promise . . ."

"Anything," Charity whispered.

Emma drew in a deep breath. "That you won't use the key to come talk to me tonight."

Seconds passed before Charity answered with a sigh. "I promise."

Exhaling slowly, Emma nodded. "Thank you. Good night, Charity, Father." And before either could bid her good night, she flew up the steps to the safety of her room, not sure she would *ever* be ready to face the people she loved. And with the turn of the bolt, she locked everyone out, hopefully to embrace a sanctuary where shame wouldn't find her.

"So . . . how'd it go?" Mitch glanced up at Charity as she entered the kitchen, his spoon poised over half-eaten cobbler that wasn't long for this world. A cleft appeared at the bridge of his nose when Father Mac followed, an untouched dessert tray in hand and a crease in his brow.

"As well as can be expected, I suppose," Charity said, "considering Emma bolted the moment I entered the room." Her lips slanted into a droll smile. "Which, oddly enough, is the same effect I seem to have on my son."

Sean stood to his feet. "Where is she?"

Charity studied her brother's ashen face, the pallor of which highlighted a crop of dark freckles she never even realized he had. "In hiding," she said quietly, "safely locked in her room." She took the tray from Father Mac and laid it on the table, then placed his coffee and dessert in front of him. Releasing a weary sigh, she squeezed Sean's elbow and dropped into a chair. "Everything was fine, apparently, until I showed up with dessert, and then Emma shot up the stairs faster than a squirrel up a tree at first sight of Henry." She sagged against the table, elbow flat and head propped to her fist. Her eyes suddenly trained on the near-empty pan of cobbler in the center of the table and she sat straight up, yanking it forward with a drop of her jaw. Her gaze snapped to her husband. "Sweet saints, how many pieces did you have?"

Mitch stopped mid-chew, swallowing hard. "Three," he said defensively. "So what?"

"So, this is not your personal pan of cobbler, Mitch Dennehy, and you know it."

He gave her a half-lidded smile while rolling the spoon in his mouth, obviously intent on licking it clean. "So I have a voracious appetite, little girl—big surprise."

Heat dusted her cheeks, and she quickly turned away, sobering considerably as her thoughts refocused on Emma. She reached for her cup of coffee and eyed Father Mac over the rim. "So, Father," she whispered, "is it true . . . about her marriage to Rory?"

"What about her marriage to Rory?" Sean folded his arms with a scowl that suggested he'd taken lessons from Henry. "And why would she be in hiding for pity's sake?"

Charity put her coffee down and glanced up at her brother, eyes soft with concern. "Because she's ashamed," she said quietly, "ashamed to face the people she loves."

"Why?" Sean asked sharply. "So she let that lowlife dupe her twice—so what? That's nothing more than a testament to her compassion and mercy."

"I'm afraid there's a little more to it than that," Charity said, her solemn gaze flicking to Father Mac before returning to her brother. "I think you better sit down."

He stared at her for several seconds, jaw tight and lips even worse, then slowly lowered into his chair. His eyes shifted to Father Mac. "What's going on?"

With a pensive pause, Father Mac laid his fork on his plate and pushed it away. Leaning forward, he leveled thick arms on the table with a loose clasp of hands. "We didn't want to say anything until Emma confirmed it, but it seems that . . ." He hesitated to draw in a deep breath, their gazes locked. "That Emma is a single woman. She is not now . . . nor ever has been . . . legally married to Rory Malloy."

No one breathed. The kitchen was deathly still except for the steady drip-drip of the sink from a new leak Mitch had attempted to fix. Charity watched as emotions rolled across her brother's features like cloud pictures in the sky—shock, hope, joy, pain, and finally anger—slowly dissolving from one image to the next until they billowed into thunderclouds, dark and threatening.

"Why?" he whispered, his voice tinged with a raw hurt she'd never heard. "Why would she lie? When she knows how much I love her, want her—why would she do that?"

A weary exhale parted from Father Mac's lips. "Horrific tragedy has a way of skewing one's mind," he said quietly, "in some more than others." He leaned back in his chair, idly fingering the scalloped design on the end of his unused fork. "Unfortunately, Emma has endured a great deal of pain in her life, pain that has, at times, distorted the truth for her. Her story is—" Father Mac lowered his gaze, his voice thick with emotion—"heartbreaking at best."

For several seconds, Sean stared, jaw stiff and mouth hard before he finally slumped back in his chair with a hand to his eyes. His voice was a hollow whisper. "So where does that leave me, Father? In Emma's mind?"

"Well, I would say that depends on you, Sean," Father Mac said slowly, "and whether or not you can forgive her."

It seemed an eternity before Sean looked up, but when he did, there was a glaze of moisture in his eyes. He unleashed a weighty sigh. "I love her, Mac. What choice do I have?"

Father Mac smiled. "None, then, I'd say." Sobriety returned as he glanced around the table. "I hope and pray that Emma chooses to share her past with each of you so you can understand the trials she's had to endure. But it's her decision, and I think it's only fair to tell you that she's running scared. The truth is, she's so paralyzed by guilt and shame that she doesn't feel ready to face any of you just yet." He nodded at Sean. "Especially you. She loves you, Sean, but I'll warn you right now—she's going to try to run like the devil, from you more than anybody, because she doesn't feel worthy."

"That's ridiculous," Sean said.

"Maybe so, but when it comes to the love she has for you, that's how she sees herself—a scarred woman, inside and out. Keep in mind that when a woman's self-image has been destroyed, both by the man she loved and the very sins that have imprisoned her most of her life, she can't see what you see. It will only be through the mirror of God's love and that of your own that Emma will finally have a glimpse of the beautiful woman God created her to be."

"I couldn't agree more," Charity said, finger pressed to her lip, "and I think I may just have the key." She squinted, formulating the plan in her mind. "Sean needs to profess his love and forgiveness for her as soon as possible—tonight, before all that shame and guilt has time to fester."

Sagging further into his chair, Sean kneaded the bridge of his nose, his lips set in a grim line. "And just how I am supposed to do that if she refuses to come out of her room?"

"You're not listening," Charity said. She slipped a hand into her pocket and held up a brass key with mischief in her eyes. "I *said*, 'I have the key.'" She wriggled her brows. "Because somehow I had a sneaky feeling I'd be needing it tonight."

A smile flickered at the edges of Father Mac's mouth. "I believe I distinctly heard you promise you wouldn't use the key, Mrs. Dennehy."

Charity's eyes widened in innocence. "Why, Father McHugh, how can you possibly think I'd break a promise, and in front of a priest, no less?" She promptly deposited the key into Sean's hand with a jut of her chin. "I promised *I* wouldn't use it—not Sean."

A slow grin traveled Sean's lips as he gave his sister a kiss on the cheek. "No matter what anybody says, sis, don't ever change." He rose and bobbled the key with a grin. "Which room?"

"Last one on the left," Charity said. "And don't take no for answer."

He strode to the door. "Don't worry," he said, holding the key aloft. "If the good Lord has opened a door, then I'm sure not gonna let anybody lock it." He winked. "Wish me luck."

"You mean blessing, don't you?" Charity called after him.

Sean grinned. *Oh, yes.* He took the steps two at time, chest heaving like a bellows, but not from the climb. He halted on the landing and closed his eyes, heart pumping faster than the adrenaline surging through his veins. *Emma is free!* The magnitude of that single thought sent shock waves through his body until he couldn't breathe. And then gratitude rose up like a rush of joy so sweet that moisture stung in his eyes. Striding down the hall, he stopped before her door, the sound of muffled crying stilling his body to stone. *Oh, Emma—let me dry your tears . . .*

He knocked, his heart ramming against his ribs. "Emma, it's Sean—can I come in?"

No answer.

He leaned in, head bowed and palm to the door. "Please don't shut me out—I need you."

"And I need to be alone," she said, her voice nasal from weeping. "Please go."

He vented with a blast of frustration. "No, I won't go. You're done spending your time alone, always shouldering burdens too heavy to bear. It's time to admit you need me as much as I need you." He rattled the knob, but it was locked as tight as her heart. "Open the door, Emma."

Silence.

"Fine. Have it your way." He unlocked the door, causing her to jolt up on the bed when it opened.

"What are you doing?" she cried, hair tousled and clothes rumpled.

He quietly closed it behind him. "Talking to the woman I love."

She shook her head. "No, don't say that."

"Why not?" He moved toward the bed, challenging her with his gaze. "It's the truth, Emma, no matter how difficult it is for you to hear."

"I'm not the woman you think I am," she whispered, inching back against the wall as if somehow she thought she could put distance between them. He took another step forward, determined there would never be distance again.

"Yes, you are," he said quietly. "Your past is over. It's your future I care about."

"Don't come any closer—please." She wouldn't look at him, head bowed and eyes squeezed shut while she clutched her arms to her waist.

"Emma." He said it softly, fervently, with all the passion he felt in his heart. "Look at me—please."

She began to tremble, and he moved closer. He knelt one

knee on the bed, and her eyes jerked open, spanning wide. "Sean—if you really and truly love me—you'll leave me be."

He stared a long time, her words a jagged barb that bled into his voice. "Tell me, Emma," he whispered, "is loving me such a painful prospect?"

Water welled in her eyes, and she shook her head, dispelling her tears. "No," she said, her voice a frail rasp, "not me loving you—you loving me." A heave shuddered in her chest as she looked away. "If you only knew . . . you would understand. I'm not worthy."

He stood rooted to the floor, comprehending for the first time in his life that God had ordained him for this. Blessed him with the privilege and the calling to love and nurture one of the wounded souls so very close to God's heart. To restore what the locusts had eaten in a woman's life who had given her life to God.

And I will restore to you the years that the locust hath eaten . . . and ye shall eat in plenty, and be satisfied and praise the name of the Lord your God, that hath dealt wondrously with you: and my people shall never be ashamed.

Wondrously, indeed. A holy reverence lighted on him that he'd never felt in any church, in any prayer uttered over a meal, or in any rote confession of faith. No, it was far deeper—a reverent gratitude for the touch of God in his life and his infinite love and mercy for those he calls by name. *Like Emma Malloy*, he thought, emotion swelling in his throat. *And me . . . the man privileged to love her.*

With slow and deliberate motion, Sean reached for her against her will . . . like God so often does with his children who are lost. Holding her in his arms, he rocked her gently while she wept, whispering his love against the tendrils of her hair. "You have it all wrong, Emma," he said quietly when her tears finally slowed. "I'm the one who's not worthy." And cupping her swollen face in his hands, he gently kissed each scar on her face, marks of beauty all for a woman who'd chosen to forgive rather than hate.

His body relaxed when she finally melted in his arms, lids

closed and her mouth parted in shallow breaths. He kissed her eyes then, tasting the salt of her tears. "My prayer is that someday these very eyes will see your beauty as I see it, Emma." His mouth wandered to her ear, warming it with the touch of his lips. "That your ears will hear the truth of your priceless worth." Slowly trailing the curve of her face, he nuzzled her lips gently, carefully. "And that this mouth will utter thanks to God every day when these very lips become a feast for our love." He deepened the kiss until their tenuous breaths became as one, then rested his head to hers. "I love you, Emma Malloy," he whispered, her cheek wet against his lips, "and I need you to be my wife."

Seconds seemed suspended in time as he awaited her answer, light-years that delayed the next beat of his heart.

"Frey," she said in a timid voice that tilted the corners of his mouth. "My name is Emma Frey."

His deep chuckle feathered the silk of her skin before he cradled her face in his hands. "What a beautiful name," he said, grazing her jaw with the pads of his thumbs. His smile was tender. "Too bad I have to change it."

21

*T*hese w-waterworks have got to s-stop," Charity said with a wobble in her voice, blinking in the sunlight that filtered through the gauzy sheers of her bedroom windows. The scent of Shalimar lingered in the air along with cousins' shrieks and giggles in the backyard from a snowball fight going on.

"I don't know how . . . ," Emma said, swiping at the wetness on her face. Despite the chill of the snow-clad New Year's Day, she had never felt so warm, so alive, so full of joy that just naturally spilled out.

Mrs. Sean O'Connor.

She closed her eyes and drank in the moment, Charity's hand warm in hers while they sniffled and swayed to Rudy Vallee singing "As Time Goes By," as it drifted from downstairs where family and friends waited to say goodbye. *You must remember this, a kiss is just a kiss, a sigh is just a sigh. The fundamental things apply, as time goes by . . .*

Emma smiled while more "waterworks" stung her eyes. *As time goes by.* In a few short weeks, a lifetime of sorrow and shame had, indeed, gone by, leaving Emma with new hope, a new husband, and a new life. *Oh, Lord, how can I ever thank you?*

Charity shoved one of ten handkerchiefs she stole from Mitch's drawer into Emma's hand, sniffling right along with her best friend. "We shouldn't be crying—this is s-supposed to b-be the happiest d-day of our lives."

Emma laughed, and then started blubbering again. "It issssss . . . ," she said, hugging Charity before trailing off into another happy whimper. She pulled back and dabbed at her face, a crooked grin breaking through. "I think this may be a record—how many is this?" she asked, holding the handkerchief in the air."

A waterlogged giggle broke through as Charity blew her nose. "T-ten t-total, including four for you and me and one each for my mother, sisters, Alli, and Bert."

"Bert cried?" Emma asked, wonder lacing her tone.

Charity nodded, her lips veering into an off-center smile. "But I'm not sure if it's because she's happy or because she's sitting next to Horace." With a noticeable quiver of her lips, she clasped Emma's hands in hers. "Emma O'Connor, do you have any idea how much I love you?"

Stroking a hand to Charity's cheek, Emma gave her a watery smile so tender that on its own it assured Charity she was loved. "Yes, friend of my heart, I most definitely do."

"Good," Charity said with a final swipe of her handkerchief. She jutted her chin. "You better send me a postcard from New York before you sail for Killarney, Mrs. O'Connor, or your name is mud. And I still can't believe it—not only my sister-in-law, but now an heiress too!" She winked. "Who knows—inheriting your aunt's estate, you may be richer than me!"

Emma grinned. "Not likely, but I do remember Auntie Chloe always gave me the most lavish gifts when I was a little girl . . ." Her lips bent in a wry smile. "Before I sullied the family name with Rory, that is."

Charity squeezed her hand. "Water under the bridge, Mrs. O'Connor. You have another family name to attend to now." She glanced at her watch. "Goodness, we need to get you out of here before my brother breaks down the door." She hugged

Emma once more. "Friend of my heart, yes, but now sister of my heart too, don't forget."

"Emma, you ready?" Sean's voice sounded along with a knock on the bedroom door, and Charity grinned. "Speak of the devil."

Ready?? No! Not yet . . . Emma chewed her lip, certain she was forgetting something. "Almost," she called while her gaze darted around the room in search of her purse.

"Here." Charity handed her the pretty peach clutch that matched Emma's tailored woolen suit perfectly, complemented by a simple strand of pearls that had been a wedding gift from Sean. "You look beautiful," she said over her shoulder as she headed for the door. "But," she said with a wiggle of brows, "not as beautiful as tonight in that *very* sheer negligee I gave you."

Heat swallowed Emma whole just as Charity opened the door. Sean's smile faded as he stepped in the room, looking so handsome in his charcoal double-breasted suit and striped tie that Emma felt like crying all over again. One look at his broad shoulders, commanding height, and chiseled features, and the heat from Charity's remark traveled to every part of her body.

"Emma, are you okay?" he asked, blue eyes squinted in concern. "You look flushed."

Charity grabbed Emma's bouquet off the bed along with the garter and moseyed back to the door, giving him a wink. "That's just the blush of love in her cheeks, brother dear. Come on, you two, there are plenty of women downstairs chomping at the bit to get their mitts on this bridal bouquet, although I'm not sure we'll find too many takers for the garter."

Sean stroked Emma's cheek with his thumb, the look in his eyes warming her all over again. "You look beautiful," he whispered, leaning to brush his lips against hers.

"Hey," Charity said with a jerk of her head, "you have a whole week in New York for that stuff, never mind the rest of your lives. And lonely single women *are* waiting, you know."

"What a slave driver." Sean strolled to the door with a grin, then snatched the garter from Charity's hand. His eyes sobered as he bent to give her a kiss on the cheek. "I don't know how Emma and I can ever thank you and Mitch for all you've done for us, sis." A sheen of moisture shone in his eyes that rivaled his sister's. He squeezed her arm with a crooked smile. "You're one in a million, kid, you know that? Love ya."

"Love ya back," she said. "Besides, it's the least I could do for my big brother and best friend, not to mention myself." Her lips squirmed to the side. "You know I can't rest until every O'Connor is happily wed."

He twirled the garter on his finger with a grin. "Yeah, I know. Poor Steven."

"You best throw that thing right at him, you hear?" Charity said, finger raised in warning.

"Yes, ma'am, but no guarantee," he said, shoving the garter high on his forearm. "Steven's even more gun-shy about marriage than I was."

"Yeah, but we got our man, right, Emma?"

Emma grinned. "By the grace of God, I'm afraid, *and* the obstinance of my sister-in-law."

"Sister-in-law . . . oh, that sounds so good, doesn't it?" Charity sighed.

Emma nodded, fresh tears threatening.

"Don't start," Charity said sternly, blinking hard to dispel her own emotion. She jerked her head toward the landing. "Let's go."

Sean looked back at Emma and winked before easing the door closed in Charity's face. "We'll be right out, but first I have something to say to my wife." With a firm click, he promptly locked it and turned, all but devouring Emma with his eyes as he slowly walked to where she stood, rooted to the floor. For the first time since Rory had thrown the hot grease in her face, she felt beautiful, sending warmth through her that could have curled her toes. "I love you," he whispered, and her heart turned over at the heated look in his eyes. Like she was the world to him—the moon, the stars—or the woman he'd love for the rest of his days.

He pulled her into his arms and kissed her, slow and deliberate, causing her pulse to sprint. With a soft nuzzle of her lips, he picked her up in his arms and carried her to the bed.

"Sean O'Connor, what are you doing?" she squealed, her heart swooping in her chest like a flock of seagulls diving over Massachusetts Bay.

He eased down on the bed with her snug on his lap, leveling her defenses with a single kiss that trapped a moan in her mouth. "Sweet chorus of angels," he whispered, exploring her throat with his lips. His hands shimmied beneath the suitjacket and blouse to grip her close with a low groan. "I've been wanting to do this all day."

Emma closed her eyes, every nerve tingling from the caress of his palms against her skin as they swept the curve of her waist, the swell of her hips. His lips kindled a heat inside far warmer than the hungry reach of his hands or the gentle mating of his mouth against hers.

"I love you, Emma," he whispered, causing the warmest of shivers to tremble her body, "and I plan to spend every minute of every day making sure you never forget." He dipped her back on the bed and kissed her thoroughly until she completely forgot about the people below.

Oh, Lord, is this how much you love me? she wondered, intoxicated by the depth of Sean's love.

More, came the answer, causing a surge of joy—and her husband's fiery kiss—to take her breath away.

"Uh, excuse me, but are you two ever planning to come out?" Charity's tease carried through the door while she interrupted them with an impatient tap. "Don't mean to embarrass you, but there's a foyer full of people who have a *pre-e-e-etty* good idea of what's going on up here, so I suggest you save it for the honeymoon."

Emma jolted up, her cheeks suddenly as warm as the rest of her body. "Coming!" she shouted, wriggling off Sean's lap and retucking her blouse with a nervous chew of her lip.

Before she could steal away, he spun her back with a devious smile and a glint of trouble in lidded blue eyes. "Once I get you alone, Mrs. O'Connor, I plan to take full advantage of that ring on your finger, is that clear?"

She cupped his face, eyes tender. "It belongs to you, my love, as do I." Giving him a kiss to tide him over, she tugged him to the door with a seductive smile that would have made Charity proud. "Keep in mind the sooner we leave, Sean O'Connor, the sooner I can give you *all* of my love."

"God, give me patience," he said with a grin, prodding her through the door as if to hurry the process.

They were met on the landing by laughter and chatter and Bing Crosby on the radio singing "Wrap Your Troubles in Dreams." With a wink, Charity put two fingers to her teeth and produced an ear-splitting whistle that would have won Henry's respect. "Listen up, everybody! We need to ship these two lovebirds off to New York pronto, but not before we lasso in another potential bride and groom with the toss of the bouquet and garter."

"Uh-oh, gotta go—I think I hear my mother calling." A lazy grin eased across Steven's face as he stood talking to his brothers-in-law at the edge of the foyer, hip to the wall.

"Your mother is right here, young man," Marcy said over her shoulder, patting her husband's arm while chuckles circled the room. "Your father's determined to trim our grocery bill one way or the other, so I suggest you belly up to the banister for a shot at the garter."

"Mind your mother, Steven," Patrick said with a loop of his wife's waist.

"Yeah, Steven, just look what our garter did for Sean," Luke said with a cocky grin, arm tucked around Katie's shoulder while Kit slept, curled against his shoulder. "The man's happily married to the only woman on earth capable of tying him down."

"Excuse me," Sean said from the landing, a possessive arm latched to Emma's shoulders, "but I prefer to think of it as untying me from the lonely fate of a bachelor."

"Turncoat," Steven said, grinning up at his brother.

"Okay, ladies, move to the center of the foyer for a chance at happily ever after." Charity waved the single women forward while Emma stepped up to the railing with the bouquet.

"Me, me, me," Gabe shouted, jumping up and down along with the older cousins, all pink-cheeked from their romps in the snow.

"When you're a little older," Collin whispered to five-year-old Abby as he tugged her off to the side with a pout on her face. He swooped her up in his arms and blew a raspberry on her neck, and she giggled, while Lizzie handed Molly off to Brady with a kiss to his cheek. Glowing like a little girl at a party, Lizzie raced to join Faith, Katie, and her parents at the base of the stairs where they awaited Sean and Emma's departure.

"Henry—freeze!" Charity's voice rang in the foyer.

Slinking through the small crowd of family and friends, Henry stopped dead in his tracks behind his cousins, eyes like saucers and snowball in hand.

"Take that outside right now before I put it—and you—in the freezer, young man!"

Mitch cinched the back of Henry's neck. "She's got eyes in the back of her head, Son, don't you know that by now?" He steered Henry to the front door. "Toss it, kiddo."

"Ready?" Emma asked, bouquet in hand.

"Throw it already," Bert called. "I'm not getting any younger, you know." She slid a sideways smirk at the woman beside her. "And neither is Michelle."

"Speak for yourself, Mrs. Adriani," Michelle said, elbowing Bert out of the way.

Gabe spun around, arms on her hips. "Hey, no catching the bouquet if you're married."

"I'm a widow," Bert said with a narrow glare. She nudged Gabe forward with the tip of her shoe. "Move it, short stuff. You've got time on your side—I don't."

"I thought you weren't interested in marriage, Mrs. Adriani,"

Sean yelled from the landing, shooting her a boyish smile that helped to soften her scowl.

"So weddings bring out the sap in me, is that a crime?"

"No, ma'am." Sean nudged Emma's arm with a hand to his mouth. "Is it, Horace?"

Emma had never seen Bert blush before, and the effect made her giggle. Sean nodded toward Horace against the wall, who was as scarlet as Bert, then leaned close. "Those two have been chatting it up all day—could be love in the air," he whispered, and Emma grinned.

"Okay, here we go," Emma said, turning her back to wave the bouquet overhead. "One . . . two . . . three!" Ribbons and flowers fluttered high along with shrieks and cheers while Gabe vaulted into the air, accidentally tipping the bouquet into Bert's waiting hand. In a knee-jerk reaction, the little girl butted Bert's hold, and the flowers somersaulted over Alli's shoulder.

"Here you go, Alli," Katie said with a quick swoop of the bouquet. "I believe this belongs to you." She delivered a sassy smile while Bert's and Gabe's groans echoed through the foyer.

"Hey, no fair, Katie, you cheated!" Gabe said with a fold of her arms.

"Talk about cheating, you little squirt," Bert groused. "You knocked it out of my hand."

Gabe peered up, fists parked on her hips. "Oh, yeah? Well, I touched it before you did. Besides, you're too old to get married."

"Gabriella Dawn Smith—apologize this instant!" Marcy was aghast.

"Sorry," Gabe said with a squint of her eyes that indicated she was anything but.

Bert matched her look, slit for slit. "Yeah, yeah, yeah." She slid Alli a begrudging smile. "Good for you, kid. If anybody got it other than me, I'm glad it was you."

"Thanks, Bert," Alli said shyly, nose buried in the bouquet with a gentle smile.

Charity whistled again, and the foyer went silent. "Okay, gentlemen, it's your turn, and you know who you are . . ." She arched a brow when Steven remained propped against the wall. "Steven . . . don't make me come down there."

Brady and Mitch laughed while Collin prodded Steven to where the other bachelors waited. "Move it, Steven," he said with a gloat. "Misery loves company."

Steven lumbered to the center of the room with his hands in his pockets. "May I remind you that you can lead a horse to water, but you can't make him drink?"

"Wanna bet?" Charity said, eyes narrowing into bully mode. "Trust me, if he wants leftover wedding cake, he'll drink."

Steven peered up at his sister, shaking his head. "Have you no shame?"

"None whatsoever," Faith piped up from the sidelines, prompting more chuckles.

Emma laughed along with the others, heart overflowing that she was now part of this amazing family that had reached out to her, loved her, made her one of their own.

"All right, gentlemen," Sean said, turning his back to the crowd, "give it your best shot."

"Aim toward Steven on the right," Charity whispered, and he grinned at Emma before letting it fly with an arm adept at sailing a baseball from center field to home plate. The garter ricocheted off the far wall with a soft thump. Father Mac looked up in surprise when it bounced off his shoulder while chatting with Brady. Stooping to retrieve it, he bobbled it in his hand. "It's a garter, Sean, not a basketball in a game to the death with your parish priest." He tossed it toward the group of men in the center of the foyer, where it landed with a splat on the tip of Steven's shoe.

All the men froze, including Steven, who stared as if it were bird droppings from the sky. With a slow and casual gait, James ambled over and stooped to pick it up, offering it to Steven.

Steven backed away, two palms up. "No thanks, buddy, it's all yours."

Applause drowned out Charity's groan, and Emma's heart took a dip when James tucked the garter in the pocket of his suit coat before shooting Alli a quiet smile.

All at once Sean looped Emma's waist with a sturdy arm. "I told you love was in the air," he whispered, then kissed her on top of the head. "We have to go." With one last hug for Charity, Sean led Emma down the stairs for final goodbyes.

Patrick embraced her firmly. "We knew you belonged to us one way or the other, Emma," he said with a chuckle, "and this certainly spares us the trouble of adoption. Welcome to the family."

Marcy cupped Emma's face with tears in her eyes. "Patrick and I couldn't be happier, Emma. You've always been one of our own."

Emma nodded, unable to speak for the hitch in her throat.

"You'll love the Statue of Liberty," Katie said with a squeeze. "Make sure you see it."

"Oh, and try to see *Show Boat* on Broadway while you're there," Lizzie breathed. "I've read it's really romantic."

Faith kissed Sean's cheek, then pulled Emma into a voracious hug. "You're one of us, Emma, no backing out now." She sniffed, desperately blinking away the tears in her eyes. "And as much as I love my family, somehow you make it more complete."

Steven rattled his father's car keys. "Come on, you two, I refuse to speed to get you to the station on time."

Slipping Emma's coat over her shoulders, Sean hustled her to the door amidst a flurry of goodbyes. Hand on the knob, he bent to brush his lips against hers, causing her heart to soar at the love in his eyes. He smiled while his thumb grazed her jaw. "Ready, Emma?"

She glanced back at the O'Connors, throat aching as Charity blew her a kiss. *How can this be? I never deserved this!* And yet, this was *her* family . . . *her* husband . . . *her* life!

I honor those who honor me.

Sweet moisture stung in her eyes. *Oh, Lord!* The warmth

of his approval embraced her and she swallowed hard, returning her gaze to Sean's while a single tear trailed into the curve of her smile. She finally nodded, heart welling with joy faster than her eyes could well with water. "Am I ready?" she whispered, squeezing Sean's hand till she thought she would burst. "Oh, yes," she breathed. *For the first time in my life . . .*

Acknowledgments

To my agent, Natasha Kern, and my editor, Lonnie Hull Dupont—treasured gifts from a very wise God who knew exactly what I needed.

To the truly talented team at Revell—I am privileged to work with each and every one of you. Mega hugs to Michele Misiak for her kindness and patience with CDQs like me, to Cheryl Van Andel and Dan Thornberg for their remarkable talent and creativity, and to Barb Barnes, whose name *always* makes me smile when it pops up in email. You guys are the best!

To my brainstorming buddies, Charlotte Vernaci and Linda Tate—thank you for always responding to my 911 calls with grace, humor, and grit.

To the Seekers, fourteen of the finest women I have ever met—I am beyond blessed to claim you as dear friends, confidants, prayer partners, and therapists on call.

To Casey Herringshaw and Michelle Tuller—not only winners of my newsletter contest to have a character named after them in this book, but two of the kindest and dearest reader friends I've ever had the privilege to meet. I cherish your friendship.

To three ladies who keep me on track and without whom I'd be absolutely lost—my precious prayer partners and best friends, Joy Bollinger, Karen Chancellor, and Pat Stiehr. Love you guys lots!

To my aunt Julie; my mother-in-law Leona; and my sisters, Dee Dee, Mary, Pat, Rosie, Susie, Ellie, and Katie; and to my sisters-in-law, Diana, Mary, and Lisa—thank you for your love and support. When it comes to family, I definitely "fell in."

To my daughter, Amy; son, Matt; and daughter-in-law, Katie—I love you to pieces. Not sure what I ever did to deserve blessings like you, but I refuse to look a gift horse in the mouth, so thank you, God!

To Keith Lessman—talk about God doing abundantly, exceedingly more than I could ever hope, think, or pray. When it comes to husbands, babe, you're a grand slam.

And finally to the God of the universe, whose unfailing love keeps me afloat. Without you, I'd be up a creek instead of white-water rafting down rivers of grace.

Julie Lessman is an award-winning author whose tagline of "Passion with a Purpose" underscores her intense passion for both God and romance. Author of the Daughters of Boston series, Julie is also winner of the 2009 ACFW Debut Author of the Year and the Holt Medallion Awards of Merit for Best First Book and Long Inspirational. She is the recipient of thirteen Romance Writers of America awards. Julie resides in Missouri with her husband, daughter, son, and daughter-in-law.

Contact Julie through her website at www.julielessman.com.

"If you're looking for an awesome writer and a story charged with romance, you don't want to miss *A Hope Undaunted*."
—Judith Miller, author of *Somewhere to Belong*, Daughters of Amana series

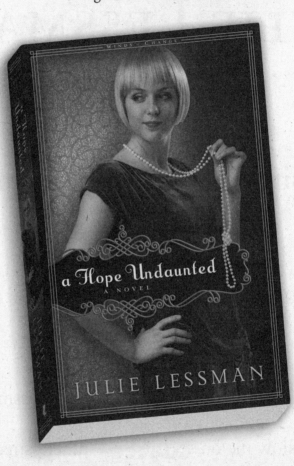

The delightful story of Kate O'Connor, a smart and sassy woman who has her goals laid out for the future—including the perfect husband and career. Will she follow her plans or her heart?

"Guaranteed to satisfy the most romantic of hearts."

—TAMERA ALEXANDER, bestselling author

Full of passion, romance, rivalry, and betrayal,
A Passion Most Pure will captivate you from the
first page. Don't miss book 1 in the
Daughters of Boston series!

No man can resist her charms. Or so she thought.

Charity O'Connor is a woman who gets what she wants. That is, until Mitch Dennehy. Don't miss book 2 in the Daughters of Boston series!

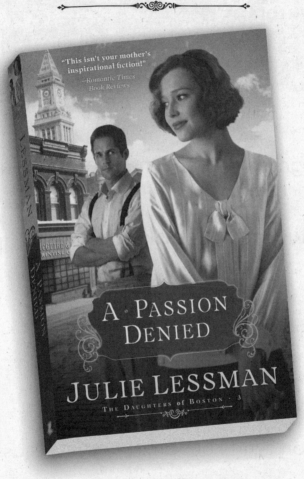